THAT DEPLORABLE BOY

THE SECOND FOOTMAN

THAT DEPLORABLE BOY

PART II OF THE MIREMONT TRILOGY

JASPER BARRY

Catullus translation by the author

Matador
9 Priory Business Park,
Wistow Road, Kibworth Beauchamp,
Leicestershire LE8 0RX
Tel: 0116 279 2299
Email: books@troubador.co.uk
Web: www.troubador.co.uk/matador
Twitter: @matadorbooks

ISBN 978 1788038 508

British Library Cataloguing in Publication Data.
A catalogue record for this book is available from the British Library.

Printed and bound by CPI Group (UK) Ltd, Croydon, CR0 4YY
Typeset in 10.5pt Baskerville by Troubador Publishing Ltd, Leicester, UK

Matador is an imprint of Troubador Publishing Ltd

My thanks to Patricia Coulson, Valerie Cumming, Martin Village and to Jed and Alex Beardmore of fightingfitfencing.com/ for their help and support.

CHAPTER ONE

A man without a wife may do much as he pleases, particularly if he is discreet. M. le marquis de Miremont had lived with his young lover, Max Fabien, for well over a year and, since the boy was officially his secretary and the marquis, besides, rarely went about in Society, not an eyebrow had twitched.

However, Armand de Miremont did have a wife. True, the couple were long-estranged, so that for months at a time he could forget her existence. But they had two daughters, the youngest of whom, Juliette, had reached marriageable age. Accordingly, Mme la marquise proposed to accompany Juliette to the Hôtel de Miremont for a lengthy visit. For what father would deny his daughter her debut in Paris?

So much for Miremont's congenial domestic arrangements. Closed doors were an invitation to Aline de Miremont, the desire for privacy a sickness. She would turn their lives inside out and shake them like old coats.

Her letter arrived when they had only just quitted Paris for their usual summer at Beauvallon, Miremont's small estate in the Yonne. They had come in from their morning swim in the lake and, still with wet hair and in their dressing gowns, were taking breakfast when Miremont's valet, Thomas, brought in the post.

Miremont put the envelope to one side, assuming this was another of Aline's diatribes about the château at Miremont-Sainte-Fleur, whose amenities, however frequently refurbished, would never merit her satisfaction. Much more to his taste was Hugo Chausson-Laurier's letter from Alexandria: the previous winter, Chausson-Laurier and his companion, Charles de Selincourt, had excavated an Amarna-period rock tomb at Luxor in the Valley of the Kings—in June, Miremont and Max had attended their lecture at the Geographical Society—and now Chausson-Laurier brought news that they had at last raised the money for a second excavation. Miremont read the letter slowly, savouring its detail. Then, passing it to Max, he poured himself another cup of coffee: he would rather ponder Egypt and the Pharaohs than the lack of a tennis court at Sainte-Fleur.

What Max Fabien remembered most about the Geographical Society lecture was the landscape revealed by Selincourt's lantern slides. Thus the letter from Egypt evoked great barren mountains lying in a waste of burning desert, a world away from the boulevards of Paris or the fields and vineyards of Beauvallon. Max was reliving this vision of adventure when he heard Armand's cup clatter into its saucer.

He raised his eyebrows, but Armand appeared bereft of words. He took Mme de Miremont's letter from the old boy's shaking hand.

Although Max had so far escaped Armand's wife, he knew her scandalous history, having received it in outline from M. de M and also, wickedly embellished, from the duchesse de Claireville. When Mlle Juliette had been no more than a few months old, madame had run away to Florence with Arturo Ogetti, a tenor much in vogue at that season's musical evenings. Later, much against the advice of his friends, Armand had taken her back, out of compassion and from the wish that his daughters should not be deprived of a mother. But not only did she show every sign of reverting to her old ways: the marriage was intolerable to both parties. Another separation was agreed, awarding her a substantial settlement and the care of their daughters but exiling her to the family's estate in Burgundy, Miremont-Sainte-Fleur. This second banishment had endured fifteen years.

But now, she wrote, she must implore her unyielding husband to relax the extreme severity of its terms. She would do all in a mother's power to find poor Juliette a suitable husband. However, though seventeen years had passed since her own misfortune, seventeen long years, there were small-minded persons in Paris whose memories might be longer. Surely monsieur would not wish to see doors closed to his dearest Juliette? Not when the poor child might be spared this shame if her noble papa were at her side and the Hôtel de Miremont were her setting. Although monsieur might continue to withhold all favour from his poor ill-fated wife, he would surely not deny his duty to his daughter...

And so forth. Aline de Miremont's hand, large, round and girlish, yet curiously difficult to construe, sprawled incontinently across thick watered paper beneath a flamboyantly embossed family crest: the effect was far grander than anything to be found in M. de M's writing desk and, appearing to gainsay the writer's wheedling tone, did not foster a heartening impression. Nor was Max unaware of the letter's implications for himself. However, faced with Armand's distress, he sought words of consolation.

"She does say she does not expect the three of you to live en famille, that it will be an arrangement of convenience."

Miremont pushed his coffee cup aside. "Darling boy, my wife has as much notion of convenience as the leopards in the Jardin des Plantes. However, she is right, I cannot refuse Julie." Here he sighed and grew wistful. "Do you know, I have not seen her since the Mother Superior allowed her a special dispensation for Agathe's christening—and the child is almost two by now. Two years! My beautiful daughter was still in short frocks. And now we are planning to offer her to the market like an issue of Panamanian bonds."

Last summer, on oppressive nights like this, they had taken mattresses out to the summer house, grandly named the Temple of Dionysus, and slept beside the lake. But so far this summer such schoolboy abandon had not seemed fitting; tonight their only concession to the heat had been to throw off the sheets. They lay in Miremont's bed, but apart, backs turned, and Miremont could not sleep. He sensed Max was awake too, yet when he rolled over the boy did not stir. Indeed, he scarcely appeared to be breathing and, although his face was buried in the pillow, the promontory of his shoulder and the long sweep of his back, pale in the moonlight, marble-still, suggested he was waiting, muscles tensed, until Miremont slept and he could retreat to his own bed.

Miremont sighed. He wanted to lean across, kiss that handsome naked shoulder and whisper that he was sorry for their perfunctory embraces. But no, better let things be. Instead, very quietly to humour Max's pretence, he swung his legs out of bed, reached for his dressing gown and took up a candle to light his way on the landing. Downstairs in the vestibule he exchanged the candle for a lamp, although, given the brightness of the moon and the familiarity of his path, he scarcely required it to cross the lawns to the lake.

As he sat in the colonnade of the Temple of Dionysus, a nocturne of tiny well-loved sounds soothed him: frogs in lusty chorus amongst the lily pads beyond the Chinese bridge; the plop of a water vole quitting its burrow in the bank of the little island that hid the grotto; the prattling of crickets in the shrubbery; the chug-chug of the water-wheel, the distant chur of a nightjar. The air was scented with honeysuckle and fresher here, despite the heat.

Home. Earlier, he had almost wished he was in Egypt with Chausson-Laurier and Selincourt, but in truth he would not be anywhere but here. He loved Max and Beauvallon would heal their troubles.

All the same, there was now the problem of Aline to be considered.

For, of course, he could hardly refuse his pretty little daughter a Paris Season. As it was, he felt sufficiently remorseful that circumstances had conspired to keep him distant from his favourite child for so long.

If he did not doubt he had acted in accordance with simple humanity when he had surrendered both girls to their mother, he still regretted it. His stiff annual New Year visits to Sainte-Fleur had only tended to remind him of the brief months they had lived with him in Paris: he recalled how Clotilde had loved a piggyback and how Julie had gurgled merrily when he had dangled his watch over her crib.

Nor could he dispel his concern that Aline was hardly an ideal influence on two growing girls. So he must suppose it was not Clotilde's fault, but his own, that she disappointed him. Granted, Clotilde was not flighty: married at eighteen, she was, at twenty-two, a diligent Society matron, who, with the first of her two children, had provided the longed-for heir to the marquisate. He was not proud of preferring one child over the other: yet, in her narrowness and petty snobbery, Clotilde was the very copy of her mother.

But then, in those awkward New Year encounters, when the girls had been brought down from the nursery to sit, as if corseted, in their best pinafores, Clotilde had always seemed the stolid one, Julie the pretty imp, coerced into subduing her vitality by some dire maternal threat. Miremont could hope her spirit and intelligence had survived intact, for she, at least, had escaped her mother. They had been painful for him, the four years she had been away in Bruges, boarding with the Sisters of Saint Augustine, but he could console himself that she had retained her innocence and received a proper education. When Miremont had last seen her, she had been the image of Aline in but one respect: she promised to mirror her mother's youthful beauty.

Clotilde had not required a season: she had found her own husband in Burgundy, Raymond Thierry-Le Puy, whose family owned a neighbouring estate. But Julie, although a month away from her eighteenth birthday, was scarcely out of the convent. With this in mind, Miremont had agreed Aline might take her to England where, watched over by his English relations, she could experience the London Season: he hoped the visit would extend Julie's education and widen her horizons. Alas—how could he not have foreseen this?—it had widened Aline's horizons too. She might concede presentation at the Court of St James's had helped 'finish' their daughter, but London was not Paris: thus, at long last, she had found the path back from exile.

Miremont sighed. If he must suffer Aline's excesses, it was a necessary sacrifice: he could hardly spurn this chance to be a father again to his favourite child. Nevertheless, the arrival of his wife and daughter filled him with dread. Its timing was less than propitious.

It was not merely that his guilt was reawakened, the guilt of a man who, having followed the path of conventional and unquestioning rectitude into middle age, one day finds himself ambushed by his own nature. He would have given much to be able to present himself to Julie as he had been in her childhood, a dull fellow perhaps and ignorant of happiness, but all the same straightforward, not someone who, to protect what he most values, must routinely live mired in deceit. By what right could he claim the respect and love that would normally be a father's due? Was it not a failure of parental duty to welcome her innocence into such a household as his?

Yet the main force of his anxiety centred, as ever, upon Max.

Leaving his chair in the colonnade but reluctant to return to an empty bed, Miremont walked out onto the short jetty from which they plunged into the lake. Tomorrow, as usual, he and Max would swim, ride and compete fiercely at the shooting gallery and, watching the boy's face, seeing his look of pleasure, he would temporarily escape the shadow that oppressed him. Beauvallon should work its magic. But if it did not, they were not well-placed to live under siege: in fact, it could undo them.

CHAPTER TWO

Often in the last year, while engaged in some perfectly ordinary task—leafing through a book, lighting a cigar after dinner—Miremont had been arrested by the extraordinary fact of his happiness. Whatever his moral qualms, he did not regret having taken Max into his house. How could he, when he still reeled from the discovery that he could love, was capable of receiving, and giving, pleasure? How could he, remembering the years with Aline or the rigid notions of Lesage, his previous secretary, regret a companion whose perceptions so closely chimed with his, to whom he could speak freely, with whom he could laugh, who would happily spar for hours over some fine point of literature or philosophy, yet was equally content with reflective silence?

After their first golden summer together at Beauvallon, they had settled into a harmonious routine at the Hôtel de Miremont. Over winter, the first chapters of Miremont's work on Ovid, copied in the boy's clear hand, had mounted into a satisfying pile on the study table. Riding in the Champs-Élysées or the Bois de Boulogne, fencing in the ballroom (under the martial eye of Captain Horthy, Miremont's fencing master, Max was coming on apace)—shared work had been leavened with shared recreation. Then, in the spring, as Miremont had promised, they had travelled.

Italy had seemed to Miremont the obvious, the only choice for the boy's first excursion abroad: not only could Max experience at first hand the glories of ancient Rome; his growing interest in Renaissance art would be amply requited and he might practise the Italian he had been teaching himself this past year. Rome, Naples to see the excavations at Pompeii and Herculaneum, then back north, via Rome again, to Florence and Venice—they had followed the route Miremont himself had taken when he was a carefree second son. Although Italy, since those far off days, had become a single nation, with Rome rightfully restored as its capital, much that Miremont recalled remained unchanged; yet, to his constant delight, he saw it all anew through the boy's eyes. So apparently self-possessed, worldly-wise in areas where his middle-aged lover was a novice, Max was still in others refreshingly unsophisticated, open to spontaneous, joyous discovery in a way no twenty-one-year-old born to privilege could ever be.

Despite a childhood spent in Normandy, he had never seen the sea and the Bay of Naples was more of a wonder to him than Brunelleschi's dome or the ruined hulk of the Coliseum. And then, of course, there was Venice: Miremont would especially cherish the moment they had disembarked at San Marco, when Max had gazed about him, quite inebriated by the beauty of it all. But the boy was keenly alert to the smaller sensations too, a flash of sunlight glimpsed from a hidden courtyard, the scent of sweet almonds drifting across a piazza.

Not that his was an uncritical eye. Miremont was amused by the way he seemed to interrogate the countless Madonnas, Annunciations and Pietas—perhaps it was his unfortunate upbringing in the cloister that made him view them with scepticism, even anger. He still despised Annibale Carracci and could not, however Miremont tried, be persuaded of the virtues of Tintoretto; but while he continued faithful to his idol, Titian, he had acquired two more gods, Michelangelo and Caravaggio; and besides, Miremont enjoyed the debate.

He could not but feel proud of the boy. Max had grown into a fine young man. He was still astonishingly beautiful—Miremont never ceased to marvel that he, forty-five and never handsome himself, should be blessed with such a beautiful lover—yet he had steadied, too, during his time in the Hôtel de Miremont, had lost much of his recklessness and that restless, feral look Miremont had glimpsed on occasion. Indeed, seeing him, tall and elegant in the top hat and alpaca overcoat Miremont had insisted he should be equipped with for their travels, it was hardly possible to conceive that, not two years since, he had worn Catherine de Claireville's livery and waited upon Miremont at table.

But then it was as Miremont had always thought: the boy's instincts were good. He never sought to exploit his situation. When Lesage had retired, Miremont was ready to consider the secretaryship a sinecure, but he had reckoned without Max's obstinate pride: although he seemed to have little regard for money and—fortunately for Miremont, who was endlessly contriving to give him presents by stealth—a hazy notion of its value, he held it as a point of principle that he should earn his increased wages.

Miremont had feared the extra duties would imperil the leisurely tenor of their life. But, within weeks, the boy's sharp mind had shrunk the tremendous load that had filled Lesage's day until it occupied a mere hour or two before luncheon. Moreover the frequent squalls that had seemed to buffet Miremont's affairs under Lesage's aegis either died down or died out altogether. Miremont felt quite spoilt by such efficiency. Even in Italy, he discovered that train timetables, tickets, papers and the other tiresome formalities of travel were now the secretary's preserve and he might do nothing more than enjoy himself: when he ventured that it should be otherwise, the boy would not hear of it.

Ah, Italy. Here, once Thomas had retired to his own quarters, they could live as they lived at Beauvallon, free from the constraints of society and the scrutiny of a large household. How Miremont had treasured the memories of those two months, until he had been forced to view them in a new and cruel light.

There had been one other aspect of their time in Italy which had lightened Miremont's heart, although it shamed him to admit it. As at Beauvallon, Max had no days off. When the boy had taken the post of librarian at the Hôtel de Miremont, he had been awarded a half-day on Thursdays and a full day on Sundays and in Paris he still made use of this freedom: Miremont could hardly object, since on Thursday evenings he himself played chess with his old friend Dr Gérard, and on Sunday afternoons Clotilde and her children paid their filial visit. Besides, the boy was young and might otherwise feel suffocated; for this reason too, and so that Max might enjoy a full night's sleep instead of making the excursion up the service stairs to his own room in the small hours, Miremont had suggested that on Thursdays and Sundays they should forgo their nightly encounters. Yet these nights were torture to him. Indeed, however he fought against it, Max's well-deserved and entirely reasonable freedom caused him acute pain.

Miremont had never thought of himself as a jealous man. He had not experienced jealousy over Aline's betrayals, merely hurt pride. But where the boy was concerned he was racked by it, crazed with suspicion, tortured by emotions his old self would not have recognised and would have roundly condemned if it had. Perhaps he should blame Achille de Tarascon for dripping the poison into his ear. But no, it was his own weakness that had heeded Tarascon's insinuations: he was mortified when he recalled the weeks of dread and suspicion he had endured, only to discover the boy was innocent, that, far from having succumbed to Tarascon's advances, Max regarded the comte with a distaste that surpassed his own.

The boy was blameless, the monster lived in Miremont's imagination. But it refused to be tamed: it ripped away reason as you might skin a rabbit. Yes, he could tell himself his suspicions were the commonplace imaginings of any man with a much younger lover; the monster countered that they were commonplace with just cause.

He retained sufficient pride not to cross-question the boy. Besides he would do well to remember, much as this pained him too, that despite their affinity Max was by nature reserved (the matter of his parentage was but one tender place Miremont had learnt not to probe). Yet, when it came to his days off, was it fair to accuse the boy of secrecy? True, he was vague as to detail, but he mentioned a Russian family he visited: although they lived in modest circumstances they held musical evenings, apparently, and Max sometimes read Pushkin to the invalid mother. This was much to his credit: Miremont was glad he still valued his former acquaintance and had not let his changed fortunes go to his head. Although Max was an accomplished liar when discretion required it, Miremont was confident he would know if the boy were lying to him.

Nevertheless, the phantoms persisted. It scarcely helped that society stood in the way of their forming common friendships. Miremont was not, as Aline maintained contemptuously, a total recluse: while he loathed the butterfly life she had once forced upon him, he had never abandoned a small circle of old friends. But, although Max was always at table when Miremont's friends dined, he was there, as Lesage had been, as Miremont's secretary: he was no more likely than Lesage to be invited into the La Marnes' box at the Garnier or included in the company at one of Constant de Sauvigny's supper parties.

Miremont had treasured greater hopes of his younger nephew Roland: a handsome, amiable boy of about Max's age, the very image of his dead mother, Miremont's sister Léonore, he had taken to making a useful fourth at Captain Horthy's fencing sessions and he and Max had warmed to each other immediately. Miremont, who knew (as it happened, from a spurned Achille de Tarascon) that he need not be jealous of Roland, could not have been more delighted. But Roland, alas, shared his father Constant's respect for the niceties of rank: his friendship with Max stayed in the ballroom, put away with the foils and masks until their next meeting.

And yet how could it be otherwise? Discretion demanded Miremont's relations with his young secretary must appear unremarkable, the straightforward dealings of the employer with the employed. Even so, it irked Miremont that the person dearest to him was consigned to the shadows.

There were exceptions of course: once Miremont's newly opened eyes could see beyond Tarascon's dangerous flamboyance, he caught glimpses beneath Society's unruffled surface of another society, unfathomed and soundless as the deeper waters of the ocean, in which, while discretion remained all, moral latitudes were broader.

No pretence was required with Hugo Chausson-Laurier and Charles de Selincourt; but, alas, even when they were not excavating at Luxor, they were often travelling elsewhere. Sadly, too, when Baroness Dohnányi and Françine de la Falaise had arrived last January, their visit had been fleeting: Beatrice Dohnányi, although appearing to consider every European capital her home, never stayed in any long—once she had overseen l'Odéon's production of her verse drama *Jaël*, she was due to lecture Vienna on Sappho.

Of course, there remained Catherine de Claireville, who knew everything about Miremont and Max's affairs, or more than was strictly comfortable. Miremont was very fond of Catherine: just as she had once been his sister's closest friend, now she was his; but, when he recalled the singular duty she imposed upon her footmen, his devotion could not suppress a twinge of what, though it was an old jealousy, could still stir pain. If only she would not take such a proprietorial interest in the boy, if only her every call did not feel like an inspection—but no, this was unfair, her concern was kindly meant. And what greater kindness than so willingly to accept Max and Miremont's love for him? Catherine would have been delighted if Max had accompanied Miremont when he called on her, would have been happy to receive him at her Thursdays; but here the difficulty was the boy himself, who scrupled to flaunt his improved lot before Catherine's servants, so lately his fellows.

Thus it was that while they were beneath the roof of the Hôtel de Miremont, Miremont and Max enjoyed the greatest intimacy but, once outside its gates, they stepped into separate worlds whose orbits never touched. Miremont must live with his shaming jealousy as best he could.

CHAPTER THREE

One Sunday in January, when Clotilde and her husband had been summoned to the sickbed of a Thierry relation, Miremont had been prevailed upon by Dr Rosenthal, his friend from the Sorbonne, to attend one of Pasdeloup's afternoon concerts at the Cirque d'Hiver.

At the end of the concert, caught up in the crowd, they were finally descending the short flight of stairs to the foyer when, on the stairs leading from the opposite side, Miremont glimpsed a familiar tall figure. His heart leapt. Then a poisonous curiosity overtook his delight. He craned his neck anxiously, but Max— Miremont felt almost faint with relief—was not with a man: he was escorting two ladies, one on each arm. Two young ladies, pretty, both chattering excitedly, their faces glowing, and Max glancing from one to the other with the same glowing look: Miremont's relief vanished. Seeing that they would escape him, that they had already reached the doors to the street, he could not restrain himself. Excusing himself to Rosenthal and his wife, he struggled forward, found a gap in the press of bodies, and was swept out through the doors by the general tide. Here he became entangled with those who had congregated outside to smoke and chat, so that it took him a moment to spot his quarry.

"Max!"

He had called out involuntarily and instantly wished he had not, for he must present an undignified and unmannerly figure. But they had turned, the three of them, leaving him no choice but to approach. As he doffed his hat, the two ladies stared at him in polite surprise: dimly he registered that one was dark and fashionably dressed, with the sort of striking looks often described as jolie laide, while the other was younger, fair and more austerely attired in a simple grey mantle and bonnet. But his attention was focused on Max.

Far from looking guilty, the boy was beaming. "Monsieur! How wonderful that you are here. Was he not brilliant?"

Miremont's suspicion struggled with embarrassment, yet still demanded to know which young woman was the danger. Although the dark girl was the obvious choice, it was the fair girl who clung more tightly to Max's arm and whose round blue eyes, having recovered from their astonishment, were scrutinising Miremont with barely concealed curiosity.

"My dear boy, I…?"

"Mitya? Was it not a triumph?"

"Yes… yes indeed."

"We are on our way round to the Green Room to congratulate him."

Shame overtook Miremont. Of course. The young unknown soloist whose performance of M. Saint-Saëns' latest violin concerto they had just acclaimed had been called Zhukovsky. But Miremont, his concentration trained upon the unfamiliar music, had noted this too absently to connect it with Max's Russians.

"But—forgive me…" Max briskly recalled his manners. "Mademoiselle Antonova and Mademoiselle Zhukovskaya, may I introduce Monsieur le marquis de Miremont? Mademoiselle Antonova, monsieur, is betrothed to my friend Zhukovsky, and Mademoiselle Zhukovskaya is his sister—" he smiled at the fair girl "—and my honorary sister too."

"Our mother would have given much to have accompanied us," Mlle Zhukovskaya added, as if she divined Miremont's need for an explanation, "but sadly she is not well enough. So we are in Maxim Alexandrovitch's care."

As Miremont stammered out his appreciation of Dmitri Zhukovsky's performance and of the concerto itself, he fancied the 'honorary sister' still studied him with a not uncritical eye. But in the end she thanked him very sweetly. After which, Miremont, whose embarrassment was now complete, recollected his need to make amends to the Rosenthals, whom he could see not far off, awaiting him patiently; murmuring farewells and apologies, he took flight.

He regretted his cowardice as he pondered the episode over his solitary dinner and later, as he lay awake listening for Max's return. He would have liked to know more of this Dmitri Zhukovsky, Max's dearest friend, and, alas, not merely because he was a talented musician; for, while Miremont might take comfort from the fiancée, the monster countered with the honorary sister: could he afford complacency about a bond so close the family thought of Max as one of their own?

Of course, this was foolish. But if he could not kill the fiend once and for all, he could at least loosen its grip.

The next morning, when Max joined Miremont for breakfast, heavy-eyed from the previous night's celebrations, it was natural to discuss the concert, while the boy's enthusiasm for the music and his friend's success made him more forthcoming than usual.

"I wish," said Miremont casually, sipping his coffee, "you would bring Monsieur Zhukovsky to call on me one afternoon."

Max, who had begun upon the post, paused in the midst of slicing open an envelope. To Miremont's alarm, he looked at him rather askance. "You want him to play for you?"

"Of course not. Although I do not mean… I mean that I should like to meet him. In fact, why not invite him to luncheon?"

"Here?"

"Naturally here." Miremont was disconcerted by the boy's reluctance. However, an explanation occurred to him. Yet, though it was generally the rule that secretaries did not receive callers, a rule that Lesage had strictly and mercifully observed, surely Max understood his own position was different? "My dear boy, he is your friend and he is clearly a remarkable young man. I should be happy to receive him—for us both to receive him—in this house."

But this did not achieve the hoped-for effect. On the contrary, Max studied the paper knife for a moment. "Very well, Armand. I shall ask him."

"Excellent."

"But don't be offended if he declines."

Miremont stared at the boy. But then one obvious and highly disagreeable notion suggested itself. "You mean he is aware that you and I…?"

It was Max's turn to look aggrieved. "Good God, Armand, do you really trust me so little?"

"Oh, my dear, I did not—"

"But even if he did know, it's unlikely he'd turn a hair. He's hardly led a sheltered life."

Miremont recalled Max had once let slip that he had met the Zhukovskys when they were all of them living in poverty. "You think he would feel awkward coming here?"

At this, at least, the boy laughed. "Mitya's people were hereditary nobles with estates and serfs. His grandfather was at court in Saint Petersburg. If he has ended up in Paris playing the fiddle for a living, it's because his father, who was a poet, offended the Tsar and died in Siberia."

"Poor young fellow."

"Mitya holds his father's views."

"After such an injustice, that is scarcely surprising… But I do not see…"

"He is committed to the total abolition of rank and privilege."

Miremont paused, uncertain whether to be insulted or to laugh. "Oh, my dear boy, if he is such a nihilist that his principles would be compromised by taking luncheon with me—then however do you and he…?"

"We avoid the subject."

"Whereas he and I could not?" Miremont noted that Max's response was to look a trifle shamefaced. All the same, he was considerably irritated by what now seemed absurd prevarication. "My dear Max, do you have some reason for not wishing me to meet Monsieur Zhukovsky?"

"No. None at all. I—I should like it."

"Then that is settled, is it not?"

Miremont was not without anxiety as he awaited his guest's arrival. His seat in the Cirque d'Hiver had been high above the concert platform and he had not worn his pince-nez, so that, while he could recall a stocky figure, not as tall as Max, with fair hair and a short fair beard, he was left with no image of the young man's face, nor any clue as to his character, except that he had stood in a workmanlike way with his feet firmly planted and, although playing with feeling and power, had eschewed the flourishes of bow and instrument taken by the cognoscenti for exquisite sensibility. All the same, his suspicions apart, the conversation with Max had left him with a picture of the young Russian as a tortured soul, burning with the twin fires of artistic temperament and political conviction, volatile, touchy and, as the decanter emptied, prone to gloom.

Max, Miremont could not help noticing, was on edge too, so that the first few moments after Zhukovsky had been shown into the Little Salon were distinctly awkward. But Miremont's preconceptions were quickly overturned. At close quarters Dmitri Zhukovsky radiated good nature and a capable energy that was as far as could be imagined from artistic anguish. His broad, plain, snub-nosed face, his smile, his eyes, which were round and blue like his sister's and alight with intelligent humour, all conveyed an attractive straightforwardness of character. He spoke perfect French, enjoyed Miremont's burgundy, but in moderation, and, during a conversation that ranged widely beyond the inevitable first topic of music, never touched upon politics once.

As Miremont watched the two young men, at ease now, laughing together, it amused him that, deprived of prior knowledge and asked to choose which was the concert violinist, his unenlightened eye would have overlooked this unpretentious and level-headed fellow and settled immediately upon Max—Max with his natural grace, his sensuous, scornful mouth, his reckless chin, the sweep of brown hair falling over his forehead to hide his scarred temple, Max, who, for all his love of music, could not play a note.

Altogether, Miremont was thoroughly reassured by Dmitri Zhukovsky. As he listened to the two friends sparring good-humouredly, he forgot his jealousy. Their affection for each other was evident, but it was indeed a brotherly affection. If Mlle Zhukovskaya were Max's young sister, Dmitri, who must be his senior by several years, was his steadying elder sibling, an influence only for good. Besides, Zhukovsky's frequent mentions of Mlle Antonova left no doubt that he was deeply in love, although they could not be married, as he told Miremont, until his future was settled.

The full significance of this remark was not apparent until later, when coffee and liqueurs were brought. Declining brandy as he was playing as usual at the Garnier that night, but accepting a cigarette, Zhukovsky drew in smoke for a moment, before leaning forward, so that, while his words included Miremont, his eyes were fixed upon Max.

"I can't—I was intending to speak when things were more definite, but you have both paid me so many compliments and you, Maxim, old chap, have always given me such encouragement—I should feel a fraud if I did not tell you now. I have decided against trying to make a career as a soloist. Lyudin and I are putting together a string quartet."

Max's look of shock and his heartfelt protests made Miremont long to stretch out a hand to comfort him. But at last the boy was persuaded to listen to his friend's explanation. Yes, Zhukovsky was abandoning what had once been his life's ambition, even though his performance had been generally well-received. He was immensely grateful to M. Saint-Saëns, who was a friend of his teacher at the conservatoire, for entrusting him with the concerto: during his long hours of practice he had taken great pleasure in the music and had felt that pleasure too while he was performing. But he had not enjoyed other aspects of the experience.

He did not think being the focus of attention suited his character. Furthermore, while the soloist was the audience's god, as leader of an orchestra he saw music-making as a collaboration: he understood why some virtuosi became egotistical monsters. Besides, he was naturally gregarious and the consequence of his success would be a life of solitary hotel rooms and strange orchestras.

His cellist friend Lyudin, as Max knew, had been badgering him for months about forming a quartet. He was to be first violin, another friend, Bogdanov, was keen to be second and at last they had found a suitable viola player. For their own amusement they had begun trying out a repertoire and he had discovered his true passion: the intimacy of the ensemble, the making and moulding of something that was greater than all their individual skills, the way the playing of the others taught him to question and rethink his own—it was early days and he had no thought yet of abandoning the Paris Opéra, but he had known, even before he had stepped onto the platform at the Cirque d'Hiver, that this was his future.

While Max still looked horrified, Miremont felt it would be hard to dispute Zhukovsky's cogent justification of a decision that seemed to reflect a remarkable maturity. "You did not consider withdrawing from the concert?" he enquired.

"I wanted to confirm my decision. And I could hardly let down Monsieur Gans, my teacher, or Monsieur Saint-Saëns and Monsieur Pasdeloup, who had all placed such faith in me. But I had another debt to repay, too." Zhukovsky grinned. "To this fellow here."

Max, who had been staring disconsolately at the tablecloth, looked up with a start. "Mitya, you owe me nothing."

Zhukovsky favoured Miremont with a gesture of mock despair. "He has enough pride for both of us, but I am allowed a little too. The autumn before last—"

"Oh, for pity's sake, Mitya!" Max was suddenly as close as Miremont had ever seen him to blushing.

"The autumn before last, like an utter fool, I had let myself be rooked by a crooked promoter who promised me a recital tour in Italy and then ran off with all our savings. We owed rent, my mother was ill, my poor sister was talking about giving piano lessons and I was ready to shoot myself. Then this fellow arrives back in Paris—"

"Damn you, Mitya," said Max.

"And while I'm telling my tale of woe, he starts behaving like a lunatic, demanding scissors and snipping away at that vile old frock coat he used to wear."

Miremont remembered the frock coat: although it had certainly seen better days he recalled it with great affection, for Max had been wearing it at their first encounter in Bordeaux.

"Then, like a conjurer, he produces from the hem a thousand-franc note. Which he insists I take."

Miremont too remembered such a banknote. At their painful parting on his departure from Bordeaux, he had tried to give it to Max surreptitiously and had eventually been obliged to force it upon him.

"Naturally," Zhukovsky continued, cheerfully ignoring Max's baleful stare, "I cannot accept it. So then what does this madman do?"

Miremont recalled that a few months later when the boy had arrived to take up the post of librarian with a second-hand wardrobe offensive to Lesage's fond notion of 'the dignity of the house', he had wondered what Max had done with the money. It was an unworthy doubt, but it had seeded the idea that the boy was heedlessly extravagant.

"He threatens to put it on the fire." Zhukovsky laughed. "And, by God, he would have done it, if Mama hadn't told us we were a couple of schoolboys. But of course he wouldn't accept repayment. Not even when by some miracle I was re-employed by the Opéra—"

Max's exasperation could no longer be contained. "Mitya, if you must tell this ridiculous story, at least tell it correctly. Do not omit that when I was ill and down on my luck at Mère Richoux's your mother and Vera Alexandrovna took care of me and you would have lent me your last centime."

"If I had had one."

"That makes no difference."

Miremont, as he looked across at Max, was overwhelmed by a mixture of emotions—pride, affection, guilt that he had misjudged the poor boy—but he was also amused and touched by Max's strenuous effort to disown his generosity.

"Anyway," continued Zhukovsky, smiling at Miremont, "I did at last extract a promise from Maxim. I might pay him back when I played my first solo."

"Mitya, you wretch, the solo *was* the repayment."

"Let's not split hairs, old chap. On arriving here I gave an envelope to the footman, with instructions to deliver it to your quarters. And, as Monsieur de Miremont will bear witness, I shall take it as a grave attack upon my honour if you attempt to give it back." Then, seeing that Max was not appeased, Zhukovsky lifted his wine glass, in which some burgundy remained. "To an obstinate idiot. And a true friend."

*

That night, when they lay in each other's arms, Miremont had at last dared to ask: "Now, my dear Max, the truth—why did you not want me to meet Zhukovsky?"

The boy had laughed. "Is that not obvious? And he claims I'm the lunatic."

"No, truly?"

"Truly?" Max shrugged. "What if you had disliked each other?"

But Miremont had been charmed by the young Russian, so charmed that he had offered him the Music Salon adjoining the ballroom for the quartet's practice. For he too had a debt to repay: Zhukovsky had shown him an aspect of Max that could only make Miremont love him the more. And as for the monster, it could still its obnoxious whisperings; if Max spent his free time with this sensible, honourable young man and his family, then Miremont need no longer fret about Thursdays and Sundays.

Poor Miremont. If he had looked for danger and found none, he had merely looked in the wrong place.

CHAPTER FOUR

The blow fell at the end of June, two months after their return from Italy, when they were already preparing to leave for Beauvallon. The agent of destruction was, of course, Achille de Tarascon.

How often afterwards Miremont had wished he had pleaded indisposition to his brother-in-law that evening. He had known Tarascon would be present—Constant's latest mistress, Fanny d'Harnoncourt, was a tremendous admirer of the noted poet and wit—but he had counted on avoiding him, which was easy at these gatherings: before supper the imposing figure with the silky black beard and medieval knight's mane, attired outlandishly in purple velvet, was always surrounded by ladies eager for his star to shine upon their salons; and at table, Tarascon, knowing what was required of him and only too ready to oblige, would scorch the early shoots of general conversation with a blaze of epigrams and searing wit.

Miremont, who knew these party tricks by heart, was more than usually bored this evening and, as soon as the chairs were pulled back from the supper table, began to think of making his escape. But, as luck would have it, he was forestalled by his nephew Roland, who—as a result, doubtless, of his latest flame, Mlle de Grès, reserving her smiles for his elder brother Edmond—looked decidedly crestfallen. Since it was in any case abominably hot in the salon, they went out onto the terrace to smoke.

For a few minutes they leant in silence on the balustrade, listening to the chatter of the fountain and inhaling the night air: Miremont fancied he caught the scent of lime blossom drifting on a soft breeze from the Luxembourg Gardens. Then his nose was assailed by a more pungent odour. Tarascon's cologne.

Undoubtedly it was taking pity on lovelorn Roland that had sealed Miremont's fate. Tarascon would surely not have shaken off his admirers except for the chance to speak to Roland alone. But, as it was, before Miremont could excuse himself, Roland was inventing his own need to return indoors at once. Tarascon watched his retreat. Then he heaved a deep sigh.

"Ah, true love! Forever sacrificing to false gods."

Miremont, who had once received Tarascon's full confession of his unrequited passion for Roland and dreaded a repetition, saw in the comte's lugubrious silence a chance to take his leave. But, before he could frame an apology, Tarascon seemed to shrug off his gloom.

"By the way, my dear Miremont," he said, smiling and taking out his cigar case, "Prince Stolytsin wishes to be remembered to you."

Miremont allowed himself a relieved smile in return. They had become acquainted with the prince, he and Max, in Venice. Although it was understood in certain circles that Stolytsin was a close companion of Grand Duke Sergei Alexandrovitch, he had been travelling with the composer Shuvalov and three youths—one a poet, Miremont seemed to recall, and the other two students. The prince, who knew little Russian but spoke perfect French, had proved an entertaining companion and Miremont was glad to have news of him.

"He is here, in Paris?"

"Alas, no, he was passing through last Sunday on his way to Nice. But naturally, wishing him to enjoy the splendours of our great city, I took him to the baths."

At this, uttered in Tarascon's normal orotund tones, Miremont glanced nervously over his shoulder, but fortunately there was no one else on the terrace and the scattered groups now strolling the garden's gravel paths were too distant for the comte's words to carry above the fountain.

"Ah yes, Stolytsin has fond memories of your time in Venice. The sight of your delightful Ganymede could not but recall it."

The breeze from the Luxembourg suddenly blew chill. "I beg your pardon?"

"The vigorous sapling you have planted where the withered trunk of old Legrange once stood."

"Forgive me, I—"

"Of course, he was too preoccupied to notice us—the young make such a business of pleasure."

"My dear Tarascon." Miremont collected himself, for it was not the first time the comte had tried this trick. "If you are saying you saw my secretary in the bathhouse, I fear you are mistaken."

"My dear Miremont, the scar on his temple is quite unmistakable— and that is not his only notable attribute."

"Monsieur, I think you forget yourself!"

But Tarascon brushed aside Miremont's outrage with a laugh. "Anyway, it was all one to us. Since the prince is partial to such things, we soon adjourned to Madame Tonton's, where the corsets and coiffeurs would have put La Pompadour to shame. Besides—" still curved in a smile, Tarascon's moist red lips, fringed by his mustachios and glossy beard, called to mind the foliage of some carnivorous plant "—Stolytsin assured me your lily of the valley had already unfurled his blossoms."

"Oh, for pity's sake! Tarascon! Why do you bother to listen to him?"

This was exactly what Miremont had expected the boy to say. And was Max not right simply to shrug it off?

"But this is the second—no, the third time he has invented some fable about you. Why would he persist in such a thing?"

"Because he's an evil old goat. Since he can't have what he wants, he can't see why anyone else should."

Miremont could never accustom himself to the notion that Achille de Tarascon might envy him. After all, to such as Tarascon he must appear deficient in every respect: a legendary duffer at repartee, blind to fashion, immune to the joys of social success; a man who, incapable of poetry himself, merely plodded in the path of poets; a dunce who, as the comte might see it, preferred the lees to the wine. Yet, of course, he was notably blessed in one way Tarascon was not. And had not Tarascon's lies about Max followed fast upon the wretched man's rejection by Roland? His chagrin had merely sought its nearest target.

Besides, the entire story was absurd. Miremont, for once, knew where Max had been on Sunday night—not at the baths but at the Zhukovskys', where they had been celebrating the naming of the new quartet. After weeks of squabbling, all four members had at last agreed to take the name, not of a Russian musician or composer as was traditional, but of one of their nation's great socialist thinkers, Alexander Herzen, who had been a close friend of Zhukovsky's father. Max had volunteered this at breakfast on Monday in case Miremont wished to congratulate the four when they assembled in the Music Room for their afternoon's practice; and when Miremont had spoken to Zhukovsky he had mentioned the previous night's celebrations.

The lie about Prince Stolytsin was also preposterous. It could not be denied that 'lilies of the valley' rang true, but no doubt Tarascon had seized on Stolytsin's singular code for pleasure to authenticate his tale. Miremont could not remember one occasion in Venice when Max and the prince had been alone together. Nor had there been the slightest opportunity for them to meet secretly: while Miremont and Max had been staying at Princess Orsini's palazzo on the Grand Canal, the

Russians were lodged across the Lagoon on the Lido; any assignation would have involved the boy in a lengthy absence that could not have escaped Miremont's notice.

Yes, like Max, he must shrug the business off. Tarascon had been taking revenge for his, Miremont's, undeserved good fortune.

All the same, after the boy left him that night he could not sleep. If Tarascon's ill-will towards Max were easily dismissed, it was less easy to account for the boy's hatred of Tarascon. And no, hatred was not too strong. Max had admitted the comte had made overtures to him while he was still a footman, but it could hardly have been the first time he had repelled unwelcome advances; it certainly could not account for his visceral loathing of the man. Miremont had believed him completely when he had denied there had ever been relations between them. But now, faced with the persistence of their enmity, Miremont's faith began to waver.

This was the monster's doing, of course, this doubt, this anxious tossing and turning; and the same was true of this other thing—not a doubt exactly, but something, an uncertainty, some occurrence in Venice Miremont could not quite remember. Reason told him to close his mind to these whisperings: was he weary of happiness, that he should be so willing to destroy it? And besides—Prince Stolytsin? In all Miremont's grim fantasies the thieves that stole Max's kisses and rifled his body were as young and beautiful as the boy himself. Stolytsin was stout, balding and older than Miremont, so he hazarded, by a good five years. Max could not have betrayed him with Stolytsin: it was quite impossible.

Dawn was not far off when Miremont, woken by troubling dreams, suddenly saw what haunted him, watched it take shape in the darkness until it was no longer clouded by doubt.

He recalled that when he had first encountered Stolytsin he had not liked him. And he remembered why.

Painfully he forced himself to relive every moment of that meeting at the Caffè Florian, forensically to examine its smallest detail. It had been mid-afternoon and for once he had been alone—Max had gone to renew his worship of the Titians in San Salvatore. Miremont had been at a table in the colonnade, sipping strega and absently leafing through a week-old copy of *Le Figaro*, barely aware of the party at the next table, when a voice had exclaimed: "*Mon Dieu*, monsieur! Is it not all so beautiful?"

As it was early March and still topcoat weather, there were few others taking refreshment outside and, besides, the speaker's use of French could leave Miremont in no doubt that the remark was addressed to him. Turning politely in his chair, he observed three youths and an elderly man with a worn grey face and a shock of white hair. It was this last who had spoken: so much was evident from the rapturous widening of his lipless mouth and from his long bony hand, which took in the basilica, the Doge's Palace, the Palazzo Correr and even the pigeons with one comprehensive passionate gesture; here was an ecstasy so overpowering it was compelled to bear witness, even to a stranger. Miremont, remembering Max's similar intoxication, could not but smile and allow himself to be drawn into conversation.

In any case, the three young men were murmuring amongst themselves in a language he recognised: since the advent of other young men punctuating the glorious emanations from his Music Room with furioso bursts of Russian, he had come to feel a general warmth towards all who spoke it. These four were from Moscow and awaiting the fifth member of their party, who knew Venice well and was acting as their cicerone.

In due course introductions were made. Miremont could not remember the names of the three youths—indeed he had struggled to recall them at the time: he only recollected that the poet was the beauty of the three and that one of the students was the nephew of the white-haired man, Vassily Shuvalov, whose opera *Potëmkin* had been acclaimed in Paris last autumn.

By now Miremont had realised it was not merely the sound of Russian that had thawed his reserve. Shuvalov's manner was as overt as Tarascon's, yet here, away from family and acquaintance, safely on foreign soil, Miremont felt less threatened by these affectations. When Max appeared they would no doubt know Miremont for one of their own, if Shuvalov had not deduced it already, but this realisation was strangely comforting: it would be a relief, just for once, to abandon pretence.

He had been indulging in these thoughts, as he recalled, when the missing member of the party, Prince Stolytsin, had arrived. Miremont remembered being struck at the time by the prince's brutal masculinity, his bull neck and his hands clad, despite his bald pate, even above the knuckles in a thick dark pelt. Again introductions were made and Stolytsin, courteous and charming, pulled out a chair beside Miremont, summoning the waiter to draw their two tables together. He said he had just been to see the Titians in San Salvatore and Miremont had been about to remark upon the coincidence, since his secretary was also visiting the church with the same purpose, when the arrival of the waiter and the business of the tables cut him short.

But anyway here was Max, walking across the square in a flutter of pigeons. Miremont had hung back from presenting his secretary until the prince had disengaged himself from the waiter: Max had smiled and bowed his head politely—and the prince had snubbed him. He had nodded a curt 'monsieur' at Max, then immediately turned to recall the waiter.

Miremont's loathing of snobbery rose up, his resentment of this false division between himself and his lover. By what right did the prince smile charmingly upon the Russian boys, yet slight Max, who was more than their equal in refinement and intelligence? And what of Max himself, whose pride must feel the insult still more keenly? Miremont was sickened by his new acquaintance; he would ask for his bill at once.

Yet, oddly, Max seemed unconcerned by the slight, seizing the chance to practise his Russian with the three boys, smiling, laughing. And stranger still—very strange, now Miremont recalled it—the prince seemed in minutes to forget his contempt for a mere secretary, joking that Max spoke his native language better than he did and showing the boy the same courtesy he showed Miremont.

And thus the prince had continued in the few days they had all spent together, so that Miremont quite forgave him. He had not flirted with Max as Shuvalov had, nor shown the slightest spark of desire. Max was clearly not—damn Tarascon!—one of Stolytsin's lilies. The prince's initial rudeness must have been the result of momentary distraction: no doubt he had been irritated by the waiter. Yet Miremont, as he agonisingly rehearsed the episode again and again, knew this would not do.

What if the prince's reaction to the boy had arisen, not from snobbery or distraction, but from surprise?

They had both claimed to have visited San Salvatore. Max had crossed the square diagonally from the Orologio, as though he had come via the Mercerie; Miremont could not be sure, for he had been talking to Shuvalov at the time, but he thought the prince had approached from the same direction. Max had appeared some five minutes after the prince and, if they had encountered each other at the church, would have been able to recognise Stolytsin as he walked across the square, so that his shock at seeing the prince in Miremont's company would long have been suppressed by the time he reached the Caffè Florian. The prince, on the other hand, had been in conversation with the waiter with his back to the clock tower and could not have seen Max until he had turned so that Miremont could introduce them. Was it Miremont's imagination, embroidering with hindsight, or had Stolytsin's eyes widened for an instant before he had responded so abruptly? Moments later, his presence of mind recovered, he would have been able to play his part every bit as perfectly as Max.

Was this why the prince had never shown interest in this particular lily of the valley? Because, as Tarascon had claimed, he had already sampled its delights?

Oh God, no! This was the monster again, in its worst incarnation. Max had been gone scarcely more than half an hour. How could he have walked to San Salvatore, studied the paintings, encountered Stolytsin, found a room, made love, then walked back again to the Piazza San Marco, all in thirty minutes? Except that Miremont remembered his own shameful encounters in the Bois de Boulogne, before his love for Max had redeemed him. Max and Stolytsin had not needed a room, they had not 'made love': they had found some cranny, some doorway, some pissoir in which they had performed a brutal cursory act. And then they had parted, two strangers who had never expected to see each other again.

Bile rose in Miremont's throat. It could not be. When he thought of their own lovemaking, its exquisite intimacies and the tenderness of its aftermath, it could not be. Did he not recall that Tarascon had lied before? If he had not believed the boy had robbed Tarascon in the Champs-Élysées, why should he believe this fiction about Stolytsin?

Yet other memories of Italy pressed in upon him, however he tried to thrust them away. In Rome, at the Palatine, he and Max had lost each other for nearly an hour; in Florence the boy had been an unconscionable time buying postcards; in Naples, too, he had unaccountably disappeared. He had always returned with a plausible explanation—he had taken a wrong turning, could not find the street seller he had seen earlier, had been distracted by a band of child musicians. Miremont had thought nothing of these absences. Why should he? The boy had never appeared awkward or guilty. And besides, Miremont had trusted him. For all his agonising jealousy when they were apart, he had trusted him absolutely when they were together.

He had trusted Max even though he knew he was a practised liar. Even though the boy was secretive and had undoubtedly told untruths about his past, even though at their very first meeting he had deceived him, like a fool he had chosen to believe the lad's instincts were sound. He had trusted their affinity, the apparent harmony of their life together, their love—for, yes, even if Max could seldom find the words, Miremont had persuaded himself the boy loved him a little—he had allowed all this to convince him that his lover would not lie to him, or that, if he did, he would know it.

Of course he had never noticed Aline's infidelity either: his first knowledge of that had come with the shock of her flight. But he had not loved or even liked Aline: they had scarcely shared a life, let alone a bed. Whereas he and Max still took increasing pleasure in each other—or so it seemed to Miremont. Yet perhaps he had been obtuse there too: for him the nightly anticipation of familiar sensations only heightened desire and remade pleasure afresh, but perhaps it was no longer enough for the boy. Perhaps, skilled dissembler that he was, Max had concealed a growing boredom, which Miremont, blinded by love, had failed to discern.

Not all his senses had been dulled: at least he now knew his jealousy was justified. Yet there was small comfort in this, for he could not but wonder if he had wished betrayal upon himself by imagining it so often. Besides, the monster's phantasms were pallid compared with the reality. For if Max, without an apparent qualm, could deceive him when he was with him, what must he do when he was on his own? Miremont's nausea overcame him.

CHAPTER FIVE

Mercifully, upon stumbling back, weak and ill, to his bed, Miremont seemed to have drifted into a fitful sleep, so that, when he heard Thomas drawing the curtains and opened his eyes to the sun's optimistic rays, he could convince himself that he had merely suffered a nightmare. All the same, after Thomas had helped him into his dressing gown, he hesitated before going into his sitting room to take breakfast with the boy.

Yet what had he feared to see? Max was unchanged: there was nothing questionable in his smile of greeting, no hesitation in his embrace. It was as if they had never spoken of Achille de Tarascon. Only after the boy had inspected Miremont more closely did his brows narrow, yet Miremont could not deny this betokened solicitude.

"A bad night?"

"It is nothing." Miremont found he was almost afraid to speak. "Indigestion. It will pass." He reached for the newspaper in terror that Max would question him further, but the boy merely grinned sympathetically and addressed himself to the post.

To speak would make it real, to speak would mean saying, hearing words that could not be taken back, that would change everything forever. Miremont remained entrenched behind his newspaper while the footman, Philippe, poured coffee. He continued silent once Philippe had taken his leave. It seemed to him that if he could refrain from speaking for long enough the mosquitoes swarming in his head would fly off and all would be as it had been before.

But Max, while he had borne the silence with understanding, could not avoid noticing Miremont's uncharacteristic distaste for his coffee and brioche.

"Armand?"

Miremont gave what he hoped was a preoccupied grunt. But Max was not to be discouraged.

"Armand, should you like me to fetch Doctor Gérard?"

This forced Miremont to lower the newspaper. "I have said—it is indigestion."

"But, dear heart, you look dreadful. Perhaps you have been poisoned by something."

This was indeed an unfortunate choice of words. But it was the way the boy reached out to touch his arm that made Miremont snap, the affection, the concern, which appeared entirely sincere but must be a callous pretence. Miremont jerked himself free. Did Max believe he was such an old fool that he could be soothed into forgetting Tarascon's allegations?

"I want you to tell me the truth about Stolytsin."

The boy seemed genuinely taken aback. "Oh, not that again! I thought we had agreed—"

"We agreed nothing."

Max sighed. "My dear Armand, we must find the antidote to Tarascon before his bite proves fatal."

"You always say that. You always blame Tarascon. But now I want the truth."

"Oh, for heaven's sake—!"

"Did you meet Stolytsin at San Salvatore and have—" Miremont fumbled for the appropriate word "—relations with him?"

Did Max's eyes flicker at the mention of the church? If they did, he recovered himself with laughter. "Stolytsin? That fat old bulldog?"

"Did you go to the bathhouse on Sunday night?"

"You know I was celebrating with Mitya."

"You came in very late."

The boy's face hardened as he drew the inevitable inference that Miremont had been spying on him. "Some of us went on afterwards to the Closerie des Lilas."

"And did you then go to the bathhouse?"

"Well, I suppose you are perfectly free to cross-question Mitya. And make us both look ridiculous."

Miremont knew that Max could safely assume he would not interrogate Zhukovsky, both because Zhukovsky, as Max's closest friend, would undoubtedly lie on his behalf and because to ask such questions would be to raise others concerning his own relationship with Max. This knowledge filled Miremont with impotent rage.

He brought his fist down on the table so that the cups clattered in their saucers. "I—just—want—the—truth!"

"The truth?" The boy's lip curled. Rising from his chair, he began gathering up the envelopes and letters beside his plate. "Since you clearly prefer Monsieur de Tarascon's version, there is no more to be said."

*

Miremont did not ride that morning and remained closeted in his study, where he took a lonely luncheon. As the hours passed he grew increasingly ashamed of himself: he felt polluted by that frightening anger of his, which he had not known he possessed until he had fallen in love with Max. It was true that Max had not given him straightforward answers, yet what else could he expect, since his manner had been calculated to raise the poor lad's defences? And besides, what answers had he sought? Had he wanted, could he have borne anything other than a denial? And was that not what Max had given him, even if it had not amounted to an outright 'no'? In any case, the more Miremont considered his suspicions about Venice, the more he could see they were the megrims of insomnia. And now the poor boy believed he no longer trusted him. It pained Miremont to recall Max's look of disdain, yet he could not but accept he had deserved it.

The boy was working at his table in the library. He raised his head as Miremont entered but his glance was without warmth.

"My dear boy—"

"If you are in need of those quotations from *Metamorphoses*, I am halfway through the list. But by all means take what I have found so far."

Miremont stared at the proffered sheets. It was extraordinary, he thought, how precious the boy was to him, so that even the sight of that familiar hand with its boldly formed letters and elegant slant had the power to move him.

"My darling boy, please forgive me. I do not know what came over me this morning."

Max's expression softened. "Clearly something disagreed with you."

"It must have been last night's lobster. Yes, undoubtedly the lobster. I shall ask Madame Mercier to speak to Madame Dussardier."

"But you are recovered now?"

"Yes, dear boy, I am quite myself again."

"Well, that is a relief." Max pushed back his chair and came out from behind his table.

As they kissed, Miremont wondered how he could ever have doubted the boy. When they drew apart he took Max's hand and pressed it to his heart.

"You must know how dearly I love you."

"And I, Armand, am very fond of you."

Fond? Miremont felt it would be a lesser cruelty if the boy could bring himself to say the words he longed for, even if they were untrue. Why was it, the monster whispered, that Max could not tell this lie when he lied readily about so much else?

Releasing the boy's hand, he took a step away from him. "You must understand, I cannot bear that there should be any deceit between us."

Max looked at him incredulously.

"All I ask, dear boy, is the truth."

"The truth, Armand, is that you would do well to give up lobster."

"Please, Max, if it is not as Tarascon says—"

"And oysters. They can be the devil for men of your constitution."

"All I require is a simple answer."

"Also anchovies, I am told—"

"All I ask from you, Max, is a simple 'yes' or 'no'!"

Thus far the boy had appeared merely exasperated, but all at once his eyes were blazing. "And if I obliged you, would you believe me? Or would you continue to lap up Tarascon's venom? Would you continue to spy on me? Would your ridiculous jealousy be satisfied if I told you I tried never to lie to you? Or would you fall upon my words and pick them to shreds like some old crow with a carcass?"

As ever, Miremont recoiled from the boy's scorn. He could not but be chastened by the justice of Max's accusation: perhaps the monster never would be appeased. Yet, at the same time, he was all too aware they had rehearsed this argument before.

"I did not ask if you had ever lied to me. I asked you to tell me the truth."

"Ah yes, the great god Truth. Your daily worship. But what truth? Whose truth? What if there is no simple truth, no 'yes' and 'no', no simple answer?"

The chill of premonition seized Miremont. "I—I do not understand."

But Max had turned away, was at the window staring out at the courtyard and, from the set of his jaw, seemed to be trying to collect himself, as if he knew he had gone too far.

Feeling an unsteadiness in his legs, Miremont slumped into Max's chair. "I do not understand you," he repeated weakly.

Max sighed. "Dear Armand, you are still such an innocent."

"If you hope, by insulting me—"

"It is not an insult. But it does mean that you are apt to…" Turning from the window, Max came over to Miremont and, shifting a pile of books, settled himself on the corner of his worktable. Miremont, staring up at him in horrified fascination, sensed that he was about to lean forward and squeeze his shoulder. But the boy evidently thought better of it.

"Look, let us suppose for the sake of argument I had—what was your exquisite turn of phrase?— 'relations with' Stolytsin—"

"Oh God, no!" Miremont turned his head away.

"I repeat, for the sake of argument. Would it matter?"

Miremont looked back at him aghast. "Of course it would matter. How can you ask that?"

"Yet it would have nothing to do with what is between us."

"We love each other. At least, I love you and once upon a time I was foolish enough to believe you might love me."

"But this is a different thing entirely. You must know that. Compared with our life together, it is quite meaningless."

A fresh access of nausea temporarily deprived Miremont of speech.

Yet the boy was smiling. "Opportunities arise and it seems a shame to waste them. But it has no more significance than—than coughing or sneezing."

Once again Miremont recalled his furtive excursions to the Bois, the boys' faces pinched with cold and distaste, the squalid impersonality of those transactions. Of course in the Bois money had changed hands. But the experience must compare in its brutishness and he recalled how it had defiled him. Max, perched, legs crossed, on the end of the table, was so close to him that the boy's left foot almost touched his calf, and suddenly Miremont could not bear this proximity. He pushed his chair back.

"That is disgusting!"

"Is it?" The boy had the temerity to laugh. "Then you do not recall our first meeting?"

Of course Miremont recalled it: the copse, the waterfall, the pool where they had swum, the outcrop of rock that had sheltered their lovemaking, the moment in which Miremont had been made whole, at last at peace with what was natural to him. He not only remembered it, he held the memory sacred and would not stand to hear it profaned.

"How dare you! How dare you suggest that this was—what was your repulsive phrase?—no more than sneezing or farting!"

"It was an opportunity, Armand, and you seized it. I grant you, it turned out rather differently. People do not discuss Racine or Catullus at the baths—or indeed talk much at all. But let us not forget you were happy not to know my name or divulge yours, and you certainly never expected to see me again."

This forced Miremont to retrieve a rather less agreeable memory—of how he had failed to recognise the footman who waited on him at table while he was staying at Catherine de Claireville's château. The boy had deliberately reminded him of this in order to mortify him, so that he would submit meekly to being betrayed and humiliated; he could not but recall Aline, how she had twisted his words and actions against him to much the same effect.

He stared up at Max. Poised gracefully on his perch, one arm extended to support himself, his head a little inclined, his long legs swinging, he seemed as beautiful as ever. But this beauty, it now appeared, was a shell.

"Why?" he burst out. "Why have you done this?"

Max shrugged. "The risk, I suppose. It's exciting. But you are not exactly averse to that yourself, old thing. Remember our bad behaviour at Madame de Claireville's? Or that time in Naples? And there have been other occasions I could mention—"

"No!" There it was again, Miremont's actions were to be turned against him, he was to be bludgeoned into believing that expressions of enduring love were no different from a crude act with a complete stranger. And all the while there was this dreadful flippancy in the boy's manner—calling Miremont 'old thing', smiling, shrugging—as if his treachery were of no account.

"No! I do not wish to know why you let Stolytsin suck your cock in some urinal. I want to know why you have betrayed me."

"Armand, I have already said that it has nothing to do with—"

"Why do you despise me so?"

"Old thing, you know I have the deepest respect for you."

The boy had swung his legs from the table and, in fear that he would try to embrace him, Miremont shot from his chair. "Do not call me that! And do not touch me! Do not come near me unless you can explain to me why you have made a mockery of the last two years and desecrated everything I hold most dear."

"Oh for pity's sake! These are big words for something entirely trivial."

"Trivial? That you are utterly faithless?"

"I am not your wife, Armand, I have not sworn eternal fidelity. And neither have you. Perhaps you should try the baths yourself. You would very likely enjoy it."

Blind fury seized Miremont. He took a step towards the boy. His right arm began to rise as if by its own volition, it was only in the nick of time he mastered himself. Pressing both arms tightly to his sides and clenching his fists, he stood transfixed by the effort of control.

Max met his eyes for a moment. Then he smiled sarcastically. "Would monsieur like me to fetch his whip?"

Once, under extreme provocation, when Max, riding headlong, had nearly killed himself and then made light of his recklessness, Miremont had struck him across the face with his riding crop. It was, in Miremont's whole life, the act of which he was most ashamed. The boy's taunt, the horrifying realisation that, in another instant, if he had not caught himself, he would have repeated the abomination, the disgrace of it—all should have stayed his anger. But, as he rushed from the library and up the stairs to his own apartments, his feelings of shame merely compounded his fury, until, careering through his sitting room into his study, he stood, shuddering, breathless, blind to the familiar comforts of his surroundings, yet looking around wildly, desperate to release his suffocating rage. Seizing a book from the table, he hurled it at the wall with a howl.

There was a crash and the sound of splintering glass as the book struck a Daumier cartoon hanging above the bookcase; another crash as the tome, rebounding onto the parquet, dislodged in its passage a porcelain figure; a third as the picture slid to earth behind the bookcase.

Miremont stared at the destruction. The book—it was Lemprière's *Classical Dictionary*—lay with its binding shattered; heaven knew if broken glass had torn the Daumier in its descent; and as for the figurine, its fragments were dispersed across the parquet, over the rug, beneath the chairs and table, the head here, an arm there, unrecognisable shards and flakes everywhere, as if in the aftermath of shellfire.

The figure, a cherub disguised in a lion skin as Hercules leaning on his club, had been of Derby porcelain and of no great value—one of the lion's paws was chipped and there was a fine crack in its base; yet it had been a treasure of Miremont's mother's, a childhood present from her own mother, his English grandmother. As a child himself, when he was permitted into his mother's boudoir, he had been allowed to play with it while she told him stories of Hercules slaying the Hydra or stealing the apples of the Hesperides; he recollected how carefully he had held it and how surprisingly light it had felt.

Heavily he got down on his knees and, despite the futility of the task, began retrieving the pieces. Pointless, mindless destruction. All because of Max—but the boy did not care. He was indifferent to the pain his heartless candour inflicted, unashamed of his faithlessness, devoid of conscience. Love? Of course Max could not say the word, he had no notion of its meaning. Affection, loyalty, understanding, tenderness—to him they were all meaningless words.

Miremont recalled how he had suspected the boy's motives at the start of their affair. Although not before his suspicions had caused much needless pain, he had convinced himself they were unworthy; yet perhaps he should have heeded his first instincts. Max had hated service, had always been anxious to better himself. Even from that day beside the waterfall, the day Miremont held so sacred, the boy's charm must have concealed calculation. He had worked upon Miremont until he had wormed his way into his heart.

Although Miremont had filled the tray of his inkwell with porcelain fragments, although his back ached and a shard had sliced his thumb, wherever he looked there were more tiny pieces. He slumped into a chair, buried his face in his bloodied hands and wept.

CHAPTER SIX

Max preferred not to frequent the bathhouse, for the very reason that it was too public. It had been his friend Hyppolite who, deciding their customary haunt, the Green Monkey, had grown intolerably dull, had persuaded him to ignore his better judgement. Of course, if he had seen the comte de Tarascon there, nothing would have prevented him from leaving at once. But he had not seen him, nor Prince Stolytsin. Curse them both for being so outrageously indiscreet! But, above all, curse M. de M: if he had been prepared to leave the thing alone, he could have continued happily oblivious. But no, as usual he must have the truth, and now there was this endless 'why, why, why?' Yet the truth was, Max did not know why. He could not explain his willingness to hazard all that was most agreeable in his life for a few trivial moments of excitement. And he was damned if he would analyse his motives as if they were a passage from Ovid.

You might look at Max as Armand de Miremont did, and see an untroubled smile and a clear brow, but nowadays these owed much to the boy's lifelong training in hiding his feelings. In fact he was torn by contradictions. Matters that had appeared simple to the sixteen-year-old who had launched himself upon Paris and relatively straightforward to his nineteen-year-old self were now fraught with awkward complications that seemed to increase the longer he stayed at the Hôtel de Miremont. He scorned virtue, yet longed for honour; he aspired to ruthlessness, but his instincts defied him; he repudiated God, yet felt steeped in sin; he yearned for freedom, yet hankered after the security of the cloister, in spite of the beatings and betrayals he had suffered there; he could say the word 'love' when he did not mean it, but it stuck in his throat if there were any danger he did. He endeavoured to deafen himself to the opposing voices that assailed him and for the most part was successful; but sometimes at night, finally alone and wakeful in his own room, he would feel their conflict as a physical sensation, as though his body could no longer endure to harbour so much chaos; and when he at last slept, the nightmares he had suffered from childhood would return with full force.

He was not lying or even twisting the truth when he spoke of his affection and respect for Armand de Miremont. He had begun by thinking the old fellow naive but had gradually been won over by his rigorous integrity. Of course, they could be infuriating, those sentimental notions of honour and duty that belonged to some ancient chivalric era, fitting no doubt in the first marquis under Henri II, but unworldly in the twelfth; yet they seemed so inseparable from the old boy's generous heart and unassuming dignity as to be the fount of his being. While Max, for his own part, had foresworn God and all moral strictures, he was not unaware of the torments of conscience monsieur had endured on his account: he had taken a vow to protect the old boy's treasured honour, and he would hold to it.

He would hold to it even though this was profoundly inconvenient, for it was not what he had planned. His life's aim had been—must still be—to seize the gift the Fates had bestowed on him in his sixteenth year. One day he would be raised high, one day—confound the haughty denizens of the Faubourg Saint-Germain!—dukes would bow to him. Thus, when he had seduced M. le marquis, he had not been solely impelled by the old boy's noble qualities: he had also hoped monsieur might use the influence of his rank to smooth his path with the illustrious personages he must eventually convince. That this would involve a degree of duplicity had not at first troubled him. But, as he had come to know M. de M better, he had seen the impossibility of it: he could not ask the old fellow to assist him in perpetrating a fraud.

Max was grateful for his life at the Hôtel de Miremont. He would have been the first to agree that he had improved under monsieur's tutelage. The fencing, the riding, the shooting practice at Beauvallon, the travels in Italy—he had entered service with the misplaced hope of acquiring the manners and habits of a gentleman, but what he had learnt as a footman would have deceived no one, still less the notables who were so essential to his grand plan; yet now he defied these faceless personages to question his breeding. As for the other defects in his education, the books, thoughts, ideas denied to him during his schooldays in the cloister, the deprivations he had sought to remedy by the light of a filched candle in the footmen's dormitory— if monsieur's love of intellectual debate were not enough, the library at the Hôtel de Miremont offered more possibilities than he could explore in a lifetime.

There was no urgent need for him to leave: the scar on his forehead might now be six years old, but if he were to pass it off as a childhood injury another year or two would do no harm. There was still much he could learn from the old boy. And, besides, it was not disagreeable to be loved, to compel something more than transient lust; and if he would not go so far as to admit to the 'weakness' of love himself, he could not deny he would miss the old fellow badly.

Yet the thought of his lost freedom also plagued him. On the rare occasions Max had possessed this jewel, it must be said its lustre had dimmed. But this he could put down to misfortune; now its brilliance mocked him for failing to pursue what should be the focus of his ambition. And there were other reasons to guard his independence.

He might not have monsieur's antediluvian sense of honour, but he was not without pride. The fencing lessons, his horse Pretender, the luxury which had attended their Italian travels, indeed the very clothes he stood up in—all were provided by the old boy's beneficence. At least the title of secretary gave evidence that he worked for his living—but when did he ever have occasion to spend his wages? He was deeply indebted to the old fellow, but indebtedness was not a comfortable condition.

Curse Fabrice! Or, he should say, Hyppolite (Max still struggled not to call his former comrade-in-arms by his footman's *nomme de guerre*). Max might brush aside his jibes and, true, in Hyppolite's case, they were more often cries of envy, yet his pride recoiled at the very notion he was 'kept'. And that Mitya Zhukovsky might share Polly's belief was too mortifying to contemplate. But what else was Max to make of that business over the banknote?

Mitya knew Max too well to be under any illusions about his relationship with the old boy. It was clear that, in telling monsieur the story of the loan, he had known exactly where the money had come from and was making some point at Max's expense. In Florence Max had spent the entire sum Mitya had repaid on a present for the old fellow, a tiny Etruscan bronze, acquired after lengthy haggling with a dealer in the Via Maggio (although he had told M. de M he had found it in the flea market). Thus he had retrieved a modicum of self-respect. But the painful certainty remained that his best friend thought him not much better than a renter.

Not that he should give a damn what anyone thought. Did his heroes—Alexander, Augustus, Napoleon—fret about the opinion of others while they were conquering empires? Had his childhood taught him nothing? Not for him attachments, scruples, duties, loyalties— throw off these restraints and the world was yours. So had thought his sixteen-year-old self. But now the world, declining to be gained so easily, had tempted and confused him.

*

Although monsieur had retired to his apartments 'indisposed', and had even cancelled chess with Dr Gérard, Max saw no reason why he should not take his Thursday evening as usual. Yet, since he still seethed with resentment, he was in no frame of mind for the Zhukovskys: although Mitya would be working, Mme Zhukovskaya, ever grateful for M. le marquis' patronage of the quartet, was bound to enquire after the old boy. It was a relief, too, that Hyppolite's new situation as manservant to a paper manufacturer out at Auteuil allowed him only Sundays off: Polly was a good fellow, but not the best company when one's nerves were on edge. Later, of course, Max would visit the Monkey, pay his usual respects to Old Jouvert, the mysterious éminence grise of the world of service whose protégé he had once been, and then see what the night offered: in present circumstances, it seemed his bounden duty to take full advantage of whatever arose.

But meanwhile he must dine. Turning his back on Montparnasse and the Quartier Latin, he crossed the river by the Pont Neuf and, skirting the Louvre, set off towards the grand boulevards in the hope that the walk might purge his anger. Yet the strolling crowds taking enjoyment of the fine summer evening curbed his stride: escaping into a brasserie in the Boulevard des Italiens, he chose at random from the menu, then was too restless to eat more than a few mouthfuls; even tobacco and his customary *mazagran* could not quell the bitter thoughts that made his temples throb. Paying his bill, he set out again, northwards, with no firm destination.

He had done no wrong. He had meant it absolutely when he had told monsieur that his adventures had no bearing on their life together: it was absurd to compare them. There were a great many things he would rather walk through fire than confess to the old fellow—Dom Sébastien, for instance, or the Father Superior's 'detentions', or how, during his first poverty-stricken days in Paris, M. de Tarascon had half-killed him—but, once he had realised his evasions were useless in the face of that maddening 'why, why, why', he had tried to tell the truth about the bathhouse. At least, it was the truth as he saw it and he had convinced himself it was something monsieur could grasp. How could he not have foreseen this was foolish?

Even so, it was hard to comprehend the old boy's revulsion. Innocent though he was, he must surely know that for most men like themselves this quick slaking of lust was normal. At least it had been for Max before their affair. Furthermore, as Max had reminded him, it was hypocritical to deny such encounters sparked a thrill the comforts of the bedroom could not offer.

Yet now Max's harmless adventures were to be given a grandiloquent name: 'infidelity'. This was preposterous. No one could have honoured their shared intimacies more than Max, no one could have guarded them with more delicacy and discretion. To talk of 'desecration' and 'betrayal' was insulting. Damn the old fellow's rosy notions of love, damn his crazy jealousy! Was what monsieur had of him not enough? Must he spy on him too, ordain what he did with his free time, claim ownership of him, mind and body, drain his very lifeblood?

"When you love and are loved, you are not free." The old fellow had said that, last summer when Max had come a cropper on Pretender, the day he had struck him with his whip. At the time it had been the blow that had rankled, the insult to Max's pride, as well as the memory it had evoked of Dom Sébastien. But now it was those words that lingered.

Freedom—that was the nub of it. If the old fellow demanded an explanation, here it was: Max was not betraying monsieur by asserting his inalienable right to freedom, for to do otherwise was to betray himself.

For what was love anyway? Words heartfelt one day, meaningless the next: Dom Sébastien's caressing hands all at once clenched into fists. Love was the betrayer, despite the claims and demands it made. Shit! The times Max had trusted the old boy, only to fall victim to monsieur's moral scruples. And yet, like a fool, he had let himself be lulled into trusting again. Damn monsieur! He was the deceiver, demanding Max give up his freedom for a will-o'-the-wisp—

Max had walked on, oblivious of his surroundings and the gathering dusk, but, as he stepped out to cross the road, his train of thought was rudely cut off by a close shave with a passing carriage. Staggering back, he slipped, fell, and watched the wheels, of terrifying dimensions, crashing over the cobbles a whisker from his nose, while from above came the whinnying of the horses and the curses of the driver and, in the gutter, when he dared catch breath, the fulsome stench of dung embraced him. Thankfully the throng in the boulevards was absent here and the lighting sparse; there was no witness to his humiliation as he picked himself up, rescued his hat and brushed himself down.

He was, he realised, where the Rue Bréda met the Rue de Laval and the Rue Frochot, near the Place Pigalle. The accident, while it had reduced his anger not a whit—indeed the indignity had stoked it—had nonetheless sobered him a little for, although he was uninjured, this brush with fate had shaken him.

There was an estaminet just off the Place Pigalle he had frequented years ago when he was baron Reinhardt's footman, mainly because its squalor was in pleasing contrast to the overblown magnificence of the banker's mansion. If he repaired there, he could rest for a while and consider his future. For, brought to himself, he saw that this raging about love and betrayal was futile. If his freedom were precious to him, there could be no argument: it might be sooner than he had wished, monsieur's insults and accusations might have forced his hand, but this was his moment to leave the Hôtel de Miremont.

The café was much as he recalled it, a coalhole of a place stinking of sweat, aniseed and *caporal*, its deficiencies harshly revealed by twin overhead globes of jaundiced light; the heavy-eyed *patron* slouched morosely behind his zinc counter; at one table a contingent of navvies, still in their smocks, was engaged in violent argument while at another a rowdy card game was in progress; with her stare fixed on some distant phantom, a solitary woman in a rusty black hat sat before her absinthe.

This drinking den had never been welcoming, yet Max was unprepared as he entered for the silence that fell. Even if he had failed to notice the hostile eyes anatomising his silk topper and the modish cut of his coat, or had hoped the residue of the gutter on his trousers would be taken in mitigation, that silence would have impelled him to leave. Baron Reinhardt's footman in his stovepipe hat and ancient frock coat, outsider though he was, had slid into a corner without comment. Damn monsieur, Max thought, as he retreated hastily. Damn, damn monsieur, he repeated, even though, whatever charges he might level against the old boy, it was hardly reasonable to condemn him for a transformation he, Max, had keenly desired.

The Place Pigalle was not lacking in other more salubrious establishments but he had lost the desire for company. He struck out north again, towards the Butte Montmartre.

If he were to go, he must not hesitate, he must go tomorrow. But where to? Obviously he could not put his grand plan into action immediately, he must take his time, use caution. Thanks to the old boy's burdensome generosity rather than any providence of his own, he had savings enough to rent a room for a while. But, in the meantime, there was tomorrow night to consider.

Once he would not have hesitated to ask the Zhukovskys to put him up. But now Mitya was in and out of the Hôtel de Miremont as if he lived there. Whatever excuse Max gave for leaving the old boy, his arrival would cause embarrassment: Mitya's opinion of him would sink still lower, for his friend would feel compromised, wondering if he were obliged to take sides; Mme Zhukovskaya would be distressed; and Vera—well, Max was already out of favour with Vera.

Perhaps M. de M could also be blamed for this, for she had been distant ever since they had run into the old boy at the Cirque d'Hiver. Or perhaps Max should blame Lyudin, for a few days later she had suddenly announced that the cellist had proposed to her and when, quite naturally, Max had been appalled, she had enquired by what right he objected. "By a brother's," had been his obvious reply. Whereupon she had given him a look he could not fathom, before turning away with a shrill laugh; ever since then, though she had rejected Lyudin's proposal, while not exactly cold to Max, she had ceased calling him 'Maxim Alexandrovitch'.

As far as he had ever felt safe, he had felt so at the Zhukovskys': they had offered him a world, far removed from the rest of his existence, in which he could let his guard down. But now monsieur had merged the boundaries of this territory with his own domain and Max was in exile.

Yet—he could not escape it—there was a shaming note of self-pity in these execrations. He had by now reached the steep flight of steps that would take him to the summit of the Butte Montmartre, while above him rose the bulk of the unfinished Sacré-Coeur, its domes pallid in the moonlight, its scaffolded bell tower like a giant mushroom in a monstrous basket. As if determined to crush all inner frailty, he pounded up the steps, and, pausing to recover his breath only for an instant, pressed on past the lighted windows of the Place du Tertre until he found solitude, a straggling tree and a low wall that afforded a view of the city. Gratefully he leant against the wall and took out his cigarette case.

Before him was Paris, a vortex of light, its distant blazing centre seeming to draw every spark from its periphery, the constellations of Pigalle, Batignolles and Clichy, the astral trails of trains shunting in and out of the Gare Saint-Lazare and, even here in the outer darkness, like tiny stars at the very edge of the hemisphere, the flicker of street lamps, the glow of attic windows, the pinpoints of carriage lanterns weaving like fireflies through the black thicket of chimneys.

From the slopes beneath came faint music, raucous laughter, revellers from Le Chat Noir and Le Moulin de la Galette, reminding Max he had intended to call in at the Monkey. Well, he had no heart for that now: the Monkey lay an hour and a half's walk away, across the river, on the far side of that dazzling light.

He recalled Balzac's Rastignac, who had looked out on the city from Père-Lachaise and challenged it to war. Max threw down his gauntlet too. He would not lack a place in the world. However false the city had played him in the past, it would yield up the destiny the Fates had promised him. First thing tomorrow he would inform monsieur of his departure, then set out to look for lodgings. That blaze on the horizon that challenged the moon and stars was the beacon proclaiming his glorious future.

Yet, now the decision was made, he felt a pang of desolation. This feebleness was undoubtedly caused by the sudden exhaustion that assailed him. It certainly could have nothing to do with a familiar nagging feeling that refused to be vanquished, as always proving stronger than the renewed fury it aroused. Damn, damn, damn monsieur! Why was it that Max could never quarrel with him without feeling he too had behaved badly?

Gazing out from his eyrie, Max no longer saw Paris, but M. de M's look when he had taunted him about the whip. That had been cruel: Max knew the tortures of remorse the poor old boy had suffered and, besides, every line and pleat of that crumpled, mobile, all-too-expressive face had declared the old fellow's resolve never to lose control again. Max wished he could unsay those words. And certain other things he had said...

But all the same... Why the hell should he feel guilty? How could he be accused of betrayal? As he had told the old fellow, he had never lied to him. True, he had not been entirely frank with him either, but then he was not like Polly, who was never happier than when confiding the minutest detail of his own affairs: restraint had always been instinctive to him, even before the need for secrecy had been driven into him like a nail by that terrible time—months, years, he could not say exactly—when he and the Other had been captives. It was natural to him to keep his life in separate boxes, M. de M in one, the Zhukovskys in another, Polly and the Monkey in a third, while a fourth, securely padlocked, contained the Other, the scar, and his life before the cloister. If he had been less than open with the old boy, it was because secrecy, like freedom, was essential to him.

Yet he could not help thinking that the old boy would have another name for it. And perhaps he had been deceitful, even if he had told no outright lies. Take his silence about Polly: however fond of him Max was, there was no denying his friend gave off the aura of the Monkey; when Max and M. de M had nearly run across him in the Luxembourg Gardens, Max had been relieved that Polly, with surprising discretion, had taken the other path. And, as for his reluctance to introduce Mitya to the old boy—the Zhukovskys had been not just his refuge, but his alibi.

Yes, of course he had deceived the old boy. And, when he had told himself M. de M would understand, he had known, deep down, that he was deceiving himself too. Shit, he had only to think back to last New Year, when monsieur had been away on his duty visit to Burgundy. As it had turned out, Max had panicked for nothing, it had been a false alarm. But he remembered his turmoil before he had steeled himself to visit Polly's quack: how was he to tell monsieur, what if he had infected the old fellow? Even now he shuddered at the horror of it.

After that he had resolved to be more cautious for a while. So why, then, had he taken such stupid risks in Italy? Had he wished to be found out? If so, the reason was obscure to him. Was he already seeking an excuse to leave? Did he want the old boy to think the worst of him? God, if he valued Mitya's good opinion, he valued M. de M's still more.

He could not share monsieur's high-minded, exclusive notion of love and he did not understand his jealousy. But, if he could not love the old fellow in the way he wanted, his heart was not closed to him: it might be a weakness, but he could not overcome it. If he did not know the answer to 'why, why, why', at least this was certain—the last thing he had intended was to hurt the old boy.

Max drew miserably upon his cigarette. He had not wanted to hurt Armand, yet he had hurt him. For that, if for nothing else, he felt ashamed.

CHAPTER SEVEN

By next morning the pleasant routines of the Hôtel de Miremont were completely suspended: M. de Miremont breakfasted alone and did not ride; Captain Horthy had been put off and a note sent to Roland; work had not proceeded on monsieur's magnum opus yesterday and doubtless would not today. Even the housemaids, as they flitted from room to room with feather dusters and polishing cloths, were subdued by the silence that hung over the great palace, a louring silence prickling with the threat of a storm.

Miremont, having passed another night of little sleep, lay on the divan in his study, impotent with misery. Although his pain was still intense, the prospect of another day shut up in his apartments was scarcely bearable; but what else could he do?

He dreaded meeting the boy, yet hoped for it too. But, when he hoped, it was with the yearning to fling his arms around Max's neck and find everything was as it had been before. Yet nothing could be as before. Nothing could change the fact of the boy's perfidy or his brazen lack of repentance. If Miremont dreaded meeting him, it was from fear his renewed suspicions would be confirmed and he would see him, in clear day, as a heartless trickster.

Perhaps it would be a relief to find the boy repugnant. For nothing that had passed yesterday had reformed his behaviour: Miremont, lying sleepless and alert to every creaking floorboard, knew too well the hour of his return last night. If only he had shown the slightest remorse, if only he had been sorry instead of sneering...

The divan let out a plaintive creak as Miremont shifted to ease his back: although it had been his grandfather's and he loved its worn leather, its springs were the likely cause of his sciatica. Stiffly he rose and drew up a chair to the table; to escape into a book would be a comfort, yet he lacked the concentration for reading. Truly this self-imposed imprisonment was becoming intolerable, and the more so because he was not alone.

Through the open doors of the enfilade came the muffled sounds of his valet Thomas passing backwards and forwards from his bedroom to his dressing room, reorganising something or other—his shirt drawers or the ordering of his waistcoats, heaven knew what! While the other servants, respecting Miremont's indisposition, did not appear unless he touched the bell, Thomas had deemed it his mission to watch over his master: since yesterday, on the slightest pretext, he had been in and out of Miremont's apartments, quite regardless of the latter's irritation, and, whenever Miremont, losing patience, had sent him away, he had retired no further than the landing, where, like a grizzled mastiff, he had remained guarding the door.

Miremont was under no illusions as to the cause of this devotion. Thomas might not speak, except in extremis—the stone that had put out his right eye during Louis Napoleon's 1851 coup d'état and ended his army service had also, for reasons impenetrable to the physicians, deprived him of all but the rudiments of language—but after twenty-nine years in Miremont's service he knew his master all too well. It had not needed the scene of destruction in Miremont's study for Thomas to discern that M. le marquis and his secretary had quarrelled. Nor could Miremont be in the slightest doubt how this would be received by his valet, even if he had failed to note the complacent clicking of Thomas' teeth as he had retrieved the porcelain fragments from the inkwell, or the new spring in his step, or the smug glint this morning in that single bloodshot eye as he had deftly swept the cut-throat over his master's cheeks.

Thomas hated Max. He had also hated Aline and poor Lesage, would doubtless snarl at anyone who came between him and his master; yet he had been given good reason to loathe Aline, while Lesage's high-handedness had been unfortunate. Max, by contrast, had always treated Thomas with great politeness. However that would weigh little against the obvious objection to the boy's presence, particularly since Thomas, despite his rough military manner and tendency to drunkenness on his days off, had recently grown devout. Granted there had been a change in his attitude to Miremont over the past two years, from dumb rebellion to silent reproach, but Max remained the incubus who had corrupted his master and any sign that this demon might be routed could be taken as answering Thomas' prayers.

Thus it was not only his valet's fussing over him that made Miremont wish to be relieved of his presence. God, if it were possible to settle to some work... It occurred to Miremont, returning to the couch and finding its springs as unaccommodating as before, that he might send Thomas to fetch Boussec, his maître d'hôtel: he could cure the divan's ills, if not his own, thereby providing himself with a distraction.

He had called to Thomas and the valet had just appeared from the bedroom when there was a knock at the outer doors. Miremont, his heart racing, jumped to his feet. But Thomas, moving with surprising speed for such a giant, was already through into the sitting room and opening the right-hand door a chink, which he barred with his formidable chest. All the same, above his growls, Miremont could hear the boy declaring he had some letters that required monsieur's signature.

Once Thomas had been prevailed upon to admit Max and take his own dismissal, Miremont seated himself at his worktable. The boy, when he appeared in the study doorway with the folder of letters under his arm, looked very pale. He stood disconcertingly straight and seemed all at once so extraordinarily young that Miremont struggled for composure.

Seeking for anything that would cover his emotion and break the awkwardness of the moment, he gestured foolishly at the divan. "I was only just now thinking of having this poor old thing reupholstered. It is high time... don't you think...?"

Max stepped forward and placed the letters on the table. Then, ignoring Miremont's nod towards a chair as completely as he had ignored his remark about the sofa, he stepped back, standing rigidly to attention once again.

"Monsieur, I wish to offer you my profound apologies. I have behaved dishonourably and I beg you to forgive me."

Miremont's first reaction was relief. He knew how difficult Max found it to apologise and, now the boy had made the effort, this wretched business was surely over, he could hold out his arms and crush him to his breast. But something kept him in his chair: it was not just the formality of the words, the use of *vous* and 'monsieur' that sounded too cold and pat for sincerity; 'dishonourably' jarred in particular. No question the boy had been dishonourable, but he had been more, far more than that. Honour might be essential to Miremont's own sense of himself, yet it was a pale thing, he now found, bloodless compared with the dark place beyond thought and reason where Max had struck: Aline had dishonoured him, but the pain Max had inflicted tore at some rudimentary substance in the depths of his being. This was not an injury that could easily be forgiven. It could certainly not be forgiven in consequence of one glib speech. It seemed to Miremont that perhaps he should not forgive it at all.

The boy, visibly disconcerted by his silence, had grown even paler. "Please believe me, if I had known how much it would hurt you—"

"You ought to have known. How could you not know?"

"Truly, Armand, I am sorry, as sorry as I can be."

But Miremont was unmoved by the boy's downcast look and his return to the familiar. Indeed, he hardly heard him. "You come here hoping you can make a pretty speech and that will be the end of it. You think you have taken me in for so long that you can take me in again. Well, I grant I am an old fool, but I'm not that foolish. I do not believe a word of it. You have proved to me amply that I should never have trusted you. How can I trust a single word you say?"

Max had spent his long walk home and part of the night considering his apology, choosing a strict formality of address in the hope that, by contrast with his previous regrettable sarcasm, it would convey both respect and humility. Now, however, he was stung.

"Armand, that is unjust."

"Unjust, is it? Well, let us consider the sincerity of your apology. By what shall we judge it? The hour you came back last night?"

"It was not as you—"

"Dear God, and you expect me to forgive you? When, even after yesterday, you cannot keep your cock in your fly?"

One reason Max respected M. de M was that during their disagreements he had always shown a generosity of spirit, a dignified willingness to subdue his pride, to concede that, even where the main fault was not his, there could be a degree of blame on both sides. Max barely recognised this angry madman who refused to listen, who ranted at him and abused him. His pallor turned icy.

"If monsieur persists in spying on me—"

"Like coughing or sneezing, was it? Another prince? Or some errand boy?"

"I'm damned if I'll explain myself. I'm not your prisoner!"

And so the two of them continued, until Max swept out.

Afterwards Miremont sat with his head in his hands, scarcely noticing Thomas' return, or Philippe's arrival to set the sitting-room table for his luncheon. As usual, he grew deeply ashamed of his anger: reliving the scene again and again, he saw Max's apology could have been genuine; he was even obliged to concede these new accusations of his might have been precipitate. Of course, a simple apology, however sincere, was not enough: much more was required for forgiveness, and even forgiveness could not restore trust. Yet that yearning for all to be as before returned—the longing for the boy's laughter, his friendship, the taste, the smell of him: it was impossible to contemplate the pain of such a loss.

Max had left his folder of letters behind. Abandoning his barely-touched luncheon, Miremont applied his signature where necessary then, taking the folder, went in search of the boy. Max was not in the library but in the picture gallery, contemplating one of Miremont's Claudes.

Claude's *Pyramus and Thisbe* had been the subject of much discussion between them, with Miremont avowing the originality of its vision and Max sceptical. As he studied it now, did Max hope for some insight into the conundrum Armand de Miremont had become? At any rate, he had lost his haughty defiance and gave a cautious welcome to Miremont's efforts at conciliation, so that Miremont was moved to suggest a truce: should they not see if they could resume their usual routine—a little work, perhaps a stroll in the Luxembourg Gardens, and then dinner together? Max did not demur; but when he let slip that he had spent the time left on his hands by Miremont's absence reading Shakespeare's tragedies Miremont was affronted: how could the boy divert himself when his own pain admitted of no distraction? Within moments the two of them were tearing at each other again, all talk of a truce forgotten.

Thus both seemed impelled to bring about what they wanted least. When Max coldly asked: "May I take it that you wish me to leave?" Miremont's hasty answer was "No." But he could not forever deafen himself to the promptings of logic: if Max could not be forgiven, this allowed of but one end. Max too, with his attempts at contrition spurned, was bound to heed his pride, which urged that here was a signal from the Fates only a milksop would ignore.

Before dinner they made a further attempt to heal their breach, meeting by agreement in the library. But this proved even less successful: embers smouldering from their previous encounters took fire and soon the flames devoured everything but their anger, so that even the cause of their quarrel was charred past recognition. Both said things they could not have imagined saying, would once have been mortified to think.

"You only ever cared about what you could get from me!" Miremont found himself shouting: "You're a vile little street arab, and I wish to God I had left you in the gutter!"

Whereupon Max, saying nothing, turned on his heel and left.

Armand de Miremont had contrived to persuade himself that, apart from Thomas, none of his servants knew the true nature of his relations with his secretary (Max, of course, indulged in no such wishful thinking). But now, it must be said, even Joseph the boot boy needed to be deaf and blind not to know that the master and M. Fabien were locked in a lovers' quarrel. The picture gallery's doorway opened onto the vestibule, allowing their angry voices to rise up the stairwell, where they mingled with the strains of the quartet's Friday rehearsal. And that was not to take into account monsieur's mysterious 'indisposition', the horses fretful with lack of exercise in the stables, the empty dining room and the interdiction placed upon callers, even Dr Gérard, as if the house were struck by plague.

Outwardly, of course, no one in the household showed the slightest sign that anything was afoot, but there was much gossip in the servants' hall and, it cannot be denied, a degree of speculation behind the discreetly closed door of the housekeeper's parlour, where the upper servants retired to take their postprandial coffee. To those longest in service, the present state of war recalled the time of Mme la marquise. That, for all its unpleasantness and the tendency of its battles to inflict widespread damage, had concluded most satisfactorily; thus hopes rose that this conflict would find a similar resolution.

For, while none of his fellows shared M. Thomas' violent hatred of monsieur's new secretary (a hatred to be deduced only from the valet's demeanour for, on this as on any other topic, he remained resolutely mute), they could not have disagreed with his moral objections. They were also bound to suspect, although they had no definite proof, that this young man, who was no better than he should be, exercised undue influence on their master, which was all the more disgraceful since everyone knew—the two footmen, Georges and Philippe, had it from an unimpeachable source—that this so-called secretary had only recently been in service himself.

Some members of the household held particular grudges against the young upstart: the housekeeper and the cook, Mmes Mercier and Dussardier, would certainly not forget that, when M. Lesage was supposedly on his deathbed last summer, after all their efforts on the invalid's behalf it was M. Fabien who had stolen the credit for getting the obstinate old man up from his bed and taking nourishment, and then only because he had resorted to underhand means; Boussec accused him of squandering monsieur's precious 1827 port; Georges blamed him for the Music Room's invasion by raggle-taggle foreigners.

It was true these were individual complaints and the generality acknowledged M. Fabien's manner was an improvement on his predecessor's, while the mere mention of him made some younger housemaids blush; but as with upstairs, so with downstairs: those with power decide the general verdict, while the generality knows its place.

Thus it was that, though hail still battered the Hôtel de Miremont, so that the Herzens spoke in whispers as they packed up their instruments and Zhukovsky, who was wont to drop into the library on the off-chance of seeing his friend, stole away with the rest, there was otherwise relief that the storm had finally broken, not unmingled with anticipation, which could only be heightened by Georges' report of events the next morning.

M. Fabien had left the house very early, even before Christine, the junior housemaid who served the top floor, had brought his breakfast— but not so early that he had been unable to find Georges. He had handed Georges an envelope with instructions to pass it to M. Thomas for M. le marquis. And he had also requested that Joseph send up his box.

CHAPTER EIGHT

The letter could come as no surprise to Miremont, yet his stomach still lurched as he opened it. No discreetly coded endearments, no reference to the poetic passions of Catullus—all this must now belong to the past. Max's resignation, although thanking Miremont for his kindness and generosity, adhered strictly to form, addressing him as "Monsieur le marquis", trusting that, by mutual agreement, there would be no requirement for him to work his notice and concluding: "I beg you, monsieur, to accept the expression of my sincere respects."

So it was done. Too cowardly to wield the knife himself, Miremont had forced the boy to do it. At first, as with those wounds which send the whole organism into a protective state of shock, he felt nothing. He could do nothing. He could not run after the boy; in any case, Georges, when sent for, informed him that M. Fabien had said he would not be returning until late. There was nothing to be done. He must accept it, must make himself see that it was for the best. It was over. It might have been the great joy of his life, but now it was nothing.

All the same, he could not bear to spend a third day imprisoned in his apartments, pondering the rightness of the outcome. Nor could he bear to look at his gaoler, Thomas, whose face—though perhaps he could not help it, poor fellow—revealed gratification in every contour. Fortunately he was engaged for this evening, to Catherine, who had invited him to her box to hear Nilsson in *La Traviata* and then to take supper. In the meantime it seemed essential to avoid thought.

Sending to the stables to have Darius saddled, Miremont rode out to the Bois, where, contrary to his usual habit, he worked the horse until its flanks were steaming. On his return, forgoing luncheon, he summoned Boussec and, having discussed repairs to the divan, they went out together to inspect some new cracks in the masonry of the west wing. Then, recollecting that he had been remiss in his attentions to his second cousin, the princesse de Vaux, who lived in the apartments facing the forecourt, he sent to see if she would receive him. Although it was less than charitable to admit it, this call was a mistake, for the princesse was not yet out of mourning for her sister, who had died last December, and conversation dwelt heavily on the comforts of religion, doing little to lighten Miremont's spirits: worse still, both the princesse and her lady companion asked after Max, whose concern they had appreciated when Mme d'Ancy-Miremont had first been taken ill;

Miremont supposed he must accustom himself to deflecting enquiries about the 'dear, kind young man'.

After that, there was nothing for it but a brisk walk, not to the Luxembourg Gardens, which were too steeped in memories, but across the river to the Palais-Royal and Miremont's favourite antiquarian book-dealer. But it seemed that the princesse, in her innocence, had torn the dressing from his wound: far from driving out painful thoughts, walking aggravated them, while, as he entered M. Grimaux's shop, the scent of old bindings, inescapably recalling the boy's days as his librarian, threatened him with tears.

Now that the pain had set in, he regretted his commitment to Catherine: she possessed such a talent for seeing through him. To make matters worse, Miremont's main reason for accepting the invitation had been that, with her usual generosity and knowing the boy's love of music, she had extended it to Max: Miremont would be obliged to find some pretext for his absence, for he could not confess the true state of affairs—not yet, not until he was hardened to it. As Thomas helped him into his tails, the evening loomed before him as an insuperable ordeal.

Yet he could not stay at home, where every object, from the curtains of his bed to the very pens on his writing desk, bore the imprint of the boy's memory. Max himself had not returned: he clearly wished to avoid a formal parting and for this Miremont should be grateful.

He should be grateful, too, for the Corvignacs and the La Rochefontaines, who made up the party in Catherine's box, as well as the strangers, mostly young gallants, who came to pay court to Mme la duchesse as she sat, regally fanning herself, as confident of the effect produced by her brilliants, décolletage and artfully dressed hair as any beauty thirty years her junior: here, at least, she could not indulge her legendary penchant for forthright questions. It was true that, after he had kissed her hand and stumbled out Max's excuses—a minor riding mishap seemed most probable, given the boy's robust health—her shrewd eyes had treated him to a searching look; but mercifully another cavalier had arrived to distract her.

Miremont's sensibilities more naturally drew him to Mozart than to the extravagances of Verdi. Yet, although Christine Nilsson was in fine voice, it must be said that, whatever had been playing, Miremont could not have fixed his attention upon it. Instead of the singers and the stage he saw Max. Instead of the music he heard Max, laughing, teasing, arguing with passion that Titian was a god and Tintoretto a journeyman, sighing at the moment of climax, breathing softly in his sleep. With his arm around the boy's waist he walked down to the lake at Beauvallon; he watched Max swing gracefully into Pretender's saddle; he scrabbled with him barefoot in the mud and loam beside a far-distant pool, hunting out flat stones for ducks and drakes.

By the first interval Miremont's agony was such that he was desperate to flee. Catherine's two footmen hovering with champagne at the rear of the box in their azure tailcoats and revealing breeches brought a fresh access of excruciating recollection. Alas, he was buttonholed by Jean-Marie de la Rochefontaine, who had been badly hit by January's crash of the Bourse and, seeking the comfort traditional in the misfortunes of others, hoped to wheedle out of him news of that renowned plunger, Robert de Sestrès, Aline's brother. But in any case he would have found no chance to make his excuses to Catherine, for her attention was continuously engaged until the curtain rose for the second act.

Again it was for Miremont as if the stage and the great gilded auditorium were empty. Perhaps he was destined always to be betrayed. Yet if Max had brought him pain, he had brought him enchantment, joy, rapture in greater measure. If Max had not loved him, he had made a generous pretence of it, he had given abundantly of himself; and, as to what he had kept back—why should that count for so much more than everything he gave? Love was greedy, it must know all, understand all, possess all, yet what was that but the extinction of what it loved? Was it not the boy's independent spirit that endeared him to Miremont, was it not his contradictions that touched him—the self-possession warmed by unexpected tenderness, the worldly wisdom betrayed by its naiveties, the reckless courage vulnerable to night terrors and a child's fear of spiders? If Miremont had loved Max, if the boy, unfathomable though he was, had let him love him, was that not a gift that deserved thanks?

Yet he was allowing Max to leave with less ceremony than he would show Georges or Philippe. Too cowardly to face him, he was letting him walk out of his house, unrewarded by the smallest token of acknowledgement for all the happiness he had given him.

And where would the boy go? Miremont remembered that he had once talked of enlisting. The thought of this, and of what the army had done to Thomas, filled Miremont with horror.

He must leave the moment the curtain came down for the second interval. He must go at once, slip out quickly, sending a note to Catherine tomorrow. Even then, it might be too late. The boy might already have gone, might have vanished forever into the ocean that was Paris.

He was on his feet as the applause began. But Catherine had turned and was beckoning to him. Bending over her chair, he whispered indistinctly about a headache. However, she was not to be deceived: patting his hand, she favoured him with a smile at once sympathetic and penetrating.

"My poor darling Armand. Of course I am grieved for you. But we both know the boy."

"No, you do not know him!" Miremont's sudden anger rose above the din of applause, startling Mme de la Rochefontaine, who occupied the next chair. "With respect, Catherine, you do not know him at all."

Miremont's carriage was not amongst those ranked outside the Garnier, for he had told his coachman Théo to return just before the final curtain. However, hastening down the Avenue de l'Opéra, he was able to hail a cab.

He could forgive Max. He knew, in the instant of his outburst to Catherine, that he had forgiven him. But could Max forgive him? He grimaced when he recalled the terrible things he had said, he covered his face with his hands.

At least the boy had not yet left. Georges, as Miremont thrust his hat and cloak at him, informed him that M. Fabien had returned over an hour ago and had retired to his room. Miremont, disregarding the need to preserve appearances, took the staircase at speed. Although the gas still burned on the second landing, the third floor, above the narrower stairway that led to it, lay in darkness; yet, as Miremont rushed upwards, he could see a sliver of light beneath the second door.

For reasons of discretion he had never before visited the boy's room. Max's bedroom at Beauvallon, communicating with his own through a connecting dressing room, was familiar territory and he had always marvelled at its spartan tidiness, more characteristic of some ascetic than a nonchalant youth scarcely out of his teens. Behind this door on the top landing of the Hôtel de Miremont, however, lay yet another part of the boy's life that remained unknown to him.

The first fleeting impression he received, when, after a short pause, his knock was answered, was of emptiness—bare surfaces, bare walls shadowed in the lamplight by the angles of the gable. But his eyes went immediately to Max, who stood at the centre of this void, in the small island of disarray surrounding the bed.

The voice that had responded to the knock had registered a wary surprise, but Max had had time to collect himself. "Monsieur," he said, in a tone that conveyed neither question nor welcome.

"Oh, my dear Max…" But, as he saw that stiff, cold face with its haughty chin, Miremont's words tailed away. He had not come too late to find the boy, yet all the same he was too late.

Slowly he took in the tin box at the end of the bed, filled almost to the top with books; he noted the jumble of clothing on the counterpane, amongst which he recognised the disreputable frock coat, Max's old Sunday best; he saw that the boy himself, who was in shirtsleeves, wore the trousers and waistcoat of the ill-fitting pale grey suit that had so offended Lesage on his arrival at the Hôtel de Miremont and which Miremont had always thought of, not without a certain frisson, as his renter's suit; and finally his eye was caught by the open doors of the wardrobe, which, unlike the empty bookshelves and despite the scattering of garments on the bed, was crammed full: the tails, the alpaca topcoat, the suit of grey worsted, all Mathurin's masterpieces of tailoring, even the long midnight-blue dressing gown that made the boy look like some Oriental princeling, remained neatly on their pegs.

Max had evidently followed Miremont's glance. "Those belong to your secretary, monsieur. I believe you have noted my resignation." Reaching for a pile of books, he turned away.

"Oh, my dear, dear boy… In the last two days I have been driven by some madness to say a great many things that were not true and which I would give the world to take back."

Max began laying the books neatly on top of the others in the trunk. He did not look up.

"Please," said Miremont, struggling to keep his desperation from his voice, "if you can, do not take them too much to heart. Please try to find the generosity I have lamentably failed to show you and forgive me."

At this, at least, the boy paused. He appeared to consider for a moment. Then, straightening his back, he again faced Miremont. It seemed to Miremont that he smiled faintly.

"I too have said things I did not mean, monsieur. And I have done things for which, I can only repeat, I am truly sorry. I am ashamed not to have understood that something of so little consequence to me would be of immense consequence to you."

For an instant Miremont felt a rush of hope, but it was quickly checked. The smile had been a brief concession: Max had spoken gravely, without emotion, and now that he had finished, while perhaps his manner had lost something of its hauteur, his expression was again impervious. This was no prelude to a new beginning, merely a sober settling of accounts. Even now, the boy was turning back to his packing.

Miremont slumped into a nearby chair. "Where will you go?"

"I have found a room just off the Place de la Sorbonne. I may move in first thing tomorrow, if that is no inconvenience."

Miremont only nodded, for he was lost for suitable words: any concern that Max would be comfortable, that he would have everything he needed and sufficient money, must, as the contents of the wardrobe bore witness, merely compound Miremont's offence.

"You will find all your *Metamorphoses* quotations, with my rough translations, on your study table. Your correspondence is also there, up to date apart from two letters that arrived today after I had gone out. I have just now drafted replies to them, but I should like to read them over. If you are agreeable, monsieur, I shall give them to Thomas tomorrow before I leave."

Murmuring his assent, Miremont glanced across at the escritoire, upon whose flap, as Max had indicated, several sheets of paper lay. Otherwise, the desk and its pigeonholes were as empty as the bookshelves, yet on top of it, Miremont noticed, was a small array of objects, including two or three jewellery cases and something that gleamed silver.

Miremont rose and went to the escritoire as if to look at the letters. He hardly need open the cases to know what was in them for, yes, they were all there, set out as neatly and impartially as the riding boots and evening pumps in the bottom of the wardrobe, all the various trinkets he had given the boy, tie pins, cufflinks, a cigarette case, even the set of pearl dress-shirt studs that had been a present last January to mark the anniversary of Max's arrival, a day that, since the boy was ignorant of the real date, they had designated his birthday. But to Miremont the watch signified the cruellest rejection.

He picked it up, letting the chain run through his fingers. It was a simple object, although pleasing, with its clean lines and clear face, and not of silver but white gold. It had been Miremont's own until he had given it to the boy the summer before last on the agonising occasion of their first parting—he had cherished a fancy, he remembered, that, whenever Max took this gift from his pocket to tell the time, he would be bound to recall the giver. And now even this was to be spurned, even this was to be fastidiously repudiated like every other token of Miremont's love.

Miremont glanced back at Max, who, bending to fold the ancient frock coat on top of the books, seemed utterly indifferent to his presence. Miremont's fingers closed protectively around the watch. This was cruel of the boy, spiteful.

But then he reminded himself that Max, although he had admired the watch, had not wanted to take it, any more than he had wished to accept the money hidden beneath it, the banknote which, as it transpired, he had immediately given to the Zhukovskys. The boy had stood fiercely on his pride, even then.

Miremont's bitterness increased, yet now it was turned upon himself. What was love, that, seeking to wound, it knew how to drive the dagger in to the hilt? All his life he had valued moderation and restraint: he wished he had been struck dumb before he could make his stupid, intemperate, false accusations.

Then, as he looked down at the watch, he recalled something else about their parting at La Boissière. Tentatively, he took a few steps towards Max.

"My dear fellow... If I cannot persuade you that you have deserved everything you have ever received from me, so be it... But you surely cannot refuse to take this?"

Max at last deigned to glance up. He stared at the watch in Miremont's outstretched palm and—although perhaps this was Miremont's wishful thinking—a shadow seemed to pass across his face. But he did no more than raise his eyebrows.

"Do you not recall?"

"Monsieur will pardon me...?"

"Do you not remember? This was not a present, you received it in fair exchange."

The boy set down the bundle of linen he was holding. "Fair exchange? Good lord, for what?"

"You truly do not recall?"

"I recall that I had nothing, so I can have given you nothing."

"You gave me a stone." A stone the size of a thumb joint, crimson veined with white, that had looked like agate when wet but, dry, was merely a pebble. Miremont, at least, would not forget how the boy, laughing, had said he would magic it into agate again and had taken it into his mouth, slowly revolving it upon his tongue.

"My God, I do remember!" Max laughed again, incredulously. "A stone. A worthless pebble."

"Not worthless to me. I have it still in my stud box, although it has taken Herculean effort to stop Thomas disposing of it."

Max stared at Miremont. Then his lips twisted bitterly. "And that is about the sum of it, is it not? You give me love and I give you stones."

"Oh, my dear boy… If that is all you think you have given me…" But Miremont was no longer equal to speech. He sat down heavily on the end of the bed.

Max continued to stare at monsieur's bent head. A dull horror came over him that he had caused this misery, followed by a foolish longing to go to the old boy. But this was weakness and anger must crush it. A pebble for a keepsake—how typical of the old fellow's sentimental nonsense! Yes, it was true he had not made the hysterical scene Max had feared at his knock; yes, granted, he seemed restored to his former even-handed self, so that it was hard not to be touched by his effort at amends. Yet it behoved Max to keep in mind the shouting and the insults.

Besides, he had determined to go. Even if the Fates and freedom did not call him, he was too far on to retreat: he had resigned in writing, found lodgings, his box was almost packed; he could not turn back without considerable loss of face. His future lay before him, if he were any sort of a man he would not be swayed by a few sentimental memories.

Yet it was impossible to look at the old boy sitting there, mute, the watch chain lacing his fingers, without feeling a pain that answered his, or without letting in, however Max fought it, the aching despair that had pursued him all day as he had trudged the streets looking for lodgings. A voice that anger could not silence—not the Other childishly screaming: "You're a filthy sinner and you'll burn in Hell", nor even the imprecations of Dom Sébastien, but a whisper, faint yet distinct, from somewhere very far off in the past—told him that this was how it would always be, that he was misbegotten, cursed, lacking in some quality essential to humanity. If he left now, it would not simply be to claim his freedom, but because, for the old fellow's sake, he must.

"You should not love me, monsieur," he said roughly.

The old boy looked up and Max saw with dismay that his eyes glistened.

"Damn you, you must understand—I cannot—I am unable—for a thousand reasons—" But here Max was appalled to realise his own cheeks were wet.

He turned aside quickly. This was mortifying. He did not weep. He had not shed tears since he was thirteen and hopelessly drunk on Brother Bernard's cider. Keeping his back to the room, seeking sanctuary at the window, which was unshuttered and open to the night air, he battled to master himself. But the tears, which he could not wipe away without betraying his lapse, continued to come.

Not that monsieur seemed deceived. From behind him, Max felt a tentative hand on his arm. He shook it off.

"Shit!... Oh hell!... I'm sorry... Oh damnation!..." He bit his lip until it bled, but his anguish mounted. "Oh God, I don't... I can't..."

He no longer resisted when the old fellow, working his arms beneath his, enfolded his chest and laid his cheek against his shoulder. "Hush," said Miremont, gently moulding his own body to his, soothing him as he soothed his nightmares. "Hush, my dear..."

After a while, when the tremors that convulsed the boy's shoulders and spine had somewhat subsided, Miremont dared press his lips to the nape of his neck. "My dear Max, do you truly want to leave me?"

The shoulders shuddered again as the boy uttered a strangled laugh. "I suppose I might miss you once in a while."

"Then you do have some feelings for me?"

"Damn you, Armand!" Wresting himself from Miremont's arms, Max turned so they were face to face. "Damn you, you old lunatic, of course I love you!"

While the immediate joys of reconciliation were sweet, the damage would take time to mend. Undertakings were given and a certain equilibrium restored, but they had lost their instinctive ease with each other: like a pair of invalids, they were constrained, considerate, each wary that a careless word or gesture might catch the other on the raw. Although Miremont could take comfort in the boy's avowal and Max, having made it, felt, not shame, but relief, as if the contrary ropes tugging him had been cut, their return to happiness remained precarious. They were still far from the point where Max could make promises he was able to keep or Miremont could accept love truly should be blind.

So it was that Miremont hoped their summer months at Beauvallon, far from the disturbing influences of Paris, would provide the necessary period of recuperation. But they had been in the country only a week when Mme la marquise's letter arrived.

CHAPTER NINE

Armand de Miremont and his eldest daughter, Clotilde Thierry-Le Puy, stood before one of the mirrors in the ballroom, he with a look of barely concealed irritation, she with a little leather-bound notebook in her hand.

"My dearest girl, it is not a simple question of resilvering."

"But, Papa—"

"These glasses are from Murano and they are backed with metal. Yes, it is true the backing has stained the glass in places, but that is only to be expected after nearly three centuries."

"However, Maman has most particularly asked—"

"Your mother should know better. We tinker with them at our peril."

Max, also armed with notebook and pencil, stood a few paces off, observing this scene. Although his expression remained suitably opaque, he felt for the old fellow. Altogether it had been a trying afternoon.

Throughout July and August they had laboured over the preparations for Mme la marquise's arrival. Max had taken dictation for countless letters to Paris—to Boussec, to Mme Mercier, to Lemoin, Armand's architect—not to mention replies to the stream of correspondence that had flowed to Beauvallon from Miremont-Sainte-Fleur. Madame's apartments had once been in the east wing of the Hôtel de Miremont, but three years after her departure, during the siege of Paris, monsieur had offered the vacant wing to his sister, the comtesse de Sauvigny, to house her hospital for the wounded: eleven years later, although the original furniture had been returned to its place, the rooms remained unoccupied and unrestored. Now, from this neglect, must be magicked habitable quarters for madame, Mlle Julie and—as Miremont learned suddenly at the beginning of August—for a lady companion, Miss Pilkington, to whom Julie had become attached during their stay in England.

While Miremont's extensive library occupied what had once been the marquis' state apartments on the ground floor of the west wing, the corresponding apartments for the marquise in the east wing remained untouched. But Aline de Miremont would not hear of moving into them: they should, apparently, be reserved for honoured guests. ("Do we expect the Prince of Wales?" Miremont was heard to mutter. "Or the Tsar of all the Russias?") Instead, the enfilade on the second floor must be refashioned into two separate suites for madame and her daughter, while the lady companion would be accommodated on the third floor, which had formerly housed the nursery.

Thus poor Boussec had seen his usual summer furlough postponed as he pored over blueprints with Lemoin's assistants or supervised the regiment of builders, carpenters, joiners, glaziers and decorators who hammered and sawed until all hours despite the suffocating heat, while Mme Mercier, likewise deprived of her customary fortnight at her married sister's, conferred with upholsterers and the purveyors of hangings and curtains.

It was now the first week in September and, while smocked figures with paint cans and ladders could still be glimpsed crossing the inner courtyard, the noise and the dust had abated, so that Miremont, returning from Beauvallon a month earlier than usual, was able to pronounce himself delighted with the results.

Yet they must satisfy a keener eye. This was not Clotilde's usual filial visit—Frédéric and little Agathe remained at home with their nursemaid—nor was it the first time she had called since her father's return; almost daily, it seemed, she appeared with a list: Maman would require a larger cheval glass, a more elegant writing desk, could not abide the smallest draught, would not countenance yellow and red anywhere together nor velvet in a boudoir, only chintz…

While Miremont felt the pull of consanguinity towards his elder child, he wished these encounters were less apt to remind him that, shamefully, he did not much like her. Clotilde seemed to own no opinion that had not been handed down, a little shiny at the elbows, by someone else: when she was not clothed in Aline's prejudices, she faithfully donned those of her husband, fifteen years her senior, a nice enough man in his way (although Miremont never knew what to say to him) but apparently consumed by a single passion, to be elected to the Jockey Club, which garland, as Clotilde never ceased to mention, he had finally won this year. Furthermore, while hers was a pinched version of her mother's beauty and she lacked Aline's flirtatiousness, she seemed to have inherited a full share of that other characteristic always to the fore when madame's wishes were thwarted: a tendency to bully.

Latterly, too—Miremont had noticed this ever since Frédéric's birth—his elder daughter had developed a grating condescension towards him. While Miremont took pleasure in his grandson and was naturally delighted that the marquisate had an heir, he was not best pleased by Clotilde's harping on the future of the line, as though what she liked to refer to as 'his bachelor existence' amongst 'all those dusty books' was a symptom of his dotage.

He supposed he should be relieved that she saw his young secretary merely as one of the props of this twilight life, or rather, since M. Fabien was a paid minion, generally chose not to see him at all. Yet it was insufficient consolation. Recalling the tiny girl who had squealed with joy when he had carried her on his shoulders, Miremont could not but be depressed by the officious matron who lectured him now. Everything must be new, must glitter with pretension: nothing held value that was not expensively à la mode. Clutching her notebook and with critical pencil poised, Clotilde appeared to feel herself invested with plenipotentiary powers. For the most part, knowing the futility of arguing with Aline's caprices and, besides, not begrudging his wife and younger daughter whatever comforts they desired, Miremont hid his annoyance and submitted. But this afternoon Clotilde's zeal had encroached beyond the east-wing apartments.

It was clear—Miremont had glimpsed the heavy underlinings in the notebook—that the ballroom had been her first target when she had demanded a tour of the piano nobile. But since this was one of the Herzen Quartet's afternoons in the adjacent Music Room and Miremont had no wish to disturb them, while Clotilde had declared she could hardly think 'with so much noise', there was general agreement that the tour should commence instead with the Empress Elizabeth Salon, working its way round to regain the grand staircase and the ballroom.

This was a dispiriting progress, which, if it had not irritated Miremont acutely, would have broken his heart. Here, told in commodes and ingenious cabinets, in chairs of every style and period, in bronze and marble statuary, in paintings, in tapestries, in porphyry obelisks and malachite coups, in Sèvres, in Meissen, jade, ivory, cloisonné, was the history of the family: here were the treasures his grandfather, Roland de Miremont, the ninth marquis, had saved from the revolution in 1789 by sending them to his châteaux in Burgundy and the Vendée, treasures which had survived the Terror and the Republic's pacification of the staunchly royalist Vendéens, and which, on the Restoration and the family's return from exile, Roland had reclaimed along with his estates.

Miremont, after his father and briefly his elder brother, the guardian of this inheritance, viewed the obligation as sacred, not merely for the sake of Freddie and generations to come, but for the communion it granted him with generations past: all these objects crammed haphazardly into room after room were precious, regardless of their material worth or pretentions to beauty—he was as content to run his fingers over his great uncle Balthazar's pipe rack as to lift the jewelled cup presented to the first marquis by Catherine de' Medici; for, pondering these relicts of better, braver men, he was reminded that, however unworthy he was, the blood which had flowed in their veins flowed in his, still infused, despite the dilutions of centuries, with the traces of a glorious ideal.

Thus, when his daughter, wrinkling her nose, proclaimed the furniture in the Elizabeth Salon ugly or asked why he had not long ago disposed of the clay pipes, it caused him pain. Indeed, there was hardly a room Clotilde entered with which she did not find fault. While struggling to show forbearance, he stood his ground. But the ballroom might be his Philippi.

He did not need the underlinings in the notebook to remind him of what had been Aline's favourite theme, even in the first days of their marriage. Clotilde's fastidious sniff at the traces left by the fencing school—chalk dust, an aroma of sweat and leather—had been but a preliminary sally. Even the contretemps over the mirrors had been a mere skirmish. But now, as she cast her eyes over the ballroom curtains, her lines were drawn for battle.

"Maman is quite right. Poor Julie. They simply must be replaced."

Miremont, letting his glance stray to the view of the inner courtyard, feigned preoccupation with some birds—starlings, he thought—fluttering around the fountain. Yet abstraction, as he knew, was no defence.

"I realise you do not notice these things, Papa. But truly, they are a disgrace."

Miremont sighed.

The ballroom draperies had gone up in his great-grandfather's time before the revolution and had survived the incendiary attack that had destroyed the east and service wings in 1792, having been saved by loyal servants from the looting which followed the fire. Once, so Miremont's father had remembered, they had been pale gold; but from Miremont's earliest childhood he recalled them as they were now, subdued by age to the colour of unburnished brass. He remembered how, when he was small, he had loved to rub his face in the trailing hem of a curtain and drink in the smell, compounded of tallow and woodsmoke and ancient dust. Nowadays the damask was too stiff and fragile for any but the gentlest treatment: the maids flicked away cobwebs with feather dusters and that was all. It was true that in daylight one could glimpse places where age had split the cloth; yet, when the chandeliers were lit, it glowed with subtle gradations of bronze, green and ochre, as though the room were hung with delicate flutes of metal.

"No," he said.

She favoured him with that annoying smile of hers, at once forgiving and cautionary. "Now, Papa, we all know how unworldly you are—"

"No, Clotilde."

"But please consider dear Julie. Her ball will certainly be the talk of Paris, but not for the reasons our poor darling deserves."

While Miremont would happily concede anything that would allow Julie her triumph, he did not think she would ask this of him. His younger daughter would possess the sensitivity to understand, to know the value of memories kept alive through generations. However, since he scrupulously avoided any utterance that might make Clotilde aware of his unfair preference, he did not advance this argument but merely repeated: "No, my dear. Now that is an end to it."

Her face stiffened for an instant before the smile reasserted itself, accompanied by a brisk laugh. "Dearest Papa. We cannot all live like savages, even if you choose to. I know you do not care to hear Maman's opinions, but you will grant, I am sure, that she has some knowledge of the world."

Miremont repressed an unsuitable retort.

"And it is not just the window-hangings and the pelmets. You cannot have looked at the side chairs recently. They will need to be reupholstered, of course, to match the new draperies, but they are also in urgent need of regilding."

"They serve perfectly well as they are. Why make them look like gimcrack reproductions?"

Now it was Clotilde's turn to sigh. "Please, Papa, I have given in to you over the looking glasses—"

"As common sense dictated—"

"But I warn you, over the rest Maman is likely to put her foot down. And if you consider the matter unselfishly, as I know in the end, dear Papa, you always do, you will see she is correct."

Miremont's heart began to pound, a roaring assailed his ears, he found himself quivering with the breathless panic and rage his quarrels with Max had unleashed. "May I remind you, and madame your mother, that this is my house."

"But it is Freddie's too. Maman is right, we cannot permit you to let his inheritance go to rack and ruin—"

"In heaven's name, Clotilde! The child is barely four years old."

"Even so—"

"And, if your mother has her way, by the time he is five there will be nothing to inherit but bric-a-brac!"

He must have spoken louder than he knew, for his daughter took an abrupt step backwards, while Max shot him a concerned glance before resuming his secretary's face.

But Miremont ceased to care that he was shouting. "These curtains, Clotilde, have survived four revolutions, two monarchies, two empires, two republics, barricades in the streets and the Prussians outside our gates. They will survive the depredations of your mother."

"Oh Papa, if, just for once, the two of you…"

However, Miremont had turned away before he could see the tears of desperation that had welled in his daughter's eyes. So far as he was concerned, he had made his final pronouncement.

The weeks before the arrival of his wife and his younger daughter seemed to Miremont at once to fly and to drag abominably. On the one hand, he must treasure these last days of freedom: on the other, with all these aggravating interruptions and the constant coming and going of workmen, he found it impossible to work himself or indeed to settle to anything.

He craved the peace of Beauvallon, resented the precious month forfeited by this early return. It had always been his habit to celebrate the vintage at the end of September and this year, as last, he felt a special obligation to the commune, for once again phylloxera had devastated the vines; yet he could not consign poor Boussec to the mercies of Clotilde, nor, for all Max's promises, was he willing to let the boy stand as his deputy, left to his own devices in Paris.

September was not entirely devoid of pleasure. In their last week of freedom they attended the Herzens' first concert, at the Conservatoire. Although Miremont was profoundly embarrassed by the speech Zhukovsky made before the quartet's final bow, thanking its generous patron, he was delighted all seemed to come off well, and even better pleased when, through Max, he learnt the performance had received favourable reviews and that Zhukovsky, although made wary by past experience, was in tentative discussions with a promoter. All the same, the Herzens' spirited performance of Haydn's *Emperor* quartet and the first of Beethoven's quartets for Prince Razumovsky had not been able to stop the increasingly agitated wanderings of Miremont's mind.

It was not in the least what he wanted, it could not be more unfortunate, but eventually he could not escape the decision: while his wife and daughter were beneath his roof, Max's visits to his bedroom must cease. Of course he feared Aline's intrusions, her blunderbuss curiosity that made everyone's business her own: indeed, it was Aline he cited when, at last, very reluctantly, he broached the matter with Max. But in truth Julie was his first concern. He simply could not imagine making unrestrained love to the boy while his daughter, in her virginal innocence, trusted to the shelter of his house. That his life was a lie, that he was derelict in his moral duties as a father, was bad enough; to persist in gratifying his base desires in Julie's very presence was a profanity.

All the same, Miremont knew the risk he was taking with Max. When, on the penultimate night before his family's arrival, he steeled himself to tell the boy, he certainly expected vociferous objection. Yet Max submitted without protest. Miremont could not prevent a deep sinking of his spirits.

CHAPTER TEN

"Don't skulk in the doorway, wretched boy. Come here, so I may look at you."

When, two days before Mme de Miremont's arrival, Mme de Claireville paid the customary call to mark her return from the country, Max took refuge in the picture gallery: he did not forget she had sworn retribution if he ever played the old boy false and, although he was certain Armand would have swallowed his tongue rather than speak of his troubles, the old fellow had been Mme de Claireville's guest on the fatal night; that face of his, so unsuited to deception, would inevitably have told her all. As Mme de Claireville had shortly afterwards left for La Boissière while they had departed for Beauvallon, Max had thus far been spared any encounter with the old witch: even now, if his relations with the servants had been better, he might have asked Philippe to say he could not be found; but Max was under no illusions—since he had raised the hopes of the servants' hall only to dash them so brutally, he could not expect the slightest favour from that quarter.

He arrived at the Little Salon to discover, to his dismay, that the old boy was absent: apparently he was speaking to Boussec about some last-minute problem with the renovations, although Mme de Claireville seemed quite unperturbed by this lapse in M. de M's impeccable manners. She sat imperiously amongst the tea things, her threatening aspect enhanced by the predatory aigrette perched in its nest of veiling above her hennaed curls.

Damn the old Medusa! She was often kind to him, Max was obliged to admit, but that did not entitle her to bring him to account. If she wished to look at him, he would look back at her, straight in the eye.

All the same he could not but feel she was divining every one of his past misdeeds and inventing several for good measure. So he was greatly disconcerted when, uttering what was neither quite a sigh nor a laugh, she said: "Oh well, since he is willing to forgive you, so shall I. Needs must under the circumstances."

"Then perhaps, madame, I may also be forgiven for being unsure what—"

"None of your monkey tricks, we know each other too well. Here!" She patted the space next to her on the chaise. "I require to have a serious discussion with you."

As he settled himself beside her, he caught a gust of her scent, the heavy musk that pervaded the atmosphere of the Hôtel de Claireville but which most of all reminded him of her bed, in which he had triumphed for eight nights: now that time had softened the memory, he tended to recall his pleasure almost as clearly as his unjustified banishment. As it seemed she did not intend to berate him, he essayed a smile.

She, however, continued to regard him gravely. "I wish to speak to you on the subject of stupidity."

Resentment crushed his pleasant memories. Would the old broomstick never let him forget the jibe with which she had dismissed him as her lover? That he was intelligent, but not yet clever. "I am sure madame will find me every bit as stupid as she has always—"

"Heavens above, the ridiculous vanity of the creature! We were not discussing you." Then, all at once reminded of her words and delighted they still rankled, she burst out laughing. "Absurd child! On the contrary, I am certain from the way you have got round my poor Armand that you are now—woe betide us—as clever as a tribe of snake-charmers. Although, I suppose, in the present case, this may be to the good."

Observing that she sighed again, Max wondered if she were not bent on lecturing him after all. "The present case?" he enquired cautiously.

"Ah yes, stupidity. Which, my friend, is by no means the same as not being clever. Stupidity is the true root of all evil."

"So it is to be philosophical, this discussion of ours?"

"Entirely practical. An intelligent man should never marry a stupid woman."

At last Max saw where this was tending, but all he proffered was: "Ah."

"Intelligent women, by exercising their genius for persuasion and sleight of hand, have been known to moderate the excesses of stupid men. But an intelligent husband is always defenceless against a supremely stupid wife. He persists, you see, in thinking she must be amenable to reason. But he might just as well address her in Mandarin—and when she does not understand, she considers it his fault, not hers. Since she is too stupid to know what she does not know, she extols her deficiency as a virtue. What she wants must be right, because it is she who wants it. And, should she stop to think of others at all, she supposes they are bound to agree—if they do not they are merely activated by malice. So it is, my boy, that an intelligent man, however generous, compassionate and long-suffering, is always in the wrong when he is married to a stupid woman."

Although Max had never heard Mme de Claireville refer to Mme la marquise without a certain edge to her voice and although she was renowned for being blunt, she had not ventured to be quite so indiscreet in his presence before. Not for the first time, he found himself questioning whether her interest in Armand had always derived from her bosom friendship with his sister.

He laughed uncertainly. "Surely things cannot be as bad as that?"

"Worse."

"I am not unaware of monsieur's misgivings, but—"

"Armand de Miremont, as we can both agree, is an extremely intelligent man. But he is not—as, without slandering the dear fellow, we may also agree—remotely clever. Otherwise why should he be so excessively fond of such a cocky, preening, faithless creature as you?"

"Madame, I—"

She stilled his protest by placing her hand on his. She smiled. "Dear silly boy. You will look after him, won't you?"

Max was obliged to smile in return. "Madame overestimates me. I cannot charm snakes."

"Oh, I do not deny it will be a trial for you too. But you must do what you can. You must promise me not to desert the poor dear man at this time of—"

But, mercifully, she was prevented from binding him to some undying vow by Armand's reappearance.

The irony of the situation did not escape Max. If the omens were to be believed, there could never be a better time to leave the Hôtel de Miremont. However, he had not needed any urging by Mme de Claireville—damn her effrontery, yet bless her concern for the old boy. Max was already pledged to stand by him.

He had not abandoned his ambitions, but, since he had given up his struggle and capitulated to the old fellow, all the other conflicts that had raged within him seemed miraculously resolved; as if the world were bathed in a pristine light, he could view it calmly and perceive that what had been muddied before was clear and simple. It was not a weakness to seize happiness when it was offered or to enjoy his present comfortable existence; neither was it an infraction of his code. When the time came for destiny to call him—and he understood this had been his previous mistake, that he had hoped to force the Fates rather than waiting upon their pleasure—he would be strengthened by this remission from struggle.

Once he had relaxed his grip upon the future, the past, too, seemed to loosen its chains. His nightmares had ceased, he was no longer visited by the Other, he rarely if ever thought of Dom Sébastien. As for that other distant accusing voice, what had it been but the voice of his own misery? He might have rejected sentiment and morality but he was not some maimed creature incapable of human feeling. He could, did love. Now he had only one concern: to make amends to the old boy. At first he had hoped his shame would be sufficient. But he grew aware that, while Armand's forgiveness was unquestionably sincere, there were signs—a sudden involuntary darkening of his brow, the occasional bleak silence after their lovemaking—which suggested that, however M. de M scoured his heart, he was powerless to erase all trace of Max's betrayal.

Once this would have provoked Max to indignation and doubt. Indeed, for a moment it did. Yet, even as he was cursing the old boy, his new clarity of vision gave him pause. What else could he expect? He could see that Armand himself rued his inability to forget: the old fellow's love was not damaged at the roots, merely pollarded, and would grow back to its full span if properly tended. If it were truly precious to Max, it was worth more than a few glib promises: however he dealt with the rest of the world, he must try to love Armand on Armand's own terms, with the same generosity, the same devotion to truth; what he had formerly taken for granted he must now strive to earn.

Thus, when Mme la marquise's letter had arrived, though Max could not ignore its long-term implications, he had been grateful for the immediate opportunity it supplied. Not only was he given countless ways to show his solicitude, but this common enemy naturally drew them both together.

In truth, Max had been puzzled by the strength of Armand's distaste for his wife. Of course, lest Max forget, there was the matter of her infidelity—might he too never win forgiveness?—but it grew apparent that in madame's case this was not the only obstacle: her letters gave evidence of how tiresome and small-minded she could be. Nonetheless, these were defects Armand generally viewed with saintly tolerance: he had put up with that mean old buzzard Lesage for over twenty-five years. Granted, it might be different with a wife. But surely Mme la marquise could not be the tartar she was painted, any more than the old boy's beloved Juliette could be such a paragon?

But that was at Beauvallon, when, swimming in the lake, making love in the summerhouse, riding out across the broad hectares of the old boy's demesne, free spirits, answerable to no one, they had been able to ignore for hours at a time the importunate letters piling up in the library.

In Paris, Max conceded, the auguries were not promising. As they drove through the gates, the pedimented windows of the Hôtel de Miremont, like so many hooded eyes, gazed out over the forecourt with their usual dispassion; yet, even as Max stood back while M. de M was greeted by the servants, he could feel the atmosphere within had changed. Everyone, even phlegmatic Boussec, seemed on edge. What with the comings and goings of the decorators, the dust, the noise and the weather, still airless and sticky in the first week of September, there was a general sense of foreboding, as in a citadel preparing for siege.

Then came the enemy's scouting party. It must be owned that Max had once agreed with Clotilde: coming fresh from the elegant appointments of the Hôtel de Claireville, he had been dismayed by this cavernous palace lying in the shadow of Saint-Sulpice like some ancient whale at the bottom of the ocean, its ceremonial rooms shuttered to protect their antiquities, its expanses of marble chilly with the silence of the crypt. Yet, as his fondness for Armand had increased, he must also have grown fond of Armand's Leviathan, for he was outraged by Clotilde's assault upon it.

Not, of course, that he had made any protest. Clotilde's visits had another disagreeable aspect, that they reminded him of the mask he must wear for the coming weeks. An equal in Italy and in the solitude of Beauvallon, at the Hôtel de Miremont, at least in public, he must keep a deferential one step behind. Although he was by now well used to these complexities, prolonged periods of equality had not sharpened his appetite for becoming a lackey again; and, while even in the Hôtel de Miremont he and the old boy could usually spend long, uninterrupted hours together, now the house would be overrun: not only would they live under the eye of the old fellow's family, but there would be At Homes, balls, supper parties, a constant stream of callers. He had yet to meet Mlle Juliette, the occasion for all this, but he must already crush down an unworthy resentment, and envy too, every time he heard the old boy speak of her—the adored daughter who might openly bask in M. de M's love and who held it with an unconditional and lasting title that foolish indiscretions could not cancel.

Ah well! In his present contrite mood, Max accepted the sacrifice. He would bow and scrape. He would do his damndest to protect the old boy. For there was no denying Armand needed protection, if not from his family, from that other danger—himself.

Max could not but agree with Mme de Claireville: M. de M was certainly not 'clever' in her sense of the word. Indeed such cleverness was not a quality the old boy esteemed, with the result that, despite Max's tutoring, he remained an unconvincing liar and, if his countenance did not betray him, was prone to forgetful gestures or slips of the tongue. He continued shockingly naive about the servants, too, as if he expected a couple of months to obliterate all memory of previous events. Although here, it must be granted, he was relatively safe: the servants might long to take revenge upon Max, but they could hardly undo him without undoing their master and, in any case, their loyalty to monsieur would be bolstered by their detectable lack of enthusiasm for madame. All the same, most servants were loyal only to a point and any lower servant was liable to be severely tested by a well-judged tip.

Thus Max was resolved to put his eyes and wits at the old fellow's disposal and to submit gracefully, whatever was expected of him. Certainly Mme la duchesse's warning was yet another ill-omen, but at least Armand seemed calmer now his family's arrival was almost upon them. As for himself—if he loved the old boy, it was a trifling thing to play the humble secretary during the day: after all, they would still have the nights.

The nights? The crazy old fellow could hardly conceive of the blow he dealt when, that very night, as they lay in each other's arms, he announced that, once Mme la marquise was in residence, they must forgo this pleasure along with everything else. It was true that before he uttered this pronouncement he disentangled himself from Max's embrace and covered himself with his dressing gown, as he always did when he had something disagreeable to impart, true also that he spoke haltingly and avoided Max's eye; yet, despite his embarrassment, it was clear his mind was made up.

"It will only be for a week or two... Just until... until we see, darling boy... how things are..."

Had he any idea what he asked? At Beauvallon it had not been hard for Max to stay true to his promise—there was little chance to do otherwise—but his days off in Paris were a very different matter. Conscientiously avoiding his other haunts, he had so far spent his time either with the Zhukovskys or wandering the Louvre (although even this last was not entirely without its dangers). However, the previous Thursday, since he was concerned about Polly, from whom he had heard nothing all summer, he had felt compelled to brave the Monkey. It had been futile, of course, for Old Jouvert had washed his hands of poor Polly (as Max had suspected, his friend had fallen out with the manufacturer in Auteuil), and no one else appeared to have set eyes on him for weeks. Nevertheless, the joshing, the camaraderie, the very smell of the place had stirred their usual excitement—indeed, through being forbidden, it was redoubled in force—so that Max had been obliged to make hasty excuses; once outside, he had hailed the nearest cab, no longer even trusting the seductive darkness of the streets.

He had told himself that a promise held little value if keeping it were effortless. He had told himself, too, that his love for the old boy would eventually teach him constancy. But now—had he escaped the cloister, only to find celibacy thrust upon him again? It was all very well for the old fellow, but he was young, his body at the height of its powers. This was preposterous cruelty.

He opened his mouth to begin his objections. Yet he could see terror of madame had rendered Armand immovable. Not only were they to live chastely for some indefinite period, they were no longer even to take breakfast together (although what indecency might be imputed to their shared coffee and brioche Max could not imagine): Max would go through the post with the old fellow, as Lesage had done, after the morning's ride.

"You do understand, dearest boy? I should give anything not to ask this of you, but there seems no choice."

A sarcastic retort hovered on Max's tongue. He bit it back. Had he not vowed to take every measure to safeguard the old fellow? Had he not accepted that a promise that could be kept without renunciation or suffering was scarcely a promise at all? If he wanted to show himself worthy of the old boy's love, to prove that he too could be generous and selfless, then here was his chance. It would be torture—but so be it.

Armand sat glumly on the edge of the bed. Putting an arm around his shoulders, Max kissed him lightly on the cheek. "Yes, of course, dear heart. I'm sure you are right, it is the wisest thing."

On the afternoon of madame's arrival Max busied himself in the library. He had been excused standing alongside the upper servants in the entrance hall to welcome the party, but he had heard the carriages from the station rumble into the forecourt and Georges and Philippe rushing to unburden the second carriage of luggage. Although he had not remained untouched by the nervous agitation that had animated the house since first light—the maids feverishly polishing and dusting, Mme Mercier's inquisitorial finger following in their wake—he was determined to appear unruffled.

Nevertheless, as he searched out references for the old boy, his eye travelled the pages blindly, while the unexpected sound of voices in the anteroom made him start and lose his place.

"Two monarchies," M. de M was saying, "two empires, the Communards, the Prussians—"

A silvery laugh cut across him, followed by a voice resembling Clotilde's, yet pitched higher and fraught with girlish vibrato. "You know, Tilda is quite right, Armand. You are a savage."

They had reached the open doors of the library and M. de M stood aside to let madame enter. A waft of sweet violet preceded her. She stood on the threshold, seeming to take in with one glance the tall shelves, the shadowed mezzanine, the pools of yellow light picking out leather chairs, reading stands, and tables burdened with stacks of books. "Ah yes," she said, with a sniff. "Well, here, for once, we need not bother…"

Mme de Miremont, despite having been the sun for so long to a galaxy of provincial ladies, had always taken the strictest precautions not to lapse into provincial habits of dress. She ordered the latest pattern books from Paris and harried her friends with letters demanding to know the newest shade for gloves or ribbons. In addition, her recent sojourn in London at the height of the Season had, she felt confident, reaffirmed her title to be considered a cosmopolitan woman of fashion. However, it has to be said that Aline de Miremont was not a woman to leave well alone. There was not a dress so precisely à la mode that she did not believe it improved by an extra string of beads or a ruffle of lace or a little frilled cape about the shoulders, nor a hat that was not the better for more feathers or a dramatic swathe of veiling. Nor was the effect of this profusion diminished by her valiant defiance of age. Although her waist no longer fitted the handspan that had measured it in the days of her great beauty, she still wore the pale colours of girlhood, even in autumn. Her complexion always evoked rose petals, although this delicate blush now owed much to a liberality of rouge and powder; her hair was always dressed in a teasing abundance of curls. She was a short woman, but this overblown extravagance, this riot of curls and supernumerary frills, somehow rendered her gigantic. She made Max think of a huge iced cake, the work of some apprentice pastry cook determined to show his mettle.

Her voice had drifted away, she was turning to sweep out, when she appeared to realise there was something she had missed.

M. de M cleared his throat. Although only of medium height, he was strongly built, with a physique that attested more to his love of fencing and riding than to his hours spent in study, and despite his retiring nature he carried himself with a dignity that was not devoid of presence; yet beside his wife he seemed to have shrunk. His face, Max noticed, was stiff with anxiety and the effort to appear equable.

"Madame, may I present to you my secretary, Monsieur Fabien."

Max stepped away from his worktable and, pausing a respectful distance from Mme de Miremont, dipped his head in a brief bow.

She peered at him. Then she turned to her husband. "But where is Monsieur Lesage?"

"He retired last summer."

"But he has been with you for years, he was with your father."

"He is blind and bedridden, poor fellow. He lives with his sister now, at Nogent."

As though reluctant to be satisfied with this information, madame peered at the new secretary again. "This one is very young."

To Max, the old fellow's embarrassment was palpable. "Monsieur Fabien has excellent Latin."

"But Monsieur Lesage was such a mine of information—"

"And serviceable Greek."

"—as well as being so very obliging…"

"And he writes a good, clear hand."

Madame continued to stare at Max—hers was the blurred gaze, he realised, of someone with myopia too vain to use a lorgnette. All at once, disconcertingly, her eyelashes fluttered. "Well, we shall see."

To M. de M's embarrassment had been added displeasure that his secretary was being discussed as if he were a chair or a table. He cleared his throat once more. "Aline, the clock is telling us we should be dressing for dinner." Under cover of ushering her out, he shot Max an apologetic grimace.

The doors remained parted, so that Max could hear the silvery laugh floating back from the anteroom. "Armand, you are such an old stick you would not think to notice. But your Monsieur How-d'you-call-him is quite passably good-looking."

CHAPTER ELEVEN

To Miremont's intense relief, Aline's first evening under his roof passed off peacefully. He had feared the worst when, instead of retiring to change out of her travelling clothes, she had demanded a tour of the piano nobile while her maid unpacked, but, apart from the expected contretemps over the ballroom, which Miremont, ashamed of having lost his temper with Clotilde, felt he had on this occasion resolved firmly but calmly, she had offered few complaints.

Perhaps a false impression had been created by Clotilde's officiousness. Perhaps, owing to his lamentable failure to put aside the past, he was being unfair. Heaven knew, he, Miremont, had changed in the last fifteen years—must not Aline have changed too? If he had seen no sign of it from her letters or his last New Year visit, was not that because he was too ready to judge? Age must have taught her a modicum of good sense: having attained her goal of returning to Paris, she understood it was politic to be on her best behaviour.

Certainly the family gathering at supper, which included Clotilde and her husband, was a somewhat strained affair; but perhaps it only appeared so to Miremont because he must reaccustom himself to Aline's constant chatter. Thierry-Le Puy's tales of the Jockey Club were summarily cut off, Clotilde could manage only sporadic interjections and even poor Julie, although urged by Aline herself to describe her presentation at the English court, had the story snatched from her when she had scarcely begun; as for Miss Pilkington, the English companion, a large plain woman in her late twenties, she spoke only when spoken to and therefore not at all, while Max followed her example, wearing his secretary's face throughout and resisting—very properly, as Miremont reminded himself—any covert exchange of glances.

Yet surely Miremont should welcome his wife's loquacity, since it spared him the burden of small talk. He must admit the real cause of his impatience: he was keen to hear Julie speak of her acquaintance with his English cousins and the month she had spent at Feltwell House, their country seat in Norfolk, a topic Aline was unlikely to dilate upon—as the Massinghams would not receive her, Julie had gone there with Miss Pilkington. Yet, fond as he was of Charles and Lavinia Massingham, even this was an excuse: the truth was he longed to have his younger daughter to himself.

*

Miremont could not be more delighted with Julie. Two long years! Even after she had left the convent he had been cheated of her presence, for last New Year Aline had thoughtlessly agreed to her joining the family of a school friend somewhere in the Alps. He had been forced to make do with his memory from Agathe's christening of a charming but coltish creature; but here, demure yet poised, and dressed with a pleasing simplicity that should have shamed her mother, was an entrancingly beautiful young woman.

She had the blonde hair, baby-blue eyes and translucent skin that had distinguished Aline's youth. Her features were perhaps not so perfect—her mouth might be judged a fraction too small, her nose was slightly tilted and her chin bore the Miremont dimple—but these small irregularities merely added to her appeal. Despite her superficial resemblance to her mother, he could see much of his own family in her too, not just the dimple, but a vivacity, a taking way of crinkling her nose when she laughed that reminded him of his beloved sister Léonore. Of course, she had her mother's way, as well, of lowering her chin and looking up at you through her lashes. But—and this was the miracle—she had escaped her mother's nature.

Admittedly, he had been taken aback at the moment of their reunion when, instead of hurrying forward to meet his embrace, she had paused, seeming to regard him coolly before enquiring: "So, Papa, we are not quite strangers?" But then she had laughed and he had understood she had been teasing.

She liked to tease him, he discovered. She would steal into his study when he was supposed to be working, sit on his lap with her arms around his neck and call him her 'dear old grey-haired Papa' (although—and this was his one vanity—his dark curls as yet showed no trace of silver). Nevertheless, unlike Clotilde, she sought his advice, seemed to value his opinions and, while he could hardly expect a girl of her age with the dazzle of Society to distract her to evince any interest in his work, he enjoyed listening to her bright chatter about boarding school and the Massinghams and the various impressions left upon her by her travels. He took great pleasure in her sharp perceptions and agile mind; and, if he privately regretted that the nuns, along with instilling the proper womanly virtues, had not seen fit to nurture this intelligence—she seemed woefully ignorant of literature and history—then, it would not be her lot in life to puzzle over abstractions. She would be a handsome prize, just as she was, for any man. (Having only just had her restored to him, it pained him to recall the true purpose of her visit.)

Yet he discerned that she had not remained unaffected by the years spent in her mother's care. From certain remarks she let slip, it appeared she had been brought up to pinching self-denial. For instance, he was dismayed by a conversation before luncheon on the first full day of her visit, when he was showing her the picture gallery.

She had fixed her gaze on one of his Fragonards, Cupid whispering into the ear of a comely young woman, and he could not resist saying: "Yes, my dear, she is very pretty. But you are beautiful."

"Dear silly Papa!" This was accompanied by a blush and a self-deprecatory moue; becoming modesty, yet, Miremont sensed, fraught also with something other.

He took her hand, marvelling at how tiny it seemed in his. "You must believe you are beautiful."

"Darling Papa, you are prejudiced."

"Am I the only one who says it?"

"Oh, people may say what they like. If you were me, looking in the glass every morning…"

"My darling child!" He had tightened his fingers around hers, horrified at what she might see that was so at odds with the truth. But, laughing, snatching her hand away, she tugged at one of the tight curls that framed her temples.

"Ugh! Mademoiselle Bonnard dresses Maman's hair exactly to her taste and that is all very well. But she is Maman's age. And besides…"

Miremont, who had thought the curls charming, could only dimly comprehend her. However she must have taken his look of perplexity for a frown, for she said:

"Oh dear, now I have made you angry."

"Angry?"

"After all, you have already given me the pearls."

This increased Miremont's puzzlement. The double strand of pearls, which had been his mother's, had been conveyed to Sainte-Fleur in September for Julie's birthday (Clotilde had also received one of his mother's pearl necklaces when she had turned eighteen). Julie had delighted him by wearing the pearls last night. But what they had to do with her offending tresses he could not see. Did it mean she was dissatisfied with them too?

"My dear girl, if you would have preferred something else—"

"Oh no, Papa. They are magnificent, far more than I deserve. That is why I can hardly expect—I know you wish us to be prudent and I am sure Maman is right, you would think it an unnecessary expense."

Although Miremont was now more lost than ever, the words 'Maman' and 'expense', coupled together, had a galvanising effect. "What can you not expect? What does your mother consider unnecessary?"

"There, Papa, now you are angry in earnest."

"I am not angry."

"Please, I shan't utter another word about sharing Mademoiselle Bonnard with Maman."

"I am not angry—with you."

"After all, why should I expect to have my own lady's maid?"

A lady's maid? He stared at her, astonished. Was this all his poor child wanted? A beautiful young woman, setting out in Society, required a lady's maid of her own, but thought it unreasonable to ask for one? When he weighed this against all Aline's requests, from the lavish furnishing of her apartments to the new landau (painted, of course, with the Miremont escutcheon), he was momentarily lost for words. It was Julie, not Aline, who was being launched upon the world, Julie who must be at the centre of their concerns, poor little Julie, who, beautiful though she was, disliked what she saw in her looking glass and even felt unworthy of her grandmother's pearls.

"My dearest girl." He took both her hands in his. "I shall speak to Madame Mercier directly. She is bound to know of some suitable young woman—I shall tell her it is a matter of urgency."

As she looked up at him, her lower lip trembled a little. "And you are certain that you are not vexed with me?"

"My dear, it is a father's privilege, his delight, to grant his daughter's wishes, in whatever way he can."

"Oh, thank you, thank you, Papa!" She flung her arms around his neck. While she planted kisses on both his cheeks he held her gingerly, feeling how small and delicate she was, this innocent creature it was his duty to protect. But, as she pulled away, she was laughing again. "Mind you, Papa dearest, you should beware what you say. I might lead you into hopeless extravagance."

"Darling Julie, if I can make you happy, nothing will seem extravagant except the happiness that gives me."

"Then…"

He was pained to see she hesitated. "There is something else?"

"Oh, Papa, I warned you…"

He smiled. "Come, my dear child, out with it."

"Maman intends to consult Monsieur Worth."

"Well, I suppose—"

"Oh, I know she is right, I have dresses enough, I ought to make do with the toilettes I got in London. And of course a great many ladies there go to Elise and positively swear by her. But—" she pulled at her sleeve with the same disgust she had shown for the curls "—as you can see, the shape is all wrong. And the cut of the skirt. It has not yet reached London that the *tournure* is *le dernier cri* again. But then in England—oh, I agree there is no one but Redfern if you need a riding habit—but in general, as you know, Papa, the English are most comfortable when dressed head to toe in tweed."

This left Miremont as out of his depth as he had been before: he had admired her costume for the way its two shades of blue brought out the colour of her eyes, he had no notion what a *tournure* could be (she would later try to educate him about the bustle, although without great success), and he felt she had been somewhat harsh about the English. But even he knew of Worth and one salient point did strike him: while his wife was to be dressed by the most sought-after couturier in Europe, his darling child was expected to 'make do'. Yes, of course she must commission from Worth whatever she needed. He would not wish her to be outshone by any woman, let alone her mother.

This conversation in the picture gallery, as may be imagined, caused Miremont bitter reflection. Aline's allowance had always been generous and, in addition, whenever she had run up debts, which was not infrequently, he had paid them, principally for his daughters' sakes. He was outraged to discover they had nevertheless been forced to make pointless sacrifices; nor was he pleased by the glimpse Julie had given him of how he had been represented to his children. Was it surprising Clotilde despised him? It was much to Julie's credit that she seemed to harbour no resentment, was still prepared to love him even while believing him a skinflint.

No, if Julie resented anyone it was evidently her mother. While she behaved impeccably to Aline's face—although without warmth, Miremont could not help noticing—she sometimes allowed herself comments in private that, whatever his own views, it was his paternal duty to discourage. The conversation about riding was a case in point.

Julie wished to accompany him on his morning rides in the Bois. "I want to be an Amazon, Papa. You must have seen them. They are the height of elegance in their severe black habits and top hats—but they ride with the daring of any man."

Miremont was half startled, half amused. "My little daughter an Amazon?"

"I ride well, Papa. If you doubt me, write to the Massinghams. We could not ride to hounds at Feltwell as it was not the season, but we rode a great deal nevertheless."

"All the same—"

"Oh, there is nothing improper in it. Amazons ride side-saddle, not like bicyclists. As I keep telling Maman, if only she would listen."

Aline, she explained, had put her foot down: aside from the expense of providing Julie with a mount, as a young unmarried girl she would appear to better advantage at her Maman's side in the landau. Miremont could not agree: he was delighted his daughter wished to join him in one of his greatest pleasures; he applauded her spirit and would be proud to ride with her, while, as for a mount, there was an even-tempered mare in his stables that would suit her perfectly. He promised to try to persuade her mother.

"Oh, Papa! On no account do that. You must let me talk to her."

"But, my dearest—"

"Dear, sweet, silly Papa, you have been married to her all these years, yet you have not the slightest notion how to manage her. I shall do as I did about my lady's maid."

Miremont raised his eyebrows. He had assumed that, once he had agreed to bear the expense, there had been no further contention over the lady's maid.

"I shall tell her you are absolutely opposed. Then she will agree to everything in an instant."

Quite apart from her conspiratorial disregard for the truth, there was something in his daughter's tone, a certain lightness, a cheerful disrespect for her mother that he felt obliged to check. But she must have found his reprimand as pompous as it sounded to his own ears, for she simply laughed and kissed his brow. And anyway, he was human: he could not fail to rejoice that one of his daughters regarded him as an ally.

CHAPTER TWELVE

Miremont was certainly in need of allies. To imagine Aline had matured with age had been folly. Yes, her second day at the Hôtel de Miremont had been spent peaceably enough, writing letters, visiting *les grand magasins* with Julie and Miss Pilkington and dining en famille with her brother and his wife, an occasion Miremont was mercifully excused, since he and Robert de Sestrès had never been on the friendliest terms. But—Miremont recalled Virgil's description of a serpent, hibernating in the cold earth, shedding its skin, then rearing up at the first shaft of sunlight, renewed in all its glory—by the third day she was rested and ready to strike.

The fires in her apartments smoked, her breakfast chocolate was cold, the servants were slovenly, the supper menus dull, the silver smeared, the napkins wrongly folded, the flowers everywhere a disgrace—did no one recall she could not abide chrysanthemums?—while the Elizabeth Salon smelled of mildew and you had only to move a cushion in the Grand Salon to sneeze yourself insensible from the dust. And as for Thomas, his deformity sickened her and, if Miremont were still unwilling to send him packing, he should have the consideration to keep the hideous creature from her sight.

An arrangement of convenience? It was clear she would not rest until she had reclaimed a wife's entitlement to oversee the running of the household.

Juliette had been unjust to her father. Miremont did have a means of managing Aline: wherever possible, he gave way. He had learnt from bitter experience the consequences of opposing her, was wearied by the very recollection of her seemingly unstoppable tirades, and he dreaded them the more now he understood himself better, knew he harboured a rage to answer hers. Of course, his yielding only increased his wife's contempt and compounded his difficulties when he was obliged to stand up to her. And, yes, he would admit to cowardice, at least where his own interests were concerned. But usually there were wider considerations: while surrender, as in the case of poor Thomas, might sometimes prove impossible, it was often the better of two evils.

Mme Mercier had run the distaff side of Miremont's household admirably for over twenty years and would not relish being superintended by madame—she knew her of old. But the alternative, that the housekeeper should be torn by conflicting orders from master and mistress, was unthinkable. For Aline would expect her word to be law whatever Miremont decided and, while she reserved her worst excesses for her husband, she had never restrained herself with the servants. Accordingly, Miremont informed Mme Mercier that she should now consult madame on any matter relating to menus and housekeeping. Mme Mercier must have foreseen the inevitable, for she did not remonstrate but accepted his instruction with a small, grim nod.

Miremont's second surrender came the next day and was unlooked-for and painful. Rejoicing in the growing warmth of his relations with Julie, he could hardly question his vow of celibacy, yet he passed restless nights imagining Max asleep overhead in the room above his study. Their occasional partings had always caused Miremont torment, but this parting in propinquity, this separation by mere lath and plaster, seemed singularly cruel. Surprising, too, how rapidly one could unlearn the disciplines and sacrifices of the solitary life; as much as sexual pleasure, Miremont missed the comfort bestowed by the boy's touch, by the boy's limbs warming his. After a lonely breakfast in his apartments, where the door was zealously guarded by Thomas, he had at last met Max at the stables. But it was only when they had returned from their ride, and when Thomas, having changed his master out of his riding breeches, was eventually persuaded to desert his post, that they could finally count on privacy. If their vow afforded him nothing else, Miremont could spend what remained of the morning taking pleasure in the boy's presence.

Alas, madame was not one of those ladies who like to breakfast languidly in bed, never emerging from their boudoirs before noon: on the contrary, she was seized by a rapacious energy from the first moment of waking. With Thomas no longer on guard, she was able to penetrate the outer doors of Miremont's apartments and would have reached the threshold of his study before he and Max were aware of her, had the yapping of her lapdog not heralded her approach. By the time she had flung open the study doors—without so much as a knock, Miremont noted—Max was standing innocently at Miremont's writing desk, while Miremont himself had seized a book and was ostentatiously leafing through it. All the same, his heart had turned over; nor was his discomfiture lessened when the little dog began snuffling around his ankles as though scenting his guilt.

Madame surveyed the two of them. "Ah, good!" she said. It seemed to Miremont that her gaze rested on Max for a moment before she cast it around the room and finally turned it back upon his own person.

"Please, my dear," he said, struggling for a smile, "do be seated."

"On that vile thing?" She inclined her head contemptuously towards the divan, whose springs, despite Miremont's good intentions, had yet to be remedied. "Armand, I swear this room has not changed in fifteen years, except to be still more lowering of the spirit. All these mouldy old books, these ugly pictures, these horrid knick-knacks…"

Did she propose to extend her redecoration schemes to his own quarters? Miremont felt a stab of fear as he saw the books, the Daumiers, his Etruscan bronzes and his grandfather's beloved couch all swept away in the quest for *le dernier cri*. But, in his effort to remain calm, he failed to perceive her attack was directed elsewhere.

"Well, Monsieur Fabien, I have come to rescue you. There is urgent work to be done."

While Max looked startled, Miremont was too taken aback for speech, so that the boy found his tongue first. "Madame will forgive me, but monsieur requires—"

"Nonsense, he cannot object to my borrowing you for an hour or two."

"Aline—my dear…" With difficulty, Miremont recovered himself. "Monsieur Fabien and I were in the midst of… He is assisting me with my chapter on the *Fasti*—"

She cut him off with her irritating laugh. "Armand, you are an incorrigible old fossil. Look at Monsieur Fabien. He is young and handsome, you cannot bury him alive with your dead Romans."

"Madame, my secretary is not—"

"Besides, this is proper work. Admit it, you can easily manage without him for a couple of hours."

She gathered up the dog, which, having raised its leg to the pedestal of the writing desk, was at present savaging the fringes of the rug. "Come, Bébé! Come, Monsieur Fabien!"

"Madame, you may not—you cannot simply…"

But, with a swish of her train, she had already turned to leave and, in any case, Miremont, much to his surprise, could see Max shaking his head.

"Better that I go," the boy mouthed. Then, lightly squeezing Miremont's arm as he passed, he followed her.

Through the open study doors, her voice, punctuated by Bébé's yaps, trailed back to him as she swept through his drawing room: "Quick, quick, young man. We must commission a photographer for my carte de visite. You must talk to the printers. And I shall require a list of the houses where I should call and those where I may send a servant with my card…"

Miremont sank heavily onto the divan. Of course the boy was right. For him to seem overly possessive of his secretary would not only provoke the usual scene: it might also invite questions. No battle could better warrant surrender. Furthermore, he should be grateful that the consuming but impermissible urge which had seized him during their embrace had now subsided. All the same, he felt like weeping.

Even Aline's innocent morning of letter-writing was, it transpired, not without consequence. She soon informed Miremont that they would be expecting a guest: Lady Telford would be arriving from England in two days and, since she had been of inestimable service to Aline during her stay in London, she must be treated royally. A dispute immediately arose about where this illustrious personage should be quartered. Rather to Miremont's surprise, Aline did not suggest the state apartments—perhaps she really was expecting the Prince of Wales—but she was most unhappy with the other guest rooms.

"They are dreadfully shabby. And they overlook the servants' yard."

The guest wing having windows in both elevations, its second floor was not served by a concealed passage but by a windowed corridor that did indeed face the rear courtyard; however, as Miremont reminded his wife, the guest apartments themselves looked out upon the central courtyard and the fountain. Aline was not appeased. Her complaint, it turned out, had a byzantine motive.

"The apartments at the front would be so much more suitable. If only you had not allowed those wretched old women to play upon your emotions. No doubt they only pay you a paltry rent."

Miremont had never charged his second cousins a sou. He sighed. "This is a large house, my dear."

"All the same—to clutter it up with poor relations…"

"As Clotilde wrote to tell you, Caroline d'Ancy-Miremont died some months ago. Poor Arianne de Vaux is now on her own."

An idea seemed to strike Aline. "What if she dies too?"

"My dear, I hardly feel—"

"Come to think of it, I am sure I saw Doctor Chevalier's carriage outside yesterday."

"The princesse suffers from lumbago."

"And a priest going in."

"Abbé Pierelle from the Institute visits her regularly. She is still distressed about her sister."

"Do you not see?" And no, Miremont was not mistaken, Aline's voice carried a note of triumph. "We should be in full mourning for a month. No parties, no balls. It would be a frightful disaster."

As so often nowadays, Miremont was temporarily lost for words.

"Surely you could persuade her to move. To somewhere quieter, in the country perhaps. There must be room for her at Beauvallon."

"For pity's sake, woman!"

"Supposing she dies just before Julie's ball? It would have to be cancelled."

"Good grief, we have not even set a date!"

"I know you will not think of me, although I am the one who must arrange everything. But do think of your darling Julie!"

"Madame, enough!" He knew what he risked, her hand had gone to her throat, her bosom was already heaving, but he was too appalled to care. "If your Lady Telford is dissatisfied with her accommodation then she may take the next boat back to England. This is Arianne de Vaux's home and she leaves it over my dead body —which, may I remind you, would put you in crape for a year. Besides, in the very unlikely event that the poor lady should suffer misfortune, I am confident that Julie, at least, will show compassion."

This last remark moved Aline to a peculiar little laugh. But, greatly to Miremont's relief, her gasping and heaving ceased before they had properly begun. He was not sure what saved him. Perhaps, thanks to a rare glimmer of reason, she had seen that, should she hope to be received by her husband's connections, throwing one of his elderly relations onto the street was not the best way to advance her cause.

Lady Telford transpired not to be English, but French. A plump woman of middle years, she appeared quite remarkably emollient: from her skin, which was as pink and unwrinkled as blancmange, to her dress, which, despite the length of her widowhood, still favoured the gentle greys and lilacs of third-year mourning, her every aspect suggested a pliant softness, a willingness to take all comers to her soothing bosom. Her voice was low and well modulated, her conversation carefully agreeable: she tried to draw Miremont out by talking to him about the Massinghams, with whom she claimed to be on close terms, and once even engaged with him bravely, if briefly, on the subject of Ovid.

She was, Miremont supposed, the perfect foil for Aline: if he found this surfeit of sympathy wearing, then he was churlish, for apparently they were in Lady Telford's debt on a great many counts. Well-placed to introduce Aline and Julie into London Society owing to her late husband's position in the higher echelons of the British diplomatic service, she had offered them the hospitality of her Mayfair house; she had found them Miss Pilkington to improve Julie's schoolgirl English and to act as chaperone on those occasions when, as the good lady delicately put it, her dear *maman* was obliged to be elsewhere; and, as she was related on her mother's side to the Polignacs, she could render further aid in Paris by advising on prospective husbands for their darling.

Nevertheless, Miremont could not help suspecting this downy pillow might conceal a brick. Julie, of course, must have seen a good deal of Lady Telford, but all she would vouchsafe was: "Oh, she and Maman are thick as thieves." Clotilde, however, although her acquaintance with their benefactress was as brief as his own, was unusually forthright. In fact, she was eloquent in her contempt for Lady Telford, who was not a 'Lady' in the true sense at all, for her late husband had been a mere baronet; and as for her being related to the Polignacs, it was a relationship so distant as to be invisible to the *Almanach de Gotha*. Poor Maman: she had been out of Society for so long and in London she must have been quite lost (for, as Papa knew, she spoke no English). It was hardly a wonder she had been imposed upon by such a person.

Miremont was untroubled by Lady Telford's standing with the *Almanach*; besides, he recognised Clotilde's true grievance: she had been displaced as her mother's confidante. All the same, the conversation was hardly encouraging. Nor did Max offer much comfort. In his opinion Lady Telford belonged to a type he knew from his time in service: expert at extracting generosity, yet stingy with tips and given to furtive meanness—Max had seen her tip an entire dish of bonbons into her reticule when she believed herself unobserved—she bore the hallmarks of the professional house guest.

"A species not unlike deathwatch beetle," Max concluded with a grin. "Once entrenched, the devil to eradicate."

Miremont groaned. Though cheated of the princesse de Vaux's apartments, Lady Telford had pronounced herself charmed by the guest wing: clearly they would endure her for months.

Aline's resuming command of the household did not produce the peace Miremont had hoped for. She had at once decided there were nowhere near enough servants: more of all kinds were required, including at least four more footmen. The servants' hall, settled in its ways and long accustomed to the foibles and shortcomings of its members, was suddenly doubled in size. The effect of so many incomers, ignorant of the house and its routines, was as might be expected: nerves jangled, footmen dropped trays or clattered silver, housemaids left their mops and buckets behind in the salons, meals were sent over late or cold.

Morale was not improved by another innovation that caused even Georges and Philippe to stalk about with a mutinous air. Aline had always found the Miremont livery irredeemably dull; Miremont, when informed gloomily by Boussec that madame desired changes, judged this was one of those matters where it would be unwise to resist and instructed his butler that she should be indulged. He had imagined his sober *corbeau* would be augmented with showier detail—say, new buttons or frogging: he had not bargained for its being replaced by canary yellow.

From now on, in addition to wearing powdered wigs like Mme de Claireville's footmen, all the liveried servants, including the grooms and the two new pageboys, would sport yellow tailcoats when in full dress, with black-and-yellow striped waistcoats and black breeches. "Wasps!" said Théo, the coachman, who was wont to be frank when he had Miremont on his own in the brougham. "We looks—pardon my language, monsieur—like a swarm of ruddy hornets."

Boussec and Mme Mercier worked grimly to discipline their troubled army, while constantly issuing it with additional orders: madame's apartments must be sprayed with eau de cologne, coals for madame's grate must be wrapped in paper to avoid noise when replenishing the fire, daily omelettes must be prepared for Bébé. Miremont could not bring himself to complain about the disarray. A few broken glasses or a stray mop were as nothing when he observed the upheaval all around him. By the time the month was out, his life had utterly changed.

His comfortable routine was swept away. His house was filled with people, many of whom he did not know or disliked. His brother-in-law Robert de Sestrès, with his endless talk of stocks and bonds and 'dead-cert' investments, became a frequent presence and Achille de Tarascon was also much in evidence, for Aline had always adored him and recognised, besides, that in capturing such a celebrity she re-established herself as a force to be reckoned with. As for Miremont's own circle, its members were either out of favour—as ever, Mme de Claireville and Aline jangled like knives in a box—or, like the La Marnes and Constant de Sauvigny, restricted themselves to a fleeting courtesy call.

Other regular visitors to the Hôtel de Miremont were banished altogether. Miremont's weekly chess evenings with Dr Gérard were disallowed: the social round left no time and in any case the doctor, with his gauche manners and shabby morning coat, was scarcely a person to be received by the nobility—not to mention the diseases he might bring into the house from his charity work. (It was notable that while Aline considered poor Gérard beneath her, she was happy to entertain Dr Chevalier, just as bourgeois but equipped with that instrument essential to a Society physician: a varnished tongue.) Professor Ricard and Dr Rosenthal, Miremont's friends from the Sorbonne, with whom he had spent many joyful evenings debating Augustan poetry, also failed to pass muster: they were not only bourgeois but, worse still, Jews.

Since Aline was usually out paying calls in the afternoons, the Herzens' rehearsals in the Music Room escaped her attention for almost a fortnight and when at last she discovered them she reacted with surprise and delight—until Miremont was obliged to explain that these were not jobbing musicians to be hired by the hour to entertain her guests, whereupon she sent them packing. Only Captain Horthy was spared: fencing, Aline opined, set the correct tone, as well as offering the advantage of Roland de Sauvigny's presence; for she still hoped to win over his father and, as Miremont was to discover, had included Constant's elder son, Edmond, on her list of husbands for Julie.

It goes without saying that these insults to good friends filled Miremont with anger and mortification. (He was mortified still further, when Zhukovsky, having overheard his conversation with Aline, offered the quartet's services gratis if ever madame should require them.) Yet, if he cared for these friends, once again he had no choice: unless he wished to expose them to his wife's prejudices, he must consent to their exile. His hope, of course, was to invent excuses that enabled him to meet them elsewhere, but Aline contrived it so that there was seldom a free evening; when they were not receiving visitors, they were being received at conversaziones, dinners, soirées, balls.

As a young man Miremont had believed himself shy, but middle age had taught him that his true problem was boredom. He lacked the energy to invent the fleeting inconsequential topics suited to the dinner table; nor did he fare better with the conversations he was expected to conduct with other gentlemen of rank, rapidly running out of stamina when it came to who was rising at which ministry, or whether South American ventures were still a sound bet. Occasionally, he would be lucky enough to light upon a gift—an eminent anthropologist who had lived for a year amongst nomads or an aged general who had fought at Solferino—and then he would sit enthralled in the smoking room for hours. But Aline would search him out to remind him of his duty, which was to cultivate Prince So-and-So, or M. le duc de Such-and-Such, whose sons might prove suitable for their daughter.

He had known it would be torture, yet he was happy to endure it for Julie's sake. To see her radiant in her Worth tulle, to count the admiring glances she attracted, hear her humorous post-mortem of last night's ball, gain her confidence and her friendship—these were his rewards. And he could easily have sustained himself against the creeping, crushing fatigue that besets a man unused to singing for his supper, if he could only have spent some hours in peace with his books; although, of course, it was not books he longed for—he had abandoned any attempt to concentrate on Ovid—it was Max; Max, with whom he was now seldom alone; Max, who for long hours he scarcely saw; Max, who seemed daily to be growing more distant.

No doubt Aline had merely desired to disrupt his work when she had kidnapped the boy, yet if she wished to be revenged upon him she could not have chosen a better weapon: what bitter irony that she could not know the wound she inflicted. A couple of hours? Soon it was every morning until luncheon, and afternoons too: even if Aline were not at home, she would find ways to keep Max occupied in her absence; at other times he was closeted in her boudoir, where she met in conclave with Lady Telford and Clotilde. Miremont might unsaddle with him in the stable yard, measure foils with him, see him distantly beyond the salt when they dined at home, but to kiss him, ruffle his hair—even in their rare private moments interruption threatened the smallest intimacy.

Wretchedly Miremont recalled the game of risk they had played at Catherine's château at the start of their affair, the unbearable excitement of illicit pleasures snatched in defiance of the Fates. But of course there was no question of that here. And besides at La Boissière the boy had been as willing as he, if not the leader in their mischief.

For this was the worst of it: Max did not appear to object to their new situation. And Miremont thought he knew why.

From the first, Aline, although old enough to be Max's mother, had flirted with him quite shamelessly. It was her way with men—the lowered eyes, the fluttering lashes, the teasing laugh—Miremont recalled how it had irritated him even in the first days of their marriage. Max might surely be trusted to greet these blandishments with the indifference they deserved. But no, the boy was flirting back. Daily Miremont grew more aware of the little smiles, the secret glances, the suggestive tone of the boy's "Yes, madame, my pleasure, madame."

When he had decided on celibacy, Miremont had known it would strain Max's resolve and foment his own jealousy. He still suffered dreadfully during Max's days off. But, as ever, his imaginings conjured up other men, he had not considered danger from this quarter. Yet now he recalled the little nursemaid who had stirred his suspicions at La Boissière; he recalled how close Max had stood to Mlle de la Falaise as she explained the rules of croquet; he recalled Vera Zhukovskaya, the 'honorary sister'; and if he tried to allay his fears by reminding himself these women were young, he had only to remember that Max, during his time in Catherine's service, must have performed the nocturnal duties that, legend had it, devolved upon all her footmen.

Dear God, was it possible? Could he doubt the boy loved him? Miremont reminded himself with a shudder how readily Max had agreed to the temporary break in their relations, how willingly, at Aline's command, he had abandoned him. Yet, even so—he would not—could not... Surely Max could never stoop so low as to betray Miremont with his own wife?

CHAPTER THIRTEEN

Max was inclined to think Mme de Claireville had been overly kind about Mme de Miremont. She was indeed an extraordinarily stupid woman. But, while stupidity, in Max's experience, was often accompanied by a predisposition to sloth, madame's was borne along by a whirling energy that could let nothing lie, that sucked everything and everybody into its vortex, so that when she had been in a room above ten minutes she had gobbled up all the air.

At first Max had not understood Armand's willingness to give in to her whims; he had been shocked by the old fellow's surrender of his household. But when his own turn came to be commandeered, he had immediately seen resistance was folly: it would not deflect madame, who might wonder why her husband, who had never required exclusive right to old Lesage, was so very possessive of his new secretary.

Besides—and Max concurred with Mme de Claireville on this point—the old fellow would always prove powerless against his wife, although it was not reason that handicapped him so much as the measureless ether between planets. In Armand's cosmos, reality was filtered through a prism of attachments, loyalties, duties, obligations; in madame's, it was concentrated within a single beam of light, in which she stood, as beautiful as when she had been a bride, as deserving of adoration and recognition; let others dare encroach and she was merciless in regaining sole command of the spotlight. If poor Armand were to enter this universe, he must imagine himself Bernhardt playing Phèdre.

Max, however, since he was frequently, if unwillingly, privy to madame's confidences, had by now acquired a working knowledge of her delusions. He had also experienced the full power of her hysteria.

"Lists, dear Monsieur Fabien! Monsieur Lesage always had lists. He always knew exactly whom we called upon and who called on us."

Max had tried, that first morning, not to look bewildered. There was no point in explaining that, unlike Lesage, he had no experience of this sort of thing, that M. de M did not bother with cards, much less keep a visitors' book. Fortunately he recalled that Lesage had preserved the visitors' books from the time before madame and monsieur's separation: the Buzzard's personal effects had long since been sent to Nogent but, to maintain the illusion that the old bird, though blind and paralysed, might one day resume his post, his study, with its meticulous records of the Miremonts' every engagement, remained untouched. But when Max had retrieved the books he was none the wiser: not only was he unfamiliar with most of the names, but death must have extinguished some of these comets, while others would have risen in their place; moreover there was the delicate question of who would be at home to madame and who might feel her past obliged them to forgo this pleasure.

Armand, as might be expected, was of little help. Max might ask Boussec or Georges, but the likelihood that either would be willing to assist him had not been increased by the chaos engulfing the servants' hall. Besides, there was only one person in Paris who knew where the social compass was set, as well or better than any duchess. That night, when everyone was at the opera (to please madame, Armand had hired a box for the season, but its privileges did not extend to his secretary), Max braved the Monkey to consult Old Jouvert.

Two mornings later, he was invited, not to the Monkey, but—and he recognised this was a signal honour—to Old Jouvert's main place of business. Although this transpired to be an unprepossessing café in the Faubourg Saint-Antoine, it was clear that, while at the Monkey the old toper was something of a pariah, sought out only by servants of a certain disposition who were down on their luck, here he was king. As at the Monkey, he had his favourite table, but here it was not in a disregarded corner; here he was honoured with napery and a willing if greasy waiter to replenish his glass, here he sat enthroned, a ledger at his elbow, a queue of petitioners hovering in his orbit, the potentate accepting his dues. While the scope of these could only be guessed at, the vassal at present in audience—a crumpled fellow, out at the elbows—must have forgotten his obligations, for Old Jouvert was counting tattered notes and shaking his head.

The *patron*, a youngish man who, if you added a grog-blossom nose and subtracted the scar running the length of his right cheek, bore a passing resemblance to the potentate himself, had meanwhile been alerted to the presence of a smartly dressed stranger; he approached Max with a none-too-welcoming air. However Old Jouvert, having written something in his ledger, waved away the crumpled man and the elderly woman in tired furs who was hoping to succeed to the vacant chair and, stowing the notes in a leather wallet at his waist, beckoned Max over.

In return for three bottles of Armand's vintage cognac, Old

Jouvert handed over three lists: the first recorded those whom Mme la marquise might count amongst her acquaintance and on whom she could pay calls without censure; the second named those luminaries as yet unknown to her, to whom she must acquire an introduction; the third—rather lengthy, Max reflected as he rendered it later into his own hand—set down those houses where her welcome had lapsed. Still naive so far as madame was concerned, for this was only his first week in her employ, he was resolved to spare her feelings by withholding this last list.

Summoned to madame's boudoir—where had he been all morning when she had been searching high and low?—he found her ensconced with Lady Telford and her daughters. Although she kept him standing, she was initially all smiles.

"What a clever dear boy you are. Monsieur Lesage could not have been more thorough." Yet, as the ladies pored over the first two lists, her voice took on a note of puzzlement. "But where are the D'Issy-Lévêques? And the Merlincourts? And the Princess of Modena?"

A small silence fell. Max waited for rescue, from Lady Telford perhaps, but since none came he heaved in breath. "Madame, I am advised—"

"These are some of my oldest, dearest friends. Monsieur Lesage would never have forgotten them."

"Madame, I fear—"

"All this time with monsieur's mouldering Romans must have addled your brains, Monsieur Fabien. Marie-Louise d'Issy-Lévêque was one of my bridesmaids. I knew Inès de Merlincourt when she was a mere Rubenstein."

"My dear," said Lady Telford in her most soothing voice, "poor Monsieur Fabien is very young and is not—shall we say he lacks our experience of the beau monde. I am sure he will be more than willing to acknowledge his mistakes."

This was too much for Max. Besides, although madame might be aggrieved now, she would be more so later—and justly—when she discovered he had failed to shield her from humiliation. He produced the third list from his folder. "Madame, it is with the greatest regret…"

She snatched the paper, peered at it, but, as usual lacking her lorgnette, could make nothing of it and was compelled to hand it to Lady Telford, who read, in suitably incredulous tones: "'Houses where Madame la marquise de Miremont cannot be received…'"

Madame's bosom heaved. "Merciful heaven, this is unspeakable!"

"Indeed it is, my dear," cooed Lady Telford. "I am well acquainted with both the Princess of Modena and the comtesse d'Issy-Lévêque and I am certain they will make you perfectly welcome."

"Of course they will." Madame essayed her bell-like laugh. "Monsieur Fabien, you will take note that I shall call on all these people and you will be sure to include them in our invitation list."

Max had not missed the hysteria in her laughter and he observed that, in spite of her defiant tone, her bosom still heaved and her eyes had widened. Sensing danger, he hesitated. "Madame will forgive me…"

However it was Clotilde, thus far so silent he had hardly noticed her, who precipitated disaster. "Maman, please. You must do no such thing. I beg you, think of the shame, consider the harm you may do poor Julie. And poor Papa, too—when you leave your card you must also leave his."

Perhaps it was the mention of 'poor Papa', but Mme de Miremont suddenly let out a dreadful scream. Her eyes rolled, beneath the layers of rice powder her complexion changed to a dusky purple, she fought for breath. Then, just as it seemed she might succumb to a seizure, she folded both arms tightly across her stomach as if in receipt of a knife thrust and, rocking back and forth, began to wail.

"Never! My own daughter! Never in my life have I been treated so cruelly. Never have I been so hurt and abused! Is it not enough that everyone has been poisoned against me? Is it not enough that I am allowed no pleasure, no happiness, no friends? But my own daughter, whom I bore in agony, for whom I almost gave my life—oh, it is too frightful, too cruel…"

Lady Telford offered her smelling salts; Bébé yelped and pawed at her skirts; Clotilde, with many protestations of repentance, tried to embrace her; Mlle Bonnard was rung for to loosen her stays: nothing stopped the flow of her plaint. Even when she rose and, screwing the offending paper into a ball, flung it at the mantelpiece, hurling other small objects after it—a novel, a cushion, a crystal paperweight—which drove Bébé into a frenzy, the words of reproach continued to pour from her.

"Of course, I should have known. You have always been just like your father. He never gives a thought to anyone's feelings. Throughout our marriage—the coldness, the selfishness—I sacrificed everything to him, my youth, my beauty—but even if I'd lived like a nun and worn sackcloth and ashes—and now, when I have suffered so cruelly all these years, he cannot bear me to enjoy a little happiness. Poisoning everyone's minds. He and that she-devil Catherine de Claireville. He believes he's the model of moral rectitude, so superior. But he's a heartless monster! If my own dear Papa had known when he signed the marriage contract, if he could have foreseen how I would suffer…"

And so it went on, until Lady Telford, Clotilde and the lady's maid had assisted her to her bedroom amidst much commotion, and Max was left alone with a howling Bébé.

Max's struggles with Lesage had taught him how to rise above such circumstances to a plane of detachment. Even so, as he bent to pacify the dog, he found his hands were shaking. Only one person had remained unmoved throughout: Mlle Juliette had spent the entire discussion staring wordlessly out of the window and the moment her mother had commenced her hysterics she had calmly left the room.

For an entire day madame's terrible energy was stilled by a sick headache and, as she lay, under Dr Chevalier's orders, in a darkened room, Max was freed to return to Armand. He cherished the hope that, since he had been the cause of her outburst, the fancy she seemed to have taken to him would vanish. But, alas, next morning she was up and about early, chivvying him to go to the printers. Clotilde was selected to bear the blame: for a week madame refused to see either her elder daughter or her grandchildren. Nor had she given up on the D'Issy-Lévêques or the Merlincourts, and the resultant snubs she suffered occasioned more tears and recrimination.

But by then Max had learned that experience taught her nothing. Even before her visiting cards went to the printers, she had determined to hold her salon on Thursdays. Max could not but be concerned: he had no wish to witness another tantrum, but in those early days he still thought it his duty to protect her.

"Forgive me, madame, but I feel I must make you aware—Mme de Claireville has her salon on Thursdays."

He waited for the explosion and was astonished when none came. Instead, like a general who has been informed the enemy's forces are badly exposed on the left flank, madame was suffused with a glow of triumph.

"Then we shall see, Monsieur Fabien. We shall see, shan't we?"

And of course she did see. Once again there was much railing against Mme de Claireville and talk of treachery. Achille de Tarascon was notable amongst the traitors and, to Max's delight, he was banished for a fortnight. But since he was the jewel in madame's crown he was soon forgiven and the Thursdays limped on as if madame expected Mme la duchesse imminently to suffer the eclipse she deserved. Max might have felt pity for her humiliation if she had understood how she compounded it, but she could no more see she was her own worst enemy than a drunk can help falling into the gutter.

Although Max became used to her extreme changes of mood, he never ceased to be appalled by her lack of restraint. She was rude to the servants, shamefully indiscreet, and her dislikes easily turned into vendettas: the princesse de Vaux was on the infamous third list and if ever madame saw the old lady climbing into her carriage or crossing the forecourt on the arm of her paid companion she would shout after her: "Parasite!", like a Les Halles' fishwife. But naturally what Max loathed most about Mme la marquise was her constant belittling of Armand: the desire to rise up and defend the old fellow sometimes gripped him so fiercely he thought it would choke him; but, of course, for M. de M's sake, he must contain himself. Now he had the measure of madame, the old boy's fears did not seem excessive.

He set himself resolutely to follow Catherine de Claireville's advice: he would try to charm madame. He would concede to the myth that she was still an eighteen-year-old beauty: when she gazed at him from beneath her lashes he would smile as if she had bestowed a gift; when she touched his hand he would not withdraw it; while never presuming, while always remaining the respectful, dutiful secretary, he would nevertheless convey that he was sensible of her favour.

Shit, it sapped the spirit! His days were consumed by her never-ending demands. When he was not arranging appointments for dress-fitters or jewellers, or hiring musicians or placing orders with the florist, he was shut up in her boudoir, outlining her engagements for the day and dealing with her copious correspondence. On those afternoons when she was paying calls, he might hope to spend some time with the old boy, but often he found himself laboriously inscribing invitation cards or replying to invitations from others—for Society was still well supplied with those who could swallow their moral objections to Mme de Miremont, or at least respected her husband's rank and wealth.

At other times he would be sent on tiresome errands: to Houbigant for scent, to Debauve & Gallais for chocolates—tasks any footman could perform. A footman, too, would be appropriate to carry the parcels madame and Lady Telford acquired as, notwithstanding the glovers, lacemakers, milliners and purveyors of other fashionable necessities who came to the house, the two ladies succumbed to the novelties of Bon Marché and Printemps; but it seemed Max was uniquely qualified to advise on the colour of ribbons or the fit of a glove—or to fill the role, for the benefit of the other lady customers, of madame's young admirer.

Max observed that madame spent a great deal of time with Lady Telford and very little with Mlle Juliette, who, if she were not obliged to pay calls with her mother, preferred the company of Miss Pilkington and her own apartments. Max could not but feel that mademoiselle took the wisest course: Lady Telford was not only an outrageous flatterer who encouraged madame in her delusions; Max would amplify the opinion he had given Armand—she was a shameless fraud who no more knew the D'Issy-Lévêques than she could recite the Upanishads.

She was, however, tenacious in her hold upon madame, not only buoying her with false assurances but preying upon her superstition. As well as being on intimate terms with every aristocratic family in England and France, Lady Telford, it transpired, was a trusted disciple of Mme Blavatsky, the Theosophist, whom she had met in New York. During Mme de Miremont's stay in London, milady had taken her to a Theosophist séance, where ectoplasm had materialised, a table had moved of its own volition and madame had received a message from her dear papa on the other side assuring her that her suffering would be rewarded.

Keen to continue madame's spiritual nourishment, Lady Telford had arranged to make trial of the planchette at the Hôtel de Miremont. M. de M and Mlle Juliette had excused themselves, but Max had been obliged to sit in candlelight with milady, madame and Miss Pilkington as they joined hands to summon the psychic energy required for the medium, Mme Neroni, to contact Mustafa, her spirit guide. This seemed to take an eternity, particularly as Max was so seated as to find himself holding madame's hand and could not escape its gentle but suggestive pressure; but in due course Mustafa heard the call and guided Mme Neroni's mittened fingers as they lay upon the planchette, until its pencil, with frantic but apparently haphazard activity, had covered the paper with scrawl. It was no surprise to Max when this was pronounced to be another encouraging message from madame's poor dead papa; rather, he was intrigued by Mme Neroni's resemblance to the crone in furs at Old Jouvert's *levée*.

Milady Telford was not only eager to make spirits materialise, she could make things dematerialise too—or so Max was convinced—and she did not restrict herself to bonbons. Other small objects began to disappear: when madame's cameo brooch vanished, a housemaid was sent packing; one of the footmen paid the penalty for a missing cloisonné bowl. The Hôtel de Miremont offered rich pickings for light fingers and Max began seriously to fear for the old boy's treasures. Of course he could prove nothing; besides, he did not wish to worry Armand, while complaining to madame was naturally out of the question. But when he chanced to find Lady Telford in the Marble Salon, standing before the unlocked vitrine that held the ninth marquis' netsuke, although he assisted her to admire the tiny jade and ivory carvings and was politeness itself as, firmly closing the case, he accompanied her upstairs, he resolved to take action: he too was not untutored in pilfery.

Opportunely, the good lady was paying calls with madame the following afternoon; once their carriage had rumbled safely out of the gate, he made a discreet but thorough search of milady's apartments. He was unable to recover the brooch or the cloisonné bowl, but in a drawer in the escritoire that easily succumbed to his lock-picking skills he found a number of objects he recognised, including two netsuke and a jewelled snuffbox, while in the bottom of the press he discovered the gilt and ormolu clock from the Tapestry Room—he marvelled how the old jackdaw had crammed it into her reticule. He did not tell M. de M what he had done but simply restored everything to its customary place: while the old boy would have been shocked by the propensities of his unwanted guest, he would have considered Max's breach of hospitality yet more shocking.

For some while, to Max's gratification, the disappearances ceased. But Lady Telford doubtless recalled the pointed manner in which he had closed the vitrine, for her benevolent smiles were now decidedly hollow. It was unfortunate, if unavoidable, to have made her his enemy, for she would seek to stir up trouble for him with madame and, out of necessity, she was observant. Max sighed: here was yet more reason to exercise discretion.

Max missed the old fellow more than he could say. No matter how often he reminded himself this slavery was a labour of love, he felt put-upon and wretched. A week or two, the old boy had said. Six weeks had passed, six weeks in which to snatch time alone with him had become an increasing struggle. If Max were fortunate enough to escape madame, he would find his old enemy Thomas guarding M. de M's apartments;

or there was madame herself, who, when she was not harrying her spouse over some domestic 'improvement', was never content to send a servant to remind him of a luncheon engagement or a call he must pay; or there was another unlooked-for obstacle: Mlle Juliette.

Nowadays, during their morning rides, it was Mlle Juliette who accompanied the old boy, while Max rode respectfully behind with the groom; if Max at last found Armand alone in his study, moments later Mlle Juliette would appear, anxious to consult her papa on some pressing matter, so that Max, minion that he was, must withdraw: it was Mlle Juliette who sat beside Armand at the opera, Mlle Juliette with whom he exchanged covert smiles at the supper table, on whom his adoring glances were bestowed.

Max was not proud of his jealousy. Given the misfortunes of his childhood, he was bound to admit a certain ignorance where parental affections were concerned, yet it was not beyond him to comprehend that, having been kept from his daughter for years, any father, and most particularly one as tender-hearted as the old boy, might rejoice at their reunion and wish to make much of his long-lost child. If he set aside his jealous thoughts, he could see that M. de M's sincere affection for his daughter need not diminish the old boy's love for him. All the same—and maybe this too was jealousy at work, although he did not think so—Max did not care for Juliette. He neither liked nor trusted her and on the whole preferred Clotilde.

Clotilde, if you could ignore her infernal snobbery, at least evinced a spark of human warmth. It was perhaps not her fault that she had become the tool of her mother: easy to see that such a *maman* as Mme de Miremont would wear down the resistance of any child. Yet Max could also see—and he wished Armand could see it too—that every time Clotilde was sent into the fray on madame's behalf she was motivated by the wish, not just to pacify her mother, but to win her father over, to bring her parents together in harmony for once. It was a deluded wish, but a conscientious one. With her sense of duty and her sentimental notions, she was not, Max thought, so unlike Armand. She even looked like him: if you discounted the receding chin and slightly protuberant teeth that recalled her mother's brother, there was something definitely reminiscent of her father in her furrowed brow and worried eyes. Perhaps that was why Armand was blind to her virtues.

Juliette, of course, was the pretty one, the one who resembled madame—or, rather, madame as she looked in the faded photographs Lesage had cherished. But apparently the resemblance was physical only, for in temperament she seemed remarkably cool and self-possessed. Max strove to find this poise admirable: the composure she exhibited during her mother's outbursts was undeniably impressive; yet he was bound to recall that, as Lesage had taught him, the prerequisite for such calm was indifference. Given madame's ruthless use of her daughter for her own advantage, Juliette might be forgiven her lack of feeling; Max noted, however, that, while in company, yes, she could appear demure and charming, this coldness characterised her private dealings and even her sister was not exempt.

For his own part, he was delighted she shared Clotilde's ability to stare through minions as if they were transparent: at least there was no fear of questions from that quarter. Yet he had other fears for the old boy. For, in the light of his observations, what was he to make of Juliette's effusiveness towards her father? He might hope that these displays of girlish affection were a just recognition of Armand's worth, but he could not avoid suspecting that Juliette, after all, was not so unlike her mother.

His suspicions were not eased by a conversation he chanced to have with Roland de Sauvigny.

The morning's fencing was over, Max had narrowly won his bout with Sauvigny and they had taken off their masks to clap each other good-naturedly on the shoulder, when Sauvigny's gaze was diverted.

"Thank the Lord, she's gone!"

Max, who had been fencing with his back to the main ballroom doors, turned to follow Sauvigny's eyes and saw only the empty doorway.

"The Iceberg," said Sauvigny.

"Who?"

"Small wonder I dropped my guard, you lucky devil, and gave you that last hit. Plays hell with the concentration, that chilling stare."

Max, who was used to Sauvigny's excuses, laughed amiably. "So it's phantoms now, is it?"

"No phantom, old chap. She was watching my every move."

"Madame?"

"Good Lord, no!" Sauvigny glanced around anxiously for M. de M, who was deep in conversation with Captain Horthy. Although the pair were at the opposite end of the ballroom and probably out of earshot, nevertheless he lowered his voice. "Mademoiselle. My cousin."

Max recalled that Juliette, under sufferance, was accompanying her mother to lunch with her maternal uncle and aunt. She must have paused to glance into the ballroom on her way downstairs to the carriage.

"The Iceberg?"

"Oh, you know, old chap—that's what my brother calls her. Icy on the surface, ten times icier beneath."

Max stared at him, then let out a burst of laughter.

Sauvigny again looked around nervously, but Armand and the fencing master had departed. "Oh dear, there I go again, indiscreet as usual. For heaven's sake, Fabien, old chap, not a word to my uncle. Still, it's apposite, is it not?"

The social ambiguity of Max's relationship with Roland de Sauvigny—they were friends, yet he was never quite allowed to forget their differing stations—constrained him to swallow his laughter and find an equivocal reply. However, a footman appeared—not Philippe, but one of the new arrivals: was it Antoine or Jacques?—and both he and Sauvigny were temporarily occupied, piling their masks, gloves and foils into the man's arms so that, on madame's strict instructions, they could be whisked out of sight.

"Anyway," said Sauvigny, when the servant had gone, "I suppose I should be grateful to Edmond for stealing Hermione de Grès."

Max had not escaped the details of Sauvigny's unrequited passion for Mlle de Grès. He raised astonished eyebrows.

"Edmond has proposed and been accepted."

"My dear Sauvigny—"

"I'm beside myself, of course. But at least I shan't have the Iceberg as my sister-in-law."

"Was that likely?"

"My aunt, I'm told, was very keen."

"So you think…?" Max began to understand why Sauvigny was discomfited by Juliette's interest.

"Good grief, I hope not! After all, I should be safe—I'm the younger son and anyway there are—difficulties."

"That you are cousins?"

"Oh, that's seen as a positive advantage." Sauvigny frowned, but was vanquished, as usual, by his love of gossip. "No, to tell the truth, Fabien old chap, Edmond popping the question has got us out of a hole. Uncle Armand is a decent sort, very decent. The Pater is very fond of him. But he draws the line at my aunt…"

Max felt a certain pity for Mlle Juliette, but it was fleeting.

CHAPTER FOURTEEN

At the start, once Max had explained that pandering to madame was the only sensible course, M. de M had sighed but had been sympathetic. In the increasingly rare moments when they could talk freely, they had even been able to laugh at their predicament. Max had taken pains to see that his work for the old fellow did not suffer, staying until all hours in the library if there were urgent letters to write or pages of manuscript to copy. But of course he was often required to badger Armand on madame's behalf: had he come to a decision about his new visiting cards, did he remember the La Rochefontaines' Winter Ball was fancy dress? And gradually—Max could not have said when it first began—the old fellow had grown tetchy and sarcastic, so that, even when Max was able to escape from madame, he would be greeted with: "Oh, so you deign to honour me with your presence…" or "Dear boy, I must not deprive you of the delights of Bon Marché…" When Max, irritated in turn, reminded him these absences were not of his choosing, Armand merely snorted and turned away.

Naturally, the old boy must feel the strain of their situation: how could he not, even though it was of his making? Late at night, returning to his room under the eaves, Max would huddle over the grate's dying embers, reluctant to face the chill emptiness of the bed. Shivering in his nightgown, he would recall the attic dormitory he had once shared with Polly and how, for warmth, they had lain on top of each other like spoons in a drawer, often chastely, sometimes not; then desire would seize him, not for Polly, not for Armand, but a general rapacious hunger to be joined with other flesh; but, when he had laboured to stave off these pangs, he felt as cold and wretched as ever.

Of course there was a solution, but it seemed the old fellow was too on edge to listen: as at other times of difficulty, he had withdrawn into himself. Foiled of the chance to explain his plan, which would run little risk of scandal, Max supposed he might repeat the stratagem that had breached the old boy's defences during the crisis over Lesage: he could take the volume of Catullus, mark an appropriate love poem and leave the book with the day's letters on Armand's study table. The obvious choice was one of the poems to Juventius, XLVIII—they added these numerals as a postscript whenever they wrote to each other. Yet his pride rebelled. The young man in the poem was promised 'three hundred thousand kisses', but he was damned if he would go whining for a kiss like some infant in petticoats when he was daily offering painful proofs of his love.

He had told himself a promise had no value unless it were hard to keep: but perhaps it had not been worth making in the first place.

Max now longed for his days off as keenly as he had during his time in service. The Zhukovskys' cluttered apartment in the Rue Boissonade was a glowing brazier in a chill world. The light of revelation that had descended once he had accepted that he loved the old boy had banished the shadows here, too: he was ashamed he had ever doubted Mitya or resented Zenaïda Antonova; Vera was her former self—whatever offence Max had committed, he had clearly been forgiven; and Mme Zhukovskaya, when she was well enough for him to read to her, made Mme de Miremont seem the figment of a nightmare. Although the Herzens were rehearsing for a tour of the Rhineland, Mitya had not yet abandoned his leadership at the Opéra, but if he were absent Max was happy to pass the time regaling Vera and Zenaïda Feodorovna with Mme la marquise's latest excesses. He felt somewhat disloyal to Armand, yet there was exquisite relief in turning melodrama into farce.

Consolation came also from an unlikely source. "Neither flesh nor fowl" was Old Jouvert's verdict on secretaries: not servants, but not masters either. And the same was true of paid companions. Max and Miss Pilkington were expected at table when monsieur and madame were dining at home even when there were guests; but when the family was invited elsewhere they remained behind, taking supper separately in their own quarters.

At first Max rejoiced to be left to his own devices. Besides, he was unsure what to make of the English miss. He was not even certain what her duties were. A big-boned woman with frizzy ginger hair, a square jaw and copious freckles, she was only a year or two past marriageable age but clearly destined for eternal spinsterhood: perhaps her purpose was to set off Mlle Juliette's porcelain beauty. As to her character, she possessed genteel manners and an obliging smile and she spoke reasonable French—when she spoke at all. Despite being La Telford's protégée, she seemed harmless: but dull, Max concluded.

Max's personal studies were devoted to the reading of *Hamlet*. Having enjoyed Ducis's translation, he had been disappointed to hear from Armand that Ducis had been rather free with the original, simplifying a good deal, removing certain 'errors of taste' and rendering the play in the French classical tradition, much as if it had been by Corneille: if Max wished to appreciate Shakespeare as Shakespeare, he must read him in English. Armand, with his English ties, spoke the language with some fluency and, while they were at Beauvallon, he had begun to teach Max. But they had not progressed much beyond the rudiments by their return to Paris, when, of course, the lessons had ceased.

Max had persisted on his own in the brief moments available to him. But English was proving more intractable than Italian. And, besides, when it came to *Hamlet*, the rudiments were laughably insufficient. When Max opened his English edition his heart sank and his brain froze.

Lighting a cigarette, he let his mind stray from the impenetrable verses. Christine, the third-floor maid, had not yet collected his supper tray; he thought of Miss Pilkington, far away in the east wing, contemplating the remains of her own solitary supper. Shit! How could he have been so obtuse?

Miss Pilkington was delighted to help him learn English: she was keen to improve her French accent, if Max had no objection to returning the favour. The first evening they met after supper in the library, but, since common sense suggested that two separate trays might more conveniently become one, thereafter they ate together in the old schoolroom along the corridor from Miss Pilkington's room.

Miss Pilkington not only proved an excellent teacher—Max thought he had much the best end of the bargain—but it transpired one of her duties, when Mlle Juliette deigned to delight guests with her shrill soprano, was to accompany her on the piano. The sparse furnishings of the disused schoolroom included an ancient upright, woefully out of tune; however, once Max had suborned the tuner who attended to the Érard in the Music Room, he was able, when their studies were over, to recline on the schoolroom's shabby ottoman and listen to Miss Pilkington playing Chopin; although she did not quite have Vera's touch, it gave him infinite pleasure to lose himself in the music.

Max would have been the first to admit that he had cultivated Miss Pilkington for selfish motives, yet he soon felt genuine liking for her and could not imagine how he had dismissed her as dull. On their first evening, once she had conquered her shyness, she had revealed herself to be a thoroughly good sort who did not flirt or play games and was impressively well-educated for her sex. Yet, though her straightforwardness was refreshing, she was a puzzle too.

Max was allowed to glean only the bare details of her past. Born in the north of England, the only child of a mother who had died young, she had been brought up by her father, a country parson who had educated her as if she were the son he lacked. This had stood her in good stead when suddenly this beloved father had also died, leaving her at the age of twenty without means. An aristocratic connection, a distant cousin of her late mother, had taken her in as a governess, and there had followed two similar posts, the last of which had brought her to London, where she had eventually become companion to the aged Countess of St Neots. When Lady St Neots had died, Miss Pilkington had once again found herself adrift in the world, until Lady Telford, a friend of the deceased countess, had kindly recommended her to Mme de Miremont.

Although Max could imagine the pain and loneliness that lay beneath this spare account, the humiliation of being passed from family to family to be used and discarded like parcel string, the puzzle of Miss Pilkington was not just that she forbore to complain about fate's unkindness: she refused to see it as unkind at all.

On the contrary, she seemed pathetically grateful (although 'pathetic', Max reflected, was not a word appropriate to Miss Pilkington). He soon learned to avoid satirical comments about the residents of the east wing. Miss Pilkington freely expressed her debt to madame and Lady Telford for giving her this opportunity to visit Paris and perfect her French, and she appeared devoted to Mlle Juliette; she spoke without envy of mademoiselle's beauty, praised her kindness (manifested by the gift of cast-off shawls and fans, and the receipt for a potion to discourage freckles), and was glad to offer support to her youth and innocence. It might be that Miss Pilkington's willingness to subdue her spirit and know her place was the product of naivety. But Max, who had never known his place and was usually ready to despise those who did, came to see that, in her case, acceptance of her lot was a matter of honour, intrinsic to her dignity.

Having saved a little of her weekly pittance, on her return to England she intended to join a friend in setting up a school. Max was gladdened by this plan for her future independence, but all the same, when she launched upon some theory about *Hamlet*, eyes bright, laughing at her own passion, he was reminded of Princess Zelenska's nursemaid at La Boissière, worth twice her mistress, yet doomed to have her vitality crushed. Endowed from birth with Mlle Juliette's good fortune, Miss Pilkington might never have been a beauty, but, with her copper hair flatteringly coiffured and her vivacity unleashed, she would have been counted a jolly, good-natured girl, appreciated, even sought after.

It had been for his own enjoyment that Max had procured the piano tuner, yet Miss Pilkington had been so touched by this gesture that thenceforward he made a point of looking out books for her and doing her what other small favours were in his power.

But, if anything lifted Max's spirits, it was the surprise he received one afternoon when he had managed to steal a couple of hours in the library.

Amongst the duties he had been compelled to let slip was the cataloguing and shelving of Armand's new books, although parcels still came weekly from the bookseller. Cataloguing required the use of his quill pen, for each entry must be calligraphed, then pasted into the appropriate ledger; but the vast room was cold despite the fire in the far grate and his fingers grew numb. Since the slightest mistake forced him to tear up his effort and begin afresh, he touched the bell for a warming jug of coffee.

It was Antoine, the longest surviving of the new footmen, who answered his summons. While he waited for the coffee, Max ran four times up and down the mezzanine steps to restore the blood to his fingers, then settled to work again. Thus, although he registered the sound of the doors opening, he was almost at the end of an entry and concentrating so fiercely on not making slips or blots that, while he was aware of a tray being settled in the empty space on his worktable, he did not look up, but merely murmured: "Thank you, Antoine."

There was a strange buzzing noise.

Max ignored it, pressing on, but it came again, louder. "Bzzzzzzz!"

Antoine had not departed, Max could feel him standing there. Had he taken leave of his senses? A stolid man not much younger than Georges, he did not look the type. With determination Max wrote the last two digits of the publication date, wiped the quill and returned it to the inkstand. Then, reaching triumphantly for his blotter, he at last glanced up.

The extraordinary spectacle confronted him of a person in

footman's livery performing a little dance, thrusting out his yellow-and-black striped thorax and flapping his tailcoat's yellow wings.

"Dear God!"

"Hornet Jacques at your service, monsieur."

"Polly, by all that's wonderful! Polly!"

"You do know, angel, in that ever-so-elegant inscription of yours you've left out the first O in Xenophon?"

Max glanced down at his calligraphy. "Curses! But who cares!" Casting his work aside and leaping from his chair, he came round the table to embrace his friend. "Shit, it's good to see you."

Polly had once been described by his admirers as willowy, but now, as Max stood back to look at him, he appeared merely thin and worn: although the wig hid the sad retreat of his blond curls, his cheeks were reddened by broken veins and his face had hardened, showing every one of his twenty-eight years; on the other hand, his malicious grin was unchanged and he breathed not a hint of alcohol.

"My dear fellow, I thought you'd been incarcerated in the Château d'If."

Polly shrugged. "I had a teeny altercation with the miserly old quean at Auteuil."

"So I gathered."

"Anyway, it seems your Madame la marquise took against the last Jacques. So here I am, angel. How do you like me?" He struck a statuesque pose. "Very à la mode. The stripes might be judged a touch unfortunate. But you should see my sting."

Max laughed, as he was supposed to. Yet what a comedown for Polly after his career as a valet. And to add to the indignity, since Georges and Philippe were long-established, he would not be first footman despite his height, nor even second.

"Fifth," said his friend, reading his thoughts. "But a girl's got to eat."

"Did Old Jouvert send you?"

"An agency, dearest. Far more reliable."

So it was true: Old Jouvert had given up on Polly. "Well, I suppose he has never been able to install a spy here."

"He's got you, angel."

Max cared neither for this remark, nor its arch tone, but Polly cut him off before he could remonstrate. "Not that Your Highness would know much about the servants' hall these days. The new suiting is exquisite. And as for that amethyst pin! I'm delighted Little Miss Mouse is still treating her girl well."

"Polly, how many times—"

"Oh, I know, petal, I know. Monsieur le marquis to me. You, I presume, are also to be monsieured. And if I ever claim to have seen you before, I'll turn into a pillar of salt. This girl knows her place, *Monsieur* Fabien."

"For pity's sake, you idiot! Not when we're alone." Max put his arm around Polly's shoulder. "Shit, one can see one's breath in here. Let's go over to the fire."

"I shall be missed."

"Have your astonishing powers of invention deserted you?"

Polly's struggle with temptation lasted no longer than it took Max to produce his cigarette case. Once they had drawn up chairs to the fire and were drinking the coffee Polly had brought, sharing the tray's single cup, Max hoped his friend would explain his previous disappearance. But apart from a florid account of his dalliance with a circus acrobat out at Auteuil, Polly was reticent, preferring to dwell on present circumstances.

"Although I only arrived last night, I am bound to say, angel, this does not strike me as a deliriously happy house."

Max laughed.

"Of course it was not the best of omens to bump into that great one-eyed brute from La Boissière, your Mouse's valet. And then, in the dormitory—or should I say, nest—my fellow Hornets are abuzz with gossip. Apparently, everybody used to be united in their hatred of you—"

Max laughed again. "That goes without saying."

"But now there are so many people to hate they scarcely know where to start. The old ones hate us new ones and vice versa. Some hate mademoiselle's lady's maid for giving herself airs—I gather she was one of the parlourmaids. Some hate Madame Mercier and that undertaker's mute of a butler for not putting up more of a fight on behalf of us serfs. Most hate the ladies in the east wing, not to mention the English guest. Everyone hates madame. And there is one thing all the Hornets can agree upon, having traipsed after the creature with mop and pail—they long to strangle madame's beloved Bébé."

Max, who had been listening unsurprised, was distracted by a sudden concern. "Polly, do you know why the previous Jacques got his cards?"

"No idea, angel. Perhaps madame decided pee-pee was not his colour."

"Nothing to do with theft?"

"Ah!" Polly gave a knowing grin. "Yes, I've heard about that."

"Then do me the favour of taking care when you are in the guest apartments or the east wing. And if you have any trouble of that sort, tell me."

"If you think it will help." Inhaling a last luxuriant draught of Turkish tobacco, Polly tossed the stub into the fire before it burned his fingers, then pushed back his chair. "Speaking of trouble, this girl must go. Or she's out on the street."

It struck Max that for Polly this might no longer be a figure of speech. He, too, rose. "Dear fellow, let's find a way to meet regularly."

They were in the midst of a parting embrace when the library doors were thrown open.

CHAPTER FIFTEEN

Miremont had hardly been in the best of tempers when he had gone in search of Max. His suspicions about Aline continued to torture him. Reason told him he should confront the boy, who would probably set his mind at rest; yet, when he recalled the previous consequences of confrontation, he flinched. In his worst moments he reflected bitterly that Aline and Max were two of a kind, constitutionally faithless. This thought had predominated as, stung by fresh provocation, he had gone downstairs to the library. He would have it out with the boy, he had told himself as he thrust open the doors.

The sight of Max embracing one of the footmen brought him to an abrupt halt.

After the first moment of shock, his clearest thought was that he must leave, that to witness this scene an instant longer would be insupportable. But Max had already detached himself from his companion and was hurrying towards him.

"Monsieur!"

Although the boy looked alarmed, as if he understood exactly what Miremont was thinking, he gave no appearance of guilt. On the contrary, he was ushering the footman forward.

"Monsieur de Miremont, may I present an old friend of mine, Hyppolite Dufour."

The footman—yet another new face, they changed footmen nowadays as Aline changed hats—stepped a few paces closer and gave a small, punctilious bow. The obligations of politeness contended with Miremont's suspicion.

"In fact he is already known to you," said Max. "From Madame de Claireville's. There he was called Fabrice."

It was true, there did seem something familiar about the fellow. Miremont applied his pince-nez, and yes, he recalled the young man, a slim blond boy whose ephebic prettiness, while not attracting Miremont, had undoubtedly appealed to the likes of Achille de Tarascon: not that Miremont would have recognised the poor fellow without prompting, for he could no longer be described as either pretty or a boy.

"Oh… Ah yes, of course… Forgive me, Monsieur…"

"Dufour," prompted Max.

"I did not realise… It was the livery…"

"Polly is the new Jacques. I had not the slightest notion he was here until I rang for coffee. Naturally I was astounded to see my old comrade."

Max's delight seemed so unaffected, so untouched by guile that Miremont began to feel ashamed. Curse the distorting glass of his jealousy. Reconsidering the embrace he had witnessed, he could not deny it had been what one might expect from two good friends suddenly reunited.

He extended his hand. "Monsieur Dufour—Jacques—welcome to my house."

All the same, as he was exchanging courtesies with Max's comrade, he was falling prey to a new concern. Although Dufour's manner could not be faulted, his gestures, his voice, the very inclination of his head plainly declared what he was. While Dufour gathered up the tray and took his departure, Miremont carried his anxiety over to the mantelpiece, where he stood, warming his calves, as if the heat might disperse it.

Max was smiling as he came to join him. It saddened Miremont that he must wipe away that smile with yet another prohibition. How many times had they stood thus, debating some point of literature, discussing the morning's ride, shoulder to shoulder, utterly comfortable with each other? If Miremont had been wrong about Dufour, could he not also be wrong about Aline? He felt a surge of heat that owed nothing to the parsimonious fire: he had only to slide his arm around the boy's waist and, for the moment at least, all else—his present concern, his duty to Julie, his fears and suspicions—would be blotted out.

But then Max, still smiling, said: "I'm glad you and Polly have been properly introduced. But were you looking for me?" And Miremont instantly recalled his original grievance.

"Ah yes." He stepped away from the mantelpiece. "Thomas has shown me the costume you have hired for me to wear at this wretched ball. I thought we had settled upon Cardinal Richelieu?"

Max seemed taken aback. "Yes, of course. Since madame is going as Anne of Austria, we agreed—"

"Doublet and hose?"

"Richelieu, as you will recall, was also a soldier."

"Are you determined to make me look ridiculous?"

"Armand, I merely thought—you have the legs and the figure for it and I thought you might prefer—"

"I know what you thought. Doubtless you and my wife found it very amusing when you hatched it between you."

"Oh, for pity's sake!"

"Anyway, we have more to concern us now than the La Rochefontaines' tiresome love of fancy dress. Your friend Dufour—it won't do, I fear."

Max had turned away in exasperation, but now he stared at Miremont. "What won't do?"

"I am afraid he must go."

"Go? Polly?"

"Polly—Fabrice—whatever you call him. He cannot stay here, under the circumstances."

Max's incredulity vanished. "Damn you to hell, Armand! Damn your preposterous, never-ending jealousy! I do not fuck Polly, he is my friend. He is my friend, he is down on his luck and he needs this situation. But you—with your saintly ideals and your endless harping upon truth and justice—you're quite happy to fling him into the gutter if that satisfies your insane delusions."

"My dear, you mistake me!" Miremont regretted that anger had made him so blunt, yet he was further nettled by these echoes of Aline's rhetoric. He must contain himself. Reason was required: Max would understand his concern if it were explained to him calmly and reasonably.

"My dear boy—although I admit I—well, you both took me by surprise at first—but I no longer doubt you. And your loyalty to your friend does you credit. All the same, you must see he cannot remain in this house. The risk is too great."

"What risk?"

"Of course I understand that the poor man's livelihood is at stake. Naturally I shall compensate him—"

"Pay him off? In heaven's name why?"

"He knows."

It was Max's first instinct to deny this, Miremont fancied; but, faced with the unlikelihood of being believed, he appeared to change his mind. "Very well. Polly knows. What of it?"

"Do you not see? He might threaten to go to Aline."

"So poor Polly is a blackmailer now?"

"I am merely pointing out, dear boy, that we cannot take the chance."

Max gave a small sour laugh. "Achille de Tarascon 'knows', as you put it. Are we to pack him off with a month's wages in lieu of notice?"

Miremont, who lived in constant fear of what Tarascon might let slip, only wished this were possible.

"Even Tarascon has to guard against scandal. Do you not think it is the same for Polly? He cannot compromise us without compromising himself. Oh, I suppose you will say he is just a servant, he has nothing to lose."

"Max, you know I do not—"

"Well, he has his place to lose. So let us suppose for a moment that your accusation is correct and Polly is a blackmailer—"

"My dear boy, you know I am not saying—"

"Polly is a blackmailer and you put him out on the street. Do you think that is likely to reform him?"

"As I have already promised you, I shan't leave the poor fellow destitute. I intend to make him a very generous settlement."

"Which, if he is a bloodsucker, will discourage him from coming back for more? And what if he isn't the scoundrel you paint him? What is he to suppose when he is suddenly sent packing for no apparent reason with a large sum of money?"

"I admit I had not thought—"

"Besides which, I should love to be there when you tell Boussec he must give an experienced footman his cards after one day's service with a settlement far beyond the usual terms. I can just imagine the whispers that will spread through the servants' hall. You might as well place an advertisement in *Le Petit Parisien*: 'Monsieur le marquis de Miremont seeks blackmailer: all applicants seen.'"

Miremont sighed. He had wilted under this barrage of sarcasm, the more so because he could not deny the boy's logic. The thought of Boussec and the servants made him shudder. Furthermore, he remembered how he had once, before they were better acquainted, wrongly suspected Max of blackmail; the shame of his craven doubts came back to him. Of course, this situation might be different. But it was true that when he had spoken of 'compensation' and 'a generous settlement', the words had sounded distasteful even to his own ears.

"Armand, Polly is honest. Please believe me. I am prepared to vouch for him absolutely."

Max's voice had softened, he had crossed the hearthrug to put his hand on Miremont's arm. Once more it struck Miremont that he had only to respond for the misery to cease, that the boy, who was dissolving in the fumes of mistrust, could be saved if he held him tightly, could be restored to him as a solid, clearly discernible presence. But in this moment of hesitation, before desire could overwhelm him, the fumes rose up again: he could not help suspecting Max's staunch defence of Dufour; perhaps, after all, there was more to it than friendship.

Brushing off the boy's hand, he turned away. "Very well. If you say so. I suppose we must live with the risk."

"Risk? Tell me, Armand—" scorn returned to the boy's voice "—why is it you won't trust Polly, when I vouch for him as my friend? After all, you think the world of Mitya Zhukovsky. But then Polly is a servant and Mitya's father was a count."

Anger deprived Miremont of an apt rejoinder. "Just see to it that you find me some cardinal's robes by tomorrow afternoon."

That night Max's nightmares returned and he was a child again, back in the cellar with the Other. The stealthy night-army crept out of its crannies and scuttled over their faces, the stench weighed upon them like a sodden blanket, the leak from somewhere up above dripped into the slops pail, ticking the relentless minutes of each endless hour.

How long had they been here, captive in the dark—weeks, years? The night was only different from the day because their tormentors never came. The night was free of shouting and beatings, but it was not peaceful. Beside him the Other, who had pissed himself again, was choking and burning with fever. Max sponged his forehead with rank water from the slops pail. The Other must not die. They must remember, they must count, count out loud everything they recalled from Before. How many Romans on plinths in the gallery, how many marble chequers in the passage to the orangery, how many coats of arms above the panelling in the Great Hall? Count, damn you, count! Buttons on a guardsman's tunic? Puppies in Freya's last litter? Lipizzaners in the Riding School? Count! Now! Or we'll both die.

For that was the truth of it. Max was not crouched over the Other's body forcing his own breath into the Other's lungs out of love or loyalty, but because it had been dinned into him, long before they had ended up huddled on the same piss-soaked palliasse, that, like two halves of one organism, he, Max, was bad and the Other good. It was the Other they wanted, the Other who was valuable. If the Other died, he would be killed.

So they must count, call up the spell of Before to save them. Count, damn and blast you, or—

But here one of the furtive creeping things, which had hidden itself in Max's left nostril, crawled out and fell into his open mouth. He awoke, retching. And there at the end of his bed stood the Other.

At least he assumed the robed figure was the Other, although the cowl kept most of the face in shadow. In the sliver of moonlight that penetrated a chink in the shutters, it stood, still as a post. But any menace it might have conveyed vanished the next instant for, although it had the height and bulk of an adult, it spoke in the Other's plaintive schoolboy tones.

"You're a dirty cheat and a snivelling coward! You swore to set me free if I gave you what you wanted. But as usual you funked it."

Max mumbled a protest, but his persecutor was unmoved.

"Our pact was made before God and the Devil and sealed with blood. You have no business making promises to anyone else."

Miremont's deepening gloom was relieved by one constant light—his dearest Juliette. Whatever the humiliations of the La Rochefontaines' ball, he was bound to feel proud of his beautiful daughter, arrayed as the young Catherine de' Medici in Worth's jewel-encrusted interpretation of sixteenth-century Florentine costume: not only was this a touching tribute to family history (for it was to Catherine the Varons owed the marquisate); Julie dressed as Henri II's bride, for whose hand so many illustrious suitors had competed, could not but inspire in Miremont poignant emotions.

Like most devoted fathers, he shrank from the thought of his daughter's marriage; but devotion also urged duty; nor was he prepared to sit back and allow Aline's absurd notions to blight Julie's future.

It was quite bad enough that the poor girl's evident virtues would not be enough in some quarters to counter her mother's reputation. Miremont would have liked nothing better than to see her married to his nephew Edmond but, knowing Constant's prejudices, he had kept his own counsel and had been mortified when Aline, without consulting him, had simply charged in: he had been as much relieved as the Sauvignys when Edmond had disqualified himself.

Then there was the advice Aline had sought from her brother. Miremont had been shown a list of suggested suitors, no doubt drawn up over one of those cosy luncheons at Robert's: he was not so unworldly that he failed to recognise most of the names as relations of Robert's plunger cronies; he did not intend that his beloved daughter should stand collateral for some speculator's debts. Whoever married Julie must value her for herself, not for her generous dowry and eventual inheritance.

Ideally, of course, the man must equal her in rank. But, most of all, Miremont hoped the successful suitor would be the choice of Julie's heart. As his own marriage had proved, love did not necessarily grow from propinquity: the lack of it could as readily point up what else was lacking—desire, companionable interests, shared sensibilities. In Miremont's more forgiving moments, he felt profoundly sorry for Aline: Eugène de Sestrès, whose own fortunes were shaky, had doubtless congratulated himself on marrying his daughter into wealth and the old aristocracy, yet, better acquainted with the bridegroom, he might have foreseen Aline's cruel disappointment before the contract was signed. Love—Miremont never knew this better than at this moment—could be agony, but nothing was more crushing than indifference.

Thus, despite his own longing to have peace restored, Miremont was determined Juliette should not be rushed. Nevertheless, although they were still more than a month from the New Year celebrations and his darling must wait weeks yet for her ball, there were signs that a well-qualified suitor had already appeared. At the La Rochefontaines', the comte de Niversac had seemed much smitten with Catherine de' Medici.

Raoul de Niversac was in his early thirties and had been a major in the Cuirassiers. An only son, he had resigned his commission upon the death of his father a year ago to take care of the family interests, which were substantial and included two estates in the Dordogne and property in Paris, as well as land and copper mines in Canada. He was therefore in the position Miremont had been when his elder brother had died, head of a family which included a widowed mother and sisters but no immediate male heirs, and must accordingly view marriage as a necessity.

In person, although not tall and not a beauty like Max, he was not unattractive: his black moustache and cavalry officer's dash seemed to appeal to the ladies, or so Miremont observed. Yet when he was not in female company there was a reassuring seriousness about his long, pale, rather sensitive face and an encouraging maturity in his manner. Introduced to him at the Corvignacs' by Edmond de Sauvigny, Miremont, who had endured supper trapped between stern Mme de Beaumont-Grammont and languid Princess Zelenska, was quite revived by their conversation in the smoking room. Niversac, it transpired, had once taken brief leave from the army to explore the wilds of Canada and spoke intriguingly of his encounters with the native Indian tribes. He had other interests too: like Charles de Selincourt, he was an enthusiastic amateur photographer, and—here was a subject dear to

Miremont's heart—he was keen to introduce modern farming methods on his estates. Altogether, Miremont received a favourable impression that was not diminished by further acquaintance. If he had to entrust his daughter to anyone, Niversac certainly seemed a decent and intelligent young man. And at least he would prove a more congenial son-in-law than poor, foolish Thierry-Le Puy.

Of course, there would be hurdles to surmount, Aline being not the least. Surprisingly, she had at first disparaged the match: doubtless Niversac had not appeared on any of her lists, for she complained he was unworthy of her daughter, only warming to him when Lady Telford pronounced him to be related to both the La Marnes and the Mortemarts. But Aline warm was as dangerous as Aline cold. The dowager comtesse de Niversac and her daughters mercifully remained in the country, safe from importunate visiting cards, for there was no knowing if they might not share Constant's scruples. And then there was the poor young man himself: he and Julie must be protected from madame's interference—although Miremont was vexed to know how.

Still, it was early yet. While Raoul de Niversac was patently in love, Julie had yet to declare herself. Miremont observed that she was not above the weathercock game played by her peers, where sunbeams capriciously alternate with frosts—alas, this artifice was deemed virtue in unmarried girls. All the same, he was not without hope: he was certain he had seen his darling blush as Niversac had kissed her hand. Meanwhile, given the young comte's friendship with his nephews, what more natural than that Miremont should invite him to accompany Roland to their fencing sessions, establishing him as an accepted caller at the house.

Ah, the house—Miremont was diverted from his matchmaking by a fresh threat to the good order of the Hôtel de Miremont. He supposed he should have made more of Aline's carping about the lack of originality in the menus; but then he had observed that, while his wife wrinkled her nose at whatever was placed before her, and even probed it with a fork, as if, like a stone, it might hide something repulsive, she usually devoured every morsel. He was slow to realise these criticisms were strategic because her objective was unthinkable. She wished to dismiss Mme Dussardier—nowadays any household of note employed a chef.

Mme Dussardier had been Miremont's cook for twenty-four years: indeed, he had inherited her with the marquisate. True, she did not go in for show—blackbird pâtés sporting the creatures' claws and beaks, sorbets masquerading as asparagus spears—but, in Miremont's view, her dishes looked the more inviting for eschewing such novelties. Admittedly his tastes were simple and he held no claim to be a gourmet like Robert de Sestrès or Jean-Marie de la Rochefontaine, but he could still appreciate the mastery of Mme Dussardier's subtle flavours and deft touch: with her silky veloutés, her creamy béchamels, her lobster in tarragon butter, her tiny tender violet artichokes poached in a broth of *jus de veau*—not to mention her chocolate soufflé, which Catherine de Claireville and Gervaise de la Marne both maintained to be beyond compare—she could easily hold her own against the latest culinary 'genius'.

Besides, this was not merely a culinary matter. Was Miremont to forget that when Prussian guns were battering the walls of the city and starving Parisians were eating rats and the elephants in the Jardin Zoologique, Mme Dussardier had mysteriously conjured up the eggs to make him omelettes? Was he to forget all the other ways she had spoiled him over the years?

And then Mme Mercier must also be considered. Although in person they were as different as could be (Mme Mercier small and spry, Mme Dussardier large, doughy and deceptively placid), and although, working together over so many years, they had naturally had their moments, they were devoted friends: Miremont recalled they were even distantly related. He had already burdened Mme Mercier with Aline. Was she also to be deprived of her closest ally?

And what of Mme Dussardier herself? Oh, she would have splendid references and would undoubtedly find a new place. But she was no longer young and had spent most of her life in the Hôtel de Miremont: he fancied she had begun there as a scullery maid. Of course, he would not be required to look her in the eye when she was given her dismissal—Aline would inform Mme Mercier, handing her the responsibility—but all the same he could not bear to think the poor woman would receive such base treatment in his house.

Surrendering the housekeeping to Aline had been one thing, done in order to save others pain, but this was another. Here was a situation in which he, Miremont, could not give in.

CHAPTER SIXTEEN

Although it was a bitter December afternoon, sufficient to deter most strollers from the Luxembourg Gardens, an elegant young man could be observed entering regardless from the Rue de Vaugirard and rounding the palace to skirt the deserted lake; while, proceeding in the opposite direction along the same path, there also appeared a footman, muffled in a black cape and walking a small white dog.

Alas, this animal was one of those excitable creatures driven to paroxysms by so much as a wind-tossed leaf: while the elegant gentleman and the footman appeared oblivious of each other and a stretch of gravel remained before their paths would cross, the dog, although portly and inclined to drag on the lead, was suddenly galvanised by the stranger's approach and hurled itself at him, barking frantically. The footman, clutching at his tricorn as he was precipitated forward, was greatly discomposed; but the gentleman bore the pawmarks on his fine alpaca with surprising good grace and even stooped to pacify the creature; more surprising still, once the animal was under control and the footman had given vent to some words of, no doubt, fulsome apology, the two men walked off amicably towards the bare avenue of pleached chestnuts, where, despite the biting wind and their differing stations, they settled together on a bench.

"Sodding pooch!" said Polly, for Bébé had momentarily been set off again by a pigeon on the wing. "Cut it, will you! Or your Auntie Polly will peel your balls for andouillette."

"Poor beast."

"You take the horrid thing, angel, if you're so fond of it."

But Max was searching in an inner pocket for his cigarettes.

Polly twined the lead vigorously around his glove, forcing the dog into submission at his feet. "I suppose I should be grateful to the flea-bitten creature. Volunteer to walk it and nobody's counting the minutes until you bring it back."

"Whereas," said Max, offering the cigarette case, "monsieur thinks I'm with madame, madame thinks I'm with monsieur. So, knowing my present luck…"

"Rather your luck than mine." Polly sniffed the unlit Muratti as if it were Château Lafite. "You know, that coat is a wonder, dear heart, and I can't fault the topper. But you simply must acquire an exquisite cane to complete the ensemble."

Although Max had lit his own cigarette, he had not proffered the match and, when Polly inclined his head towards it, he pointedly blew out the flame.

"Oh, la-di-da! Pardon me, Your Serene Highness."

"Don't be an idiot."

Polly pulled a face. There might be few people about and his cloak might cover all but a glimpse of identifying yellow, but, as he well knew, if he were spotted smoking in livery he would instantly get his cards. This did not lessen his resentment as he stowed the cigarette away in his waistcoat pocket, nor was he mollified by Max's concern for his welfare.

"Still," he said, "it's hardly surprising you're on edge, angel. Given the rumour that's abroad."

Max exhaled smoke. "Oh Lord, what now?"

"Word is that Little Miss Mouse—"

"For pity's sake, Polly, for the hundredth time—"

"No need for the vapours, dear heart. *Monsieur*, if you must. Either way, it's all over the servants' hall that you and she have had a tiff."

"That's utter nonsense. True, he's a little out of sorts at the moment. But who can blame him?"

"More than a little, by all accounts. Apparently it will be madame who stumps up for that silver-topped cane of yours."

"Oh, for God's sake!"

"Truly. According to Simon—"

"Who the hell is Simon?"

"Our sixth Hornet—as Your Highness would know if she hadn't grown too grand to notice the hoi polloi. Although you must have noticed La Simone—she's eighteen and delicious."

"Ah, that one."

"And no, darling heart, you keep your sticky fingers off! Anyway, the darling girl knows all the gossip and last night she informed the dormitory that your Little—*monsieur* had caught you and madame in her boudoir. *In flagrante*."

"He—what?" Max, who had been lounging on the bench with his legs outstretched, sat up so violently that he kicked Bébé, who loosed a volley of indignant yelps. Once they had calmed the animal, Polly by swearing at him and Max, more successfully, by patting his rump, Max buried his head in his hands. "Shit, should I laugh or cry? Or garrotte this cretin Simon? Surely nobody believes this nonsense?"

"Well, naturally I don't, sweetie. I never believed your heady passion for Princess Zelenska, if you recall. However, I'm not the entire Hornets' nest."

"But no one in his right mind…"

"Alas, petal, that's just the trouble. None of us *is* in our right mind. In fact, I shouldn't be surprised if there were bloody revolution in the servants' hall. You should hear the mutterings about Madame Dussardier."

"What has she done? Poisoned milady, I should hope."

"Monsieur must have told you."

Max saw that Polly read his discomfiture. "As I said, he has been out of sorts."

"Then you don't know that madame is talking of giving Madame Dussardier notice? Rumour has it she is trying to lure our old friend Quintivali away from Madame de Claireville."

"Quintivali, who uses footmen to hone his knife-throwing skills?"

"When he's not making ragout out of the kitchen maids."

"Shit, the poor old boy!" Max put his head in his hands once more. "No wonder it's been as if the Furies were after him for the past few days. But why in heaven's name didn't he tell me?"

Polly greeted this with tactful silence.

"Well—" with determination Max recovered himself "—you may assure the servants' hall there is no cause for concern. Monsieur thinks highly of Madame Dussardier. He is bound to make a stand."

"Oh, they know he will, petal. Before he thinks better of it and scuttles back to his hole."

Max seemed to lack the heart to counter this.

"Of course," said Polly, after a small pause, "you could always try your influence with madame."

A short sour laugh was his friend's only reply. Polly, however, was undeterred. "I've told you, I don't credit the gossip. But I have observed her batting her eyelashes at you and you, angel, batting shamelessly in return."

Max sighed. "Flattery may be madame's elixir of eternal youth, but she regards it as no more than her due. I have less influence than Bébé here."

At the sound of his name, the dog, who had been whimpering listlessly, leapt up, wagging his tail and pawing at Max's trousers. As Max, instead of discouraging the beast, patted its head and went so far as to let it slobber over his glove, Polly looked on in disgust. For it must be granted that, while Bébé had perhaps been charming as a puppy and was not yet advanced in age, his appeal was already sadly diminished: should you forgive his rheum-caked eyes and the yellow stains in his beard, as if he had been chewing tobacco, it was hard to ignore his characteristic smell.

"Serves you right," Polly said, "if you come down with mange."

"Poor little wretch. It's not his fault. Look at him."

"Oh *please*, angel!"

"He's miserable. Just like the rest of us. It's as you say. We are none of us in our right minds."

This moved them both to depressed silence. When Max produced his cigarette case again, Polly turned aside with a sniff; but, on finding not one but three Murattis held out to him, he was somewhat appeased; by the time he had concealed this booty about his person, pure luxury to be consumed in the sluice room in place of meagrely-rolled *caporal*, he had brightened considerably.

"Angel, this Dussardier business—I've had an idea—well, more of a glimmering really…"

Max raised his eyebrows.

"They say madame is given to superstition."

"If La Telford said she was being called from the other side by Marie Antoinette, she'd believe it."

"I can't promise spirits. But one of the junior housemaids tells the cards."

"I'm not certain—"

"No, truly, dear heart, she's a dab. Apparently your Auntie Polly is set for fame and fortune, if she can heed her better nature and ignore temptation."

Max let out a guffaw.

"No need to mock, sweetest. Truth to tell, I wouldn't know my Major Arcana from my Minor. However, she's very convincing, little Christine."

"Christine?"

"Though you've doubtless failed to notice her, she brings your hot water every morning and makes your bed."

"Of course I've noticed her. She's a nice girl. Very helpful when I was having difficulties with old Lesage."

"And since she's one of the few of us not to regard you as close kin to the Antichrist, I'm certain she'll assist here too. Once you've persuaded madame to see her."

The wind had penetrated Max's topcoat, Bébé was shivering, and even Polly's countenance was acquiring a bluish tinge: Max was not inclined to optimism.

"Might it not seem a trifle suspicious if the cards say 'Do not sack your cook'?"

"The Tarot shuns your crude literal-mindedness, angel. It speaks in loftier terms of a moral and spiritual journey. Such as, 'If you wish to avoid the disaster forecast by this Tower I see here, or that reversed Hanged Man, but yearn for the happiness promised by this Queen of Cups, be guided by the wise instincts of the Empress and avoid even the smallest decisions this week.'"

"Very impressive, Gypsy Queen. But how can Christine predict which cards will come up? Since she, poor girl, clearly believes in this taradiddle, we can hardly ask her to cheat."

"From what I can see, it's not the cards so much as their interpretation. Furthermore—" here Polly grinned slyly "—if you, with one of your adorable smiles, chanced to slip her the wherewithal for a new hat, I'm sure she'd be happy to finesse The Devil or Death or any number of threatening Swords. Everybody's fond of Madame Dussardier."

Max remained sceptical of Polly's scheme, which was, in any case, overtaken by events. That same afternoon, when madame returned from her calls, monsieur informed her that he would, under no circumstances, countenance the dismissal of Madame Dussardier, and, despite his wife's sobs and screams, he remained immovable.

The upshot was as the household had come to expect: madame retired to her bed, the doctor was sent for and a tense hush gripped the east wing. But there was also an expectation that she would reappear in the morning to return with verve to the fray. Yet on this occasion she did not; neither on that morning, nor the morning after, nor the next; and, by the fourth day, Dr Chevalier, when taken aside by monsieur, hinted at brain fever. Although her absence had at first afforded relief, the gloom of the east wing seeped like floodwater into all corners of the house.

Throughout madame remained incommunicable: enquiries after her health went unanswered, visits from her daughters were rejected, solicitous baskets of fruit and flowers ignored; even Lady Telford was relegated to the boudoir. Only Dr Chevalier and madame's lady's maid, Mlle Bonnard, were admitted to the bedroom; and, from the first morning, Max.

It could not be said that Max considered himself honoured, for he had hoped to be free to patch things up with the old boy; nor, as he quickly understood on speaking to Mlle Bonnard, was any honour intended: he had been summoned from necessity. There were excuses to be sent for invitations already accepted, cancellations of dress-fittings, the postponement of this week's Thursday and madame's musical evening, planned for two days hence—in short, countless urgent notes to be written and rearrangements to be made.

Mlle Bonnard was of indeterminate age and, unusually for a lady's maid, without hauteur: Max fancied madame had run through a good few maids before being compelled to settle for this obstinately loyal woman, who spoke in reverential whispers and was given to wringing her hands. She made him pause while she vanished into the bedchamber and when he was at last admitted he found the curtains were closed. However, as the ample fire precluded total darkness, he was quickly able to discern the reason: madame's face was naked of rouge and powder and, although *en déshabillé* she customarily wore her hair in two girlish lovelocks, it was at present free of false pieces and altogether undressed. Yet, if Max were shocked barely to recognise the woman lying amongst the pillows, this was not the sole cause: she had also been divested of her trying vigour. Dull-eyed, sunken-cheeked, she stared into the middle distance and seemed unaware of his presence.

The room was oppressively hot and freshly sprayed cologne failed to mask the smell of feminine perspiration, admixed with Bébé's distinctive aroma, which lingered like his shade even when he was not present. Max fidgeted, then coughed.

A feeble voice at last came from the bed. "Monsieur Fabien? Is that you? I cannot… It is all too difficult…" An uncharacteristic lisp, suggesting that madame, along with her other accoutrements, was bereft of her teeth, made her words at first hard to catch. "I cannot explain to Bonnard. But you know… what needs to be done." And when Max assured her that he did, she did not contradict him or seek to multiply his tasks, but merely said: "You are a good dear boy," before turning her face towards the pillows.

After a day or two of this, it was hard to doubt she was genuinely ill. Max could not avoid a degree of pity and M. de M also expressed concern, although he recalled she had suffered spells of prostration before and always recovered. For now, though, her melancholy continued unabated.

On the third morning, when Max came to report his progress,

Bébé leapt out of the rumpled bedclothes, wagging his tail. Max was ruffling the animal's ears and allowing his hands to be licked, when the voice from the bed remarked plaintively: "He loves you. He loves you, Monsieur Fabien, more than he loves me."

"Indeed not, madame." Gathering up Bébé, Max carried him over to the bed and deposited him on the counterpane. "Look, he's settling next to you. Good dog. There, you see, he's curling up happily."

But madame continued to stare into the distance. "No one loves me. No one has ever loved me. Only my darling Papa, who has been dead these many years."

"Madame, I—I am sure that's not true. Think of your daughters. And your grandchildren. And your good friend Lady Telford."

But she waved this away with a limp hand—women, Max realised, were beside the point.

"When I think how I have given of myself, all my life. Given and given, while others take. Do you think he feels guilt? Do you think he cares that he has made me ill?"

"Madame, I assure you, Monsieur de Miremont is—"

"Oh, pray don't bother, I know him better than you. And are other men different? One gives so much of oneself that one has nothing left and can only ask—where did I go wrong? Why is everything not enough? Why is all that I have nothing? If I am so worthless, what does it matter if I die?"

"Madame, you should not—"

"No one has ever loved me, no one ever will. How can I bear to contemplate such a future?"

The word 'future' reminded Max of Polly's ridiculous scheme. Given madame's present state of mind, it no longer seemed quite so ridiculous: true, it had been designed for a battle already won, but, knowing madame, there would be other battles, and besides it might bring her comfort. If nothing else, it would be a plank Max could fling into this spate of embarrassing confidences in the hope of diverting its flow.

"But, madame, you do not know what lies ahead. What if you could see the future? It may hold all manner of good things."

"That is what Lady Telford says. But none of the messages from my dear Papa have come true."

"Perhaps it is too soon. My dear madame—" Max dared the liberty of sitting on the bed and reaching for her hand "—you must not talk of dying."

"Oh, Monsieur Fabien, if you only knew…"

"You must not give up. Dear madame—I pray you will not think me impertinent—but there is a young woman in this house who tells the Tarot."

"In this house?"

"Believe me, she is of gypsy blood and has remarkable powers—"

"In this house? A servant?" Although she had previously offered no resistance, her hand withdrew from his grasp.

Max endeavoured to smile. "The spirits often favour the humble, madame—think of Jeanne d'Arc. And this young lady is very discreet. If she could confirm your father's predictions, would it not give you hope?"

He could see her hesitating. But, alas, she shook her head.

Of course—how like Polly—the idea was absurd. Nevertheless, if Christine had been able to establish an influence… *Tant pis*, Max reflected: it had been bound to come to nothing.

So when madame announced next morning that she had thought long and deeply about the servant girl, and yes, she was prepared to see her—"In one's pain one must try anything"—he was hard put to restrain his glee. Fortunately he came upon Polly in the boudoir collecting Bébé for his morning walk and immediately despatched him to find Christine.

It must be confessed Christine made an improbable gypsy—she was a rosy-cheeked, blue-eyed country girl from the Ardennes—and, as Max led her into the darkened bedroom to be presented to madame, he could feel her trembling. However, when he had impressed upon her: "No decisions, madame must be discouraged from decisions of any kind," she had nodded approvingly. And, although he withdrew at once and had no notion what took place, her talents must have vindicated Polly's high opinion, for he was summoned later, told he was a 'good, dear boy' and instructed to bring the girl without fail the next day.

Christine's daily Tarot readings worked no instant cure: madame's melancholia lingered and Dr Chevalier opined that, while the threat of brain fever had receded, she would continue an invalid for some weeks. Nevertheless she had grown strong enough to receive her daughters; Lady Telford, too, was recalled from exile, although grudgingly, Max thought, as if there had been a falling out: at any rate her tender commiserations were brushed aside, nor was she invited to try Christine's powers. When madame spoke glowingly of her 'little gypsy', milady, much to Max's delight, could barely conceal her pique.

CHAPTER SEVENTEEN

The following Tuesday, when madame had been laid low for over a week, Max was startled to report for duty and find she was not in her apartments. Although the day before she had seemed as fretful and listless as ever, this morning, according to Mlle Bonnard, she had risen at six full of energy and, having breakfasted early, was at present closeted with monsieur. Max would be sent for when he was required.

This did not augur well. Since he could not present himself to the old boy either, Max had no choice but to retire to the library. To occupy this enforced idleness he resumed his struggle with *Hamlet*, but concentration was impossible. Perhaps he should be delighted by madame's miraculous recovery, but he could not help thinking of Armand, his leisurely coffee and brioche interrupted—for what? Had Christine forgotten to give madame the usual warnings? Hoping Polly would appear to enlighten him, he touched the bell, but instead it brought Simon. The boy, tall, with broad shoulders and muscular calves, was handsome, no doubt of it, but the thought of the fanciful tales he would concoct forestalled Max's enquiries. Besides, as it transpired, Simon had not come in answer to the bell but to inform him he was needed by madame.

Mme de Miremont was certainly restored to her old self. In a pink cashmere wrapper encrusted with frills, looped with ribbons and topped for good measure with a lace pelerine, she sat at her escritoire scribbling vigorously and, although she failed to glance up when Max entered, he was able to note that her cheeks were plump and painted and her hair was once again copious and already dressed playfully *en frisette*. Yet these improvements did not extend to her temper. No fluttering eyelashes, no 'good dear boy': having brushed aside his felicitations for her return to health, she proceeded to batter him with orders, before folding the note she had been writing, sealing it with her wafer and thrusting it at him.

"Once you have seen to everything else, be so good as to go to Boucheron. It is weeks since Monsieur Legrand took my diamond and emerald bracelet to repair the clasp. If this note will not suffice for him to give it into your hands, get him to send it this afternoon."

After he had been dismissed as if he were the boot boy, Max did not obediently descend to his worktable in the library but made instead for Armand's apartments: while madame's commands required him yet again to excuse himself from the morning ride, his most pressing concern was to discover the cause of her vile temper. But, as he arrived at the piano-nobile landing to take the stairs to the west wing, he was astonished to see the old boy descending, not in riding boots and breeches, but in his topcoat and carrying his hat and cane.

"Monsieur?"

The old fellow could not have failed to hear him, despite being in such a rush, and indeed Max fancied he gave a start; but he continued, grim-faced, taking the main staircase with resolution and leaving Max to watch his retreating back, while any thought of calling after him was quelled by the presence of Georges in the foyer, waiting to hold the door open for his master.

In the hope of returning from the jeweller's in time for luncheon, Max had taken a cab to the Palais-Royal. But, although ledgers were checked and rechecked, Alphonse Legrand was summoned in person and an assistant was sent to the workshop, Boucheron could find no trace of madame's bracelet. It did not help that Max could not describe it, for he was not generally present when jewellers called at the Hôtel de Miremont, madame preferring to explain her requirements herself. However he was obliged to accept Legrand's word: Boucheron had certainly executed commissions for Mme de Miremont, but not this one. Had madame perhaps employed another firm?

Max had made appointments in recent weeks for Bapst and Falize, and Louis Cartier: he set off for Bapst and Falize, since their premises were nearest, in the Rue d'Antin. But here too he drew a blank. Cartier's workshop was in the Rue Montorgueil, towards Les Halles, but unless he wished to aggravate madame's temper by returning empty-handed he had no choice but to trudge there. Already he was beginning to wonder whether the bracelet truly existed and, when Cartier also denied possession of it, his doubts were increased—perhaps Lady Telford had snaffled it before it could ever reach the jeweller's. But then Louis Cartier recalled the piece: it had come to the workshop along with several other items, all of which—and his ledgers confirmed this—had been returned three weeks ago.

Was madame growing absent-minded? Or was this fool's errand punishment for whatever crime Max had committed? His mood was black as his hansom deposited him in the forecourt of the Hôtel de Miremont at a little after three o'clock, and he was disagreeably surprised to be pounced on by Georges. Did he know where M. le marquis was? Monsieur was needed urgently.

Exasperated by all things Miremont, Max's first inclination was tell Georges to go to hell, but he could not avoid noticing the fellow lacked his usual air of jovial cynicism. And, as irritation gave way to misgiving, he was yet more unsettled to find that Georges was joined by the improbable pairing of Polly and Thomas. It seemed all three had been lying in wait for him, for Thomas immediately fixed him with a baleful eye, while Georges and Polly began talking at once.

There had been no sign of monsieur since he had left in such haste this morning. He had been expected to take luncheon with the comte de Sauvigny (so much Max could confirm) and a page had been despatched to the Rue de Condé, but monsieur had sent the comte his excuses. Everyone was from home: madame was out in the carriage with Lady Telford; Mlle Juliette, with Miss Pilkington, was at Lebas' studio, sitting for her portrait; he, Max, was gadding about somewhere; M. Boussec was taking his afternoon off. The La Marnes and Mme de Claireville had also been sent to, also in vain. Yet monsieur must be found and brought back urgently.

"Or," Thomas rasped, finding his voice suddenly, "too late!"

"For heaven's sake," said Max, "will someone tell me, what is the matter? Is it Madame Dussardier?"

"The ballroom!" said Polly, seizing his arm as if to drag him to the stairs.

"No time!" growled Thomas. And he flung open the servants' door under the staircase.

The old boy's precious ballroom. If Max was amazed that the Cyclops, his arch enemy, should demand his help, this explained what had forced the old brute to such extremity. Still, Max was unclear why they were careering off in the opposite direction, along the underground passage that led beneath the courtyard to the servants' wing. He had little time to observe these unfamiliar surroundings: coal, wood, wine, barrels and sacks of provisions—all flashed past as they rushed through the vaults, Thomas, his head almost brushing the highest point of the ceiling, setting a fierce pace, with Max close behind and Polly, breathless, at the rear.

"I don't understand," Max shouted over his shoulder at Polly. "What does he expect me to do?"

"Stop Madame Mercier."

"From what?"

"Obeying madame."

"We need Boussec for that. Or better still, monsieur."

"If they were here."

"Then what about Christine? She knows her instructions—"

"No good."

"Why the devil—?"

"Sent packing this morning."

"What?" Max stopped in his tracks.

"Madame's emerald earring," gasped Polly as he narrowly avoided colliding with him. "Found in her apron pocket."

"Curse milady Telford! May she suffer all the plagues and torments of—"

But Thomas had glanced back and was barking at them.

The stairs at the far end of the cellars brought them to the servants' quarters; racing past the kitchens and pantries, they reached the end of the wing, turned into a shorter passage and at last burst out through the door that gave onto the servants' courtyard.

Afterwards, Max found himself thinking: 'If only it had rained'. It had rained relentlessly the previous day and even been inclined to sleet. But today, as fate would have it, the weather had been clear and sunny. Mind you, it was bitterly cold in the servants' courtyard, despite the sheltering wall of the stables, but that was insufficient excuse for Mme Mercier's minions to abandon their work.

The ballroom curtains, Armand's treasured relics from before the revolution, symbol of the Hôtel de Miremont's steadfast continuity, lay neatly piled in several baskets. That is, all save one, which, hanging on a line strung across the yard, was being belaboured with carpet beaters by two housemaids. Just out of range of the clouds of dust stood the small severe figure of Mme Mercier, bemittened and with a shawl thrown over her black dress.

"No!" roared Thomas as they ran across the cobbles. "You—tell her." And, forgetting all propriety, he pushed Max forward.

It was pointless for Max to retort that, as monsieur's secretary, neither flesh nor fowl, he had no authority over anyone in the household, let alone Mme Mercier. Besides, Thomas knew that. What he required of Max was to do what he, tongue-tied, could not: plead Armand's cause. Normally Max would have had his teeth pulled before going on his knees to the housekeeper, who had always treated him with suspicion and contempt, and he doubted his voice would have the slightest influence. Still, for the old fellow's sake, he must try.

"Please, madame. You know—we all know—this is against monsieur's wishes. This is his house, we all serve him—you yourself, as he has often said, have always served him unstintingly. I know I have no right to ask anything of you, but at least let me appeal to you on monsieur's behalf. For pity's sake don't do something that will cause him great distress."

This, however, merely had the effect Max feared: like any good servant required to follow to the letter a distasteful command, Mme Mercier stood upon her dignity. "I am under madame's orders, monsieur. On Monsieur le marquis' instruction. And madame requires that, if these draperies cannot be renewed, they must have the dust and dirt beaten out of them."

"Then please at least wait until monsieur returns."

"We cannot delay any longer. Another hour and we shall lose the light."

It was true the sun had vanished behind a pall of grey that was gathering weight. But in any case further protest was pointless. For there was light enough to observe how the length of material on the line had sustained its beating. With every stroke, the brittle threads, glued together by a century's dust, tallow fumes and smuts, had frayed and split, until the silk hung in tatters like an ancient grave cloth. Madame's work was done. Now one of the ballroom curtains was destroyed, they must all be replaced.

"Dear Papa, I know she can be impossible. But she has been ill, you cannot be too harsh with her."

Miremont had returned at close on half past five and had immediately been taken by Thomas and Georges to the ballroom and shown its bare windows, after which he had retired to his study, intending to nurse his anger alone. But Julie, sweet, thoughtful Julie, had knocked moments later. He was touched that she should be the first to console him and, although scarcely in a frame of mind to receive her well-meant kisses, had scrupled to discourage her from her usual perch on his knee. All the same, he was bound to protest at her defence of Aline.

"Your mother was expressly told—"

"Oh, but you know Maman. Sometimes I wonder if she's not just short-sighted, but hard of hearing as well. Besides, she probably thought she was acting for the best."

Here Miremont unwound her arms from his neck. While it had displeased him that Julie sometimes spoke slightingly of her mother, this was quite unreasonably charitable under the circumstances.

"No, no, darling Papa. You know she is not practical. She wanted to make the curtains clean and pretty again. She was thinking of me."

"You?"

"For when I have my ball."

"But you would not have wanted this desecration?"

"Of course not, Papa. Although they were dreadfully old and shabby—I heard Madame de Corvignac and Madame de la Rochefontaine remarking on it at Maman's last soirée. But I truly did not care. They are only curtains, after all."

"Only curtains!"

"Unless…" Her face fell, her hand, which had begun to stroke his cheek, dropped away. "Oh Papa, will it cost a great deal to replace them? How thoughtless of me! When you have already incurred so many expenses on my account…"

If there were one thing calculated to divert Miremont's anger, it was the thought that his beloved daughter still feared he was mean. "I have no notion of the cost. It is of no matter. Do you truly think I would begrudge you?"

"Dear, sweet Papa." She flung her arms around his neck once more and kissed him. "So you must try to be lenient with Maman. It is not as if she has burned down your beloved library. And besides—" her fingers began to play affectionately with the curls of his forelock "—I know how you can take your revenge."

"My darling girl, I hardly—"

"Hush. It is very simple. Maman is thinking of pink for the ballroom. Or perhaps gold. Which do you prefer?"

"Well—old gold. Like the originals."

"Then you must tell her that you strongly favour pink."

"I cannot see…"

Juliette laughed. "Of course you can, darling Papa. You know, whatever you prefer, she will choose the opposite."

Max had resolved to be the first to speak to Armand; but, by the time he had been apprised of his return and had hurried to his apartments, the old boy was already engaged. Damn Mlle Juliette—for, through the chink Thomas allowed in the open door, Max had glimpsed her entering Armand's study. Curse the Cyclops, too: as if they had never formed their alliance in the servants' yard, the old brute was reluctant to let him wait in the drawing room and remained, a surly presence, while he sat and cooled his heels.

When Juliette at last emerged from commiserating with her dear Papa, she was not solemn but smiling. And, to increase Max's distrust, she, who had never before deigned to notice him, allowed the smile to play briefly in his direction, as though informing him of some triumph. Poor old fellow. Max, when he had closed the study door, was already extending his arms to embrace him.

But Armand did not move from his chair by the fire. "Oh, it's you, is it? I cannot think why you troubled to come."

This was hardly the welcome Max had expected. His arms fell to his sides. "I came because I knew you would be wretched."

"And you wanted to gloat? Report back to my wife?"

"Dear God, Armand, not again! You know this is mad."

The old boy paused to stare into the fire, then favoured Max with a long, cold look he was unable to fathom. "Yes, I suppose under the circumstances… Even so, you did nothing to stop it. But why should you care?"

"Of course I care. But there was nothing I could—"

"You were not even there."

"Neither were you. Madame had me chasing thin air across the first and second arrondissements. But you were supposed to be two minutes away. If you had come when they sent to you—"

"If I had not been obliged—if remaining in my own house had not become intolerable—" The old boy struggled for breath as if he were choking. "And then you come here, pretending to be sorry."

Max gaped at the injustice of this.

"But in any case, what is the point of this ridiculous fuss? Good heavens, they were only curtains. This afternoon, Gérard took me on his rounds at the Hôtel-Dieu—the fever ward—and here are we, lamenting curtains! Now, I fear—" Armand rose from the chair "—my wife has decided to celebrate her recovery at the opera and afterwards we are to take supper at Le Grand Véfour with the La Rochefontaines. My daughter informs me it will be remarked upon if I do not attend, so—if you will be so good—Thomas is waiting to dress me."

Max stared at him. What seemed the more astonishing about this volte-face over the ballroom was the tone in which it had been expressed: not philosophically, but with contained fury, which, taken with the manner in which he was being dismissed, left Max angry in turn and not a little affronted.

"Am I to understand, Armand, that you are blaming me for this wretched business?"

"I blame myself. I was a fool to believe you when you said you loved me."

Max considered him levelly. "You are certainly a fool."

Max carried his rage and hurt down to the library. Damn all Miremonts, wife, daughter, husband! Damn Gérard too! If the old boy had spent the day with the good doctor, it would hardly assist Max's cause, for Gérard, having mesmerised himself into denying his own inclinations, while he did not condemn Armand outright, disapproved of Uranians in general and Max in particular. Shit, shit, shit! The only small consolation was that the entire troupe including milady would be out of the house until midnight at least, leaving him with Miss Pilkington and Chopin to calm him.

However, when he entered the library he was greatly surprised to see none other than Miss Pilkington, who appeared much in need of calming herself.

"Oh, Monsieur Fabien, I hope you are not in trouble on my account."

Max summoned a grin. "My dear madame, I am forever in trouble. But never on your account."

"Then no one has spoken to you? You do not know? Oh, dear friend, I am so dreadfully sorry."

"I can't imagine your needing to apologise to anyone, let alone to me. But come, you had better tell me."

Concerned by her agitation, he tried to lead her to a chair, but she snatched her hand away as if it might burn him. "No, I cannot stay. I should not be here now. But I am glad I came, since you did not know. You are not to come to the schoolroom tonight. Madame de Miremont expressly forbids it."

"Forgive me?"

"Madame has found out how we spend our evenings when no one else is at home. And she thinks it improper."

"Improper? Chopin and Shakespeare?"

"I am unmarried and you are a young unmarried man."

"Oh, for Christ's—pardon me, but we are not exactly—" Max paused before he could add a lack of gallantry to his profanity.

"I tried to explain that our sole interest was the pursuit of knowledge. But madame is quite immovable."

"Damn that old crow Lady Telford!"

"Lady Telford? You think it was she who…?"

"No doubt of it."

"But she seems such a kind, well-intentioned person." Miss Pilkington hesitated. "I had not thought…"

"I fear she has taken a particular dislike to me."

"Then I suppose you must be right. It could not be anyone else." She seemed grateful to have the enemy identified, even a little relieved. "But you, my friend—if I have unwittingly helped to increase her prejudice against you, I am so very sorry."

Max cursed milady afresh. However hell-bent on revenge, she might have thought to spare this good-natured Englishwoman, whose earnest face was excruciated on his behalf, although it was she who might suffer most damage.

"Please, my dear Miss Pilkington," he said, "it is I who should apologise to you. I did not imagine—forgive me for thoughtlessly putting your reputation at risk. And your place."

"As to that—" Miss Pilkington managed a smile "—you must not be concerned. Mademoiselle Juliette spoke up for me."

Max was glad to hear Mlle Juliette was not completely without humanity.

"But," continued Miss Pilkington, "it did not matter how often I insisted to Madame de Miremont that you had never been other than a gentleman, she was adamant monsieur must be told."

Max contrived what he hoped was a carefree laugh. "If that is what concerns you, madame, you may rest easy. Monsieur would never believe such absurdities."

So now Max knew why he was no longer madame's 'good, dear boy' and why Armand had been so insufferable. Perhaps he should take something rare that would instantly be missed, like the Medici cup, secrete it in La Telford's rooms and then expose her. For he was reminded, when an unfamiliar housemaid delivered his supper tray, that Miss Pilkington was not the only innocent victim of milady's machinations, although admittedly, in the matter of poor Christine, he and Polly must bear some of the guilt.

Then there was Armand himself, with his mad delusions and

equally insane vow. Albeit that Simon was a ninny, if Max thought there were any chance of luring him from the servants' wing he would seduce him this very night and to hell with the repercussions.

But in the end, drained by his anger, he grew too tired for fantasies of revenge. He should listen to the Other, who still plagued his sleep nightly. He should never have let himself be infected by the old boy's sentimental notions. Love was a fool's business—the greater your investment, the worse you were repaid.

CHAPTER EIGHTEEN

Gérard was as perceptive as ever. Miremont would not have confided in him even if frankness had been possible, but the doctor, returning home from his last call of the morning to find his friend awaiting him, had clearly sensed his distress. Although Miremont had often expressed interest in Gérard's work, he was certain the invitation to visit the Hôtel-Dieu that afternoon was not coincidental: how could he, Miremont, look at those rows of iron bedsteads with their emaciated occupants without gratitude for his own exceptional and undeserved privilege? But even before that, as he had sat down to luncheon with the doctor and his sister, the solid comforts of his surroundings, the unpretentious meal and unaffected conversation had soothed the frenzy whipped up by the hours he had spent blindly pacing the streets until he had found himself in the Rue Poissonnière, at Gérard's door.

Miremont's long separation from Aline had allowed him to forget her madness was catching: it was not simply that he must guard his anger; the daily strain imposed by her unpredictable moods left its mark too. In the end, as you tried to anticipate her, you absorbed her unreason like the poisons in foul air, you started unwittingly to share her delusions, her sense of persecution, her trivial obsessions; you could not begin to understand her, yet somehow she sucked you in and swallowed you up, as a toad flashes out its tongue to ingest a fly.

After an hour or so in Gérard's company, Miremont found his faculties returning. It seemed obvious to him, all of a sudden, that if Max and his wife were lovers, Aline would not have interrupted his breakfast to insist he reprimand 'his' secretary for improper behaviour: she would have summoned Max himself and thrown a spectacular tantrum. Oh, her pride was hurt that the handsome young man she considered her courtier was dancing attendance on someone else, and she took malicious pleasure in telling Miremont yet another person in his employ had been found wanting; but that was all. His jealousy was not merely needless: it was deranged.

And what of Max's supposed impropriety with the poor lady companion? Reason assured Miremont this too was fanciful. True, the boy was not above flirting with young women, but Miss Pilkington was a confirmed bluestocking past marriageable age, who seemed, in any case, far too sensible to let her virtue be assailed. On the contrary, Max's enthusiasm for Shakespeare convinced Miremont the 'English lessons' were precisely that.

The reminder that he, Miremont, had once been Max's English teacher brought acute pain. God, it had been less than three months, but now they seldom saw each other alone, rarely spoke without arguing, were virtually estranged. And whose fault was it? He might have had no choice but to bind them to celibacy; but, for the rest…

Such were the thoughts he carried back with him to the Hôtel de Miremont. Yet Georges had scarcely helped him out of the cab when the madness reclaimed him. Why? Why had Aline done this? Was it revenge for her defeat over Mme Dussardier? Or a petty act of spite? Or fury that her *chevalier servant* had deceived her? She had organised it very cleverly, with everyone out of the house. Could she have succeeded without connivance?

He did not trust himself to confront his wife directly—besides, this would add to her triumph. All the same, his rage was hard to contain, the more so because Gérard's tuition had rendered its cause trivial—he had not needed Julie to tell him that. Yet he could not vent his anger upon his daughter, whose love, regained after prolonged separation, seemed rare and precious, with the inherent fragility of all exquisite things. With Max, however, he felt no such constraint. And the moment he gave way, all the doubts and suspicions, like chaff stirred by wind, came whirling back.

He retained a clear memory of the boy's parting shot, but an even clearer picture of his expression. For Max had not raised his chin or curled his lip, had not manifested outrage, contempt or even pain: on the contrary, his face had been quite empty, as if Miremont no longer merited the smallest expenditure of emotion.

'Fool'. The word rang in Miremont's head throughout the entire unpleasant evening, through the performance of Massenet's *Le roi de Lahore*, through supper's false bonhomie, through the draining charade of appearing to be at his wife's side while studiously avoiding all contact with her. Yes, he was a fool indeed. For could he not remember another evening at the Garnier, spent in torment, blindly staring at the stage? And did he not recall that, then as now, it had ceased to matter who was right or wrong? He ached for Max in mind and body. He could not live through the misery of last summer all over again.

*

It was past two o'clock by the time Thomas had undressed him and the house was still. Taking the lamp from his bedroom, following the route Max had always used on his nightly visits, he passed through the concealed door to the servants' passage and made his way to the back stairs. When he had last ventured onto the third floor he had been guided to Max's door by the light beneath it, but now everywhere was in darkness—the boy must have retired. Miremont found what he was confident was the right door and softly knocked. Silence: evidently Max was fast asleep. He hesitated. He was conscious that he presented the picture of indiscretion, stealing about in the small hours in his dressing gown; furthermore, these were precisely the circumstances to put his vow under strain. This very thought prompted an image, at once familiar and fraught with loss, of the boy lying on his stomach amongst the disordered sheets, his arms flung out, his sleeping profile guileless, oblivious to the rucked nightgown exposing the curve of his buttocks and the shadows at their cleft. Miremont let his hand fall away from the doorknob. But for no more than an instant.

The bed was empty. Nor had it been slept in, but was just as the maid had left it when she had turned it down.

Miremont's lamp explored the rest of the room: Max's copy of *Hamlet* and an English dictionary lay on the table; on the flap of the escritoire were his cigarette case and watch; but beyond that, the room appeared hardly less spartan than on Miremont's last visit, when its shelves and drawers had been cleared for packing. Although the fire had been banked up and still glowed feebly, it was dreadfully cold: as he stood, lamp aloft, surveying the plumped and smoothed linen of the empty bed, he began to shiver.

A sudden influx of light cast a second shadow across the wall and made him turn. Max, also in his nightclothes and carrying a lamp, stood in the doorway.

They considered each other briefly, Max with raised eyebrows, Miremont appalled.

"Which is it?" he burst out. "My wife? Or the lady companion?"

"Oh, both, naturally. But don't distress yourself—I still have enough energy for you. Except, of course—" Max paused to settle his lamp on the table "—I was forgetting we don't do that kind of thing nowadays."

Although Miremont winced at this last, he refused to be deterred. "I hardly think your tone is—"

"Oh, I agree, this is decidedly not a joking matter. Shit, it is freezing in here." Seizing the poker, Max began stabbing the recalcitrant fire. "It is definitely no—joke—when the master—of the madhouse—is its—biggest—lunatic." He flung the poker aside. "How many times have I told you I have become madame's indentured slave for one reason alone—that it is politic? Dear God, the idea of anything more—even if she were not your wife, gallantry would forbid me to speak further. And as for poor blameless Miss Pilkington... Yet you, Armand, a man whose intelligence and honour I used to respect, still sneak around spying on me in the middle of the night like some wronged husband in a third-rate comic opera."

"My dear boy, I was not spying. I came—I—I wished to apologise for speaking harshly this afternoon."

"A curious start for an apology."

"But then I saw your bed was empty—"

"So, naturally, I was in someone else's?"

"No—I—it is very late—and I..." Miremont, already feeling stupid, longed to retreat.

"Pray go on," said Max remorselessly. "I know you are dying to ask it."

"Really, dear boy, there is no need..."

"I was in the library."

"At this hour?"

"I couldn't sleep. I was reading Catullus."

The poet's name so strongly evoked the joys of life before Aline that Miremont's throat tightened. But Max had picked up the poker again and was resuming his assault on the fire.

"I trust, Armand, that your curiosity is satisfied. Having dared this sortie into the netherworld, you must be only too anxious to return to your bed."

"My dear boy..."

"Well?"

Wound untidily round Max's neck and curiously at odds with the splendour of his dressing gown, was a woollen muffler that had seen better days, while on his hands, Miremont noticed, were the sort of fingerless mittens worn by street vendors and market women. These prophylactics against the pitiless cold of his room should have seemed absurd, yet taken with the swirling skirts of his robe, his dishevelled hair and the streak of coal dust on his right cheek, they lent him on the contrary a brigandish air: true, the brigand, as he swung round from the grate, was armed impromptu with poker and tongs, but he still gave off the reckless energy, the spark of something wild and other that Miremont found so exciting.

He should take his dismissal—the boy was right. However, that would not clear the air between them: he must not forget the true purpose of his visit. Ridiculously, he was still holding his lamp aloft. Setting it down on the side chair next to the bed, he cleared his throat.

"My dear Max, I cannot blame you for your anger. I treated you most unfairly this afternoon."

"Only this afternoon?"

"Oh, that is—" Unjust, Miremont had been about to say. But, when he recalled his earlier reflections, he saw he had no right of dispute. Unfairness, mistrust, unwarranted hostility—he was guilty on every count.

"I am not the enemy."

"Oh, my darling boy, I know."

"I have tried to help you."

"I know. Forgive me. You are right, Aline has not only turned my house upside down, she seems to have overturned my wits. If you can begin to imagine…"

Miremont was about to elaborate upon his misery—the inability to work, the alternating periods of fury and boredom, the crushing insincerity and triviality of it all, the anxiety, the loneliness—but he could not bear to hear himself intone this threnody of self-pity. He longed to sit, but the nearest available surface was the bed with its suggestively turned-down coverlet. The fire was also dangerous, although by now he was chilled to his bones, for that would bring him into close proximity with Max, who, to make matters worse, was regarding him not unsympathetically, as if he had heard and understood his unspoken complaints.

"I've missed you," the boy said.

An embrace, a few innocent kisses, to touch, be touched—it was not in strict contravention of his vow, Julie would not begrudge him. "Oh, dear God, darling boy, I've missed you too."

"When I found you here—before you started accusing me of rampant fornication—well, you will know what I thought."

Already, in his imagination, Miremont had torn away that obstructive muffler, already his tongue had skimmed the boy's throat and found the triangle of sweet-smelling skin the unbuttoned neck of the nightshirt laid bare; already, while his mouth feasted, his hands, too, foraged urgently: of innocence there was not the least hope.

He reached for the lamp. "My darling Max, I love you, I miss you. But we both know what present circumstances require." And, not trusting himself further, he made for the door.

All the same, he could feel the boy's eyes upon him. He heard a brief sarcastic laugh.

"Sixty-three," Max said.

The strangeness of this compelled Miremont to turn.

"My reading in the library. It seemed appropriate."

Miremont flinched. For he needed no reminder that Catullus's sixty-third poem recounted the torments of Attis who, castrating himself in frenzied worship of Cybele, came bitterly to lament the loss of his manhood.

"My dear, dear boy… Is that how you feel?"

"Ego mei pars, ego vir sterilis ero?"[1]

Miremont's horror increased. "But you were… I thought you agreed it was advisable. You made no objection at the time."

"You said it would only be for a couple of weeks. And I suppose…" Max turned away. "I suppose I wanted to show you I could mend my ways."

"Oh, my darling boy—"

"Though the irony is exquisite, is it not? While my cock atrophies from lack of use, I'm accused of being an incorrigible seducer, so crazed with lust that no woman, whatever her age and attractions, is safe in my—"

But here Max broke off and began to laugh.

Miremont stared at him.

"Do you not see? It is perfect."

"I fear I—"

"It has worked. All those dreadful weeks of playing charades with madame. So appalling is my reputation that no one in the east wing will give a thought to the nature of my relations with you. We are safe, you and I."

"Oh, but…"

"We are free to leave the cloister."

"But I…"

"To hell with celibacy—which is where it belongs."

Miremont wanted to object that danger was not the only consideration, there was also paternal duty. At least, one voice wished to say this; but it was drowned by the other, whose clamour, not content

---

1   Shall I be a fragment of myself, a barren shadow of a man?

with its troubling insistence ever since he had entered the room, had gained further strength from the thought of Max as Attis, which, though itself horrific, had spawned compensating images of agonising eroticism. He began to shiver again, and not from the cold.

Max gently released the lamp from Miremont's grasp and set it aside. Then he took his face in his hands and kissed him hard upon the mouth. After that, mercifully, all thought vanished. There was only need and feverish grappling with obstacles, the shedding of Max's muffler and gloves, the fumbling with dressing-gown cords and the tails of nightshirts; Miremont shuddered when Max's hand slid between his legs, and again when the boy thrust himself between his thighs, but if he were conscious of any thought it was only that he must find the willpower to hold back a little longer; when the other thought visited him, he was quite unaware of it. Yet suddenly his muscles froze and his blood ebbed.

"It's this damnable cold," said Max. "Let's get into the bed."

But the bed made no difference. Granted it was not much warmer beneath the blankets, yet Max's efforts to revive him should not have been without avail.

Miremont, who now understood his trouble, heaved a sigh that was close to a sob. "Oh, my darling boy, I am so very sorry."

"You're out of practice, dear heart. Or perhaps I am."

"No, no... Dear God, it's not you." Miremont shifted so that they faced each other. "I wanted to desperately, I still want to. But I can't."

Max attempted a grin. "Madame has yet to see through walls, let alone all the way from the east wing."

"It's not..." Both from embarrassment and because it seemed a profanity, Miremont could not bring himself to mention the vision of Julie that had been his undoing; he preferred to let the misunderstanding lie. "I just can't."

"Never?"

"Not under this roof."

"Ah." Max paused to digest this. "Well, if that's the case..." He worked his arms around Miremont's waist and drew him closer. All at once he seemed extraordinarily cheerful. "Are you engaged for luncheon today?"

"N-no—not that I am aware."

"Excellent. Madame is bound to send me to the printers again, but I shall say there was something wrong with the order and I had to wait until they had put it right."

"Forgive me, dear boy... We are to lunch together?"

"In a manner of speaking." This time Max's grin was altogether unforced.

The happy understanding that slowly dawned in Miremont was succeeded by a frown. "She'll want to know who I'm meeting. I suppose I could say Constant, to offer my apologies for yesterday."

"Too easy to check."

"Catherine, then. Aline would go a long way to avoid speaking to Catherine."

"No, it must be someone madame does not know and is never likely to meet." Max thought for a moment, then uttered a hoot of triumph. "Of course. Our old friend Doctor van Zuylen."

Dr van Zuylen, a venerable expert on the Augustan poets, had, as Miremont well remembered, played a central role in the fiction that had installed Max in the Hôtel de Miremont: most generously, he had recommended the boy for the post of librarian, despite being innocent of his very existence. The elderly scholar possessed a signal qualification for his part: he resided in Reims and, being an invalid, never came to Paris.

"By the way," said Max, "how is the poor old chap? Still a martyr to stomach catarrh?"

"I suppose so. I have not heard from him recently."

"Well, I'm sure it would cheer his sickbed to do us further service."

CHAPTER NINETEEN

With its oak doors and well-maintained shutters, the house in the Rue Mazarine looked entirely respectable. Miremont, in some trepidation, not knowing what to expect, reread the note Max had left concealed in the pages of Catullus, but yes, he had found the right number.

The young servant in tails who admitted him seemed respectable too, and so did the concierge, with her widow's bombazine, old-fashioned lace cap and stately embonpoint. In the lobby the chequered tiles appeared freshly washed and there was a cleanly aroma of lye, while an open door afforded a glimpse of Second Empire sofas and potted palms. Under the circumstances, Miremont almost scrupled to use the absurd alias Max had chosen, but not a tremor shook the concierge's several chins as she replied that M. Hamlet had already arrived and directed the servant to show monsieur to Room 7. It was only then Miremont noticed that for a respectable widow she wore an unusual quantity of powder, through which, nevertheless, a blue shadow crept over her jowls and lip.

Miremont reflected upon this while the servant conducted him up two flights of stairs. Yet all around him was the hush of propriety: no voices echoed from the stairwell, every door he glimpsed was closed, even the sound of their own footsteps was muffled by the stair carpet, so that by the time they had reached the second landing and turned off into a corridor—more silence, more closed doors—he began to think that, apart from the remarkable widow, he and the servant were the only ones in the house. Thus he was greatly taken aback when the nearest door was flung open, disgorging a gust of raucous laughter and a red-faced gentleman, copiously moustachioed and whiskered but otherwise attired only in a cavalry corset and what was surely a tutu.

Miremont glanced away quickly, but not quickly enough to avoid catching the eye of the ballerina, who, exclaiming: "Ooops! A thousand pardons, monsieur!", rapidly retreated and shut the door. The servant, on the other hand, for all that he was still inclined to adolescent pimples, was not a whit disconcerted. "Directly, monsieur!" he called after the closing door, meanwhile continuing to escort Miremont to the end of the corridor: at Number Seven, pocketing Miremont's tip so discreetly he seemed to do it by sleight of hand, he slid off with equal circumspection.

Miremont opened the door—and almost forgot to close it behind him, for he hardly knew where to look. He was overjoyed to see Max, already in his shirtsleeves and stretched out nonchalantly in an armchair, smoking. Yet the room too, begged, nay, screamed for his attention. Even despite the ballerina, the journey upstairs had conditioned him to expect more plush sofas and palms; but here were walls tented in swagged satin, a bed canopied by a flying coronet trailing brocaded and tasselled draperies, a bedhead supported by two enormous gilt swans, and all, from carpet to coverlet, in every imaginable shade of red—crimson, vermillion, scarlet, madder, maroon. Someone had attempted to recreate the Empress Josephine's bedroom at Malmaison and had refused to be discouraged by the space available, which, aside from not being a rotunda, would have fitted into the original fourfold.

It must be said, however, that, splendid as this creation would have looked by candlelight, when the gas chandelier was supplemented by sharp winter sun from the partly open curtains it showed to less advantage. Even as Miremont's vision reeled, he was conscious that not all the shades of red were happily matched, that the carpet was stained in places and the draperies, although not shabby exactly, had the air of having been breathed over and thumbed by countless previous occupants; likewise the coverlet, which had been smoothed beneath the bolster as if in haste. There was also a faint but readily identifiable smell that set him wondering whether the sheets were clean.

"I shouldn't think so for a moment," said Max, who had been watching him with amusement. "Now—there is lunch." He gestured towards a commode on which stood some platters and a champagne bucket. "Or we could continue where we left off. There is no absolute need for you to remove your topcoat, dear heart, but at least let me relieve you of your hat and cane."

In the looking glass thoughtfully installed within the bed canopy, Miremont considered his reflection: a dazed, naked, foolishly smiling man sat propped up by the bolster, drinking champagne, while beside him the sheet still bore, warm to his touch, the imprint of his lover's body where they had finally collapsed like beached swimmers. But now their two hours were almost up and Max, beyond the range of the glass, was soaping himself at the washstand.

Miremont was much taken with the looking glass. He had been amused, too, by the ceiling fresco, which rewarded a second glance by revealing the antics of its cherubs. He would admit the bourgeois decency he had encountered on first entering this house had been somewhat disappointing: Room 7, on the other hand, after the first bewildering moments, had more than gratified his expectations.

The recollection made him laugh. "This place is paradise. I don't care about the sheets."

"I doubt we've improved them," said Max, grinning, as he approached with hot water and towels. Setting down the basin beside the bed, he took the glass from Miremont's hand and kissed him. Then, as Miremont rolled over with a sigh, he began to bathe him, just as he had the first night they had spent together, under Catherine de Claireville's roof at La Boissière.

"So you approve this arrangement?"

"Oh, my darling boy... My only question is, how often may we come here?"

"As often as we can manage. Of course, madame cannot always guarantee the bridal suite."

"Madame?" Miremont remembered the curious creature downstairs.

"Madame Tonton."

"But I thought—Achille de Tarascon gave me to understand..."

"The lunchtime clientele prefers discretion. At night, though, it's certainly a different story, particularly when there's a ball."

"Good heavens!" Although Miremont had just received telling proofs of Max's love, a familiar voice, like a tic that can never be completely cured, enquired how the boy had acquired this knowledge.

But Max was laughing. "Don't worry, old thing. I have yet to develop a taste for false bosoms. And as for flagellation, I had quite enough of that at Saint-Pons. But you on the other hand—" he flicked the wet towel across Miremont's buttocks "—well, they do say Madame T's more mature customers—"

"Wretched boy!" Miremont grabbed Max's wrist and they grappled with each other until it was clear they would soon be oblivious of the clock.

"Oh shit!" said Max, kissing Miremont on the lips and pulling away.

The sight of the boy, still aroused as he searched for his clothes, was almost too much for Miremont. "Two hours... What cruelty."

"It's not just Madame T. It's Madame de M. You may take as long as you please to lunch with poor old Van Zuylen. But I shall get a roasting if—oh, shit! Curse this confounded thing!" Max, in reaching to extract his trousers from their tangled clothing, had stubbed his toe on the parcel from the printers.

This at least had the effect of rousing Miremont from the bed. But his consoling embrace was frustrated, for Max was pulling on his shirt.

"With any luck," said the boy when the shirt was over his head, "she will be out when I get back. But if we're to do this regularly we'll need a better excuse."

Accustomed for years to the ministrations of Thomas, Miremont was befuddled by the business of dressing in a hurry. "Should I invent a mistress?"

Max laughed. "Apparently the comte d'Issy-Lévêque has ended his arrangement with Princess Zelenska."

Catherine, who, until better informed, had shared the general view that Miremont needed consolation after the rupture with Aline, had once intrigued to spirit Iphigénie Zelenska into his bed. The memory forced him to repress a shudder.

Max was still laughing. "Alas, though a delightful thought, it would not serve."

"Indeed not, wicked boy. My wife is on friendly terms with the princess."

"More to the point, what man takes his secretary when he visits his mistress? Dear heart, we need an excuse for both of us."

"Ah… yes. Of course." But, distracted by the struggle to fasten his collar stud, Miremont could think of nothing helpful.

"Supposing—supposing you and old Van Zuylen were engaged in some enterprise which required me to take notes? Editing a manuscript, perhaps? Or starting a new scholarly journal."

"You know what Aline thinks of that sort of thing. I should never hear the end of it."

Thomas could fasten the stud in one swift movement. Miremont was irritated and shamed by his incompetence, the more so since he could see that Max observed it. He was damned if he would ask for help. However the boy had the tact to avert his eyes.

"Darling Max, forgive me." At last, seemingly of its own volition, the stud snapped into place. "I agree we must think of something. Only I cannot see what."

By now Max was fully dressed, even to his topcoat, and was lifting the lids of their untouched lunch platters. After offering a dish of foie gras to Miremont, who, engaged in pinning his cravat, shook his head, he larded a hunk of bread with the pâté and stood, munching thoughtfully. Mid-mouthful he gave a muffled exclamation.

"I have it! The Trust."

"I beg your pardon, dear boy?"

"Your mother's trust. When you attend trustees' meetings, I go with you to take minutes."

Miremont recoiled. The Marquise de Miremont Trust, established in memoriam to continue his beloved mother's charitable work among distressed young women, was for him a sacred duty, no more to be profaned than his obligation to Julie: it was unthinkable to use it as a cover for visits to a *maison de passe*, let alone such a particular *maison* as this. However, he was also conscious that he had contributed little towards resolving their difficulty. Rather than utter a shocked rejection, he seized upon the practical obstacles that came to mind.

"But, dear boy, the board only meets twice a year."

"Then it must embark on some venture that demands weekly meetings. At your last, you discussed setting up a school."

"Besides, Aline loathes the very mention of these unfortunate girls. She thinks Monsieur Worth more deserving."

"The Trust imposes legal obligations. Even madame can't expect you to shirk those."

"And then there's Constant." This was Miremont's trump card. Of the three trustees—himself, his brother-in-law and Gérard—the latter, having been banished, posed no danger. But Constant, although not very diligent in his trustee's duties and no friend to Aline, presented a ready magnet for awkward questions.

"Could you not ask Monsieur de Sauvigny to say he was at the meetings—or at least knew of them?"

Miremont stared at the boy, appalled. "You wish me to ask my brother-in-law to tell lies on my behalf?"

"He might be happy to do so."

"Truly, dear boy—to say I am shocked is to—"

"I was merely wondering," said Max, undeterred and indeed smiling, "what a man like the comte de Sauvigny is likely to think if you ask him confidentially to cover your tracks for a couple of hours each week."

The boy was right, of course. Constant, assuming that Miremont had at last taken the advice he had been giving him for years, would co-operate gladly, no questions asked.

"So there you are." Max applied foie gras to another crust of bread. "You have your imaginary mistress after all."

"No, darling boy. I'm sorry. It is impossible."

Max considered him for a moment, then gave a wry smile. "Dear heart, you could actually set up a school. Afterwards. As a penance."

Miremont shook his head.

Their time had more than elapsed, particularly since Miremont must delay his departure until the boy had left the house and vanished into a side street. Max discarded the bread and retrieved his parcel while Miremont struggled into his topcoat.

"Forgive me, dear heart," said Max, as they embraced. "It was only that it seemed the perfect solution. But we'll think of something."

Yet, as they kissed and Miremont again tasted the joys of the last two hours, he could scarcely feel reconciled to their usual wretched existence. Of course that changed nothing. The boy's idea was out of the question. Miremont could not tell himself his mother would forgive him, for, understanding as she had been, she would scarcely have understood this. And as for deceiving Constant, persuading the poor fellow to lie under false pretences, casting still wider the net of falsehood in which he himself was enmeshed—it was indeed unthinkable. Yet... Two hours? Two miserly hours, and then a return to celibacy for months to come? And if he, Miremont, could bring himself to suffer for his tender conscience, was it fair to force Max to suffer too?

As it happened, life at the Hôtel de Miremont, while still by no means easy, did temper its rigour over the next few weeks.

Although madame continued to require Max to organise her diary and run errands, he was no longer commanded to pay court in her boudoir. For this he had not only his supposed faithlessness to thank; it emerged that, the day before madame's startling recovery, Lady Telford had received a telegram from Dieppe: a second cousin of hers by marriage had just disembarked from England and hoped to pay his respects when he was settled in Paris. The familial bond must have been strong despite the distance of the relationship, for Lord Stilorgan called at the Hôtel de Miremont not two days later.

Tall, fleshy and in his late thirties, Jack Stilorgan wore the careless air of a man who has sunk much grand cru claret, vanquished many foxes, and held many good hands at chemin de fer. Clotilde, visiting at the time, observed that his was merely an Irish peerage, but madame, who, it turned out, was slightly acquainted with milord from her time in London, appeared charmed by his tawny whiskers and tales of derring-do. Lady Telford was restored to full favour, particularly as his lordship's attentions to his distant relative, which were very assiduous, usually embraced madame too: most afternoons he and the two ladies were out in the carriage, paying calls or enjoying some jaunt or other.

Miremont might have taken the assiduousness of the noble lord as an assault on his honour for, though he and Aline were formally separated, she was at present beneath his roof, but instead, so long as he were not forced into the fellow's company, he resolved to be pragmatic: he and Max were frequently left to their own devices, while the meetings of the Marquise de Miremont Trust went unremarked. Indeed, much of their normal routine was restored, for Max was free to ride again and resume regular attendance at the fencing sessions, and in the afternoons they sometimes even managed a little work on Ovid. It was not enough for contentment—they could never be certain of privacy and their weekly two hours brought as much frustration as pleasure—but affection and trust flowed freely once more.

This encouraged Max to reveal milady Telford's little weakness, for he was concerned that it was far from cured. Although Miremont, as expected, was horrified by Max's search of milady's rooms, he was yet more aghast that his house had been stealthily pillaged and his first instinct was to ask the good lady to leave. But of course that was impossible: if Miremont tried to expel the convenient second cousin of the attentive Lord Stilorgan, he would face a war with madame that would make the affair of Mme Dussardier seem a scuffle. Scandal might be piled upon scandal: better to have a quiet word with Boussec about their guest's interesting habit.

As for Christine, Max was relieved to hear she had not left Paris but had taken refuge with an aunt in Ménilmontant. As well as sending her a sum to augment her 'hat' money, he took care to recommend her to Old Jouvert, who would find her a situation, supplying the references she lacked.

Of course there were shocks and reversals to be borne. Aline was not so preoccupied with her milord that she forgot to set the redecoration of the ballroom in train. For the remainder of December fencing was relegated to the Marble Salon, while dust sheets were laid and the precious Venetian mirrors taken down, for apparently, if the ballroom draperies were to be replaced, the ancient wall hangings must be renewed as well. Miremont kept his distance while the work was in progress, for he retained confidence in Julie's ruse. Alas, her trust in Aline's perversity transpired to have been misplaced. "Poor Papa," she said, as he stared, appalled, at the finished renovations. "But I suppose you mustn't blame Maman, considering you said you preferred pink."

Apart from this, however, the New Year festivities passed without disaster. Miremont was delighted to observe the growing affinity between Julie and Raoul de Niversac. While the young man had protested modestly that he was no Nadar, he had brought his camera to the Hôtel de Miremont and had made several studies of Julie that everyone judged enchanting and certainly to be preferred over her portrait in oils, which, although it now hung with the other family paintings, sadly failed to capture the singular sweetness of her beauty. Watching the couple, heads bent close as they leafed through Niversac's album portraying the wild Canadian landscape, Miremont felt both joy and regret: it would surely not be long before Julie consented to an engagement.

In the second week of January came Max's twenty-second birthday. This year's celebrations perforce took place in secret: as Miremont's present was too large to be got out of the house unnoticed, an emergency session of the Trust was followed by a more restrained meeting held just before midnight in the boy's room.

Determined that Max should have a picture to enliven his barren walls and noting that the boy had begun to take an interest in the avant-garde, Miremont had consulted his usual dealer, Korsakov, who had acquired for him, through Durand-Ruel, a painting by Manet (Miremont recollected the name in connection with some past brouhaha at the Salon). Its subject, though inconsequential, was charming—a blond boy in a straw hat on a bicycle—but Miremont was surprised at the price, not because he begrudged Max, but because the daubed brushwork and sketchy background struck him as untutored. Max, however, was as overwhelmed as if it had been a Caravaggio. His joy continued to warm Miremont when, not long after, he retired to the virtuous chill of his own bed.

He was still smiling at the recollection the next morning when Boussec arrived to interrupt his breakfast: Aline had instructed Mme Mercier to give Mme Dussardier her notice.

"He's utterly bewildered, poor old fellow. After all these weeks, when he was so certain she'd conceded defeat…"

It was too cold and wet to smoke. The snow that had begun not fifteen minutes earlier was already blanching the Luxembourg's lawns and crowning the statues with silver lace; Max and Polly had sought the inadequate shelter of the bandstand, where, shoulders hunched, they paced back and forth, trailing a petulant Bébé.

"You can blame that old tart Quintivali," said Polly. "She wouldn't drop her bloomers until the price was right."

"So we're definitely getting Quintivali?"

"According to Victor—you remember Victor, angel?"

Max nodded: Victor had been sixth footman during his time at Mme de Claireville's.

"Well, I chanced upon the dear girl this morning. She happened to be coming out of the Hôtel de Claireville on an errand just as I was taking the doggie for a stroll."

"To the Rue de Varenne? Poor beast. No wonder he's exhausted." And indeed Bébé had hunkered down obdurately on the damp floor, forcing them to halt their pacing and shiver.

"Anyway, Victor says La Quintivali gave notice yesterday. Double her wages was too good to resist."

"Double? The greedy bastard. That's probably four times what Madame Dussardier gets."

"But naturally dinner will be four times as tasty."

Max sighed.

"Victor reports that the servants' hall is celebrating but Mme de Claireville is less than delighted. And as for my fellow serfs—well, the mood is black."

"Wait for the flying meat cleavers and saucepans. That should—"

But Max was interrupted by Bébé, who, seized by some vision beyond the veil of snow, was suddenly goaded from lethargy. As his leash dragged Polly to the perimeter of the bandstand, a shadowy figure rose up—another footman, by the outline of his tricorn and cape—walking a lean, long-muzzled dog that picked its way through the snow like a duchess in satin slippers. The footman, warned by the sounds of canine frenzy, turned back into the blizzard towards the Medici Fountain, the borzoi following to heel in silent disdain, and moments later both were obliterated. But this seemed insufficient for Bébé, who continued to yap and snarl.

"Cut it!" screamed Polly. "Cut it while Auntie finds your medicine! Angel, take him, will you?" Thrusting the leash into Max's hands, Polly rummaged beneath his cape, finally bringing out a waxed-paper packet.

The sight of the chocolate worked a transformation: the dog gazed up at Polly, whimpering expectantly.

"Good doggie! Yum yum! Here, have another."

"For pity's sake!" said Max.

"Violet creams. From Debauve & Gallais. Mademoiselle Bonnard keeps me supplied. Enough, doggie dearest, leave one for Auntie." Helping himself, Polly proffered the packet to Max, who shook his head.

"You're killing the poor creature."

"Nonsense," said Polly, returning the sweetmeats to the inner recesses of his cape. "They're just what the doctor ordered. See! Oh yes, good doggums."

Max was forced to concede that Bébé was settling, albeit with resignation, at Polly's feet.

"Anyway—" Polly licked a smear of chocolate from his glove "—to return to La Dussardier, this girl's had an idea."

Max groaned. "If it's like the last one—"

"Now that's unfair! You can't blame me because that old bawd milady—"

"All right." A change in the wind was blowing the snow into the bandstand and flakes as large as centimes were beginning to sting Max's face. "Quickly, before we get frostbite."

"It's very simple, dear heart. In fact it hardly takes a girl of my genius to—"

"I said 'quickly'."

"Oh, have it your own way. La Dussardier is without a situation and the Empress Catherine is without a cook. And your Monsieur Mouse is bosom friends with the Empress."

"That's all very well, but it hardly solves the problem. He doesn't wish to part with Madame Dussardier—even supposing Madame de Claireville will employ her."

"But what if it were a loan?"

"I don't see—"

"Madame isn't going to be with us forever, is she?"

"Dear God, I pray not. Monsieur expects her to return to the country when Mademoiselle Juliette is married."

Polly grinned. "Well then, there you are, angel."

Miremont was unsure. He agreed the idea was ingenious and would guarantee Mme Dussardier's immediate future; yet the poor woman might object to being lent out like a set of plate. Besides it seemed unfair to blight the new chef's prospects before he had even joined the household, although Max suggested Catherine might be prepared to forgive Quintivali by the time Aline departed. After some reflection Miremont decided to call on Catherine and, much to his surprise, whether through appreciation of Mme Dussardier's talents or the pleasure of outwitting Aline, she was delighted to comply. Mme Dussardier, once she had received Miremont's assurances, was also willing. Thus, three weeks later, as M. Quintivali was haranguing the kitchen servants at the Hôtel de Miremont, Mme Dussardier was taking a welcoming glass of muscat with Mme Pinet in the housekeeper's parlour at the Rue de Varenne.

Miremont hoped, now his wife had her chef and her way over the ballroom, she would feel the supremacy of her power: there surely could be no cause left for conflict.

CHAPTER TWENTY

Letting fall the letter she was reading, Juliette de Miremont drifted to the window to gaze down at the courtyard, where snow had spread its quilt over the gravel walks and beds of box. There would be another fall by the look of the sky: although the gas in the piano nobile would not be lit until midday, there were lights burning opposite in her father's apartments; there was also, she could not help noticing, a solitary lamp glowing below, in the library. She caught herself uttering a disconsolate sigh.

Pulling her wrapper more tightly around her, she turned away. It was nothing, this restlessness, this dissatisfaction: ennui was to be expected now the entertainments of the New Year were a distant memory, and today even riding was precluded by the weather. M. de Niversac would make the perfect husband: he was rich, of rank, and worshipped her. Had it not been for the truce with her mother, which stipulated a stay of maternal interference so long as she postponed her marriage until the end of the Season, she would probably have accepted him long since. But Maman must have her salon and her Worth toilettes and her assignations with that beastly Lord Jack, so she must play the obedient daughter: the engagement would be announced at her ball and, allowing for the time it would take to draw up the contract, she would become Mme la comtesse de Niversac by July.

Naturally she had received other proposals: there had been two in England, although she had refused both; Colonel Lord Urchfont might be heir to the Duke of Wardour and his mother a princess from one of those quaint German principalities, but Juliette had no wish to be an English army wife, even as a prospective duchess, nor was there much promise in the Waldavian connection, since the princess's branch of the family was in exile; besides which, Aubyn Urchfont was years older than her and spoke barely a word of French; and the same could be said of her other suitor, Sir Jonas Smythe, whose offer was anyway little less than an affront, since, despite being related to the Massinghams, he was only a knight and a widower with three children into the bargain. Besides, who would choose to live in England, a country full of people whose necks were stiffened by the perpetual damp? With M. de Niversac came Paris and Society (admittedly there was also Canada, but Juliette would soon wean him from that).

Once again she enumerated Raoul de Niversac's virtues: he could dance without treading on her train; he was not a pompous bore, like Clotilde's Raymond; now that he had ceased to point his camera at dull landscapes and horrid savages, he took charming photographs; he was even reasonably good-looking—Mimi de Sainte-Foy swore his moustache turned her to jelly, while Manon de Merlincourt had been as sour as a crab apple since realising her moonstruck glances were quite in vain.

Granted, he too was old, not as old as Lord Urchfont and nowhere near as old as Sir Jonas, but still twelve years her senior. Yet young men were so conceited—take Roland de Sauvigny, who had thought he could step into his brother's shoes without troubling to make the slightest effort to please. Whereas the right sort of older man showed you respect, treated you with reverence, knew he must earn the smiles you granted; and if he also regarded you as a pretty little doll, believed innocence meant stupidity, well, that was not necessarily a disadvantage.

A good marriage was the prerequisite for any sensible girl. Love could come later. A married woman of rank was free to direct her affections where she pleased, provided—and Juliette had not failed to learn from her *maman*—she did not lose her reputation along with her heart.

Thus comforted, she was able to refrain from going to the window again and instead, retrieving Nettie du Vivier's letter, settled herself on the chaise. Poor silly Nettie. Here, in these lines from her school friend, was ample confirmation of her own good sense.

Ah, Emilio Baldoni. Oh yes, he was young and very handsome— those soulful brown eyes, that thick dark hair curling romantically over his collar—but Juliette had remained unmoved, she was not in the least put out when it was clear his attentions were focused on her friend, even though she herself was generally judged the beauty of the two. She did not forget that Signor Baldoni was merely the drawing master.

Certainly the elopement was dreadfully exciting (although afterwards it had been no easy task for Juliette to convince Reverend Mother that, despite being Nettie's bosom friend, she had known not a single thing); doubtless it was the longing to revive this thrilling drama that had lured her into accepting Nettie's invitation to visit the newly married lovers—that and the daring adventure of travelling to Lugano, of striking out on her own, undercover, as it were, so that the nuns believed she was joining her mother, while Maman, absorbed in her own concerns, did not question the letter from Belgium in which Mme la baronne du Vivier invited Juliette to accompany a family party to take the Alpine air.

But of course that was the end of the excitement. It was painful to watch poor Nettie, plain Signora Baldoni now, cut off by her family and fast losing her waistline, making do on a pittance from a compassionate aunt and what Baldoni could earn from his paintings. She might pretend she enjoyed playing housewife in a garret, the couple might shower each other with endearments, but Juliette was too clear-eyed to be deceived. Life with Baldoni was coarsening Nettie: naturally, as the son of a teacher and grandson of a peasant, he could not be expected to display the manners that came with breeding, so perhaps ought to be pardoned for failing to show her, Juliette, the attention due to a guest, but Nettie too seemed disposed to forget a visitor's wishes should be paramount. Altogether, it was exceedingly uncomfortable to find oneself a wallflower; only the certainty that things must turn out badly lent Juliette the strength to forgive her friend.

That was a year ago. The baby had come long since, although how Nettie managed with only a maid-of-all-work to look after it, Juliette could not imagine. And now the silly creature wrote that she was again in an interesting condition, as if she expected Juliette to rejoice for her.

Poor Nettie. She had paid a high price for excitement. In five years' time she would have six babies, no figure and a life of squalor, while Juliette de Niversac would be queen of Paris. In five years' time Nettie would be begging her father to relent, while Juliette de Niversac would be free once and for all of her parents, free to forget the injustices of her childhood and enjoy any indulgence she craved.

Clotilde maintained you were bound to love your mother and father whatever their faults, not simply from duty but because blood forged a bond that could not be broken (no doubt her own motherhood encouraged this optimistic view). Juliette, on the other hand, could honestly say she felt nothing in particular for either of her parents.

Her misfortunes had begun with being the younger daughter in a household where money was always short. While Clotilde had been given new dresses, she had worn cast-offs like an orphan; even her dolls were the tattered creatures her sister had tired of. Added to which, dull, obedient Clotilde was the yardstick against which she, Juliette, was measured: Clotilde did not get grass stains on her pinafore or leave inkblots in her copybook; Clotilde paid attention to her sums and her reading, even if she were a plodder; Clotilde was not rude, did not tell lies, leave her embroidery silks in a tangle, spit out her castor oil, smuggle frogs into the nursery or pour honey over the keys of the schoolroom piano.

Oh yes, Clotilde was the general favourite of nurses and governesses. And there was a steady succession of those, universally old and ugly, selected for their hairy lips and onion breath: Juliette remembered with clarity only the worst of them, Grosch, the Swiss nursemaid who had tied them to their bedsteads to prevent them getting dirty, and later Mme Carnot, the Protestant governess from Caen who had made them recite Bible verses day and night. But what did she care for these vile old hags? She was certain she was Maman's favourite—beautiful, fragrant Maman with her melodious laughter, who would rescue her from these monsters.

Yet in truth they scarcely saw Maman. Sometimes she would appear in the nursery just before bedtime in a cloud of tulle and scent, but mostly she was a distant figure, drifting across the lawns beneath a parasol in the company of other elegantly attired figures. Once, when Juliette was ill, Maman had arrived at her bedside dressed for a ball and had bent as if to kiss her forehead; but then—Juliette could not help herself—she had been sick, all over Maman's gloves and fan: the screams of outrage and disgust still seared her memory. After that she had begun to hate Maman as passionately as she had idolised her.

Then, when she was about seven or eight, things changed. Someone—probably M. de Tréville, Maman's admirer at the time— must have suggested that charming, attractive children were not an encumbrance to a beautiful woman, but an ornament. Clotilde and Juliette were both equipped with dainty new frocks and pinafores and, with their hair curled into ringlets, were brought down to entertain the visitors taking afternoon tea: Juliette, as the baby and the pretty one, sang and improvised a little ballet, while Clotilde provided a stumbling piano accompaniment and Maman, despite her modest blushes, lapped up the compliments. Afterwards, of course, they were shooed back to the nursery and changed out of their finery, but such was the success of this tribute to Maman's motherhood that their performance became a requirement whenever there was company.

At first Juliette was merely delighted to have eclipsed Clotilde. But later she began to study her performance and the art of charm. Naturally she took her mother for a model and, after much practice and observation, was able to mimic her every gesture: the eyes glancing up from beneath lowered lashes, the vulnerable flutter of one hand to the throat, the girlish moues, the silvery laugh—she had it all pat. One day, when she was left alone for a moment with M. de Tréville, she put her accomplishments to the test—and was overjoyed to find that henceforth his glance was no longer reserved for her mother.

Here was her revenge. The entertainments had ceased by then, since neither she nor her sister could continue to be passed off as enchanting little children—Clotilde was almost fourteen and inclined to pimples, while she would soon be eleven. But, for the same reason, they could no longer be sequestered in the schoolroom every hour of the day. Although M. de Tréville tired of Maman, he was succeeded by other admirers, not all susceptible, but some exceedingly so. Mind you, Juliette learned to be careful: the repulsive, slobbery, wine-laden kiss planted directly on her mouth by old Dr Colombe was lesson enough; she became as spry as a bird, quick to anticipate wandering hands and dart away with a skip and a giggle. Maman, she knew, watched her suspiciously, but she was careful there too: so far as she could see, her mother's main fear was of being outshone by her growing beauty. But then, when she was thirteen, she was caught in the arbour sitting on M. Ferrier-Lalange's knee and summarily packed off to Bruges.

To be put away in a convent with fusty old nuns, as if this were the Middle Ages—how she had loathed her mother. But when she was allowed home for her niece's christening and saw that Clotilde, even though married, was still under Maman's thumb, she realised banishment was a gift: her mother was a ridiculous fat old hag with fewer brains than a powder puff, no more worthy to be dignified by hatred than by love; she, Juliette, was in the ascendancy now.

Since mother and daughter alike were less than delighted when Juliette returned home for good, it was easy to reach an accommodation. In London, although Juliette knew very well who was paying the rent on Lady Telford's fine house in Albemarle Street and had not failed to note Lord Stilorgan's frequent presence, she was happy to turn a blind eye; let Maman be thoroughly fleeced by the old baggage and her so-called cousin if it kept her quiet. Indeed, Juliette scarcely saw her mother, for it was Lady Massingham who superintended her entrance into London Society and presented her at court; and, if the countess were not available to chaperone her, there was always Miss Pilkington, who was naive to the point of stupidity and easy to win over.

In Paris, the arrangement continued: Juliette might do as she pleased so long as her mother's interests were not threatened; however, there was a further proviso, that she should ensure her papa paid all her expenses.

Clotilde could remember—or said she could—the time when Maman was in Florence and they had lived with Papa, before Maman had returned and then left again, taking them both to the country. Clotilde maintained he had been quite different then: she recalled him kneeling on the nursery floor, showing her how to spin a top and, another time, lifting her up in his arms, laughing as he swung her aloft, promising he would one day swing her up to touch the clouds.

Juliette had been in her cradle then, of course. The Papa she remembered was the man who had visited them every Christmas and New Year, a chilly, stiff, silent personage who seemed uncomfortable when he accompanied Maman to the nursery and who later appeared to take scant interest in his offspring, bringing them presents they had already grown out of or dull books without pictures, and only bothering to speak when he could ask them stupid questions about their schoolwork.

Clotilde might cling to her illusions and Maman might be wrong about very many things, but on this Juliette was bound to agree with her mother: her father was a cold, unfeeling, selfish man. For yes, of course she could see that, like M. de Tréville and all the others, Papa had in the end found Maman intolerable; but why, when they had parted, had he also parted with his daughters? If, as Clotilde claimed, he had loved them, why had he given them up, consigned them to Maman's mercies knowing quite well what she was like? Why, if he wished to punish Maman by keeping her short of money, had he not cared that he was punishing them too? Why, if he loved them, had he never once stood up for them?

Juliette could hear him now. "You must show respect to your mother." "You must obey your mother." "If that is your mother's wish, I may not interfere." Even when she had written to him, begging, pleading not to be sent to Bruges, he had refused to stand up for her as a father should. There could be no moral objection to his taking her side, since Maman, who had her own motive to lie, claimed the purpose of sending her away was educational, but he still did nothing. She might resent the hand-me-downs and Nurse Grosch and Mme Carnot and all the other childhood miseries he could have relieved had he cared to, but Bruges was beyond mere resentment. Bruges was proof positive that he did not care.

So what was she to make of him now, when it was "Darling Julie" and "My dear sweet daughter"? Had he undergone a miraculous change of heart? Perhaps, after the disappointment of Clotilde, whose marriage had made no great splash, he was suddenly alive to the prestige of having a beautiful daughter who would marry well and create a sensation in Society, further distinguishing all those long-dead Miremonts he seemed to love more than the living. Or perhaps Clotilde was right and age was softening his brain—it was certainly amazingly easy to pull the wool over his eyes.

Whatever the reason for these sudden displays of fatherly affection, it did not matter. He could tell Juliette she was beautiful as many times as he liked; it would always be meaningless. When she had longed for him to praise her and adore her, he had been silent. And now it was too late.

Besides, in many ways he had not changed one jot. In company he remained tongue-tied and clumsy, an embarrassment when you compared him with M. de Tarascon or M. de la Rochefontaine or even aged M. de Cressy. And he was still mean, despite his protests. His stinginess over the ballroom was no exception. Had he not thought, for instance, that a beautiful young girl might like a new and fashionable piece of jewellery for her eighteenth birthday, not her grandmother's old pearls (and then not even the finest string—that, of course, had gone to Clotilde)? Then there was his 'generosity' over her maid: she had expected a proper experienced lady's maid, not an under-servant promoted from the ranks according to some stupid tradition, an uncouth girl to whom she must teach even the basic rudiments of style. No wonder that, for all his avowed devotion, he was so keen for her to marry, thrusting her into the arms of M. de Niversac at every opportunity. He must bear the expense of her wedding and dowry, but after that she would cease to be a drain on his purse. For a moment she was tempted to turn down Raoul de Niversac, just to spite him.

Still, she could not complain that he loved Clotilde any better— she was favoured as the eldest, nothing more. He had never loved their mother, so he could not love her daughters. And yet—sometimes Juliette wanted to believe in his smiles and his kisses—even though she knew it was a delusion, she wanted—she longed… Unbidden came the image of Emilio Baldoni when Nettie had tripped on the stairs, how he had rushed out of the parlour and scooped her up, pressing his lips to her cheeks and hair, begging her to tell him she was not hurt or in pain, his voice filled with such concentrated tenderness, as if there were no one else in the world. Of course, Nettie had only missed the bottom step and had come to no harm, besides which it had been entirely her own fault, since she had been laughing and not looking where she was going. But Juliette, watching Emilio from the stair above, had thought suddenly: 'No one has ever loved me like that.'

Stupid! She found her handkerchief and wiped her eyes. She was cool, she was calm, she was sensible. She would settle for M. de Niversac. All the same, she could not prevent herself from turning back to the window. But the snow was falling again, so heavily that she could no longer see across the courtyard, let alone make out whether a light remained in the library. For some reason, this filled her with such uncontrollable frustration she almost screamed. It was ridiculous. She was not a girl who read novels or indulged in silly fantasies. What in heaven's name had come over her? If it had not been for that goose Euphemia Pilkington—yes, it was all Miss Pilkington's fault!

CHAPTER TWENTY-ONE

It had started weeks ago, at the beginning of December, when Juliette was about to leave for her final sitting with M. Lebas. She was ready early, since there had only been her hair and jewellery to attend to—the artist had used a model to execute the Catherine de' Medici gown, adding his subject's head afterwards, so that all the portrait required now was some finishing touches to the face—and rather than sit about, restless, in her apartments, she had sent Drouet, her maid, to instruct Miss Pilkington that they would wait for the carriage in the foyer, while she went downstairs in her furs to the picture gallery.

She was not quite happy with the portrait. Lebas was Maman's choice and, although he was an Academician who, according to her, had painted everyone from the comtesse de Paris to Princess von Metternich, Juliette found him vulgar and did not trust him. She recalled the picture of the beautiful woman with the cupid and how Papa had said she was even more beautiful; if she scrutinised it carefully, perhaps she would be able to tell M. Lebas where his portrait had gone wrong. But she had scarcely found the painting when she heard voices and laughter echoing in the foyer and was astonished to recognise the usually solemn tones of Miss Pilkington.

Edging to the half-open doorway, where she might observe but not be observed, she saw her lady companion and her father's secretary coming from the anteroom that led to the library. Whatever they had been doing amongst Papa's dreary books, it must have been singularly amusing, because they were still laughing when they paused near the stairs. Juliette was struck by their easy familiarity, how directly they looked into each other's faces, how close together they stood. Miss Pilkington, with her bright eyes and flushed cheeks, seemed to have forgotten she was an old maid and M. Fabien, although he was half her age, was smiling as if he had forgotten it too.

He was carrying some books and, as Juliette watched, they engaged in an amiable dispute as to who should transport these upstairs. Although the slim volumes made a small pile and Miss Pilkington was scarcely a fragile blossom, M. Fabien insisted it would be his pleasure to deliver them to the third floor, while she countered that she must go up in any case to fetch her mantle and reticule. Eventually she succeeded in claiming possession but, as the books changed hands, the topmost volume slid sideways and began to fall; whereupon both reached out to

166

save it and, for an instant, their fingers touched. And—shame on Miss Pilkington—she blushed; there was no doubt about it, she blushed to the roots of her unfortunate hair.

At least she had the grace to look embarrassed, but the secretary was laughing as he restored the book carefully to the pile in her arms. "There, my friend. What did I say?"

"My dear Monsieur Fabien, you have been too kind already."

"Not at all. It is pure self-interest. I am impatient for you to read them and give me your opinion. *À bientôt?*"

"*À bientôt.*"

He had called her 'my friend', she had called him 'my dear' and evidently this assignation in the library was a regular occurrence. Well might Euphemia Pilkington blush—it was disgraceful. And as for Papa's secretary, was it not enough, the way he carried on with Maman, without his making eyes at Juliette's paid companion, a middle-aged Englishwoman with a dismal complexion and huge feet? Perhaps he was the type who preyed on desperation. Juliette could not say, for until now she had never given him much thought; she was bound to note in passing that he was tall and not ill-looking, but that was hardly of moment: he was a menial, her parents' creature, of no more interest than a groom or a footman.

Yet, now this sordid little scene obliged her to consider him, Juliette could not but grant he was handsome—if you ignored the scar on his forehead, that is. At any rate, he did not look the sort of young man who preferred to consort with elderly women. Of course he probably had little choice but to make up to Maman—even shop assistants were required to endure that charade. But Miss Pilkington? What possible interest could he have in Euphemia Pilkington? It was intolerable. Juliette should be thankful he had never had the impertinence to flirt with *her*.

In fact, now she reflected on it, in all the weeks she had been at the Hôtel de Miremont, they had scarcely exchanged a word—and then only the banalities enforced by politeness. If you set aside his dealings with her mother, he had otherwise seemed sober and dutiful, leaving the room without prompting when she visited Papa, never speaking at table unless addressed, riding at an appropriate distance when they went to the Bois. She was not even sure he had ever smiled at her—if he had, it was certainly not the smile that had mesmerised Miss Pilkington. She was not even sure he had ever spared her a glance.

168

Deceitful creature! Pretending to be respectful, when really he was as conceited as Roland de Sauvigny. Well, now Juliette had discovered the truth, he would be sorry. She knew just how to punish him. But first she must deal with that noodle Pilkington.

Unlike her mother, Juliette had learned that it was politic to conciliate the lower orders: in Bruges, engaging smiles and small gifts to the servants had bought all manner of freedoms—even a couple of the novices were not immune to charm. Thus, while Drouet was a blockhead, Juliette exercised patience as best she could, together with judicious presents of cast-off gowns and gloves, for unflinching loyalty was essential in a lady's maid.

Nothing of Juliette's would fit Miss Pilkington apart from the occasional shawl, but in her case largesse had not been necessary: the Englishwoman, like those spaniels her countrymen were so fond of, had been devoted to Juliette from the start. As with a lady's maid, devotion was the prime requirement of a paid companion and nothing to inspire gratitude; nevertheless Juliette had been grateful, for her time in England had not measured up to her hopes.

Even her presentation at court had been a frightful anticlimax, an absurd proceeding during which, with three plumes nodding in her hair as if she were a carriage horse, she was obliged to curtsey to an old woman with a head like a turnip, before walking out backwards without tripping over her train. Then, quite apart from the cold and the damp, there was the hideous language, which she had never been able to grasp, even in the schoolroom—why should she when French, the beautiful language of diplomacy, was spoken by everyone of any breeding? But not, it seemed, by the young Massinghams, who at Feltwell used their deficiency as an excuse to ignore her, while even the earl and countess, who had appeared welcoming in London, reverted to their true chilly English colours.

Altogether, she was miserable, and had it not been for Miss Pilkington she did not know how she could have borne it. Miss Pilkington not only spoke French and acted as her interpreter, she understood, she sympathised: how could Juliette, in her innocence, have realised Sir Jonas Smythe had been intended for the Massinghams' third daughter? She stood, solid, homely Miss Pilkington, a bulwark against the tide of Anglo-Saxon treachery, as unquestioning in her adoration of Juliette as she was sincere.

Thus Juliette, in the matter of impertinent M. Fabien, must tread with care. She could not approach the subject as they returned from M. Lebas' studio since Drouet was also in the carriage. But later, in her boudoir, when they had finished deploring both the artist and the portrait and the maid had been dismissed, she brought the conversation round to M. de Niversac and his recommendations as a husband. Then, reaching out across the sofa to place her hand on Miss Pilkington's, she said:

"But, my dear Euphemia, a little bird whispers that you too have lost your heart."

Miss Pilkington looked startled, not to say alarmed, although it was true she did not blush. "I? Oh, my goodness. Mademoiselle Juliette—"

"Come now, I have confided in you about Monsieur de Niversac. It is very unfair of you to hold back."

"But I—"

"After all, who can blame you? He is very handsome. And most attentive—so my little songbird says."

Here poor Pilkington tried to defend herself with an astonished laugh, but Juliette merely squeezed her hand more tightly.

"Well, in truth, my little finch is Drouet." Everything Juliette knew of her companion's character assured her she would shrink from cross-questioning a lady's maid. "I sent her to find you before we left for the studio, but you and Monsieur Fabien were so deep in conversation she feared to interrupt you."

"Monsieur Fabien? Oh, but—oh dear, I'm afraid Mademoiselle Drouet is quite mistaken. We were talking about poetry." Yet, despite the poor creature's defensive smile, her complexion betrayed her at last.

"Poetry? How romantic!"

"Yes—no." Miss Pilkington's blush deepened. "I told Monsieur Fabien I should like to read some modern French verse, so he has looked me out a selection—Baudelaire, Verlaine, Mallarmé…"

"How I adore love poems!"

"No, they are not—Mademoiselle Juliette, it is not at all what you think."

"My dear Euphemia," said Juliette, twining her fingers with Miss Pilkington's in spite of their reluctance, "do not imagine I disapprove. On the contrary, I am delighted for you."

"Truly, you must not—"

"Only you and he should take care. According to Drouet, the servants are already gossiping about your tête-a-têtes."

This was but a chance thrust. However, to Juliette's delight, Miss Pilkington turned a yet brighter shade of scarlet. "But it was partly because of the servants—to save two trays…" And then, poor guileless creature, she let it all tumble out—the meetings in the schoolroom when everyone else was from home, the dinners à deux, the so-called English lessons, the piano serenades.

"So you do see?" Now it was Miss Pilkington's turn to grasp Juliette's hand. "My dear mademoiselle, you do see it is quite harmless?"

Juliette nodded, smiling sweetly.

"Dear me, how could it be otherwise? Even if I were… Monsieur Fabien is hardly more than a boy."

"But he is still a Frenchman."

The silly goose looked perfectly horrified. "Mademoiselle, I can assure you, he has never been anything but a gentleman."

"Of course, dear Euphemia, I do believe you. But others may not."

"Others?"

"My papa, as you know, holds very old-fashioned views. And even Maman has been known to ride her high horse on occasion."

"Oh, my goodness!"

"If only gossip did not spread like plague through this house. It merely takes Drouet to drop a word to Maman's Bonnard. Or to whichever maid attends Lady Telford…"

"Oh, good gracious!"

By now Miss Pilkington looked so thoroughly wilted that Juliet leant across to kiss her cheek. "But do not worry, my dear. It may not come to that, so long as you and he are more discreet. Still…" She sat back to regard her companion somewhat sadly. "You know, he is not worthy of you."

Miss Pilkington looked startled again.

"Oh, I admit Monsieur Fabien cuts a good figure. And he may be charming."

"He is a good, kind friend."

"But, as you say, he is just a boy. And a nobody. If your thoughts have turned—well, with all this talk of my own marriage it is hardly surprising—we could find you someone so much better. Doctor Vionnet, Doctor Chevalier's nephew, is recently widowed. Or there is Maman's notary, Maître Marquand, who, although he is old, is—"

"No!" Miss Pilkington was scarlet once more. "I have no thought of marriage. Or—or anything else. There is nothing between Monsieur Fabien and me except innocent friendship. I thought you believed me."

Juliette saw she had gone too far. "Oh, I do, my dear Euphemia, I do."

Miss Pilkington also recognised she had overstepped the mark. "Mademoiselle Juliette, forgive me, I know you mean to be kind. But my ambition remains unchanged—to set up a school for girls with my friend Miss Stokes."

"Of course, the English school. Well, when I am Madame de Niversac and we must sadly part, I am sure I can persuade Papa to be generous." Juliette patted Miss Pilkington's hand. "Meanwhile, rest assured, my dear. I shall not speak again of Monsieur Fabien or utter a word about this conversation. And if I catch any hint of gossip, I shall silence it at once."

When Juliette visited her mother's sickbed that evening, it was fortunate the telegram that was to cure the invalid had not yet arrived. One hour later and Juliette would have had the greatest difficulty in distracting her mother from the imminent Lord Stilorgan; as it was, persistence was required to pierce Maman's lethargy; but, when she could at last be brought to hear Juliette's concerns (or, rather, what Juliette, in strict confidence, relayed of what Mlle Drouet and other servants had reported), her reaction to M. Fabien's duplicity was as her daughter could have wished.

Juliette did not fear Maman's breaking her confidence—she most certainly would: but she would not say: 'Juliette tells me…' or 'The servants are saying…', preferring to stamp such reports with her own authority. If there were anything that would upset Juliette's plan, it was that horrid telegram, which might obliterate all else. But, thank goodness, restored to health, Maman was as vigorous in avenging slights as in chasing pleasure.

Thus Juliette had dealt out justice in several directions: she had punished her mother; she had discommoded her father; she had humbled silly, sentimental Miss Pilkington for daring to dream that a young man like M. Fabien could ever regard her with the slightest affection.

Now for the young man himself. Juliette would teach him to play games. She would show him what it was like to flirt with a real woman, a young beautiful girl, close to him in age but far above him in station, a prize someone of M. Fabien's ilk should tremble to aspire to. She would make the arrogant boy love her. Then she would break his heart.

CHAPTER TWENTY-TWO

Although Juliette had embarked upon her campaign the very next day, she had been surprised, not to say piqued, to achieve little result. This could partly be blamed on the season: in the flurry of engagements to celebrate Christmas and New Year she was often out and, even when Maman and Papa were entertaining at home, M. Fabien was a shadowy presence, so far down the dinner table as to be beyond her glance. All the same, on the rare evenings they dined en famille, things were no better: he seemed not to notice her looking at him beneath her lashes and, when she went so far as to address him directly, he responded with a polite commonplace that invited no reply.

Papa was another obstacle. How she wished he would call his secretary back when, despite her friendly greeting, M. Fabien made his usual retreat the moment she entered the study. How she wished Papa would not monopolise her so when they were out riding or she had stolen in to watch the fencing. And if it were not Papa, it was M. de Niversac. How could she possibly train her full attention upon M. Fabien when she was constantly being distracted?

Yet she was compelled to admit that even when she was alone with her quarry, passing him on the stairs or the east-wing landing, she might smile all she liked—while he was never less than courteous, he appeared unmoved.

How dare he! She had done all she could, the very utmost her dignity would allow. How dare he ignore her! Did he expect her to throw herself at him?

And here was the worst of it: by studying the upstart as she had never troubled to before, she had made herself constantly aware of him. She knew now, off by heart, every detail of his person from the colour of his eyes—they were a clear grey-blue—to the shape of his hands and feet, which were long and elegant; she was forced to note that, while he was broad-shouldered, he was not a clumsy bear like some tall men, but slim and rather graceful in his movements; his smooth brown hair, sweeping his brow from a side parting, was free of pomade and he was rigorously clean-shaven (Juliette, unlike Mimi de Sainte-Foy, was not turned to jelly by whiskers); he had good teeth, a straight nose, a firm jaw, and in evening dress you might mistake him for a gentleman; the scar, when he absently revealed it by pushing back his hair, did not detract from his looks, but rather added a dash of glamour, like a duelling scar. Yes, she was obliged to concede he was handsome, quite as handsome as Emilio Baldoni.

Yet there was something cold and impenetrable about him too. In all her watching she had never once seen him drop his guard. Oh, sometimes with Papa he seemed to unbend a little, but she had never seen the M. Fabien who had stood in the foyer affectionately teasing Miss Pilkington. He was two people. How she hated both of them.

Well, she would waste no more time on hateful M. Fabien. She would never speak to him or smile at him again.

Then an extraordinary thing happened.

Her portrait, varnished and framed, was delivered from Lebas' studio just after Christmas. Although Maman proclaimed it was 'to the life', Papa, who at least knew something about art, even though all the artists he admired were dead, was of Juliette's view that it was hideous and unflattering, the eyes lifeless, the mouth too small, the colours gaudy. Nevertheless Maman insisted it must be hung with the other family portraits and Papa, as usual, gave in.

The hanging was not attended with any ceremony but left to Boussec: however Papa must have sent his secretary to ensure it was satisfactory; when, wondering whether the picture might not be improved by its setting, Juliette made her way to the Empress Elizabeth Salon, Boussec had gone and two footmen were gathering up their tools; M. Fabien alone remained standing before the painting.

Indeed, he was studying it with such fixed concentration that he did not hear Juliette approach. She hesitated before interrupting him.

"Everyone says it is not a bit like me."

He turned, startled. For a moment his face was unguarded and something quite unexpected flashed in his eyes.

Juliette was so astonished she took a step backwards.

"Mademoiselle," he said, recovering himself.

"I—I agree with Papa, don't you? Monsieur Lebas is very second-rate."

"You compliment him, mademoiselle." With a small abrupt bow but without another word, he took his departure.

Juliette stared after him. He had been angry. He had looked at Lebas' travesty of her beauty and it had made him angry. Her smiles and glances had not been in vain. He was not indifferent. Far from it.

*

All the same, it was hard to know how to proceed for, although he had vouchsafed her this brief revelation, he continued as distant as before. It occurred to her that she had grievously misjudged him. Yes, it was true that he was not above flirting on occasion. But only when it was of no consequence. His dalliance with Miss Pilkington, could that simpleton but see it, was as meaningless as the games Maman had forced him to play. If his passions were engaged—well, then it would be a very different matter, he would naturally behave with the greatest caution.

Perhaps he already loved her. Perhaps she had conquered him before she had ever noticed him. She gave a shiver of triumph. Yet what use was a conquest without a declaration? And how could he declare himself if they never spoke? Oh, she might ask him about her ball: she and Maman had decided the theme, *fête galante*, and Papa had approved it, but it would fall to M. Fabien to execute the detail. However, when she next encountered him in the east wing, he was reluctant to be drawn—it was impossible to arrange anything until New Year was over—and Maman must have burdened him with some irritating chore, for he was almost short with her. In any case, he would hardly speak his heart on the east-wing landing; she must engineer a proper conversation somewhere they could be alone.

Here she found herself in as much perplexity as before. She could not summon him to her boudoir without an excuse that was both pressing and practical: her ball would have sufficed, but he had declined to discuss it and she could think of no other pretext that would not seem forward. Then, as she was waltzing with Raoul de Niversac at the Merlincourts' on New Year's Eve, inspiration struck her. Not her boudoir, the library. She had noticed, as she gazed out over the courtyard on these dark winter mornings, that a light sometimes burned there before luncheon. Who else could it be but M. Fabien? On the days when there was no fencing, after returning from the morning ride and attending upon her parents, he must retire there to work. Oh yes, the library was quite perfect. It even relieved her of racking her brain for excuses. For what had he and Miss Pilkington seemed so fond of discussing? She too would talk to him about books.

*

Three days later, once the New Year had ceased to disrupt routine, Juliette, having instructed Drouet to change her speedily out of her riding habit, was rewarded by a propitious glow from the ground floor of the west wing. In a new house dress of salmon pink Sicilienne trimmed with lace and rosettes of ruby ribbon, and with her hair piled high above an amber comb that released a fetching tumble of curls at her brow, she descended confidently to the foyer, passed through the anteroom and pushed open the library doors. But then—perhaps her mind's eye had seen him waiting for her appearance as for an unhoped-for gift, so that when he glanced up she was bound to be startled by his look, which seemed not to express joy so much as irritation—at any rate, she succumbed to an uncharacteristic flutter of nerves.

But she was mistaken, he had been surprised rather than annoyed, for in an instant he had put aside his pen and was on his feet, smiling.

"Mademoiselle?"

This was not the smile with which he had favoured Euphemia Pilkington, it did not part his lips or travel to his eyes; yet it was a smile, nonetheless. She smiled back.

"I fear I have interrupted you, monsieur."

"Not in the least. How may I help you?"

It was cold in the library despite the fire at the far end, and she wished she had brought a shawl. Still absurdly disconcerted, she almost forgot the opening lines of the ingenious scenario she had contrived on her way downstairs. "I—I am without a thing to read. I wondered, monsieur, if you might recommend something."

"I shall do my best, mademoiselle. A novel, perhaps?"

"I prefer poetry."

Here the scenario required him to ask: 'What kind of poetry?' Whereupon, fixing her eyes upon his, she would say: 'I find love poems very beautiful, don't you?'

Alas, he failed to oblige. "Do you have a particular poet in mind?"

"Yes, I…" She struggled to recall the names Miss Pilkington had mentioned. "I think—Baudelaire."

He raised his eyebrows.

"They say he writes so tenderly of love."

"Do they, indeed?"

The smile had certainly reached his eyes now, indeed had broadened into a grin. Yet was he secretly laughing, did he have the effrontery to mock her? However, his tone was solemn as he said: "I do not think I would recommend Baudelaire."

He had recommended Baudelaire to Miss Pilkington. Juliette was vexed in earnest. "Why not, pray?"

"Because I doubt you would care for him."

"Perhaps, monsieur, I should decide that for myself."

"As you wish, mademoiselle. May I fetch you *Les Fleurs du mal?*"

The flowers of evil. That did not sound tender or beautiful. She faltered. It had been no part of her plan to quarrel with M. Fabien. Perhaps he spoke in good faith; perhaps Baudelaire's poems were horrid and he was merely protecting her; while he had not bothered to protect Miss Pilkington, he understood her own sensibilities were more delicate.

"No—no, you may be right." She offered a conciliatory smile. "I may have been under a misapprehension."

"I sense there are other poets you might prefer. Malherbe? Lamartine?"

These names so strongly evoked the schoolroom that she could not repress a shudder.

Although he laughed at this, out loud this time, he seemed not unsympathetic. Yet he crushed her with his next words: "Perhaps, after all, we should consider novels."

It had been dinned into Juliette by successive governesses and the nuns that only empty-headed girls read novels. Reading poetry was acceptable, a sign of intelligence and discrimination, but novels—one had only to think of Maman, propped up on her pillows, devouring chocolates and romances with equal avidity, to know that, while most of what one had learned in the schoolroom was not worth a sou, this dictum, at least, had the ring of truth. And now, just because Juliette had made a silly mistake about Baudelaire... She did not mind being thought naive when this had practical advantages, but she did not wish M. Fabien to think her stupid, let alone more stupid than Miss Pilkington.

"I don't care for novels."

"Truly? Why ever not?" His surprise could not be considered flattering.

"They are ridiculous. Quite unrealistic."

"All of them?"

"Most of them, certainly. Maman is very fond of Aristide de Bellac. All those plain girls of humble origin who win everyone's heart with their simple virtue and end up married happily ever after to a rich handsome nobleman—it is utterly absurd. In real life, the girl would not be received anywhere and the nobleman would be cut by all his acquaintance if he expected their wives to call on her."

M. Fabien was regarding her with an expression she could not quite fathom. "Well, mademoiselle, what else may I recommend? History, topography, heraldry, the natural sciences…?"

Following his gesture as it swept the packed shelves, Juliette felt both angry and deflated. This was not how her playlet was supposed to end: she had imagined him taking down a slim volume and, at her invitation, reading aloud—to his other attractions could be added a beautiful voice—while, as they listened together to these exquisite stanzas of agonised love, they too would exchange sighs and glances, they too would feel understanding blossoming between them. Who knew, he might even have declared himself then and there. Instead of which, he had refused to speak his lines, odious M. Fabien, and had left her looking ridiculous.

It had been a mistake to talk about books, however opportune a subject it had seemed. For, truth to tell, Juliette had never been an enthusiastic reader: while she liked the idea of poetry, in practice she cared for it no more than for novels, indeed even less. She had been liberated from books when she had been liberated from the convent. Yet now she stood in her father's library surrounded by them, tall books, short books, blue, red and green books, shabby books the colour of mud, smart books tooled in gold, books lining the walls, books on the mezzanine—how many? Too many to count, surely thousands. And she could be certain there was not a single one she wished to read. So must she retire humiliated and leave the conceited creature to enjoy his victory?

But no; an object she had glimpsed far away at the other end of the library gave her an idea.

"Monsieur, I am interrupting your work. Let me explore the shelves—I am bound to find something."

While he settled at his table again and took up his pen, Juliette worked her way down the room, trailing her fingers over bindings, pausing to stare with concentration at the shelves, even once or twice taking down a volume and briefly scanning its pages. She avoided the staircase to the mezzanine—its narrow wrought-iron spiral looked too dangerous—but, when she reached the rosewood library steps drawn up to the final section of shelving, she could see they were perfectly suited to her purpose. Grasping the pole with her left hand and gathering up her skirts with her right, she ascended the four stairs, teetering a little when she reached the top.

In case M. Fabien was watching her—her climb had surely granted him a teasing glimpse of ankle—she pretended for a moment to scrutinise the upper shelves. Yet the room was very still: only the ticking of various clocks and the shifting of coals on the fire broke the silence and, when she dared at last to glance over her shoulder, far from being distracted by her presence, he was plying his pen as if she had ceased to exist.

Well, he would be distracted now. Clutching her skirts and feeling for the step below with her right foot, for she was obliged to proceed backwards, she began her descent.

She had only intended to miss the bottom step, crumpling sideways in graceful disarray: however, catching the heel of her right shoe in her petticoats, she missed two. For an instant it seemed that, staggering backwards, she must crack her head on the parquet and pull down the steps on top of her. Managing somehow to fall to her right, she landed with her bosom and ribs crushed against the stairs while the rest of her slid to the floor in a heap, legs sprawled, skirts twisted. The scream she uttered was unfeigned.

"Mademoiselle!"

She could hear him running and when he reached her, although he did not take her in his arms as Emilio had Nettie, she could not doubt his concern.

"Are you hurt?"

"No, I... I am not sure..."

"Are you able to move?"

"I think so."

He extended his hands and she took them. They were cool and dry, she noticed, as, taking the weight of her body, they raised her to her knees, then gently drew her upright. Their touch filled her with the strangest sensation.

"You are unwell?"

"A little faint."

"We must find you a chair."

Although obliged to relinquish his hands, she might console herself with the arm he offered as he guided her to one of the armchairs by the fire. They went slowly as she deemed it judicious to limp a little, which, to her delight, redoubled his concern.

"You are hurt after all?"

"It is nothing. A slight twinge in my ankle."

"Shall I send for your maid? Or Miss Pilkington?"

"Thank you, but it is sure to pass."

"Then a glass of water perhaps? Or smelling salts?"

His voice was gentle, his eyes—which were more blue than grey, she thought—had shed their veil of reserve and were looking down at her with an anxiety every bit as tender as Emilio Baldoni's. For an instant that curious giddiness overwhelmed her again—perhaps she did need smelling salts. But then she remembered to summon a small, brave smile.

"Truly, monsieur, I shall soon be quite myself." She glanced up at him through her lashes. "You are most kind. I do not deserve it, having been so very foolish."

"The blame is all mine, mademoiselle. I should never have taken my eye from you."

She could not help it, she caught her breath. "Oh, Monsieur Fabien, you must not—"

"Indeed, mademoiselle, I must. But, if you will rest here for a moment, I shall make recompense."

Trapped in her chair and blinkered by its wings, she heard his steps retreating but could not see what he was doing. Had he stopped at his worktable, was he writing? Now this intimacy had been forged between them, was he committing to paper the words he still lacked the courage to speak?

But when he returned it was with a book.

Attempting to disguise her disappointment, she revolved it in her hands. "*Madame Bovary*?"

"You should not despise all novels, mademoiselle. You will not find Flaubert in the least like Aristide de Bellac. Humble girls do not triumph."

What could she do but take it? She seemed to recall Maman had begun it once but had not liked it, which perhaps was promising. Besides, he had presented it as his tribute and, if he did not yet understand her completely, he would soon learn. Allowing him to assist her from the chair, she smiled and folded the book to her bosom.

"I must go, monsieur. I have disturbed you long enough."

"If you are certain you are quite recovered. At least your ankle seems to be on the mend."

"Oh—oh yes. Thanks to you I had quite forgotten it. You have healing powers, Monsieur Fabien."

He laughed at this. "Well, at any rate I am most relieved. If you had come to any harm I don't know what I should have done."

Her heart fluttered. "No?"

"How would I have told your father I had let his daughter plunge to her doom from the library steps?"

Afterwards, when Juliette considered those parting words of his, she realised she had been foolish to take them as a blow. They did not gainsay his gentleness, his concern, his manifest tenderness. He had laughed, made a joke of his feelings, because his heart was too full. At least they had established a mutual sympathy, when they met again they would feel its warmth.

In fact, at this juncture, it behoved her not to be too warm: she must stand back, let him suffer a little. He should not think her easily won. The more distant she was, the greater his anguish, the more likely he was to abandon all reserve.

Perplexingly, however, he seemed not to have grasped these rules. Oh, it was true he did not fail to smile when they crossed paths in the east wing or saddled up in the stable yard, but they had returned to the brief exchange of small talk as if their encounter in the library had never occurred. Nor were their chances of coming upon each other alone any more plentiful than before. He should be the one to seek her out this time, but he did nothing. Was he pretending a lack of desire or did he simply want the courage? It was altogether most provoking.

More provoking still, she had spent so long thinking about him that he refused to leave her thoughts. When she was wearing a new toilette or Drouet had dressed her hair for the evening so that little enticing tendrils caressed the nape of her neck, she would find herself wondering if he approved. Even when he was not there, she saw him; when she was chatting to Papa or playing solitaire with Miss Pilkington or sitting tête-à-tête with M. de Niversac in the Little Salon, he would all at once appear to her; she saw him in her dreams. But, curiously, when she saw him in the flesh, she was troubled by an irritating malaise: she knew the moment he entered a room because she began to tremble and then everything she had formerly done without thought, lifting a glass, opening her fan, turning her head, became a nerve-racking effort; but nothing was so much effort as training her gaze steadily and unblushingly on M. Fabien.

He, on the other hand, appeared quite unafflicted. Yet he was the one in love, he was the one who should be suffering immoderately. It truly was an intolerable state of affairs.

Needless to say, she did not fail to notice whenever a lamp was lit in the library. But what was she to do? She could not compromise her dignity by paying a second visit. And then there was the book: he would expect her to have read it. Granted she had brought herself to struggle through two or three pages and she could already tell it was not like Aristide de Bellac, but even more tedious, about cloddish boys in some dreary provincial school and no mention of any Mme Bovary, who would probably transpire to be the schoolmistress; when Juliette had said she preferred realism, she had not meant that sort of reality. Yet he would want to discuss it—what had he said to Miss Pilkington? "I burn to know your opinion." Juliette supposed if she read the last page as well as the first two she might pretend to know the whole, but she was bound to admit this had never served her wonderfully at the convent.

The book was a curse, for it meant she could not return to the library. Yet it was also blessed, for he had touched it. She liked to stroke the binding, fancying it might transmit that delicious but frightening sensation when he had taken her hands in his. Once she went so far as to press her lips to the cover.

Then at last she understood. He did not expect her to read *Madame Bovary*. In fact it would not have mattered if it had been some other work. She recalled how he had bent to bestow it on her like an offering. The book was a sign, a pledge of his love, a surety she might keep with her, even when circumstances forced them apart. She had only to wait and he would come to her.

But now a full week had passed and here she was, alone in her boudoir, staring out at the falling snow. No, of course she was not despondent, not in the slightest. Who cared for signs and pledges? He was a coward. Lord Urchfont and Sir Jonas Smythe had been brave enough to press their cause, even though they must have known it was hopeless. But M. Fabien, her father's lackey—why should he guard his heart so closely?

Well, she, Juliette, hoped he might be crushed by an avalanche of his wretched books. It had been a game anyway, to take it seriously was beneath her. She was a realist and she would marry M. de Niversac, even though he did not have slender fingers and his touch was somewhat clammy. She would marry M. de Niversac, she would rule Paris, and she would not call Drouet to dress her, quickly, while the light still shone in the library.

Besides, when she looked again it was possible to see, despite the snow, that the lamp had been extinguished.

CHAPTER TWENTY-THREE

By Sunday it had ceased snowing and word was that the lakes in the Bois de Boulogne were frozen. Juliette sent to M. de Niversac, who was due to call in the afternoon, warning him to come prepared to go skating. Although obedient, he was doubtful: as it was a Sunday the world and his wife would take to the ice; tomorrow would be better. But Juliette was not to be discouraged: she was an accomplished skater and knew her skating costume of blue velvet trimmed with astrakhan showed her to advantage, but she was also sorely in need of something to lift her spirits; she was quite ready to brave the masses, for spending the afternoon closeted in the house would drive her to distraction. In any case, if she had cared about such a thing—which of course she did not—M. Fabien would not be in the library, since, along with others of his class, he had Sundays off.

The roads were icy despite the straggling bands of workmen wielding shovels and brooms but, since there was little traffic and, on Papa's orders, the sleigh had been harnessed, they arrived at the Bois in good time. Nevertheless, M. de Niversac's prediction was fulfilled. Both lakes, Le Petit and Le Grand, were thronged with skaters, while spectators crowded the banks and a mêlée of coaches and gigs hazarded the treacherous carriage paths. However, Juliette, wrapped in a fur rug and conscious that the keen air had brought becoming colour to her cheeks, had felt her heart lift as they had glided across the snowbound river and through the muffled, deserted streets. The sun shone, the ice gleamed, her feathered hat suited her to perfection. They chose the Grand Lac and, leaving Miss Pilkington, who did not skate, on the bank, Juliette and M. de Niversac set their course for the islands.

Agility was required to dodge their fellow skaters, the beginners slithering perilously, the small boys racing, the stately matrons, the tradesmen in bowlers, the dowager, complete with lapdog, propelled by her crimson-faced lady companion in a chair equipped with runners. Once, Juliette thought she spotted someone from her circle—was that Manon de Merlincourt and were those two boys her brothers? No matter: she did not mind being out of her usual element; it was exhilarating, like the dazzling whiteness and the air that seared her lungs and the sensation of her skates crisply cutting the surface of the ice. Irritatingly, M. de Niversac had no difficulty keeping up—she supposed he must have become a proficient skater during his sojourns in Canada.

When they had gone the length of the lower island, they paused to catch their breath. And that was when M. de Niversac, who had offered her his hand although she did not need steadying, let out his fateful exclamation.

Not that she made anything of it at first, for his words were drowned by the laughter and shouts of nearby skaters and anyway, far from paying attention, she was gazing idly at the Emperor's Kiosk, whose dome rose like a snowy moon through the rimed trees.

"Yes, by Jove, it is! It's Fabien. With a pretty girl in tow."

She turned her head so suddenly she nearly overbalanced them both. But she only gave way for an instant—later she was able to tell herself she had behaved with commendable control.

A pretty girl? Although she was very fair like Juliette, she was an insignificant little thing in a dowdy grey mantle and a hat Miss Pilkington might favour. Nevertheless, he, faithless M. Fabien, had stretched out both his hands to this house mouse, just as he had to Juliette. The pair stood, marking time on the ice, not four metres away.

"Oh yes," said Juliette. "I see now. Well, you did say we should be rubbing shoulders with all sorts."

The two lovers were engaged in playful debate—lovers they must be, for, to judge by their laughter, they were on teasing terms. Soon they would shift their gaze and notice Juliette. What would he think, M. Fabien, when he saw her? Would he have the grace to feel ashamed?

But just then the girl released one of her hands to wave and another couple sailed into view, a sturdy bearded man and a dark-haired girl more fashionably dressed than M. Fabien's inamorata but ugly, with a face that was all angles. After some raillery, the foursome linked hands and, without so much as a glance at Juliette and M. de Niversac, sped off towards the arch of the footbridge between the two islands.

Certainly Juliette's sangfroid had been miraculous. She had managed a desultory conversation with M. de Niversac and even skated a little further before announcing she was tired and chilled to the bone. True, on returning home, claiming the cold had brought on a headache, she had retired immediately to her own apartments, but she had bravely borne the universal concern and the ministrations of Drouet and Miss Pilkington. It was long after she had been put to bed, when, declining supper on a tray, she was at last alone, that she had finally broken down.

She sobbed, she screamed, she tore her handkerchief with her teeth, she beat her pillows. How dare he! Did he think now he loved her he could still continue in his old treacherous ways? How could he betray her, Juliette de Miremont, with some grey little nobody? Was there a woman in Paris beneath his notice? Well, he would be sorry. She would make sure of that.

Sniffing, she crushed the shredded handkerchief into a ball. She would not cry, he should not have that satisfaction, she had never wept over a man, not even Emilio Baldoni. She would not let two-faced, heartless M. Fabien reduce her to tears.

Yet she continued to sob and wail. It was as if a burning liquid were rising within her veins, swelling them, tearing them, consuming her with a pain that would not stop, but only grew stronger. She knew he loved her—she would not forget his face when he had looked at her portrait. And here, beneath her disordered pillows, was the book he had given her, the pledge of his devotion. He must love her, he must. She could not bear to lose him, could not bear that she would never feel his touch again.

But how could he be so tender one minute, so cruel the next? Deceitful, odious wretch! She hurled *Madame Bovary* across the room.

She did not need the book as an excuse, for it appeared the snow had not prevented the printers delivering the invitations for her ball. Or, more likely, Maman had sent M. Fabien to collect them, regardless of the icy streets. There he sat at his worktable, surrounded by piles of cards and envelopes, inscribing names and addresses. As before, that disconcerting expression crossed his face when she entered, but this time she did not falter, for she knew what prompted it: guilt.

Her intention had been to slam the book down on his table and stalk out without a word, but there was no space available, unless she were to damage her beautiful invitations. Instead, she thrust it at him as he was rising to his feet. She could see this upset him because he failed to return his pen properly to the ink stand and it rolled out of the tray onto the envelope he had been addressing; for a moment it seemed he might give vent to his emotions, but, manfully attempting concealment, he became fully occupied with pen wiper and blotter.

All the same, she did not see why she should soften, particularly as she was left holding out the book. "Please, monsieur, take it."

Tearing up the ruined envelope clearly brought him relief; by the time he had tipped the pieces into the wastepaper basket, he had regained his composure. "Mademoiselle?"

"I wish to return your book. It is not to my taste."

"I am sorry for that. May I find you something else?"

"No. Nothing. Thank you."

Since there was nowhere to set down his despised offering, he was obliged to return it to the shelves. Was there a hangdog droop to his shoulders as he walked away from her? Well, she was by no means done with him yet.

Craning her neck, she scrutinised his worktable. Formerly to find him thus devoted to her service would have filled her with delight, but now she reflected sourly that he was in her debt, for at least the work was more interesting than his labours for Papa. Reaching for one of her invitations, she made as if to study it; and indeed it was gratifying to feel again the thickness of the card, to admire the embossed crest and the elegance of the type. However, on his return, she cast it aside with a sigh.

"Oh dear, I truly believe I could not have held out any longer."

"Mademoiselle?"

"Maman wishes it to be announced at my ball, but that is weeks away."

He must have known what was coming, for he avoided her eyes, attending instead to a spot of ink he had missed.

"Oh yes." She gestured that he might sit; at least he might be granted this small mercy, that he should take the blow sitting down. "I have written to Monsieur de Niversac accepting him."

Of course, it was not a mere secretary's place to protest, whatever his feelings; she supposed she should admire the heroic way he continued to dab at the ink and the steady tone in which he said: "Please accept my felicitations."

"Naturally, the engagement will not be official for a week or two. His mother and sisters will doubtless need to come up from the country to inspect me. On your honour, Monsieur Fabien, you must not tell a soul, not even Papa until I have spoken to him. I have only confided in you because I regard you as a friend."

He gave her a curious look, which somewhat mitigated her disappointment. "You have my promise, mademoiselle."

But, though he made to salve his wounds by returning to his work, she was still not finished. "And I shall keep your secret too, monsieur."

This startled him, there was no question. Yet it was evident he would not fall into her palm as neatly as Miss Pilkington, for in a moment he had recovered himself. "What secret is that, mademoiselle?"

"Monsieur de Niversac saw you yesterday, out skating—"

"In the Bois? Were you with him? Was it not marvellous?"

"Yes—yes indeed. Although I did not—" Infuriatingly, he was once more forcing her to deviate from the lines she had written. "That is to say, by the time Monsieur de Niversac drew my attention, you had gone. But he said—"

"I should win no laurels for my skating? Sadly that is no secret. My friends are without mercy. But then, they are Russians and could skate before they could walk."

This confused her. Determinedly she smothered her irritation. "Come, come, monsieur. You shan't evade me."

"Mademoiselle?"

"Monsieur de Niversac said you were with a young lady."

"Ah."

"I did not see her myself. But he said she was very pretty."

"You must mean Mademoiselle Zhukovskaya." He smiled. Juliette sensed—no, she was certain—he was relieved.

"Monsieur de Niversac wondered if she might be your betrothed."

There could be no doubt of it—however disposed he had been to fence with her before, he had dropped his guard: as though he had made a conscious decision, his shoulders relaxed, his expression became candid, his smile broadened and gave way to laughter. "Mademoiselle Zhukovskaya is the sister of my closest friend. She is accomplished and charming and I have the fondest regard for her, but I have known her since she was in short skirts."

"Even so…"

"It is good of you, mademoiselle, to take an interest in my affairs, but I have no thought of marriage."

Did she believe him? When she recalled his relief, she thought she did. Evidently Mlle Whatever-She-Was-Called was not the secret he guarded. What was it, then? Why, when he was too clever to be pumped like Pilkington, had he chosen, of his own accord, to be frank about the little grey miss? Because he had grasped why she, Juliette, was angry, and keenly desired to correct the misunderstanding. Was his true secret so hard to guess?

Her spirits lifted. "Oh, monsieur, you must forgive me, my mind is so full of marriage at present."

"Naturally."

"And love, of course."

"Of course."

"Have you ever been in love, Monsieur Fabien?"

"No, mademoiselle, I fear not."

Yet his answer was too rapid and too categorical. She was sure it was a lie. Her heart soared. "Not even the least little bit?"

"As I say, mademoiselle, I have no thought of such things. My circumstances do not permit it."

She would have liked to have enquired further on this point but Maman chose this moment to burst in and give them both a scolding, M. Fabien for not concentrating on his work and her, Juliette, for distracting him.

All the same, she left the library with a light step. "My circumstances do not permit it." It was not treachery or cowardice that held him back: she rued her charge of arrogance, for he was clearly all too conscious of the difference in their stations. But he was honourable, unlike Emilio Baldoni; regarding his feelings as hopeless, he would lock them deep within his breast.

Even so, might not the two of them indulge in a few bittersweet pleasures, the tender brush of fingers, stolen kisses? Since Dr Colombe, she had disliked the idea of kissing, indeed it disgusted her, she could not imagine being kissed on the mouth by anyone, certainly not M. de Niversac, yet now, when she thought of—

But here, halfway up the staircase to the east wing, she froze in horror. What in heaven's name had she done? She had quite forgotten her letter to M. de Niversac. M. Fabien would never declare himself now she was betrothed to another. Of course it was all his fault: if he had not made her angry, she would never have acted so rashly. If he suffered, he had only himself to blame. Except that she must suffer too. She, who prided herself on her cool head—whatever had he done to her? He had even made her return his love-token and now she had nothing.

One afternoon a few days later, on one of her impromptu visits to her father, Juliette was relieved not to find his monstrous valet in attendance, but somewhat surprised to hear voices drifting into the salon: usually when Papa was working with M. Fabien the study doors were closed, but today by an oversight they had left them open a chink.

Since the sound of M. Fabien's voice always made her heart turn over and her arrival would only prompt his dutiful departure, she paused to listen.

"So you do not think he is merely pretending, you think he truly is mad?"

"My dear Max, he has lost faith in reason. You must agree that is a kind of madness."

"Lost faith? Oh come, Armand, he is reason's prisoner. The more he thinks, the less he does."

"Exactly so. He can only act on impulse."

"Because he has reasoned himself to a standstill."

"Because, as young men are apt to, he sees in black and white—no, dear boy, don't pull that face. While his father—his Jove, his Hyperion—still lived, he believed reason ennobled mankind. But now he is convinced of the other extreme—mankind is rotten to the core. Men are brute beasts, driven only by passion, their flesh is corrupted, the quintessence of dust…"

If Juliette had wondered to whom they referred, whether this portended some scandal amongst their acquaintance, she had rapidly been arrested by the tone of the discussion. It had never occurred to her to speculate about her father's relationship with his secretary: Papa could be short with M. Fabien, although less so recently perhaps, but in general they seemed to observe the usual formalities between master and menial. Yet here they were addressing each other as '*tu*', while M. Fabien took the shocking liberty of using Papa's given name: indeed, although they were arguing, in Papa's case with some heat—in fact, Juliette had seldom heard him so eloquent—there was an amiability to the exchange which suggested the ease of friends.

"Oh, he knows what honour and duty require," her papa continued, "but the consequences appear as black as everything else. Despair prevents him from balancing judgement and passion. That is his madness."

Whereupon M. Fabien laughed. "You know, it occurs to me the outcome would have been much the same if, instead of torturing himself, he had simply done nothing."

"Dear boy, that is absurd."

"You forget Fortinbras. On his return from defeating the Poles, would Fortinbras not still burn to avenge his own father's death? He could have killed Claudius and Gertrude, settled the whole business.

Doubtless Hamlet would have had to die, just the same. But order would have been restored. With fewer fatalities."

"And there would have been no play."

Not some interesting scandal after all, only a book—Juliette supposed she might have guessed. Everyone seemed to be reading *Hamlet*. Had not Miss Pilkington told Maman that was M. Fabien's excuse for learning English? They had pored over it, the two of them, when they were not reciting Baudelaire. And now Papa was engrossed in it too.

Still, even if it were dreadfully dull like Corneille and Racine, its promise was obvious. And to find M. Fabien on such friendly terms with Papa—once she had recovered from the shock, was not this consoling too? It was with a lightened heart that she pushed apart the doors to interrupt their laughter.

CHAPTER TWENTY-FOUR

Max could not but notice he had suddenly become the object of Mlle Juliette's interest. This did nothing to warm him: although he owed it to Armand to try to share his admiration for his younger daughter, the more he saw of her the more he disliked her.

Of course he might continue to attribute this to envy, but now he and the old boy trusted each other again the indignities of his situation rankled less. Or he might blame Lebas. It was quite bad enough that Achille de Tarascon was received at the house, but at least he usually came to madame's Thursdays, when it was Max's evening off: Lebas was present any day of the week Max chose to visit the Elizabeth Salon, Lebas and his tawdry portrait; and all at once Max was sixteen again, not in the studio half-naked, holding some classical pose (for in those days the noted Academician painted tableaux in the manner of David), but in Lebas' Blue Room, bound to the bed. They had relished tightening the thongs around his wrists, Lebas and Tarascon, his screams had only stoked their excitement, while all he could think of in his agony was the Spanish boy, how the word was at the Monkey that it was not the pain that did for you but the painless wound that followed. He supposed he should be grateful to Lebas, who, suddenly alive to the risk of scandal, had put an end to it. Yet, forced to watch with Boussec as Philippe and Antoine hung the portrait, he felt sick with rage.

Still, he could hardly dislike Mlle Juliette because he loathed the artist who had painted her: it was not she who had commissioned the painting and, to do her justice, she seemed displeased with it too. And, if Max could draw back and view the wretched thing objectively, he could only agree it was a shoddy piece of work, undeserving of the fee Lebas' reputation commanded now he had abandoned Olympus for the Faubourg Saint-Germain. The pillars, draperies and even the dress itself were probably executed by his assistants while, for the face, the Master had undoubtedly adapted one of a series of templates into which the physiognomies of most Society ladies could be made to fit.

All the same, while it was not a literal likeness, by some accident the portrait seemed to capture the essence of its subject. That tight little mouth was the mouth that snapped at Miss Pilkington; those hard blue eyes betrayed precisely the calculation that extracted the last pinch of advantage from her father's devotion. The rigidity of the pose; the chilly artifice of the marble pillars intended to complement the sitter's costume with a crude reference to the Renaissance; the unforgiving orange of the gown itself and its overdone highlights, which rendered the folds of fabric stiff as drainpipes: all combined, in Max's view, to give a very accurate account of Mlle Juliette.

As to why he was unexpectedly honoured with her favour, he at first assumed it was yet another burden that came with organising her ball. His heart sank. Although everyone, most particularly madame, appeared to think a secretary must know to the last detail what was required and certainly old Lesage would have fallen upon the task with the zeal of Alexander marching against the Persians, Max's only experience of such occasions had been as a footman; swallowing his pride, he would be obliged to lean heavily upon Boussec and Mme Mercier, but their knowledge would be rusty, for the Hôtel de Miremont had not seen a ball for nearly twenty years. The last thing he desired was to find Mlle Juliette peering over his shoulder, yet he fancied he recognised those sweet smiles and winsome glances—did she not lavish them upon Armand when she needed new gowns or brilliants for her hair? From now until the beginning of April, Max would find himself chasing her every whim and, unless he wished to upset the old boy, he must return the smiles and submit.

This was what he had thought to begin with. Only gradually did he understand there was something more. After all, the accident with the library steps could have been genuine. And as for her strange fury over *Madame Bovary*—years ago the novel had been accused of offending public morals and perhaps Armand would have deemed it unsuitable for his virgin daughter. But then Max had only offered it as a means of getting rid of her; he had certainly not expected her to read it.

However, he was bound to be unsettled by the rest of their conversation. Of course it was absurd to imagine she truly knew his secret. All the same her curiosity about Vera had set him on treacherous ground: what if she related the encounter to Armand with the same leaden innuendo, reigniting the old boy's mad suspicions? Max had been obliged to clarify matters; but, alas, in doing so, he had laid himself open to that interrogation about love.

Mlle Juliette's playfulness had the delicacy of a siege gun. Yet he was bewildered, for, in almost the same breath, she announced she would be marrying Raoul de Niversac. Perhaps he was wrong, perhaps she really was teasing.

*

It was Max's ambition to defeat the fencing master, Captain Horthy. This morning success had come unexpectedly close when, in a moment of overconfidence, he had mistimed a feint, giving the sinewy old cavalryman the last, victorious hit. Roland de Sauvigny was on hand to commiserate.

"Hard luck, Fabien. Thought you'd finally got the bridle on the old Warhorse. Doubtless you were put off by the sudden chill."

Although you could see your breath in the ballroom, as on most winter mornings, Max's brow was wet from his exertions and he could feel sweat trickling beneath his shirt. He stared at Sauvigny.

"The Iceberg." Sauvigny affected to shiver.

"I thought she'd given you up long since."

"So she has, old chap—heaven be praised."

"She must have been hoping to watch Monsieur de Niversac."

"Who was not expected today."

"No doubt she forgot."

"She doesn't come to watch Niversac."

Max looked at Sauvigny. Sauvigny held his glance.

"That's nonsense," Max said. "She's accepted him."

"It's still unofficial. Besides, who can tell the ways of women?"

"Oh, for pity's sake!"

Sauvigny laughed. "All the same, my friend, I'd be careful if I were you. You know what they say—like mother, like daughter."

It was true the pointed glances had not ceased, nor the smiles, although they alternated puzzlingly with scowls. Max had played up to madame, for she had merely required flattery, but—Sauvigny was wrong—the daughter, Armand's jewel, was a different proposition. From his time in servants' quarters, Max was not without experience in such matters: there had been baron Reinhardt's valet and a couple of the maids at Mme de Claireville's; on the whole, although sterner measures had been required with the valet, he had found that being pleasant but distant had worked perfectly well.

Yet perhaps there was no need for concern. In company, the newly betrothed Mlle Juliette hung upon her fiancé's arm, appropriately radiant. Raoul de Niversac, too, appeared delighted, poor chap, all but overwhelmed. While somewhat earnest, Niversac was, from everything

Max had seen, a perfectly decent fellow, courteous, modest and, unlike Roland de Sauvigny, quite without side: he did not deserve the fate his title and estates had bought him. But from Mlle Juliette's point of view he was the ideal match and, now she had made up her mind to accept him, she would have plenty to distract her from whatever flight of fancy she had entertained. For the first time in his life, Max was grateful he could be considered a nobody. Sauvigny had been joshing him as usual.

But the next day before luncheon there she was in the library, demanding to read *Hamlet*.

"Miss Pilkington forever has her nose in it. So does Papa. And you, Monsieur Fabien. If I don't read it myself, whomever shall I talk to?"

"Mademoiselle, I am not certain—"

"Oh, not in English, it's so ugly. Surely you have a translation."

Inwardly Max groaned. In fact, he had three, but two were of little use to him. Owing to the French desire to make Shakespeare less barbarous, the Ducis version, with which Max had begun, was not, as Armand had pointed out, a translation at all, but an entirely new play in rhyming couplets after the manner of Corneille: it not only excised Shakespeare's indecorous comic scenes, but cut the cast of characters to eight and left Hamlet alive at the end. Max had acquired a more recent version by Alexandre Dumas, but that was no better as a crib—Hamlet again survived. Then Miss Pilkington—how he missed her—had found him the François-Victor Hugo translation, which, while it was in prose and could not replicate the untranslatable richness of the language, was otherwise faithful to the original. Max would be lost without it.

Meanly, he thought of giving mademoiselle the Ducis. It was likely she would not read it. But had he not made that assumption about *Madame Bovary*? Supposing she seriously intended to discuss the play with Armand? Even if he lent her the Dumas, the old boy would soon realise how little he had gone out of his way to help her. He would have to surrender the Hugo.

Then he was struck by a cheering thought. The Hugo was not in the library but upstairs in his room. He would promise to send it to her apartments and with luck she would have forgotten it by tomorrow.

"Oh, but we may send for it now." She laughed the silvery laugh that was so much like her mother's. "Heavens, it is not as if we lacked servants and most of them do next to nothing."

When he returned from touching the bell, she had commandeered his chair and was peering at the translations he was making of the old boy's chosen quotations from the *Fasti*.

"Oh dear. Papa's Great Work. Will it ever be finished, do you think?"

"Of course."

"He has been writing it ever since anyone can remember. Maman says it is his excuse to avoid civilised people."

"Forgive me, mademoiselle, but you underestimate your father. He has a fine mind, his work is respected by scholars. And if it were not for—"

Max was saved by the appearance of Antoine. By the time he had given instruction as to where the Hugo could be found, he had recalled his obligation to remain polite and charming.

Mlle Juliette, however, did not seem disconcerted. "You are very loyal, monsieur. But, all the same, it must be dreary for you."

"Not a bit."

"Papa is an old man. But you? Buried in this mausoleum, deprived of the pleasures of life? Oh, I know there is my ball to look forward to—"

"I am flattered by your concern, mademoiselle, but I am quite content."

"Still, you are clever. You must have ambitions."

"My present ambition is to light the al fresco ballet you require for the ball without burning the house down."

This pleased her, it was evident. But it did not distract her as he had hoped.

"I suppose your people are too poor to do much for you?"

"People?"

"You say your circumstances do not permit you to marry."

Max hardly knew whether to be angry at the intrusive turn of her questions or alarmed at this echo of their previous conversation. "I do not have 'people', mademoiselle."

"You are an orphan?"

He thought it safest, despite the intrusion, to tell her the official story of his arrival at the Hôtel de Miremont: how he had been a seminarian (he remembered not to mention Bruges, since, unlike him, Mlle Juliette had been there), and how, when he had lost his vocation, the ever-useful Dr van Zuylen had recommended him to M. de M.

"So you see, mademoiselle, I owe everything to your father and I could not be more grateful to him. He has shown me great kindness and generosity."

"Oh, I know Papa is very fond of you."

Max was momentarily dismayed. Had he spoken too hotly in

Armand's defence? But, as before, he was able to reassure himself: even if she could circumvent the old boy's neurasthenic precautions, she was too blinded by her own concerns to perceive anything approaching the truth. And so her next words proved.

"Oh yes, Monsieur Fabien, I can assure you of that. He has often told me so. But he has not been as generous as he might be."

"Mademoiselle, I cannot—"

"Poor Papa, you must not blame him, he simply does not think. But he could do so much more for you."

"Truly, I—"

"No, monsieur, you must listen. Papa may play at being unworldly, but he is not without useful acquaintance. The duc de la Marne knows everyone who is anyone, Monsieur de la Rochefontaine has the ear of ministers. A post in the civil service could easily be—"

"No, mademoiselle."

"Or the law, perhaps. Maître Ladurie could—"

"Please, mademoiselle. I am unsuited to be a lawyer. Or a civil servant."

"With your education? You could rise to the very top. All you need is ambition."

"I have none."

"Oh come, Monsieur Fabien. How can I believe you? If you do not care to ask Papa, I will gladly talk to him for you."

"No, mademoiselle! You must not do that on any account."

Again he was rescued by Antoine, who had returned with the Hugo translation —none too soon, Max thought, for this time mademoiselle had not ignored his outburst: she was pouting and inclined to be tearful.

"Please," he said, when they were alone once more, "I am sure you mean well. But, mademoiselle, you must promise never to speak to monsieur on my behalf. He has been so generous already that—that I should be mortified." As indeed he would be, if Armand believed he had been scheming with his daughter to acquire some venal advancement.

"You are proud, monsieur. Too proud." She rose from his worktable and came round to where he stood. "You must not let pride hold you back."

Max thought it best not to reply. Instead, he proffered the Hugo. "I must beg you, mademoiselle, to take good care of this. It is invaluable to me."

Although her eyes still glittered, she was all at once smiling as she hugged the book to her breast. "Oh, I shall, monsieur. I shall."

CHAPTER TWENTY-FIVE

"But what is my friend to do? Surely this lady cannot believe he will ever return her feelings when he has given her no encouragement— rather the reverse?"

To Max's surprise, Zenaïda Feodorovna let out a laugh that was more like a bark, whereupon Vera, who was usually so even-tempered, glared at her ferociously. Max sometimes suspected Zenaïda Feodorovna did not like him—perhaps she resented his friendship with Mitya; he had rather hoped she would be absent this Thursday for, although she usually waited at the Rue Boissonade for Mitya to return from the Opéra, he was at present with the Herzens on their tour of the Rhineland. In truth, what Max had most wished for was a moment alone with Mme Zhukovskaya: instead of turning his predicament into an amusing story he could have confessed it openly, and she would have given him sensible advice. But when he arrived she was propped up on her pillows with both girls at her bedside, playing Hussar.

Nonetheless, they had all, even Zenaïda Feodorovna, expressed delight at his presence, urging him to draw up another chair to the bed and abandoning the cards in favour of conversation; and after a while he had foolishly decided three women could advise him better than one. But even to his own ears his story had lacked the froth which might have redeemed it: indeed it was clear from the atmosphere that he had committed a solecism, although it was not clear what.

"My dear," said Mme Zhukovskaya gently, "as your friend must be aware, men can be just as persistent. I remember a young officer in Petersburg, a lanky fellow with an eyeglass—Koligin, Kutchinsky?— well, no matter—he was turned down by my sister four times, yet even when she was safely married he trailed in her wake and when she was in her coffin, God rest her soul, he wept throughout the liturgy inconsolably. Perhaps the fact that she could not love him made him love her the more. Some natures are fated to love the unattainable, but thank heavens they are rare."

"But women must suffer their fate in silence," said Zenaïda Feodorovna. "Men can shower women with poems and proposals, but women must bite their lips and cry into their pillows. Yet it's not a woman's fault if a man doesn't have the sense to value her love."

Vera, Max noticed, was gathering up the cards as though she had ceased to listen, but for all that her cheeks were scarlet.

"And besides, Monsieur Fabien," continued Zenaïda Feodorovna, "how can this friend of yours be so sure he has not encouraged the poor girl? If he is handsome and knows it, but does not know the difference between flirting and making himself agreeable, then how is she—?"

"My dear," said Mme Zhukovskaya, "I am quite tired. Perhaps we may continue this another time."

But she was too late, for Vera, snapping shut the box of cards, pushed back her chair and left the room without a word.

Max watched her go with confusion and dawning horror. He recalled how cold she had been to him last winter, and her manner when he had objected to the notion of her marrying Lyudin. But she could not—she surely did not…

He rose. But Zenaïda Feodorovna had also risen and, no longer combative but flushed with mortification, was hastening after her friend. And when he made to follow, Mme Zhukovskaya called him back.

"Please, dear Maxim, stay and read to me."

"But I must—I cannot—"

"Shush! The least said… Now, where is our book? You know I sleep better when you read to me."

Pushkin. Thankfully this was *The Queen of Spades* and not *Eugene Onegin*, not Natasha's letter of love, so despised by its recipient. Max understood how Mme Zhukovskaya would recoil from discussing her children's private affairs: he should be content that she seemed not to share Zenaïda Feodorovna's opinion of him. All the same, his agitation and the sound of raised voices somewhere beyond the closed door made it hard to concentrate on Pushkin's expressive Russian: he stumbled repeatedly and once or twice was on the point of giving up. Then, distantly, a door slammed and silence fell; and when he next looked up from the page Mme Zhukovskaya appeared to be sleeping— at least she was breathing deeply and her eyes were closed. Replacing the book quietly on the night table, he tiptoed from the room.

The kitchen was empty, the maid long gone, and there was no one in the salon: Zenaïda Feodorovna must have taken her departure. Max eventually found Vera in the tiny box room next to the scullery, where she kept her loom.

As he had searched for her, a profusion of words had jostled in his head, but now he did not know what to say. He watched as she worked the treadle, passing and repassing the shuttle through the warp, adding a stripe of turquoise to blue, crimson and purple.

"Please, you must believe me, Vera Alexandrovna, I did not mean you."

"I know. Zenaïda Feodorovna was mistaken."

"If I were not a complete fool, if I had realised… There is no other woman in the world whose love I would value more. Please forgive me for being a blundering idiot—"

"If I was angry, it was not at you." Setting the shuttle aside, she looked up. Although it was evident she had been crying, she seemed composed. "Zenaïda Feodorovna may have intended well, but she does not understand and spoke out of turn. In any case, what is past is past."

"But I have hurt you. Stupidly, thoughtlessly, I have hurt the one person who least—"

"Oh come, Maxim Alexandrovitch. Life hurts but we do not die of it. Please, stop wringing your hands and sit down."

She was smiling, even if it were a somewhat watery smile, and for the first time in months she had used the patronymic she had invented for him. Amongst the hanks of yarn, raddles, shuttles, and discarded lengths of weaving that were piled everywhere in the space not taken up by the loom was a single deal chair: carefully clearing it of some sketched designs, Max obeyed her command.

"I used to worship you when I was fourteen," she said. "You were so handsome and so clever. I thought, when I'm grown up I shall marry him—"

"Oh, Verotchka, I—"

"And even when I was grown up and you went to work for your marquis, I thought, I'll wait. One day he'll be tired of running errands for the nobility and we can be married. But then—do you remember, the day Mitya played the Saint-Saëns?— I met your marquis."

Max grew pale.

"And I knew then that I shouldn't wait."

He struggled with the urge not to understand her or, if he must, to find a comforting lie. But her directness transfixed him, all he could do was stutter. "D—did Mitya—?"

"Of course not, he would never do that. I knew from the way your marquis looked at you. And at me, Baba Yaga, come to eat you up. And then I watched your face when you spoke of him. So I knew."

He stared at her, chilled. "Good grief, you must have—"

"Hated you? I didn't understand what I knew at first, but when I did, yes, I hated you. And your Monsieur le marquis. But—oh, Maxim Alexandrovitch, don't look like that—I couldn't seem to hate either of you for long. Monsieur de Miremont has been so good to Mitya. And how could I hate you for what brings you happiness? Perhaps one could hate a husband forever, but not a brother."

Max could not speak. He was not sure which affected him more, that she should find him out or that she should forgive him so readily. Yet he was also conscious of another, contradictory sensation, the lightness of relief.

In the end, he reached for her hand. She gave it to him without demur, returning the pressure of his fingers; but after a moment she withdrew it again.

"Maxim Alexandrovitch, I should never willingly have confessed any of this, had there not been some point. You must tell me who this woman is—the one who is so persistent."

When he told her, she frowned. "I thought as much. But you said she had become engaged."

"It seems to make no difference."

"Then I understand why you are anxious. If she is in love with you, she will see what I saw."

Max laughed. "She is not you, Vera Alexandrovna."

"She is a woman in love. Sooner or later—"

But she was interrupted by the little handbell her mother kept on the night table. As she rose from the loom, she said softly: "Be careful."

It had been a vain hope that Mlle Juliette would not read *Hamlet*. She soon reappeared in the library and, although by her own confession she had skimmed the last act, she was definite in her views.

"I cannot see why you all make so much of this play. It is nonsense from beginning to end and the hero is perfectly stupid. Of course he should kill his uncle at once, and not just to avenge his father. Hamlet is the crown prince, Claudius has stolen his throne. I do not understand why he hesitates for a moment."

"Perhaps," said Max mildly, "he is concerned about his mother."

Mlle Juliette laughed. "His mother? An ageing woman who is only interested in having some man at her side? She cares nothing for Hamlet, why should he care about her? No, he should become king and marry Ophelia, instead of pretending he doesn't love her and driving her mad."

"Do you not think she goes mad because he has killed her father?"

"Oh no. Her father is a silly old fool and no loss. He would have died soon anyway."

Max's heart went out to Armand. Nevertheless, he managed to keep his voice pleasant and even. "So you do not care greatly for Shakespeare, mademoiselle?"

She pulled a face. "He is even worse than Corneille and Racine. Although I suppose the play does have a useful motto."

He did not like the way she paused significantly or the sudden intensity of her gaze.

"Do not listen to ghosts?"

"That we must be brave, Monsieur Fabien, and let nothing stand in the way of our destiny."

It was only after she had gone that he recalled she had not returned the Hugo translation and, in his disquiet, he had omitted to remind her.

As the Empress Josephine's bedroom was unavailable that week, Madame Tonton had allotted them Room 5, which Armand, noting its boat-shaped bed, gauzy draperies and classical statues, had pronounced to be the bedchamber of Mme Récamier. Not that they wasted further thought on the lady or her famous salon: the days of famine between these brief feasts were becoming ever longer and harder to bear.

Nevertheless, Max was haunted by Vera's warning and must manage to speak to the old boy before they left. Armand would have noticed nothing untoward, given his daughter's public portrayal of a happily affianced maiden. Yet, for all that, whenever Max was in her presence, even when she was with poor Niversac, he could feel her eyes upon him like a cat's before a mouse hole; and, while he was confident he would give nothing away, Armand was another matter: Vera's account of the old boy's transparency merely confirmed what he already feared.

Still, it would be a difficult, not to say disagreeable, conversation, and for several days Max had been troubled as to how to begin it. But then, this morning, a letter had arrived from Calvert, the steward at Beauvallon, reporting a fire in one of the labourers' cottages Armand was continuing to build on the estate. The flames had not spread and the cause was not mysterious—the culprit was Plibou, the village drunk, who had since fled. However, as the model cottages were the old fellow's pet obsession, the matter must warrant a visit. Max's relief was unbounded. He could avoid any mention of Mlle Juliette.

But Armand barely heard him out. "Of course not, darling boy. How can I spare you? I am being driven to distraction as it is."

"It seemed to me that if you could not go yourself—"

"I should not go even if I could. Calvert has it in hand. In any case, you are busy with Juliette's ball."

"I've made most of the arrangements, the rest can be left to Boussec."

This was a mistake. The old fellow had pulled Max closer, but now he drew back in alarm. "Only for a day or two, I understood you to say?"

"Well—" Max endeavoured to smile reassuringly "—I know you have faith in Calvert but he has never been enthusiastic about the cottages. I thought I might stay for a couple of weeks. Just to see how the work was progressing."

"A couple of weeks?"

"Perhaps a month."

"Why, Max? Why do you want to leave me?"

"I don't. I—"

"I realise this life of ours is torture. But the madness will cease when Juliette is married."

The looking glass in Mme Récamier's bedroom was not in the canopy, but framed by the gauze draperies on the wall next to the bed, so that, although Armand had turned away, once Max sat up he could see beyond his lover's shoulder to a clear reflection of his anguished face.

"Oh, for pity's sake, dear heart." Max rubbed the old boy's shoulder with his chin, then pressed his lips to it. But the mention of Mlle Juliette, while it had made him flinch, had strengthened his purpose. "I am not deserting you. I'm merely asking you to send me to Beauvallon for a while."

Armand, too, sat up. "But why, in heaven's name?"

"Please don't ask me to explain—just accept it's for both our sakes."

Even as he said this, Max knew it expressed a vain wish. The old fellow was immediately filled with concern: it had not escaped him that Max had been on edge recently, but he had put it down to this tiresome business of the ball. But now, if there were something else troubling him…? With a sigh, Max climbed out of bed to fetch his cigarette case.

Inhaling deeply, he passed the cigarette to Armand. "I think your daughter…"

"Juliette?"

There seemed no words that would not affront both the old boy's devotion to his daughter and his notions of gallantry. "I think... I believe she has developed a—a liking for me."

"Well of course she likes you, darling boy. She has told me how kind you have been, discussing Shakespeare with her and recommending novels. And I must say, I am grateful to you—the nuns have left her education sadly wanting in that regard."

Max retrieved the cigarette and drew on it again. "No, Armand. That is not what I mean."

The old boy considered this, first with bewilderment, then incredulity. Then his brows contracted, his jaw clenched, every sinew in his face seemed to quiver. "I see! So that is how it is. First my wife, then the poor Englishwoman. And now my daughter. My unspoilt, innocent daughter. Dear God, even though she is betrothed! Is there no end to your iniquity?"

Although he was obliged to clamber over Max in order to do so, Armand hurled himself from the bed and strode towards the chair draped with his clothes. "Well, my boy, you flatter yourself. My beautiful Juliette—if you think, even for a moment—she loves Raoul de Niversac, a fine, honourable man, and if you imagine she would pay the slightest attention to your vile tricks—God in heaven, it is not just that you are constitutionally incapable of keeping your trousers buttoned, your mind is diseased."

Max had been framing a savage retort for the instant any reply was permitted him but, as he sat watching Armand frantically pulling on his clothes, he was suddenly too despairing for anger. What else could he have expected? The old boy would sooner gouge out his eyes than see any defect in his Juliette. And as for warning him—since he could be no other than he was, had not the notion been futile? All Max had achieved was to make a new breach between them, which, judging by the old fellow's anxiety to flee, would last until they had another chance to talk freely to each other—and that might not be for days.

Discarding the cigarette with a sigh, Max slid from the bed. "Armand, you misunderstand me."

"Oh, I understand you all too well, my boy."

"Please, listen to reason for a moment."

"Reason? How reasonable should a man be when his lover plans to betray him with his own daughter?"

"Dear heart, if I truly planned to seduce Mademoiselle Juliette, why on earth would I tell you?"

"Because you—you—Oh, damn this thing!"

Their weekly visits to Madame Tonton's had taught M. de M a degree of command over his collar stud but, in his present agitation, this mastery had deserted him. As, with gritted teeth, he was peering through his pince-nez into the glass above the commode, his fumblings had contrived to dislodge the stud entirely, so that he was left, collar flapping, vainly plucking at his shirt front.

With keener eyes, Max discerned the offending object beneath the rim of one of their lunch platters. Armand thanked him grudgingly, snarling: "For God's sake, do not watch me!" as he returned to the struggle; yet Max observed the interruption had calmed him somewhat.

"I thought we had agreed my challenge to Casanova was a trifle overrated."

The stud at last safely in place, Armand was reaching for his cravat. "Then, in heaven's name, dear boy, why did you tell me—what you told me?"

"Mademoiselle Juliette seems to visit the library a great deal. I wondered if she were forming some kind of attachment to me—if that were true, it would present obvious difficulties. But I may very well be mistaken."

The old fellow turned to look at him. "More than mistaken, sadly deluded—I am surprised at you, darling boy. Of course Juliette would wish to talk to you. Quite apart from her splendid new interest in literature, there is her ball to discuss. And if, unlike her mother and sister, she is pleasant and open—well, that is her nature, she makes no distinction, she is charming to everyone."

In the interests of reconciliation, Max offered no objection. At least Armand was smiling.

"Dearest Max," said the old boy, putting his arms around him, "you must keep your vanity in check. Not quite everyone who sees you falls distractedly in love with you. I like to think that divine misfortune is mine alone."

CHAPTER TWENTY-SIX

Max resolved to make the best of it. He even found himself wondering whether Armand was right and he had simply misinterpreted Mlle Juliette's manner.

He was permitted to cherish this illusion until his next encounter with mademoiselle, early the following morning in the stable yard, when, as he was reining in Pretender so that her bay could precede him, there was no mistaking the smile she shot him behind Armand's back.

That morning, too, alas, Captain Horthy chose to match him with Raoul de Niversac. Surprisingly perhaps for an ex-major in the Cuirassiers, Niversac was a moderate swordsman and, being the more aggressive fighter and doubly advantaged by youth and height, Max frequently beat him. Indeed, he had already scored the first hit, when, returning to his line on the piste and taking guard, he glimpsed something that made his spirits sink. A flash of pale blue, over in the far corner of the ballroom, near the doors. Immediately he became determined that today Mlle Juliette should not see him win: today her fiancé must reap the honours.

But how to lose? Already Niversac, whose instinct was defensive, had been slow to take advantage of his opponent's hesitation: while he had claimed right of way, his attack was easily parried and during Max's riposte he laid his left side open so invitingly that to ignore it argued with every competitive fibre of Max's being. Fortunately this brief wavering had its effect; before he could strike home, Niversac had counter-attacked and seconds later Max could announce he was hit.

Yet damn the fellow! If Max were to lose he must not make it so obvious—that would be more humiliating for Niversac than defeat. All the same, it would take the experience of old Horthy to wield a foil so as to contrive a defeat subtly. Then Max recalled the Warhorse's lecture after his last encounter with Sauvigny, when a particularly daring *flèche* of his had not only missed its mark but cost him a hit by sending him careering off the side of the piste. "You are not in the circus, monsieur. Discipline and precision, if you please." That was what he must do—eschew flamboyant lunges and bravura feints, play as Niversac played, defensively. If he were challenged, he could claim he had taken the captain's words to heart.

It could not be said this strategy brought immediate results.

Niversac seemed first disoriented, then suspicious of his opponent's changed tactics, reluctant to be forced constantly onto the attack. Although Max's unease with his new role accorded Niversac further success, he was grateful when Horthy called for them to break and change ends.

But gradually Niversac lost his suspicion. Perhaps he was fired by the sight of his fair Juliette. Perhaps he recalled that, as a nobleman and former cavalry officer, he had no business being intimidated by an upstart. More likely, the sportsman in him finally recognised his opponent's new strategy, not as the precursor to some mercurial display of aggression, but as punishable weakness. At any rate, he began to relish the attack. By the time they had taken the second break and again changed ends, he was fighting with formidable speed and calculation, and although Max, abandoning the struggle against his own instincts, retaliated in kind, he was no match for him. When Horthy declared the comte the winner by seven hits to three, it was a well-deserved victory; Max, despite counting it the most exhausting bout of his life, could not have shaken his opponent's hand more wholeheartedly, albeit that Horthy darted him a cautionary look.

As Max brushed the comte's victorious chalk marks from his jacket, he observed that Niversac was receiving the congratulations of his intended. Thus it was with pardonable self-satisfaction that he quitted the ballroom and went upstairs to change. He was forgoing luncheon to attend to further arrangements for the ball; with luck, since the family was at the opera this evening, he would see no more of mademoiselle till tomorrow. His air remained jaunty as, in his topcoat and carrying his hat, he descended towards the foyer.

But, as he reached the second-floor landing, a figure was lying in wait for him in the shadows of the east-wing corridor.

"Monsieur Fabien!"

"Mademoiselle? I thought you were taking lunch."

"Oh yes, yes I am. But I said I was cold and needed to fetch my shawl. I had to see you."

"Mademoiselle—"

"I must apologise."

"Forgive me, but I don't—"

"Oh yes, Monsieur Fabien, I must. I distracted you. No, please do not deny it. You were fighting with your usual brilliance. But then you saw me. And I smiled at you—and sent your thoughts flying elsewhere."

She had crossed the landing by now and was looking up at him, so that, if he harboured any doubt about her meaning, her eyes disabused him. The irony of it might have provoked him to laughter, were he not aghast.

"Oh, I am touched, monsieur, very touched. You are my valiant knight. But your heart was in the fight until your fair lady stole it away. It mortifies her that she made you lose to Monsieur de Niversac."

"Monsieur le comte won quite fairly, on merit."

"Nonsense, you always beat him."

"Today he was the better man."

She laughed. "Such false modesty! You know you are twice the swordsman, have a better seat on a horse, are in every way more—"

She had put her hand on his arm, but he stepped aside to escape it. "Mademoiselle, I cannot possibly—"

"Oh, please don't tell me it is not your place!"

"It is certainly not for me to pass an opinion on Monsieur de Niversac. But if it were, I should say that he is a thoroughly decent fellow and you have the greatest good fortune to be betrothed to him. Now, if you will forgive me…"

But she was not one to lose the last word. Her voice drifted back to him as he strode downstairs. "You and your maddening honour! Monsieur, honour is not everything!"

Even after his meeting with Levchenko, the friend of Mitya's who was designing the grand scheme for the ball, Max remained unsettled. Although he had promised M. de M he would join him in his study for what remained of the afternoon, he could not face the old boy and instead slipped into a dingy café off the Place Maubert where, hunched gloomily over a *mazagran*, he used one cigarette to light the next.

Mlle Juliette had never expressed herself so plainly before. Nor had she dared be so indiscreet—true, the family were safely in the dining room, but a conversation on the landing could be heard by any passing servant. But what troubled Max most was the revelation that in her eyes this was a folie à deux: she had not simply developed some crazed fancy for him, but believed it was requited. He racked his brains as to what he might have done to encourage this delusion but could think of nothing; yet she believed it, so firmly that harsh words could not shake her.

Where was this insanity leading, what did she want of him? Surely not an affair? She, the virginal bride-to-be? She was certainly prone to vexing contradictions, praising 'realism', yet in thrall to the clichés of novelettes; still, she seemed sufficiently realistic where it served her interest, not to say calculating and ruthless. He was safe enough; having enslaved Niversac, she would surely do nothing to weaken the poor fellow's chains.

All the same, Max's dislike had turned to loathing: he hated her depreciation of Niversac, hated her mulish ignorance and her snobbery and every hollow cadence of her gushing, teasing girlishness—the very tinkle of her voice set his teeth on edge. But above all he loathed her contempt for Armand. If he remembered anything of their fatuous discussion of *Hamlet*, it was that chilling dismissal of her parents: perhaps in the case of madame she might be forgiven, but her father, who adored her, who would go to any length for her happiness—how did he deserve her scorn?

When Max thought of what the old boy had surrendered, of what he himself had been forced to endure during these celibate months, he burned with rage. And now, if he did not take care, she would drive them further apart. For, of course, in one sense she was right—Armand was certainly an old fool, to love her so blindly. Yet Max had learned his lesson yesterday: unless he mastered his loathing, it was he who would feel the old boy's displeasure.

Confound M. de M—so wise in some respects, so damnably stupid in others! To forbid Max even to go to Beauvallon? It was not as if he were threatening to leave for good. Or that he paid any heed when the Other, who continued to plague his nights, shrieked that he, Max, had broken their pact and denied his destiny and would stay a lackey for the rest of his days.

As Max watched his smoke curl upwards, shake out its coils and melt into air, he felt the familiar urge for flight. But, if he had any love for Armand, he could not abandon him, not now, when the old boy most needed protection.

Perhaps he should try to think of Mlle Juliette as if she were Vera—although even with Vera, as things stood, he was bound to feel a certain constraint. In any case, the two could not be more different. Yet, if he failed to discern in mademoiselle a single one of Vera's agreeable traits, he must surely find some point in her favour. As one not unskilled in the art himself, should he not admire her capacity for deception? And was her disdain for her parents after all so shocking? Was it natural to honour your father and mother? He was scarcely one to judge. Of his own parents, his real parents, he admittedly had few memories, but none fond: his mother he recalled seeing only once, when, aged six, he had been sent home ill to the family estate and she had stood at the end of his bed, emanating fumes of camphor and distaste; what he remembered of his father, beyond the flat of his hand, was also tainted with shame, a sense he had absorbed from the ether that this man, puffed up in his uniform, bedizened with braid and buttons like an overstuffed chair, was nevertheless to be held in contempt, esteemed as little as his newly bestowed 'von'.

Curious. These memories always whetted Max's appetite for righteous anger, but today, like the dregs in his coffee glass, they tasted sour and spent. Besides, mademoiselle did not have a shrill bullfrog for a father; what possible resentment could she feel towards Armand?

The wretched girl was mad, as simple as that. From now on he must avoid being alone with her, work in his room when he was not in the old fellow's apartments and visit the library only out of necessity. Of course, there was the accursed ball! But if she used the preparations as an excuse for further meetings, he would insist that her mother was present: this would be tiresome, only encouraging madame to change her mind yet again about the flowers or the paper lanterns, but there was no alternative. In fact, he should stop cursing the ball and be grateful for it; whatever its toll on his time and nerves, it would keep him from the house a good deal during the next month and provide him with an excuse to forgo riding and fencing.

Meanwhile, M. de Niversac's mother and sisters were expected in Paris. If they approved the prospective bride—which Armand, of course, thought a certainty—the engagement would be public knowledge by the time the ball took place, and notaries would be drawing up the marriage contract. Should all proceed according to plan, mademoiselle would embrace reality and Max might rest easy.

He summoned the waiter and paid his bill. As he extinguished his last cigarette, he even smiled to himself: at any rate, Vera was wrong, Armand and he were quite safe. For there was one advantage to Mlle Juliette's delusion. If she believed so obstinately, against all the evidence, that he returned her passion, she would never perceive the truth.

Max commenced his new routine the next morning, sequestering himself in his room to catch up with M. de M's correspondence. Despite the spring sunshine sidling in through the dormer windows, the room was still cold but, having stoked the fire and poured the fresh coffee the maid had left him, he settled to work. Nothing stirred on the third floor.

No madame, no Lady Telford and above all no mademoiselle—just peace and solitude.

So he was considerably startled when, after he had been at the escritoire for an hour or so, his door was unceremoniously thrown open.

"Aha! This is where Her Highness is hiding herself these days."

It had been agreed that, for the sake of discretion, Polly would never come to Max's room. But Max had scarcely opened his mouth, let alone framed any objection, before his friend forestalled him.

"Oh, up your sweet arse with that! You weren't in the library. One of the stable boys assured me you weren't out in the Champs-Élysées masquerading as one of the nobs. And the Cyclops, with typical charm, ejected me from the Mouse's quarters. So where else, tell me, angel, was I supposed to find you?"

Since Max's ever-multiplying duties had kept him from the Luxembourg Gardens, several days had passed since he had last met Polly. Then, as he had watched him trying to teach Bébé tricks, his friend, for all his usual banter, had struck him as subdued. Now, on the contrary, he was wild-eyed, the very picture of animation: the jacket of his morning livery flapped, his waistcoat swung, unbuttoned, his collar jerked; as he paced—no, careered—about the room, he radiated ill-contained fury and a stench of anise.

"My, hasn't Her Highness done well!" He whirled, arms outstretched, in the tract between the escritoire and the bed. "You could fit ten Hornets in here—more if you weren't particular about Mathieu's impetigo and Antoine's feet. Not that I care a toss. I buzz no longer."

Max stared at him. "You mean you've given notice?"

"I mean I've been squashed, petal. My wings are crushed, my sting is drawn."

"Shit! But why? By whom?"

"By madame. She swatted me when I went to collect the doggie for his morning constitutional."

"Damn milady Telford! May the old hag—"

"Oh, it wasn't that."

"Thank God! But then—why…?"

"Madame no more needs a 'why' than Genghis Khan. She'll take her scimitar to anyone. It wouldn't surprise me, sweetie, if you were next."

"Please, be serious."

"She had the nerve to accuse me of being drunk."

"But you *are* drunk." Max put his head in his hands.

"Of course I am, now. But not then. I'd only had the teeniest fortifying snifter."

"Oh, for pity's sake, Polly! Bébé has more brains. Well, you shan't leave without a proper settlement. I shall talk to monsieur——"

"Yes, angel. You will certainly talk to him."

Max was so taken aback by the change in Polly's voice that he thought he had misheard. But Polly, he saw, was suddenly still, no longer whirling and feverish but fixed as a pillar in the centre of the room, his face set, his eyes stony.

"You will tell Little Miss Mouse I need five thousand francs."

"Oh, for heaven's sake——"

"You will tell her. Or your Auntie Polly will tell madame where you both go every Wednesday lunchtime."

"Not that it's any of your business, we attend a regular meeting of——"

"Oh *please!*"

Max was pulled up briefly. Then he summoned a laugh. "You idiot, there is no need for this."

"Or, if you think your lunchtime frolics are not enough, I have plenty of other delicious titbits."

"Don't you see? Monsieur knows you are my friend, he would not have left you destitute——"

"Madame might like to know how you came by that sublime alpaca coat of yours. And your amethyst pin. And that pretty boy with his velocipede gracing your wall over there."

"Damn you, Polly! I vouched for you. I swore to Armand you could be trusted."

"More fool you, angel."

Max considered him in silence for a moment. "You're right. I am a confounded fool. I thought we were friends. I thought, halfwit that I am, that we stood by each other. When you had your run of bad luck, I was even stupid enough to feel sorry for you——"

"I don't want your pity. I want five thousand francs."

"Go and hang!"

"Very brave, petal. And I'm sure the Mouse will be equally courageous." Polly smiled unpleasantly. "Five thousand. Tomorrow afternoon."

*

Max did not tell Armand: the effect on the old fellow did not bear contemplating. Instead, he spent the rest of the morning and much of the afternoon emptying his bank account of two years' savings, pawning three cravat pins, some cufflinks, his spare cigarette case and second pair of riding boots—he could not pawn his watch, for M. de M would notice its absence—and finally selling to a book dealer in the Palais-Royal a first edition of Constant's *Adolphe*, a lucky find weeks ago from a rummage through the *bouquinistes*. The fruit of these endeavours was nowhere near five thousand francs: in fact, the sum he counted into a manila envelope was one thousand, four hundred and twenty-two francs, forty-seven centimes. But he would remind Polly there were certain habitués of the Monkey who not only shared the general view of blackmailers, but were handy with knives. Polly should take what was in the envelope and think himself fortunate.

In the Luxembourg Gardens, although the chestnut branches were still bare, the beds had been planted out and the almond trees were in blossom. But Max, numb with rage, did not see these signs of spring. He picked out from afar the figure huddled on the usual bench and strode towards it.

The figure, as Max neared, let fall the *caporal* that had burned down to its fingers and, lurching to its feet, began flapping its arms. "Oh angel! Angel heart! Thank God you've come."

But Max had no desire to hear it, or even to see it; furthermore, he could already smell absinthe. He extracted the envelope from his inner pocket. "It's not what you asked for, but it's all I have. You can sing for the rest."

"Oh angel, forgive your Auntie Polly. I don't know what came over her, the Green Fairy must have stolen her mind. To think that she would ever—of course she was desperate, but to stoop so low, after all you and she have been through together—she begs you, implores you on her knees—please, dear girl, please forgive her."

Surprise forced Max to look at his erstwhile friend. He saw that Polly's face was yellow and his eyes red-rimmed; that he shivered without a greatcoat; that his shoulders were bony beneath his flimsy jacket, which, once so à la mode with its single button, was now stained and creased; that, indeed, the entire rig-out, from topper to spats, in which he had strutted on his Sundays off, a glorious gentleman of fashion, had succumbed to incautious use of the benzene bottle and the depredations of rain and dust, as an orchid succumbs when the hothouse door is left open. Max saw this, but anger left him indifferent.

"Take the money!"

"I don't want it, angel. I tell you, it was the Green Fairy talking. All I want is your forgiveness."

Polly's lip was trembling, to Max's disgust. He threw the envelope onto the bench. "Take it, damn you! And let me forget you exist."

When Armand, noticing Polly's absence, enquired what had become of him, Max said he had tired of service and gone back to his family in Lyon.

CHAPTER TWENTY-SEVEN

While resolved to obliterate all thought of Polly, Max could not help missing their illicit jaunts. He continued to miss Euphemia Pilkington, too. Although they were daily under the same roof and free to exchange conversation in company, this had obvious limitations; besides, now he was confined to his room in the mornings, evenings spent between the same four walls held few attractions—he had even laid aside *Hamlet*, since mademoiselle had forgotten about his crib and he would hardly risk asking for it. Yet, however he longed for Chopin and genial debate, however he argued that, given the passage of time, no one would be the wiser, Miss Pilkington was adamant. It was not that she had been persuaded their soirées were improper—on the contrary—but she had given her word to madame. And Miss Pilkington's word, like Armand's, was not given lightly.

Again he cursed milady Telford. Granted, she ensured madame was occupied most afternoons with Lord Jack, but otherwise she had much to answer for. Recently he had found her by the Music Room mantelpiece fingering one of the bronzes and, although she had naturally claimed to be struck by its beauty, she had reminded Max of the pawnbroker pricing his worldly goods. Of course he spoke to Boussec, who swore he checked the piano nobile every day, but Boussec nowadays was as busy with the ball as he was.

Nor was Max reassured when, taking the back stairs to his room to avoid the second-floor landing, he had an unexpected encounter: Mme Neroni, descending in her mangy furs, carrying a carpet bag. She expressed no alarm, conceding him an unworldly smile as he stood aside to let her pass: yet he could not help noticing the carpet bag seemed heavy.

But perhaps she had only been preparing for Lady Telford's latest séance. They were all summoned: Armand was able to make his excuses and Max was about to follow, when mademoiselle, who, as he recalled, had once scorned the spirits, implored him not to let them down—the greater their number, the stronger the psychic energy; and since her plea was made while M. de M was still present, Max was obliged to give in or seem churlish.

He was comforted that Raoul de Niversac, who had dined with the family, had been similarly dragooned: his presence would allow Max to evade Mlle Juliette as they gathered in the Little Salon to take their seats at the round table. But, while Niversac chose to sit at mademoiselle's right, the left-hand chair still beckoned and, although Max strove to yield the place to Miss Pilkington, he found himself outmanoeuvred.

The lights were extinguished save for a single taper; incense perfumed the shadows; they joined hands, silent, scarcely breathing, willing Mustafa, Mme Neroni's spirit guide, to appear. Mustafa was taking an unconscionable time of it, Max thought, as, sustained by Miss Pilkington's cool grasp of his left hand, he tried to ignore the fingers caressing his right. But eventually Mme Neroni began to rock to and fro, emitting a soft but eldritch crooning. Then her eyes rolled upwards so that only the whites were visible: Mustafa had deigned to tear himself away from the spirit world.

His first message was inevitable. Madame's papa stood at his side and was anxious to reassure his daughter her present happiness would last (Max assumed the late M. de Sestrès, not without impropriety, was referring to Lord Stilorgan). This communication took time as madame had further questions, which she put to the spirit in suitably hushed tones.

To shut out that other message, impressed stealthily upon his right hand, Max directed his thoughts towards Mme Neroni. She wore heavy earrings, many bangles and flowing robes of scarlet and purple, embroidered with gold thread: oriental robes—but from which part of the Orient precisely? Her nose was hooked, her wrinkled face the colour of China tea; her hair, loosely covered by a gauzy veil, was black, streaked with silver at its parting. She spoke with a faint foreign accent, although it was not one Max could place. Was she Indian? A princess from an ancient Berber tribe? A gypsy? Or was she a peasant's daughter from Languedoc, who, on arriving in Paris, rather than settle for life as a flower girl or a seamstress, had decided to capitalise on her swarthy Catalan features? And what was her business with—?

But unfortunately at this moment his fingers received a violent squeeze, while the toe of a slipper probed his right foot. The late M. de Sestrès had not forgotten his granddaughter and was promising her enduring love. Was she simultaneously crushing Niversac's hand, Max wondered, was she also nudging the comte's foot under the table?

Grimly, he returned his thoughts to Mme Neroni. Naturally such a woman would have recourse to a moneylender from time to time, but did she have other business with Old Jouvert? If Theosophy had become fashionable, then La Neroni must be in demand—according to madame, she could count Mmes de Corvignac and de Grès amongst her disciples. In which case, she was ideally placed to furnish the old rogue of an ex-butler with those intimate details of goings-on in grand houses that were the very wellspring of his mysterious power. Or was there more? Did Old Jouvert's labyrinthine dealings extend further? Was it possible that he—?

Max was jolted to attention by Mustafa's warblings. "… to a certain young man in this room. The Other is here and has a message for you."

The Other? Max froze. It could not be. No one knew about the Other, not even Armand. It was impossible.

"It is not for me," came Niversac's voice from his right. "I have never been blessed with a brother."

Brother. Of course. Damn this senseless panic! Lost in his speculations, Max had simply misheard.

"Your brother, Pierre," intoned Mustafa.

Pierre. The Other's name in the cloister. Pierre and Paul. Small wonder they had often been mistaken for twins. Was the Other dead? Had he 'crossed to the other side', as they liked to put it? Max had no way of knowing. Even so, it was ridiculous. A hoax of some kind. No cause for the sweat that had broken out on his forehead. Yet they were all gazing at him, faces cast by the single candle flame into grotesque relief, madame, milady, with the old crone between them, swaying and muttering in her eastern robes.

"Monsieur Fabien?" prompted Lady Telford in a stage whisper. "You are the only other young man present."

Max summoned a smile. "Alas, like Monsieur de Niversac, I have no brother."

"But you are an orphan," whispered mademoiselle, squeezing his hand again. "You could have a brother without knowing it."

"Your brother, Pierre, has a warning for you," continued Mustafa relentlessly. "Seek not to cross the spirits, or your future will be your past."

This pronouncement, uttered in sepulchral tones, stilled the entire circle. Max, hearing an echo of the Other's nightly predictions, felt his skin prickle. Yet only for an instant, before he caught a decidedly false note. Had he been Raoul de Niversac, he might have braved madame's wrath by bursting out in a gale of laughter that declared the whole thing poppycock. But, as the ever-obedient secretary, he merely freed his hands and sat back in his chair.

"I fear Mustafa is mistaken. I have no brother, living or dead."

"Shhhh!" hissed madame. "You will wake the medium."

"As it is," said Lady Telford, "he has broken our circle. The energy is fading. Oh dear, it is not good for poor Madame Neroni to come out of a trance suddenly."

On cue—or so it seemed—Mme Neroni's eyes rolled, she began to shake as though in a fit, then fell back, apparently fainting. Milady delved into her reticule for smelling salts, Niversac, muttering "Brandy!", went to touch the bell, madame scowled at Max unforgivingly. But, after a twitch or two, the medium raised her head and, uttering a sigh of profound exhaustion, came to herself.

As Mme Neroni was led away to rest by madame and milady, and the company broke up, Miss Pilkington shot Max a sympathetic smile. Rather less consoling was mademoiselle's whisper when Niversac's back was turned: "It is good, the message. It means you must take courage."

Of course it had been nonsense. Max was ashamed that he, who prided himself on his unbelief, could have credited it, even for a second. He was convinced the Other was still living—he might be weak, but he had a keen will to survive; as ivy seeks an oak, he would have found some other fool's strength to sap. But, aside from that, the portentous ring of the so-called message was quite unlike his usual juvenile utterances. Nor should it be forgotten that the Other was devout: he would no more speak of 'spirits' than curse the Pope.

No, it was all clear now, Max knew exactly which spirits he was not supposed to cross. Mme Neroni had noted his suspicious glance at her carpet bag and reported back to milady. It must be generally known that he was an orphan—it was central to the myth of how he came to be at the Hôtel de Miremont—so that he would find it hard to challenge an invented brother; and as for Pierre, it was a common enough name, there was a Pierre in most families. But in truth Max was not required to believe in Mustafa but only to understand the crude warning: if he continued to interfere in milady's business, he would find himself in trouble—doubtless of the same sort as poor Christine.

He smiled to himself. He would love to hear milady telling M. de M he had snaffled the Music Room's Apollo. But Lady Telford's kleptomania was no longer his only concern. Aside from the bogus séances, did milady find other uses for Mme Neroni? And what exactly were the dealings La Neroni had with Old Jouvert?

Max suffered a wretched night, during which mademoiselle joined forces with the Other to pull him this way and that, screeching about 'courage' and 'destiny'. But, though he awoke mired in sweat, he did not abandon his suspicions; when his next evening off came, he risked a visit to the Monkey.

Old Jouvert had not always been the scaly-fingered, greasy-bearded, purple-nosed toper he was now. He had once been a very grand butler, in command of a ducal house until the key to its wine cellars had undone him, and, whatever trade he plied in the Faubourg Saint-Antoine, he would forever view those times in the Faubourg Saint-Germain as his glory days. Indeed he was wont to expatiate upon them at elaborate and repetitive length, so that, although there might be one or two acolytes at his table, mostly junior servants hoping to draw upon his power to magic references out of air, the generality of the Monkey preferred to give him a wide berth. Max, on the other hand, remembering how the old soak had saved him from destitution, felt a certain affection for him, which the ex-butler, despite his protégé's failure to follow in his stead, seemed to return.

All the same, there was a limit to the favours Old Jouvert would bestow: lists of noble houses were one thing; Max's present request could be taken as prying into the old rogue's business, which was quite another. Max went delicately, tendering as bait a full description of the arrangements for the ball, which the old toper gobbled, belching forth a stream of reminiscence and advice. Only when the second bottle of wine was uncorked did Max venture upon the subject of Mme Neroni.

At first Old Jouvert denied any knowledge of such a person; when Max mentioned seeing the lady at his son's estaminet in the Passage La Boule-Blanche, he brushed it away like a fly; a hint that further supplies of Armand's fine brandy might be forthcoming failed to move him; and when Max began to think some financial inducement might assist and was wondering how to broach this, he was anticipated by the gurgle of phlegm that served the old chap for a laugh.

"Other—men's—*soupe*—*de poisson*." Old Jouvert's tones were always weighty with drink. "I do not—eat theirs, my lad, they—do not eat—mine."

This could only increase Max's frustration. As to what this 'fish soup' was, he prayed it was not blackmail: although he had always assumed the old soak would jib at bleeding one of his own kind, Polly had taught him to mistrust such assumptions. Still, whatever the fishy brew, Max would be foolish to press the matter. Had he forgotten that, ever a butler at the bone, Old Jouvert worshipped respectability? The

218

old rogue might teeter at the perimeter of the law, but he would never confess to putting a toe outside it.

Thus Max, thoroughly disheartened, was about to order a farewell bottle and settle his bill when Old Jouvert, who had been studying the depths of his glass, all at once put a bony hand on his arm.

"I am given to understand that Monsieur Boussec is a butler who honours our fine traditions."

"Yes. Yes indeed." Max was not only surprised but wary. Old Jouvert, contrary to his usual custom, had always remained content with what Max volunteered about the Hôtel de Miremont and had never before attempted to pump him. But he was further disconcerted when the old fellow bared what remained of his blackened teeth in a smile that was the more grisly for being strangely wistful.

"Monsieur Boussec and I once had the distinction of serving the comte de Polignac. We were young lads then, junior footmen. But my!—he was a handsome boy, Xavier Boussec, turned all the housemaids' heads. And, by Jove, though it shames me to confess it, the larks we got up to—"

Max was not to learn what these were, for Old Jouvert's rattling laugh had turned predictably into convulsive coughing, but he was already sufficiently astonished. While he was on somewhat better terms with Boussec as a result of their present labours, he could not conceive of the gloomy, ponderous fellow he knew as a 'handsome boy', let alone fond of a jape.

"Perhaps," said Old Jouvert, wiping his lips with a surprisingly clean handkerchief and becoming solemn again, "perhaps, my lad, you would be so good as to ask Monsieur Boussec if he would do me the honour of calling upon me. Not here, of course. At La Boule-Blanche. At his convenience."

When Max relayed the message, Boussec was doubtful: he regretted his former comrade's mode of living and love of the grape; nor was he keen to venture into the shadier purlieus of Saint-Antoine. But once they had both conferred with Armand, it was decided that he should go. Max was given no report of the meeting and, from M. de M's silence, he assumed he too knew nothing. Evidently there were confidences only to be exchanged between butlers.

CHAPTER TWENTY-EIGHT

If Max had been asked to set the scene for a *fête galante* at Beauvallon, his task would have been easy: Armand's Yonne estate, with its lake, follies, picturesque ruins and wooded hills, possessed all the ingredients for an open-air festival of courtship in the manner of Watteau and Fragonard. But it was rather more daunting to create Arcadia at the Hôtel de Miremont, where 'open-air' meant the central courtyard, admittedly sizeable, but already furnished with four formal flower beds and a fountain, and where the ballroom, though gracious in its proportions, was so newly refurbished, so cosily pink that it hardly evoked a raffish air of masquerade. Nor would this be the Côte d'Or in high summer, but Paris on the fourth day of April, when clement weather could not be guaranteed.

Max was profoundly grateful to Zhukovsky and his connections at the Opéra. It was one thing to hire a band for dancing or a string orchestra for the dining room, but, when it came to staging the themed ballet madame required before supper, he was entirely at a loss. As it was, thanks to Mitya, he had found a specialist in the music of the period, who had adapted selections from one of Rameau's long-forgotten operas, *Les fêtes d'Hébé*. Accordingly, Max had acquired a third orchestra, a baroque ensemble complete with lute; he had engaged a choreographer, a troupe of dancers, a wardrobe mistress and two limelight operators; and last of all—this extra touch was suggested by the designer, Levchenko——he was employing a group of actors, suitably costumed, to play an audience picnicking at the foot of the stage, as if the entire performance were a Watteau brought to life.

But Max's biggest debt to his friend was Ivan Levchenko himself. A short, untidy man with a puckish face and a sardonic wit that was balm to Max, he was never discouraged by madame's endless demands and changes of mind: if there were a problem he simply set about solving it.

The stage for the ballet would be constructed on the side of the courtyard opposite the ballroom and behind it, dropping from the eaves of the mansard across the central section of the guest wing, would hang a painted backcloth, which, although replicating the architecture it obscured, would portray it in ruins with ferns and saplings sprouting from its cracks, until, at its centre, it crumbled away entirely, revealing a perspective view of a sunlit lake and, in the far distance, a classical temple. There would be various pieces of stage furniture including a plaster statue on a plinth (Levchenko had wanted a mausoleum, but madame had insisted upon Venus and Cupid); shrubs and young trees in planters would form the wings and hide the limelight machines; to the left of the stage would sit the orchestra, before the open flaps of an authentically extempore Arcadian tent.

The rest of the courtyard would be transformed in similar fashion. The fountain presented no problem, except that it must be turned off during the ballet to avoid obscuring the view from the ballroom. Levchenko's solution for the flower beds was to build platforms over their low, topiaried plantings of box, on which, behind balustrades, would stand more saplings in planters—holm oaks, olives, cypresses and junipers. Wires would be strung at various heights from the east wing to the west to carry lanterns. As for the windows, doorways and the ballroom balcony, all these would be festooned with foliage and flowers.

Leaves and flowers would form the main decoration indoors too; they would climb between the ballroom's Venetian mirrors, arch over the ballroom doors and burgeon like a hanging garden over the balustrade of the main staircase; in the dining room, which would be tented in silk to give the illusion that Chef Quintivali's elaborate supper on Sèvres china was indeed an al fresco picnic, they would be entwined with the creeping tendrils of ivy and the vine.

Max had negotiated with various florists to commandeer most of the city's daily supply of fresh-cut blooms for next Tuesday, the day before the ball. But the garlands would need to be made up and, given their sheer quantity, some must also be hung in advance, with the risk of blooms wilting or dying—madame's reaction could be imagined— before the evening had even commenced. To reduce this problem, Levchenko had suggested silk flowers for the courtyard. As for the garlands indoors, Mme Mercier must ensure two housemaids patrolled them, culling and replacing offending blossoms.

But this was the least of Max's concerns. What if it rained? He had arranged for the courtyard to be netted to keep out birds and perhaps this would allow tarpaulins to be thrown across, shielding the stage and the area nearest the ballroom. But supposing there were a downpour? And that was not his gravest fear.

"Always ensure the fire buckets are at the ready," Old Jouvert had advised him, wagging a gnarled finger. With the number of tapers and torchères that would be lit, the braziers to warm the night air in the courtyard, the lanterns at the mercy of breezes or lodged precariously in trees, not to mention the firework display planned for midnight, he might, after all, be grateful for a downpour. Of course the fire buckets were Boussec's charge, but Max could hardly absolve himself if Levchenko's representation of the Hôtel de Miremont in ruins ceased to be just a witty trompe l'oeil.

Armand and he seldom talked about the ball. The old fellow had been unusually tolerant of the time it stole from their afternoons; he had even, albeit grudgingly, accepted the need for fancy dress— he would wear whatever Max and Thomas provided for him—but, as for the other details, he was content to leave those to his wife and daughters: though the ball was in his house and at his expense, it was as if he expected to be no more than a guest.

Max suspected, indeed knew, that the old boy was protecting himself, that, if he were forced to acknowledge the conspicuous extravagance of it all, he would be pained by its vulgarity. Max himself, in his dealings with Mme Grillo, the purveyor of silk flowers, had been unable to banish the memory of Josette, with whom he had lived when first in Paris and who, to make ends meet in the latter months of her pregnancy, had worked by candlelight fashioning roses to order; and he could not help thinking of those hundreds of other girls at present straining their eyes in the garrets of Belleville, the Marais, the Latin Quarter.

Of course they would be paid their pittance after Mme Grillo had taken her cut. The women who sat up all night assembling the garlands, the dancers, actors, carpenters, scene-painters, musicians; the carters who were transporting the trees, some from as far away as the orangery at Miremont-Sainte-Fleur; the extra servants Mme Mercier and Boussec would need to hire for the night—they would all be paid; Levchenko too would be paid, and handsomely. But this was as nothing compared to the cost of the thousands of cut flowers, the hundreds of bottles of champagne, the foie gras, the caviar, the lobsters and game, the fruit out of season, the pyramids of sweetmeats, Chef Quintivali's planned ice sculpture of cherubs... And all that remained of this huge endeavour would be mere debris by the following day.

So much to honour one eighteen-year-old girl who did not begin to know how to make a silk flower.

On the whole, Max's strategy had been successful: it had been three weeks since he had last found himself alone with mademoiselle and, this morning, when madame had summoned him to discuss some trivial detail of the ballet, he had been relieved to see that Mme Thierry-Le Puy was also present. But, alas, just as he was taking his departure, madame was detained in conversation by her elder daughter, allowing mademoiselle to slip out after him.

"Dear Monsieur Fabien. We have become quite strangers, have we not?"

"Mademoiselle, I fear I—"

"Oh, I know it is painful but I understand. Do you think I have not noticed how devotedly you are working on my behalf? And you shall have your reward."

"That is generous, but—"

"Yes, you shall. I am saving at least two dances for you."

Max had feared something of this sort and was prepared. "Mademoiselle, I am honoured, but you must save them for Monsieur de Niversac. Sadly, I am unable dance with you."

"Nonsense. I'll be expected to dance with all sorts of people, probably even with old Monsieur de Cressy, although he can barely hobble. No one will think anything of it."

"I cannot dance with you, mademoiselle, because I cannot dance."

"Oh, but surely—"

"I'm afraid I have never learned." This was not strictly true. Although his life with Armand had furnished little opportunity to acquire the skill, during his time as a footman there had always been dancing in the servants' hall at New Year, in addition to which there were hops upstairs at the Monkey where you could polka and mazurka into the small hours.

She struggled with her astonishment. "But you are so clever at everything... Well, never mind. I shall teach you."

"Mademoiselle is too kind, but—"

"We shall start now. We'll go downstairs to the Music Room. Pilkington can play the piano for us."

The idea of putting his arm around her waist, of holding her even in the lightest embrace, filled him with distaste. "I fear there will not be time—"

"Oh, the waltz is easy. You will pick it up in an hour."

"Mademoiselle, you mistake me. I meant, during the ball. I shall be too busy making sure all goes according to plan and nothing spoils your enjoyment."

"Oh, my dear Monsieur Fabien…" She was beginning to pout. "I am grateful for your devotion, but if you truly wish for my enjoyment… Surely, one little dance?"

"That will be the moment the heavens open or the supper tent collapses. Mademoiselle, you do me honour. But I should not dance, even if I could."

At least it was Wednesday. Next Wednesday being the day of the ball, the meeting of the Marquise de Miremont Trust must be rearranged, but today Max and Armand were free to follow their usual routine: while they would make a point of departing together, Max with a document case under his arm, they would split up once they reached the Rue du Four, arriving at the house in the Rue Mazarine a few minutes apart and leaving in the same fashion. At first they had always met up again in a café in the Rue de Seine; nowadays, however, since it was not vital to their pretence that they should return together and Max often had business in the afternoon, Armand would use his escape from the house to visit those of his friends it was no longer comfortable to receive there; last week he had called on Dr Gérard, today he was taking tea with Mme de Claireville.

Later, Max reflected that if the old boy had not paused in the vestibule to chat with Georges they might have averted disaster, if only for the present. But he could not fairly blame Armand. That wretch Simon—the dimwit with the noteworthy calves—must have been lying in wait. Georges had barely opened the doors to let them into the forecourt before the cry of "Monsieur Fabien!" rang out.

Max turned.

"Madame la marquise requires your presence."

Armand, who already had one foot on the cobbles, also turned. "My dear fellow," he said, smiling at Simon, "I fear madame must speak to Monsieur Fabien on his return. We are already late."

But Simon was undaunted. "Madame is most insistent, monsieur. The matter is urgent."

Armand's brow darkened, Georges' tongue clicked—Simon would be reprimanded for his disrespect. Yet the fellow stood firm, his impressive shoulders squared, his chest puffed with pride in this fearless execution of his orders.

"Come, Fabien," said Armand. "The others will be waiting."

All the same, was it worth tempting providence? Max recalled

Simon's penchant for gossip. Whatever madame required, it could not take long—in a quarter of an hour she would be sitting down to luncheon.

"Forgive me, monsieur." He shot Armand a look he hoped Georges could not fathom. "If I may, I shall catch you up."

As he followed the shapely calves upstairs, Max occupied himself with the thought that stupidity blighted beauty. But, rather, he should have marked the spring in Simon's step, the air the fellow failed to suppress of gleeful anticipation, for he was quite unprepared, on entering madame's boudoir, to encounter her rising like a Fury from her escritoire to brandish a piece of paper.

"Aha, young man! You have been found out!"

Max stared at her.

"Oh yes, I know your game. I know where you and my husband go every Wednesday afternoon."

A chill stole over him. "We attend a meeting of—"

"Ridiculous lies! Oh, I have had my suspicions. But here is the proof."

As she flourished the paper triumphantly—it was writing paper, a letter—the chill grew. Polly. Evidently his repentance had not lasted. Max searched for a convincing denial but his mind had frozen. Even when madame, realising Simon still stood smugly by the door, paused to wave him away, invention failed. But, after all, was not silence safer? Better to find out first what Polly alleged.

"Proof?" Max ventured.

"Young man, I am not the fool you and monsieur seem to take me for. It was not difficult to get my brother-in-law to confess these meetings of yours do not exist. He did not say outright that my husband has a mistress, but he certainly implied it—indeed, I found his comments highly insulting."

A *mistress?*

"But that is Constant de Sauvigny for you, and quite by the by. Now, at last, I know who she is."

So overwhelming was Max's relief that he could barely repress insane laughter. The effort rendered him speechless.

"Of course a great many men keep mistresses—I ought to be relieved, it is natural and healthy, unlike those dead Romans of his. But that it should be her! An ugly, vulgar old witch who might be his mother. And to think it has been going on all these years. That pretence of hers, that she was his sister's best friend. She always had her eye on him. I should have known, I should have seen it. I should have understood why I was banished. To think that I was betrayed, vilified, sacrificed—for the sake of an old hag like Catherine de Claireville!"

Madame had worked herself into such a passion that she was oblivious to Max's astonishment. "Madame de Claireville?"

She had been dabbing her eyes with her handkerchief, but now she drew herself up. "Do not try to sound surprised, young man. I have had quite enough of your lies. This arrived this morning." Snatching up the letter, which she had cast aside during her tirade, and fumbling with the ribbon of her lorgnette, she began to read: "'My darling Armand...'"

While she adjusted the distance, first of the paper and then of the lorgnette, Max had time to spot the torn envelope on the writing desk. Shit, she was opening Armand's post. Unstamped, delivered by hand, the missive must have been intercepted before it could reach Thomas. Simple Simon was sly as well as stupid.

"'My darling Armand, you cannot know how I long to see you this afternoon. I have missed you dreadfully and am only grateful you have been able to escape from the toils of...'" Whatever followed could not have been entirely complimentary to the reader, for she let the words trail away. "And so on and so forth. It is all in the same vein. She even has the gall to gloat over his lavish presents to her—presents he does not deign to give me."

"Presents?"

Madame adjusted her lorgnette again. "'I continue to treasure the jewel you sent me. Every time I sit down to dinner, I think Aline's loss my gain.'"

It took Max a second to interpret this. But then he could no longer hold back his laughter. "Madame, she does not—it is not what you—"

"How dare you laugh! Have you the nerve to deny it?"

Max pulled himself together. He should not get carried away by his relief. It was pointless to explain that Mme de Claireville's 'jewel' was Mme Dussardier, the cook she, madame, had sent packing. Pointless and dangerous. For, much as he would like to defend Mme de Claireville, what would be served by correcting madame's mistake? The question of the fictitious trust meetings would once again require an answer.

At least, as it was, their Wednesdays were safe. Indeed, a glance at the mantelpiece clock told Max that if he walked with speed they would have lost only fifteen minutes of their two hours. Besides, he had had enough of madame and her farcical suspicions. If she were angry with Armand, why in heaven's name did she not, as was proper, have it out behind closed doors with the old fellow himself?

"Madame, I am merely monsieur's secretary. I cannot deny or confirm anything relating to his private affairs. May I respectfully suggest you take the matter up with monsieur. Now, if you will excuse me—"

"Not so fast, young man!"

Max, still clutching his bogus documents, had nearly reached the door.

"Much as I abominate his choice, I cannot prevent my husband visiting his mistress."

No, Max supposed she could not. Not if she hoped for Armand's continued tolerance of the egregious Lord Stilorgan.

"But I can forbid you to visit yours."

Once again, Max was stunned to silence.

"Or am I to suppose that, while my husband is cavorting with Mme de Claireville, you wait obediently at the bedroom door?"

"Madame, I—"

"Some little chit of a Russian, I gather."

Shit, the tittle-tattle in this house! What business of Lady Telford's was his friendship with the Zhukovskys? Confound her, was there no end to her malice?

"May I remind you, Monsieur Fabien, that you are in our employ. We allow you generous—overgenerous—days off. You will not take advantage of my husband's unfortunate weakness to pursue your own dalliances in the time we pay you to work."

Their assignations safe? This was their death knell. Max heard it with anger and incredulity. Was she to set spies on him now? 'Our employ'? She did not employ him, she had no right. He would talk to Armand. They would think of something. Meanwhile he must make his escape and warn the old boy.

But madame was relentless. "As it is, you have used the excuse of the ball to let your other duties slide—do not imagine I have not noticed. Well, you shall start remedying matters now. My correspondence urgently needs your attention. Then, when I return from luncheon, there is a pile of invitations to be gone through…"

Max and Miremont sat by the lake at the Luxembourg. It had been a bright spring day and strollers were taking pleasure in the mild afternoon air and the green tips proffered shyly by trees and bushes. Summer was not so far away, Miremont told himself in a vain effort to lift his spirits.

This week at the Rue Mazarine they had been allotted Mme de Pompadour, to judge by the rococo gilding and the bed in the alcove. But Miremont had quickly become blind to these splendours when Max failed to appear. Nor had his apprehension been soothed when, realising the unwisdom of returning home if their subterfuge were to be maintained, he had arrived at Catherine's to be handed Max's cryptic note, apparently delivered by a street urchin (distrusting anyone in livery, Max had slipped out while madame was at lunch to bribe the saddler's apprentice in the colonnade). Miremont had been prey to the darkest thoughts when, in accordance with the note's instructions, he had entered the palace gardens.

His relief, like Max's, had been succeeded by fury. Perhaps he should not be surprised that Aline opened his letters—had he not suspected as much in the past?—but it enraged him nonetheless. He was appalled by the insult to Catherine and unamused by the irony that Max had only been released from incarceration when the carriage had arrived to take Aline on one of her so-called jaunts. But what angered him most was his wife's presumption.

"I shall tell her you have my permission to visit this mistress of yours—this fictional mistress…"

Max shot him a pained look.

"Forgive me, dear boy, of course she is. Anyway, I shall make it plain to Aline that what you do with your time is my business."

Max shook his head. "She has put her foot down. There will be a scene. Her suspicions may be alerted."

"But—? Darling boy, I can't bear…"

"We shall think of a way."

"But what?" Receiving no answer, Miremont sighed. "Well, at least I shall ask Boussec to get rid of that despicable footman."

"No. Tell Boussec to ensure all your letters go straight to Thomas. Wait till things die down." Max laid his hand discreetly upon Miremont's. "I shall come up with a plan, I promise, dear heart. Besides, we can't do anything much until after the ball."

After the ball. Miremont squeezed Max's fingers, then reluctantly let them go. Of course the boy was right. He would not challenge Aline or risk dismissing her minion: quite apart from the need for caution, there was the very real fear that a week of sobbing and sulking would blight Juliette's great occasion. He would do as he always did—crush his anger and give in.

CHAPTER TWENTY-NINE

The day of the ball dawned sunny and it would be pleasing to report that the Hôtel de Miremont awoke with joyful anticipation. But it is one thing to attend a ball and quite another to give it.

To the servants' hall such occasions bring limited blessings. True, for the distaff side and even for some footmen, they offer the chance to peek at celebrated ladies in their gowns and jewels, while fancy dress is an added attraction—it was rumoured Princess Zelenska would come as Aphrodite and the comte de Tarascon as a turbaned Turk. And, for a well-ordered house (if you credit Old Jouvert), there is also the satisfaction of knowing every task has been unobtrusively, unstintingly performed to perfection, delivering the triumph the mistress deserves.

However, the Hôtel de Miremont was no longer well-ordered. Extra duties stirred up old quarrels, while the additional staff imported to shift chairs, man the cloakrooms and attend to sundry tasks in the kitchens and pantries merely aggravated the discord by rushing about at cross-purposes and getting under everyone's feet; and that was not to mention the foreign artist's team of assistants hanging garlands everywhere you looked, shedding petals and leaves that would need to be swept up before they were ground in a slippery paste into the marble floors.

Yes, Mme Mercier had quite enough to contend with, marshalling her usual forces—one of the housemaids deputed to tend the flowers was already laid low by paroxysms of sneezing—without the secretary's insistence that his dancers, actors and musicians would all need somewhere to change into their costumes; not only that, but they and the stagehands and the two other orchestras would of course require suitable refreshment at different points during the evening, prompting Chef Quintivali to announce that his kitchens were too busy creating works of genius to feed saucisson to the rabble. But at least M. Fabien, although not all he should be, was polite and had warned Mme Mercier in advance; not so madame, who was wearing the housekeeper to rags with constant and contradictory instructions—when she was not bothering M. Boussec, that is, about the supplies of champagne or the order of precedence for going into supper.

Then there was the noise, which had been going on since yesterday. First there were the carts, horses whinnying, wheels crashing over the cobbles as they jammed both the servants' courtyard and the forecourt, unloading basket upon basket of provisions and timber in great quantities, and today bringing trees, too, in pots that left a trail of earth as they were dragged on trolleys through the crowded servants' passages.

But this was as nothing to the sawing and hammering in the inner courtyard. It had been hard to prevent junior servants pausing to gape at the scaffold rising to cover the central section of the guest wing (Georges, who should know better, had opined that, as the pièce de résistance, madame was to be guillotined during the fireworks); and, although the carpenters had completed the construction of the scaffolding and stage, this morning they were still hard at work covering the flower beds, while other workmen, balanced on ladders or leaning from upper windows to affix wires or hang festoons, added their banging and shouting to the general din.

Nor should it be said that suffering was confined to the servants' hall. The commotion tried the noble ladies' nerves and had driven Bébé to such a pitch of hysteria that he had comprehensively disgraced himself on madame's coverlet, after which Simon, commanded to take the animal for a lengthy walk, had dragged him to the servants' wing and shut him in the sluice room, where, amidst the general hullabaloo, his howling could scarcely be heard.

Milady Telford could count herself doubly afflicted, since the windows of her apartments, while not actually obscured by the scaffolding, were in close proximity: as she told madame in her most emollient tones, she was not one to complain, but the construction gave off inimical vibrations and she dared not predict the consequence for her health unless it were removed.

As for madame herself, had she not worries enough? The incompetence of the servants was hardly unexpected, but Worth, too, had brazenly ignored her instructions: she was to appear *en rustique* as Marie Antoinette at Le Hameau, but her milkmaid costume was positively drab; Bonnard had been sent to Bon Marché for ribbon to add extra bows. And now, to crown everything, for the second day running she had seen Dr Chevalier's carriage near the door to the princesse de Vaux's apartments. Armand, who had called there yesterday to apologise for the upheaval, claimed that, far from breathing her last, his cousin had a slight chill. But supposing the old parasite took a turn for the worse? Once the ball was underway she could be ignored, but for her to die on them this morning, or even this afternoon—oh, it would be too cruel...

*

All was silent for the moment. A wide bale of canvas was being winched up the scaffolding and everyone paused to look as it unfurled itself, fold by fold. Miremont, watching from his study window, had an oblique view that showed the men on the near side of the scaffold carefully guiding the folds to prevent them catching or tearing. Below, too, if he glanced in the opposite direction, he could see Max and his friend Levchenko, one tall and one diminutive figure, standing by the fountain, staring upwards; the winches stopped and Levchenko covered his eyes, but Max—Miremont felt a twinge of jealousy—patted his shoulder, saying something that made them both laugh, and at that instant the canvas resumed its progress. Then, at last, to the applause of the courtyard, it reached the top.

By the time Miremont had moved to the furthest window in his sitting room for a clearer view, the onlookers had returned to their work, Max had vanished and Levchenko was gesturing to the men on the scaffolding, now left, now right, until he was satisfied the canvas hung true. The backdrop was no surprise to Miremont—Max had shown him a sketch, in case he disapproved—but, as he surveyed the finished work, he was impressed by how cleverly it matched the building, not merely its proportions but the stone-carving of the pediments and the ashlars framing the windows. Altogether, the conceit was ingenious and its execution of a high order.

The fall of the House of Miremont. He smiled grimly. Had it not seemed in the past week that his wife was determined to bring that about? He had controlled his anger over last Wednesday with the greatest difficulty. Catherine, although she restricted her exchanges with Aline to the leaving of cards, was too illustrious to be omitted from tonight's invitation list and had promised to attend for his sake: thus it had been his embarrassing duty to warn her of the reception she might receive. Mercifully she had taken Aline's misapprehension as a tremendous joke, but his chagrin was scarcely diminished. And on top of this, three days ago, had come news from Boussec that had left him so furious he preferred not to speak of it, even to Max. Of course the matter would have to be dealt with, but since it promised the most disagreeable consequences, it too must wait until after the ball.

As it was, observing Aline's rising hysteria—this morning she had burst in upon him three times on one ridiculous pretext or another— he could not but fear anew that Julie's celebration stood in peril. But since nothing he could say would calm his wife, and since he abhorred further discussion of poor Arianne de Vaux's unlikely demise, Thomas was at present posted at his door of his apartments to inform madame that monsieur was suffering from dyspepsia and could not be disturbed.

In fact he had not touched the luncheon laid out in his sitting-room (a cold collation in view of the turmoil in the kitchen). It was not so much that he dreaded the ball: while his presence had too often been required at such occasions recently, this one by no means promised to be the worst. At least his duties were clearly defined. While Aline, as hostess, must stand at the head of the staircase receiving their guests and then generally officiate, he had two brief tasks to perform, to make the formal announcement of Julie's engagement and to take the most senior lady into supper—Boussec would tell him which. After supper, when Julie and Niversac had led off the dancing, he might steal a waltz with his daughter, but then he was free to seek sanctuary. The brocaded coat and waistcoat Max and Thomas had provided for him were not uncomfortable and he was not required to sport a queue: indeed, although he would feel a trifle ridiculous in breeches, this costume was a distinct improvement upon cardinal's robes. Added to which, there was the promise of seeing Max in breeches again.

All that remained was to pray Aline did nothing shaming; fortunately Clotilde was arriving early and could be deputed to soothe her. And then, by tomorrow, thank God, it would all be over. True, there was the unpleasantness to be gone through, but after that... As he stared out at the backdrop, Miremont focused on the little golden temple glowing beyond the ruins: it seemed to symbolise his future return to happiness. Yet he was torn.

Dear Lord, he longed for Max. Not Max the dutiful, efficient secretary, who so often nowadays wore his servant's face, but Max his lover. Desire was not diminished by incapacity—rather the reverse. Nor had the weekly two hours in which his inhibition was lifted salved his pain. Oh, he could praise the boy for his hard work, he could thank him for his sacrifice, he could even, so long as Thomas was not about, tell him he loved him. But he could not show it without dread of interruption. These days, he was almost grateful that the boy was frequently absent in the afternoons. For what were they to do? Miremont had long ago given up the struggle to work and, although he had tried to teach Max chess, neither could muster the required concentration. Instead, they sat like prisoners in his study, making desultory conversation, while his desire grew until it seemed a third presence in the room; often, in desperation, he would suggest taking the air, in the Luxembourg Gardens or even in the courtyard, where, although they could be observed, they could not be ambushed nor overheard above the play of the fountain.

He understood what the scene-painters' temple recalled: the Temple of Dionysus at Beauvallon, the summer nights when they had feasted on each other at leisure, when he would lie, exhausted, feeling the weight of the boy's leg indolently cast across his, smelling his sweat mingled with the scent of the honeysuckle, tasting him, astringent, on his lips.

Nor did he merely dwell upon their lovemaking. The riding, the swimming, the rivalry at the shooting gallery; the heated debates, the shared silences, the irrepressible laughter: it was not just desire that was constrained by their present situation but the very stuff of friendship, crushed by the fear he would forget to address the boy formally or a gesture of affection would be misjudged.

But soon, the backdrop's temple reminded him, they would be back at Beauvallon. Given that hope, he might endure even the loss of their Wednesdays. Although the weeks might stretch before them, it was after all not so very long now. The middle of June, if they were lucky.

Yet here Miremont was once again riven with guilt. For, while he loved Max, he also loved his daughter. And, in wishing for one, he was wishing away the other.

Why, after all, had these painful sacrifices been made? Not so that Aline might think herself the faubourg's leading hostess. They had all been for Julie, the daughter who had been kept from him for so long, in order that he could at last be a proper father to her. And had she not, his beautiful Juliette, amply rewarded him? Could he begrudge her the time she stole from his afternoons with Max? Dear child, with her teasing and her guileless affection—how could he not adore it when she threw her arms around his neck, how could he not be touched when she sought to widen her reading, just to please him, her old fossil of a father?

But that was her way, as he had told Max at Madame Tonton's. Of course he had watched Julie afterwards to see if Max's fantasy had any foundation, but it was as he had said: she made no difference between people: Raoul de Niversac, Max, Miss Pilkington—she was charming and open with everyone. Whereas he, himself—often, when he saw her taking delight in some new gown, or heard her laugh, or caught her innocent blue glance, he would feel the shame of his own life of deceit and know he did not deserve such a daughter.

And now, when he had scarcely found her, he was losing her again. Tonight, when she stood beside him, on Niversac's arm, and he made his brief speech announcing their engagement, this would be the first step, the first formal recognition that she was moving away from him. He liked and trusted Niversac; Niversac's mother and sisters, when he and Julie had met them, had struck him as kind and unpretentious, the sort of people who would welcome his darling into their midst and cherish her virtues; Julie was marrying a man she loved, who loved her and would ensure her future happiness: how could he, Miremont, regret any of this? And of course it was not as if he would never see her again: they would live in Paris during the winter, she would visit him every Sunday like Clotilde, sooner or later bringing her children to perch upon the old fossil's knee as she had done.

When he contemplated this, his eyes grew moist. Yet what did he expect? Would he want to be one of those fathers who held on grimly to their daughters, expecting them to minister to paternal senescence as they shrivelled in spinsterhood? He was not—he had no right to be—a tyrannical father. Children could not be denied their futures. Niversac would be Julie's life, as Max was his. The more reason not to count the days she remained to him.

Two aproned men were gingerly manoeuvring a harpsichord across the courtyard, followed by a straggle of musicians carrying their instruments. Up on the stage, beside the statue, a gentleman in a top hat was using his cane to demonstrate some sequence to the dancers, who were muffled in everyday jackets over their hose and practice skirts.

Now she had sent Pilkington away, Juliette was at liberty to stare out of her window as often as she pleased. However, since the focus of her interest was absent, the activities in the courtyard had quickly lost their allure. Instead, she was contemplating her engagement ring, which she would wear for the first time tonight.

A heart-shaped diamond, set within a larger heart of brilliants topped with a bow, the ring had originally belonged to Raoul de Niversac's paternal grandmother. It was quite pretty and of a good size: what a shame Manon de Merlincourt's mother had to stand on her principles, but at least Mme de Sainte-Foy was not as particular, so Mimi would be present to go green as a gooseberry.

Yet the jewel, having invoked this delightful picture, disobligingly summoned another: frumpy Mme de Niversac and her three dreary daughters. Thank goodness Juliette would be spared them tonight— some indisposition of the comtesse's kept them in the Dordogne. All the same, as she twisted the ring on her finger, she seemed to smell lavender bags and cobwebs. Oh, why did everyone set such store by hand-me-down jewellery? What was wrong with something new and fashionable?

Besides, the tradition was so unfair: as usual, the eldest got everything decent. That had been her thought this morning, as she had wondered what other jewellery to wear. Her own grandmother's second-best pearls? There were the Miremont diamonds, but they went to Clotilde, to pass to Freddie's wife—or so tradition decreed, although Maman still clung onto them. There were also sapphires, which a younger daughter might hope for; they would certainly suit Juliette's blue eyes and rose-petal complexion, but Maman had kept possession of those too, although she never wore them.

But then, just as Juliette was looking into her glass and frowning at the pearls, Pilkington had announced that Papa was in her boudoir. With a package from Boucheron.

Seven flowers, the centres pink diamonds, the petals brilliants, on a linked chain of diamond leaves, with delicate swags of brilliants suspended between the blossoms. What a surprise—the more so that Papa had thought of it himself, without her having to wheedle it out of him; perhaps he at last understood what was owing to her. Not only was the necklace new—she, and only she, would wear it—but it was quite soigné, considering what a fogey he was, and there was a frame to adapt it as a tiara if she fancied, as well as earrings to match. So it was not difficult to throw her arms around his neck and kiss him on both cheeks: she was quite touched to see how embarrassed he was, her stiff old Papa, by his pleasure at her pleasure.

Afterwards she realised he deserved his embarrassment: this expensive present would absolve him of his eagerness to get her off his hands. And anyway a choker would have been far more fashionable. But she must grant pink diamonds were better than sapphires, since they suited her costume to perfection; its wide, ruched, white silk skirt was decorated between the ruching with trails of pink rosebuds, with a garland of the same flowers crossing the bodice from neck to waist. She would wear the necklace at her throat and more pink roses in her hair, held in place with a diamond-studded comb. Pilkington and Drouet had seen her in the gown and proclaimed that she would outshine everyone. And so she would. No one would look twice at Maman, it would be her triumph, hers alone. A certain person would surely not be too busy to notice.

Strains of music drifting up from the courtyard announced the ballet rehearsal had begun. The dancers had cast off their jackets, the top-hatted gentleman was watching from beside the fountain and—yes, there, standing next to that ugly little artist, there he was. M. Fabien—Max—Maxime. She remained at her window until, having inspected the clumps of trees, he and the little man walked back into the house.

Goodness, there was still an age to wait before Drouet could dress her hair, let alone fit her into her costume. Dearest Maxime. He might not dance, but he should not fear, she would find a way they could be together. Going into her bedroom, she took from beneath her pillows the book he had given her and pressed it to her lips.

CHAPTER THIRTY

The fireworks were over and the first guests were taking their departure, relieving the crush on the dance floor and the press of carriages in the forecourt and neighbouring streets. It was already cooler; at one point the heat in the ballroom had been such that two young ladies had fainted, while the all-pervading scent of the flowers, which had become more oppressive throughout the day, had prevailed over the competing stench of sweat and tallow to thicken the air like glue. But, on the whole, Max could tell himself things had gone well.

The ballet had come off satisfactorily, despite the ballerina cast as Terpsichore falling ill and the harpsichord's proving inaudible to all but the front rows of chairs: the dancers, at least, could follow the music and the stand-in Terpsichore had performed admirably. Two of the platforms supporting the trees were threatening collapse but, now Georges and he had shifted some of the planters to redistribute the weight, they would probably hold out until the guests were gone. It had not rained. And there had been only one small fire, when a taper had been knocked into the tent in the supper room; and that, by the time he arrived, heart pounding, had already been put out by quick-thinking guests.

Of the ball itself, he had seen very little—to avoid mademoiselle, he had kept himself as much as possible behind the scenes, using the servants' passages to come and go and eating with the performers in the servants' hall. However, on brief excursions to the piano nobile, he had been driven to observe that eighteenth-century gowns with their wide padded skirts did little to ease the congestion in the ballroom; and as to the gentlemen, he smiled at his own resentful donning of stockings and breeches, for quite a number of them looked as if they might be in livery, and some had even powdered their hair—the real footmen were mainly distinguishable by their much-loathed yellow cutaway coats.

True, there was a sprinkling of Pierrots, a Harlequin or two and a black-robed Dottore clutching his beaked mask, and Max had spotted Achille de Tarascon, turbaned as promised, with his silky beard waxed into a fork. But the sensation of the evening, word had it, was not M. le comte, nor Princess Zelenska in her clinging Grecian drapery, but the duchesse de Claireville, for she too was in breeches: as commedia dell'arte's young gallant, Mezzetin, from her short cloak to the soft beret worn at a dashing angle over her vivid red hair, she was attired in old-rose crushed velvet, set off by Mezzetin's traditional white ruff and the plum-coloured stockings that revealed her slim but well-turned calves for all to see. Certainly no one would mistake her for a footman: the duc de la Marne was heard to exclaim: "By God, she was the most elegant woman in Paris when I was a boy and there's still no touching her!" No wonder Mme de Miremont, already pink and perspiring as she had greeted her guests, had been crimson down to the line of her décolletage the last time Max had seen her. Of mademoiselle, he was pleased to say, he had caught only the occasional glimpse, as a flash of white on the dance floor or surrounded by admirers.

Less than two hours to go. As Max returned from the servants' courtyard, where he had tipped the firework master and his firing team, he felt suddenly exhausted. Since he had nothing immediate to do, he would seek out Armand, who was ensconced in the smoking room with Gervaise de la Marne and old General Darrioux.

Unable to bear the stifling servants' passages again, he decided it would be safe by now to cross the central courtyard and go in through the library doors, taking the main staircase to the piano nobile, but turning right to avoid the ballroom. In the library he paused to retie his stock and discard his queue. Then he passed through the anteroom into the foyer—where at once he ran into Simon.

"Ah, Monsieur Fabien. I wondered if you might be in the library. I have searched everywhere for you. You are wanted in the picture gallery."

If Simon himself were not enough to rouse suspicion, this summons to the gallery certainly was: it was not one of the rooms given over to the ball and Max was under the impression Boussec had locked it.

"Monsieur requires me urgently. Please attend to whatever it is yourself."

But he could already see a pink-and-white figure hovering in the gallery's doorway. Perhaps she even called out to him, but, since there were two groups of guests in the foyer waiting for their carriages, as well as Boussec at the main doors, she was prevented from raising her voice. Max's instinct was to take the servants' door under the stairs, where she could not follow; however, since she stood not far from it, he would be forced to acknowledge her presence. Instead, he headed for the staircase, observing as he turned into the first stair that, damn her, she was pursuing him. Climbing as fast as he could without appearing to run, and consoled by the thought that she was impeded by her skirts, he was nevertheless compelled to flatten himself against the wall to accommodate two ladies descending to the cloakroom. No matter, they would hold mademoiselle back too.

Yet, as he reached the top stair, he could sense she was still behind him. Would she so far forget her dignity as to chase him all the way to the smoking room? Then he was blessed with a stroke of luck. There on the landing, coming out of the Music Room, was old M. de Cressy, in black and a periwig like a magistrate, with a slender boy on his arm. But no—although Max knew the *succès fou* of the evening only by report, there was no mistaking that hennaed hair beneath the beret, or those decisive features, still handsome despite the unkind failure of powder and rouge to veil their wrinkles.

"So there you are, wicked boy. Why have you been hiding from me all evening?"

Max gave a little bow to Mme la duchesse and then to M. de Cressy. He could feel the presence of mademoiselle somewhere behind him and was seized by an idea. "Forgive me, monsieur," he said to M. de Cressy, "but I should like to take the liberty—madame, would you honour me with the next dance, if it is not promised?"

M. de Cressy, who, even if he failed to recall that Max had once been his cousin's footman, stood very much on his dignity, looked not in the least forgiving. Mme de Claireville also hesitated. But then she smiled. "We were on the point of leaving. But I suppose, now you have deigned to make an appearance, I should be ungracious to refuse you."

The orchestra was playing a waltz as he led her through to the ballroom. Placing his hand on her bony shoulder blade, feeling her thin arm upon his, he thought this was not so different from partnering some skinny grocer's boy at the Monkey. But smelling, even above the toxic aroma of the flowers, the musk she wore, the scent that had lingered in every room she passed through in the Hôtel de Claireville, he was also bound to recall how he had held her when they were lovers. Her frailty was deceptive: he smiled as he remembered the skills that sinewy little body had taught him. Although her costume for this evening must have been chosen out of mischief, it suited her, flattered her unfashionably small breasts and slender hips; she was the one woman in the faubourg who could carry it off, and how well she knew it.

"What are you smiling at, you rascal?"

"I hear you have scored another well-deserved triumph."

She laughed. "I could not outdo our hostess. Although, when Marie Antoinette dallied in the fields with her milking stool, did she wear every single one of her diamonds?"

She had not entirely foresworn diamonds herself: above the ruff, her ears glittered discreetly. He grinned. "I should say you were revenged."

"Oh, I do not in the least mind being thought Armand's Madame de Montespan. On the contrary, I am honoured. If I must take revenge on anyone, it is you, stupid boy."

"Me?"

"Deserving young women, indeed? I thought you were the past master when it came to lies. And then to expect Constant de Sauvigny to bear you out! Ah well—" she feigned a tragic look "—I shall no doubt survive Aline's displeasure, much as I have for the last twenty-five years. But need you subject me to the opprobrium of the entire family? Even Armand's little princess was scowling at me just now."

"Mademoiselle Juliette? Scowling?" Max endeavoured to sound innocent.

"I could see her standing behind you when we were talking on the landing and she looked positively venomous. There you are, she is doing it again. You will see for yourself if you turn us a little."

Out of the corner of his eye, Max glimpsed the pink-and-white gown. Far from ceasing her pursuit, mademoiselle had found poor Niversac and hauled him onto the dance floor. Indeed, now there were fewer dancers, the pair were only separated from Max and Mme de Claireville by one other couple. Soon they would be waltzing side by side.

"There, you see? Decidedly that is a scowl."

Max could not disagree that mademoiselle was glaring balefully over Niversac's right shoulder.

"Although, do you know," said Mme de Claireville, "I do not think it is me she is scowling at."

As Max span them round and whirled them off to the far end of the ballroom, she gave him a cautionary look. "Have you been up to your tricks again, you deplorable boy? Despite your promise?"

"What tricks? No, of course not."

"Flirting with poor Armand's little rosebud?"

"Madame, I can assure you, I would rather... It is a misunderstanding, that is all."

"A misunderstanding, eh?"

"I told her..." Max sighed. "I told her I couldn't dance."

"Well, as you have stepped on my toe twice in the last two minutes that is not, strictly speaking, a falsehood."

"Forgive me."

"For my ruined slippers, yes. But for the rest—do I take it, you wretch, that you asked me to dance in order to offend Princess Rosebud?"

"No! No, madame, I asked you to dance because it would give me pleasure." But while this was true—in part, at least—she seemed far from mollified; furthermore he had once more caught sight of the rosebud gown gliding in rapid circles towards them. "Although I am— you could say, in something of a difficulty... Do you think perhaps we might take the air for a moment?"

It had proved a clear night; a hint of gunpowder from the fireworks still spiced the light breeze—by no means disagreeable after the suffocating atmosphere within. All the same, it was cold. Although the rows of lanterns appeared magically to float in the darkness and even the forests looked almost convincing, only a few hardy guests remained in the courtyard, mostly clustered around the braziers. Max was concerned for Mme de Claireville, but she laughed.

"I have been abominably hot all night—at last I see why you gentlemen end up in such a lather. What I would have given for bare arms and a daring décolletage! But now—" she took his arm and they began to walk "—you will be so good as to explain yourself, my boy."

CHAPTER THIRTY-ONE

"How dare you! How dare you lie to me! How dare you refuse to dance with me, when you were quite able to dance with that horrid old cat, who is not only Papa's mistress, but who ruined my entire ball by making an exhibition of herself like some vulgar actress in a low cabaret—and I don't care if she is a duchess! How could you treat me like this? Can I help it that Papa and Maman are forcing me to marry Monsieur de Niversac? How dare you punish me, when it is not my fault! I hate you, do you hear? I hate you and your stupid honour. I hate you, I hate you and I never wish to speak to you or see your face again!"

The morning after the ball had not been quiet, for the workmen were in the courtyard demolishing all they had built the previous day; it had been peaceful, however. Mme de Miremont was confined to bed with nervous prostration, brought on in part by Catherine de Claireville's indecent display but in the main by Lord Jack, who, not content with ignoring her all evening, had danced nearly every dance with Princess Zelenska; milady Telford, out of favour in consequence, was skulking in the guest wing; and Mlle Juliette, apparently, was sleeping late to recover from the night's excitements.

As Miremont and Max had ridden out to the Champs-Élysées, contentedly alone, each had found private cause to welcome the ladies' absence. Miremont, having earmarked this morning for dealing with 'the unpleasantness', had not been sorry to postpone it until tomorrow. Max had pondered Mlle Juliette's fatigue. Miss Pilkington had reported that mademoiselle had retired to her apartments for the rest of the day, putting off all callers, even M. de Niversac. Was this a good sign? Surely it could not be bad?

It had been humiliating to relate his predicament to Mme de Claireville: once again he had caught himself wondering if the delusion were his and not mademoiselle's, for he struggled to explain his inability to extricate himself; there were the limitations of his situation to consider, as well as Armand's feelings, but even so… However, contrary to his expectation, Mme de Claireville had not mocked him; rather, she had patted his arm with a sigh.

"As I have said before, poor Armand is not clever. And I fancy he longs to believe something good has resulted from his miserable marriage. But his little princess is Aline's daughter. It is Sestrès blood. Look at the brother. And Eugène de Sestrès was as vile an old curmudgeon as you could wish to meet. It is not you who are mad, silly boy. They are all fit for the asylum, every one of them."

He had been grateful for her understanding, but when she had offered to speak to Armand his pride had recoiled and he had sworn her to secrecy. In any case, there might be no need. Perhaps his calculated insult would have the desired effect. Yet, if proclaiming her engagement to the whole of Paris had not deterred the wretched girl, who could tell? Still, he could comfort himself that the library was safe, if only for today.

He had not been there above ten minutes when the doors had been flung open. In her wrapper with her hair flying wildly about her shoulders, red-eyed, her face contorted, she had presented an extraordinary vision: gone was Mlle Rosebud; rather, she had put Max in mind of an irate gargoyle. Words had poured from her, leaving no pause in which he might have defended himself, had he cared to. Then, with a final "I hate you!", she had vanished.

He stood, mildly stunned. But only for a moment. He reached for his cigarette case and a celebratory Muratti.

Next morning the only reminder of the ball was the crushed topiary in the flower beds. Madame was still laid low, Lady Telford continued unforgiven and mademoiselle, although recovered according to Miss Pilkington, had duty letters to write and would take luncheon in her boudoir. Miremont and Max again rode out alone and afterwards, since fencing had resumed, they joined Captain Horthy and Roland de Sauvigny in the ballroom.

This calm lasted until half an hour after luncheon when, well-nigh simultaneously, two incidents occurred. Max, visiting the library to collect a book Miremont needed, found a note on his worktable. And, in the east wing, an outraged scream rent the air.

"Don't you struggle with me, you little hussy! You'll tell your father what you have done. And you, you repulsive creature, out of my way! I know monsieur is in, I am his wife, your mistress, what do I care if he is not to be disturbed? This is his fault for spoiling her. After all I have suffered during the last few weeks, the toil, the worry, the sick headaches, the palpitations, just so she, the ungrateful minx, can wear Worth, and bat her eyes and think herself the greatest beauty that ever dazzled Society—"

Alerted by the din, Miremont had come out of his study to find a distasteful spectacle. Aline, in a tea gown and other assorted draperies, by the look of them hastily donned, had Julie by the wrist and was elbowing poor Thomas aside as she dragged the girl over his threshold.

"Madame!" Though Miremont raised his voice until he was shouting, it took him several attempts before he was heard. "Let go of Juliette, this instant!"

"If you knew what—"

"Let her go!"

After much prevarication, Aline obeyed. Julie immediately stepped away from her mother, but, although she shot her an angry look and was massaging her wrist, otherwise, Miremont noted as he glanced at her solicitously, she seemed remarkably composed.

"She is a grown woman now, not a schoolgirl."

"Oh, is she? I can see no sign of it. And neither will you when you hear what she has done."

"Well, what has she done, for you to treat her so disgracefully?"

"Send that brute away."

Miremont nodded to Thomas. The moment the door had closed on the valet, both Aline and Julie opened their mouths to speak. Aline got in first.

"She has jilted Niversac, that's what. An only son, with a title dating back to Louis XIV, and two estates and a fortune in stocks and mines in Canada. After the months I spent, poring over lists, cultivating acquaintance, to find her the most eligible man in Paris, and then she—"

"Madame, please be quiet!"

"She has disgraced us. Before everyone. What am I to say to Hélène de Corvignac and Amélie de la Rochefontaine? I shall never be able to hold my head up again—"

"Be *silent!*" Miremont, still scarcely understanding what he heard, turned to his daughter. Her composure did not waver.

"I have broken off my engagement, Papa."

"But you—my darling girl, why?"

"I do not wish to marry Monsieur de Niversac."

"There, you see. She has shamed us all but she stands there, the bare-faced hussy, without even the grace to say sorry!"

"Madame!"

"She is her father's daughter, she cares for nobody's feelings but her own."

"Madame!"

"And where is she to find another suitor, may I ask, before the Season is over? Where is she to live if she does not marry? Not under my roof, she may be certain of that—"

"*Madame!*"

Yet Miremont raised his voice in vain: only when, red in the face and short of breath, Aline seemed to have exhausted herself, was he able to suggest he talk to poor Julie alone. This met with the contempt he might have predicted, but eventually, pressing a hand to her temples, his wife gave a martyred sigh. "Oh, do as you please. My head is on fire. She will be my death!"

Miremont led his daughter over to a sofa and settled beside her. Despite his shock at her announcement, he was resolved to be gentle, the more so because, now her mother had left, her composure, which had no doubt been hard-won, had all at once deserted her and two tears, perfect as tiny crystals, shone on her lower lids. He drew his handkerchief from his sleeve and she accepted it with watery gratitude.

As he watched her dabbing at the two clear rivulets that, like dew, moistened rather than stained her cheeks, he sought to fathom their cause. Two days ago she had been radiantly happy. Had she and Niversac had a quarrel? Had Aline said something unfortunate? Or perhaps the poor girl was still fatigued, perhaps the world seemed flat after the ball's vertiginous peak.

"Dearest child," he said, clasping the little hand not occupied with the handkerchief, "I know marriage is a big step. And I realise your mother and I have not—we are perhaps not a shining example. But that should not make you afraid. Most marriages—well, it is natural to have the occasional falling-out…"

He paused but, since she did not take him up on this, he was forced to plough on. "But most couples, even if they have differences from time to time, manage to live in harmony. Think of—" here he was about to cite the example of Léonore and Constant, who had loved each other deeply, despite his string of mistresses, but he realised that Julie would not remember his sister, whom she had scarcely met and who had died when she was twelve "—think of Clotilde and Raymond. They have Freddie and little Agathe and are very happy together."

She surprised him by smiling. "But you don't care for Raymond, Papa."

"I admit he and I share few interests. But he is a decent fellow for all that, and good to your sister. As Niversac will be good to you, even if you do not always—"

"Oh, I have not quarrelled with Monsieur de Niversac, Papa." She returned his handkerchief. "I simply do not wish to marry him."

There was no trace of the tears now, her eyes were bright, her tone matter-of-fact, and, in the tilt of that delicate dimpled chin of hers, he saw a determination he found thoroughly disconcerting. "But, my darling girl—this is not something—two days after the announcement—this is a decision that requires thought. Who knows but that tomorrow you—"

"I do know, Papa. I have already written and sent back his ring. My letter was delivered to him this morning."

Miremont stared at her, horrified. "But—my dear—"

"I do not love him."

"But you seemed so happy together. And there is no doubt he loves you—"

"I tried to love him, darling Papa, for your sake, because you wished it. But I find I cannot. And you said I ought not to marry without love."

"Well—perhaps I did. But nevertheless—"

"I know he is a good match. But you yourself said that is not everything."

"I—I may have done. And of course it is not. All the same, I—"

"You said you did not mind whom I married so long as I was in love with him. And he was someone you liked."

"Did I?"

"If I loved him and he loved me and you thought well of him, you would be happy no matter who he was. Even if he swept the streets."

"I definitely never—"

"Well, not a street-sweeper, naturally. But someone who was not of rank."

She might, of course, be teasing Miremont in her usual way. But, throughout this last exchange, there had been an intensity to her brightness that, after the shock of her jilting poor Niversac, was bound to alert his suspicions. Even before she had raised the matter of rank, he had remembered his argument with Max. Dear God no, it could not be possible!

He endeavoured to keep his voice even as he asked: "And is there such a man?"

"Oh Papa!" Though she blushed prettily, she did not avoid his eyes as she spoke. "When there is, my dear darling father, you shall be the first one I tell."

Once she had disentangled her arms from his neck and left him, he sat immobilised by conflicting bewilderment and rage. It grieved him that his beautiful daughter should throw away her future; it perplexed him that he had not seen she was unhappy; yet the conviction also grew that he was being deceived. If she had doubted, if she had hesitated—but no, her certainty was absolute. There had even been in her parting smile a hint of—what, exactly?—triumph? So who could he be, this man without rank she favoured over poor ill-used Niversac? And who was the deceiver? Surely not his innocent affectionate daughter. Whereas Max—

But here, despite his fury, he again recalled their quarrel at Madame Tonton's. Had he been wrong to brush aside the boy's warning? He remembered how Max had greeted his accusations with genuine incredulity. Yet this could have been a blind. Except that he did not believe Max, whatever his past failings, would stoop to these depths of betrayal. But then neither could he believe it of his beloved daughter. How was he to accept that the two people he loved more than life had deceived him utterly? And if not both, one or the other. He no longer knew what to believe.

The envelope on Max's worktable was sealed with a Miremont wafer and inscribed with his name in a bold but childish hand that he took for madame's—but only at first glance. His heart was already sinking as he tore it open.

> 'My darling Valiant Knight,
> Your Fair Lady forgives you. You were harsh, but she understands now that you were cruel to be kind. Fear not, you shall have the reward you long for. Wait and see.
> Your ever-loving Fair One.'

Max's disbelief gave way to despair, then rage. Cursing, he tore the note into shreds and consigned it to the fire.

It took him but a moment to realise his mistake. Even if it were sickening twaddle and mentioned no names, it was in her hand; it still proved he was not being fanciful. And of that he must urgently convince Armand. For it was clear that, whatever he, Max, did, she would never give up, he would never be free of her.

Alas, though he rushed to the grate and seized the tongs, the paper had caught and all he gleaned for his efforts were a few singed scraps. There was the envelope, of course, but that, since the missive had undoubtedly been delivered by a servant, was addressed, with due propriety, to 'M. Fabien'. He rose, brushing the ash from his trousers. Yes, he had been foolish to act in passion, but the note was proof, to himself at least, that he could no longer afford to hold back: if the old boy's sensibilities were injured, then so be it.

Seizing the book Armand had wanted, he strode upstairs. However, the entrance to the old boy's apartments was barred by Thomas, who glared at him and shook his head. And, indeed, through the stout double doors, some sort of fracas was audible—he could hear both Armand and madame shouting. Poor old boy, he thought, what now? But when he raised his eyebrows, Thomas' glare only grew more ferocious.

Ah well, whatever it was, it would probably be over in ten minutes or so, when Armand had brought himself to concede defeat. There was little point in Max going upstairs to his room, he might as well return to the library.

That, as he was afterwards to reflect, was his second mistake—by no means as stupid as destroying the note, as events were to transpire, but still foolish. For he had just glanced at the clock and concluded that ample time had elapsed to permit a second foray upstairs, when the library doors opened.

"Darling Maxime!"

She was at his worktable in a whirl of skirts almost before he could rise to his feet and he feared for one dreadful moment she would fling herself into his arms. But instead she let forth a breathless torrent of words.

"My dearest, I cannot stay more than a minute, Maman is in a fury and will hunt me down, but I wanted you to know that I have spoken to Papa and while he was a little put out at first—you know what a stickler he is for convention—I know he will come round—"

"Mademoiselle!" Max could make no sense of what she was saying, in fact was barely listening. "This must stop. This minute!"

"Juliette, dearest—you may call me Juliette now. And there is no need to look so stern. It has stopped. Did you not get my letter?"

"Yes, and I did what any sane man would do—I tore it up."

"Oh, my darling, how like you, always thinking of my reputation. But there is no need now. I have done as you wished."

"Mademoiselle, what I wish is—"

"I am no longer engaged to Raoul de Niversac."

This struck Max dumb.

"Of course I did not mention you to Papa by name in case we need to elope. But I think he may suspect. If he says something, you must tell him how much we love each other and then I can do the rest—I shall wind him round my little finger, as always. And now—I know you long to take me in your arms and I long for it too—but I must go."

"In heaven's name, will you please—"

"Just try to be patient, my darling. *À bientôt!*"

She blew him a kiss as she left. There was no point in shouting after her. She did not heed what he said or even his tone of voice. Elope? Mme de Claireville was right: the wretched girl was stark mad. With a groan, he slumped into his chair.

Scarcely five minutes had elapsed when the doors flew open once more. Max started, but was relieved to see Armand—until he read his face.

"Is this your doing? Do you know what my daughter has—?"

"Please, Armand—"

"So you do know. She has done your bidding."

"Dear God, no! She told me moments ago—"

"I did not want to believe it, I wanted to think my first instincts were wrong. But I see I should have—"

"For pity's sake! Listen to me!" Max had risen from his chair and was on the point of gripping Armand by the shoulders when he was arrested by a loud cough: Georges was standing in the open doorway.

"Monsieur le marquis de Niversac has called, monsieur, and wishes to see you."

Armand turned, startled.

"Shall I say you are not at home?"

"No—no, obviously I must… Please show Monsieur le marquis into my study and say… say I shall be with him directly."

Dread of facing Niversac had thrown Armand off balance. Directly Georges had departed, tactfully closing the doors, Max seized his chance.

"Armand, you must listen. You declined to listen before but you cannot refuse to hear me now. It is absolutely imperative that I go to Beauvallon. I know you worship your daughter but she has no grounds,

I swear to you, no grounds whatsoever, for this—this hallucination of hers. Please, dear heart—you may still save the situation, if I am no longer here to—"

But he was silenced by the doors being thrown open again.

"Forgive me for interrupting, monsieur," said Simon, "but, as you were not in your apartments, madame sent me to find you. She requires to speak to you immediately."

This momentarily rendered the old boy incoherent. Max, however, retained his presence of mind. "Perhaps," he said, addressing Armand, "you would prefer to discuss this Beauvallon business later?"

"N—no, no. You—whatever your name is—Simon—you will tell madame an urgent matter has arisen in the country—and—and I shall be with her once I have decided what steps to take."

"But, monsieur—"

"Is that understood?"

This time Max scarcely waited for the doors to close. "Armand, now we have our excuse. I can catch an early train tomorrow. Believe me, it is the only…"

But the old boy was shaking his head. "It is no good."

"Damn you, then I'll go anyway!"

"Aline. She will not give up, she is doubtless on her way here this minute. And poor Niversac is upstairs. Dear God, held at bay in my own house!"

"Then—quickly!" Max unlatched the French windows onto the courtyard.

To escape Maman, Juliette had been forced to lock herself in her bedroom and install Pilkington in her boudoir to guard the door. And now, according to Drouet, M. de Niversac had arrived, so that she was even more of a prisoner. But, when she saw the two figures walk out into the courtyard, her heart leapt.

Her brave, true knight! How touching that, having gallantly destroyed her letter, he had saved the envelope: it had been there on his table—he must have been gazing at it, postponing the moment he must hide it in his breast pocket, next to his heart. And then, how he had looked at her—wild, even despairing, when she had told him he must wait to cover her throat with kisses. Yet even so, she had feared those ridiculous scruples of his: perhaps the duty he claimed he owed Papa would make him hesitate to speak.

But no, here he was, her hero, charging into battle. It was true that, as they walked round the fountain, their voices were drowned by the splashing water; nor, when the circle took them to the opposite side of the courtyard, could she always see their faces: all the same, the set of their shoulders and their gestures spoke volumes, she could tell they were arguing, Maxime with great passion. She watched, one hand to her throat, as they went round and round; and, gradually, though she hardly dared believe it, her papa's resistance seemed to abate, their manner grew calmer, their circles slower, like a wheel anticipating its final revolution. When at last that came, it left them to the right of the fountain, near the library doors, standing in profile, facing each other. Then Papa did a strange thing. He did it very quickly and the conclusion of the gesture was partly hidden by his lapel, but she was certain she saw it. He took Maxime's hand and laid it over his heart.

She was dizzy with joy as she watched them vanish into the library. Papa had given his blessing! Now she had only to wait until her conquering hero came to her.

CHAPTER THIRTY-TWO

Max had taken supper in his room and ideally he would also have avoided the library; yet, if he were packing for what might be a longish stay in the country, there were books and papers he needed. The gas had been extinguished, the shutters were closed and the only light he allowed himself was a single dimmed lamp, but nevertheless he was on edge, working as rapidly and silently as a burglar and escaping discovery with as much relief. After that, there was only the second-floor landing to be dared. His guard relaxed as he climbed the west-wing stairs to the third floor: even though the light beneath his door was unexpected, it did not alarm him—Armand, in spite of all that was on his mind, must have been persuaded by tomorrow's parting to throw discretion aside. Max was smiling, already framing affectionate words, as he turned the doorknob.

The words died. She stood in the centre of his room as if she had been pacing the floorboards, her arms folded angrily across her bosom.

"What in heaven's name—? Mademoiselle, you should not be here. You must leave immediately."

"Tell me, do you do everything my papa orders you to do? Are you truly so spineless?"

Max had entered the room no further than would enable him to put down his books and lamp. He was careful not to close the door. "Mademoiselle, you compromise yourself every minute you remain here. Please go."

"I thought you had won Papa over, I waited and waited for you to come to me. Even when you were not at supper and Papa refused so much as to look at me, I still hoped—Maman was absent too, perhaps you had fallen into her clutches, perhaps Papa was vexed on account of explaining to Monsieur de Niversac. And then, when Lady Telford asked where you were, and Papa said something about a fire at Beauvallon, and you were to go there first thing tomorrow—it was all I could do not to faint away. I was so certain when I watched you from my window, I thought I had seen Papa give you his blessing—"

Shit! Max had hoped the old boy's impulsiveness had gone unobserved.

"—but no, he was blessing you for being obedient, for letting him banish you—"

Thank God she had misinterpreted it, as she did everything else.

"—and now I come up here and what do I find?" Tearfully she gestured at his open valise and the clothes laid out on the bed for packing. "You are prepared, at one word from him, to sneak away, forget everything between us."

"Mademoiselle, there is nothing between us. Now—I repeat— please leave."

"What has Papa done to deserve this obedience? Does he treat you well? Look at this mean little room, there is hardly any furniture, only one tawdry picture on the walls—" the sweep of her hand took in the Manet "—and that is not even finished. He makes you live like a servant, he keeps you slaving all day over his boring books—"

"Mademoiselle, I will not—" But such anger was dangerous, Max pulled himself up. "Your father has given me no orders. I am going to Beauvallon at my own request."

She stared at him. But to his dismay her face, instead of crumpling, suddenly brightened, as though with understanding. "Oh, my darling, forgive me. How could I forget your devotion to honour? Pardon your Fair Lady, please, for being angry. It is noble of you to defend Papa— but you must see there are limits. If you do not betray your duty to Papa, you will betray our love?"

She had come closer, would have seized his hand if he had not moved aside.

"I do not love you."

Yet she seemed not to hear. "Anyway, now I think of it, Papa's sending you to Beauvallon is all to the good, it makes everything easier. Once you arrive at the station, you must wait for me. I shall get Drouet to pack first thing, then pretend I am going out on an errand with Pilkington—she will lie for me, she is utterly devoted—but of course I shall take the carriage to the station and meet you under the clock—is there a clock at the Gare de Rungis?—well no matter, we will meet and take a hansom to the Gare du Nord or the Gare Montparnasse, whatever you decide, and—"

"No! I do not—"

"Oh, I know you have no money, but I have a little and we can sell my jewellery. And as for Papa, he will not disown me, he will soon relent, he will find you a post in the civil service—" she tried to take his hand again "—and you, my clever darling, will rise to the top and gain honours, and we shall be received everywhere and live quite comfortably."

He tore his hand from her grasp. "No! Must I say it again? I do not love you, mademoiselle. I do not love you and I have never loved you. Now—please—you must leave."

She was silent at last. She surveyed him with a look of complete astonishment. "No. That is not true."

Recalling his obligation to Armand, he endeavoured to speak more gently. "I am afraid it is."

"But—no—how can that be? You have always loved me, you loved me from the first moment you saw me. You cannot deny it—I feel it, I see it, in your touch, your smile, in the way you hardly dare look at me. I breathe in your longing every time I kiss the beloved talisman you gave me, I tremble at the power of it whenever you enter the room. I know you suffered when I was engaged to another, but you never stopped loving me. I am your Fair One and you are my Valiant—"

"Please! Mademoiselle! If I have ever done or said anything to encourage you in this belief, then I am truly sorry for it. Whatever it was, it was entirely unintentional."

"B—but…" She stared as if he had spoken in some foreign tongue. "But I do not understand. Maxime darling, have you decided to stop loving me?"

"I repeat, I have never—"

"You cannot decide. There are two of us. We love each other."

"Mademoiselle—"

"You cannot just decide to stop. I have not stopped loving you."

"Mademoiselle, this is—"

"You made me love you. You must love me."

The certainty with which she said this chilled Max. All trace of Princess Rosebud was gone: a cold, pale determination sharpened her chin and narrowed her eyes, willing him into submission. Of course, she was quite mad and the situation was farcical. But just for an instant, for all his masculine advantages of height and strength, he shivered, as if he had thrust his hand into potpourri and met teeth.

There was only one thing he could do—fool that he was, he should have done it sooner. But as he turned towards the door, she caught up with him and barred his way.

"You cannot leave me!"

"Mademoiselle, if you will not go, I must."

"You cannot leave me. You love me. You know you love me."

She clung to his arms. He shook her off. She hurled herself at him and began to pound his chest with her fists.

"How dare you deny it! You must love me! You must! I gave up

Raoul de Niversac for you! You promised to love me forever! You promised we should elope! You must love me! You cannot leave me! You promised! You promised!"

His instinct was to catch her wrists and hold them fast to her sides but he managed to remember she was the old boy's daughter. He stood, unresisting, as she punched and pummelled him. At last her shrieks gave way to sobs and she slid slowly to the floor, clutching at his clothes in her descent and finally locking her arms around his calves.

Carefully, and despite her howls of protest, he detached her fingers and stepped free. He looked down at the heaving, wailing bundle at his feet. He loathed her all the more because she had forced him to be brutal; yet pity made him wonder if he should try to raise her. Thinking better of it, he reached for the lamp. Although he half-expected her screams to have roused the household—they must surely have been audible below, in Armand's quarters—the landing remained dark and quiet. He set out to fetch Miss Pilkington.

Thank God, M. de M had missed the commotion. Consumed with anxiety about his daughter, he had gone for a walk after dinner and had ended by calling upon Dr Gérard. He appeared in Max's room shortly after Max had felt able to return to it himself—not knowing how long Miss Pilkington's errand of mercy might take, he had retired for an hour to the library, where he had struggled to rid himself of his anger and repugnance and, above all, any thought of the thing, the creature, the bolus of claws, hair and teeth that, for a split second, had snarled at him from mademoiselle's baby-blue eyes.

At least Armand seemed easier in his mind; perhaps he had confided in Gérard. At any rate, he had convinced himself his daughter was suffering from a missish infatuation; once Max was gone, she would soon be reconciled with Niversac, who still loved her and would take her back.

"Three weeks, darling boy, two if we are lucky. I shall be wretched without you, but we must pray it works the cure."

Max did not mention mademoiselle's visit: quite apart from wishing to spare Armand's feelings, his only desire now was to bury the incident, not to be forced, yet again, to recount his own powerlessness, still less to confess that unmanly instant of fear. As they lay fully dressed and chastely in each other's arms, they talked of Beauvallon. Yet M. de M sensed his disquiet. Attributing it to their parting, he held Max closer.

"Never forget, dear boy, how much I love you."

Love? It was not a word Max wished to hear for the moment, even from Armand.

"You will do as I tell you! Get rid of him! At once!"

Max had shaved with an unsteady hand this morning, for he had managed little sleep, but the thought that he would soon be on his way to the station buoyed him as he went to pay Armand a formal farewell. He was disconcerted to find madame in the open doorway of the old boy's apartments, indeed nearly to collide with her as, having screeched her commands, she whirled round to make her exit. And he was still more unsettled by her expression when she saw him.

"Monster!" she spat. Raising her head as if it were a breach of her dignity even to note his presence, she swept past him.

Unusually, there was no Thomas to bar the door. Bewildered, Max went in.

Armand sat in his dressing gown at the sitting-room table before a breakfast he appeared to have left untouched. Gone entirely was his previous air of calm resignation. He looked—there was no other word for it—thunderstruck. Worse still, when he saw Max he recoiled for an instant.

"Dear heart? For pity's sake, what has happened?"

"Are the doors closed? Then please sit down."

Armand's voice was very quiet, almost devoid of inflection. With increased misgiving, Max pulled out the chair opposite him.

"Did my daughter visit your room last night?"

Max's spirits sank. Since it was clear Armand already knew the answer, he had no choice but to say yes. "But I—"

"Did she come at your invitation?"

Dear God, what had the wretched girl been saying? "No, of course not. Armand, in heaven's name! I thought you believed me yesterday."

The old boy's face seemed to soften slightly. "Then why did you not tell me?"

"Because I didn't want to distress you. Because it was..." He struggled to find words for mademoiselle's conduct that would not offend Armand's notions of gallantry. "She asked me to elope with her. I was forced to tell her bluntly that I had no feelings for her. Not surprisingly, she became upset. It was an unfortunate episode and I would much rather forget it."

"So you deny luring my daughter to your room?"

"Luring? Is that what she says?"

"You deny touching her lewdly and trying to kiss her?"

"Is that what she has told you?"

"You deny flinging her down on the bed and tearing her dress?"

"For Christ's sake! Of course I deny it. Armand, what do you take me for? Forgive me—she is your daughter, you love her—but, if she has told you this, it is another of her fantasies."

"She has told her mother, who has just now told me."

"Then ask her yourself. Ask her to her face."

Armand sighed. "Naturally I shall. But first I must be certain…"

"Certain of what? Damn you, Armand! Certain of what?"

The old boy sighed again. "You swear you did not touch her?"

"Of course I do."

"You did not touch her, improperly or in any other way, while she was in your room?"

"No, I did not. At least…"

"Then you did touch her?"

"Not in the way she says. I was obliged to… I…"

"Please, dear boy." The furrows in Armand's cheeks had never seemed deeper. "I need you to tell me the truth."

It was Max's turn to sigh. Even setting aside the humiliation of it, he doubted an accurate account of mademoiselle's visit would win him much credit, since the old fellow, hearing it with a father's ears, would find it so disagreeable he would rather not believe it. Max had the bruises for proof—they had emerged by this morning in weals across his chest—but the shame of owning to them, particularly to his lover, was beyond thought.

As expected, Armand's face darkened while, haltingly, seeking judicious phrases, Max described mademoiselle's attack upon him and her collapse. "So you see," he ended lamely, "the only time I touched her—of my own accord —well, she was clinging to my legs, so I was forced to… I did wonder if I should pick her up. But instead I fetched Miss Pilkington."

"Miss Pilkington?"

Apparently, while concocting her vengeful lies, mademoiselle had omitted to mention Miss Pilkington. "She collected Mademoiselle Juliette from my room. I did not watch her, I stayed well away, but perhaps that was when mademoiselle's dress was torn."

Armand studied him for a moment, then nodded, although

whether this was a nod in his favour Max could not tell. A painful silence ensued, during which the old boy rubbed the fold of his napkin with his thumb as if the damask might engender some Solomonic judgement. Max, unable to bear it, was on the point of interrupting when at last Armand looked up.

"The carriage is waiting to drive you to the station?"

"Yes, but—"

"Then take it."

"No!"

"Go at once."

"No." Max stared at Armand in horror. "Do you not see? It is out of the question for me to leave now, I must stay to defend myself."

"My dear boy—"

"You must allow me that chance. My honour is at stake. I can't run away like a coward."

"My dear Max, you cannot fight madame, you do not have equal weapons. You must trust me to defend you."

"But I—"

"Please. Go now or you will miss your train."

They looked fixedly at each other across the table. Still holding the old boy's gaze, Max pushed back his chair. "Then you do believe me?"

"Yes. Although, as a father, I wish I did not."

Max's eyes continued to search Armand's. "You swear it?"

"I do believe you. Now, please, dear boy—go."

CHAPTER THIRTY-THREE

As the train drew out of the station and Paris began to slide past him in drifts of steam, Max was unsure what he felt—relief, or disgust at this craven retreat. Besides, might it not be taken as an admission of guilt? Yet Armand was right: how would he, Max, a mere secretary, fare if he told Mme la marquise her precious daughter was a liar? No better than poor Christine, found with that earring in her apron.

At least he had managed to convince Armand of the truth yesterday, at least, even faced with this vile new turn of events, the old boy still believed him. Max remembered something M. de M had said in their early days together—it had been, Max fancied, during one of their quarrels about Lesage: "My dear boy, if you ever meet with injustice in this house I shall defend you with everything in my power."

Armand did not always give in to madame. He had stood firm over Thomas, and even over Mme Dussardier, although madame had outflanked him. And now, when so much more was at stake—even if the old fellow's love fought with his fear of discovery, his code of honour would hold firm. Max smiled as he recalled how frustrating he had found it in the days of Lesage, this meticulous fairness, this religious obsession with truth and keeping one's word. But now it should be a comfort. Armand had sworn to defend him against mademoiselle's lies and Max should trust him to honour his pledge.

As soon as a hastily summoned Thomas had dressed him, Miremont set out to see his daughter. But she was in bed, with the door firmly closed: Dr Chevalier had already visited, according to Miss Pilkington, and had administered a sedative that would keep Julie in a deep sleep for several hours. Miremont had not anticipated this check. Nevertheless, here he was, face-to-face with the lady companion; if he were to get to the truth as quickly as possible, he must question her too. However, he had scarcely opened his mouth to address her when Aline burst into the boudoir.

"Monsieur! I hope your presence at poor Julie's sickbed means you have done your duty—you have taken steps against that evil brute."

Miremont contained himself with difficulty. "Madame, if you refer to Monsieur Fabien, he has gone to Beauvallon as planned."

"Gone to—? When I ordered you—?"

"It is not for you, madame, to tell me how I may treat my secretary."

"Merciful heaven!" Aline's bosom heaved. "I knew you were heartless. But to do nothing? Not even to send him packing? A criminal! A Bluebeard! A monster who has ravished your daughter!"

"Ravished? Half an hour ago he was charged with attempting a kiss."

"Oh, my poor little Julie. She will never marry now. It is bad enough that the whole of Paris knows she has jilted Raoul de Niversac. Think of the scandal when this gets about. She will have no reputation left. And when everyone hears that her father would not even..."

But, at the word 'scandal', Miremont ceased to hear his wife. For Julie, for all of them, there was something he must do, something more urgent even than speaking to Miss Pilkington. He had put it off the day after the ball, the broken engagement had distracted him yesterday, but now the unpleasant business could wait not a minute longer.

He raised his voice to cut off Aline's monologue: "You will say nothing. And you too, Miss Pilkington. You will speak to no one about our daughter's troubles." Then he turned on his heel and went to find Boussec.

Lady Telford had never before been invited to visit Miremont's apartments and she seemed a little surprised to find herself conducted through the salon into the confines of the study. But, if her surprise turned to alarm when she was offered a seat opposite Miremont at the study table or noticed Boussec standing in a far corner, she did not show it. In lavender wool, her pale hair neatly dressed, her plump, pink hands folded decorously in her lap, she appeared as complaisant as ever. She even permitted herself a sweet smile as she surveyed her surroundings—was she hungrily eying the Etruscan bronzes?

"Ah, monsieur! Even if I did not know you, one glance would tell me—this is the sanctum of a learned man."

Miremont cleared his throat. It must be done. The repercussions would be fewer than he had feared, for Lord Stilorgan had not left Aline so much as his card since the ball; yet that made the task no more agreeable. "Madame, I have asked you here... There is a matter—a very grave matter—which I am afraid—"

"Oh monsieur, no more!" The lady's chins trembled with sympathy. "Aline has told me all. Poor darling Julie. You were right to summon me and I assure you I shall bring her what consolation I can. That wicked, wicked young man!"

This last strengthened Miremont. "Madame, you will say not another word on the subject."

"Oh, of course, of course." Although his tone had clearly startled her, she was not to be put off. "I understand your distress, the very thought must be dreadfully painful to a father. And your own secretary, too, a viper in your bosom. Although forgive me, monsieur—you are the soul of charity, but others might have been warned by his conduct towards poor Pilkington. A young man of that type, an orphan, of no character. I have not liked to say this, even to Aline, but there are other respects in which his honesty is—"

"Madame! Not only must I ask you to refrain from discussing my family's affairs. It is my distasteful duty to request that you leave this house."

"I beg your pardon?"

"I require you to leave my house. Madame Mercier has sent a maid to pack you."

As she stared at him, Miremont fancied that, despite her show of amazement, she was no stranger to this turn of events; he thought he could detect her wavering for an instant: how much did he know? But, of course, injured innocence must be her opening gambit.

"Well I never—goodness gracious!" The plump hands went to her reticule for a handkerchief. "I have never been so insulted! By a gentleman of rank. A man who poses as the very model of honour." She applied the scrap of lace to her eyes. "I wonder what Aline will say when she hears how her dearest friend has been abused. But I shall not call her to my defence, I have my pride. Do not concern yourself, monsieur. I shall not stay to be further insulted."

"Please, madame, remain seated a moment."

"Not one moment, monsieur. Not one second longer in this house of savages. You may send my boxes on in due course."

Very clever, but she would not make her escape: even as she had risen and adjusted her train, Boussec had moved to the doors; and, although he opened them, it was to admit Thomas.

Finding her way barred by the bulky figure of Boussec and the yet heftier presence of Thomas and doubtless noticing, besides, that the latter carried two sacks, milady Telford whirled round.

"This is an outrage! Let me pass! At once!"

"Please, madame." Miremont motioned her back to her chair. "I agree this is highly disagreeable. Let us have done with it as quickly as we can."

"Done with what? More insults? This is false imprisonment. When my cousin, Lord Stilorgan, hears of it..."

Yet, although her complaints continued, she could hardly avoid observing that Boussec, having taken the lighter of the sacks from Thomas, was laying out a series of small objects upon the table: three snuffboxes, a jade amulet, a magnifier with an ornately carved ivory handle, a Bohemian glass goblet, a Russian toasting cup and grape scissors, both of silver, and the bronze Apollo from the Music Salon. She might have forgotten to be emollient, but she seemed still to believe innocence her best course, for as the array grew she ceased protesting and began to laugh.

"What sort of a man are you, monsieur? Would a mere bourgeois stoop to searching his guest's rooms? And this is not the first time— even my locks were picked. Oh, I should have spoken up, but I did not wish to distress Aline. She likes me to have lovely things about me."

"You maintain my wife gave you these things?"

"Lent them, monsieur. And that little bronze I took into my protection, to save it from the light fingers of your secretary."

With great effort, Miremont subdued his anger. "Boussec!"

But the butler had already fetched the larger sack: its hessian bulged at awkward angles and it clanked as he settled it by the table. With no more expression than before on his heavy yellow face, he first extracted a parcelled-up shawl, which proved to contain a Dutch still life more usually gracing a remote corner of the east wing; then came two candelabra, then an epergne, then a marble and gilt lyre clock from the marquise's state apartments...

As the objects gradually covered the remaining surface of the table, milady watched with a satirical smile. "My goodness, monsieur! Are you planning a bazaar for some worthy cause?"

"I assume you do not claim my wife lent you these."

"Certainly not. I have never seen them in my life."

"Then you do not know a woman called Marie Cordier?"

"No. Is she one of your housemaids?"

"She also goes by the name of Madame Neroni."

"Madame Neroni?" Lady Telford commenced the pantomime of horror she had probably been rehearsing since the second sack had been opened. "But she is the most spiritual person. She was once blessed by Madame Blavatsky. You are surely not suggesting—even you would not dare…"

"Madame Neroni is at present in Saint-Lazare, awaiting trial for theft."

"Oh, the poor dear soul! There must be some terrible misunderstanding."

"She was apprehended five days ago trying to sell the clock and the painting to a dealer in bric-a-brac in the Passage des Panoramas."

"Surely not!"

"This gentleman, who is entirely respectable and was delighted to co-operate with the police, testifies that he has received several visits from Madame Neroni in the past weeks. While it has not been possible to trace everything that was stolen from this house, we have at least recovered these things you see here—"

"Madame Neroni? I cannot believe it!"

"—and also these."

While milady was exclaiming and dabbing her eyes, Boussec had handed his master a shallow leather case. Miremont opened it.

Did Lady Telford wince? The sudden radiance of the Miremont sapphires was certainly dazzling.

"Madame Neroni has used her time in gaol to reflect. She has made a statement, implicating you, madame, in all these thefts. She claims that, in selling the spoils, she merely acted as your agent for a percentage of the profits."

Rather than listening, milady appeared to have been studying the sapphires. When she raised her eyes, her tears had vanished, along with every trace of the accommodating house guest.

"Lies!" she snarled. "It's all lies."

"Perhaps you would care to say that to the police."

"You wish me to shame you, monsieur? You wish them to know the truth? Your wife asked me to sell the jewels."

Miremont's mouth tightened, but otherwise he retained his composure. "Come, madame, that is laughable."

"You will not be laughing once the whole of Paris knows it. Your wife was desperate for money. She gave me the necklace because she wanted it sold in secret."

"Forgive me, but that is impossible."

"Then ask her."

Miremont endeavoured to hold milady's gaze coldly and steadily. "There is no need, madame. My wife knows, as you evidently do not, that these are family jewels and not hers to sell. I can guarantee she will deny your allegation."

For the first time, Lady Telford seemed taken aback. But she quickly rallied. "Incredible! Monstrous! After I have bled my very soul to show her kindness. Well, you shall see, monsieur." She pushed back her chair. "I am related to the Polignacs, my cousin is a peer of the English realm, I am received by all the best families. Neroni, Cordier, whatever she calls herself—a petty thief—is there anyone in Paris who will take her word against mine?"

"On the contrary. The Sûreté regards the matter very seriously. Commissaire Macé is showing a personal interest."

"Then I dare you to let him arrest me. I shall tell the world how you have treated me—Monsieur le marquis de Miremont, who pretends to be such a saint! Society shall see what a hypocrite you are. Everyone shall hear about your trollop of a wife and your ruined daughter."

Miremont willed himself to stay calm. "No one will hear you, madame."

"Oh? And how will you stop me? You ordered me to leave and I am leaving."

"Most certainly you are."

"Then tell your man to move away from the door."

"You are right in one respect. I no more want a trial than you—I hardly wish it advertised that my family has been living with a common criminal in its midst. Fortunately Monsieur Macé and I have reached an accommodation. You will not face prosecution if you leave the country."

Milady seemed, for the first time, to falter. But then she tossed her head. "And if I do not care to?"

"You have no choice. Boussec and Thomas will escort you downstairs, where the carriage is waiting to take you to the Gare du Nord."

"You cannot force me to go anywhere!"

"Inspector Roger of the Sûreté is also waiting for you downstairs. He and Thomas will travel with you on the train and ensure you board the boat at Calais. Once you have reached England, you would be wise to stay there. Set foot again on French soil and you will be arrested."

Would Max have been proud of him, Miremont wondered? His performance must have been convincing, for Boussec, returning with a rare smile on his face, assured him the lady had gone off quietly in the end. Perhaps he had been helped by the certainty that he was lying in a good cause—by that, and Boussec's thorough briefing. For, of course, he had never met Commissaire Macé or anyone from the Sûreté: 'Inspector Roger' was in fact Boussec's brother, head waiter at a restaurant in the Boulevard Saint-Germain.

In truth Miremont had no idea how his family's possessions had been recovered, what pressure this shady fellow Jouvert had applied, or upon whom: he only knew that, while it had cost a pretty sum, it had saved the Hôtel de Miremont from police intrusion. Furthermore, he doubted Boussec, despite his role as go-between, was any wiser. There was only one certainty to be relied upon in the entire business: the police had actually arrested Neroni-Cordier, although over another matter, apparently after a tip from some obliging informant.

But, in any case, now was not the time for idle speculation. Ridding the house of Lady Telford and her poisonous gossip had taken most of the morning. Yet it was but a preliminary to Miremont's other urgent tasks.

CHAPTER THIRTY-FOUR

Aline lay on the chaise in her boudoir with a cold compress applied to her forehead. She barely stirred when Miremont entered and seemed not to notice that, instead of taking a chair, he stood, stiff and set-faced, with his hands behind his back.

"Oh dear," she wailed, on hearing Lady Telford had suddenly been called back to England. "Is someone unwell? A relation? Will Lord Jack be going too?"

"Madame," said Miremont, ignoring this enquiry, "last Monday, I asked you for the set of sapphires so that I could give it to Juliette to wear at the ball. You, as I remember, told me some of the stones were loose and you had sent it to Cartier."

"Last Monday?" Aline moaned and adjusted the compress. "I don't recall…"

"And when I asked if it could be got back in time, you said it would not be ready."

"Oh, my poor head. Yes, I remember faintly, but do not bother me with it now."

"Did Lord Stilorgan have gambling debts? Or bills due to be called in?"

Aline sat up so suddenly the compress fell into her lap. "I do not know what you mean. And I do not know how you can cross-question me about jewellery at a time like this. How can you be so unfeeling when your daughter is suffering?"

"At least I do not sell what rightfully belongs to her."

"Sell?" She stared at him. "I did not—I certainly never…"

He was obliged to acknowledge she seemed genuinely shocked. "Well?" he said, after a pause.

"I—I pawned them. I have the ticket." She rose and began rummaging in the top drawer of her writing desk. "I know I put it in a safe place."

"And when Lady Telford gave you the ticket, did she also give you the money?"

"She said it would be more discreet if she took it directly to…" Bursting noisily into tears, Aline subsided onto the chaise longue. "Oh, I see now… I trusted her, I was generosity itself to her… Oh, how I was betrayed!… And anyway it was too late. He was already in the clutches of that scheming Génie Zelenska. Not that she has a sou, the prince has

265

frittered away his fortune trying to raise Poland from the dead. He'll find out soon enough, Lord Jack—after everything I've given him…"

Miremont did not care to enquire how much that was. "If it is of any interest to you, we have found the sapphires. Not a moment too soon—I am told the criminals who deal in stolen jewels prefer to do so stone by stone, but fortunately both the necklace and the earrings were still intact. They are locked in my study and I shall give them to Julie when she recovers."

This brought a fresh explosion of tears. "When? Should that not be 'if'?"

"I believe it is as I told Niversac two days ago—she has suffered some sort of nervous collapse. The moment I am permitted to talk to her—"

"Oh, my poor Julie, my poor baby girl. Is there no end to our misfortunes? Lord Jack, Marguerite Telford, now this! Merciful heaven, how strong must one be to bear it? How can a mother not bleed when her daughter has been—?"

"Stop crying, woman! This instant!"

If Miremont surprised himself by this show of force, Aline too was taken aback. She exchanged tears for a look of injured dignity. "Have you no sympathy, no compassion?"

"Madame, I should be accustomed to your foolishness after all these years, but since you insinuated yourself back under my roof, you have surpassed yourself. I care little for your extravagance or your pretensions or your squalid affairs, I can expect nothing else, but I will not have you bringing thieves and swindlers into my house—no, don't interrupt and don't start weeping again—nor will I tolerate your using property that belongs not to you, or to me, but to future generations of this family, in order to buy the affections of some reluctant lover—I repeat, do not interrupt me! I am inclined to send you back to Burgundy with as little ceremony as I showed your so-called friend. And I shall do so at once if you continue to interfere in this business with Julie. Is that clear?"

"You are one to talk about thieves and criminals, when your secretary is—"

"I said, is that clear? I shall get to the truth of this affair in my own way. And, as for Max Fabien, he is not guilty unless that is proved beyond doubt."

*

The ordeal of Lady Telford and the confrontation with his wife had left Miremont drained. However, he had high hopes of his interview with Miss Pilkington. She seemed a sensible woman: whatever had occurred last night, she could be relied upon to give an honest, unbiased account.

He was somewhat disconcerted by her sorrow at Lady Telford's abrupt departure. "Oh dear, I hope it is not a matter of life or death. I should have liked to wish her well. She has been so very kind to me."

He told himself Miss Pilkington was one of those people who strove to see good in everyone—was this not a principle he also tried to honour, although he had rather fallen down lately? But what troubled him more was her evident unease. He had settled her comfortably in an armchair in his sitting room and had offered her refreshment—tea, if she would like. But not only had she declined, albeit most politely; as he took the chair opposite her, he could see she was pale beneath her freckles, while her hands were knotted together so tightly in her lap that the tips of her fingers were crimson.

"Madame," he began gently, "you will know why I must talk to you."

"Yes, monsieur. I understand. Although I wish—it is so extremely difficult—I would give anything not to..." She bit her lip. "I have always had a high regard for Monsieur Fabien, indeed I have thought of him as my friend."

Miremont smiled encouragingly.

"Despite the concerns that were expressed about the evenings we spent together—perhaps you remember?—"

Miremont nodded.

"—despite those concerns, he was never other than a perfect gentleman. If anyone had asked me if I believed he was capable of—of the sort of conduct that is described—I should have vehemently denied it."

Should have? Miremont's heart lurched.

"But I am afraid I placed too much confidence in my powers of judgement."

Miremont stared at her. Clearly it had distressed her to say this; she was biting her lip again and her gaze had dropped to her fiercely clenched hands. Yet all the same she had said it, uttered what he least hoped to hear. He was momentarily at a loss.

"B—but... You cannot... You truly think...?"

She raised her eyes. "Why would Mademoiselle Juliette—why

would any woman invent such a thing? Something so shaming, even to speak of. Especially for an innocent young girl…" She trailed away, blushing scarlet.

Miremont strove to collect himself. She could not be—she must be mistaken. Of course, as his daughter's friend and companion, she was bound to be partial, it was even to her credit. But surely if he pressed her…? Yet her integrity was patent, his seeming to doubt her would only aggravate her distress. And what of his own partiality, the danger of being too passionate in Max's defence? Oh God! Although manners forbade it in her presence, he longed for a cigarette.

He cleared his throat. "Perhaps it would best if you could tell me— if you can bear it—what happened last night."

Her blush had receded, he was relieved to see. "I shall try, monsieur. Although I know only my part in it."

"I am told you found my daughter and put her to bed."

"Yes. Yes, I was reading in my room—Mademoiselle Juliette had kindly said she had no need of me after supper—and there was a knock on my door. It was Monsieur Fabien. I was very surprised. He had never been to my room before, and given the trouble over our previous meetings… But he said he urgently needed my help. Mademoiselle Juliette had been taken ill. Then he gave me directions to find his room and left."

"His room? Did he offer any explanation?"

"No. I was shocked, I could not understand it. Why would mademoiselle go to his room, why was she ill? But he gave me no time to ask. He went away and never came back."

"And—when he was telling you this—how did he seem?"

"Not at all his normal self. Tight-lipped. Pale, as if he had seen a ghost. But there was something else, too." Her brow was furrowed by her struggle to be exact. "I think he was angry."

Inwardly, Miremont sighed. While her account broadly endorsed what Max had told him, for others—Aline, for instance—the cause of this anger might beg interpretation.

"So you went to Monsieur Fabien's room and found my daughter?"

"Yes, I—" Miss Pilkington caught her breath as if reliving the experience. "Of course, I have witnessed hysterics before, but never anything… I had not thought to bring my sal volatile, but I doubt it would have helped. I could hear her screaming and sobbing when I reached the top of the stairs—"

"Monsieur Fabien had not closed the door?"

"No, it was wide open."

"And was she lying on the bed?"

"She was face down on the floor, quite near the door."

These details mercifully accorded with Max's version. "And did she tell you what had happened?"

"Monsieur, she could barely speak. I put my arms around her, but I could not calm her. It was as much as I could do to raise her. Even now I am not sure how I managed to get her back to her rooms. I rang for Mademoiselle Drouet and we put her to bed. Fortunately I keep Chlorodyne in my medicine chest and after I persuaded her to take a little she gradually stopped sobbing and fell asleep. I was not present first thing this morning—Mademoiselle Drouet sat up with her—but I gather on waking she asked for her mother and was at last able to tell her the whole dreadful story."

"So she said nothing to you at all?"

Miss Pilkington savaged her lip again—perhaps she still retained a vestige of friendship for Max. But having weighed it in the balance, she felt obliged to discard it. "When I first found her, she kept screaming 'I hate him, I hate him! How could he do this? How could he do this to me?' Over and over. Until she ran out of breath."

They were both silenced by this. Once again Miremont longed for the comfort of tobacco.

"Madame—my dear Miss Pilkington—you must forgive me for asking this, but has my daughter ever shown any—any inclination towards Monsieur Fabien?"

"No. She was grateful for his advice about books. But no, otherwise not."

"You seem very definite."

"Mademoiselle Juliette is quite private, she does not often confide in me. But she was set on Monsieur de Niversac, no one else, that was most apparent. Besides, she was clear, even when she wrongly believed I …" Here inexplicably Miss Pilkington blushed again. "She was very conscious that Monsieur Fabien was—well, not her equal."

'Beneath her', she had been going to say. Miremont silently thanked her for sparing him that. "Then she did not break off her engagement because of Monsieur Fabien?"

"My goodness, no. I think—I did not see Mademoiselle Juliette for most of the ball, I was in the sitting-out room with Madame de Cressy and the dowager comtesse de Corvignac, but she was upset at the end and I think she had had some difference with Monsieur de Niversac."

"He says not."

"Forgive me, monsieur, but gentlemen do not always know when ladies are upset."

This made Miremont smile. Yet there could be little to smile about when, instead of exculpating Max, this pleasant, honest woman appeared to damn him at every turn.

"Still, we have not resolved the question of why my daughter was in Monsieur Fabien's room. You must know he adamantly denies having invited her there. I suppose you will say he is bound to, under the circumstances."

Miss Pilkington nodded sadly.

"But, if he did invite her, why did she accept?"

She sighed. "I have been exercising myself about this ever since I found her. Mademoiselle Juliette was in a strange mood yesterday, up, then down—perhaps she was regretting having broken with Monsieur de Niversac—and she was angry with madame, who would not leave her in peace—"

"So she decided to do something reckless and indiscreet?"

"No, not consciously. But Monsieur Fabien is—can be very charming and perhaps she was not thinking properly."

"About visiting a young man alone in his room at night?"

"Monsieur, in some ways your daughter is worldly, but in others not. She led a very sheltered life with the nuns—" Miremont fancied he caught a hint of Protestant disapproval "—and I did notice, even in England, she was quite unaware of the effect her beauty can have on men, regardless of her own indifference. I think she trusted Monsieur Fabien, your secretary, someone she had grown used to, and saw no danger."

Yes, Miremont was disappointed, not to say shaken, by this conversation. But, to counter it, he still had, clear in his memory, Max's flabbergasted look on hearing the allegations. Besides, as Miss Pilkington had admitted, Julie did not confide in her. And, in any case, the accusations came at second hand, from Aline, who, having wrought them in her usual lurid colours, was seizing every chance to embellish them. If Miremont hoped to absolve Max, he must talk to his daughter. This time he would not be put off.

In Julie's boudoir, her maid Drouet was assiduously tending a blazing fire which, even given the requirements of an invalid, seemed excessive for a pleasant spring day and scarcely to merit further chivvying with the poker. Miremont longed to loosen his cravat and Drouet herself was scarlet in the face as she rose from the grate.

Mademoiselle was still sleeping apparently, but Drouet was happy to fetch her torn gown, if monsieur wished to see it. Miremont had forgotten to ask Miss Pilkington about the dress and Miss Pilkington had not mentioned it: all the same, as Drouet displayed the strip of lace ripped from the décolletage, it seemed to him quite possible that, as Max had suggested, the lady companion had caused the damage when she had struggled to convey Julie back to the east wing.

Miremont did not expect Julie's lady's maid to be anything but partisan; thus, although she struck him as a pert young woman who rather relished exhibiting the dress, not to mention the entire drama, he was prepared to overlook her freely expressed view that "The man who did that, monsieur, was a fiend" and "Given half a chance—begging your pardon—most men are beasts". However, he was not prepared to be kept from his daughter a moment longer. If she were asleep, he was her father, he would sit by her bed until she woke.

The bedroom was not, as he had expected, in darkness: although, in contrast to the blaze in the boudoir, the fire was damped down, the shutters were open and the curtains partly drawn back; yet all he could see of Julie was a huddle beneath the bedclothes, a very small huddle, it seemed to him, as if his grown daughter had been exchanged for a child. A glimpse of blonde hair disputed this, but otherwise, curled towards the wall, veiled by the sheets, she was motionless, absent; even her breathing produced no audible sound.

However, when he tiptoed to pull up a chair, she stirred. "Papa?"

"My dear girl…" His words died, for, as she turned, he could not conceal his shock. There, gazing up at him from the pillows, lay a girl he scarcely recognised, eyes bloodshot and rimmed with scarlet, nose swollen, lips raw, no longer his bright, beautiful, playful daughter, but a waif, struck down, inconsolable.

"Oh, Papa!" Her voice was ragged with weeping. "Oh Papa, Papa!" Rising up suddenly, she made to throw her arms around his neck.

As he sat on the edge of the bed, holding her, he thought once again how little and frail she was, how fragile the angles of her shoulder blades seemed beneath her nightgown. Her heart fluttered against his, her tears wetted his neck. The instinct to protect her overwhelmed him, the furious urge to destroy whatever had wreaked this devastation. Then, perforce, he remembered Max.

Gently unwinding her arms, he laid her back upon the pillows. "My darling girl—"

"Please tell me he is gone!" She clutched his hand. "Please, Papa, tell me he is no longer in this house."

"Yes, my dear. But—"

"Tell me, tell me! Say he won't come near me again, say you won't let him."

"Yes, he is gone." He squeezed her fingers. " But… My darling, you know I must—we must—"

"Oh no! Do not ask me!" She tore her hand from his. "Do not ask me to tell you. It is too frightful—too shaming—I cannot—please, you cannot make me!"

To his horror she began to cry in earnest, not the pretty crystal tears she had shed on breaking off her engagement, nor the hot tears that had just now trickled into his ear, but huge gasping sobs that convulsed her, that shook phlegm from her nose and choked her mouth with saliva. Helplessly, he thrust forward his handkerchief, but she was blind to him: he could only watch in consternation.

He found her hand again and stroked it. To cross-question her now would be the height of cruelty. He must wait until she was more composed.

CHAPTER THIRTY-FIVE

Miremont passed a troubled evening. He had made little progress in furthering Max's cause. Worse still, when Philippe came to dress him for dinner—for Thomas, of course, had gone to Calais—he was reminded that in his valet's absence no word of the boy's arrival had been sent to Beauvallon, an omission that must be rectified first thing tomorrow when the telegraph office opened; still, Miremont reassured himself, Madame Rose, his treasured housekeeper, was fond of Max and could be relied upon to welcome him.

Philippe's services, as it turned out, were not required. Lady Telford was gone, Julie was confined to bed and Aline, predictably after the confrontation over the sapphires, was also an invalid (for two pins Miremont truly would despatch her to Burgundy, were it not that Julie, in her present affliction, might need her mother). Thus the only person sitting down to dinner, other than Miremont himself, would be Miss Pilkington, a situation awkward enough on both sides for him to feel no compunction in taking supper in his apartments.

Alone, Miremont thought of Max at Beauvallon, saw the boy setting out his stud-box and razor in the bedroom that connected with his own, and felt both longing and loss. Yet these feelings were not unclouded: what had been clear in his mind at the start of the day had grown murky, like a lake when its depths are churned; as he recalled his broken daughter, he even wondered if he were not shamed by such longings, whether a better man would renounce them. Oh God! If Miss Pilkington found it hard to learn to hate Max, how in heaven's name could he do it?

Of course it would not come to that. Julie was ill, temporarily driven out of her senses by the overexcitement of her engagement and the ball. Nevertheless, although it was Miremont's custom to write to Max every day when they were parted, tonight he had not the heart for it.

"Oh Papa! You promised. You promised you would not make me!"

If Miremont had hoped to find Julie's condition improved by a night's sleep, he had been woefully optimistic. Just as before, she lay, limp and shrunken, with her once-glorious hair trailing in rat's tails across the pillows; her face was still blotched, her eyelids swollen, her eyes bright only with imminent tears. He had watched as she had listlessly waved away her untasted breakfast and had felt once again that to question her would be cruel. Yet it must be done, for her own sake as much as anyone's. Having bent to kiss her forehead, he had settled in the chair beside the bed and taken her hand.

"My darling girl, I realise how difficult this is—and I would not ask you, except that—"

But instantly, as if he had scorched her with a hot iron, her protests began and her tears poured forth. "You promised me! Papa, how could you?"

Although fearing a repeat of yesterday's storm of sobbing, he steeled himself to persist.

"You must understand that all I know of this dreadful business is what I have heard from your mother."

"Then why can you not talk to her? She knows everything."

"My dear, I think we would both agree your mother is prone to—well, to get a little confused over detail. So perhaps you could tell me in your own words."

"Oh, Papa—"

"I know it will be painful. But then I can see what needs to be done."

This temporarily stilled the tears. "You promise?"

"Yes, I shall do whatever is necessary."

She sniffed, then blew her nose. Miremont took this as consent to continue.

"My darling girl, I suppose the first thing—what none of us can quite understand—is why you went to Monsieur Fabien's room."

"He said he wanted to show me a painting."

She must mean the Manet. Miremont was stung. His birthday present to Max was part of their hidden life, a secret expression of their deepest intimacy. For Max cavalierly to show it off, even to Julie… He swallowed hard. "A painting?"

"We had talked about my portrait. He said Monsieur Lebas was second-rate, not a real artist."

Alas, that rang true: Max had shared Miremont's criticisms of Lebas' effort. "He said—"Julie began to sniffle again "—he said he had a much better portrait he wanted to show me. And then, last night—no, it was the night before, wasn't it?—he…" She took a shuddering breath. "He said as he was going to Beauvallon this would be my last chance to see it. Because it was in his room…"

As her tears welled, Miremont's paternal instincts cried out. Could he justify adding to the poor child's torment? Was it really so vital to find the truth, which, in any case, would be unbearable, whichever way it fell out? Yet doubt was unbearable too. No matter how heartless it seemed, he had no choice but to go on.

Besides, she was dabbing her nose and had collected herself a little. "I didn't think—I never dreamed…"

"Did he show you the painting?"

"Oh, Papa! I had barely got into the room when he locked the door."

Had not Max sworn he had left it open?

"Then he seized me by the shoulders and tried to…" Her voice dropped to a whisper. "He tried to kiss me—and I struggled—and then he—oh Papa, I can't bear it—he …" She buried her face in her pillow, so that he lost her last words.

"My dear?"

"He… touched me."

"Touched you?"

She turned her head to gaze up at him imploringly. "Papa, I cannot…" Pulling the sheet up to her neck, she pointed dumbly to where it hid her bosom.

"He touched you there?"

"He said now I was no longer engaged to Monsieur de Niversac, I should be his. I fought with all my strength, but he was stronger, he tore my dress. And then he threw me on the bed… Oh, Papa…"

"Did he—" Miremont could hardly bring himself to ask this "—did he… touch you… indecently?"

"Yes, I said so."

"I mean… elsewhere?"

To his relief, she shook her head. "He tried to hold me down, but I was struggling."

"On the bed?"

"Yes."

"Miss Pilkington told me you were on the floor."

"He flung me onto the bed. But as I struggled, I must have fallen to the floor. I was trying to escape."

"And did he not try to stop you?"

"No—not by this time. I was screaming, I suppose he was frightened someone might hear."

"He suddenly gave up?"

"I don't remember—I think I fainted."

"And, all this while, the door was locked?"

"Yes, he wouldn't open it."

"Miss Pilkington says it was open when she found you."

She stared at him. "He had run off by then, of course it was open. Papa, why are you cross-questioning me like this? What does it matter? Do you not believe me? You required me to tell you, I have tried—even though to think of it makes me sick—and you, my own papa, do not believe me!"

Her own papa. It was agony enough that he had made her sob again, that even the little dimple in her chin quivered with misery, the Miremont dimple, the beloved quirk in her beauty that marked her as his flesh and blood. He needed no reminder of what a father should feel when a daughter recounts what she had just recounted; he felt the pain and the anger in every sinew. He loved her more at this moment than he had ever loved her.

He had earned her reproaches. Why these senseless questions? Who cared if Miss Pilkington had found the door open or shut? It did not disprove Julie's account. In fact, it proved nothing.

"My darling girl, forgive me." He leant over to touch the dimple, then stroked her cheek. "Shush, now. Don't cry. Your stupid old papa only wanted to know... Well, he felt he should make sure... Do you remember when you told me you had broken things off with poor Niversac?"

She sniffed. "But this has nothing to do with—"

"I know, I know. It is just that, as I recall, you said you would marry a street sweeper if you loved him, so long as I liked him."

"I was teasing, Papa."

"You did not mean...? For some reason, I wondered if you might mean Monsieur Fabien."

"Someone no better than a servant?"

"My dear, I—"

"How could you, Papa? How could you think—?" She rose up from the pillows in outrage. "That vile man, that beast? You brought him into this house. Why did you let him near me? Could you not see what he was? Look! Look what he did to me!" Whereupon, casting aside modesty, she threw back the sheet and pushed up the loose sleeve of her nightgown.

Miremont could not but stare in horror, for there, on her upper arm below the shoulder, pale blue as yet, but showing distinctly against the translucent pallor of the flesh, was a row of bruises—injuries that could only have been inflicted by the brutal grip of a hand.

Sunday being the day of his grandchildren's usual visit, Miremont was forced to spend the afternoon with Clotilde, who took her sister's ordeal as a ready occasion for platitudes. He strove to contain his impatience; later, downstairs in the ballroom, he even managed a smile as, with forced gaiety, they applauded Frédéric bowling hoops and little Agathe toddling valiantly in his wake; even so, the visit was an agony scarcely to be endured. Yet, when Miremont was finally alone, the pain grew worse. Often walking helped him order his thoughts, but he had no heart for it. He lay on his divan staring at the ceiling and, when Thomas, back from Calais, arrived to put him into his tails, he found the very thought of dinner abhorrent and sent the poor fellow away.

Yes, he had reassured Clotilde, yes, the situation required the sternest measures and he would certainly take them. But how could he choose between the two people dearest to him? As he tried to sift the evidence from their conflicting stories, his head swam.

When Max had told him weeks ago that Julie had taken a liking to him, the boy had offered nothing to justify this fear—but then, how could he, since Miremont had refused to listen? Last Friday, when they had argued in the courtyard about his going to Beauvallon, he had been more specific: Julie had engineered meetings with him on several occasions, had been angry that he would not dance with her at the ball and had claimed he was the reason she had broken off her engagement; she had even sent him a letter, although foolishly he had burned it. Miremont had no more wanted to believe him than before, but, finally convinced by the boy's desperation, he had agreed his departure might be expedient. And, yesterday morning, although still with reluctance, he had again been persuaded by Max's denials.

Or had he been persuaded because he loved him? For where was the evidence? He had only had the boy's word; even the letter had been conveniently destroyed. And yesterday, too, there had been nothing to support Max's version of events.

Whereas Julie had proof: true, the dress might have been torn in some other way, but the bruises—Miremont was still haunted by the sight of them. Neither should he ignore Miss Pilkington's account; she too was certain Julie had never felt anything for Max, while Julie—sadly, for Miremont had thought her free of snobbery —had confirmed she considered the boy beneath her.

In any case, who was most likely to be truthful? His innocent daughter, brought up by the nuns to know right from wrong, or Max, who considered lying an accomplishment, like having a good seat on a horse? Did Miremont forget Italy? And, even now, despite his promises, there had been constant rumours—Aline, Miss Pilkington, and more lately, if Aline were to be believed, Zhukovsky's sister. Could anyone who was constitutionally faithless be relied upon to tell the truth?

Yet Miremont pulled himself up; he was unjust. The rumours had been baseless. He could not fault Max's loyalty over the past few months; in fact, considering the harsh conditions he, Miremont, had imposed on their love, was it not treachery to doubt him?

Just as Miremont had watched Julie after the quarrel at Madame Tonton's, so he had watched Max; yet with the same results. He had observed no signs of impropriety; the boy had never failed to observe the formalities due to her; indeed, this unbending politeness had rather saddened Miremont, for in the last weeks it had taken on a perceptible chill—but did not that, in itself, bear Max out?

Moreover, Miremont knew the boy. He was reckless, impulsive, not cold-blooded; however he liked to mock morality, he was not without honour. To betray Miremont by despoiling his dearly loved daughter, to inflict a wound far deeper than the cut he had dealt in Venice—Max would not do that, he would not be capable of it.

Yet, if Max had not been acting a part all these weeks, then it must be Julie who was the consummate actress. But at this Miremont balked. His marriage had thoroughly acquainted him with the manifestations of hysteria but he had never observed anything to resemble this sobbing of his daughter's, unremitting, inconsolable, aggravated by a word or gesture as the pain of a grievous injury is by the slightest jolt. She could not be pretending. When he recalled the girl who had entranced Raoul de Niversac and everyone who saw her and had altogether delighted in her life in Paris, he could not reconcile this vivacious, joyful creature with the pitiful child he had found cowering under the bedclothes; it would have taken more than the art of a Réjane or a Bernhardt to work this transformation.

He had told himself before that he knew Max—and how wrong he had been! Even if one set aside the boy's evasions about his past, he was still not honest about other aspects of his life. Take the sinister M. Jouvert: although Boussec had managed the recovery of the sapphires with commendable finesse, thanks were undoubtedly due to Max for smoothing the way with this caesar of the underworld. Yet how did he come to acquire such a friend?

No, Miremont did not know the boy. He might believe there were some acts he was incapable of committing, but he could not swear to it. No matter that the thought of life without him filled Miremont with despair: he must not allow his love—this guilty, improper love of his—to corrupt his judgement. He owed it to Julie to look at the boy's account of Friday night with a cold, clear eye. And if he did, he would be forced to note its omissions.

Why, for instance, when Miremont had come to wish him goodbye, had Max not mentioned Julie's visit to his room? Although they had lain in each other's arms with every semblance of intimacy, the boy had uttered not one word about it. Oh, he had claimed the next morning he had not wished to add to Miremont's troubles by describing a scene he himself would rather forget. But then, when Julie's allegations had forced him to describe it—Miremont could not help recalling how carefully he had chosen his words, so that, even then, had it not seemed that he was holding something back? Yes, as Miremont reviewed the conversation, over and over, the more convinced he became: Max had not told the whole truth. In which case, it was possible no part of his story was true.

"Something shameful for any woman to speak of," Miss Pilkington had said. "Would an innocent girl invent such a thing?"

Miremont again saw the bruises. Once again he recalled how Max had seemed on edge as they had embraced that night. And he remembered another detail he had tried to brush aside, although at the time it had hurt him: when he had told Max he loved him, the boy had responded only with a kiss, and that almost as an afterthought. But now—oh God, now—Miremont sat up, choking as if the air had been punched from his lungs—now it was obvious. Of course Max had been silent. Even Max was not so cynical, so devoid of feeling, that he could feign love for Miremont, there, on the very bed where he had tried to rape his daughter.

CHAPTER THIRTY-SIX

The train had been delayed just outside Montereau by cattle on the line, so that Max had missed his connection at Laroche and had arrived at Auxerre hours late; thus he supposed it was no surprise that Beauvallon's ancient barouche was not there to meet him. Since, to compound his troubles, it was pouring with rain, he had some difficulty hiring a fiacre. Nevertheless, as he set off into the early dusk precipitated by the rainstorm, he contrived to feel optimistic. Yes, he was cold, wet, begrimed with smuts from the train, exhausted by the boredom of an interminable wait on a drab station platform, but he had always loved Beauvallon; and now, in addition to the pleasures of clean air and open country, it offered other advantages: no madame, no milady and, above all, no Princess Rosebud. Had Armand succeeded in worming the truth out of her yet, had he tumbled to her tawdry little scheme of revenge?

Poor old boy. Although Max was thrown about by the jolting of the carriage wheels over the rough roads and the rain had seeped through to his skin, he could not but feel he had the best of it. Still, there was work to be done too. Tomorrow morning, after his ride, he would root out Calvert, make the sneaky fellow show him the burnt-out cottage and insist on a detailed inspection of Armand's entire building project. Doubtless progress would have stalled. What would it be this time—green wood, a delivery of faulty drainage pipes, thieves making off with the bricks? Armand, trusting as ever, was inclined to tolerate his steward's cussed resistance to innovation, not to mention certain other irregularities, on the grounds of the fellow's loyalty: his father had served Armand's father, his son would follow in his stead, and so on and so forth—it was old Lesage all over again. Well, that was as maybe. Max wondered what Calvert's mistress in Soures cost him, how much he lost at bezique to M. Saint-Séverin up at the Maison des Vignerons. Although Armand would not approve, here was the perfect opportunity, one day when Calvert was off cavorting, for Max to go through his books.

Yet, for all his confident expectations, he was still dogged by that sense of shame. He should not have fled; whatever M. de M had said, he should have stood and fought his ground. He hoped Armand's telegram had given a credible reason for his visit but, all the same, his arriving at Beauvallon without monsieur—would that not seem odd? Might it not appear he had been sent away in disgrace? Of course this was not so, far from it. Nevertheless it would be hard to explain his sudden departure from Paris, particularly as the fire damage he had come to inspect had occurred weeks ago. Naturally he would hold his head up, but the ambiguity of his situation bothered him somewhat.

This discomfort was to increase. Perhaps it was understandable there was no one at Beauvallon to open the gates, obliging Max to stagger out in the dark and wet to perform this labour himself; perhaps it was the moonless sky and the rain's heavy veil that rendered the darkness so impenetrable as they drove up the long avenue of limes; yet, even when the château came into view, there was no light anywhere. When Max had caught his first glimpse of Armand's Palladian treasure, the *geste d'amour* built by the eighth marquis for his Anglo-Irish mistress in the style of an English country house, its sandstone had glowed like honey in the sun of a cloudless afternoon; but now what rose up out of the dark was a shapeless hulk, like a lost ship barely distinguishable from the black waves consuming it; nor, when they grew closer and the dim light of the carriage lamps began to pick out detail, was this desolate impression dispelled: the stonework, where it was visible, was a grim, drowned grey and every window a dead eye, firmly shuttered.

His spirits plummeted. Turning up his coat collar and climbing out of the carriage, he sprinted across the gravel and up the steps to the shelter of the portico; but, though he rattled the doors twice, the second time violently, he knew it was pointless. Behind him, he could hear the rain and the horse snorting and shaking its harness, but within the house the silence was absolute.

Confound it! Had the old boy's telegram miscarried? Now Max must call Mme Durand out, in the dead of night and in this vile weather, to open up. If he hoped to escape embarrassing questions, this was hardly the way. Yet there was nothing for it. Prevailing upon his driver to draw up the fiacre as close as he could to the eastern corner of the building, Max edged his way along the path that separated the château from the walled garden, soon losing the benefit of the carriage lamps but at last grateful to see the lighted window of the Durands' cottage.

It was of a piece with the rest of Max's luck that Durand, not his wife, should answer his knocking. A small man with the eyes of a weasel and a jutting Adam's apple, Zacharie Durand drove the barouche and did whatever odd jobs were required—when he was not stirring up trouble, that is, or spreading gossip. Even Armand thought him untrustworthy and Max was under no illusions as to his views on monsieur's interesting relationship with his secretary or his eagerness to promulgate them in the village tabac.

"Whadyerwant?" the fellow said. "We don't expect callers at this hour."

Max was aware he did not appear at his best: his coat was sodden and water streamed from the brim of his hat. All the same, he judged this to be calculated insolence for, as Durand looked him up and down, the sly gleam in his eye was decidedly at odds with the tone of surprise in which he exclaimed: "Blow me! If it's not Monsieur Fabien! Who'd have guessed it? My love, it's Monsieur Fabien, sprung out of nowhere."

The door gave directly onto a room that was both kitchen and parlour and, beyond Durand, in the pool of light shed by an oil lamp, Max glimpsed two figures huddled round the table, an ancient, shrivelled man and an equally decrepit old woman, both swaddled in shawls: Mme Durand's parents, M. and Mme Thomas. Rosalie Durand had been spooning something from a bowl into her father's mouth, but now she turned. Her face lit up.

"Monsieur is here?" Casting aside the bowl, she hastened to displace Durand and usher Max over the threshold.

Rosalie Durand, Armand's 'Madame Rose', was a big woman, composed of many curves: buxom bosoms, billowing hips, huge rounded forearms, cheeks like peaches, ripe and softly furred; Armand always said her smile made him think of newly baked bread or the taste of raspberries filched from the cane, and this was the smile she was now lavishing upon Max.

"What a lovely surprise, monsieur! Gracious, you're half drowned. Come to the stove before you catch your death."

Bowing his head to avoid the lintel, Max stepped in gratefully. His anxiety had been needless: even if her husband were a brute, Madame Rose's good nature could be relied on. "Thank you, madame."

"I hope Monsieur de Miremont is keeping dry in the carriage."

"He is not here, I'm afraid."

"Not here? But..."

"I have come alone. Did you not get monsieur's wire?"

Her smile died, every sweet, generous, motherly trace of it. "So monsieur is not with you."

"I had expected he would telegraph..."

"We got no telegram. Durand," she called over her shoulder, "was there a telegram?"

Max could see Durand shaking his head with unwarranted emphasis.

"No," she said, folding her arms. "There's been no telegram."

"It must have gone astray."

"So it must."

"Monsieur has sent me to report on the building works. He would have come himself but, with Madame la marquise and Mademoiselle Juliette staying at the Hôtel de Miremont, he has been fully occupied."

She continued to favour him with a hard look. "The château is shut up."

"I realise I am causing you great inconvenience."

"We do not open it until the summer. And then on monsieur's orders."

He should have heeded his instinct: after all, on initial acquaintance he had distrusted Madame Rose. She could not be oblivious to the rumours about him; why should she fuss over his comforts and honour him with the Smile, unless to curry favour with monsieur? But time and Armand's endlessly singing her praises had dulled his suspicions, he had grown used to her ensuring his shirts were laundered with exquisite care and pandering to his weakness for frangipane. Now—yes, it was a shock to find she was as two-faced as her weasely husband, but it was no surprise, why should it be? Did he forget his arch-enemy, the Cyclops, was her brother?

"I apologise, madame. But, as you can see…" He gestured with his eloquently dripping hat.

"There are no fires, the beds aren't aired, the roof is leaking. And I'm on my own here—it's far too late to get Pélagie or Josephine up from the village, even if it wasn't coming down cats and dogs."

What could he do? Without the accursed telegram, he lacked any authority. Remembering the cab still waited outside, he was about to give up and return to Auxerre when she slowly unfolded her arms.

Perhaps she reflected that, deprived though she might be of M. de M's presence, word would surely get back if she mistreated his favourite; at any rate, she heaved a grudging sigh. "Well, now you're here, we'll have to make the best of it."

He awoke the next morning, freezing cold, in an unfamiliar bed within unfamiliar walls. Pulling the blankets up to his chin, he struggled to take stock of his situation. Then he remembered that, according to Madame

Rose, his usual bedroom, part of the master suite and connected to Armand's via the doors of the dressing room, had been put out of commission by a leaking ceiling. The narrow bed he occupied belonged to an isolated room at the extreme eastern end of the landing.

Was it still dark? Distantly a bell was tolling. The Angelus? Unless he lit the candle on the chair beside the bed, he could not read his watch; rather than fumble with matches, he made a cape of the coverlet and braved the clammy air to unlatch the shutters.

A pewter sky greeted him. Although it was long past daybreak, the downpour had not let up. The magnificent view from the garden front was one of the joys of Beauvallon, but this morning the wooded hills, the Gothic tower, the Moorish kiosk and the other lunatic glories of Armand's Arcadia were lost in thick mist, while the lake, what little Max could see of it, was turbid and pocked with rain, and the Temple of Dionysus had been stripped of all pretension to classical grandeur and cruelly revealed for what it was: a wooden shack with a puddled roof and sagging walls, badly in need of paint.

Far off and muffled by the rain, the bell of the village church continued to toll. Of course—it was summoning the faithful to morning mass, today was Sunday. Damn, damn, damn! No wire would arrive, the telegraph office in Soures was closed until tomorrow.

Turning disconsolately from the window, Max surveyed the dingy walls and sparse furnishings of his new quarters. The room was a quarter the size of his own and had probably been intended for a lady's maid or a valet. Last night, tired, chilled to the bone and famished, he had not protested, for at least Madame Rose had taken his wet clothes to be dried and, while there had evidently been no question of a hot meal, she had deigned to serve him bread and cheese. But now, as he kicked his valise under the washstand to clear a path to the wardrobe, he was suddenly furious. It was not so much that he minded the shabby puce-striped wallpaper or the iron bedstead—he could live without luxury—or that the air was rancid with damp: the gloomy stripes were peeling in places and the wall next to the bed appeared porous. What riled him about this mean little room was that it felt like a demotion, a reminder that, in the eyes of Madame Rose, damn her, he, Max, without M. de M, was nothing. Why in heaven's name had the old boy not sent the wire? Was something wrong? That absurd sense of shame assailed him again but he crushed it angrily. He was not suspect, he was not in disgrace. Once he had made himself presentable, he would seek out Madame Rose and put her right on that score.

But, of course, before he could wash and shave he needed hot water, which no one had thought to bring him. And coffee would not go amiss either—he must touch the bell. Yet, though he searched, he could not find one. Curse Madame Rose, this was the final straw! Throwing off the counterpane, he snatched his dressing gown from the hook on the door. He would go downstairs, this minute, just as he was, and demand she move him immediately. Drips and buckets would be preferable to this cupboard that reminded of him of the footman's dormitory he had once shared with Polly.

However, even as his hand was on the doorknob, he heard a timid knock and, when he tore the door open, there was one of the housemaids. A large, plain girl with thin hair and a nose as flat as a button, Pélagie was solemn and painfully shy; confronted by his fury, she stepped backwards abruptly, nearly dropping the can of water she was carrying.

Max was instantly abashed.

"B—begging your pardon, monsieur."

"No, Pélagie, it is I who should beg yours." For, after all, none of this was her fault; she, at least, had always seemed without malice. "Here, please—" he held out his hands for the can "—let me."

But she was still trembling as she released her burden. "Madame says to say she's sorry but she's had trouble getting the copper going and breakfast is served at your convenience." Then, having gabbled her prepared message without once looking him in the eye, she scurried away.

Max did not protest about his room. It was not simply that the continuing absence of the telegram left him on shaky ground; or that he regretted having upset Pélagie, who had sacrificed a day off on his account; or that his mood was tempered by the coffee and brioche laid out for him in the breakfast room. True, Madame Rose did not apologise or honour him with the Smile, but when he wandered through to the kitchen he found her gutting a pullet, which augured well for luncheon, and besides, though he still loathed her duplicity, he began to understand why she was so put out by his arrival.

Armand's apartments were not locked and he had been able to confirm the truth of the dripping ceiling. Furthermore, after breakfast, drifting idly about downstairs, he found every room as dank and cheerless as his own. According to M. de M, the house had been gutted during the revolution, but then lovingly restored by his great-uncle Balthazar; however, that had been sixty years ago and precious little seemed to have been done since. It was with good reason, Max realised, that Armand, much as he loved the place, never ventured here earlier than June and left directly after the wine harvest in September.

In summer the absence of modern comforts was easy to bear, indeed not without appeal. In mellow sunlight, old Balthazar's worn Gobelin upholstery possessed a faded charm; but now, as Pélagie stripped off the dust sheets, it exuded melancholy and more than a whiff of decay. On long summer days the lack of gas was no hardship; but, as Max came upon Durand with a ladder up to one of the chandeliers, he was reminded how many candles, in this, the Grand Salon, and throughout the piano nobile, must be trimmed and lit before nightfall.

And the damp—given the position of the château, in a valley and overlooking a lake, Max supposed it was an inevitable hazard, even without the failings of the low-pitched roof; in August, he remembered, its wraith still hovered in some of the unused upstairs rooms, but at this time of year, with the rain lashing the windows, it crept in everywhere, a manifestation that refused to be exorcised, abetted by draughts from warped window frames and doors. Although the other maid, Josephine, was on her knees, lighting fires in every grate, it would take weeks before the house felt warm and dry. Max could see that if the old boy himself had descended without warning at the beginning of April, Madame Rose, though greeting him in a very different manner, would still have struggled to furnish the welcome he expected.

Max had not forgotten the hardships of service; reluctant fellow feeling stifled his complaints. In any case, he would not be here long— with luck, for no more than two or three days. He even choked back his pride and consented to eat all his meals in the breakfast room; although laying up the dining-room for one person would be Madame Rose's bounden duty if that person were M. de M, Max recoiled from wasting her effort merely to prove a point; he could manage without the full panoply of glass, silver and napery and besides (though he doubted that wretch Durand would be grateful) it saved the nightly toil of two chandeliers.

These signs that he was prepared to be accommodating thawed her somewhat and he was able to ask her about an incident that had intrigued him. When he had wandered into the Yellow Salon, he had come across a strange little figure, standing on a chair to pose in front of a looking glass as she draped herself in a dust sheet. Persephone?

Aphrodite? He was reminded, ridiculously, of Princess Zelenska at the ball, as the child adjusted her draperies, roguishly exposing an imagined bare shoulder. While she was pouting seductively at her own reflection, her eyes caught his in the glass. She stuck out her tongue. He found himself laughing. But, before he could offer any further riposte, she had nimbly disentangled herself from her costume and jumped from the chair. Grabbing a pile of other dust sheets from a sofa, pausing only to pull a hideous face, she rushed past him and was gone.

She could be no more than twelve or thirteen, but her serge dress and apron suggested service. Max could not recall Beauvallon having a between-maid. Even so, something about her—the wild hair, the defiant eyes—seemed curiously familiar.

Madame Rose sighed. "Oh, that'll be Madeleine Plibou."

The daughter of the village drunk and arsonist. Max recollected her now. He remembered her, under Calvert's monitory eye, dragging back a stolen cow to its rightful owners, the Robinots. That had been two years ago and he had scarcely seen her since. She had been skinnier then, and dirtier, but she had not lost her audacity, the impish refusal to be quelled by authority that, as he recalled, he had rather admired at the time.

He laughed. "I should have known. One of the local hobgoblins."

"A flibbertigibbet, more like." Madame Rose sighed again. "It was Monsieur de Miremont's idea to take her on. They owed rent again, the children were hungry, and poor Fernande Plibou works her hands raw doing washing, but, what with that husband of hers taking her last sou—"

"I thought Plibou had run off. After the fire."

"Oh, he's back. Not living there, mind. But still calling in for his drinking money. So if the girl can help put bread on the table… Well, that was monsieur's thought, anyway."

Max smiled to himself. He had seldom seen a girl less suited to service than Madeleine Plibou and he almost felt sorry for Madame Rose: it was typical of the old boy that, in wishing to rescue a lamb from the thicket, he rarely thought that others must suffer the attendant thorns.

"Well, madame, I'm sure you'll lick her into shape eventually."

Madame Rose gave a third, even deeper sigh. "We all have our crosses, monsieur. Just keep your valuables under lock and key."

*

Since it was Sunday, Max could not pursue his business with Calvert; it was too wet for a ride; and Josephine, for all her best efforts, could not get the fire in the library to draw: "Must be a bird's nest," she opined, sooty-faced, as smoke billowed from the chimney, "but we won't get no sweep till tomorrow."

Huddled over the fire in the Yellow Salon, Max fretted at this enforced idleness. Although he had found himself a book, he struggled to concentrate, for his thoughts, with the determination of homing pigeons, kept flying to Paris. Magpie Madeleine recalled milady Telford; but mainly he dwelt with rage on Princess Rosebud. Had she confessed by now? Was Armand furious, was the entire house in uproar? Was that why no one had telegraphed? Was the missing wire perhaps the best possible omen?

But, worst of all, he was pricked by the demon that always began to torment him when he was apart from the old boy. He did not want to, it was a ridiculous weakness—but, confound it, he missed the old fellow. He could blame Beauvallon, of course, for, even in its present inhospitable state, there was not one cranny which failed to remind him that, if there were such a thing as happiness, he had been happy here.

He should not forget he had his daily letter to write. The inkwell in the Yellow Salon's escritoire was dry and there were no nibs, but even when Pélagie had remedied these deficiencies, he sat for a while before picking up his pen. Correspondence with Armand was subject to severe constraints: no endearments, no familiarities, nothing inconsistent with a dutiful secretary writing to his master, nothing at all that might prompt speculation. In the past Max had considered these strictures overcautious and even Armand had slipped from rigid observance on occasion. However, now that madame had taken to opening the old boy's post, the rules were in full force. Max could mention his missed connection and the lack of the telegram, he could say that it was raining and he had not yet seen Calvert; but he could not enquire about Princess Rosebud or write of anything that was in his heart. He must content himself with saying that Madame Rose regretted monsieur's absence and, with everyone at Beauvallon, hoped to see him as soon as his affairs in Paris would permit.

Nonetheless, it seemed safe to assume that Mme de Miremont was not a devotee of the poems of Catullus: at the bottom of the page, beneath his formal respects and signature, Max added the numerals XLVIII.

CHAPTER THIRTY-SEVEN

Euphemia Pilkington was troubled. She wished she did not keep thinking about the book. It had slipped from beneath the pillows when she had put Mlle Juliette to bed that dreadful night. The Hugo translation of *Hamlet*, which she had given to M. Fabien. Too preoccupied with mademoiselle to pay it much heed, she had picked it up from the rug and placed it on a side table. With the turmoil of the following day, she had quite forgotten it.

However, it recurred to her that night, as she lay awake trying to understand how she could have been so wrong about M. Fabien. How odd that Mlle Juliette should keep the book under her pillow? Miss Pilkington recalled that it had fallen open and in the act of closing it she had glimpsed notes in mademoiselle's hand filling the margins and even scrawled over the type. Although Mlle Juliette had subjected her to a barrage of questions when she had decided to read *Hamlet*, Miss Pilkington had formed the view that she did not care for Shakespeare—her interest seemed to have waned as quickly as it had arisen. But perhaps this was to do her an injustice. And, if so, did it not rather touchingly explain why the book had been where it was? Miss Pilkington recalled the childhood superstition: to learn something by heart, you put it beneath your pillow and you would remember every word when you awoke the next morning.

Miss Pilkington did not wish to dwell on the matter because it reminded her too painfully of M. Fabien. Yet, when she was finally admitted to Mlle Juliette's bedroom the next morning, she could not help noticing the book was no longer on the side table. As for the impulse that made her search the boudoir—she could not explain it. But search she did, in vain. She was still examining the bookcase when Drouet came in bearing hot milk and biscuits.

"That horrid book? What you want that for?" Drouet struggled to summon the gentility required of a lady's maid at the best of times, and with such as Miss Pilkington she spared herself the bother.

Still, it was a reasonable question. "I—I don't. I just wondered where it was."

"Gone up in smoke, if you must know. Every last page."

"You burnt it?"

"Yesterday afternoon. On mademoiselle's orders. And a good thing too. She don't want the nasty thing reminding her of that monster."

"No. No, I'm sure she doesn't."

"Well, he'll get what's coming, don't you worry. Monsieur's been again first thing this morning. Proper upset, he was. It was bad enough yesterday when I showed him the gown."

"The gown?"

Drouet looked at Miss Pilkington as if she were simple-minded. "Where the brute tore it to shreds with his bare hands. Then this morning mademoiselle, poor thing, forced herself to show monsieur the terrible bruises on her arm. White as a sheet, the poor gentleman was, when he left. I tell you what—" here Drouet, as she balanced her tray to open the bedroom door, gave Miss Pilkington a knowing look "—I wouldn't be surprised if they bring the ruffian back in handcuffs and turn him over to the magistrate. I wouldn't be surprised at all."

A torn dress? Bruises? Miss Pilkington went away to her own room, puzzled. She had helped Drouet undress Mlle Juliette and put her to bed, but she had not noticed her evening gown was torn— crumpled, perhaps, and even a little dirty from the floorboards, but not torn. And, while bruises took time to make their appearance, there surely would have been red marks already visible on mademoiselle's bare arms.

Perhaps her concern had blinded her. Or, more likely, Drouet was exaggerating—she was very young and this dreadful situation seemed to prey on her imagination. And, as for the book, naturally Mlle Juliette would have wanted it destroyed: if the sight of it was painful to her, Euphemia Pilkington, how much more so to M. Fabien's victim.

Nevertheless, there was the writing—Miss Pilkington could not shake that glimpse of it from her mind. Notes on *Hamlet*? Quotations to be memorised? There was another reason girls kept things under their pillows.

Miss Pilkington had seldom heard Mlle Juliette talk of M. Fabien with less than contempt. Yet could it all have been a pretence? In England, where mademoiselle had been out of her element and at a loss with the language, Miss Pilkington had felt they had become close; but here, in Paris, it was as she had told monsieur: his daughter no longer regarded her as a confidante; now Mlle Juliette was the centre of attention with her every whim indulged, she blew hot and cold towards her and, unless it were as a chaperone to houses where madame was not invited, seemed to have little time for her. Miss Pilkington was in no position to divine any secrets she might have. Or say what she might do.

But then she could not say what M. Fabien might do, either. He had lulled her suspicions by being the one person at the Hôtel de Miremont with whom she had felt at ease; yet that might be only in consequence of their shared situation—neither fish nor fowl, as he put it. Still, she could not help feeling—oh, he had not said so, apart from one outburst about Lady Telford he had always, as was proper, kept his opinions to himself—however, she had gained the distinct impression that, for all his courtesy and willingness to choose books for her, he had not taken to Mlle Juliette.

Miss Pilkington stood by her assertion that no woman in her right mind would invent the sort of allegations Mlle Juliette had made. To describe such a thing to another person, in intimate detail—the very thought of it made her shudder. Yet a woman spurned... a spoilt young girl, self-absorbed and shallow, accustomed to getting her own way—

But here Miss Pilkington reined herself in abruptly. Her dear father had taught her there was good to be found in everyone. "Dwell on the good, my dear. Dwell on the faults and you punish nobody but yourself." He could not know it, poor Papa, but after his death, when she had found herself thrown upon her own resources, moving from one situation to the next, this advice had proved as invaluable as the education he had given her; in fact, it had enabled her to survive. Life at other people's beck and call was not easy. But how much harder if you let yourself be hurt by every slight, which in any case might stem from want of consideration rather than malice. Better to cherish what kindnesses were shown to you; better to be uncomplaining and retain your self-respect than let grudges corrode you.

The Miremonts were not without their foibles—madame's behaviour would cause a scandal in England—but then this was France, a country both irreligious and prone to Catholic laxity. Besides, any affront to Miss Pilkington's rectitude was far outweighed by her debt to the family. She was living in Paris, in great luxury and with everything found. She had been given a wonderful opportunity to perfect her French. And, more than that, her savings from her generous wages had turned her dream of setting up a school with Mina Stokes into a realistic prospect. She owed firm loyalty to the family. And to no one more than to Mlle Juliette, whose paid companion she was.

It did not serve—it threatened the very premise that sustained her—how could she paint the poor girl in such unforgiving colours? Perhaps she liked Mlle Juliette less than she liked M. Fabien, but it was not her business to like or dislike. Mademoiselle, despite her fashionable airs, was still a child, poorly educated, in want of maternal support. If she were thoughtless sometimes, if, although forever chattering about M. de Niversac, she had never shown much depth of feeling for him, finer sensibility would come to her as she matured.

In any case, whatever had occurred in M. Fabien's room, there was no doubt the poor girl was wretchedly unhappy. When Miss Pilkington visited her again in the afternoon with the offer to read to her—which was declined—she looked so pale and pathetic that Miss Pilkington was immediately mortified by her uncharitable thoughts. It was her duty to comfort mademoiselle, not suspect her.

She had glimpsed the writing in the book for no more than a second: was it not presumption to conclude it was a secret diary? She might speculate that it was Drouet who had torn the dress, that mademoiselle had sustained her bruises when she had fainted. But that was all it was— unworthy speculation.

Yet what if this were not a question of charity, but of right and wrong? Her dear Papa would not expect her to condone injustice. She might shrug off wrongs done to herself, but what sort of person would she be if she knew M. Fabien had been falsely accused and, to preserve her own equilibrium, stayed silent?

She tried to pray, as her father would have, but God seemed to have deserted her. She longed to confide in someone, but the only friend she had in Paris apart from M. Fabien was Mme Radescu, the princesse de Vaux's lady companion, and that was not an intimate friendship; besides which, since the poor princess was unwell, Mme Radescu had other, more important concerns.

She longed for Mina. She longed to be back in England with Mina's arms around her, to lay her head on her friend's breast and blurt out her pain and confusion. Mina would see it all clearly and know what she should do. Of course she could write, explain her quandary in her weekly letter. But though she made several false starts, the words, which would have come so readily in Mina's dear presence, seemed to shrink from the chill of ink and paper.

She must try to still her conscience. She must think of M. de Miremont, who, although somewhat distant, had always treated her with the utmost courtesy. Was he not distressed enough already, poor gentleman? And, if she told him Mlle Juliette was lying, would she save M. Fabien? True, M. de Miremont had seemed fond of him; but a secretary, like a paid companion, was always dispensable: not so a beloved daughter. Better to live with her doubts as best she could.

Miremont knew what he must do, but he did not know how to do it. Should he go to Beauvallon? Should he summon the boy back to Paris? Or would it be better—and easier—to write? Yet how could he send such a letter to someone who had been the joy of his life for the past three years? And here was the nub of it: no matter what anger and outrage urged, let alone love for his daughter, he could not seem to shake the habit of loving the boy. When Max's letter arrived, he was enraged by its postscript—how could someone who had done what Max had done insouciantly promise him three hundred thousand kisses?—but, at the same time, the words of Catullus poignantly evoked the afternoon they had become lovers, excruciatingly roused, not just memory, but desire. Worse still, with desire came jealousy. But, dear God, to be jealous of your own daughter! In such circumstances?

Miremont's self-loathing hardened his anger. There could be no argument, no havering, no compromise. His duty was quite straightforward.

However, before he could set out for Beauvallon—a letter was cowardly—there were other troubles to preoccupy him. At least Max was out of the way and a telegram had finally been despatched on the Monday, out of consideration for Madame Rose. Juliette's reputation, on the other hand, was of pressing concern. While the poor child was still an invalid, moving no further from her bed than to a chair, Aline had regained her vigour and was talking of paying calls and reviving her Thursdays. There was doubtless gossip enough about Julie's broken engagement. If Aline went about in Society again, but without her daughter, would not questions be asked? To say Julie was laid low by some mysterious illness would be merely to feed greedy tongues, even Miremont could see that.

It had certainly not been sufficient to banish Lady Telford, as he was soon to discover. One afternoon, not a week after her departure, Raoul de Niversac called upon him.

Entering the Little Salon, arms outstretched to greet the young man, Miremont faltered. Niversac stood as if to attention before the fireplace, white-faced and unsmiling.

Miremont let his arms fall. "My dear fellow…?"

Niversac marched two short paces towards him, then cleared his throat. "Monsieur, I am here to inform you that I shall be sending you my seconds."

"Your...?" Shock and astonishment made Miremont laugh. "Forgive me, but... You are challenging me?"

"I regret I have no alternative."

"But, in heaven's name—why?"

"Although Mademoiselle Juliette is no longer my fiancée, her honour remains dear to me. It is my understanding that this honour has been despoiled—"

"My dear Niversac—"

"I cannot challenge the guilty man, because he is not of my rank. So, since the swine was in your employ, I must challenge you, monsieur. Please be so good as to appoint your seconds."

As Miremont continued to gape at Niversac, confused thoughts assailed him. What a shame protocol prevented the poor fellow from killing Max. Although, since Max was a better swordsman and probably a better shot, the reverse was more likely. If he, Miremont, had to fight, what would he do? Choose pistols, of course, and fire into the air—in present circumstances death would not be unwelcome. But then what would become of Juliette without a father? What would become of poor Niversac himself, fleeing a criminal charge, trapped for the rest of his life in some godforsaken spot abroad? And all this, while the real malefactor—

But his mind cleared and common sense reasserted itself. "My dear Niversac, there is no need for this."

"I never took you for a coward, monsieur."

"I should certainly not insult you by declining your challenge, if it were justified. But, thank heaven, it is not. Let me assure you my daughter's virtue remains intact." No matter what fictions might be necessary to pacify the young man, Miremont could console himself that this at least was true.

"But I heard—"

"Whatever you heard, it is vile gossip. Please, my friend... Let us not stand on ceremony..."

Niversac looked doubtfully at the chair Miremont proffered. "You are certain?"

"Absolutely certain. Poor Juliette is still unwell. But it is as I told you before—a nervous collapse brought on by too much excitement. However, I have had occasion to ask Lady Telford to leave my house.

Out of animus, she may have—how shall I put it?—embroidered the cause of Juliette's indisposition."

This mention of Lady Telford seemed to hit home. Niversac's military bearing deserted him; indeed, it appeared for an instant he might faint from relief. "Thank God!" He slumped into the chair. "Thank God. And Fabien, too—I've always found him a very decent sort."

Miremont, settling himself in a chair nearby, studiously ignored this last comment.

"I have wronged you, monsieur. Please forgive me."

"My dear Niversac, your regard for my daughter's honour does you credit."

"Would she—may I see her?"

"I'm afraid it is early days yet."

"I understand that she might not—in view of…" Niversac hung his head.

Miremont regarded him with pity and affection. Shorn of his warlike manner, he seemed, from his wan cheeks to the circles beneath his eyes, the copybook image of a rejected lover; even his splendid moustache drooped tragically. It touched Miremont that he still cared for Juliette despite her capricious treatment of him.

"Girls of my daughter's age have delicate constitutions. Doctor Chevalier has recommended rest and seclusion. But he assures me that in due course she will recover her joie de vivre. Of course, I cannot promise anything, my dear fellow…"

Niversac nodded sadly.

"But in the meantime we must scotch this poisonous rumour. Perhaps, if you do not mind, you will tell me where you heard it." Where indeed, since Lady Telford had been escorted directly to Calais?

"From your nephew, Roland."

"Roland!"

"He had it from Lord Stilorgan."

Of course. No power Miremont possessed could stop Lady Telford writing letters. An appalling thought struck him. If Niversac had been prepared to fight over Julie's ruined reputation, should not her father take similar action? Once again he shrank from the notion of firing shots in anger, he who deplored even the shooting of game. But if it were to save his daughter, if the person concerned were a rat like Stilorgan, perhaps he should not let principle stand in his way.

But Niversac had already leapt to his feet with fire in his eyes. "That scoundrel Stilorgan! That cad, that sharper. I should have realised. Well, he shall pay for his filthy lies."

"My friend, I do not think—surely, it is I who—"

"No, monsieur, I beg you. It will be a privilege and a pleasure. I shall go to the swine directly."

Miremont could not delude himself that the gossip would cease, particularly if Niversac held to his resolve. But the family was all at once sequestered from it by the obligations of mourning.

The princesse de Vaux's chill had turned to pneumonia and, although she had seemed to be rallying, a sudden relapse had claimed her with barely time for the last rites. Aline, inevitably, was furious: no Thursdays, no opera, no theatre, no receptions: instead, a whole month of purdah, relieved only by dreary condolence calls; the latest thing in *crêpe anglais* mourning toilettes was no consolation. Miremont, who had been fond of the princesse, was forced to post Thomas at his door again to escape his wife's complaints. But then a second death silenced her.

The day after the princesse succumbed, Bébé vanished. Aline accused Simon of losing him in the Luxembourg Gardens. But, two days later, one of the housemaids dusting the Elizabeth Salon noticed a smell, which she traced to a marquetry cabinet in a far corner. Beneath it, silenced for once, defeated by his diet of chocolate or by sheer misery, Bébé had sought his final refuge.

All the tears another might have shed for the princesse, Aline poured out for Bébé's loss. She took to her bed and Dr Chevalier was sent for.

CHAPTER THIRTY-EIGHT

For several days, while the princesse de Vaux's children and other distant Miremont relations gathered for the vigil and her Requiem Mass at Saint-Sulpice, Miremont was much occupied. Even after her coffin had finally left for Picardy to be interred beside her husband's in his ancestral mausoleum and the family gathering had dispersed, there were letters of sympathy to be answered and calls from friends to be received, the burden of which should properly have been Aline's but, given her indisposition, naturally fell upon Miremont.

As a result, he had yet to take action against Max. Every day he made time to visit Julie and, as each visit still found her unimproved, frail and dwindling as a fern starved of water, his guilt mounted. It was he who had brought the boy into the house, who had let lust corrupt him, who had even deluded himself that temporary abstinence would restore his moral probity and shield Julie from his sins: he, as much as Max, had done this to his daughter. And now, if that were not enough, he was failing in this paramount duty. If the princesse's death prevented him from setting out for Beauvallon, then he must write.

He had in fact already written, but only as the Gauls might have sent ambassadors to Caesar, to win time and stave off the inevitable. The boy himself had by now written three times and his last letter had tellingly omitted the Roman numerals; Miremont's silence might put it into his head to return to Paris, which must be prevented at all cost. Accordingly, Miremont had sent the briefest possible missive, informing him of Lady Telford's departure and the princesse's passing. But the real letter, the letter of dismissal—oh, he had tried several times but had not yet got further than a stumbling opening sentence, promptly scratched out.

Catherine de Claireville lowered her teacup. "Where's the boy?"

Clotilde, who had been assisting her father with the condolence calls, had excused herself fastidiously when the duchesse was announced, obliging Miremont to receive his supposed mistress alone. And, of course, having duly expressed sympathy for the family's loss, Catherine had fixed him with the look he had been dreading.

When he did not immediately answer her question, she settled her cup in its saucer and asked again: "Well? What have you done with him?"

"For the moment, he's in the country—"

"For the moment?"

"Until I can... until I..." Catherine might be renowned for her bluntness but, since she must certainly have heard the gossip, it behoved her, Miremont thought, to exercise tact for once. "Forgive me, but I prefer not to discuss it."

She cocked her head so that even the beady eye of the small black bird adorning her hat seemed to regard him askance. "Am I to understand you believe this nonsense?"

"Please, let us not—"

"You, who profess to care for him?"

"Catherine, I beg you..." For a moment the grief he had managed to subsume in the general mourning for the princesse rose up and threatened to unman him until, recalling how unseemly it was, he was able to crush it. "If you could see my poor Juliette..."

"I did see her. The night of your ball."

The ball seemed so firmly to belong to a distant, simpler past that he stared at her, bewildered.

"I saw her fury that he was dancing with me."

As far as Miremont knew, Max had not had time to dance—yet another thing the boy had concealed. "Well—doubtless she believes Aline's absurd notion."

"She was furious because he was dancing with me to avoid her."

"Oh, but that's surely not—"

"Most unchivalrous, I agree. Particularly as I have always thoroughly spoiled him. So naturally I took him to task. And he told me everything."

"He told you...? What did he tell you?"

"I had to force it out of him and afterwards he swore me to secrecy. So I am not at liberty to say."

"For pity's sake, Catherine—"

"But I am free to tell you what he did not say. He did not say he cherished a burning desire for your daughter. He did not say her obsessive passion for him gave him pleasure. And he did not say that, when he tried to warn you weeks ago of a situation which might prove disastrous, you listened to him willingly or, indeed, listened to him at all."

A sliver of hope taunted Miremont, like a light beneath a forbidden door. Determinedly he closed his eyes to it. "My dear Catherine, those are the same lies he told me."

"I do not think he was lying."

"But you, yourself—how often have you said to me 'You know what the boy is?'"

"To tease, perhaps. Because he is such a cocksure rascal. But, darling Armand—" she reached across the tea-table to grasp his hand "—he was not cocky then. He was as I have never seen him before—thoroughly shaken, not himself at all."

The locked door flew open, Miremont was dazzled as hope flooded in. But almost instantly a shadow obscured it, the image of Julie, red-rimmed eyes apathetic, fragile hands laid limply upon the rug that covered her knees. He disentangled his fingers from Catherine's.

"So it is Juliette who is lying?"

She merely looked at him.

"But you cannot—if you knew, if you saw my poor broken child, if you sat by helplessly, as I must, and watched her suffer, you would never... Good grief, Catherine, where is your heart? Where is your womanly understanding, that you can bring yourself to insinuate such a thing?"

"Might it be womanly understanding that prompts me?"

Miremont's outrage overwhelmed him. "How dare you! In all the years of our friendship I have never thought you hard. But to traduce a wronged and innocent girl? That is hard, madame, hard as stone. I cannot forgive it."

Catherine de Claireville gathered up her gloves and reticule. "In all the years of our friendship, Armand, I have thought you intelligent, but not clever." The swish of her train as she rose rattled cups and dislodged the sugar tongs. "But I see I was wrong on both counts. You are a complete fool."

No, Miremont would not forgive Catherine, either for the hope she had stirred, or for defending Max, for which the unregenerate part of him still craved to love her. Anger was his best recourse, prickly, tormenting anger, a girdle of thorns to purge unsuitable thoughts.

Consolation during these troubled days came from an unexpected quarter: Clotilde. Practical and sensible, she proved a more than adequate substitute for her mother in carrying out the social duties mourning imposed, earning Miremont's gratitude and appreciation; although it was true she still spoke to him as if he were in his dotage, he felt remorse for his previous antipathy.

One afternoon, as they sat together in the Little Salon after the last callers had gone, he ventured to seek her advice, for he was in despair about her sister.

To his surprise, she favoured him with an indulgent, even pitying look, and patted his hand. "Poor dear Papa. You are too soft-hearted."

Miremont was instantly indignant. "But she is gravely ill, Chevalier speaks of brain fever."

"Nonsense. She is a little anaemic, no more. It is high time she pulled herself together."

"Pulled herself—? Clotilde, I am amazed at you! After all your sister has been through!"

But Clotilde was unabashed. "Dear Papa, she is not the Lady of the Camellias, just a spoony schoolgirl."

"Whatever do you mean by that?"

"Oh, Papa!" She shot him another of her patronising looks.

"Are you saying … Are you saying she encouraged him?"

"I shouldn't be at all surprised."

"Clotilde!" Once more Miremont drove out hope with rage. "Have you no sisterly feeling? Poor innocent Julie! Of course, I realise you have always been jealous of her."

"I—jealous of Julie? Gracious, Papa, why should I be? I have two beautiful children and a husband I adore, if I could persuade you and Maman to stop bickering I should be quite content. I do not in the least envy Julie."

Her astonishment seemed so genuine he was immediately ashamed of himself. "But then, why…?

"Poor Papa." She patted his hand again. "It is you who are innocent. Ask Maman why she sent Julie to Bruges."

The moment Clotilde had gone, Miremont set out for his wife's apartments, but on the way he encountered Miss Pilkington, who wished to speak to him urgently.

Ever since their previous conversation, Miremont had felt towards the Englishwoman that unjust coldness which muddles the messenger with the message; yet there was at present something curious in her manner, not agitation precisely, but a kind of heroic determination, so that he found it impossible to turn her away.

However, once installed on a chair in his salon, while she did not blush—on the contrary, she was deathly pale—she seemed to find it hard to begin.

"I—I wanted to thank you, monsieur, for your kindness to Madame Radescu."

Poor distraught Mme Radescu had been left homeless and destitute by her mistress's demise, for, although the will promised her a bequest, the princesse had died penniless; with the assistance of Clotilde, Miremont had found her a place with the elder Mme de Corvignac.

"Madame Radescu served my cousin with devotion," he said. "It was the least we could do." Yet, while he knew the two lady companions were friends, he was puzzled: the determined set of Miss Pilkington's jaw promised more than politesse.

Nor was he mistaken. Miss Pilkington visibly squared her shoulders, then took a deep breath. "It was kind, monsieur. And—now my friend is settled—I must trespass on your kindness again. I must ask you to accept my notice, with immediate effect."

"My dear madame—"

"I realise I have not given you due warning. But I beg you to take whatever wages are outstanding to me in lieu."

"Madame—Miss Pilkington…" Miremont stared at her, bemused. "In the first place, I do not employ you. You should properly speak to my daughter or Madame de Miremont."

"No. That is—it is better I speak to you."

Given present circumstances, this was probably sensible, but Miremont was still disconcerted by Miss Pilkington's resolute jaw. "Very well. But then I must ask—have we in some way offended you?"

"No, it is I who—that is to say, I am needed at home. By my friend Miss Stokes. We are setting up a school."

"Ah yes, I think Juliette mentioned your school. Well, my dear Miss Pilkington, we shall be very sorry to lose you. Very sorry." Miremont found his coldness had vanished; he would indeed miss this pleasant, willing Englishwoman who had brought to his household the calm good sense that was so often lacking. "Of course we do not expect you to sacrifice any money owed to you and we must pay your passage back to England. And, as for your school, it would be my pleasure to contribute—"

"No!"

Her cry startled them both. To Miremont it sounded like a cry of pain.

"No. I am sorry, but you should not…" Colour spread from her throat until her very ears burned scarlet. "I have done wrong."

To Miremont's dismay, her eyes filled with tears. Miss Pilkington did not weep like Julie, freely and copiously; her tears were clotted, ungainly, impeded by a strenuous but futile clenching of her eyelids.

"I was wrong to question my judgement of Monsieur Fabien. He is not—he has never been—anything other than a gentleman."

"My dear Miss Pilkington—"

"Please, monsieur, I cannot say more. Do not ask me."

"Woman, for—!" Miremont only narrowly stopped himself from swearing. He had been in this stuffy room for half an hour now, sitting in semi-darkness on the uncomfortable chair he had drawn up to the bed and listening to Aline's endless prevarications. "I just want you to tell me the truth!"

"Do not shout. My head is splitting."

"Am I to take it you knew all along that things were not right with Julie?"

"Have some mercy. It is not my fault."

"Not your fault? You let our daughter risk her reputation, you even exaggerated the business until it was the talk of Paris, yet you knew it was a figment and an innocent man had been accused."

"Innocent? She may have led them on but they were none of them innocent."

"What do you mean? They—who are they?"

"I am not to blame. I thought the nuns would drive it out of her. Please, if you have any compassion, let me have a dab of cologne."

With a sigh of exasperation, Miremont reached for the bottle from the nightstand. He watched impatiently as she sprinkled her handkerchief and then pressed it to her forehead. God, she was weeping again. He was tired of womanly tears; he was tired of sickrooms, whether it were Julie's, cold and arid with self-abnegation, or this one, oppressive as a hothouse, smelling of scent and overripe flesh; he was tired of evasion and melodrama: he dreaded the truth for what it might reveal about his daughter, but he was determined to hear it if it permitted him to love Max.

Aline mopped her face with the handkerchief, then, wincing as if valiantly suppressing intolerable pain, fell back upon her pillows. "You always blame me. Always. Yet what could I have done?"

"You are Julie's mother, for pity's sake!"

"And you are her father. Who discarded me, packed me off to the country so you could have your way with that evil witch—"

"Madame, how many times must I tell you, Catherine de Claireville has never been—"

"I was young, I was beautiful, I was bound to have admirers. She was jealous of me."

"Julie? She was a child."

"She was thirteen. Of age. She envied my beauty, how men fell madly in love with me."

"Oh, for heaven's sake!"

"She was always difficult, even in the nursery she did everything to spite me."

"If this is true, why did you not tell me?"

"You? What did you care? You wanted sons, not daughters."

"Aline, that is not fair."

"Yes, she is your beloved Julie now. She thinks she has you dangling from her little finger, she thinks she can wheedle anything out of you— gowns, jewels, servants—"

That a mother should be so brazenly jealous of her own child— Miremont was all at once unable to contain his distaste; his only wish was to quit this fetid room and hear no more. But, though he pushed back his chair, Aline was not to be silenced.

"But little does she know, she's only beloved for as long as it takes to marry her off. Oh, my own dear Papa—"

"Madame!" Miremont rose. "I have heard quite enough about your father over the years to realise I do not merit comparison, so if you will forgive me—"

"On the contrary. She'll see. You are just like him—two-faced." Aline's tears recommenced, but quietly, as though she were suddenly overcome with fatigue. "Do you want the truth about my Papa? He had no time for me, it was always Robert, Robert, Robert. Then one day he noticed I was a beauty, and I hoped—I started to believe… But he only wanted me off his hands. If you must know, I was just a thing to be traded and you were a great coup—an old title and rich enough not to be too particular about the dowry. I adored him, I wanted to please him, but he didn't care what pleased me." She had reared up, stretching out her hand as if to drag Miremont back to her, but now she collapsed upon her pillows. "Oh, I've tried to pretend to myself—I even wanted to believe Madame Neroni's stories about the spirit world. But the truth is, Papa never loved me. In all my life no one has ever loved me or cared about my happiness. Not you, with your vile hag of a mistress. Not my daughters, not my so-called friends. I have given unstintingly of myself, given and given until I am wrung dry—but, do you know, there is only one soul who has ever truly loved me, one creature in the world." Her hand drifted to the space beside her on the coverlet where Bébé had always slept. "And now, poor lamb, he is gone!"

Miremont resumed his chair. His flight had been arrested by her extraordinary admission that venal old Papa de Sestrès had been less than a paragon, so that, whereas he normally deafened himself to his wife's tirades and there was much in this one that was, as ever, self-serving, he could not avoid hearing its genuine despair; nor, despite the bathos of her final outburst, could he deny her agony was heartfelt.

He stared down at her—the doughy flesh, the flaccid toothless cheeks, the handkerchief still plastered to her temples like a dead leaf to dank paving. Yes, she had been a beauty once, more beautiful even than Julie. Was it her fault if he had not desired her? With renewed guilt, he recalled the clumsy humiliations of their wedding night and her look of disappointment and disgust. If he had known about himself what he knew now, would he have continued to dwell on his inadequacy, would he have let his revulsion, his dread at each necessary but inglorious attempt, remake her beauty in the image of his own shame? Poor thing, beauty was all she had possessed. Perhaps, if he had been wiser, less solipsistic, kinder, he might have coaxed out of her more enduring virtues, sensitivities her upbringing had stunted. But, in his self-loathing, he had failed her.

He found her hand and took it in his. "My dear, I am sorry."

She gazed up at him, her puffy eyes glittering with astonishment. "You? *You* are sorry?"

"I know I have not been a good husband to you."

She continued to stare at him. Then she let forth a throaty laugh. "You? Armand de Miremont. The pillar of virtue. You at last admit what a hypocrite you are, that you and that harpy—?"

"Please! Aline!" Although she had withdrawn her hand, determinedly he regained it. "I don't know how you acquired this notion, but you must believe me, it is fanciful. Catherine is not and has never been my mistress, she is a friend, no more. If I have been less than… If I have seemed unfeeling, it is because I… because I am unsuited to marriage. I wish I had known that before I married you, and I blame myself that I did not."

The watery eyes took on a glimmer of uncertainty, even puzzlement. "You blame yourself? Then why have I always been to blame for everything?"

"My dear, you have not."

"Two minutes ago you were claiming Juliette was all my fault."

"If there is something amiss with Julie, it is my fault as much as yours. You are right, I cannot ignore my responsibilities as her father. Now please…" Although her fingers were damp and flabby, he endeavoured to knead them between his, for she had begun to sob again, whether from relief or renewed consciousness of her wrongs it was hard to tell. "Please, my dear, try not to distress yourself. Please, if you can, forgive my failures and let there be a truce between us."

All the same, Miremont returned to his study angry and sickened. His sweet innocent daughter? She had deceived him, treated him like a fool—and that was not to consider her treatment of Max. Well, it was, as he had said, a father's responsibility, his pressing duty to curb this laxity—flirtatiousness, licence, whatever it was—to drum it out of her, ensure she did not go the way of her poor benighted mother. He would confront her and force her to admit the truth. Then, in a week or so, when the situation was calmer, he could send for Max.

CHAPTER THIRTY-NINE

There was a smell of pine and the Other was screaming. They were inside a tree trunk, both of them, trapped, able to see out but unable to get free. They were in a forest. There were other trees with people inside them. These people were screaming too, screaming, shrieking. The forest was on fire, the trees were blazing. The Other yelled: "They want to kill me, but they'll kill you too!" Then a face rose up, white as the moon. Their nurse Fromchen, who was kind to him and smelt of aloes. He thought she would tell them it was time for bed, but when she opened her mouth a serpent slithered out and slid over her bosom. The Other was clinging to him. He tried to shake him off, but the Other had wrapped his arms and legs around him like the Old Man of the Sea. He twisted, turned, lashed out—

There was a crash. Then darkness.

For some moments, such was his terror, Max thought the steady drip, drip, drip was blood. Then he fancied he must be back in the cellar, hearing the gutter leaking into the slop bucket. But no, when at last he came to consciousness and struggled to sit up, he discovered that in trying to disentangle himself from the sheets he had knocked the water carafe from the chair beside his bed. Even then, he might have lit his candle to check the Other was not lurking in the darkness, but the discovery that his matches were soaked through brought him fully to his senses. The screaming he had heard in his dream was only the wind shrieking round the eaves and whistling through the ill-fitting window frames. He was crouched, shivering, in his room at Beauvallon and it was still raining.

On the Monday after Max's arrival, the telegram legitimising his mission had finally been delivered and he had received a visit from Calvert, during which it was agreed they should make a tour of the building works the following morning.

Unlike Madame Rose, the steward was affability itself. He could not have been more contrite about the roof, offering an assortment of excuses from the weather and the notorious unreliability of contractors to the difficulty obtaining the right texture and thickness of slate; and, as for devoting several hours of his day to M. Fabien's concerns, well— his broad shoulders shrugged expansively, his black eyes twinkled with conscious charm, his gold teeth glittered—what task could be more important or more pleasurable?

Max was duly shown the fire-damaged cottage, from which most of the charred timber and brick had by now been hacked away. It was not the Plibous' dwelling or the one adjoining it, but the home of the jobbing carpenter, Cagot. However, Calvert had no hesitation in naming the guilty party: granted there were no witnesses nor other evidence to speak of, but, even if you ignored Plibou's being behind most of the village's petty crime, he was known to hold a long-standing grudge against the Cagots; besides, why else had he run off that night?

Max nodded his agreement. Today, although the rain had thinned to drizzle, it remained constant and dispiriting. Yet he was determined to match Calvert's apparent indifference to the cold and damp, resolved to meet the challenge thrown out by his adversary's knowing smiles with a confident counter-attack.

The footings for the new phase of cottages, the drainage works, the home farm fields newly sown according to Armand's experimental rotation scheme, even the old fellow's latest toy, a Ransomes threshing machine, the most up-to-date model specially imported from England, a monster of wood and iron, which, with its shiny black steam engine and towering elevator, occupied most of the Great Barn—Max scrutinised it all with what he hoped was an air of authority. He would show Calvert he was not the effete city-dweller he took him to be. Had he not spent his schooldays in the Normandy countryside, enduring frequent spells of penance working with the lay brothers in the monastery fields? And, after two summers at Beauvallon, was he not thoroughly conversant with Armand's projects?

But, in truth, none of this availed him, neither what he had learned pulling turnips for Brother Bernard, nor his discussions with Armand, which had generally centred, not on the practicalities of the works, but on the benefits they would bring. If Max were to catch Calvert skimping or bodging, he required an eye trained in the technicalities of construction. Whereas, watching the men labouring in the sodden drainage trenches, although disagreeably reminded of his own stint as a drain-digger during his first months in Paris, he could not have told if the trenches were deep enough or the clay tiles of suitable quality. And it was the same everywhere. He asked questions, of course, but, lest he betray his ignorance, they must be restricted to the circumstantial kind: "How long will it take? How much will it cost?" When Calvert informed him that the threshing machine's bewildering array of cogs, chains and wheels could thrash four hundred bushels of wheat a day, he could only nod sagely.

It did not escape him that Calvert failed to be deceived. Indeed, to his chagrin, with every proof of his deficiency his foe's charm grew oilier. Still, Max would shake the old swindler's complacency yet. When Calvert suggested they take lunch together in the steward's room and afterwards go through the accounts, he accepted with alacrity.

The account ledgers occupied one wall of the steward's room and, judging by the faded spines on the upper shelves, were ranged chronologically, meticulous records of the Calvert family's dealings on behalf of the estate dating back to old Balthazar's time. Max had only to apply himself to the most recent volumes and, if there were the smallest inconsistency, the slightest evidence of malfeasance, he would surely root it out.

Accordingly, when they had consumed Madame Rose's onion soup, cassoulet and baked custard, Pélagie had brought coffee, and Calvert, having dabbed his moustache with his napkin, was pushing back his chair, Max stayed him with a gesture. "Monsieur, I fear I have taken up enough of your valuable time already. Shall we look at the accounts another day?"

"Of course, monsieur." Calvert reached into his breast pocket for his cigar case. "Whenever you prefer."

"Or perhaps I need not trouble you at all. If the key is readily available."

Had Max rattled the fellow? Did he falter for an instant? If so, he was to be commended for his bravado, for his teeth winked genially as he proffered the cigar case, the points of his moustache positively twitched with pleasure. "My dear monsieur, this room is never locked. Please, I beg you, make free."

In fact, Max never did examine the ledgers. Reflection told him he would find nothing questionable: Calvert was far too shrewd. But in any case he had lost heart for the endeavour.

It was not just that the rain continued, battering the white petals from the pear trees in the orchard and bearing down like a bully on the apple boughs and their pink buds, bent on draggling their finery before it was ever unfurled.

Nor was it merely because, having admitted defeat over the accounts, Max had nothing to do. Oh, he accompanied Calvert on a couple of his routine inspections of the estate and the park, visited the Maison des Vignerons, where M. Saint-Séverin's report on the phylloxera was pessimistic, and rode out on his own several times, in spite of the weather. But the grass was like sponge, the road puddled, even awash in some parts, and every bridle path a quagmire, while, in Armand's absence, the only saddle horse in the stables was a stolid chestnut mare resentful of going above a canter, a distinct comedown after his usual mount, Pretender. There was the shooting gallery, of course, out by the ruins of the Old Manoir, but in this weather it was less than inviting. And, as for swimming—even if the temperature were to rise, the area of the lake he and the old boy frequented was clogged with weed and never dredged until the beginning of summer.

Neither was any distraction to be found in the village itself. Now he was no longer wafted on the warm breeze of sycophancy stirred by monsieur's presence, he was all too aware that the villagers, not to say the entire commune, shared Madame Rose's judgement: without the old boy he was nothing; at best a stranger, against whom the village clenched its muscles like an oyster resisting the knife; at worst, a spy, with an unsavoury reputation to boot. Calvert, though disliked, merited a greeting and a doffed cap, but those passing Max on the road either stared at him balefully or looked aside, while at the village tabac, which was run by a Thomas (half the villagers, even the local policeman, seemed to be related to the Cyclops), Max's entrance met with a silence worthy of the Pigalle's roughest estaminet. He had managed to invite ill will, too, during his visit to the vinery: somehow, in the company of Armand, M. Saint-Séverin had overlooked Max's customary abstinence, but on this occasion it was clear his refusal to taste Beauvallon's prized vintages had given offence.

Max took it as a point of principle to appear unconcerned. After all, he was only here for a few days. Still, there was no harm in making himself less conspicuous. The only country clothes he possessed were intended for high summer, while this was overcoat weather; yet he could hardly complain of attracting stares in his alpaca coat and topper. He found an old felt hat and an oilcloth cape in Armand's wardrobe and adopted the gaiters the old boy wore instead of riding boots.

Alas, to little avail. The smaller Calvert boys, a trio now the youngest had grown, and a ragamuffin bunch despite their father's social pretensions, were given to mimicking Max's supposed Parisian airs: one even dared take aim at the felt hat with his catapult, although they all ran off fast enough when Max swung round to glare. Even

Plibou, whom Max had encountered out by the Old Manoir, had let forth a stream of abuse: a wild, emaciated figure, still limping from the injury he had sustained two winters ago falling into the path of a cart, he had rolled his yellow eyes and wagged a threatening finger—although Max, who could only distinguish the words 'tyrant' and 'revolution', wondered if the wretch had not mistaken him for Armand: Plibou, like the village schoolmaster, M. Crépin, was one of Beauvallon's fervent Jacobins.

Yet it would all have been bearable if there had only been a letter from the old fellow—dear God, Armand could usually not restrain himself from writing every day, but now there was not a word and Max's own letters went unanswered. Of course, the old boy would not find it easy to challenge his little princess and no doubt madame would compound his problems. Max should make allowances. Hadn't the telegram arrived eventually? Perhaps it was the same with the lack of post—a mischance, not an omen. Nevertheless, Max's innocence should be established by now; again he bitterly regretted not staying. He might recall the old boy's promise to uphold justice, but he was bound to find the silence depressing.

When at last a letter did arrive, it scarcely reassured him. He was sad to learn of the princesse de Vaux's death (although his acquaintance with her was slight, he knew the old boy would be grieved); equally he rejoiced to see milady had departed; but there were no thanks for his own part in her leaving, nor indeed any hint of encouragement in the single curt page, however minutely he studied it for hidden meanings. No mention was made of La Rosebud. Or of his return to Paris. And, bleakest sign of all, there was no postscript.

His instinct was to write a savage reply: not the anaemic account of doings at Beauvallon he was supposed to send, but a full-blooded expression of his rage and disgust. Why had the old boy sworn he believed him, when that was clearly a lie? Was this the sole reward he, Max, deserved for the deprivations and humiliations of the past six months? Love? If this was what Armand's hypocritical twaddle amounted to, then he could... But gradually Max calmed himself. Mme de Vaux's death would have caused all manner of upheaval. If he had not been pronounced innocent, he had not been found guilty; perhaps he should give the old fellow the benefit of the doubt. Besides, there was a very real risk of madame intercepting his letter. Two weeks, the old boy had said. He had not been at Beauvallon above ten days. He should restrain himself and wait.

Yet the old boy's chilly tone continued to disturb him. And, when his dutifully written report of the latest village trivia received no response, not for mere days but for over a week, his anger mounted again, together with a misery that crept through him like slow fever.

However, life at Beauvallon had improved somewhat. The rain had stopped, the apple trees were in blossom, every field and verge was all at once abundantly green; and Max was in Madame Rose's favour at last.

He had been walking back from the stables when he had found her in a state of some fury and screaming for Durand. The Calvert boys had let the home farm piglets out and chased them into the walled garden, where the creatures were rooting up the asparagus and trampling her precious herbs. There was no sign of Durand. While Max might be no expert in other agricultural matters, he had learned much about pigs from Brother Bernard, who had shared his hut companionably with Juno, the Saint-Pons sow.

The first two were easy: their little black rumps were towards Max as they truffled in the salsify bed and he was able to snatch one by the hind leg, then swing it, trotters dangling, over his left forearm while his right hand grabbed the other. On the path beyond the doorway, Madame Rose had the largest Calvert boy by the scruff of the neck and was marching him towards the scene of the crime; Max decanted the beasts into the hands of the miscreant, who, on pain of having his ears boxed, would restore them to their pen.

The element of surprise was gone, however. The other five piglets, squealing joyfully, raced around the garden, churning up earth and plants, darting down paths and behind bushes, here, there, in every direction except towards the open doorway. Attempting the groinking and he-hons Brother Bernard had favoured, Max captured a third. And he was chasing a fourth around the raspberry canes when he grew aware that someone else had joined him. Not Durand. This was a fellow closer to his own age, improbably dressed in a suit and bowler. Separately, they accounted for the fifth piglet and the sixth. But the seventh, the wiliest, undoubtedly the Napoleon of the litter, eluded their joint efforts.

Max had been irritated by the stranger's incursion, for the chase was a rare peak of exhilaration in the flat futility of his days. Yet his unwanted helper seemed to have caught his mood. True, the fellow cursed roundly when, narrowly missing Napoleon's hindquarters as he pursued him along a border, he was pitched flat onto his respectable suiting; but he was chuckling as he struggled to his feet. For an instant their quarry seemed to have vanished entirely and they stood, out of breath and muddy, bereft of their hats, exchanging grins. Then Max spotted the fugitive at the other end of the garden, emerging jauntily from a gooseberry bush to play toss with his new comrade's bowler, and they were off again, Max to attack his rearguard, the stranger to cut off his advance. But, outwitted every time by the little Corsican's dodges and feints, they soon abandoned finesse, giving themselves up to the joy of the chase, whooping, swearing, thundering between cucumber frames and through beds of young lettuces like charging Cossacks. At last Napoleon found himself cornered behind the water butt; as he shot out on Max's side, they both fell upon him and the stranger seized his hind legs.

Madame Rose could not have been more delighted when they emerged with their captive. Max, going back briefly to retrieve their hats, fancied she might be less effusive on inspecting the garden, where the pursuers had wreaked more destruction than the pursued. Still, he accepted her praise for rushing into the breach and her rueful exclamations about the state of his clothing; he was even rather pleased, against his better nature, to find himself once again worthy of the Smile. His comrade, to whom he had yet to be introduced, was not so favoured, he noticed. Indeed, though he shared Max's elation as they walked back to the house, clapping him on the shoulder and laughing cheerfully at the sight of his mangled bowler, he did not seem unaware that he was under a cloud.

The reason was made evident once they were in the kitchen and Pélagie and Josephine were divesting them of their muddy boots and jackets.

"I've said it before," grumbled Madame Rose, emerging from the pantry with one of her pear and frangipane tarts. "Those little devils of yours! Never at school, running riot like weevils. High time your father took the strap to them and meant business."

"Madame, once again I can only..."

While his new comrade was promising faithfully that the damage would be rectified, Max was overcoming his surprise. Of course. He had wondered how a stranger had felt free to give the boys such a tongue-lashing. But he might have recognised the hook of the nose and jut of the jaw, even if the complexion were fairer and not shot with veins and the thatch on the upper lip modest compared with the paternal mustachios. Palmyre Calvert. The steward's eldest son, whom Armand had sent to be educated at the École Normale Supérieure and who must now be in his first year at the Institute of Agronomy at Grignon. Unfairly perhaps, Max's comradely feelings cooled.

"That's all very well," said Madame Rose, as she set the sliced tart on the table. "But what am I to tell monsieur if there's no asparagus to be had this summer? Why, if it hadn't been for Monsieur Fabien here, dashing to the rescue…"

"Monsieur Fabien?" Now it was Palmyre Calvert's turn to look at Max sharply, even with puzzlement, as though struggling to match what he saw with some fixed preconception. Then a reciprocal coldness stiffened him too. "My old man mentioned you were here."

"More than he did you," said Madame Rose, conveying a large slice of tart onto Max's plate, but pointedly angling the server for Palmyre to help himself. "Popping up out of nowhere. Quite a stranger, you are. Still, you'll have fancy new friends in Dijon, I don't doubt."

"If you must know, I've come to see my mother. The governor wrote that she's taken a turn for the worse. The doc says it's consumption."

Max had not seen Mme Calvert since his arrival, but then she was rarely visible at the best of times, a wisp of a woman, walled up in that overly grand house beyond the farm buildings, beset not only by the ragamuffins but by the needs of her two daughters, one simple by all accounts, the other in callipers. And now she was ill, wretched downtrodden creature, although you would not guess it from her husband, who went on swaggering and gambling and visiting that expensive mistress of his: Max appended callousness to his list of charges against the steward.

The son, however, was apparently made of different stuff, or at least not devoid of filial affection: his voice had trembled as he had spoken the word 'consumption'. Yet he seemed to regret this weakness, for, though Madame Rose, softening at once, sat down beside him and even patted his hand, he shrugged off her commiserations and turned the talk elsewhere.

And perhaps he was not so different from his father after all. Max could not but observe, as they talked about the course at Grignon, that the caution which had chilled Palmyre's manner on learning his identity had not relaxed. To the contrary. Whereas, when they had first faced each other across the table, Palmyre had slouched forward in friendly fashion, now he sat upright, rigid, withdrawn; although his conversation was amiable enough and his tone not unpleasant, when Max passed him the cake slice he took ostentatious care to avoid their hands touching. Monsieur's spy. Monsieur's *petit jésus*. Did he believe Max too stupid to guess what he was thinking?

Thus, when Pélagie had returned with their jackets and they were rising to leave, Max was greatly surprised to hear Palmyre say casually: "According to the governor, you shoot a bit. How about me showing you how it's done one of these days?"

Although Max was at first disposed to throw the invitation back in Palmyre's face, he missed the competition Armand provided at the shooting range. And besides, did he not have time on his hands?

At any rate, it was his pleasure the next morning to demonstrate to the fellow that he required no lessons in aiming a pistol. To his credit, Palmyre took defeat with good grace, even unthawed somewhat as if his prejudices were shaken; since Max could hardly deny him the chance to even the score, they spent most of the morning at the targets and parted on good enough terms to agree to meet again the next day.

It transpired that Palmyre, too, had time to spare, for Mme Calvert had fortunately come through her crisis. He and Max spent much of the next week together, shooting, riding, climbing the hills in Armand's Arcadia, taking out shotguns on a couple of nights to bag rabbits. At first Max was surprised Palmyre did not join his father on his rounds of the estate, but one or two chance remarks suggested father and son might not always see eye to eye. Palmyre, it seemed, had advanced ideas on agriculture and was keen to see the estate and the entire commune more productive; while he had enjoyed the École Normale he had disliked Paris and was glad to be back in the Côte D'Or, one step closer to his goal, which was to bring farming out of the dark ages; and, who knew, his scientific notions might prove more effective than Armand's woolly philanthropy. Max liked his enthusiasm and his commitment to improving the lot of agricultural workers—he was reminded of Mitya Zhukovsky (God, he missed Mitya, sometimes more than he missed the old boy).

While it was true Palmyre had never again gone so far as to clap him on the shoulder, as they galloped across the park together, recklessly jumping culverts, digging their heels furiously into their horses' flanks, Max felt they had recovered the camaraderie of the piglet hunt; when Palmyre returned to Grignon, which he must now Mme Calvert had been declared out of danger, he would be sorry to lose his company. So he was all the more unprepared, on Palmyre's last day, after they had climbed to the battlements of the Gothic Tower and were contemplating the view of the house and lake, when his companion turned to him with a smile and asked: "Well? Have you found out all you wanted?"

For a moment Max was too staggered to answer. So much for fellow feeling, so much for friendship!

Palmyre continued to smile. "Come off it, old chap. Everyone knows why you were sent here. You being in Monsieur de Miremont's pocket—as it were."

What made this worse was that it was said quite amiably, even with a hint of amusement. Here was the smug assurance of someone so confident in the righteousness of his own prejudices that he expected his victim to assent to them too. Damn the fellow for a duplicitous little shit! But then, what should Max have expected? Like father, like son.

Yet contending with his rage was the need to repudiate the sneer and save his pride. He, Max, was not a lackey. Whatever he was to Armand, he was not the old boy's poodle.

With effort, he returned Palmyre's smile. "That's not why I'm here."

Palmyre raised his eyebrows.

"The truth is, there was a spot of bother with monsieur's daughter."

Max watched himself slowly transforming in Palmyre's eyes.

"Well, I'll be damned!" The fellow let out a hoot and Max's shoulder might have been rewarded with that friendly slap, had he not turned away.

He had seldom felt so disgusted with himself. Yes, he had many times lied by omission when good sense had required it, but he had never before directly denied his nature. How had he sunk so low as to give a fig for the opinion of a worm like Palmyre Calvert? And, as for spying, why had he not realised Calvert Père would use his son to play tit for tat? Was he really so lonely, so desperate for friendship that he was losing his wits as well as his backbone?

Letters from Armand now arrived once a week, but they were still curt and businesslike, Max continued to search in vain for any mention of La Rosebud or his return to Paris. Reason told him that, if Armand had found him guilty as charged, he would not write or, rather, would have sent a different sort of letter. But reason battled with his knowledge of the old boy: these letters could well be a prelude to Armand's shamefaced confession that he had done as he usually did under family pressure and caved in.

Of course, by now, owing to the stupid impulse that had driven Max to betray his very sense of himself, everyone in Beauvallon would know he was in disgrace: he had not asked Palmyre to honour the confidence—what would have been the point? He watched Madame Rose, waiting for the Smile to vanish. To his astonishment, it did not. But then, she was none too fond of the Calverts.

All the same, although the roof was mended and the ceilings freshly distempered, he did not move from his servant's cubbyhole into the comfortable bedroom next to the old boy's. It was not simply that it seemed more and more like tempting providence: the thought of lying there, recalling happier times, was just too painful. He despised himself for this as well, he resented Armand savagely for inducing this weakness.

At night, he slept badly. He was plagued by the Other and the usual dreams; yet the people inside the trees also recurred, and Fromchen and horses with manes of fire, rearing, screaming; when he awoke the horror still clung to him like the stench of sulphur. Now that the nights were clear, too, sounds carried across the fields, often from far off, so that even when he had managed a return to fitful sleep, he would be woken again by horses restless in their stalls or drunks staggering home from the tabac. One night when, for a change, his sleep had been dreamless, he was roused by what sounded like heavy machinery being moved close by; but when he lit a candle and found his way to the window, he saw nothing untoward—the noise must have drifted from one of the tenanted farms kilometres away.

It was the first week in May. He had been at Beauvallon a month and he had had his fill of it. Curse Armand and his so-called justice. He would give the old boy another week, no more.

CHAPTER FORTY

Miremont had approached his daughter's apartments fully determined to do his paternal duty: he would be stern but calm, and he would not leave until he had the truth. Yet when he saw her he could not but falter.

At least, although still in her wrapper, she was up and sitting in a chair at the window of her boudoir, but she seemed thinner and paler than ever. A wan glance acknowledged his presence; then her eyes returned listlessly to the view of the courtyard.

He remembered the bruises and his heart misgave him. If Aline and Clotilde were right, she must have inflicted them herself. Surely that was inconceivable—this frail child would not possess the strength, let alone be capable of the frenzy required. Of course one might tell from the location of the bruises, whether they were towards the inner or outer part of the arm; at the time he had been too shocked to notice and he could hardly ask to inspect them again, apart from which they would by now have faded. In any case… Oh God, it was impossible, he should simply accept that Max was guilty.

"Papa?" She had turned from the window. "Why are you scowling at me? Have I done something wrong?"

Well, had she? Was she loose and deceitful, this waif, this brittle shell of his beautiful daughter? Or was she the innocent victim of malice? Yet, even if her mother and sister, and Catherine too, were united in their ill will, could he set aside Miss Pilkington's tearful admission?

He sighed. "My dear, we cannot go on like this. Look at you—you are all skin and bone. And next week, when we are out of mourning, we shall have to go about in Society again."

"I don't care about Society, Papa. I'd rather die than go to another ball."

He drew up a chair to sit beside her. "I'm sure that's not so. Just as I'm sure your Maman will revive once she can start receiving again. We must get the colour back into your cheeks. And we must…" He had not planned to take this line—had he not done all he could to shield her from the gossip?—but he could see now that severity would be futile. "We must put a stop to any talk."

"Talk, Papa?"

"This story about you and Monsieur Fabien—"

"It is not a story!"

He must let this go for the moment: at least she was alert, finally

317

giving him her full attention. "For unscrupulous people with evil tongues—"

"Horrid old Lady Telford?"

"—it is a heaven-sent chance to make mischief. Thankfully you have friends to protect you. Monsieur de Niversac has even called a man out on your account."

This, admittedly, was a slight exaggeration, for although Niversac, true to his word, had challenged Stilorgan and the Englishman had declared nothing would please him more than to thrash an ex-major of the Cuirassiers, his seconds had never materialised and it was discovered that milord had been urgently called back to London. Nevertheless, if the detail were wanting, Miremont hoped the broad brushstroke would have its effect.

Julie, however, turned her head languidly towards the window again.

"So you see, my dear—" he reached for her hand but found it elusive "—for your reputation... and your peace of mind... I think it would be advisable... if you withdrew your allegation against Monsieur Fabien."

Her languor was gone in an instant. Miremont was horrified to see tears spring to her eyes, fearing another sobbing fit; but these, as her outraged gasp made clear, were tears of indignation. "Are you suggesting—?"

"I am simply saying it would be sensible—"

"Are you asking me to pretend it never happened? To forget what that man—that beast—did to me?"

"Dear girl, I merely think—"

"You swore you believed me. You promised to stand up for me. Yet you want me to forget I was abused and humiliated. I thought you were my own Papa at last. I thought you loved me."

"Oh my dear..." Miremont looked down at his hands. This was proving far more painful than he had anticipated and once again he was tempted to give up. But no, for Max's sake he must press on. "My darling Julie, you know very well how precious you are to me. But sometimes a loving father must... My dear, all this weeping and fasting is doing you no good. I beg you, take your Papa's advice and let there be an end to it."

If he had wished for colour in her cheeks, that was certainly granted: her eyes, too, blazed with fury. "My doting Papa? And to think I imagined you had changed. You are just as you always were, cold and heartless. You never stood up for me, you never defended me, even when I was little—"

"Julie, that is not—"

"Even when I wrote you letters drenched in tears, begging and pleading not to be sent to Bruges, you never stood up for me!"

Bruges. Wounded though he was by this unexpected onslaught, and near to surrender, the word brought him up. "Juliette, your mother has told me why she wished you to be sent to the convent."

"For my education? It was all lies, so she could—"

"Yesterday she told me the truth."

"And you believed her? A jealous old—"

"Juliette!"

"I made her look her age, that's why she—"

"Young lady! You will speak of your mother with respect!"

The violence of this silenced them both for a moment.

Juliette sniffed petulantly. "You believe her, but you won't believe me." She dabbed her eyes with her handkerchief. "You swore you believed me about Monsieur Fabien. Even Maman believed me. But now, on one of her whims, she's changed her mind. And so you say I've made it all up. Yet you can see how I've suffered, you can see what that brute did to me…"

Her eyes filled, her hand went to her throat; with her scarlet face and heaving bosom she had never looked to Miremont so like her mother; he knew in the next instant one of her paroxysms would start, he could hear the first sob rising in her throat.

"No! No more weeping! I've had enough of it, do you hear?"

Much to his surprise, she choked back the sob. Perhaps she was shocked by this second unexpected display of forcefulness—at any rate, she confined herself to shooting him a wounded look. For his part, he was hard put to conceal the fact that his hands were shaking.

He took a deep breath, then strove to make his tone calm and level. "My dear, all I want is the truth."

"I've told you the truth." She began sullenly to twist the handkerchief in her fingers.

"There are… there are elements in your account that I can't help finding… questionable. I still don't quite understand, for instance, why you went to Monsieur Fabien's room."

"I've told you why."

"Because he asked you to?"

"Yes."

"To look at a picture?"

She was silent, her eyes intent on the handkerchief. Then, just as he despaired of answer, she shook her head. "You were sending him away. He asked me to say goodbye to him before he left. Oh, Papa…" Casting aside the crumpled lace, she raised her head and looked Miremont full in the face. "I was such a fool. I only wanted to be kind. I knew it was improper for me to go, but I took pity on him."

"Pity?"

"He was so in love with me. Of course it was quite impossible, but I could see he was suffering so much. His eyes followed me everywhere. He used to lie in wait for me in the library or on the upstairs landing, hoping I would spare him a few words. He said I was his Fair Lady, and he was my Valiant Knight…"

Miremont's mouth opened in astonishment, but he quickly silenced himself.

"His hands were strong, but so gentle. I didn't think he could mean me harm. But when I went to his room…" Tears were rolling down her cheeks again but she seemed unconscious of them; though her gaze was still directed at Miremont, it was as if she were elsewhere, seeing and reliving the event in exact detail. "He was… Passion overcame him. He said we must elope. He said I should meet him at the station in the morning. He said if we sold my jewellery we would have enough to live on for a while and you would come round, you liked him and adored me, you would find him a post in one of the Ministries and we would live happily ever after. And when I said no, he said—he said he knew I loved him, if he loved me then I must love him. And then he…"

Her chin puckered and words deserted her. Miremont waited to see if she would recover. When she did not, he asked gently: "So that was when he tried to kiss you and threw you down on the bed?"

She could do no more than nod. For a long moment, she gazed at him bleakly. Then, in a strangled voice, she cried: "He was so cruel! How can anyone be so cruel?"

Burying her face in her hands, she at last gave way and wept inconsolably.

Miremont watched her with a mixture of amazement and alarm. Of course it was all untrue. He could no more imagine Max talking mawkishly of knights and fair ladies than he could credit the boy's eagerness to join the civil service. Yet at the same time his daughter had spoken with absolute conviction and her tears, for once, had been devoid of hysteria. Although her story might be fiction from beginning to end, he could not doubt she believed every word of it. Somehow, just as Aline had managed to convince herself that Eugène de Sestrès was the cynosure for fatherhood, Juliette, during the time she had spent prostrate in her apartments, had gradually recreated the night of Max's departure until the drama unfolded in the only way she found bearable.

Miremont was angry on Max's behalf; he was angry with himself for his disloyalty to the boy; he was cut to the quick to learn Julie's kisses and 'darling Papas' had been mere pretence, sickened to find in her Aline's taint, perplexed as to how his beloved daughter could have turned into a girl he barely recognised; but he was also profoundly sorry for her: he knew all too well the pain of loving Max and believing him lost forever.

Getting onto his knees, he tried to put his arms around her, but this only reignited her fury.

"You don't believe me!"

"My dear, I—"

"If you did, you would understand. You would see I would rather die than do what you ask."

Yes, to his despair, he did see. How could he hope she would take back lies that alchemy had turned into sovereign truths?

"In any case, what would it serve? I don't care about gossip. And, as for him, you've already sent him packing." Perhaps Miremont's face betrayed him, for something wild flared in her eyes—fear, panic, even contrary hope? "You have, haven't you, Papa? As you promised. You've dismissed him without a reference and he can never show his face in Paris again?"

"Yes. Yes, of course, my dear." What else could he say?

Miremont decided his best plan was to follow Max's advice to Hamlet— do nothing. At first he had thought of sending both his wife and daughter back to Burgundy to convalesce, which would enable him, if not to reinstate Max, at least to join him at Beauvallon. However, as he might have predicted, the approaching end of their month's mourning had hastened another of Aline's remarkable recoveries: it was a shame she had been forced to miss Varnishing Day at the Salon, which always fell on the first day of May, but they would be out of crape just in time for the Poule d'Essai at Longchamp, where, thanks to her son-in-law, she would be a guest of the Jockey Club; and then of course there were her Thursdays to be revived and Amélie de la Rochefontaine was giving a conversazione... But, even if Miremont had deafened himself to all this, there was soon a weightier reason for his family to remain in Paris.

Although Juliette had seemed indifferent to the news of Raoul de Niversac's duel, a day or two later, much as if she were enquiring about the weather, she had said: "I suppose you don't see much of Monsieur de Niversac nowadays, Papa. Doubtless he has gone to Canada." To which Miremont was glad to reply to the contrary, and to mention Niversac's wish to be allowed to call. She shrugged this off and turned the conversation elsewhere; but, after another day or so, she announced that, while relations between her former betrothed and herself could never be as before, it was her duty to thank him for defending her honour: she would see him, provided it was not for long and he did not tire her.

The visit duly occurred. Miremont was pleased to observe that Juliette wore a pretty lace-trimmed day dress and had taken trouble with her hair; but as to the encounter itself, she was non-committal: any hope of a reconciliation was evidently vain. Formerly, of course, the fencing had given Niversac a ready excuse to call at the house, but alas no longer—Max was gone, Roland was sulking in consequence of the lecture Miremont had read him on spreading gossip and Miremont himself lacked the heart for it. However, just as he was racking his brains for some other way of furthering the business, he discovered Niversac had been commanded to call the following week. This second meeting seemed to bring no more joy than the first: Juliette still refused to leave the house and mostly remained cloistered in her apartments. Nevertheless, it was a step forward; all was not entirely lost.

Meanwhile, greatly to his surprise, his truce with Aline was holding up: at any rate she neither interfered with his pursuits nor harried him to join in hers. She did confront him with one demand that at first outraged him: since she was back in the social swim with invitations flowing in daily and not even Miss Pilkington to direct the tide, he must hire a new secretary. It was unthinkable that anyone, even temporarily, should replace Max. Yet reflection persuaded Miremont it was politic to concede—indeed, he might do so with every appearance of generosity: the nice young man recommended by the Merlincourts should be employed exclusively to serve Aline's needs.

A new secretary, new excitements—perhaps, if fate were kind, renewed hope of a wedding: since his family believed Miremont had dismissed Max, the boy would soon be forgotten. All Miremont need do was wait.

Dear God, it was torture. Now he was free again to think fondly of his lover, he could think of little else. When he reminded himself of the letters he had sent, stiff with repressed anger, written only to keep the boy from returning to Paris, he was ashamed. Small wonder Max's replies had grown perfunctory and sporadic: it was remarkable he had replied at all.

After his fruitless interview with Juliette, Miremont had sat down to pour his heart out to the boy. But, as he had read over his three pages of love and longing, he had realised they would not do. Although, to evade Aline, Thomas took his letters to Max directly to the postbox, he still harboured a suspicion, passed down by his father from the bad old days of political unrest, that mail could be tampered with en route; but, more to the point, he worried how Max, ever wary of incontinent emotion, would respond to such outpourings. And besides, what right had he to speak of his own loneliness, his own needs, when he had not yet kept his promise? He might no longer entertain the slightest doubt of Max's innocence, but he had failed to achieve the formal pardon the boy deserved, nor could he set a date for his return to the Hôtel de Miremont. How could he write of his unqualified joy at the prospect of their reunion when his failure would, of necessity, qualify its terms?

With a sigh, he had picked up his pen again.

'My dear Monsieur Fabien,
Thank you for your last letter, which, as always, was a pleasure to receive. I am grateful for your continued patience in a difficult business and be assured your place in my regard remains unchanged. As I trust you know, I love Beauvallon, have it ever in my thoughts and miss it beyond measure. Indeed, it is my firm intention to join you there and, although I am not yet able to name a precise date for my arrival, I can promise it will be very soon…'

CHAPTER FORTY-ONE

There had been another reason for Max's return to Madame Rose's good graces. He had undertaken to teach Madeleine Plibou to read and write.

If the child were sensible of monsieur's beneficence, she failed to show it. She was rarely around when she was wanted and, if she deigned to turn up for her duties—scrubbing floors or skivvying in the scullery—she was slapdash and readily distracted. Although she never passed a looking glass without striking a pose, her appearance was an affront to good order, her dress creased, her apron stained, her cap, when she bothered to wear it, at an angle that failed to conceal her slatternly hair. And she was stealing, of course—two loaves and a chicken leg had vanished from the larder that morning. But what was Madame Rose to do? She appreciated poor Fernande Plibou, with that sot of a husband and so many mouths to feed, could not make ends meet on what she got from taking in washing, that it was a godsend to have someone in the family bringing in a wage; she respected Monsieur de Miremont's wishes. But even so—scolding was wasted breath, all you got for your pains was a giggle or the pulling of a hideous face: by rights, the little chit should have been out on her ear weeks ago.

This was in Max's first week at Beauvallon, when his own relations with Madame Rose were still distinctly under strain. Thus he had been surprised, as he was settling to his breakfast, to find the coffee pot brought that morning, not by Pélagie or Josephine, but by Madame Rose herself; and his surprise grew when, having refilled his cup, she stood, immovable, beside his chair and launched into her plaint. Possibly she felt it beneath her to vent her frustration before the maids; more likely she hoped his next letter to monsieur would plead her case for a dispensation.

Max was not unaware of Mme Plibou's plight, which, if you excepted their different stations, mirrored that of Mme Calvert: a disregarded wife with a swarm of disorderly offspring. The ragamuffins specialised in thuggery, while the Plibou brood, down to the youngest, had been trained by their reprehensible father to thieve; the ragamuffins, so far as Max understood, by virtue of their imposing house and their father's status, were held in some respect by the other village boys; the Plibous were by common consent vermin. All the same, Max seemed to remember an incident last summer when the ragamuffins had set upon the thieves to teach them a lesson: the Calverts were larger and better fed, but the Plibous, superior in numbers and agility, had given them bloody noses and made off with their catapults. Madeleine, as the eldest, must have led the gang: Max could not help smiling at the thought.

"Of course," Madame Rose was saying, "I know full well why she's stealing food. It's that father of hers. If you ask me, he's living up at the Old Manoir, made himself a hideout in the cellars."

Max recalled his encounter with Plibou near the shooting gallery.

"It's where my poor brother hid when he lost his eye and they discharged him from the army."

"Your brother?" Max's polite indifference vanished. This was an insight into the Cyclops' past history Armand had never vouchsafed.

But Madame Rose ignored his sudden interest. "So I suppose I ought to be sympathetic. But Arthur wasn't a drunken good-for-nothing, he was ill, not in his right mind. And I always asked permission. Madame Bruin—she was housekeeper then—she knew I was taking the food for Arthur. Monsieur knew, the old marquis knew. If that young madam would only ask me! But stealing comes natural to her. Lord knows what else she's pinched."

Madame Rose's heavy sigh led Max to think she had finished her peroration and he was preparing to thank her for the coffee, thereby encouraging her to take her leave, when she suddenly began all over again.

"And you know what? When I gave her a piece of my mind yesterday—do you know what she said? She couldn't care less because, if you please, she wants to go on the stage."

Max repressed a grin. You could not deny the girl had spirit.

"I ask you! She hasn't even the makings of a between-maid. I told her—actresses have education, you can't even sign your name."

"Was she never at school?"

"Plibous? School?" Madame Rose uttered an acrid laugh. "The only time that little hussy showed her face in the schoolhouse was when she and one of her brothers put a snake in Monsieur Crépin's desk."

"A snake?"

"I don't think it was a viper, more likely a grass snake. But the schoolmaster's from the town. Anyway—" frustratingly, Madame Rose brushed the rest of the story aside "—I got to wondering... Of course she'll never be an actress, no more than she's a tweeny. But they do say it's never too late, don't they?"

Max raised his eyebrows.

"To get a bit of learning."

Max could not but nod.

"And if there was someone, an educated person…"

She was fixing him with such a pointed look that it was impossible, however he strove for incomprehension, not to catch her drift.

"Oh, good Lord… I really don't think—"

"Of course, if you're too busy with whatever it is monsieur sent you here for…"

Which she knew full well he was not. Nonetheless, while he might be amused by Madeleine Plibou's antics, a hobgoblin was scarcely the ideal pupil and he was not encouraged by the snake.

"Madame, you flatter me. But sadly I lack the skills."

"You should give yourself more credit, monsieur. Aren't you always in the library, reading and writing? You're almost as learned as Monsieur de Miremont. And it would get the little baggage out from under my feet."

At the time appointed for the first lesson, Max settled in an armchair in the library to continue *The Country Doctor*, the latest volume in his progress through Balzac's *La Comédie humaine*. He suspected his pupil would not appear, indeed hoped she would not. His optimism grew as the clocks passed the hour and ticked relentlessly onwards. But, alas, they had not yet struck the half when he was roused from his book by the sound of a throat being theatrically cleared, followed by: "Oi, monsieur!"

Since she was scowling as if he were the one who was late, he thought it pointless to reprove her. Although he had scant notion how to go about his task, wishful thinking had encouraged him to prepare no further than to print the letters of the alphabet on cards; now there was nothing for it but to settle her in a chair while he spread out his handiwork on the library table. Yet he had not advanced beyond E when all of a sudden she leapt up and stood straight as a ramrod; taking a deep breath, she rattled off the letters, in order and without hesitation; then she plumped herself down again, triumphantly sticking out her tongue.

It seemed she had paid more heed to M. Crépin than the tale of the snake would suggest. She had not merely learned the alphabet by rote but could identify individual letters and even knew most of the sounds they made in combination. Since the lesson could be judged an unlooked-for success and Max had even rather enjoyed it, he suggested a second the following morning. Again, confounding his expectations, she turned up and this time was only five minutes late.

Max was obliged to give serious thought to his duties. For the moment, he could present her with simple sentences copied out in his own hand, but he needed to accustom her to print. The small library at Beauvallon did not offer much that might serve as a reading primer. However there were several volumes of La Fontaine's *Fables*, and he recalled Armand mentioning that his mother had read them to him when he was a boy—perhaps the Hobgoblin, too, would be taken with the rhymes and the animals, even if the moral endings passed over her head.

She was by no means a model student. Her concentration was patchy, she sought diversions as a bee seeks pollen: Max learned to dodge her endless questions about Paris and he rued having let slip that he had seen Bernhardt—not that Madeleine had heard of the star of *Phèdre* and *La Dame aux Camélias*, but she was agog to know every detail of the theatre itself, from the lighting to how the curtains rose and fell. Yet she was highly intelligent, no doubt of that. The village might view the Plibous as only one grade above the *crétins* tended by Balzac's country doctor, but Madeleine was no dunce. Granted, writing was a grim labour, attended by shattered lead, scored paper and much unladylike language. But in reading, like a fledgling jumping from the nest, she had found her element. She rolled her R's and spat out her S's with gusto; her grimaces as she uttered vowels were worthy of M. Saint-Séverin capturing every complex note in a bordeaux; awkward, uncooperative words she bludgeoned until she forced them to yield up their sound and sense, after which she would look up with such a victorious grin that Max could not but be touched.

Although he still thought of her as the Hobgoblin, she was a pretty little thing. When he had first seen her two years ago, she had been a scrap of skin and bone, but now, although she could not be more than twelve, she had filled out remarkably around the bosom and hips and her cheeks, too, were plump and rosy. Her nose could be judged rather too broad and the line of her mouth too jagged, but if you scrubbed her fingernails, washed that incorrigible hair of hers and ignored her swearing, she had the makings of beauty. As he had with Miss Pilkington, Max reflected on the inequity that found comeliness only where it was born to enjoy the services of a clever lady's maid.

Altogether, he was rather proud of his pupil. None of the difficulties he had expected had materialised; in fact they appeared to get on surprisingly well. Perhaps that was because, as outsiders, they held common cause. Recognising this and understanding her instinct for rebellion, he had quickly resolved not to treat her as a child, addressing her as Mlle Plibou, despite the giggles this initially provoked, and never rebuking her: if she felt under no compulsion, she would have little to gain from revolt. But, as their first week wore on, he began to see there was another far less pleasing reason for her diligent attendance.

He should have been warned by their exchange at the conclusion of the second lesson, when he had asked why she had given up school, since she seemed to have a natural aptitude for it.

"Didn't like Old Piggy Guts."

Max struggled with this until he added an E to Crépin: *crépine*, he recollected, was the fatty pig's caul that encased sausages. "He seems to have done a good job, as far as you let him."

"Ol' Piggy? He's bandy and his breath stinks. He ain't half the teacher you are."

He should have been alerted by the mischief in her dark eyes as she said this, by the way she ran her tongue over her lower lip. But, shit, she was only a child. A child who got herself up in dustsheets as Aphrodite, who primped and posed in the looking glass, a child playing at being an actress. But as the days passed and the game intensified, his discomfort grew. Now it was she, not Pélagie, who brought his morning hot water. Madame Rose professed to be delighted with this sudden dedication to duty, but, whereas Pélagie had left the can outside his door, as was usual, the Hobgoblin came in and slammed it down on the washstand; one morning he awoke to find her staring down at him—she fled with a wicked giggle the moment he rose from his pillow, but he was not consoled.

Dear God, it was Princess Rosebud all over again. True, there was nothing mad or predatory in the Hobgoblin's come-hither looks, indeed her very lack of subtlety might have had a certain charm, were it not so precocious. Perhaps it was hypocritical of him to be shocked: he had been even younger when he had fallen in love with Dom Sébastien. Yet, when he recalled how that had ended, he was the more determined to put a stop to this business. Damn the child! Mixed with his irritation was disappointment. He had convinced himself there was a measure of trust between them and he hesitated to shatter it. But the ghost of La Rosebud pursued him.

That morning they were due to start on La Fontaine. Max read out the chosen fable, but then, as there was only one copy, the Hobgoblin must sit beside him as she attempted the first line. No matter how he drew back, she seemed to nestle ever closer; her hair tickled his cheek; as she bent over the page her breast brushed his arm. He snapped the book shut and stood up.

"Mademoiselle, this must stop! This instant!"

Although startled, she seemed not remotely abashed. "Go on. Don't be scared."

"Scared?"

"From what they say, you ain't never had a woman. So it's only natural."

He stared at her, speechless. But there was no insane glint in her eye, only a look of sisterly concern so absurd his outrage vanished. "Haven't ever," he said mildly.

"Eh?" It was her turn to stare. "You poking fun?"

"No, of course not—"

"Cos if you are, you can shove your shitty—"

He deftly retrieved Armand's cherished La Fontaine just as she was reaching for it to hurl at him. "Please, mademoiselle. I didn't mean to upset you, it's the last thing I want. Now, please, sit down."

She obeyed, but sullenly and only after he had taken the chair opposite. "I thought you liked me."

"Of course I like you."

"But you don't want to fuck me?"

"I don't want to fuck you precisely because I like you."

"What you do with old monsieur—you can do it with me too."

"Oh, for heaven's sake…" Although he reminded himself again of life in a boys' dormitory, he was still shocked that a girl-child should possess this sort of knowledge. "Look—" he felt for the right words "—I should like us to like each other. But without all this. Setting apart the fact that you're not of age—"

"I am so!"

"And I'm the Emperor of China."

To his relief she permitted herself a giggle.

"Setting that apart, I can't bear to see you doing what stupid girls do. All this mooning and pouting and simpering. That's what stupid girls do to get themselves admired. But you don't need to. You're Madeleine Plibou and you're not stupid."

She looked at him doubtfully. Then she pulled a face. "Nah!"

330

"You have a quick mind. You learn fast. Look at the progress you've made in such a short time. You're sharper than most of the little princesses in Paris."

This seemed to impress her, but she still shook her head. "Ain't what he says."

"Old Pig—Monsieur Crépin?"

"My pa. He says all women are stupid cunts and I'm the stupidest cunt of the lot."

Once again, Max felt he must tread carefully. However contemptible Plibou might be, she was evidently a devoted daughter: Max had twice on his wanderings seen her scuttling off in the direction of the Old Manoir with something parcelled up in a napkin, just as Madame Rose had described.

"With due respect to your father…" he began.

But she cut him off with a hoot of laughter. "Don't you respect him, he ain't no brain hisself." A thought seemed to strike her, she bit her lip. "And don't you go telling him I'm reading books."

"Cross my heart."

She grinned. He grinned back.

"Sure you don't want to fuck me?"

"All I want, mademoiselle, is for you to read me the first two lines of *The Cat and the Fox.*"

He was delighted to see her grin broaden; indeed, he could swear she was relieved.

After that lessons went smoothly—or at least with only the usual digressions. He had said she should try reading in her spare time, so long as she did not take the book from the library, and he was pleased to find her there on occasion, hunched over the page, her lips working as her finger traced the words.

Max was not above congratulating himself; yet he was also smitten with guilt. What would happen to her when he returned to Paris? Without encouragement, could her passion for words survive a life scrubbing floors, ministering to her repellent father and overseeing her obstreperous siblings while her mother slaved at the washtub? But one day he received a shock that made such speculations irrelevant.

The Hobgoblin was at the library table, but apparently taking a break from her endeavours for, although the book lay open in front of her, she sat back in her chair, eyes half-closed. Perhaps she was dreaming of greasepaint and spotlights; loath to disturb her, he stood in the doorway, quite still. Then, as he watched, her right arm stole beneath her bosom until it came to rest where her apron billowed. He stared, disbelieving. But there could be no mistaking that gesture or the significance of her fingers gently moulding themselves to the curve. Shit, how many times had he seen Josette in just that pose? Although it had been long ago, during his first year in Paris, he did not forget the months he and Josette had spent in that suffocating room in the Rue Mouffetard as her belly had swelled with the seed of his predecessor, M. Pintard, until she was too stout to pull on her stockings and there was no longer room for him in the bed.

The Hobgoblin sighed. Afraid that she would turn her head and see his horrified expression, he quitted the doorway and went noiselessly back down the enfilade.

He told himself he should shrug it off. She was a Plibou, what else could he expect? At least here was the explanation for her premature curves and her startling precocity. She had learned all she knew from squalid games in fields and ditches with the village lads, one of whom—who could say for certain which?—was to blame for her predicament. He should just be thankful that, for once he, Max, could not be accused: she was too far gone for that.

All the same—she was a child, for Christ's sake!

But the next morning his anger had abated and he felt only pity for the poor little creature as she stumbled through *The Lion and the Rat*, concluding with her usual grin of triumph. There was a dreadful pathos in the contrast between her child's face and her gravid body. And what would become of all her dreams? Josette, to ward off disgrace, had insisted on introducing him to all and sundry as her fiancé, despite his being six years her junior, in truth not yet seventeen; yet in the end marriage had proved redundant, for her two-day travail had engendered only a tiny white coffin. Disgrace or misery? Either way, it was unlikely that Madeleine Plibou would perfect the arts of reading and writing, let alone stand before the footlights of the Comédie-Française receiving acclaim for her Phèdre.

Once he had noticed her condition, it was almost impossible not to notice it; at the end of the lesson the muscles of his face and neck were stiff with the effort of not looking, not betraying by a flicker that he had divined her secret. Perhaps she was unaware of it herself; but no, that was impossible, she had watched her mother's belly swelling often enough. Did others know? What about Madame Rose?

Max could scarcely ask the housekeeper directly for fear of getting the Hobgoblin into yet more trouble. But a few days later, when Madame Rose was again praising the remedial effects of his teaching, he thought he saw a way to sound her out.

"The girl shows definite promise," he said. "I had thought of asking monsieur if he would pay for her to go to school in Dijon—I know he has done as much for other promising children. But in this case…" He paused strategically. "Well, her future prospects seem uncertain…"

He let the sentence hang for Madame Rose to snatch up however she chose—after all, the child's being a Plibou was sufficient uncertainty in itself—but it was clear she immediately understood him, although the look she gave him was at first surprised, then seemed to reappraise him.

"You're very observant. For a young gentleman."

"What will become of her?"

"Oh, when her time comes her mother will see to things, then bring it up as one of her own. Poor Fernande Plibou—" and here, despite her sympathetic words, Madame Rose's mouth hardened "—what other choice does she have?"

CHAPTER FORTY-TWO

What Palmyre Calvert's false friendship had begun Madeleine Plibou's foolish incontinence had finished—Max's disillusionment with Beauvallon was complete. The sun rose amidst a balmy drift of cumulous cloud and set behind the hills of Armand's Arcadia in a splendour of turquoise, amethyst and burnished gold; in the fields, the spring wheat stood calf-high, in the parklands the may trees were afroth with blossom; the gardeners had begun to dredge the weed from the lake, carpenters and painters were restoring the Temple of Dionysus to glory. But Max scarcely noticed. What he saw instead, all around him, was poverty—not merely poverty of means, but of hope and spirit. What joy did they get for their hours of toil, this army of Robinots, Cagots and Plibous? Their children ran amok, their wives dwindled to shadows over the copper and the cook pot, while they, brows narrowed, faces pinched with ignorance and prejudice, thought of nothing when their day's labour was over but drinking themselves incapable in the village tabac. But Max did not blame them for their brutish existence. He blamed Armand.

At first Max had taken encouragement from the changed tone of the old boy's letters and the reappearance of the postscript. Yet the coded endearments must be balanced against the ominous reference to unfinished business and the fact that no date was given for his return to Paris: on the contrary, Armand proposed coming to Beauvallon—but declined to say when.

Although the letters now arrived almost daily, Max continued to search in vain for clear answers and solid promises. One way or another, the old boy must take him for a fool: either Armand's expressions of affection were merely to sweeten the air until he gathered up the nerve to come and dismiss him; or, more likely, given his wish to be fair and his tendency to capitulate, the old fellow had reached some shabby compromise. Curse Armand's so-called honour, which in truth was mere weakness. Max had been promised justice and justice was what he required.

Shit, had he not earned it? All these months, pandering to the old boy's foibles, bowing and scraping, allowing his life, his real life as an equal with rights and freedoms, to shrink into two hours a week at

Madame Tonton's: he had paid in full for his trivial misdemeanour in Venice.

That was the trouble with Armand's 'goodness' and obsession with 'truth'. They drew you in, whether you wanted it or not; they corrupted you, so that you lost your bearings. Had not Max always known this? Yet time after time he had let himself be deluded. As deluded as the old boy—for Mme de M was right for once, Armand was a prize hypocrite.

Take Beauvallon. Max usually avoided political discussions with Mitya Zhukovsky: he was no nihilist, having his own reasons for favouring hereditary rights. Indeed, so long as he had seen Beauvallon through the old boy's eyes, he had rather admired the way Armand ruled his fiefdom as a benevolent despot. It had seemed of a piece with the old fellow's chivalric code: whereas in Paris he was a museum keeper guarding the family heritage, here in the country he came into his own; here, dispensing charity or dreaming up new projects for the welfare of his villeins, he was truly M. le marquis, and his fastidious sense of duty, instead of bearing down upon all those around him, took on a practical and estimable purpose.

But he was a despot nonetheless. Almost a century had passed since the storming of the Bastille; yet, despite Robespierre and the Terror, despite three more revolutions, including the Paris Commune, the twelfth marquis de Miremont was the feudal overlord of Beauvallon, as if the blood of the ancien régime had never welled from the guillotine.

Yes, of course, the Third Republic was now firmly established and France enjoyed democracy: Beauvallon was a commune with a mayor, elected by universal male suffrage, who reported to the prefect in Auxerre. But M. de M owned the land. The château's home farm, the two large tenant farms at Rougefort and Les Sturnelles, the numerous smallholdings yielding a subsistence to peasants like the Robinots, the stone quarry, the vineyards, the parklands—apart from a small stretch given over to vines at the western extremity of the commune, the entirety of the land which furnished the four hundred-odd souls of Beauvallon with their livelihood belonged to M. le marquis. As for their mayor, elected recently for a further term, he was none other than Hubert Saint-Séverin, with whom M. de M spent convivial sessions at the Maison des Vignerons. All three municipal councillors were the old boy's tenants, not to mention the curé, who was indebted to Armand for the new church bell, and M. Crépin, Old Piggy Guts, who, despite passing for the Robespierre of Beauvallon, would lack a schoolhouse were it not for monsieur.

Furthermore, if you looked beyond Armand's good works, if you stood where the denizens of the commune stood, if you noted, that, for all his concern and enthusiasm, the old boy arrived in July and left at the end of September, consigning his beloved estate to the mercies of Calvert for a full nine months of the year—well, from this perspective, you would struggle not to conclude Beauvallon was merely a rich man's plaything.

And indeed, when you glanced about you, so much was alien and experimental, not traditional to the region, not even French. The eighth marquis had begun this incursion, of course, when, instead of restoring the ruined medieval manoir, he had pandered to the tastes of his Anglo-Irish mistress by building a new château that eschewed mansards and conical turrets in favour of the Palladian style, and had then, into the bargain, commissioned the garden Max thought of as Armand's Arcadia—thirty hectares of lake, wooded hills and follies, artifice imitating untrammelled nature in the manner of the English landscape architect, William Kent.

Armand had inherited this taste for English innovation. It was curious, now Max thought about it, how in Paris the old boy worshipped tradition, cherishing the relics of his ancestors and resisting such improvements to the Hôtel de Miremont as electricity and modern plumbing; yet in the country he was all for playing with the latest agricultural notions gleaned from his Norfolk cousins. When Max looked at the model cottages—two-storey tiled and gabled red brick, not only radically different from the wattle-and-daub thatched hovels they had replaced, but at variance with the masonry and render that prevailed elsewhere—he could begin to understand why Calvert had taken against them. Then there were the cropping schemes that defied traditional wisdom, and Armand's English monster of a threshing machine.

If Calvert were sceptical, he with his fine house and excellent stipend, what of the ordinary working people of Beauvallon? Had they asked for any of these so-called improvements, had they even been consulted? The thresher would doubtless put some of them out of work. And surely it should be their choice whether they slept upstairs or downstairs or drew their water from a tap instead of the pump. Armand would claim the commune's funds were already too far stretched to afford the drainage scheme or housing that accorded with the best scientific principles of health and hygiene. But what if its members were not compelled to pay Armand rent? What if the promise of the revolution had been fulfilled and they owned the land, as of right? Then *liberté, égalité, fraternité* would resound with its true meaning; then these men, these mere villeins with their ingrained scowls of discontent, would acquire the dignity and purpose to make their own destiny. Looking around with his newly jaundiced eye, Max was inclined to agree with Piggy Guts: the people's will should be paramount.

No doubt that other Jacobin, Plibou, considered himself Marat to Piggy's Robespierre. To Madame Rose's annoyance, he was making his presence felt closer to the house; she surmised he found the Old Manoir's cellars stifling now the weather had turned warmer and was sleeping in huts or outhouses: Fillon, Calvert's overseer, had twice chased him out of the home farm yard, and Max himself had seen the wretch, apparently berating the poor Hobgoblin, behind the Great Barn where the thresher was kept, while on a further occasion, as he was making his way from the stables, the drunken brute had lurched into his path and treated him to another of his harangues. As usual, while it was hard to make out the words—perhaps he was claiming arson as a revolutionary act—it was not difficult to grasp their drift.

Max walked on with a shrug. He was accustomed to hostility by now, although by no means inured to it. If Durand sidled up to him once more with his "Still here, Monsieur Fabien? I'm surprised monsieur can manage without you for so long" he would be tempted to ram the scavenger's gobbling Adam's apple down his scrawny throat.

All the same, Durand was right. It was a fortnight since Max had given Armand one more week. Nearly the end of May. He sat down to write to the old boy:

> 'Dear Monsieur,
> I feel I can be no more use to you here and, since your promised
> arrival has not materialised, I am proposing to save you the
> journey by returning to Paris at the end of the month…'

Whatever the answer, he would go back to Paris. If he were no longer welcome at the Hôtel de Miremont, the Zhukovskys would put him up while he determined his next steps. Meanwhile, he could scarcely endure another minute in this place. He would take the sluggish mare and ride to Auxerre. Although his savings had gone as blood money to that traitor Polly, Armand had given him a liberal purse for his expenses, which he had not so far drawn upon and which his pride would rather leave untouched; but, since some of this money was in lieu of wages, he might surely justify a night or two in a cheap hotel. On his return he would doubtless find the old boy's letter waiting.

The sluggish mare had not welcomed such prolonged and vigorous exercise. As Max led her to the ostlers in the yard of the Hôtel du Commerce to have her steaming flanks rubbed down, she halted, hooves glued four-square to the cobbles, refusing to go one more pace; but since she lacked the spirit and energy for heroic struggle, she was eventually coaxed into a stall. The groom who had held her bridle while Max had unbuckled his saddlebags was a well-built, fair-haired boy of seventeen or thereabouts with a freckled nose and a pleasant grin. When Max returned from depositing the bags in his room and changing out of his breeches, the boy was out in the yard again, slouching against the door to the tack room. He grinned his pleasant grin. Max smiled in return.

He had been remarkably true to his promise to the old fellow. Yes, he admitted one or two lapses—the night he had gone to the Monkey to sound out Old Jouvert about Mme Neroni, and another time, in Montparnasse, on his way to see the Zhukovskys—but he had, after all, resisted Vanya Levchenko when, no longer inhibited by any business relationship, they had dined together the Thursday after the ball. Mind you, Levchenko would have been a different thing, altogether more serious, not to be contemplated as matters had stood then. As they stood now, however...

The boy glanced around to ensure they were not observed, then Max followed him into the stables.

At the port, the smells of the waterfront mingled in his nostrils with the aroma of hay and dung still clinging suggestively to his clothes. He felt extraordinarily light-hearted. His limbs were elastic, his head was held high, as, leaving the broad expanse of the Yonne, he climbed the hill, back into the heart of the town. This was not Paris, but here at least, instead of blank sky and fields, was the clamour and jostle of civilisation: he revelled perversely in the huddled medieval streets, in the tightly packed half-timbered buildings that obscured the horizon and hemmed in the sloping cobbles, thrusting street vendors in upon genteel matrons, tilting downward-bound schoolboys into curés puffing upwards to the cathedral. He had slipped the shackles of the last two months, the days of misery and boredom, the nights rent by appalling dreams; he swung his arms, sang the odd snatch of *Don Giovanni* to himself; *non voglio più servir*—he was his own man again and nobody's serf.

He should not forget Madame Rose had entrusted him with various messages—ribbon, buttons, embroidery silks. He found a draper's and, having executed these commissions, added a length of lace on his own account as a farewell present: she, at least, had shown him kindness. Then he sought out the second-hand book dealer Armand frequented on his rare excursions to Auxerre.

For all Max's disappointment in the Hobgoblin, she continued to prick his conscience. He had not forgotten the true purpose of the Marquise de Miremont Trust and had contemplated writing to Armand about the girl's predicament, until he recalled the trust's stipulations about 'distressed young women': governesses, shopkeepers' daughters—at a pinch, parlourmaids—were 'distressed'; a child of Plibou's was 'fallen'. Still, Max did not wish his departure to cut her entirely adrift. She had done well with La Fontaine but, while she liked his fables about venal priests and crafty merchants, she was critical of his animals; deaf to Max's explanation that the poet was satirising the follies of Louis XIV's court, she protested the fellow knew nothing about the country: foxes, rats, frogs, cats—they would not live long if they carried on in that fashion. Max thought something more bloodthirsty might keep her reading once he was gone: she might like *Bluebeard*, for instance.

Although the shop was a cavern with dark crannies in which it was hard to descry titles, let alone read print, and although no obvious organising principle seemed to prevail, Max found Perrault's *Fairy Tales* without great difficulty, an illustrated copy, handsomely bound. Then he was free to pursue his own interests amongst the dusty shelves and the teetering piles of books rising from the floor and a rickety assortment of tables.

At the very back of the shop was a stack of volumes a metre high and six books deep that reminded Max of the multicoloured sarcophagi the cataloguing of M. de M's library had created. The books must be newly acquired—when Max ran his hand over the topmost volumes it came away relatively free of dust. And indeed the dealer, a white-haired, finicky fellow wearing an apron to protect his frock coat from grime, confirmed they had been delivered this very morning and had not been sorted yet: he had bought them from the estate of the late comtesse d'Alberac, in her day a celebrated figure in Paris, who had owned a château nearby.

A first glance at such spines as were visible revealed nothing sufficiently interesting to justify the prolonged crouching minute scrutiny would require. But then Max's heart lurched. Three books down in the fifth pile, a title held his glance and would not let it go. He put out trembling fingers to touch it. He felt sick, breathless. Very slowly and as carefully as his shaking hands would allow, he removed the two books above it and extracted it from the stack.

The Lost Prince of Waldavia. It took him a moment to realise he had read this with ease. It was not, as he might have expected, in the language of his birth, which, having been beaten out of him in the cellar, always brought on suffocating panic; the author had considerately penned his work in French. Udo von Westenholz, whoever he was, had apparently gone to some trouble and expense over the production of his book: the binding was of soft laurel-green leather, the gilding lavish, both of the title and the emblem on the front cover. Twin swans, necks entwined. How could Max forget that insignia, imprinted everywhere—on the buttons of his uniform, the nursery counterpanes, the fingerplates of doors?

There were photogravure illustrations too; as Max nervously opened the book what drew his eye first was not the elaborate font of the title page, but the frontispiece: the Other, aged about five by the look of it, posed stiffly in a sailor suit, all but dwarfed by Freya the wolfhound, who sat to attention at his side. 'HRH Prince Maximilian Sigismund Lothar Maria von Hohenau, heir to the Grand Duchy of Waldavia.'

Where in hell's name was he now, Max wondered? On his knees in some cloister no doubt, praying to the God he loved better than his country.

On the title page, Baron von Westenholz styled himself former Waldavian Ambassador to the court of His Late Imperial Majesty Napoleon III. There was also a handwritten dedication to the comtesse d'Alberac: in impassioned black strokes that were already fading, the baron expressed gratitude for the favour she had shown him and her gracious sympathy for the plight of his Fatherland. The next page offered a foreword, dated 1875, which struck much the same note:

'Good people of France, you who know what it is to suffer beneath the iron heel of Prussia, yet who have emerged bloodied but unbowed, I offer you this humble volume in the hope that your universally extolled love of freedom and justice will move you to take pity on my country, your former loyal ally Waldavia, and to cry out against the great tragedy that has befallen us since the heinous murder eight years ago of our rightful sovereign, Grand Duke Sigismund I, and the callous abduction of his only son, our beloved Prince Maximilian…'

There was more in this vein, but Max read no further. He could see from the facing page that Chapter I began with a history of Waldavia, much of which he could have recited without the baron's help. Besides, for all Mme d'Alberac's professed sympathy, she had neglected to cut open more than the first four pages. And anyway Max must calm himself.

The baron's name now seemed vaguely familiar from yellowed newspapers. Clearly he had not returned to Waldavia after Sigismund's death, when his diplomatic mission must have ended, but had remained in France, even during the war with Prussia and the siege—at least, he was still here in 1875. Was he still living? Did he reside in Paris? Was he, at last, the long-sought-after personage to whom Max must present his case?

The questions, the excitement, the sudden glorious hopes—these must be contained until Max was alone with the book in his room at the Hôtel du Commerce. Meanwhile he feared the bookseller, who hid shrewd eyes behind his bottle-glass spectacles, would observe his agitation, assume he had unearthed some rarity and demand a price beyond his reach. Although it was agony to let go of his prize, he made a performance of discarding it, walking away from the stack, then pausing, shrugging and wandering back to retrieve it. But the book dealer, while he greeted the Perrault with an appreciative smile, was as indifferent to *The Lost Prince of Waldavia* as Mme d'Alberac had been, and it was Max's for no more than a few sous.

With the parcel under his arm, he walked out into the glow of the late-afternoon sun and stood for a moment, breathing deeply. La Rosebud, Armand's treachery, the nightly torture of his dreams—they had all been leading him to this point. He had told himself that he could not hurry the Fates, that when the time came they would announce their intentions.

CHAPTER FORTY-THREE

"What is the meaning of this? Why is that scoundrel still writing to you? What does he mean when he says he will save you a journey and return here at the end of the month?"

Aline had ambushed Miremont while Thomas was still attending to his toilette, had burst into his dressing room without the slightest regard for propriety. Sitting with a napkin about his neck, his right cheek still lathered for shaving, he could only gape at her, befuddled, as she thrust the letter under his nose.

"Well? Answer me!"

The pause occasioned by his valet's withdrawal allowed him to collect himself somewhat. Anger fought with his dismay. "Madame, if that letter is addressed to me, you have no—"

"On the contrary, I have every right. You promised me you had sent the fellow packing, you swore it on your honour to poor Julie. So why is he still at Beauvallon? Why is he expecting a visit from you? Why are you engaged in correspondence with him?"

"Monsieur Fabien is attending to some important—"

"I do not wish to hear your excuses, monsieur. Or any more of your lies. You will write to him this very minute in the strongest possible terms to confirm that you have dispensed with his services. We have employed Monsieur Rossignol as his replacement. And if he still takes it into his head to darken our doors we will throw him into the street."

M. Rossignol, the agreeable young man recommended by the Merlincourts, had arrived yesterday and proved to be neither young nor very agreeable. A short, plump, red-cheeked fellow, he wore a bumptious air and a pedantic manner, while his voice, despite the expectations aroused by his name, no more evoked a nightingale than a rusty hinge. However, he must possess the knack of flattery, for he had impressed Aline when she had instructed him in his duties. Whatever the nature of those instructions, the new secretary had felt impelled to rise early and apprehend Philippe as he was sorting the post, insisting, despite the footman's protests, that, since most of the letters were bound to be for madame, he would take charge of the entire pile and distribute the rest later.

M. Rossignol was now fully aware he had exceeded his authority—

Boussec had seen to that. Miremont's post would be given directly into Thomas's hands and no other's. But it was too late. The hope Miremont had invested in his simple plan of inaction had been snatched away. There was no chance now of the boy's existence being forgotten, still less that the two of them would be reunited at Beauvallon. Miremont instructed Thomas to telegraph to the country immediately, lest Max lose patience and set out for Paris without waiting for his reply.

And yet, once Miremont's anger had cooled a little, he could see the situation was absurd. It had been a misjudgement to let things lie, for this had only bred difficulties where none should have existed. But it was not too late to be as he should have been all along—frank and forthright. Aline would soon see that her outburst had been uncalled for.

The first object to meet his eye as he entered his wife's boudoir was the resplendent glass case that had been delivered two days ago and, standing upon a gilded commode, occupied the place of honour beside her escritoire. While M. Rossignol haughtily took his leave, Miremont was able to study Bébé's apotheosis: planted fiercely on all four paws, his head thrust forward, his plumed tail curled, he managed, despite this challenging pose, to remain a downtrodden beast, the pathetic rictus of his jaws and the mute plea in his glass eyes defying the taxidermist's ambitions.

Aline stroked the case tenderly. "See how beautiful he is? My darling love. Now he is mine forever."

Miremont thought angrily of his own deprivations but calmed himself. "Madame—"

"I hope you've come here to tell me you've done your duty at last."

"No, madame, I have not." Seeing her bosom heave, he went on hastily. "I have come because I wish to know why you persist in calling Monsieur Fabien a scoundrel."

She seemed taken aback. "Because he is one, of course. He laid hands on poor Julie."

"I thought we had agreed he did nothing of the kind."

"We agreed she might have led him on a little—"

"Madame, we agreed he is innocent."

She blinked at him doubtfully. "That's as maybe. It is not what Julie says."

He wished she would be seated, so that he might sit too. He would never persuade her to be reasonable if he stood over her, hectoring her. "My dear, Juliette has suffered a nervous collapse. We both know her version of events is not to be relied on."

She sighed. "Perhaps so. Although I really cannot see why it matters."

"It matters because you are asking me to punish an innocent man."

"But you have no further need of his services. We have a new secretary."

A terrible panic gripped Miremont, a great welling up of his longing for Max and his fear of losing him, so that he struggled not to explode. With difficulty, he reminded himself that he was on dangerous ground. He must press his case, but not so vehemently as to provoke suspicion.

"Your Monsieur Rossignol?" He essayed a laugh. "My dear, I'm sure he's an excellent fellow. But I can't imagine he'd be much help with Ovid."

"Oh, Ovid! That great book you pretend to be writing?"

"Besides, that's not the point. Monsieur Fabien has done nothing wrong and I cannot treat him as if he has."

"But you promised Julie."

How Miremont rued his former cowardice. "If I gave her any undertaking, it was before I understood the truth of the matter."

"She will be greatly distressed."

"Not if the boy remains at Beauvallon."

"She is bound to find out." Which meant, of course, that Aline would tell her, if she had not already done so. "In any case, what help is the creature with your precious dead Romans if he's stuck away in the country?"

Again the chasm yawned before Miremont. "It is a point of principle. He is blameless and I will not dismiss him. Let that be an end to it!"

She looked him up and down. Then she whirled upon him, every bead jangling, every excessive ribbon and frill of her overdressed person quivering with outrage. "Your principles? Oh, we never cease to hear of them, do we? You have more principles than the Pope—except where your family is concerned. Is it not bad enough that all our married life I have had to endure the sight of that deformed manservant of yours, because you must honour some promise you gave to your father, who has been dead these twenty-five years? And then I was worn to a limp rag by your ridiculous devotion to a cook who disgraced me with every meal she served. And now some secretary is more important than your daughter because your principles are at stake. I realise you care nothing for my feelings, but at least you should think of Julie."

"Of course I—"

"You will drive the poor girl to a relapse, she will take to her bed again and any hope of her marrying Raoul de Niversac will be gone. What kind of father are you, that you put a menial before your own daughter? Who cares if he is guilty or innocent? It is your duty to dismiss him. It is your God-given duty as a father to put Julie first."

Miremont retired from this encounter much shaken. How could he have fooled himself yet again that Aline would be susceptible to reason? Their truce, it appeared, had been but brief.

And yet, of course, she was not wrong. He did have a duty to his daughter. It did not matter that Julie had lied, for her lies were in consequence of her illness and deserving of his compassion; it did not matter that she might not be the sweet, affectionate girl he had thought her, for she was still his child and the love he owed her set no conditions. But he also loved Max, loved him so that the notion of perpetrating such a squalid betrayal would be unthinkable even if it were not bound up with fear of losing him. Yes, he had a duty to Julie; but he had a duty to Max too.

The next day was Sunday, when Clotilde was due to bring his grandchildren on their usual visit. In the past two months, as he had softened towards his elder daughter, he had come to regard her as a repository of practical good sense. She would surely agree that her mother was being unreasonable.

But when he took Clotilde aside, she merely favoured him with one of her condescending looks. "Oh, poor Papa! Maman has told me all. And of course she is quite right."

"But you must see… If the boy is innocent—"

"Truly, Papa! What can you be thinking? How does that make the slightest difference?"

"It would be unjust."

She gave a little laugh. "Dear, darling Papa, we all know my sister is inclined to be fanciful—and we need not look far, need we, to see who she gets it from? Must I really recall to you that Julie is a Miremont? Whereas your Monsieur Whatshisname is a glorified servant."

If Miremont were affronted by her tone, which she might have employed to address Frédéric or Agathe, he was yet more enraged to be reminded of her infernal snobbery. "I thought better of you, Clotilde."

"Oh, come, come, my dear. Like all servants, he is dispensable."

"Monsieur Fabien is not a servant. He is a fine young man,

intelligent, educated, a companion in my work, altogether someone I—" But here, just in time, he saw the danger. "He… His knowledge of Greek and Latin is invaluable."

She patted his arm. "Then you may write him a glowing reference and he will soon find another place."

It sickened Miremont that his very love for Max prevented him from defending him. In his battle for Thomas all those years ago, and more recently, when he had fought Mme Dussardier's cause, although he had loathed the endless arguments, he had been certain of his ground, there had been no morass into which one incautious step might plunge him and, if he had lost the war over Mme Dussardier, it was not from holding his fire, but because Aline had scorned the rules of engagement: in both battles he had resorted only to the truth. But here, where there was so much more at stake, he was constantly undone by the need to lie.

In despair, he thought of confronting Juliette again. But since his turpitude had been revealed she generally avoided him: clearly such a conversation would be futile. Should he simply hold out against the storm, maintain his resolve to do nothing? After all, in another month the Season would be over and Aline would be obliged to return to the country, taking Juliette with her, regardless of any reconciliation with Niversac. If he could persuade Max to patience for one more month…

He had followed his telegram with a letter that repeated his faith in the boy's innocence and offered Julie's illness as the reason for delaying his return. Subduing his fear of post-office spies, Miremont had expressed himself more openly than usual; if Max still loved him, was there not every hope he would understand? Yet over these past months he had made unremitting demands on the boy's understanding.

In his rage at Aline and Clotilde, Miremont longed to fling the truth in their faces, to shout out: "This is who I am, this is whom I love, this is how I must live!" And yet the fact that he could not—rather, was paralysed by dread of the words coming unbidden—should not this serve as a caution?

Could he honestly say Aline's contempt for his principles was not justified? Could he lecture her on justice and honour when deception was intrinsic to his existence? And what sort of fellow was he to pontificate about duty, when his duplicity made him question his duty to his own daughter? As he deceived others, so, most of all, he deceived himself.

Whose fault was it, after all, that Julie had this—this failing? If he had been a better father, more sympathetic towards Aline, better able to endure the bleak indignities of his marriage—if he had been a man like his own father, not a weakling lacking the backbone to control his shaming urges…

He buried his face in his hands. What would his father say if he knew what he had become? He could see the kindness fade from those grey eyes, the stern brow furrowed, first with disbelief, then horror.

There could be no doubt how his father would judge him, how he would view his temporising and his deceit and his attempt to shirk the blame for Julie's neurasthenia. As clearly as if he heard his father speak the words, he at last understood the truth of his situation.

It was not for him to defend Max's innocence or fret about losing the boy: it was for him to conquer his own base desires. Between what affronted nature and the natural duty a father has to his child there could be no contest. If he hoped one day to see Julie bright and laughing, his beloved daughter again, if he did indeed have any principles left, any remnants of honour, there was only one course he could take.

CHAPTER FORTY-FOUR

Max hardly knew how he rode back from Auxerre. The sluggish mare had her virtues, for, if not chivvied, she was placid enough to carry her rider safely, even when he was too troubled to pay their progress proper heed.

He had come back to Beauvallon because he could think of nowhere else to go. Telling Madame Rose he was exhausted, fending off her expressions of concern, he shut himself in his room.

He had begun yesterday evening in such a fever of hope and excitement. Having gulped down a warmed-over boeuf bourguignon in the Hôtel du Commerce's gloomy restaurant, he had armed himself with a paper knife and retired to his bedroom. He had not cared that it overlooked a dank courtyard and smelt of mice or that you could only reach the washstand by sidling crabwise along the side of the bed. The book. That was his only concern.

Impatiently he slashed open its pages, passing quickly over Waldavia's medieval glories, its sufferings during the Thirty Years War, its renewal as a beacon of cultural refinement in the eighteenth century: this century was his pressing interest.

As had been dinned into them in the schoolroom until he and the Other knew it by rote, the Grand Duchy had not only survived the French wars which, at the turn of the century, had ravaged Germany's patchwork of principalities like the moth; owing to the astuteness of the ruling Grand Duke, Otto, it had increased its lands. Although he had lost the hereditary title of Elector when Napoleon had abolished the Holy Roman Empire in 1806, he had acquired two small neighbouring states as a reward for supporting the French against Austria, and later, after switching sides, saw his territorial gains confirmed and enlarged in 1815 by the Congress of Vienna. The following year, when he had died without male issue, his younger brother Maximilian had inherited a much-enhanced Grand Duchy.

Their governess, Baroness Zetter, had been keen to emphasise Maximilian III's splendid cultural achievements, in particular his transformation of the Residenz, the Summer Palace and the entire centre of Waldavia's beloved capital city, Rittenau, all of which he had rebuilt in the neoclassical style to outdo Vienna and Paris in elegance.

However, she had passed rather quickly over the end of his reign: being very old by then, and in poor health, His Royal Highness had given up the ducal throne to enjoy a well-earned retirement.

Baron von Westenholz, Max was intrigued to find, was more forthcoming. Maximilian had not retired of his own free will. Waldavia's master-builder Grand Duke had not been best suited to his time: disregarding the anti-monarchist rumblings the French Revolution had stirred throughout Europe, he had insisted upon absolute rule, repudiating any notion of a constitution, let alone an elected assembly. His costly architectural projects had also alienated his subjects, as had his increasing eccentricity (for all Westenholz's attempts to be diplomatic, it was evident that Maximilian had been prone to very public adventures with unsuitable women). When the revolutionary impulse had erupted throughout the continent in 1848, Waldavia had not been spared. The monarchy was only saved by Maximilian's abdication in favour of his heir. Westenholz hailed Sigismund I with enthusiasm:

> 'His Royal Highness was twenty-six when he came to the throne, in the prime of his manhood. Handsome and unmarried, he quickly became his people's idol, winning our devotion and loyalty with his charm, his easy manner with all conditions of men, his concern for his subjects in our poorer lands in the north...'

Here Max's thoughts were diverted, so that he gave only half an eye to the baron's encomium to Sigismund's virtues. It bothered him that he had no precise memory of this godhead. He could remember so much from the time before the cellar. It had been a point of principle to remember, it had kept them alive, him and the Other, during their captivity— "Go on, count! How many marble squares from the gallery to the orangery, how many pups in Freya's last litter, how many buttons on a dragoon's tunic, chairs in the schoolroom, cowry shells in the mantelpiece in the grotto? Out loud, damn you, count!" He could still smell the sulphurous baths in which they had soaked their chilblains, hear the crunch of boots drilling below in the courtyard, see the crack that ran like the Danube from the bedroom cornice, throwing out tributaries above his pillow; yet, of this man, of this living embodiment of the ever-present emblem, this swan of the House of Hohenau embracing the swan of Waldavia, this being whom, in accordance with his pact with the Other and the will of the Fates, he must claim as his father, he could recall nothing.

The man's presence perhaps—how, when his arrival at the Residenz was expected, everywhere fell silent and even the old footman who served the nursery stood to attention; and how the Other and himself, instead of being allowed to slide on the marble tiles leading to the orangery, were dressed by Fromchen in their scratchy serge uniforms, after which Baroness Zetter, the twin knots of gristle at the tip of her nose glinting whiter than usual, made them sit stock-still in the schoolroom for what must surely have been hours. But of the man himself Max had no picture. A dark form, tall, perhaps in a uniform. A shape, a shadow.

Although Max no longer felt pleasure in his recollections of Before, since they were more properly the Other's—he, Max, was always one servile step behind, the boy in the truckle bed in a corner of the prince's bedroom—he had clung to them tenaciously, for their unquestionable use in the furtherance of his destiny, and also because he took pride in his memory. It shook him, this blank where the image of Sigismund should have been. It reminded him that his pride was false, that these details were fireflies in vast tracts of darkness.

And if that were true of Before, it was even truer of After. He could remember the cellar vividly, yet he could not say why or how they had got there, when they had left it or where they had gone. He remembered a succession of stuffy apartments, where they lived with the blinds drawn and were not allowed outside; he remembered them sitting on a bed, while beyond the locked door they could hear their Pretend Mother arguing with their second—or was it their third?—Pretend Father. But he did not know in which places they stayed, or how they afterwards came to Saint-Pons: the rough flannel nightgown, the nit comb scraping his scalp, his bewilderment at his first sight of the dormitory and its twin rows of iron bedsteads—that was all his mind retained of his arrival in the cloister. Yet these greater events ought not to be lost to him. He would be expected to talk about them when his time came.

He had hoped for illumination from the Bibliothèque Française. No longer in livery and enjoying new freedoms at the Hôtel de Miremont, he had resolved to spend hours there, poring over papers and pamphlets. But his visits had gradually dwindled. Waldavia, although it had kept its autonomy within the new German empire, was a small, insignificant state: French newspapers would take longer than a mere decade to forget Louis Napoleon's rout at Sedan, the siege of Paris and the ultimate insult of having Wilhelm I's hubristic empire proclaimed at Versailles; they remained preoccupied with Prussia and the machinations of Bismarck. From slim paragraphs at the very bottom of columns on less-frequented pages, Max gleaned only that Waldavia, after Sigismund's death, had been ruled by a regent, Prince Friedrich, a Hohenau cousin. Nor had he fared better with the catalogue of books. He could discover nothing devoted to Waldavia, past or present, although, in desperation, he had almost been willing to confront his horror of German.

Sometimes he wished he could talk to the Other. Although the Other's memory was capricious and usually self-serving, he would surely recall things Max could not. Hadn't Max scoffed at his claim that a document recording their admission to Saint-Pons was hidden in the Father Abbot's office? True, once Max had braved another of the Reverend Father's filthy 'detentions' to find it, the paper had turned out to be worthless, its names and signature false. But it had existed, nonetheless, and the Other had remembered it.

And what of the Other's constant presence in Max's dreams? Did he have some purpose beyond plaguing him? Did he drop hints that would help Max piece together what was lost? If he did, it was futile, for here Max's memory failed him again: such nightmares as he recalled were often nonsensical; more frequently they fled his grasp the instant he awoke, leaving only a slick of dread in their wake.

Yet now, by some freak of fate, he had Baron von Westenholz's privately published plea for justice and his questions would be answered.

The light was beginning to fade; reaching out from the bed, where, for lack of an armchair, he had stretched himself out fully dressed, he lit the candle on the washstand. The baron was keen to list Sigismund's reforms: Max skimmed through the setting up of a constituent assembly and the relaxation of censorship, but in the midst of Waldavia's entry into the Zollverein, the German Customs Union, he was obliged to cut another page.

And there he was. Grand Duke Sigismund I. A tall man in a black-and-silver uniform—wasn't that the dress uniform of the Deathwatch Hussars? A tall, dark, haughtily assured man, his left hand on the tasselled pommel of his sword, the sash bearing the familiar star of the Royal Order of St Hugo slanting across his breast, the cross of some other order glinting at his collar. A tall, dark man, turned slightly to the right to display his noble profile, but not so far as to obscure the rest of his...

Max, who had brought the candle closer, pulled back suddenly.

The candle flame shook. Something cold and hard gathered in his throat, his heart was pounding, only with effort did he get the candle to safety. He tried to swallow the thing in his throat but his muscles were numb. It could not be. He must look again, force himself. But the book slipped from his hands.

Fear. Paralysing fear. He could not remember the pain, not then, nor later when, in bed at his father's country estate, he lay flat on his stomach waiting for the poultices to do their work. But he remembered the fear. And he remembered that face. Not composed, as it was in the portrait, but contorted with fury. The Other was bleeding and howling. And then the tall figure was upon him too, arm raised, eyes blazing, eyes where a monstrous thing crouched, roaring. Then he fell and the whip's next blows came down upon his back.

Here, in this grubby little hotel room, the terror once more rose like a gale within him.

When his hands were at last steady enough, he lit a cigarette in the hope of calming himself. He should be ashamed to be unmanned by a child's blind fear.

Yet it had, he now understood, lived in him, unrecognised, all these years. It had stalked his dreams; he had felt it like an insect crawling on his skin when Dom Sébastien had struck him, when Armand's riding crop had stung his mouth; it had chilled him when he had seen the frenzy in the Rosebud's eyes, but he had still refused to own it. He did not wish to own it now: he was angry, both for his six-year-old self and at his present self-pity; yet there was deep shame too, not just for his fear, but in the very memory of the incident, as if he, not the dark man, were to blame.

Shit! He refused to dwell on it, he would thrust the memory back into the depths. All the same, he remained bathed in sweat. And there was something else troubling him, a suspicion—no, a realisation—that he could not fend off, however frantically he tried.

It took a determined effort to reopen the book, find the right page and confront the portrait again. But, although he stared at it as long as he could bear, the troublesome thought did not vanish. The hair was darker, almost black, and the mouth, so far as Max could see beneath the moustache, was thinner; but the chin, the nose, the brow, the set of the eyes…

Squeezing between the bed and the washstand, Max lifted the

candle to illuminate the smut-speckled mirror. He knew others thought him handsome and would not deny trading on it on occasion, but there was something about his face he had never liked. And now he was sickened to see why. No, he could not pass it off as a distortion of the candlelight: the face in the glass defied him.

But it was the Other who was Sigismund's son. He, Max, was the son of the Bullfrog, with his pouter-pigeon chest and puffed-out cheeks.

A fantastical notion seized him. From his earliest memory, he and the Other had lived as though halves of a single organism, sharing the same room, playing the same games, learning the same lessons; when the Other broke a plate in the nursery, he, Max, was punished, when the Other's copybook was full of errors, his was sent to His Highness in its place. Good and bad, contrary forces animating one spirit. One being, split yet indivisible; one life in the cellar, survival hanging on that unity. Perhaps this scar on his forehead truly was the Other's scar, a childhood disfigurement, the result of being thrown by a pony. Perhaps he had taken the name Max, not out of recklessness on first coming to Paris, but because he really was Maximilian von Hohenau and the Other was a figment.

He began to laugh wildly at the absurdity of fate. Yet a dart of reason punctured his hysteria. He remembered when he was eleven peering into the shaving glass in the monks' lavatorium because Dom Sébastien had told him he was beautiful and he had wanted to know what that meant; he had not seen beauty, on the contrary had been struck by that sense of something alien which was now shockingly explained; but it had also been the moment he had first properly understood himself as a separate being, for, although they were constantly mistaken for twins and there were certain similarities— height of brow, colour of hair and eyes—he and the Other did not look identical. His fingers touched the scar at his temple. In spite of their pact, the Other had been too squeamish to do it: he recalled the firmness with which he had gripped the knife, the sharp downward thrust, then the moment of stillness, of absence, before the pain came and blood ran into his eyes.

All the same, he grabbed the book and began frenziedly cutting the remaining pages. Towards the end, he found it: a photograph of two boys, four or five years old, blank, unformed faces focused rigidly on the camera. Two boys, not one—although Max himself could not have told them apart had the boy in the white uniform not been perched nervously in the saddle of a Yakut pony, while the boy in the darker uniform held the bridle; how he had loathed that bottle-green tunic with its chafing high collar.

'HRH Prince Maximilian, mounted on his pony Bobik, attended by his page, Christian von Wolfsberg.'

Christian von Wolfsberg, son of the Bullfrog, Count Albrecht von Wolfsberg, formerly Albrecht Klopfer.

But how—why—if he, Max—Christian—was the image of…? His last memory of the Other, at sixteen or thereabouts, when they had left the burnt-out farmhouse near Versailles to go their separate ways, was of someone shorter and plumper than himself, with a receding chin. Why did the Other not look like Sigismund, while he resembled him so strongly? Shit, it was ridiculous—impossible. Memory not only hid things, it also played tricks.

Suddenly he doubted everything. Perhaps it was he, after all, who had ridden Bobik, and the loathsome tunic belonged to some other time. Perhaps during the upheavals of After—the cellar, the lodgings in unknown towns, Saint-Pons—perhaps during these years, when they had gone by so many different names, their identities had become muddled. Yes, he could go back to the glass and stare at the scar. But what if it had been the other way round, he who had been too lily-livered to use the knife, who had vomited noisily afterwards? What if… what if…? Dear God, could he trust anything he remembered?

Close to sobbing with confusion, he resorted to the book again. There had been other photographs: Maximilian III and his duchess, Marie-Elisabeth—like the picture of Sigismund, the reproduction of a portrait, showing the couple in middle age; a photograph of Marie-Elisabeth in old age with her eldest child, also Elisabeth, by now a grown woman; Sigismund's younger brothers, Lothar and Leopold, probably in their twenties; Viktoria, the other sister, still in a short frock with her hair down.

Bloodlines were not even-handed. While Sigismund, Leopold and Viktoria were all possessed of striking good looks, having inherited their high cheekbones and fine profiles from their father, to Elisabeth and Lothar their mother had bequeathed fleshy cheeks and weak chins. Evidently the Other took after his grandmother and, if he resembled anyone in the next generation, it was Lothar, whose pious air he also shared. Besides, he must have received some traits from his mother, the Grand Duchess Katarine: all Max could remember from her portrait in the Residenz was the foam of a white dress, and in the photograph here she remained elusive—young, still a girl, with a wide-eyed empty face—but yes, full-cheeked and plump. The Other might not take after Sigismund but there was no doubting a family likeness, he was indisputably a Hohenau.

Had Max hoped to be comforted by this? He could not even recall now what he had sought from the photographs. One more wild hope, one more fantasy to distract him from the obvious? He had not imagined the Other, he was not the Other, their identities had never been confused. He might jerk and thrash like a fish on a line, but the barb held fast. The Other was Sigismund's son and heir and he was the page, Christian von Wolfsberg.

But who was Christian?

The cruel face with the mad eyes rose up before him. Bile surged into his throat. Fate was savage in her irony. All these years he had schemed and planned to pass himself off as this monster's son. Only to find it was the hideous truth.

CHAPTER FORTY-FIVE

Sleep would have brought oblivion, but his brain would not rest. He had hurled the book aside, for he was damned if he would read any more of the baron's disgusting hagiography. But his room was too small to pace and his cigarette case was soon empty. Desperate for distraction, he was forced to retrieve the book. After all, it had not answered any of his burning questions, which had only multiplied with the sickening revelation about his birth.

Impatiently he leafed through wordy passages detailing Waldavia's new constitution and parliamentary procedures. But, as he read on, he discovered Baron von Westenholz, despite his unbending loyalty, would concede his sovereign was not without fault.

Apparently, along with his looks, Sigismund had also inherited his father's appetite for indiscretion. Despite the need for an heir, he was reluctant to marry—he drove his ministers to distraction by turning down three suitable German princesses—and Max inferred from the baron's account that, while the succession was at stake, there was also a need to scotch rumour. However, when Sigismund was thirty-eight, he agreed—principally to assert Waldavia's independence from Prussia—to sue for the hand of a junior Russian Grand Duchess. The marriage to Her Imperial Highness Yekaterina Konstantinova took place on her eighteenth birthday, the following year, and five months later the duchy rejoiced at the news that Katarine, Grand Duchess of Waldavia, was in an interesting condition.

'Thus began 1861,' Westenholz wrote portentously, 'a year of great tragedy.' Sigismund was devoted to his sixteen-year-old sister Viktoria, the baby of the family, an unexpected late blessing—indeed, he had been a father to her after their parents had died—but, alas, that February she had been taken ill with anaemia. On the thirteenth of May, when the Grand Duchess's confinement began, he was far away in the south, at a convent in the mountains, where his sister was on her deathbed. By the time he arrived at the Residenz, his wife, although delivered of a son, had also breathed her last.

What happened next, Westenholz maintained, was so completely at variance with Sigismund's usual character that it must have been brought on by intolerable grief. In blind fury he ordered both the dissolution of the convent and the punishment of everyone who had attended his son's birth.

356

'At the two state funerals, which took place on successive days, His Royal Highness was gaunt and pale and spoke to no one. We, his grieving subjects, prayed the Blessed Virgin would help our beloved sovereign recover from his great loss, but it was as if the knot of grief within him were turning to stone. Alas, he was deaf to pleas for clemency towards those he had summarily jailed or banished. He quarrelled irrevocably with his favourite brother, Prince Leopold, who sought sanctuary in Vienna. He lost interest in his plans for improving the lot of his subjects and scarcely listened to his ministers, preferring the counsel of his chamberlain, Albrecht Klopfer, whose elevation to the nobility aroused much understandable resentment. Although it was his people's dearest wish that our Grand Duke should find happiness in a second marriage, he declined to gratify our hopes and, when journalists echoed the popular disappointment, he closed down their publications and reintroduced censorship.'

Day by day, it seemed, Sigismund was turning into his father. Max was unsurprised to read that questions began to be raised about his soundness of mind—his second brother, Lothar, had already been committed to an asylum. However, Westenholz insisted Sigismund was suffering from a bodily affliction brought on by the strain of his double loss. He had become a martyr to neuralgia, dyspeptic attacks and other aches and pains, to the extent that, in the last days of his life, he was no longer the magnificent presence captured in the famous Lenbach portrait, but had aged beyond his years.

Doubtless that was why he had become increasingly reclusive. As a result rumour abounded and, unsurprisingly, the political situation deteriorated. The Leftist elements that had caused such trouble in 1848 began stirring again: secret societies with fanciful names multiplied— the Flaming Sword, the Red Fist, the Torch of Justice. Rigid censorship spawned illicit printing presses and the widespread distribution of pamphlets: some urged a united Germany, others a workers' revolution; yet others mocked Sigismund and his hated Court Chamberlain. A mine disaster sparked rioting in Nordstadt; in the east, poor harvests stoked violence, and in Rittenau the university students protested. Westenholz cautioned his reader not to assume these agitations were genuine signs of popular discontent; in his opinion most were fomented by Bismarck to weaken Sigismund by alarming the Right and thus provoking the nobles in the Upper House of Waldavia's Diet to restrict his power.

Relations between Waldavia and Prussia had long been less than cordial. When the North German Confederation was established in 1866, Sigismund refused to recognise it. This was a popular stance with his subjects, who forgave his eccentricities when they saw his determination to hold out against Prussia's ever-encroaching power; but to his ministers, and particularly to his Chief Minister, Baldur von Leckwitz, it was the height of folly. This was also the view of Leckwitz's close ally, Prince Friedrich von Hohenau.

Friedrich was not, as Max had supposed, a Hohenau cousin, but Maximilian III's eldest son. Before inheriting the duchy, Maximilian had rashly married his mistress, Louise von Ötter, who was neither from a royal house nor the upper nobility. This being a mismarriage under Waldavian law, it had been annulled when Maximilian became Grand Duke, leaving him free to take Marie-Elisabeth von Hesse-Darmstadt as a more eligible consort. Louise's one-year-old son, Friedrich, thus disinherited, went with his mother into exile, first to Saxony and then to Prussia.

In 1856, after a military career which had earned him an entrée to the Prussian court, he returned to Waldavia, generously welcomed back by Sigismund. Friedrich bore no apparent resentment towards his half-brother; rather, Sigismund came to regard him as a trusted friend and eventually appointed him Army Chief of Staff. But that was before what Baron von Westenholz continued to describe as the Tragedy.

After 1861, Sigismund grew increasingly suspicious of Friedrich, who was rumoured to have the ear of Prussia's King Wilhelm: he distrusted Friedrich's enthusiasm for enlarging and re-equipping Waldavia's token army, rejecting all but the most trivial reforms and finally dismissing Friedrich as commander-in-chief, although, owing to the controversy stirred by his replacement, an elderly general touted by Albrecht von Wolfsberg, he was persuaded to reinstate him— most unwisely, according to Westenholz, who would rather have seen Friedrich languishing in the Teufelsturm, the grim fortress in which political prisoners were confined.

Matters came to a head in 1868. A new and yet more comprehensive bill for the reform of the army came before the Diet and was passed by both chambers. Sigismund refused outright to sign it into law. There was uproar in the Diet and mutiny amongst regiments stationed in Nordstadt. Leckwitz—out of frustration, he was afterwards to claim, not any treacherous intent—put a bill to the Diet requiring the sovereign to abdicate if he would not accept the will of his parliament. When this was carried, unanimously by the Council of Nobles and by a narrow margin in the General Assembly, Sigismund, made rash by fury (here Max could imagine Baron von Westenholz with his head in his hands), dissolved the Diet and suspended the constitution, thus precipitating the coup he had for so long feared.

In Rittenau, the students took to the streets, pro-Leckwitz mobs fought royalists, troops called out to quell the rioting took sides; as news travelled from the capital, disorder spread throughout the country. Meanwhile, Leckwitz and Friedrich rode out to the Summer Palace, where Sigismund had retreated, bringing with them a deed of abdication.

What happened next, Westenholz averred, would forever be viewed by the civilised world as an abomination.

> 'The two traitors were met by officers of the Royal Guard, who at first denied them entry, but after some parlaying and once they had made a great show of being unarmed, their smooth words prevailed and they were escorted to the Grand Duke's private apartments. They entered His Royal Highness's study and the servants withdrew, closing the doors. After ten minutes a single shot rang out. The traitors claimed Sigismund had suddenly taken a pistol from his desk and put it to his temple.'

Yes, Max recalled someone, he did not know whom, saying the duke had shot himself, it was the only thing he did remember from that time.

> 'But all those loyal to their rightful sovereign were not deceived then and are not deceived now. This was a vile, brutal murder. And I cannot but detect behind this evil act the shadow of Bismarck.'

Alas, grieved Westenholz, there was worse to come.

> 'Albrecht von Wolfsberg had accompanied Sigismund to the Summer Palace. When he heard the disturbance and was told the Grand Duke was dead, he telegraphed the dreadful news to the hunting lodge at Himmelsberg, where Prince Maximilian was, then immediately set off at speed to bring His Royal Highness to Rittenau to be proclaimed sovereign. Doubtless he feared for the young Grand Duke's safety; but, also, it must not be forgotten that Wolfsberg's own son was the prince's page.'

This last brought a sour laugh from Max.

'The household at Himmelsberg attested that Prince Maximilian's party had left hastily in two coaches, escorted by the detachment of the Royal Guard stationed at the hunting lodge. In the first coach were the Court Chamberlain, the prince's governess, Baroness Zetter, and the commander of the guard, Major von Eisen, in the second His Royal Highness, his page, his physician, Dr Jacobius, and his nursemaid, Frau Fromlich. Fearing the imminent arrival of soldiers sent by Count von Leckwitz, the party set off straight away, in the small hours: although expediency dictated a circuitous route, in summer the mountain passes are generally clear of snow and the moon was almost full.

'Although it is even now the source of much contention, not to say recrimination and sorrow, no one can know for certain what happened next. Those guardsmen who survived reported that when they were halfway down the mountain a volley of shots rang out, apparently from close by. Major von Eisen halted the cavalcade and sent the guard on ahead to investigate, while he remained—one might have said injudiciously, but retrospect urges far harsher words—with only one junior officer and two guardsmen to protect the young Grand Duke. The investigating troops found no hostile forces, although they continued their descent for some considerable distance. But when they finally rode back up the pass they encountered a scene of devastation and horror.

'Albrecht von Wolfsberg lay dead on the road, along with three of their comrades. The driver and horses of the first carriage had also been shot, while the carriage itself had been set on fire and contained the charred bodies of Major von Eisen and Baroness Zetter. As for the second carriage, carrying our beloved Prince Maximilian and his attendants, although it was as yet too dark to tell for certain, only the worst could be assumed—that it had plunged over the edge of the pass into the ravine below.'

Max paused to digest this. So that was how they had taken them. He could remember nothing of the ambush, nothing at all. But, sitting here, reading by a guttering candle, was he not living proof that he and the Other had not hurtled into the ravine? While as for Major von Eisen and Baroness Zetter...

And yes, as Westenholz went on to recount, from early on there was hope that by some miracle Maximilian was alive. Rescuers searching the mountainside found wreckage from the carriage and the dismembered carcasses of horses, but no bodies, either of children or adults. Then Prince Friedrich, who, with Leckwitz's support, had been declared Regent, received an anonymous letter offering to exchange the young prince for Georg Hauser, the suspected leader of Red Fist, who had been held in the Teufelsturm since the riots in Nordstadt. In fact Hauser, along with other political prisoners, had already been executed the day before, as one of Friedrich's measures to restore order. Besides, the anonymous demand was assumed to be a hoax—Red Fist, so Leckwitz's spies informed him, could be regarded as a spent force.

Yet rumour of a kidnap plot persisted. The burnt remains in the first carriage had originally been identified by certain personal effects only partly consumed by the flames; however, closer examination revealed the deceased were in late middle age—very likely the doctor and nursemaid—and had died from gunshot wounds. (Max grieved for poor Fromchen.) Furthermore, although the catastrophe had at first driven it from their minds, several of the guardsmen subsequently remembered that, as they had ridden back up the mountain, they had passed a woodcutter and his wife with a cartload of logs travelling downwards.

But if Eisen and Zetter were the kidnappers, they could not have executed their plot alone. Who had helped them? On whose behalf had they acted? The names of various Leftist and nihilist groups were bandied about, while some blamed the Illuminati, whose sinister secret manoeuvres had been the stuff of legend for well-nigh a century. Westenholz, inevitably, saw the hand of Bismarck once again—was not Friedrich an obvious suspect, given the circumstances of Sigismund's death and the speed with which he had claimed the regency?

Yet—as even Westenholz was forced to acknowledge—a seven-year-old Grand Duke required a regent and Maximilian's immediate family members were in various ways disqualified: his aunt, Elisabeth, had married an English duke; Lothar had been declared insane; and Leopold, having sworn allegiance to the Austrian Emperor Franz Joseph, was a traitor, besides which, fighting in the Emperor's defeated army at Königgrätz, he had been so gravely wounded that two years later his health was still despaired of. In any case, what would Friedrich gain from Prince Maximilian's death? Alive, he guaranteed Friedrich's power and averted a dispute over the succession. And as for abduction— surely uncertainty was the last thing Friedrich desired.

Even so, the wildest notions were promulgated in the cafés and beer halls. But, as Friedrich's newly strengthened army began to crush dissent and Leckwitz developed his network of spies, the chatter was silenced. In 1871, Friedrich's troops joined Prussian forces in the defeat of France and Waldavia agreed to become a state within the German Reich; a year later, Friedrich, advancing what Westenholz viewed as wholly spurious evidence that his mother was related to the Wettin of Saxony, succeeded in persuading the Waldavian Diet to overturn the annulment of her marriage; the newly legitimised Friedrich, with the support of Prussia, became Grand Duke Friedrich II of Waldavia. Prince Maximilian was disinherited and, in 1875, seven years after his disappearance, officially declared dead. (Of Christian von Wolfsberg's fate, Max noted, there was not a word.)

Yet, asserted Baron von Westenholz, writing one year later, matters could not, did not end there. During his Paris exile, the baron had been corresponding with Prince Leopold, who, though he had been gravely wounded, was not the failing invalid of report. Apparently, a year after the disaster at Himmelsberg, a box had been sent to Leopold in Vienna, containing a lock of brown hair and a small white-gold locket bearing the intertwined initials S and K, Sigismund and Katarine, worked in diamonds and rubies (Max recalled the Other had once worn it beneath his shirt, although he could not remember seeing it in the cellar). Also in the box was a letter, promising to give Prince Maximilian into Leopold's care in return for a substantial payment and signed 'The Red Fist'. But when Leopold and his manservant, in obedience to the letter's instructions, went to the appointed meeting place in the Prater, no one came.

Leopold might have dismissed the letter as a piece of mischief, had it not been for the locket. He employed agents, who duly reported that, on the night he had been supposed to meet Red Fist's intermediary on the north bank of the Danube, a man—a gentleman, from his dress— had been discovered with his throat cut in one of the alleys leading down to the south bank. The dead man, being without papers, was never identified and the gendarmerie assumed he had been the victim of a violent robbery. But the coincidence left Leopold unconvinced. It was hardly in Friedrich's interests that Prince Maximilian should be found: Leopold already suspected Leckwitz's spies operated far beyond the frontiers of Waldavia. Certain his nephew was still alive and in danger, he instructed his agents to investigate Red Fist, first by picking up the trail of Major von Eisen and Baroness Zetter.

Years had passed. Of Eisen no trace had ever been found, but

Leopold's men had fared somewhat better with the governess. Almost certainly she had returned to her native country, Belgium: a woman resembling her had lived for a while in a manor in the Liège countryside, near Herve; but, although she had a husband, there had been no sign of a child and the couple had vanished long since. Later, however, the investigators had found evidence of her reappearance, in the Ardennes and then in France, at Reims; furthermore they reported, to Leopold's joy, that on both occasions, claiming to be a widow, she had been accompanied by two children—both, it was thought, boys. But Leopold's hopes had been dashed again. From 1870 onwards, she and the children had vanished; in all likelihood they had fled France at the outbreak of the war with Prussia, but as to their whereabouts thereafter, his agents had as yet found no clue.

So near, so far, Udo von Westenholz had mourned in 1876.

'Yet, as I put pen to paper, Prince Leopold's investigations continue, albeit with the utmost discretion, lest they leave a trail for our enemies. His Royal Highness's letters remain hopeful and his hope cannot but nourish mine...'

CHAPTER FORTY-SIX

In his cubbyhole at the Hôtel du Commerce, Max had longed for his once-despised room at Beauvallon; its shabby furniture and stained wallpaper had held out the consolation of the familiar, the promise of safety. But now he was here, sitting on his bed with the door firmly closed, it was merely another small room in hell. He had left it as one person and come back as another. But who? What was he? How was he to live with what he was?

His head was burning, his chest felt as if it would burst. He walked to the window, he sat in the armchair, he returned to the bed. He found comfort nowhere.

It was indignity enough to know you were a bastard. He had been unsurprised to discover he was not the Bullfrog's son, he supposed he had sensed it all along; although he had felt an instant's pity for the old amphibian when he had read about him stretched out bloody and dead, he could not otherwise recall any filial feeling. Yet better to be the son of the former Albrecht Klopfer with his venal ambition and bullying falsetto than to be the son of this other man, Sigismund.

Had Sigismund known who he was when he had beaten him half to death? Or when he had set him to serve his legitimate son? According to Westenholz, the Other had been a sickly, nervous child and, when he was two, Dr Jacobius had suggested the company of another boy of his own age might be beneficial. So what more natural than to choose the son of the Court Chamberlain, His Royal Highness's favourite? Except that it could not have been fortuitous. The Bullfrog must have known what this boy was—he and Sigismund, they must both have known. Presumably this was how the Bullfrog had earned his estate and his 'von'.

What had Sigismund intended? Was it his pleasure to see his by-blow abased, treated little better than a servant, forever the other boy in the corner, the shadow cast by his legitimate brother's sun? Or was it punishment? Who, Max wondered, was his mother? Assuredly it could not be the Bullfrog's wife, the heavy-jawed matron who had loomed disapprovingly over his sickbed at Wolfsberg; was it some whore, was he the leavings of one of Sigismund's random debaucheries, was he held to blame for the sordid act of his conception? But why then keep him in the Residenz, in plain sight? Granted he had been effectively invisible, yet what would they have done as he grew older and his origins more obvious? Would they have sent him abroad? Or might they have found a less merciful solution?

Max shivered. Again he saw the brute with the raving eyes. Mad. The brother, Lothar, too—locked up. And their father, Maximilian III, so erratic in his behaviour that his subjects had toppled him. Did insanity blight the Hohenau as phylloxera cripples vines, generation upon generation? Or was it another sort of madness? The decline in Sigismund's health that Westenholz had described, the loss of his looks, his premature ageing—Max had not been a denizen of the Monkey in vain, he knew about the pox.

Congenital insanity or syphilis—was this his inheritance? As he thought of what he might become, his skin began to itch, so violently that he threw off his jacket and began to scratch; pushing up his shirt-sleeves, he surveyed the naked flesh of his forearms with revulsion; he tore at them until they bled.

Then, all of a sudden, he burst out laughing. He laughed until his ribs hurt and he fought for breath. His destiny. Oh, the irony of it. Shame, madness, decay—surely not too great a price to gain what he had schemed for since he was fifteen? For he need not have wasted all those years, watching, learning, waiting for the scar to whiten, searching for a noble patron, turning himself into a gentleman. They would not question the scar or care about his manners, and, as for the sponsorship of an illustrious personage, he had only to find Westenholz, or better still seek out Leopold in Vienna, and he would need no recommendation to smooth his way. HRH Prince Maximilian Sigismund Lothar Maria von Hohenau to the life. They had only to look at him.

Except that they would be denied the privilege. Damn his pact with the Other! Nothing, nothing on earth, would persuade him to honour it now.

It was not just that the notion of claiming any kinship with the Hohenau revolted him. Nor was it even the danger. For yes, his situation was dangerous, more dangerous than he had ever realised. "Not in German! Say it in French, unless you want the strap again!" "Do not speak to strangers, do not look anyone in the eye, or the evil men will come for you!" The idea of the Pursuers had been beaten into them, in the cellar and later behind the shuttered windows of their various lodgings. After Brother Bernard had spotted two mysterious strangers at Saint-Pons, he and the Other had taken fright and fled; yet reason had taught him to dismiss these fears—such talk was how the major and their governess had kept them docile.

But was memory playing another of its capricious games? He had retained the brutality of the threats; yet, if what Westenholz wrote was true, it had been as much to protect them as to serve their captors' ends, while Baroness Zetter, with her minatory nose, far from being the vile witch of recollection, had preserved their lives.

Max recalled that Major von Eisen had vanished quite suddenly—he and the Other had been glad at the time, particularly as it must have been shortly afterwards that they were moved from the cellar. But now it seemed beyond doubt that the major was the unidentified corpse in Vienna and Prince Leopold's suspicions were well founded: Leckwitz's spies had hunted them for years, had even got wind of their presence in the cloister.

Were they still hunting? It all at once struck Max as extraordinary that his likeness to Sigismund had never attracted attention. Of course, as a labourer, an artist's model, a servant, he had been one of the faceless multitude. At the Hôtel de Miremont, too, as the old boy's secretary, even when Mme de M had plunged them into Society, he had retained his invisibility; and, thank God, when they had travelled they had gone far south to Italy. Yes, there had been the odd occasion in Paris when some fellow in the street had fixed him with a stare, but he had assumed the intent was lubricious rather than sinister.

Still, what did he care if he were in danger? What price his life? What was he to do with it now it had lost all point?

When he had parted from the Other, his actions had been guided by a single purpose; his study, his going into service, his seduction of Armand, even his use of the name Max to lay a trail (stupidly, as he now saw) which would authenticate his story—all had furthered what he had called his grand design: his revenge against the world. Sometimes, when he had been younger, this vengeance had been petty: those who scorned him would grovel before him when he had a royal title and power. But mainly, even then, the glory of his grand design had been its giddying edifice of ingenuity and deceit. He had not wanted to be Prince Maximilian half as much as he had wanted to fool the world.

But now—when it was so easy, when he had merely to walk into a room, when only a few trivial lies would be needed—where was the glory, or the revenge, in that? Besides, it had been a deluded fifteen-year-old's dream. The reality was different; even the Other had known that. The reality was a prison, more luxurious than the cellar, but a prison nonetheless. He had not bothered with the conclusion of Westenholz's book and its lengthy lament for the sufferings of his oppressed nation, but he had read enough. Even if the Hohenau were not abhorrent to him, would he rejoice to be pretender to a tinpot principality that was a client state of Prussia, living in exile, closely guarded for his safety?

In any case, he no longer believed in hereditary rights and titles. And, besides, he had ceased to be a Waldavian, he spoke no German, his first language was French. He was a Frenchman, a Parisian. Waldavia was part of an empire that was his country's sworn enemy.

Destiny? A schoolboy's grandiose fantasy. He had grown out of it. When he thought of his half-hearted research and how often he had postponed putting his scheme into action, he realised he had been growing out of it for years. Yet, at the same time, it had informed his life, so that he had given no thought to any other future. What was the point of his existence now? What was he to do? Indeed, who was he?

Was he Max or Christian? Or Albert Fabien, as his false papers declared? Or Paul, as they had called him at Saint-Pons? Or any of the names imposed on him as a footman or when he and the Other had sat on the beds of those lodging houses? Was he Waldavian or French? Was he a Hohenau or a Wolfsberg? Who was his mother? Why could he remember so much and yet so little?

With a scream of rage and frustration he began to beat his head with his fists. He was a bastard. Beyond that, he had no idea who he was.

He saw no one. He had offended everyone but he did not care. Madame Rose, finding her solicitude and her offer to fetch a doctor spurned, had folded up the Smile and pocketed it in high dudgeon. Pélagie deposited meals and hot water outside his door, then scuttled away without knocking.

The Hobgoblin, of course, had felt no temerity in bursting into his room. The night following his return from Auxerre had been another devoid of sleep, although he had eventually stretched out on his bed in desperation, yet next morning his eyes must have closed briefly, for they were jolted open to find her leaning over him, swinging his watch like a pendulum in front of his nose: lazy beggar, did he know what time it was, where was her lesson? He had snatched back the watch and told her to clear off. But then, remembering the Perrault, he had gestured at the parcel, which lay amongst the clutter on top of the chest of drawers. Though she had grabbed it, she had pelted him with a volley of curses he could still hear puttering on the landing like distant fireworks long after she had slammed the door. Naturally, she had not returned.

There had been a letter too, that morning, left with his brioche and coffee, but he had not opened it: he had been foolish enough to tear open the telegram that had awaited his return. So he was not on any account to come to Paris? He was not surprised. Indeed, now he was enraged about so much else, it hardly angered him. Had he truly expected Armand to defend his honour? Besides, what honour? What honour could Sigismund's bastard conceivably claim?

In any case, it was over now, his time with Armand belonged to a life that had vanished. Perhaps it was no more than he deserved. Yet, although he had entered into the affair with ignoble motives, he had grown fond of the old boy, had even persuaded himself that he had come to love him. Another delusion, of course. He had tried to love in the way Armand wished to be loved but it had never been enough, had never convinced the old fellow. And the old boy, damn him, was probably right. Now Max knew his ancestry, he no longer wondered why he struggled with fidelity.

He had pitched the letter into a corner by the window, where it lay unregarded. Yet, from force of habit, he still carried the old fellow in his head: he would rather have slit his throat than tell Armand what he had discovered, but, in his solitude, as he rehearsed his pain and confusion, it was the old boy who listened to his ravings.

He had ceased to wash, shave or change his shirt and at night, despite the heat, would fling himself onto the bed fully dressed. At first his rank smell disgusted him—he had always fastidiously soaped and scrubbed himself and it had been one of the joys of leaving service that he could change his linen twice or even three times a day. But he soon came to derive a grim satisfaction from the sweat-stiffened fabric that chafed his skin and the rasp of his unclean stubble, as though his bodily filth were an emblem of his tainted birth and presaged his eventual decay. Besides, one benefit of not shaving was that he had no need of the glass and could cover it with a napkin to banish his reflection.

His rage against his fate had not diminished but had turned inwards, so that it gnawed at his gut like a worm. He was afflicted simultaneously with physical torpor and a terrible restlessness of mind that forbade the solace of sleep or, if it did permit him a moment of unconsciousness, taunted him with indescribable nightmares, the more horrific because, though he could not recall their substance, they left him paralysed by apprehension and panic.

Although he was hardly keen to advertise his shaming state, often he was stifled by the confines of his room; his own mad thoughts seemed to shiver and sway, palpable as cobwebs, in its fetid air. In the hope of exhausting himself so sleep would come, he went out on Delphine, the sluggish mare. Or he would walk for hours in the hills above the lake; in his enfeebled condition he could sometimes barely hold himself upright on his way back to the house, yet he returned to no greater hope of oblivion.

At other times he resorted again to Westenholz's book, as if, should he turn the pages often enough, some comfort pupating within them would burst from its cocoon. Sometimes, daring himself to probe his raw wound, he would study the plates, the faces of grandparents, uncles, aunts, all unknown to him but in varying degrees resembling his own. Heredity, he observed, threw up variations that must go back to the third or fourth generation. He had not noticed it before, but Princess Viktoria, the little sister, while possessed of the Hohenau nose and cheekbones and the Hesse-Darmstadt chin, had a mouth all her own, over-wide with a full upper lip. Yet—no, not all her own—he stared at it, he shivered—it was his mouth too, almost exactly.

Sigismund's beloved little sister. According to Westenholz, Sigismund had devoted much care to constructing memorials to his sister, enlarging the chapel at the Neues Palast, where she had lived with their mother, and creating a fountain featuring the twin figures of Artemis and Apollo in her honour at the Summer Palace. If he had gone to similar lengths to commemorate his dead wife, the baron did not mention it. A notion occurred to Max, so horrific his mind blenched. But at the same time a voice, a voice he had heard before—it belonged to the Bullfrog's wife, he now realised—whispered savagely: "You are misbegotten, an offence against nature."

Max snapped the book shut. In his present state, he was given to wild imaginings. Common sense said that, like the little sister, he had received his mouth from some past generation, while the Bullfrog's wife, as she had stood over his bed, had been castigating his illegitimacy, nothing more. As if things were not bad enough—if he carried on this way he would enter into his inheritance sooner than expected.

Yet, however he tried to pull himself together, the pain did not lessen. One day, riding Delphine, he contemplated finding some obstacle, some jump she could not possibly clear—he thought there was a suitable wall out at Les Sturnelles. But they were not halfway there when a moment of sanity made him wheel round and head back: he might kill himself, but he could not kill poor Delphine. On another day he took a pistol and went out to the firing range. If possible he would try to make it seem an accident—he had tripped and the gun had gone off. But, as he approached the targets, he saw Plibou close by, squatting on a tree stump and swigging from a bottle. He was damned if his last moments were going to be witnessed by that drunken brute: however low he had sunk, he had too much pride for that.

All the same, the disgusting old sot had given him an idea. Was it really death he wanted? Wasn't it, rather, oblivion, sleep, respite from the constant torment of thought?

He never drank wine—in fact no alcohol of any kind ever passed his lips, because still with him was the humiliation of the one and only time he had tried it. In his fourteenth year, after he had fumbled his first attempt to run away from Saint-Pons, he had sat in Brother Bernard's hut, confiding in the old fellow and drinking the cider Bernard brewed for the monks. He had no notion how much he had drunk but it must have gone to his head, for he recalled becoming defiant, even bellicose; until suddenly without warning he had begun to vomit, to be wrenched by a nausea that would not stop even when he had nothing left to disgorge. Before unconsciousness had mercifully intervened, he had lain there in the straw, moaning and retching, mired in his own muck.

In truth, he had taken drink on one other occasion: the night Old Jouvert had saved him from destitution, when, as well as insisting he ate an omelette, the old toper had forced a glass of brandy upon him. Once again it had gone straight to his head, although thankfully this time nothing worse had occurred. All the same, so greatly did he dislike not being in control of himself, he had forsworn alcohol ever since.

However, in his present state, to lose himself, to be free of the ratchet that screwed his nerves ever tighter—the notion no longer seemed so repellent, particularly if oblivion followed. He had been a child when he had drunk the cider, sixteen when he had swallowed Old Jouvert's brandy; now he was a man he was surely unlikely to suffer spectacular ill effects.

He knew where Durand kept the key to the cellar. He took what first came to hand, not caring whether it were vin ordinaire or one of Beauvallon's choicest vintages, only knowing it was a burgundy from the shape of the bottle.

Upstairs in his room, when he removed the cork, the very smell knocked him back. The first glass tasted disgusting: after a couple of cautious sips, he downed it in one gulp like medicine. The second glass, taken more slowly and accompanied by a cigarette, was less disagreeable. By the third glass, he was willing to grant he might acquire a taste for the stuff; furthermore, although he was perfectly in control and entirely sober, he had begun to feel the wine's beneficial effects: his misery was lifting, the future no longer looked so bleak. He remembered what agitation and eagerness to return to Beauvallon had quite driven from his mind as he had crossed the yard of the Hôtel du Commerce at first light to saddle Delphine—his encounter, the afternoon before, with the stable lad. He smiled to himself. Life was not without its pleasures. He might be a bastard, a nobody now. But he was not without ability; he would find a way, he would show them all, he did not need the filthy Hohenau and vile Sigismund to show the world what he was made of.

Night had fallen without his noticing. Continuing to promise himself future glories, he went a trifle unsteadily to replenish his glass, and was on his way back to his chair when he happened to glance at the window. What he saw there stopped him short. Peering in at him from the darkness was a face. The evil old devil! Although the sash bars somewhat obscured him and he was not the suave figure Lenbach had painted—the pox was clearly upon him, for his hair was unkempt, his chin unshaven and his eyes staring—it was him, no doubt of it. Come to spy on his bastard son, had he? Come to gloat over his bastard's ruin? The piece of shit! The mad, perverted, pox-ridden piece of poxy shit! Well, he, Max, would show him what he thought of that!

He raised his glass, smiling. "Here's to you, my dear Papa! May your filthy syphilitic bones roast in hell!"

But, to Max's fury, Sigismund was smiling and raising his glass too. Mock him, would he? Dare to mock him? Max hurled his glass at the window and, when it shattered against the sash bars, grabbed the bottle and hurled that too.

He was vaguely aware of splintering glass and that some part of him—his cheek, his neck?—was bleeding. But just then the floorboards began to undulate, the walls to rock and the ceiling to billow and flap like a sail. He had neither time nor capacity to reach under the bed for the chamber pot before the nausea struck.

CHAPTER FORTY-SEVEN

'My darling Armand,
I grieve that we are still daggers drawn—or at least that is what
I must assume from your failure to call on me these past weeks.
So there is nothing for it but to pocket my pride and sue for
peace. Besides, our dear friend Beatrice Dohnányi has arrived
in Paris, is staying with me and longs to see you. While you
might disdain an invitation from me to take tea at the Hôtel
de Claireville tomorrow afternoon, I know you will not refuse
her...'

Miremont set aside Catherine's missive to mop his brow. It promised
to be a hot day for mid-June and he was already regretting that when
he had settled by the lake at the Luxembourg he had chosen a seat in
full sun. Nor did he feel the relief he had expected from his escape from
the house, for, of course, he carried his guilt with him.

When he had announced to his family that he had at last dismissed
Max, Miremont had not intended to lie: he knew his duty and he
had been determined to do it. Every morning he awoke with the task
hanging over him; yet when he retired to bed it hung over him still.
Evidently he required a period of mourning before he could muster
his strength. At any rate, while his resolve had not weakened, he found
himself prey to indulgences which did not speed its execution.

He could not forbear going to his stud box and taking out the small
pebble, reddish-brown shot with white, that was Max's reluctantly
granted memento of their time at La Boissière; nor, recalling how the
boy, claiming he would turn it into agate, had taken it into his mouth
and caressed it with his tongue, could he prevent himself reliving his
excitement as he touched it.

He had also begun to haunt Max's room. On his previous rare
visits he had always thought it spartan, but now the boy's abandoned
belongings—the shelves of books, the copy of *Hamlet* with its annotated
margins, the worn comb twined with a few stray hairs, several centimes
and a single cufflink cast negligently into a dish—all filled it richly with
Max's presence, so that Miremont, roaming here and there, running
his fingers along the flap of the escritoire or the curved back of a chair,

felt that, if he too might take possession of it, they might inhabit it together in defiance of physical separation.

Sometimes he would take Max's disreputable old frock coat from the press and bury his face in it, or wrap it around him and stretch out on the bed, cocooned in the boy's smell. Sometimes he sat and gazed at the Manet. The boy on the bicycle. He would remember Max's delight as he had taken the painting out of its packing, but more often he recalled when he had first seen Max himself: a hot afternoon of primary colours, a distant child in a sailor suit learning to ride a bicycle while a footman held him in the saddle—and then the instant the liveried figure had let go, his body arching gracefully upwards, his arms thrown out, all the exuberant vigour of his youth expressed joyfully in one movement. Miremont had absorbed this unconsciously, until the knowing voice of Achille de Tarascon had drawn attention to his interest.

Each time he performed these valedictory rituals, Miremont assured himself this would be the last. He should not think of the boy, but of what he owed poor Juliette. Nor should it trouble him that Max had not replied to his wire or his letter. Yet daily he badgered Thomas about the post and daily his heart sank when Thomas shook his head.

He began to wonder—could Thomas be trusted any more than Aline? Perhaps the servant had taken it upon himself to do the master's duty. Thomas had loathed Max from the outset—it had taken strong words to end his attempts to purge the stud box of that pebble. And these days, given the dogma the priests at Saint-Sulpice were doubtless stuffing into the poor fellow's head... Was he throwing away Max's letters as he had tried to throw away the stone? Did he destroy Miremont's letters too? (For yes, such was Miremont's madness that, while his pen would not write the letter duty required, that same pen, as if in the hand of another, still scribbled Max loving messages.)

Watching Thomas go about his duties, subjecting the collar drawer to martial discipline, brushing invisible specks from the sleeves of jackets, Miremont searched for indications of duplicity, but the rocky terrain of his valet's face remained impenetrable. Miremont thought of Arthur, his boyhood hero, the handsome giant who had taught him to ride and shoot, who had known where hawks roosted and sundews flourished. His number had not come up, he had enlisted as a volunteer; why had he broken Miremont's thirteen-year-old heart, only to return mad, mute and half-blind? Miremont had not understood Arthur Thomas then and, thirty-three years on, could not say he had progressed much further.

Still, that he should doubt thirty-odd years of loyalty—Miremont did not like himself the better for it. Besides, what was this but a cowardly attempt to avoid the obvious? If there were no letters from Max, he was no longer at Beauvallon. Miremont should feel relieved—there was no need for his own wretched letter, it was Max, not Thomas, who had done his duty for him.

Yet surely Max would not leave him without a word? There must be some hope—not, not hope, of course, but certainty—it behoved Miremont to make certain the boy had gone. But how? He could hardly write to Rosalie Durand: even if he could phrase his enquiry so as not to provoke speculation, Rose was barely lettered, as was her brother, for all that his nose was constantly in his missal. In the end Miremont had found a pretext to write to Calvert—some trivial concern about the drainage works—adding, as if incidentally, that the steward was doubtless keeping M. Fabien informed.

Calvert's reply had arrived this morning. Miremont's hands had trembled as he had opened it. The steward gave copious assurances about the works, but made no mention of Max. It took Miremont some moments to comprehend the true purport of this omission: if the boy had left, Calvert would surely have said so.

He took off the straw hat Thomas had insisted upon for his excursion to the Luxembourg and mopped his brow again. The sun had almost reached its zenith but he had lost his chance of moving to a shadier seat unless he were to go through the performance of hiring a chair, for all the benches were occupied. Indeed, quite a congregation was strolling the gravel walks: ladies in lawn, hanging on the arms of gentlemen in light suits or gossiping with acquaintances, their parasols bobbing; nursemaids pushing baby carriages with fringed sunshades; spectators crowding the perimeter of the lake to watch boys of assorted ages and sizes racing their toy yachts. Everyone seemed to be smiling or laughing, out to get the best from the balmy weather. Miremont felt the great weight of his loneliness.

The power of *Hamlet*, he reflected, was not merely its portrayal of man's struggle to reconcile reason with inclination; running beneath its sublime verse, piercing straight to the heart like a phrase of music, was the expression of the inexpressible, the ineffable anguish of failure.

In any other circumstance he would have sought out Gérard, who would have offered solace. But Gérard, usually so charitable, disapproved of Max. Having subdued his own urges, he lived in contented celibacy and, although it remained unspoken and did not blight their friendship, Miremont sensed the doctor's disappointment that he had failed to take the same path. Without doubt Gérard would have supported him in his resolve: of course decency required him to stand by his daughter and put the boy aside. But, in the face of such certainty, how was he to confess his despicable hesitation?

Catherine would be as dogmatic, although on the opposing side. Retrieving her note, he snorted at 'daggers drawn'—how she loved these dramatic exaggerations. Well, as to the boy's innocence, they were now in accord; yet she would hardly approve his present position. In fact, given her own flexible morals and singular domestic arrangements, she would think him no less foolish than before.

All the same, Baroness Dohnányi was in Paris so seldom, he should be sorry to miss her. When he had first met her, at La Boissière, he had considered her a horror—a vast woman, dressed in flowing Grecian garments and improbable headdresses, who was apt to subject the gentlemen of Catherine's house party to stentorian inquisitions on the Woman Question, and whose poetry, though apparently lauded throughout Europe, had, when Catherine had persuaded her into a recital, proved rather too florid for Miremont's taste. But when she and her young niece, Francine de la Falaise, had accompanied Catherine to Beauvallon, he had been obliged to revise his opinion. When not called upon to perform or make small talk, she was the most agreeable companion, perceptive, intelligent, immensely knowledgeable about art and literature, a woman who had met many of the great figures of the age, yet who was as happy to listen as to hold forth; furthermore, there was no need for pretence with her—she accepted his nature without comment, because she shared it.

Deprived, as he had been since Max's departure, of any talk that did not concern Juliette's crisis or the doings of Society, Miremont thirsted for civilised conversation. He would like to hear more of the baroness's anecdotes and engage in literary debate again; perhaps he would even be allowed a passing mention of Ovid. He had been cooped up with his misery for too long: a little distraction would settle his nerves and give him the strength to act at last.

Since Mlle de la Falaise was visiting relations at Clichy before she and the baroness departed for Budapest the next morning, Miremont and

Catherine had Beatrice Dohnányi to themselves. Catherine was on her best behaviour: she made polite enquiries after Juliette's health but did not dwell on the topic and neither she nor the baroness mentioned Max, which left Miremont relieved rather than suspicious; clearly Catherine had decided they must agree to disagree.

In consequence, they spent a very pleasant two hours. Miremont had forgotten Beatrice's guttural laugh, which, shaking every one of her chins and migrating to the billows beneath her Grecian folds, was as infectious as it was unladylike; it seemed a long time since he had last laughed spontaneously. Thus, sitting back in his chair and permitted to smoke—both Catherine and Beatrice were enjoying small cheroots— he had dropped his guard completely; even when a footman appeared and Catherine excused herself for a moment, his suspicions were not alerted.

Beatrice was travelling to Budapest to oversee a production of her latest play, *Lilith*. She talked fondly of the city—although she had been born in Vienna and spoke with a faint Italian accent, and although she never referred to her husband, the baron, who was generally supposed long-dead, it was a Hungarian title and perhaps the place held sentimental memories for her. But when Miremont ventured as much, she laughed her gravelly laugh.

"Not especially. Although last time I had an unexpected encounter with my son."

"Your son?" Miremont had always assumed she was childless.

"Francine and I were coming out of Café Gerbeaud when he was passing. He cut us, of course."

Miremont could not be other than disconcerted. But she drew calmly on her cheroot.

"We do not speak. We have not exchanged a word in twenty years."

" I—forgive me, I had no notion."

"He does not care for my way of life. In particular, he does not care for Francine. He knows, of course, that she is not my niece. He also knows she was once my maid. But, just as we do not own our children, they do not own us. I am not suited to sitting in a widow's cap sewing Bargello. So we are strangers."

Miremont stared at the baroness. How cunningly Catherine had set her trap. Yet he could only wonder how Beatrice, usually so humane and passionate, could make these appalling admissions in such a cold-blooded tone.

"But do you not—you have no regrets?"

"Naturally I do. He is my only child. He has a wife I have met once and four children I may never see. But that is of his choosing. I hope I was a reasonably good mother to him, but now he has his own life. I am told he is happy. I doubt his happiness would be greater if he had destroyed mine."

Miremont struggled with this. "Perhaps so. But it is not the same with daughters."

"No? Do not daughters also marry and have children and make their own little worlds? In fact it is more true of a daughter—a wife is expected to devote her whole being to her husband's home and hearth. I do not say this is right, but it is the present way of things."

He could not help but be reminded of Clotilde and her dutiful Sunday visits, of how she brought Frédéric and Agathe to the Hôtel de Miremont as if it were a museum and he, their grandfather, one of its quaint relics. He no longer knew what to say.

Beatrice Dohnányi's wise brown eyes were smiling at him kindly. She put her hand on his. "Francine is my blessing, your beautiful boy is yours. We should not throw our treasure to the winds."

He had sat up all night, but could come to but one conclusion: he must have it out with Juliette again.

He was relieved to find her up and dressed. Although she was still too thin, she looked very pretty, he thought, in a cream dress striped with cornflower blue, which brought out the colour of her eyes. She seemed, however, less than delighted to see him.

"Oh, Papa, I have only a moment. Raoul is calling for me and we are driving out to the Bois to see the horses he stables there. He says he has found the perfect mount for me. When I am stronger, of course."

"Which will not be long now, we pray." Miremont smiled. "I miss our rides. I look forward to resuming them."

She offered no response to this; rather, she reached for her parasol and gloves. "Papa, unless you have something particular to say to me, I'm afraid I must—"

"No, my dear, I—"

"Then in that case…"

"I mean, yes. Please—I am sure Niversac will wait for a few moments—I do have a particular thing to ask you."

"Oh, very well. If it is only a minute or two." Sighing, she subsided into an armchair.

He settled in the chair opposite her. He steadied himself. "My dear, I think it is time we rid ourselves, once and for all, of the slur that was unfortunately cast on your reputation."

She appeared genuinely astonished. "What slur, Papa?"

"The business with Monsieur Fabien——"

"Oh, that! The silly tittle-tattle of one old biddy? She is gone, he is gone, it is all in the past. Raoul doesn't care. Nobody cares anymore."

Miremont licked his lips. "I care, Juliette."

"Oh, Papa, you are such a fogey——"

"I care, because we both know that what you said about Monsieur Fabien was——well, if there was truth in it, perhaps not the entire truth."

She looked at him. All at once her face was scarlet. "How dare you! How dare you bring all this up again! You come here time after time, you harry me, you interrogate me. Even when I was on my sickbed, you accused me. And now, when it is over and forgotten and your vile Monsieur Fabien has been punished as he deserved, you are still accusing me, you still cannot let it be."

Miremont's hands were clenched in his lap. He carefully unclenched them. "Dearest Julie, all I ask is for you to pardon him."

"Most certainly not. And anyway, what purpose would it serve? He is gone and thankfully we shall never see his horrid face again. Unless..." She gazed at him incredulously. "Papa, you cannot wish to bring him back?"

"My dear, he is an excellent secretary."

"You cannot. Not while I am in this house."

"But soon you will be married to Niversac."

"That is by no means settled. I have agreed to nothing yet."

"But supposing you do——as I hope you will. Your mother will return to the country. And I shall be on my own again. What can it matter to any of you——?"

"The insult! Do you not see the insult?"

"My dear child, have pity on your foolish old father. Monsieur Fabien is more than a secretary to me, he is a friend, a companion. You will have a husband and children to brighten your life, and I shall have someone to brighten mine. You need never..."

But he tailed off, for a strange expression was spreading over her face. She muttered something he could not hear. Then she said it again: "Now I see it."

"My dear——?"

"Yes, I see it. I've been over and over it again and again and I could never make sense of it, but now I see it."

"Do you think I shan't miss you? Of course I shall."

"I believed you were giving us your blessing."

Miremont stared at her, perplexed.

"That day I watched the two of you in the courtyard. The terrible day you ordered him to the country. If you weren't giving him your blessing to marry me, why would you do such a thing?"

"Julie, my child—"

But she had risen and was backing away from him with a look of growing horror. "You put his hand on your heart."

Had he done so? "I don't recall—"

"You did. You put his hand on your heart. Because you didn't want me to have him, you wanted him for yourself. You let him call you 'tu' and 'Armand'. You love him."

A great chill seized him.

"You never loved me. Or Maman or Clotilde. You don't even love that horrid Madame de Claireville. But you love him. You wouldn't let him love me, as a man naturally loves a woman, because then he wouldn't love you. You, my own father! You're a monster!"

CHAPTER FORTY-EIGHT

Max was woken by the pain in his head. He grew aware of a filthy taste in his mouth, an even worse stench and then of something else odd: movement, water splashing, a rhythmic grating sound. This invading presence troubled him. Opening his eyes at the cost of intensifying his pain, he discerned a female form on hands and knees with a bucket and scrubbing brush. The Hobgoblin. But as he levered himself onto his elbows to demand that she desist, the sickness came from nowhere and overpowered him once more.

His mortification was complete. Later, after he had slept again for a while, she had arrived with hot water and clean bed linen. In the face of protest, she had manhandled him out of his befouled clothes, tended the small gash on his neck inflicted by the broken wine glass and helped him wash; then she had sat him in a chair while she remade the bed.

Watching this scrap of a girl with her heavy belly tussling with the mattress, vigorously tucking in sheets, he felt he could sink no further: he would never be able to face her again. Yet she showed no disgust; rather, she seemed amused by his moans and groans, as if his plight were in the everyday run of things. And perhaps for her it was, considering her father was Plibou.

Seeming to read his thoughts, she laughed. "I'll give my pa this—he always empties bottles before he throws them."

It was true that, while the Hobgoblin's mopping and scrubbing had erased all evidence of Max's personal incapacity, she had been less successful with the wine stains. Although the sash was raised to let in much-needed fresh air, he could see that the bottle itself had flown directly through one of the central panes and cracked two others besides; yet it had done less damage than the wine disgorged by its passage. The stains might perhaps come out of his clothes, the Hobgoblin had scrubbed the floorboards, and he sat in the bentwood chair so that her efforts with the armchair's upholstery might be left to dry—the smell of vinegar mingled with the room's other odours. However, around the window and on the wall beyond the chest of drawers, the dingy wallpaper's map of damp had been redrawn in crimson.

The Hobgoblin shrugged. "Looks like you've been killing the pig. Maybe madame will have a receipt for cleaning it."

At the thought of Madame Rose, Max winced. "Does she…?"

"I told her you was liverish. Ain't that what you nobs usually say?"

He made an unsuccessful attempt at a grin.

She giggled. "Oh, come on, Monsieur Cheery-Chops. It ain't as bad as all that. You could at least get into your nice clean bed, now I've made it. Or—" her eyes twinkled "—if it'll make you feel better, I can get in there with you."

He was certain she was joking—well, almost certain.

She must have left him to sleep for hours, for when she appeared again the shadows had lengthened. He groped for his watch on the chair beside the bed, but she reached it before him.

"Half past eight. I've brought you some dinner."

Bouillon and a plate of biscottes. The very sight made him shudder. He could not eat, he would not care if he never ate again. But when she threatened to feed him, he was forced to comply.

She stood over him as he sipped the bouillon, lifting the bowl gingerly to his lips since his hands shook too violently for a spoon. But after a few minutes, observing his slow progress, her natural tendency to fidget overcame her and she wandered about the room, testing the dampness of the armchair, inspecting the books at his bedside, picking up his watch again. The latter seemed to exert a special fascination: now she was suspending it from around her neck like a pendant, now she was trying it as a bracelet, twining the fob round her wrist, extending her arm to observe the effect.

"Pretty, ain't it?"

"Enchanting. But if you don't mind—"

"Just you get on and finish your dinner." Reluctantly she unwound the chain. "If you're good and eat it all up, I've got a message for you."

"A message?" Remarkably, the bouillon had made him feel somewhat better; thus his first thought was that Armand had telegraphed.

Her answer dashed this hope. "From madame. Somebody came asking for you this afternoon."

"Somebody? Who?"

"A stranger."

Max suddenly recalled Prince Leopold's warning about spies. The biscotte he was munching turned to sawdust. "Well—did he leave a card, give his name?"

"If he did, madame didn't say."

"Then what was he like? Was he a gentleman? Was he French—or a foreigner?"

"Didn't see him myself." Concerned by his change of tone, she endeavoured to soothe him. "All madame said was she didn't like the look of him—she thought he was a tramp. So she said you was indisposed and sent him on his way."

As Max's physical miseries retreated, so his mental agony returned. However often he told himself that Leopold's letter to Westenholz had been written years ago, that it was absurd to spend one's life cowering at every mention of a stranger, he passed a wretched night, in consequence of which, although he was well enough the next day to be up and about, he remained in bed, alternating lassitude with fitful bouts of sleep.

During one of these, voices came to him. And no, it was not another of his hideous dreams. He heard the Hobgoblin's giggle and other tones, not a stranger's but, alas, all too familiar, belonging to someone he had hoped never to see again and who, furthermore, was the last person on earth who should witness his present degradation. For pity's sake—Polly!

He buried his face in the bolster, but it was no use. The Hobgoblin's excited hand agitated his shoulder.

"He's back! I caught him peering in through the scullery window. And he says he's not a stranger, he's your closest friend."

"Not any longer."

Polly sniffed. "That's not very kind, angel."

"Just go away."

"After I've walked from Auxerre? And spent the night in a nasty smelly barn, having been chased from the door by your bloodthirsty ogress of a housekeeper. In fact, if this charming sprite hadn't rescued me..."

The Hobgoblin giggled.

Max rolled over with a groan. He and Polly studied each other for a moment.

Max was not surprised Madame Rose had taken Polly for a tramp.

The fashionable coat was now white at the seams, the knees of his trousers shone and the buttons missing from his waistcoat revealed he had descended to a dickey: indeed, when you included the flapping sole of his right boot, presumably in consequence of his long walk, his entire ensemble suggested the night in a barn had by no means been his first.

However, if he were to judge from Polly's expression, it was as he had feared—he, too, was making a less than favourable impression.

"I can't say, angel, that this girl is one for beards. A nicely trimmed goatee perhaps. Or a Van Dyke. The Robinson Crusoe is dreadfully déclassé. But perhaps it will look better when it grows."

"Look—" Yet Max broke off, for, although he noted Polly carried the dented topper, which he doubtless continued to sport at a jaunty angle, he also saw that his former friend was sunken-cheeked and now lacking two lower front teeth. He must have turned twenty-nine this year—nearly thirty. For all his animosity towards him, Max could not but pity him: age was cruel when looks were your stock-in-trade.

"What is it you want?" he asked, less roughly. "Tell me, then be on your way."

"I came, dear heart, to make amends."

"Oh, for heaven's sake—"

"When I heard what had befallen you—how the Mouse had…"

At least he possessed the sense to tail off when Max frowned and looked pointedly towards the Hobgoblin, who, having lost interest in their reunion, had drawn back the napkin from the washstand glass and was playing with the watch again, dangling it in the centre of her forehead like some Oriental adornment.

"Mademoiselle, if you would be good enough…"

She did not seem pleased with this demotion from ministering angel; she stuck out her tongue as she left. But it could not be helped, for Polly was bound to be indiscreet.

The latter, meanwhile, was surveying Max's quarters. "Not quite the height of luxury I had imagined. And it smells, if you'll pardon my mentioning it, like a wine shop in Saint-Antoine. I thought you were too saintly to indulge in stimulating drink."

"Just say what you have to say."

"Yes—yes, of course, dear heart." Polly settled on the end of the bed. "Well, when Simon told me—you remember Simon, don't you? A sweet girl—although of course, she's no longer chez Mouse, she got the blame when the doggie died."

Armand's letters had failed to mention Bébé was no more; Max felt a pang for the poor beast.

"Well, anyway I happened to run into La Simone at the Monkey, and she told me you'd been brought low. Just before she got the push herself, she said. A frightful scandal. The Mouse found you having your wicked way with that ghastly daughter of his—you'd pinned her to one of the library tables, apparently, while you relieved her of her bonbon—"

"You believe this?"

"I was disinclined to, given the maiden in question has the appeal of an arsenic soufflé. But one never knows with you, petal. Here you are frolicking in your nightshirt with a serving wench and she, if I am not mistaken—"

"For God's sake Polly, I've only been here two and a half months."

"Whatever you say, angel. I'm sure you've been the soul of fidelity to Little Miss Mouse, and there's no justice in this world. So when I heard you'd been banished and then given your cards—"

"That's nonsense. Monsieur sent me here to supervise a construction scheme."

Polly favoured him with a pitying look. "Then why has he hired another secretary?"

"That's—that's just another of Simon's fairy tales."

"I wish it were, dear heart. But she still keeps up with Antoine, who gives her all the gossip. The new man is firmly in place. Name of Rossignol, according to Antoine—but more like a turkey than a songbird, not a patch on you for looks or physique…"

But Max had ceased to listen. His eye drifted to the little pile of unopened letters in the corner. One of these burgundy-splotched envelopes evidently contained his dismissal, doubtless more ornately embellished than an archbishop's cope, but for all the weight of Armand's excuses, a dismissal nonetheless. Somehow, while reason had repeatedly told him the old boy was not to be depended upon, a part of him had continued naively to believe…

A last hope gripped him. Although Polly was still talking, he cut across him. "If I've been sent packing, how come you expected to find me here, at Beauvallon?"

"Oh, I didn't, angel. But I thought if I started here, someone might know where you'd gone. That's how important it is to me, you see. I never wanted the money. You remember, dear heart, I didn't want to touch it? If it had been Little Miss Mouse's—but it was your life savings. All these months I've wanted nothing more than to give it back to you. And when I heard you'd been brought down—"

"For the last time, will you—"

"Well, there's no point in denying it, dear, when you're lying there looking like something from *Les Misérables*. And so..."

He got up abruptly and, while Max watched in astonishment, began rummaging through his pockets, finally depositing on the counterpane a sprinkling of small change and several crumpled notes.

"I know it's not the whole sum. I tried not to spend any of it, but I haven't had a regular situation myself recently—"

"Please, pick it up."

"—but when I get work, I promise faithfully to pay you the rest. On my life."

"For Christ's sake, I don't want your money!" Leaping from the bed Max began to gather up the notes and coins.

"But it's your money, angel. My amends."

"Here, take it. I don't want it, or your amends."

"Dear heart—please. Then we can forgive and forget."

Max stared at him.

"Fate has cast us both down—didn't your Auntie Polly warn you not to trust the Mouse? No girl can rely on being kept forever. But now's the time for friends to—"

"Friends?" The fact that Polly was right about the old boy, far from damping Max's anger, merely stoked it. "You are not my friend. No one who did what you did can call themselves a friend of mine!"

"But I didn't mean it, angel, it was only the Green Fairy talking. And I've said I'll repay you—"

"You're a nasty little blackmailer. I do not forgive it, I do not forget it. Now take your damned money—go and buy yourself some more absinthe and drink yourself to death—I don't give a toss what you do, Polly, so long as you leave me alone."

Afterwards, when he was calmer, Max began to regret his anger. Polly had made a pathetic figure, clutching his rejected peace offering, his chin beginning to quiver. He had been too harsh and should go after him. But then—he was not dressed.

By the time he had smoked a cigarette and then another, his anger had revived, soaking up his own humiliation, the shock of Armand's perfidy and his general misery until it swelled with self-justification.

Hang Polly! Could he not understand that he had betrayed more than their friendship, that he had been a traitor to every member of their brotherhood? As was Armand, curse him—a lily-livered traitor to his own kind.

Meanwhile it had grown dark. The prospect of night appalled Max. Suddenly he could not bear another moment in this squalid room, cooped up, waiting for elusive sleep. If he walked, at least he might tire himself. Besides, he had almost run out of tobacco. But when he had lit the lamp and pulled on his clothes, he could not find his watch; it was not on the chair or the chest of drawers, nor even under the bed. Then he remembered the Hobgoblin playing at being a houri.

Damn her, she had pinched it. She had been kind, far kinder than he deserved, he would admit, but she had clearly thought herself due some reward. So she had stolen his watch. Never mind that it was his most treasured possession; never mind that it would soon be all he had left to recall his time with the old boy. It was bright, it glittered: so she, little whore, had filched it.

Shit! He hated Beauvallon.

His anger drove him at speed along the footpath through the fields to the village. Even so, when he reached the square most of the houses were in darkness and the Tabac and Café was empty apart from a group of men playing cards and the proprietor, César Thomas, desultorily sweeping the sawdust in the corner near the door. Max's entrance was greeted with the usual inimical stares. Amongst the card players he recognised Durand and the day labourer, Leboeuf, and nodded to them curtly. But, as César, tall like all his family, but corpulent too, lumbered reluctantly to the zinc counter to fetch the tobacco, Max was aware of Durand trying to catch his eye.

"Your friend was in earlier."

Max might have known Polly would flee to the nearest source of refreshment. "Forgive me?" he said.

"That townie hanging about yesterday, asking for you. Fancy manners but looks down-and-out."

"I fear he was mistaken. I don't know the fellow."

"Well, he was here most of the evening. Until Plibou came in."

"And then there was a proper set-to," interjected Leboeuf. "Isn't that right, César?"

César Thomas nodded lugubriously. "I've just now swept up the broken glass."

Max hid his alarm and astonishment with a shrug, but the three were now so well launched into their story that neither his indifference nor their dislike of him could hold them back.

Apparently Polly had been sitting on his own getting steadily but harmlessly drunk when Plibou, despite being banned from the establishment, had lurched in and demanded anisette on the slate. As César Thomas was moving from behind his counter to expel the intruder, Plibou had staggered backwards into Polly's table and spilled his drink. Whereupon Polly, like a fool, had remonstrated. Plibou, seeing a stranger and taking marked exception to his 'fancy manners', had promptly accused him of being a bourgeois oppressor and an enemy of the revolution and, as Polly had risen unsteadily to edge towards the door, had tipped over the table, seized a broken bottle and barred his retreat.

Fortunately, Plibou had been easily disarmed by César Thomas, who had gripped him in a bear hug, manoeuvred him to the door and flung him into the square. Polly, much shaken, had shortly afterwards settled his bill and gone too. But, although César Thomas had opened the door and looked out into the square to check the coast was clear, Plibou must have been lurking in the shadows; suddenly they all heard shouting and, when César flung open the door again, there was Polly running across the cobbles for his life, with Plibou, though impeded by his game leg, still in vain pursuit and continuing to pour forth curses.

Having heard this tale through with a forced grin in concession to its tellers' gales of laughter, Max paid for his twist of *caporal* and set off back to the château. Polly was an idiot, but at least he had escaped and was no doubt seeking shelter for the night: it was hardly Max's concern.

As the moon was almost full, he had not troubled to bring a lamp, but now clouds had begun to gather and on occasion he was forced to give full attention to the path. Nevertheless as he approached the farm he had sounds and smells to guide him, cows shifting in their byre, a horse whinnying, the ripe aroma of the midden. Then, once the path had skirted a small copse, it widened into a track, the dark mass of farm buildings came into view and to his right a dim light shone from one of the back bedrooms of Calvert's house. A moment later the veil was lifted from the moon, illuminating the stone curve of the dovecote, its pigeonholes like rows of supplicant mouths, and beyond it the sloping pantiles of the pigsty. And in that instant, too, a scream rang out.

Max halted abruptly. The cry seemed to come from somewhere ahead of him, perhaps the main yard. Straining his ears, he caught angry voices—Plibou, he fancied, and—no, not Polly, a girl. The

Hobgoblin? Instead of turning into the path that brought him past the Durands' cottage to the servants' door of the château, he continued along the track between the yard and the stables, quickening his pace.

"No!" yelled the Hobgoblin. "I won't, I tell you! Not anymore. It hurts me."

He could see them now in the shadows of the Great Barn, her a pale shape in her maid's summer dress, him a gaunt form, dragging her by the arm, cursing her as she struggled. An unspeakable thought came to him. He tried to shake it off but it grew to a realisation. The Hobgoblin, poor little thing, was not a whore, had not dispensed favours to the local lads. What had Madame Rose said? That Fernande Plibou would bring the baby up as one of her own. "What other choice does she have?"

He broke into a run. But as he ran the moon was once more obscured and, though he charged on, the figures vanished into shadow and the voices ceased. By the time he reached the far end of the barn's back wall there was moonlight again, but Plibou and his daughter were nowhere to be seen. Max stood to catch his breath and take stock. He could hear the stirring of sleeping livestock and the other usual nocturnal sounds, but nothing more. They could have gone anywhere—the main yard, the stable yard, the path from the lake that led to the park and the Old Manoir.

What had got into him, anyway, but a grotesque fancy? It was like his wild notion about the Little Sister, merely another of the megrims that plagued him these days. Damn the Hobgoblin. She had stolen his watch. And besides, it was none of his business.

He must at last have fallen into a deep sleep, for the persistent banging on his door had been absorbed into his dreams. He awoke to find the room illuminated by a flickering orange light and Durand pummelling him.

"Fire! Get up, damn you! Think you're too grand to do your bit? All hands to the pump! The barn's on fire!"

CHAPTER FORTY-NINE

The fire had begun in the end bay of the Great Barn where hay was stored, but had roared through the space beneath the rafters like a train in a tunnel, devouring the ancient timbers despite all efforts to check it and tearing into the double bay that housed M. le marquis' new threshing machine. Someone had ridden to Soures to fetch the fire brigade, but no help could be expected from that quarter for at least an hour, probably far longer. Meanwhile, the entire village had been alerted; every able-bodied man and every bucket, pail and pan had been drafted into service to douse the flames; under the direction of Calvert's foreman Fillon, some drew water from the well in the yard, but most made a human chain from the nearest bank of the lake. By the time Max arrived, the barn was burning from end to end and frantic work was in progress to stop the blaze spreading to the outhouses on either side; an open shed for machinery was being demolished, while the team at the well had switched to soaking the granary, which stood at right angles to the barn.

Max was only aware of chaos: the intense heat, the suffocating smoke, the noise, drowning the shouts of the fire-fighters and the bellowing of the cows being driven out of the byre. Nor did he have time to reflect. A bucket was thrust into his hands and he ran for the lake.

The world receded. Beyond the stench and the eerie light, there was only the man behind him and the man ahead, the arms of one passing him the bucket, the arms of the other as he passed the bucket on. Take, lift, pass, take, lift, pass. The movement was seamless. The man in front was Boniface Thomas, the blacksmith, the tallest and strongest of his breed of giants, naked to the waist, his torso soaked in sweat, his enviable muscles gleaming. The man behind was older, dark and wiry with pockmarked cheeks: Max had not encountered him before, but the blacksmith had called him Jacquot. Yet it did not matter who they were or what they were called: they were parts in a perfectly calibrated machine.

Take, lift, pass. Near the lake it was cooler; as they moved closer to the yard the heat grew unbearable and they pulled wet handkerchiefs over their mouths to protect them from the smoke. Yet the machine maintained its steady, disciplined movement. Only when you found yourself at the front of the chain and it was your turn to hurl your burden into the flames, getting as close as you could, then jumping back smartly to avoid the scalding steam, were you alone for an instant, an autonomous being. But then you were running back to the lake with the blacksmith in front and Jacquot behind, one link welded to many again, filling your bucket, lifting it, passing it.

No matter that they might have been using thimbles for all the good they did: no one grumbled or rebelled, nor did anyone show fear. The first time Max had neared the front of the chain, there had been a thunderous crash as the roof above the hayloft had fallen in, hurling out a shower of sparks and burning debris. But Fillon had held them back only for a moment: when Max came forward with his bucket, the flames were soaring skywards and the air was still thick with their fiery rain. For an instant Max knew terror, although he hoped he hid it, while the blacksmith, turning to run back, was struck on the shoulder by a white-hot shard. Yet the man brushed it off and carried on running and when Max, sprinting behind, yelled out to him, he shook his head and ran on.

Max did not know how he had ever called these men brutes. His comrades shamed him. Even if he had not let misery deplete him, the relentless motion of the machine would have begun to tell. His hands were too soft and soon chafed raw by the bucket handles; his back ached and his muscles cried out from the endless twisting to and fro. Yet if Boniface Thomas could work on despite the angry burn on his right shoulder, he, Max, could not weaken. Nor did he forget Durand's earlier sneer—he was damned if he would justify it, or the contempt of other oafs like Palmyre Calvert.

From his drain-digging days, Max had learnt that if you held out against physical pain you could rise above it, reach a state in which your body seemed to fall away and you were strangely exalted. But now it was not just pain he fought. The terror he had felt approaching the flames returned in force; even when he was far off, down by the lake, the towering wall of fire was all he could see. Waves of panic battered him. Take, lift, pass. Take, lift, pass. He was blinded, he could not breathe. Above the general commotion came the frightened whinny of horses.

"The wind's changed," Jacquot shouted. "They're clearing the stables!"

But Max did not hear. He heard, he saw only flames. A flaming carriage, horses on fire. Then, suddenly, Fromchen.

She rose up before him, not spectral as in his dreams, but a distinct, solid presence, pink-cheeked, heavy-bosomed, as if he might touch her. Her kindly blue eyes were staring at him in bewilderment, her hand clutched her throat, she opened her mouth as though to ask him a question, but where her teeth should have been there was blood, bright blood, pouring over her chin, spurting between her helplessly clutching fingers, soaking her breast. Her eyes rolled upwards. Then she fell into the darkness.

Although he tried to slink unnoticed into the house the next day, Madame Rose apprehended him, all concern: it was past noon, where had he been, was he hurt?

In truth, he could scarcely remember. When he had woken up in the shrubbery near the Temple of Dionysus, he only knew that his eyes were caked, his mouth seemed full of cinders and his throat was parched. But, as he stumbled down to the lake to wet his lips, the stench of the fire still soured the air.

Even then, he remembered only fragments—feeling giddy, sick, faint, and Jacquot asking, not unkindly, if he needed to rest; and how, abruptly coming to himself, he had snatched Jacquot's waiting bucket and thrust it blindly at Boniface from some wild hope of salvation in the steady, unthinking motion of the machine. Take, lift, pass. He must have worked in a trance. He vaguely recollected the fire wagon arriving, and the buckets being diverted to refill the tank feeding its hose. And he recalled the deafening crash, which he had supposed was the rest of the barn roof collapsing; but seconds later scissors of light rent the sky and great wet drops began landing on his skin. They cheered, his comrades, they held their blackened faces up to the rain as it pelted them, threw their buckets aside and flung themselves down where they were. And he, no longer able to choke back the bile in his throat, had run to the lake, concealed himself beneath the branches of a willow and emptied his stomach.

Still, he could not have entirely disgraced himself, for Madame Rose seemed to have quite forgiven his recent misanthropy: she even anointed his blistered hands with one of her special potions. The fire was completely extinguished, apparently: the thunderstorm had done its work. As to how the conflagration had started, while nobody could be sure, suspicion was bound to fall on Plibou, who was nowhere to be seen—he must have run off as he had the last time. At any rate, this time he would not escape justice: monsieur's valuable threshing machine had been destroyed and the barn was in ruins.

"Monsieur Calvert's face was a picture, they say, when he saw it this morning. Well, he was away last night, wasn't he? Off in Soures, as usual, enjoying himself. Even with Madame Calvert being so poorly…"

While Max was grateful for her solicitude, he listened to her absently and, as soon as he could, escaped to his room. Peeling off his filthy clothes, he sat naked on the bed and, with some difficulty on account of his injured hands, rolled a cigarette.

He had seen Fromchen shot. That night fifteen years ago on the Himmelsberg pass, in front of his eyes, they—whoever they were, Major von Eisen, the Red Fist—had cold-bloodedly killed poor blameless Fromchen, the only person in his childhood to show him affection. The memory had worked its way upwards into his dreams until the flames and the screaming horses had drawn it, as heat draws a boil. Last night he had been in dread of the vision recurring; but, although it had not, he understood it had not left him. Like the image of his father, it would never leave him, would manifest itself at its own choosing for the rest of his days. Nor could he tell himself with any certainty that it would be the last of such horrors.

Nevertheless, he shortly fell into a deep sleep, which, for the first time in many days, was dreamless.

"You know they've found a body?"

Waking early the next morning and thirsting for coffee, with as yet no sign of Pélagie or the Hobgoblin, he had decided to dress and go downstairs, where he had found Madame Rose already busy in the kitchen.

"A body?"

"In the barn." She began to fill the cup she had set for him at the kitchen table. "Where the hay was. They found it yesterday evening."

"But…" Max all at once thought of Polly, seen staggering away from the village the night before last, doubtless in search of shelter. The relative calm bestowed by prolonged sleep abruptly deserted him. "Do they know who it is?"

"Well, they can't say, can they, monsieur? On account of…" Madame Rose gave an eloquent shudder. "They called my cousin to come and look at it—" Max understood she meant Malo Thomas, the village policeman "—and he found a kerosene can, so it's most likely Plibou."

"But he's not certain?"

"Oh, he thinks Plibou set the fire all right. But you've got to ask yourself, haven't you—I know Plibou's not right in the head, but is he daft enough to stay and let himself get burnt to a cinder?"

Max's coffee tasted bitter.

"Anyway, the doctor's coming from Soures this morning. Maybe he'll be able to say who it is."

Max had no stomach for the brioche she offered him. He asked her to tell him if there were further news and, rather than retreat to his room, settled in the Yellow Salon to be on hand.

He should have forgiven Polly. He should not have spoken so harshly. True, within walking distance of the village square there were any number of outhouses, sheds and huts in which Polly could have spent the night—no reason to suppose he would have chosen the Great Barn. But Fate, as Max now knew too well, was arbitrary. He should have forgiven Polly while he had the chance. After all, Polly himself was mortified by what had been a moment of drunken folly. And had he not been right about Armand? The old boy was not worth protecting.

The hours passed slowly and painfully until, at around eleven, just as Max felt he could stand it no more, Madame Rose showed in Officer Thomas.

The doctor had identified the corpse as Plibou. On examination, the right femur of the deceased was found to be shorter than the left—consistent with the injury Plibou had sustained from his encounter with the cart two years ago. But that was not all. The examination had also yielded an explanation for Plibou's failure to escape the fire: embedded in the corpse just below the ribcage were three curved iron spikes, the tines of a pitchfork, an injury that would very likely have proved fatal in itself.

Overwhelmed with relief, Max had not paid full attention to the latter part of the officer's account but now, aware of a significant pause, he looked at him, startled. "Are you...? Do you think this suspicious?"

Malo Thomas, the shortest of his clan but with the family's heavy shoulders and broad chest, was a square, imposing figure in his uniform. Nevertheless, his countenance was genial; although he clearly took pride in his office, like a graft imperfectly taken it did not prevent his common-sense peasant rootstock asserting itself when required.

"Well, Monsieur Fabien, we can't pretend Plibou didn't have his enemies. So, when you make your report to Monsieur le marquis, please say I'm looking into the matter. I shall tell Madame Plibou the same, to observe the formalities. But, if you want my frank opinion, it was an accident. And the doctor agrees. Plibou lit the fire, then, full to the bung as usual, he stumbled on his way out, fell flat and impaled himself. Anyway, the doctor's signed the death certificate and I can tell the widow there'll be no problem with the burial. Not to speak ill of the dead, but it'll be a merciful release for the poor woman. And no loss to Beauvallon, if you want the truth. There'll be a deal less thieving now he's gone."

Max, still rejoicing over Polly, certainly shed no tears for Plibou. Yet he was bound to think of the Hobgoblin. He had hoped to confront her about his missing watch, but, according Madame Rose, she had not turned up for work yesterday and who could tell if she would today? Then had come news of the body and his fear for Polly had temporarily put her out of his mind. Now, instead of accusations, she deserved his sympathy. Remembering what he had witnessed on the night of the fire, he was unsure whether the death of her father would leave her grief-stricken or relieved, but, whatever the case, he owed her his condolences.

Yet she must be staying at home to look after the other children while her mother was burdened with the funeral preparations, for the following day still brought no sign of her. Max did not relish paying a formal call upon Mme Plibou, for he was not even on nodding terms with her and, in her constrained circumstances, a visit from someone she would perceive as 'from the château' would be an embarrassment and an intrusion. All the same, he set off down the avenue and along the road, past the drainage works, where labourers wielded half-hearted shovels, and the new row of cottages, whose construction was still not complete, until he reached the original, occupied row. The Plibous' was easily found, for two neighbours were departing after paying their respects and the door was open; Max was afforded a glimpse of the parlour's dim interior, and, beneath festoons of washing, a closed coffin draped in a white cloth with candles at either side, their flicker illuminating the Widow Plibou's drawn face as she sat with other villagers keeping watch.

As Max hesitated in the road, he was saved by one of the smaller Plibous, a child of perhaps five, who, emerging from the ditch opposite with several frogs in a jar, imparted the news that his sister was out and, upon further prompting, that she had gone to the village.

Max met her fifty metres down the road; or rather, he first saw an approaching handcart piled high with bundles of dirty laundry, and then, almost invisible behind their load, pushing it jointly, the Hobgoblin and another of her brothers.

Max shouted a greeting, but she did not acknowledge it. In fact, it appeared she was not even disposed to stop; but as the cart neared him one of its wheels lurched into a pothole, tipping a couple of its bundles into the road. She let go of her handle and hurried forward to retrieve them, but Max was there before her.

Seeing her close to, he was shocked. She wore a white blouse with a black armband and a limp black skirt which must once have belonged to somebody's grandmother and did nothing to conceal her pregnancy; her hair was tamed by a grubby kerchief, her feet were in sabots. Yet it was not this slatternliness that alarmed him, but her eyes: in them was neither sorrow nor relief, nor indeed any discernible emotion. He might search in vain for the spark of rebellion he had always admired; apart from the sullen downturn of her mouth, her face was as firmly closed as an icehouse door.

She took the bundles from him one by one and heaved them awkwardly onto the cart, using only her left hand, so that he realised it was not her heavy belly that had enforced her brother's assistance; her right hand was swathed in an untidy bandage which extended beyond her wrist beneath the sleeve of her blouse.

She caught the direction of his glance. "What you want?" she demanded.

"I was sorry to hear about your father."

She snorted. "Get on home, Pierrot!" she yelled at the boy.

Pierrot, like the child in the ditch, was puny, with arms like sticks, and his legs wobbled uncertainly as he gave the cart a first push. But his second effort showed surprising strength and, resolutely thrusting out his tongue, he was soon underway.

As they watched the cart recede, Max wished there was somewhere they could sit so that he could talk to her properly, but there were only brambles on one side of the road and the ditch and a field of ripening barley on the other.

"Madeleine…" he began.

Reluctantly she withdrew her eyes from the departing cart. "It's 'mademoiselle' to you."

He endeavoured not to be disconcerted. "Mademoiselle. What happened to your hand?"

"I burnt it on the copper. What of it?"

"Look... I only wanted to ask if there was anything I could do to help."

"More of your stupid lessons? More of your stinking fairy stories?"

He was taken aback by this virulence against Perrault.

"You know what you can do, Monsieur high-falutin Fabien? For me and my ma? You can tell that old gander Malo Thomas to stop bothering us and go and arrest the person who murdered my pa."

This time he was more than taken aback. Again he wished there was somewhere they could sit down. "My dear—mademoiselle—your father's death was an accident."

"He was murdered. And everybody knows who did it."

"Madeleine, the doctor is quite certain—"

"Calvert murdered my pa."

"Calvert?"

"Calvert burned down the barn and killed my pa."

"Oh, for pity's sake!" As he stared at her pale, implacable face, he felt sudden unease. "You must see that's absurd. I know your father's death was a shock and things are very difficult for you and your mother—"

"My pa didn't burn the barn, Calvert did. My pa was sleeping there and he killed him."

"Calvert was in Auxerre the night of the fire. He went to fetch a doctor for his wife." This fact had been established by Madame Rose—Mme Calvert had taken another turn for the worse and her husband had called in a specialist. Unfortunately it made no impression on the Hobgoblin.

"He didn't need to be here himself, did he?"

"It's still a nonsense. Why would Calvert, of all people, want to burn down the Great Barn?"

"Ask that pig Fillon. Ask Robinot or Leboeuf. Ask Durand."

This was arresting, but it did not quell Max's unease. "Madeleine, it's admirable to want to exonerate your father—if that's what you intend. But, please, take care—stop and think before you make wild accusations."

Alas, she had ceased to listen and was already turning away. A few paces down the road, she turned back, but only to shout: "Calvert burnt down the barn, Calvert killed my pa!"

CHAPTER FIFTY

'Calvert burned the barn, Calvert killed Plibou.' Whether it had begun with loose talk in the tabac or had been in the air all along, the accusation took hold and spread like scarlet fever.

Max remained immune to the general infection. True, he pondered certain questions. How likely was someone who tripped over a pitchfork to land neatly on all three of its tines? Why would Beauvallon's Marat pick the Great Barn for his revolutionary act, when there was another, far more obvious target? Was the Hobgoblin's distaste for Perrault so surprising if you recalled the tale *Donkey-Skin*? But he cast these musings aside, for the affair was nothing to do with him and he should take care to keep it so. Besides, he had other preoccupations.

A calm had come over him, not the calm of resignation, still less of equanimity, but of grim resolution. To hell with the Fates and Destiny—it was up to him to decide the course of his life.

He began changing his linen again and persuaded Pélagie to trim his hair, which had not seen a barber for four months. The urge to shave was almost irresistible, for his chin itched abominably, but he must endure it as best he could; from now on he would have no choice but to be bearded, to hide his face, both from others and himself.

He rode Delphine out into the park, but mostly he walked the hills of Armand's Arcadia, finally settling on the stone bench in the hermit's hut, where, gazing out unseeing at the lake below and the hills opposite, in a stillness broken only by the hum of insects and the rustle of birds in the canopy of larches, he sat in deep reflection.

It struck him now as obvious that Armand, forced to make a choice, would choose his daughter, so obvious that it was hard to understand why he had not grasped it from the first. It was not a question of guilt or innocence, or who was loved more, or even of love at all. The old boy's rigid notions of honour and morality permitted him to do no other. He, Max, should not resent this code, for its dictates were beyond reason or reflection; it ran in Armand's veins, was as much a part of him as the cleft in his chin or his habit of thrusting back his forelock when perplexed: it had irritated Max immeasurably on occasion, yet it was also part of what he had loved in the old fellow. But now, because of it, Armand had cast him out and he must accept this without rancour.

There was no point in his dwelling on their life together; there was no point, even, in regretting his missing watch—in fact, the Hobgoblin had done him a favour, for he must eschew all reminders of the old boy: memories, as he had discovered, were poisonous flowers. He would allow his pride one concession: since Armand's letter of dismissal still lay unopened in his room, he could tell himself he did not slink away like a criminal, but went freely, of his own accord.

As to where he should go or what should become of him, he had no notion. He had disposed of Udo von Westenholz's book in the disused well near the model cottages, but its pages still mocked him. The clever deceiver, unfettered by the world's petty notions of right and wrong, the man of the future? He was a prisoner of the past. It had cramped his vision, stolen his peace, destroyed his very sense of himself, and the only future it promised was blighted by fear and disease. Somehow he must escape from it, by whatever means he could. He must reinvent himself.

The outward trappings were easy enough—assume a new name, continue to grow his beard, never acknowledge, even to himself, that he was anything other than a true-born Frenchman. The inward transformation would prove more difficult, as chastening as submitting once again to the rule of the cloister; he must replace pride with humility, rebellion with acceptance, resentment with equanimity; above all, he must rid himself of the idea that had buoyed him even when he had worked as a labourer—that he was somebody. He was nobody, indeed, given the circumstances of his birth, lower than nobody. He would find another labouring job and live simply as an ordinary working man.

He winced when he recalled his condescension to the men of Beauvallon. He not only admired their strength and courage; he envied their rootedness, their powerful certainty of who they were. Although Fillon, as Calvert's foreman, was generally hated, during the fire they had set aside partisanship; they had worked willingly, hour after hour, not for Fillon, not for Calvert, not for their overlord, M. le marquis, but because the home farm labourers were all local men, joined to them by ties as old as the land itself that conferred an obligation to act when a neighbour's livelihood was at stake. He had felt their solidarity and briefly shared their comradeship.

He had devoted too much time to books, valued too highly things of the mind. If he followed the instincts of muscle and bone and blood, he would find the same primordial connection with the earth, the same salvation in belonging.

*

Max's vision of commune life might have lost some of its glow had he been privy to the general swell of opinion. From the village to the outlying hamlets, from the fields to the vineyards, even as far as the stone quarry, it was quite forgotten that Plibou had been a drunken ne'er-do-well; he was now a martyr and Calvert had blood on his hands. In vain might Malo Thomas continue to repeat the doctor's verdict: even when he announced the discovery of a second canister of kerosene in the Old Manoir's cellars, all ears were deaf. Everyone could recall some instance of Calvert's past villainy, if it were only that he rode too fine a horse and gave himself airs.

Fernande Plibou was prevailed upon to delay the funeral until a subscription could be raised to save the martyr from a pauper's grave. Thanks to a generous contribution from the tenant farmer at Les Sturnelles, who was in dispute with the steward over a rent increase, Plibou would no longer take his last ride in a deal coffin on a farm cart but would enjoy all the pomp the undertaker in Soures could provide: a silk-lined casket with brass handles, borne on a *corbillard* drawn by a pair of black, plumed horses, attended by top-hatted mutes and followed by his heavily veiled widow in a closed carriage. Six of Beauvallon's finest men, including Boniface and César Thomas, would carry the catafalque into the church, which, it was expected, would be unable to contain all the mourners, since it would be a point of principle to attend the funeral mass.

Meanwhile the cry for Malo Thomas to arrest the malefactor grew ever louder. The atmosphere in the tabac, fomented by such as Durand and Leboeuf, became increasingly febrile and M. Crépin, the schoolmaster, the commune's Robespierre, addressed a spontaneous gathering in the village square, during which he declared Plibou a victim of the tyrannical nobility and accused the Republic, in its failure to purge these corrupt remnants of the ancien régime, of betraying the will of the people and the glorious ideals of 1789.

Max was too preoccupied to notice that Madame Rose, while still favouring him with the Smile, had otherwise grown tight-lipped. But he would have been startled out of his trance, had he heard her berating her husband in the privacy of the kitchen.

"Of all the stupid, addled-brained—!" To this Madame Rose appended an expletive Max would not have supposed could pass her lips.

"My love, you've always said you wanted to see the back of those thieving Calverts."

"It'll be the back of us, more like. Going round stirring things up, making mischief. When you're as guilty as he is."

"Now that's a—"

"You took his money. You'll do anything if there's a couple of sous in it. What happens if monsieur finds out?"

"Oh, *monsieur*. Always bloody monsieur."

"And it's not just us. Where'll Ma and Pa go if we're out on our ear?

"Oh, for Christ's sake, woman!"

"Go on, get out of here. You still haven't mended that window in Monsieur Fabien's room. Go and do something useful for a change, I can't stand the sight of you."

Up in his eyrie, Max no longer dreamed of becoming a son of the soil. His second day of reflection had compelled him to recognise this was romantic folly—as foolish as the idea that had once seized him, during a previous crisis, of running off to enlist. It was not that he shrank from the physical and mental endurance it would require—far from it. But he understood there was not a commune, from the Ardennes to the Midi, in which he would belong; he might live there until his death, but he would always be other.

He had never truly belonged anywhere: not in the Residenz or the cloister or the servants' hall, although there had been moments of camaraderie amongst the footmen and yes, there was his friendship with Polly—but then, Polly, too, was an outsider. Sometimes he had managed to delude himself: the Zhukovskys had seemed to offer a haven, but Mitya was drifting away, increasingly absorbed in the affairs of the quartet; he had fancied for a time that he belonged at the Hôtel de Miremont until the arrival of the old boy's family had abruptly disabused him; only at the Monkey did he truly feel at home, and even there his social commerce had been curbed of late by the strictures of fidelity.

Not that he cared, he was safer on his own. It suited his tastes and temperament, accorded with that other urge forever in contradiction to his craven hankering after comradeship, the longing to be free. Besides, now that he knew his history, it seemed natural, fitting, that his path in life should be solitary.

Of course, there was one place where he did belong, where he could lose himself like a flea in a rag heap. The ache for Paris he always felt when he had been in the country for over a month had been subdued by his other troubles, but not dissipated. On this sunlit June morning he yearned to be strolling along the *quais*, browsing amongst the bouquinistes, or sitting with a cigarette and a *mazagran* outside a café in one of the grand boulevards.

But that was his past life, and, if he were to extinguish memory, slough off his old self, it would not do. He must go abroad. But where? Italy would remind him of the old boy and, setting aside his repugnance for the German tongue, anywhere further east in Europe brought the danger of recognition. Russia? He knew the language and it would be easy to vanish in the steppes or the Siberian tundra. Or North Africa? If tales in the Monkey were to be believed, the Arabs of Morocco and Algeria were not averse to Greek love: he would be foreign there, but not other.

Then a vision appeared to him. It was early afternoon and he had come down from the hills and was standing on the Chinese Bridge looking across the lake; but, instead of the garden front of the château, what rose before him out of the shimmering heat were great outcrops of limestone. They lay, huge prehistoric beasts, slumbering where subterranean gods had cast them up, their backs worn smooth by the winds of millennia, the ancient skin of their flanks abraded into folds and ridges like scales. Aside from the filament of a path that rose from the plateau to the nearest peak, there was no sign of humankind nor any vegetation to sustain life, while in the distance stretched the limitless desert.

The Valley of the Kings. The lantern slides from the lecture at the Geographical Society he and Armand had attended a couple of years ago. He remembered little of Hugo Chausson-Laurier's account of the excavation in the East Valley and the burial goods the rock tomb had disclosed, but he could perfectly recall Charles de Selincourt's flickering black-and-white images of an immemorial landscape that seemed to disdain the kingly relics it sheltered as the sun is impervious to the passing of a gnat.

This was where he should go. He had no idea whether Chausson-Laurier and Selincourt were still in Egypt—it must be the best part of a year since they had gone out to excavate a second tomb—but in any case he would not try to find them: aside from this being at odds with starting anew, it would be embarrassing to explain his rift with the old boy, and, although they had very decently forgotten they had first encountered him in Catherine de Claireville's livery, they were Armand's friends, not his.

There must be other archaeologists in Luxor glad to take on a solitary adventurer who was willing to wield a spade or a trowel, to toil all day in the desert heat and rejoice in proving his mettle.

Having at last come to a decision, he awoke the next morning feeling surprisingly light-hearted. There were the practicalities to be sorted out: he still had a little money left, enough to cover his train fare to Marseilles and whatever equipment he required—not much, he thought, nothing that would not fit in a knapsack. As for the voyage to Port Said, if he asked along the dockside at Marseilles, he was bound to find a captain who was short of a hand and would let him work his passage.

His sense that everything was finally falling into place was affirmed by the letter from Polly that had come in this morning's post. It went on at some length, but its gist was that, whatever Max thought of him, Polly had his honour and remained determined to pay his debt; to that end, he had given up drink and had taken a situation at a draper's in Soures; from now on Max should expect weekly payments, starting next week. However, for Max, the letter's true gift was that it included a return address. He had written back immediately after breakfast:

> 'My dear friend,
> I am deeply ashamed of my unkindness. Yes, of course I forgive you, with all my heart. Please, I beg you, do not send me your hard-earned money. I shall always think of you with the greatest affection, and if you can bring yourself to think of me fondly sometimes, that will be sufficient return.
> Warmest regards,
>   Max'

His feelings for Delphine were also benevolent. As they cantered out into the open spaces of the park and he spurred her to a gallop, he reflected that they had come to work together well. She might have her eccentricities, she might lack the spirit and strength of Pretender, but she was nonetheless an excellent creature and he would miss her.

Absorbed in the pleasure of the ride, he did not at first notice the ominous quiet everywhere. Yet, when he rode out of the park and along the bridle path towards Les Sturnelles, he saw that the fields were empty: while yesterday there had been men out clearing dykes and building haystacks and lines of women and children weeding the crops, today there was no one. Then he recalled that, in the park, distantly, he had heard the church bell tolling. Of course—today was the seventh since the fire and the sixth since the discovery of the body. Everyone had either gone to Plibou's funeral, or was staying indoors out of respect.

It was the same when he and Delphine turned onto the road on their way back to the château. Near the cottages, the smallest Plibou was once again playing in the ditch and, while the Hobgoblin was not visible, Max fancied he could hear her shouting from the back yard—it was doubtless her task to restrain the fatherless brood while her mother followed the coffin—but otherwise there were only closed shutters and silence. There was no one at the gatehouse, so that Max was obliged to dismount and open the gates himself. As he rode down the avenue, the arch of limes cut off his view of the parkland, yet the eerie emptiness still lapped his progress like an insidious tide.

Thus it was all the more startling, when the trees gave way and the house came within sight, to see a carriage drawn up not far from the front steps. His first thought—that it was the old boy—made his heart lurch (but only, he reassured himself, from force of habit). However, as he drew closer he could see the vehicle was a fiacre, with a driver waiting on the box and a bored nag listlessly flicking her ears to ward off flies.

"Excuse me, monsieur!" A second stranger had appeared from the eastern corner of the house, where the path led to the Durands' cottage. "Would you by any chance be Monsieur Fabien?"

This fellow was middle-aged with a grey walrus moustache, and dressed with such formality in a black frock coat, grey waistcoat and plush topper that Max wondered if he had strayed from the obsequies.

"The maid from the steward's house said I should find you here. But there's no one about."

"They're all at a funeral."

The stranger inclined his head respectfully.

Delphine was growing restless; Max patted her neck. He did not know this fellow from Adam and he could not imagine why the Calverts' old Euphrasia might think he did. "Monsieur, naturally I should be happy to help you. But I fear there has been—"

"Alphonse Grandier." The man tipped his hat. "A.M.A."

"I'm afraid I—"

"If you will allow me to present my card…"

Was the fellow some sort of travelling salesman? All the same, he had a pleasant smile and a mild manner. Reluctantly, Max dismounted.

'M. A-J Grandier,' the card read. 'Loss adjuster, Assurances Mutuelles Agricoles, Auxerre Branch (Fire).'

"Yesterday," said Grandier, "the office received notice of a substantial claim—a barn and a new Ransomes, Sims and Head threshing set. Since this is the second claim for fire damage made by this estate in under a year, it was felt—in accord with sensible procedure—that I should come and inspect the site."

In spite of his attire and mournful moustache, Grandier had delivered this speech without the relish habitual to officialdom: indeed, he sounded almost apologetic. Max warmed to him, particularly since he could now reassure him the matter had nothing to do with him. "You should speak to Monsieur Calvert, the steward. I assume it was he who sent in the claim."

Grandier sighed. "The maid informed me he was not at home. He must be at the funeral."

"I doubt it."

The bell had begun tolling again. The mass was over and the funeral procession would be winding its way slowly through the village and out to the walled cemetery, set apart on a hill beside the road to Soures, where the martyred Plibou, instead of taking his rest amongst the paupers in the furthest corner of the graveyard, would slumber beneath marble beside solid citizens.

"Anyway," said Grandier, "it is better that I speak to you."

Max laughed. "Monsieur, I hardly think—"

"The damaged property belongs to Monsieur le marquis de Miremont, the claim is in his name. And I am told you are Monsieur de Miremont's secretary."

Max was prevented from outright denial by Delphine, who, having grown increasingly fidgety, had put back her ears and was tossing her head.

"She's a fine animal," said Grandier. "I'll wait while you take her to the stables, then we'll go together to look at the damage."

"You wish me to show it to you?"

Grandier smiled his amenable smile. "I've already seen it. There's something I need to show you."

Max had not visited the main yard since the fire. He was surprised how little effort had been made to clear the wreckage: bricks from the barn's rear wall, which had collapsed into the track between the yard and stables, had been collected up and piled where the machine shed had stood, while other debris had been swept into a heap near the midden, but the floor of the barn appeared to have been left untouched.

The charred and gutted skeleton of the building seemed immense; the sunlight slanting in through the gaping rafters lent the blackened cavern of the interior a sacerdotal air, as if they were profaning the fire god's temple: Max was gripped for an instant by the fear of seeing Fromchen again. But Alphonse Grandier pressed on briskly, undeterred, despite his shiny boots and immaculate frock coat, by the ash and cinders and the crackle of shattered pantiles underfoot. And it seemed his agreeable manner hid a merciless eye.

This, he pointed out, indicating the hulk of what had once been a steam engine, was not the latest model from Ransomes, but looked to be at least twenty years old and of German manufacture. The spars of wood that had escaped total incineration had never been part of a thresher, but were most likely the remains of an ancient farm cart. And as for the tempered steel parts, which ought to have survived the flames— "This probably came from an old plough," he pronounced, nudging the rim of a wheel with his glossy toe. "Rubbish, like everything else here, I'm afraid. Where's the conveyor belt, where are the fans, where's the crankshaft…? I shall be obliged to report, monsieur, that there was no Ransomes threshing equipment in this barn on the night it caught fire. If indeed there ever was."

Max could testify that the machinery had existed, yet of course he had not seen it recently—not since early April, nearly three months ago. So this was what had prompted the Hobgoblin's accusations.

Through what had once been a window overlooking the yard, he observed that Fillon had appeared and was watching them. However, when they came out into the sunlight, the foreman did not bother to ask them their business; as if he knew it well enough, he merely shrugged and walked away. They had all deserted their master, had they? Even his right-hand man was leaving Calvert to his fate.

Still, this was no more Max's concern than it had been before. Determined that Grandier should confront Calvert in person, he accompanied him first to the steward's office at the château, then, finding no success there, to Calvert's house once again.

There must be someone at home. Mme Calvert, on her sickbed, would require a nurse, while the invalid daughters never went out. And what of the ragamuffins? By the looks of the black cat curled up on a low wall and the bantams scratching peacefully in the garden at the side, the boys and their catapults, like the little Plibous, had been shut in for the duration of the funeral. Yet when Max knocked, no one came, not even Euphrasia. He and Grandier waited on the steps, knocked again. But apart from the gentle clucking of the hens, there was only silence, the same uncanny silence that lay everywhere.

They had turned away and were walking back down the track towards the château when Max chanced to look over his shoulder. Just for an instant, at one of the upstairs windows at the side of the house, there was a face, a face so unexpected, so little recognisable that Max wondered fleetingly if he had imagined it. The glittering smile was gone, the moustache drooped, the cheeks were yellow and sunken, the eyes red-rimmed; yet—although, yes, it was Calvert—Max did not call Grandier back. Much as he loathed the steward, he could not but feel compunction, for the fellow had the look of a broken man.

CHAPTER FIFTY-ONE

The disappearance of the threshing machine had shaken Max. It seemed to overthrow all his assumptions and indeed he even experienced a few brief moments of relief. Was Calvert stricken because he truly did have Plibou on his conscience? However, Max had only to remind himself of certain facts to think again.

Thankfully, Grandier remained eminently reasonable. Once Max had told him about the body and Plibou's reputation, he was prepared to accept that, while the claim for the threshing machine was highly questionable, there might be convincing evidence that the destruction of the barn was an unconnected act of arson; accordingly, Max gave him directions to the police house so that he might talk to Malo Thomas.

And that was that, so far as Max was concerned. It was the last service he would perform for Armand. Now that he had made his plans, there was nothing further to keep him here: he would leave for Auxerre tomorrow.

It was late afternoon when, returning from a stroll by the lake, he was informed by Pélagie that Palmyre Calvert was in the Yellow Salon, waiting to see him. Max's heart sank.

The steward's son wore the respectable suit he had sported at their first encounter; his hands clutched the rim of the same bowler; he strode in with his usual swagger, the confident assertion of superior masculinity that Max found so offensive. And yet a second glance detected something forced in this confidence. Indeed, now he was face-to-face with Max, Palmyre hesitated, seeming all at once confounded by a welter of pent-up words, like a man trying to breathe underwater.

Max broke the silence. "I suppose your father sent for you?"

"I've come home because my mother is dying."

Whatever Max thought of Calvert, his pity for Mme Calvert was unreserved. "I'm very sorry to hear it."

"Thank you, Fabien. But the fact is—well, I've not come looking for sympathy, I need your help. My governor wants me to assure you he didn't kill this fellow Plibou."

So here it came, the son's passionate defence of the swindling father. Max groaned inwardly.

"He says he saw you with the man from A.M.A. He knows what

you found, but he swears he didn't burn down the barn. He isn't in any way responsible for Plibou's death."

"I know."

Palmyre had begun pacing as he talked, but surprise halted him.

"Your father didn't burn down the barn. But he intended to. I'm only amazed he left it so long. Doesn't harvest start in the next couple of weeks?"

"Look, I realise you don't—"

"Anyway, I assume he got a fair price for the thresher."

"Damn you, Fabien. Just because you're from Paris and have some book learning—do you always have to be so confoundedly superior? I thought we were friends."

Max was greatly taken aback by this.

"I know you've never thought well of my old man, but he's—he's not… As his son, I should…" But Palmyre's defences seemed suddenly to fold. He slumped into a chair, head bent, as if he were fighting tears. "Oh hell and damnation! We owe everything to Monsieur de Miremont, I owe him my education. And, at a time like this, with my poor mother the way she is…"

Watching him, Max could not but soften a little. Yet he remained suspicious: perhaps sympathy was exactly what Palmyre wanted, despite his denial; perhaps he hoped to whitewash his father with special pleading.

However, when Palmyre raised his head, it was evident he had been choking back anger, not grief. "My governor's not a bad man. It's just that he thinks only of his own pleasures. Last March, he says, his debts were pressing and he was desperate—if only he'd talked to me, for pity's sake, but, no, in his view I'm still a boy, what would I know? So, damned fool that he is, he hit upon the idea of selling the thresher. That would relieve his immediate difficulties and, if he had a barn fire, he could blame Plibou and the insurance would pay out, as it did with the Cagots' cottage. Then he could replace the thresher in time for harvest."

Max settled reluctantly in the chair opposite. "In March? Four months ago?"

"There was hardly a day without rain. And then, at the beginning of April, you came."

"Monsieur's spy?"

Palmyre had the grace to smile wryly. "He thought you'd only be here for a week. But you showed no sign of leaving and he was being harried by the moneylender in Auxerre. He had a buyer for the thresher, so he paid some of the men to move it."

Max recalled the Hobgoblin's list of names. "Fillon, Robinot, Leboeuf and Durand."

"You know?" Palmyre sighed. "I suppose the whole of Beauvallon knows. That's the trouble. Mind you, he says he thought you had your suspicions from the start."

"I did?"

"They moved the machinery in secret in the small hours, but apparently it wasn't possible to do it quietly. The fellow who was keeping watch—Durand, I think—said he saw a light at your window, and the next morning you made some remark about the noise to Madame Durand."

Max recalled marvelling how sounds seemed to travel at night. "I had no idea."

"Well, the governor thought you'd relayed your suspicions to monsieur and you were under instructions to keep an eye on him."

"I didn't see him from one day to the next."

"He'd got the wind up by then. He couldn't risk anything till you'd gone."

"And I didn't go."

Palmyre laughed bitterly. "God, it's all so stupid. One thing I'll say for my old man—he's always been shrewd about business matters. But now my mother's so poorly—the specialist who came last week says it's only a matter of days—well, perhaps he hasn't been the best of husbands, but he loves her in his way and he seems to have gone to pieces. It was idiotic enough to hope that if he paid Fillon and his cronies they'd be loyal and keep quiet—"

"Durand? The wretch is a weathercock."

"—but to put in that insurance claim! Assurances Mutuelles didn't send anyone last time and he didn't think they'd bother now. So we'll lose our home, our livelihood, everything. And the entire commune seems to be baying for his blood."

"Things will calm down."

"Will they, though? Marianne Leboeuf—she helps Euphrasia nurse my mother—she said at the funeral that little runt of a schoolteacher elbowed the curé away from the graveside and made a great speech about justice being due, not in the hereafter, but here on earth. And he was rallying everyone to protest in front of the *Mairie* tonight."

Max recalled that Madame Rose had seemed out of sorts on her return from the cemetery. Nevertheless, while he was bound to admit the silence during the funeral had been unnerving, during his stroll everything around him—the cowman calling the herd in for milking, a gardener's boy cutting back reeds by the lake, the grooms mucking out the stables—all suggested the steady tenor of life at Beauvallon had resumed.

"Passions were likely to run high at the funeral. But there's no evidence your father set the fire or paid anyone to do it, and plenty to suggest Plibou was up to his usual tricks. Malo Thomas will make sure reason prevails."

"Good grief! To pray the world understands your father isn't a murderer, just a common thief." All this time Palmyre had been holding the bowler between his knees, twisting its brim in his large, blunt fingers, but now he began to assault it in earnest. "Look, old chap, I know my governor will have to pay the price for what he did. And it's my shame as much as his. But, whatever his faults, I can't stand by and hear him wrongly accused of having blood on his hands. And supposing it's not as you say, and things turn ugly. I don't have your faith in that dolt Malo Thomas. Isn't there something you can do?"

Max's hostility wavered—he could hardly see someone else brought low by a worthless father without a smidgeon of fellow feeling. But, as he reminded himself, this was no longer any of his business. And besides, as Palmyre of all people must know, he, Max, had never possessed the slightest authority in Beauvallon.

"I'm sorry, but I can't help you. I am no longer monsieur's spy. Or monsieur's anything."

Palmyre stared at him.

"I've resigned. I'm leaving tomorrow."

"But—damn it, man—you can't just…"

Max looked at Palmyre pathetically clutching his bowler, all cockiness gone. He might still hate that cocksure swagger for goading him into self-betrayal, yet he must concede no whisper of his craven admission about La Rosebud had ever got out. Palmyre had respected his confidence: perhaps, after all, he was a half-decent fellow.

Nevertheless, though Max was inclined to reach across and press the poor man's shoulder, past history restrained him. Instead, he said: "Go home, my friend. Look after your mother. This Plibou business is bound to blow over."

*

Yet it did not. That night the windows of the police house were smashed and the walls daubed with slogans and, when M. Saint-Séverin stood on the steps of the *Mairie* to address the crowd, no one forgot his failure to attend the funeral or even to send his carriage: they shouted him down and pelted him with dung.

Coming in from the village the next morning, the maids were full of it. Josephine, always the more talkative of the two, regaled Madame Rose with a vivid account of the schoolmaster's fiery rhetoric and the mayor's ignoble retreat, while Pélagie added a punctuation of nods and grimaces. When Max appeared for breakfast and announced that he was leaving, he could not have chosen a moment less propitious: even though he had let Madame Rose assume he was merely returning to Paris, her horror was astonishing.

"Leaving? But you can't, Monsieur Fabien. Bad things are happening."

Nor was Max given time to remonstrate, for the next instant Palmyre was shown into the breakfast room. Last night someone had crept into the Calverts' garden and thrown a rock through the French windows, narrowly missing the elder daughter's invalid chair. And, this morning, laid out neatly on the front steps, were the severed heads of three geese.

"Poor old Euphrasia—Madame Leboeuf had to revive her with smelling salts. As it was, we'd scarcely got over finding Élodie covered in broken glass. It took half an hour to pick the splinters out of her hair and even longer to stop her screaming."

Max refused to acknowledge he was shaken. "Please—at least sit down for a moment and calm yourself. Let Madame Rose pour you some coffee."

"Dammit, Fabien, we need to do something!"

"You've called in Malo Thomas?"

"I think you should send for Monsieur de Miremont."

"Oh, for heaven's sake!"

"If you'll excuse me saying so, Monsieur Fabien," said Madame Rose, appearing with a second coffee cup, "for once, I agree with Monsieur Palmyre."

"But I don't see…" The last thing Max wanted was the arrival of Armand. His plan had always been to vanish without trace. No explanations, apologies, recriminations; he might accept that Armand did not, could not love him, but he had no particular desire to hear it from his lips. "Anyway, I doubt he'd come."

"Monsieur wouldn't desert us," said Madame Rose indignantly. "Not in our hour of need."

Max again reminded himself all this was none of his business. He fixed Palmyre with his gaze. "Well then, why don't you wire him?"

"Me? In present circumstances—hang it, old chap, I'm hardly in the position… It would be much better coming from you."

"Of course it would," said Madame Rose, with some surprise.

"I doubt—" But Max bit back the words, for he was damned if he would reveal the true ignominy of his situation. Yet this left him with no choice: he downed his coffee and set off for Soures.

At the telegraph office, he was vexed as to what to write. He had no idea how Armand would receive this untimely reminder of his existence; nor did he wish to advertise the commune's difficulties over the wires. In the end he wrote: 'TROUBLE-STOP-PLEASE-COME-AT-ONCE-STOP-MF'. Then he kicked his heels on a bench outside the telegraph office while he waited for a reply. If it came promptly he could easily take his departure before Armand arrived. But after an hour he was forced to give up and ride back to Beauvallon.

There he found Madame Rose in a state of some agitation. The schoolmaster had sent Malo Thomas an ultimatum: if the policeman had not arrested Médéric Calvert by sundown, the people of Beauvallon would come in a body to the steward's house and take him into custody themselves. Madame Rose, although no fonder of the Calverts than Max, wrung her hands when she thought of the family.

"Those two poor helpless girls. And the boys—little tykes they may be, but for all that they're only children, motherless children very soon, too. And poor, poor Madame Calvert…"

"But surely," said Max, "if Madame Calvert is on her deathbed—wouldn't Crépin and his henchmen have more respect?"

Madame Rose emitted a mirthless laugh. "They don't believe it. Oh, you may well look amazed, Monsieur Fabien. But she's been taken bad before and always recovered. Marianne Leboeuf's tried to din it into her lummox of a husband that there's no hope this time. But he won't listen. None of them will. They think it's just Monsieur Calvert, hiding behind his wife's skirts."

"Then perhaps he should let Malo Thomas arrest him."

"Not if he's innocent."

"He'd be safer locked up in the police house. Just till the outcry dies down."

"They'd see it as admitting he's guilty, so Monsieur Palmyre says.

Anyway, he wants to be with his wife." Madame Rose sighed. "We must hope monsieur can talk sense into them. When he gets here…"

Max went into the library to wait for Armand's telegram. With every minute it did not arrive, he saw the possibility of his own departure dwindling, for he could not simply abandon Madame Rose. But he also began to feel guilty. He, too, thought of the frail sisters and their dying mother, walled up in the steward's house, awaiting catastrophe, and of the ragamuffins, who, however obnoxious, hardly deserved to witness their father strung up by a mob. He recalled the broken face at the window, his last glimpse of Calvert. Suddenly he was ashamed of himself. How much longer did he hope to go on ignoring the inconvenient truth? This was very much his business. If he chose, he could stop it now. He could ride to the police house and tell Malo Thomas what he knew and that would be an end to it. But, to save Calvert, he must sacrifice another, and that was something he could not bring himself to do.

He began to wish, after all, that Armand would come. But the more he wished it and the more time passed, the greater grew his certainty that the old boy would ignore his plea. The pile of letters in the corner of his room had not grown for a fortnight: clearly Armand had washed his hands of him, had no more desire for further communication than he had. He should have insisted Palmyre sent the telegram, even if it had meant confessing the humiliating truth. And now… He must do something. But what?

By three o'clock even Madame Rose had given up hope of monsieur's arrival. He always wired to tell them when his train got into Auxerre so that Durand could be there to meet him with the barouche. But now, even if he telegraphed, it would be too late for him to be here by sundown. And besides, Durand was nowhere to be found—off plotting with his fellow conspirators, no doubt.

Max thought for a moment. Then he went to the writing desk in the Yellow Salon, found paper and envelopes and began to scribble furiously. Half an hour later he was at the stables, giving two notes to one of the grooms with instructions to deliver them as a matter of great urgency, one to Malo Thomas and the other to M. Saint-Séverin. Once he had seen the man ride off, he mounted Delphine and set off himself, to Soures again.

They came from the village along the path through the fields. Crépin, the schoolmaster, marched at their head, pink and portly, not an impressive figure at first sight; yet his diminutive stature was offset by the fire of righteousness burning behind his spectacles, and by ursine César Thomas and barrel-chested Manu Leboeuf marching with him, shoulder to shoulder, on either side. Behind them came some two hundred men, with a scattering of women. None of them bore firearms: Crépin had told Malo Thomas they would come peaceably— provided Calvert surrendered of his own volition, there would be no trouble. Yet they were not altogether unarmed. Since the plan was to avoid the narrow, easily barricaded facade of the house and approach it from its vulnerable flank, where the extensive garden gave onto a terrace and a run of tall windows, some had equipped themselves to batter down the rickety door in the garden wall and any further obstacles they encountered: Robinot had a pick, while Grosjean, the monumental mason, carried a lump hammer, as did Jacquot Godin, the wheelwright (Max's amiable comrade in the chain). Other men had randomly snatched up pitchforks, scythes and staves. Then there were the flaming torches to light their way, borne aloft by César Thomas and Leboeuf and by others midway in the procession.

Nonetheless, even after Crépin's powerful exhortations in the village square, they had set off almost in a holiday mood, straggling and exchanging jokes, while two or three drinkers from the tabac had burst rowdily into song. But soon the need to follow the footpath pressed them into formation; the blazing torches, votive flames against the night sky, imbued them with the solemnity of their mission; the steady, purposeful rhythm of the leading marchers coursed through them, catching them up like a wave, bearing them on, exhilarating even the drunks and the stragglers. Now, as their blood beat to that tune, they became one: the bond Max had admired, the solidarity which had made them heroes during the fire, now made them a mob, they advanced with the heedless certainty of a ploughshare cutting a furrow. To the rhythm of their steps, they began to chant: "Calvert, Calvert! Justice, Justice! Murderer, Murderer! Justice, Justice!"

As they neared the crumbling wall of the steward's garden, Crépin brought them to a halt while the wooden door was smashed and the loose stones surrounding it quickly torn away to widen the gap. Then Crépin, raising a torch aloft, cried in his shrill voice: "Let the will of the people prevail!"

"*Calvert!*" they shouted, as they poured into the garden. "*Murderer! Justice! Justice!*"

CHAPTER FIFTY-TWO

In the servants' hall of the Hôtel de Miremont it was agreed that monsieur had given up. Yes, he had often given in to his wife, but now he had altogether surrendered. When Boussec had gone to enquire whether the unthinkable were true—that he, Boussec, should in future take his orders from madame—monsieur, avoiding his eye, had nodded gloomily.

Madame held her Thursdays; the landau, emblazoned with the Miremont escutcheon and with two footmen in canary yellow on the back, bore her on calls or to the opera; mademoiselle, now she was recovered, went out riding with M. de Niversac; Mme Thierry-Le Puy continued her usual visits: outwardly, the life of the house went on. But M. de Miremont played no part in it. Indeed, all communication from madame and her daughters came to him via the servants and, if guests invited to partake of one of Chef Quintivali's exquisite dinners happened to enquire after the master of the house, they were to be told he was unwell.

Nor could any end be seen to this discomfiting state of affairs. True, madame would depart, along with the rest of Society, for the country next month; but whereas she had been expected to resume her exile in Burgundy, she was talking of redecorating the Elizabeth Salon—she had already viewed wallpaper samples—and there were numerous other indications that she was set on returning to the Hôtel de Miremont in the autumn.

The servants' hall was divided: its newer members were inclined to think madame's rule could be beneficial—M. Quintivali opined that, if her Thursdays were at last to take off, it would greatly add to the prestige of the house, while for the footmen the prospect of more dinners and balls promised more tips. For the old guard, however, many of whom remembered madame's previous reign, the omens could only be gloomy. M. Boussec spoke of retiring to live with his brother and sister-in-law; Mme Mercier, too, thought of retirement, and of setting up home with Mme Dussardier, whose reinstatement at the Hôtel de Miremont could no longer be hoped for. M. Thomas, of course, said nothing; but, given his master's subjugation and his loathing of madame, the older servants were unsurprised when, within a few days of her ascendency, he went on one of his periodic drinking sprees, from which he had yet to return.

However, if the advantages of the new order were disputed, its cause was not. Everyone down to the boot boy knew what had brought about monsieur's downfall—his attachment to that nefarious former secretary of his. Mlle Drouet, who had grown very uppity since her promotion to lady's maid, demanded to know what kind of man M. de Miremont was, that he could see her mistress, his own daughter, ravished, without flogging the culprit to within a hair's breadth—but then, monsieur was not a real man, was he, and that brute Fabien knew no limit to depravity. The new Simon, who, besides assuming his predecessor's name, as was the custom, had also donned his gossipmonger's mantle, swore madame had been sent correspondence by a blackmailer, letters of such obscenity that it would scorch your eyes to read them. And Philippe, who was deputising for Thomas, could not help but overhear madame use words to monsieur he would rather not repeat.

Of course, the secretary's immoral influence upon their master was already well-known to the old guard and they had always deplored it. Indeed, they deplored it still. But, nonetheless, the house had run smoothly, monsieur had been happy and M. Fabien himself, although no better than he should be, had never overplayed his advantage. Whereas now—well, they searched for a good word about M. Rossignol. Besides, there were worse things a master could do than discreetly share his bed with his secretary: M. de Miremont was no marquis de Sade. His greatest fault was not immorality but his failure to stand up to his wife.

In anger, in pity, they saw how he sequestered himself in his apartments, never receiving visitors, going out only for long, aimless walks. Philippe said he barely spoke, ate little and no longer even went down to the library, but lay on his divan, staring at nothing in particular, like a man diagnosed with a fatal disease.

While Miremont did not relish being ostracised by his family—it hurt him particularly that his grandchildren were no longer permitted to see him—he could not deny he deserved it, that he merited every slur on his character as a husband and father, every belittlement of his manhood, every contemptuous word Aline had hurled at him. None of this could be worse than the moment Juliette had divined the truth.

He supposed his reputation would be destroyed—a few days ago, when he had encountered Niversac on the main staircase, the young man had merely nodded and hurried on. Yet Aline would probably not parade her misfortune amongst her wider acquaintance: it was, in its way, as shaming to his wife as it was to him—one thing for him to betray her with Catherine de Claireville, quite another for him to reject her for someone of his own sex. He pondered the irony of Aline's fawning on Achille de Tarascon during his rare appearances at her Thursdays, Tarascon, a man whose rococo indulgences made his own sins seem tepid.

Yet they were sins nonetheless, and it was vainglorious—nay, deluded—to worry about his reputation. Honour or inclination? He had hesitated, temporised, lied, procrastinated—anything but make the choice that would protect his innocent daughter, anything but give up his sinful desire. Only when it was too late and the worst had happened, did he fully understand there had been but one course of action and, though he had failed to take it, he must not fail now.

He had ordered Thomas to throw away the stone in the stud box and pack up the contents of Max's room. There was to be no more longing for Max or writing to him or agonising over the boy's failure to reply (in any case, after Thomas's disappearance and with M. Rossignol now in charge of the post, no letter would reach Miremont); nor should he continue to fret about Max's whereabouts—he might be in Beauvallon, he might be long gone: it was immaterial. The boy's beauty, his love, all the pleasures they had enjoyed together—these could no longer remain cherished memories, but must, whatever the struggle, be expunged from Miremont's mind. He would take Gérard as his model, crush his degenerate urges and live celibate: in due course, when he felt stronger, he would, like the doctor, channel his energies into his work, finally finish his opus on Ovid.

Meanwhile, surely he should devote his concern to the absence of Thomas. His manservant had been missing for well over a week, far longer than usual, and Boussec, Georges and Philippe, despite their combined efforts, could find no trace of him. To Miremont's wonted fears—that the poor fellow might be lying in the Hôtel-Dieu with knife wounds or on a slab in the morgue—was added another: that this time he had gone for good. To lose Thomas as well as Max—true, Miremont's relationship with his valet was hardly founded on perfect understanding, yet, all the same, there was a bond between them, a lasting connection that could not be severed without the anguish of bereavement.

Arthur Thomas, the fourteen-year-old groom at Beauvallon deputed to ease eight-year-old Miremont's transition from his pony to horseback. Arthur Thomas, at nineteen a handsome giant, capable of any feat of strength or endurance, the twelve-year-old Miremont's hero. Yet was it merely hero worship? There came to Miremont a long-buried memory: he had gone to find Thomas at his parents' cottage and discovered him stripped to the waist, bending to wash himself in a tin basin. Miremont had stood in the doorway, unobserved, watching him: the corded sinews of his forearms, the thick hair in his armpits, the way the muscles of his shoulders moved as he soaped himself, how the shaft of sunlight from the little window traced the curve of his wet back in a gleaming arc. It was a mere moment before Thomas looked round and quickly reached for his shirt, but Miremont had felt such excitement he could barely breathe.

He had been wrong all along. These urges had not come upon him in middle age, had not flared up suddenly at the sight of Constant's arrogant young American visitor—what was his name?—sprawled indolently in an easy chair. He had not only worshipped Thomas; he had desired him with every atom of his pubescent being.

Had Thomas understood? Was that why he had run off to enlist? Had he felt it too? Miremont brushed this aside—no, not for a puny boy. But in the barracks, with men of his own age…? Did that explain Thomas' descent afterwards, his refusal to speak, his rejection of his family, his drunkenness, his vagrancy, his retreat to the cellars of the Old Manoir, where he had lived like an animal until Miremont, desire long forgotten, subsumed by a sixteen-year-old's callow idealism, had managed to coax him out? Did Thomas regard the stone that had put out his eye as punishment for his sins? Was that why he had willingly left the countryside, the world of nature he had inhabited as if the sweet scent of the earth sang in his blood—because it reproached him for his own unnatural urges? Had his thirty years of sewing on buttons and regimenting Miremont's collar drawer been a grim penance? Perhaps his eagerness for the mortifications of religion was now easily understood.

This was speculation, Miremont reminded himself. Yet his own shame deepened. If Thomas had suffered so much to purge himself of degeneracy, surely he, Miremont, should face his own struggle with more fortitude.

Miremont's walks took him randomly all over the city, often to quarters whose poverty was a stark revelation. But generally he walked without attending to his surroundings, to escape from the house and to stave off the wish for death.

It was hot for late June and mingling with the other smells that assailed him—rotting vegetables, horse dung, the meaty stench of tanneries—there was already a detectable whiff of bad eggs, the stifling reek from the sewers that would drive Society from Paris during July; even so, ignoring the heavy air and the thirst and exhaustion it induced, he preferred not to stop. Yet, that afternoon, in the Boulevard Beaumarchais, he did come to a halt, quite suddenly. His eye was caught by a yellow poster on a Morris column. Or rather, by a name in bold black type. The Herzen Quartet.

He should have continued on his way, but he could not help himself. They were giving a concert at the Temple Sainte-Marie, the Protestant church in the Rue Saint-Antoine. A quartet by the Russian composer Tchaikovsky, followed by Beethoven, Opus 131. At 7.30pm, Thursday 28th June. Tonight.

That end of the Rue Saint-Antoine was only a short walk away. It was madness, of course, a breach of his vow. But his memories of the four young Russians and the glorious sounds drifting from his music room were surely harmless. Besides, he had no wish to go home. He turned off into the Marais, found he was in the Jewish Quarter and, going into the first café he saw, whiled away the time until seven o'clock with an early and unaccustomed dinner of borscht, blinis and *lekach*.

At the church door it occurred to him that he should have returned home after all, to change into his tails. But his worry was needless: his frock coat did not look out of place in an audience of bourgeois couples, elderly matrons and students. Their number was not large, but then it would have required quite a crowd to fill this echoing basilica, which seemed all the emptier for its stern lack of adornment; a chilly twilight prevailed, despite the sunshine outside.

He chose a seat towards the back on the aisle, from which he could see the glow of the torchères illuminating the music stands. And, yes, it must be admitted, he felt a pang as silence fell and Mitya Zhukovsky led the others into that pool of light: gangling Lyudin with his cello, the red-haired violist, the fair, consumptive-looking boy who played second violin—benign ghosts, all of them, from an unimaginably happy past.

He bit his lip. But it seemed his fears were groundless: he did not know the Tchaikovsky quartet and, while he was touched by the haunting second movement, he was well able to survive it. The Beethoven would be more of a challenge: deaf, sick, nearing death, the composer seemed at last to open his heart in his late quartets and Opus 131 was regarded as his greatest. Miremont recalled pausing, enthralled, on the landing outside the Music Room as the Herzen had rehearsed it.

Although the Russians, defying the smallness of their audience and the austerity of the venue, played with more passion and delicacy than he had ever heard from them before, Miremont withstood this without difficulty at first. He became lost in the music, no longer harried by memories, no longer conscious of pain. But during the last movement something seized him—it pricked his throat like a mote of dust—a yearning in the tension between the fierce first subject and the lyrical second—a longing, an agonised reaching out for transcendence—and he could not see for tears. Fearing he would sob out loud, he stuffed his handkerchief in his mouth until the final, muted chord had died away. Then, as the applause began, he rushed for the door.

He felt too low to walk the next day, and thus was at home to receive Dmitri Zhukovsky when he called that afternoon.

This call could not be coincidence. And indeed the young man seemed uncharacteristically diffident, even embarrassed, so that Miremont, who had always deluded himself that Zhukovsky was unaware of his true relations with Max, was obliged to confront reality: of course the fellow knew, he was Max's best friend, he knew the boy's ways.

Conversation was strained: how could it be otherwise when the obvious topics, the concert and Max, seemed to lie between them like craters? Miremont spoke vaguely and untruthfully about his writing. Zhukovsky thanked his host for enquiring after Mme Zhukovskaya's health, then spoke of the Herzens: tours of Northern Italy and Bohemia were planned for the autumn but at present engagements were scarce, so they were playing for a pittance anywhere that would have them; it might not pay the bills but they had all found other work—he himself was teaching part-time at the conservatoire—and besides, it was enjoyable and excellent practice. At this point, Miremont felt certain Zhukovsky would mention the concert, but thankfully he did not; indeed, it seemed likely that, whatever he had come to say, he would leave without saying it. But when Miremont asked if there was anything he could do to assist the Herzens' fortunes, his visitor was galvanised.

"Monsieur, you have already been more than generous. That is not why I have come. I…" Zhukovsky's determination appeared momentarily to falter, but then he pressed on. "My sister was sitting quite near you last night. She saw you leave."

"Ah… Well—it was no criticism, may I assure you, I have never heard you play better. I had eaten a somewhat experimental dinner, it must have disagreed with me."

Zhukovsky hesitated again and Miremont, reading his broad, open face, saw his embarrassment came, not from disapproval, but delicacy, from a punctilious dread of intruding. "Vera thought—we both thought… We had a letter from Maxim yesterday. A strange, wild letter. Perhaps you already know this, in which case forgive me—but he says he's going to Egypt."

Miremont froze.

"He plans to work his passage to Port Said, then join the archaeologists at Luxor."

Countless times Miremont had imagined hearing news of this kind, yet he was still unprepared for it. "When?" he asked faintly.

"The letter said in a couple of days."

Zhukovsky paused, but Miremont's inability to speak obliged him to continue. "The fact is, Vera is concerned… Several months ago, while I was in the Rhineland, she noticed Maxim was troubled by something. And eventually, in that way women have, she managed to worm it out of him. She wonders—she worries there has been some sort of misunderstanding."

Several months ago. When Max had first voiced his anxiety about Juliette? The boy had talked to Zhukovsky's sister because he, Miremont, would not listen. Dear God, if he had only heard Max out, if he had not been such a blind fool…

Then he recollected himself. There was no point in 'might-have-beens', no sense in the questions that pounded his skull—when was the Egypt letter dated, how long was 'a couple of days', if he took the first train could he catch the boy before he left? He was done with all that. He should bless Max for rescuing him from further temptation. Yes, it was agony now, but he would be grateful in the long run.

"If there has been any misunderstanding," he said, "it has not been Max's fault. Please reassure your sister and thank her for her concern."

Zhukovsky nodded. "If he writes again, should I…?"

Miremont shook his head.

He must take pride in this renunciation, he told himself after

Zhukovsky had gone: it was, at last, a constructive step forward. All the same, when Philippe came to say that Thomas had been delivered to the servants' door by a waiter from a tavern in the Rue Monge, drunk as a fish and with his forehead bleeding but otherwise unharmed, while Miremont was naturally relieved, his gloom was not lightened.

Thomas' only sign of repentance after these delinquencies of his was an unusual attentiveness. Indeed, this morning, perhaps because of the length of his absence, he was exceptionally solicitous, shaving Miremont without a single nick despite his shaking hand, patting on cologne with exaggerated gentleness and removing the napkin from his master's shoulders as if unveiling porcelain. Held captive in the chair, obliged to look up into that craggy face with its bandaged forehead, Miremont reviewed his shaming speculations about the poor fellow and dismissed them as nonsense.

Doubtless preoccupied by other tasks—he had just now hurried off with three pairs of trousers for pressing—Thomas had left Miremont's stud box lying open on the dressing table. Miremont had not once looked into the box since he had told his valet to throw away the stone—he had not been able to bear it—but it could only be salutary to overcome this weakness. Yet the siren call of absinthe must have driven his instruction from Thomas' mind, for, to Miremont's astonishment, the small red pebble was still there. He closed the lid hastily. Thomas must be reproved when he returned; indeed, here came his footsteps.

However it was not Miremont's valet who stood in the bedroom doorway but a less-than-welcome figure in a point-device morning coat, carrying a small pigskin bag.

"Doctor Chevalier?"

The dapper little man seemed not a whit disconcerted by Miremont's tone. The impertinence of barging into Miremont's apartments unannounced and at this early hour had turned not one hair of his distinguished silver poll, if his ingratiating but unapologetic smile were to be gone by. "I did knock, monsieur. But your man was not there."

"Has my wife been taken ill again?"

"Oh dear me, no. Madame de Miremont is in excellent health."

"Then, may I ask…?"

"I have come to see you, monsieur. I am told you are under the weather. And indeed, I can see at a glance you are not eating well and sleeping badly. Perhaps if I might take your pulse—"

Miremont recoiled from Chevalier's outstretched hand. "May I remind you that you attend my wife. My physician is Doctor Gérard."

"Ah yes, the good Gérard. An admirable fellow with all his charitable work. But not, I think, well up in the latest scientific research. Is he conversant, for example, with the great strides made in neurology by my eminent colleague, Professor Charcot?"

"I neither know, nor care. Now please, if you would be so good…"

But Chevalier was unmoved by Miremont's ill temper. On the contrary, he tapped his tongue gently against his too-perfect teeth. "My dear monsieur, no one knows better than I that this is a matter of extreme delicacy. But we shall get nowhere unless we are frank. Madame de Miremont has confessed to me in tears that you suffer from an affliction that has blighted your marriage—"

"She has no right!"

"—a certain deviation from the libidinal norm that laymen call paederasty but we physicians nowadays term 'inversion'."

"That is none of your damned business!"

"But indeed, monsieur, it is. As a doctor, it is my business to cure disease."

Miremont gaped at him. "Cure?"

"Thanks to the magnificent work of Professor Charcot at the Salpêtrière, it is now possible to redirect your degenerate impulses and return you to normal healthy manhood."

Miremont continued to gape. If there were a cure—if he need no longer endure this misery…

"What afflicts you, my dear monsieur, is—forgive the use of another scientific term—a fetishistic attachment. Professor Charcot commends the traditional prophylactic—when boys reach a certain age, fathers should take them to a house of pleasure to ensure their instincts attach themselves healthily. It may be that your esteemed father neglected this precaution. But it is not too late. Charcot's treatment has successfully cured grown men."

What choice did Miremont have? He could not continue living as he lived now. He sat on the ottoman at the end of the bed as directed and, although Chevalier's hands smelt sickeningly of rose water, submitted to having his pulse taken, his tongue and eyes inspected and his chest listened to, while the doctor alternately nodded and tut-tutted to himself.

Chevalier sighed as he removed the stethoscope from his ears. "It is as I suspected—degeneracy takes its toll on the nervous system. But you need not fear. Comply with a strict regimen of mental and physical hygiene and you will soon see improvements."

"How soon?"

"No time to start like the present. I have already been in touch with the clinic at Passy and they can admit you this afternoon."

Passy? Miremont recalled the poet Gérard de Nerval had been confined to Passy during his spells of insanity. And the Salpêtrière, where Charcot worked, was also an asylum.

"You think I'm mad?"

"My dear monsieur, 'mad' is not a medical term. We prefer 'neurasthenic'. Your nervous system is deranged and you have a libidinal weakness. But, as I say, with the right course of treatment and complete abstinence from vicious excesses…"

But Miremont had ceased to listen. He had been roused from his torpor. He saw how useful Aline would find it to have him put away in an asylum. Yet he saw something else too, with still greater clarity: he did not want this cure. He did not wish to be cured of Max. And even if Max were lost to him it would make no difference—he did not wish to be cured of what was a fundamental part of his being and had brought him his life's greatest joy. If he suffered from any affliction, it was the denial of this truth, it was his readiness to accept the shame heaped upon him. And as for acting honourably—what honour was there in abjectly conforming to society's notion of the normal, when for him it would always be a degrading lie?

Dr Chevalier was still pontificating about bromide and cold showers, but he tailed off in alarm as his patient, whom he had always considered a rather ineffectual man, rose from the ottoman and advanced upon him menacingly.

"My wife put you up to this."

"Monsieur, Madame de Miremont is only concerned for your health and happiness—"

"You are a charlatan, monsieur, an obnoxious little quack. Get out! Now! Or I'll ram your precious stethoscope down your conniving gullet!"

If you believed the new Simon's version of what followed, madame had foamed at the mouth and torn out hanks of her hair. Mlle Drouet maintained monsieur had laid hands on his wife in the most violent manner. And even Mlle Bonnard, a meek soul, who (albeit from behind the closed door of her mistress's bedroom) had actually witnessed the scene, gave a highly coloured account of how madame had suffered one of her turns but monsieur, nonetheless, had remained like steel, laying down the law about the terms of their separation and threatening to withhold her allowance should she refuse to observe them.

Certain facts, however, were beyond question: monsieur had instructed M. Boussec to close up the house for the summer; both ladies' maids were packing their mistresses for Miremont-Sainte-Fleur; M. Rossignol had been given his cards; M. Thomas, heaven preserve us, had smiled; and he and monsieur were already en route to catch the next train for Auxerre.

CHAPTER FIFTY-THREE

The mob had broken into the Calverts' garden to find lanterns ablaze on the terrace and four figures waiting: Palmyre Calvert, who was ready, if it came to it, to offer himself up in his father's stead; the policeman, Malo Thomas; M. Saint-Séverin wearing his mayoral sash; and a thin, balding, nervous-looking stranger in a hand-me-down black suit.

After M. Crépin had reiterated the will of the people, M. Saint-Séverin replied that it was only fair to hear all the evidence first, particularly as new facts had come to light. But, although the schoolmaster grudgingly consented, the crowd was restive. As Malo Thomas reported afterwards, they were crammed in, shoulder to shoulder, and he did not like the whites of their eyes. He was heckled as he rehearsed the doctor's report and Médéric Calvert's alibi—they had heard it all before, and would have shouted him down, had he not bawled above the din: "Monsieur Calvert paid somebody to light the fire? Then it must have been one of you. Who was it?" This silenced them for a moment. Feet shuffled. Sidelong glances of suspicion flashed here and there. But then someone laughed, and the commotion recommenced.

Shouting that he had a new witness, Malo Thomas pushed the stranger forward. While he had not been recognised in his drably respectable attire, the men who had been drinking in the tabac on the last night of Plibou's life knew him the moment he opened his mouth, even though his voice quavered and he struggled to make himself heard. They could attest that Plibou had attacked the tramp with the la-di-da Île-de-France accent inside the tabac, and then again when he had left. So when the tramp swore that Plibou had not only cursed him but had vowed to wreak revenge on Beauvallon with a glorious conflagration, goading him to doss in the Great Barn that night so he could roast in the fires of hell, it did not seem improbable. There were sceptical voices—it was too convenient, a put-up job—but there were other murmurings too: the Plibou the tramp evoked was not the people's martyr, the Plibou of rhetoric, but that other Plibou the village knew too well, the ragged yellow-eyed drunk who taught his children to steal, who had not done a day's work since anyone could remember, who had burned down the Cagots' cottage in a dispute over a cheese.

Malo Thomas began to like the eyes of the crowd a little better. All the same, the jeering started again when it was M. Saint-Séverin's turn to speak. But the hullabaloo subsided once the mayor had made it clear he brought a message from M. le marquis, and, when M. Crépin objected, he was the one shouted down.

M. de Miremont's letter, transcribed for convenience in his secretary's more readily legible hand, was not long; nor did it contribute a great deal that was new. In fact, it said much of what M. Crépin had said (although in shorter words with fewer abstractions), emphasising the people of Beauvallon's proud ties to the land, generation through generation, and the bond this gave them, a sacred duty to act together in times of trouble. However, monsieur felt certain they would wish to honour their precious tradition of unity with their customary courage, good sense and respect for the law: if there were grievances, he promised to hear them in person and endeavour to set matters right.

The crowd listened in silence, and Malo Thomas observed that quite a few were nodding—M. de Miremont might live in the château, but his family, too, had been here for generations, he shared their traditions; furthermore, he was a plain man who spoke as he found, as folk did in Beauvallon—whereas the schoolmaster was a town-dweller from Rouen who had lived in the commune a mere nine years.

Nevertheless, despite the nods, despite the uncertainty Malo Thomas now noted in many faces, he felt, as he told Max later, that the affair still teetered on a knife-edge—one jeer, one mocking laugh, and Palmyre could yet be called upon to sacrifice himself. And, of course, M. Crépin, appalled by his followers' slavish credulity, did not hesitate to rally them. But he had scarcely opened his mouth when, from somewhere within the house, a wailing arose and the curé, who had been giving Mme Calvert the last rites, appeared on the terrace to announce that her soul was with the angels. Had they no respect? They should all be ashamed of themselves. Some made the sign of the cross, others bowed their heads. Silently, in ones and twos, then in a body, they turned and went away.

Max had considered it politic to keep well out of sight. In fact, his first thought, since Durand was as usual nowhere to be found, had been to protect Madame Rose and her parents: although two gendarmes from Soures were stationed behind the Calverts' French windows to back up Malo Thomas, if they failed to prevent a riot and the disorder spread, both the Durands' cottage and the château would be threatened. However, when Max arrived at the cottage, Boniface Thomas and one of his brothers were already standing guard. Since the prefect had promised Malo Thomas a detachment of troops from the barracks at Dijon to guard the château, Max returned there to meet it. Taking a revolver from the gun room, he had sat on the steps, listening to the distant shouts of the crowd. The soldiers had never materialised; but nor, much to his relief, had the riot.

Thereafter, once word had come to confirm that, apart from the sad death of Mme Calvert, all was well, Max's night had been filled with activity. When he could be certain the village was finally abed and there was no one to observe him, he saddled Delphine and rode to the police house, where Malo Thomas gave him an account of events and he collected Polly, whom he conveyed back to Soures the way he had brought him, on horseback, riding double. At the door of Polly's lodgings, as they parted, it was agreed Polly owed Max no further amends.

Dawn had broken by the time Max rode back to Beauvallon. The last day of June. He had vowed to be gone by the end of the month, but there were certain things he must do before he could take his departure. Amongst them was a report for Armand of yesterday's happenings and the situation that had led up to them. As well as laying out the facts, he had decided to offer some recommendations: he would not mention giving the land to the people, for, while he still believed in the principle, he had come to see that the practicalities might be more complicated; but there were other recommendations, which, since they had not been arrived at in accordance with Armand's exacting moral standards—they excused a fraud and concealed a murder—would not be as easily dashed off as those impassioned lines about the traditions of Beauvallon. Not only that; he would need some sleep first. He settled with himself that he would pack and say his goodbyes tonight. Then he would leave for Auxerre at first light tomorrow.

In the kitchen, to his surprise, he found Madame Rose already at work kneading pastry. He was not only surprised but amused. For she worked on, vigorously pummelling the dough, seemingly oblivious of the thumps and shouts emanating from somewhere down the passage.

Last night, returning from her cottage to the château, Max had reflected on Durand's disappearances. He was prompted to recall the night of the fire: despite the insulting manner in which the little weasel had roused him from his bed, he had not seen Durand amongst the fire-fighters. Curious how, when there was mischief to be made, the wretch was in the thick of it, but any hint of danger and he melted away.

Later, as Max was prowling the house before going outside to await the troops, he had heard muffled footsteps in the vicinity of the kitchen, then a click, as if of a door latch. The key to the wine cellar was missing from its hook and when he rattled the door it appeared to be locked from the other side—not only that, but he detected scuffling within.

"A rat," he said loudly to an imaginary soldier. "Oh well, at least we'll be rid of them if the house burns down."

Aside from the lock, the door was furnished with two heavy, ancient bolts, top and bottom, stiff with disuse; with effort, Max had shot one home, then the other. After which, despite outraged yells from the cellar, he had gone on his way.

In fact he had quite forgotten the incident until hearing the racket this morning. Madame Rose could not but have heard it too and recognised the cries. All the same, as they discussed last night's happenings and she busied herself making him coffee, she showed no recognition of anything untoward. Max grinned to himself. If she chose to ignore the rat's plight, who was he not to do likewise?

After conveying his condolences to the Calvert family and taking leave of Palmyre, he had one more task to perform before he could finally snatch some sleep.

The Hobgoblin was back at work. He found her in the Grand Salon, flicking an erratic feather duster over the mantelpiece with her left hand, while her useless right arm remained dangling at her side. She looked round but did not greet him.

She was still wearing the white blouse and shapeless black skirt, he noted—how had she explained the loss of her maid's dress? Destroyed in the wash? From what he could see of her bandage, she needed a doctor, but, in the unlikelihood that the Plibous could afford such a thing, that too would require awkward explanations. Altogether, from her colourless face to the way she held her body, as though fighting pain, she was the picture of misery, her spirit not merely crushed, but extinguished.

Yet, as he smiled and came towards her, something did flash in those dull eyes of hers. She was afraid of him.

"Mademoiselle, I have only come to say goodbye. I'm leaving tomorrow."

Was she reassured? She said nothing, only shrugged.

He sought for a snippet to cheer her. "You know old Piggy Guts has been arrested? He's under lock and key at the police house."

She did not smile. "Your friend—he's a fucking liar. Letting that crooked Calvert get away—"

"Shush! Enough of that. There's no need for it any longer. It's now accepted your father's death was an accident."

He waited for some change in her expression, but her face continued bleak.

"Please, mademoiselle—Madeleine—come and sit down."

Although she glanced at the place he indicated on the nearest settee, she remained where she stood, clutching the feather duster to her breast like a weapon.

"Your father's death was an accident, for which he had only himself to blame. Even if he didn't trip over the pitchfork—even if someone—someone who was frightened, who couldn't bear what he did any longer—even if that person picked up the pitchfork to ward him off and somehow he fell on it, that would be self-defence. Not a deliberate act. Just as much an accident, in its way, as if he really had tripped over it."

She did not move.

"I think he had the kerosene up at the Old Manoir because he planned to burn down this house."

After a moment, faintly, she nodded.

"If there was any crime, it was the fire. But I can understand her terror, the person with the pitchfork. She thought—and who's to say she's not right?—that she would never be believed."

Two tears spilled from her lower lids.

"In *Donkey-Skin* the princess is saved from marrying her father. But it is a fairy tale."

The tears trickled slowly down her stony cheeks. Pity urged him to go over, ease the duster from her grasp and lead her gently by her undamaged hand to the sofa. But the bond he felt with her warned she would not care for pity.

"Should you like to go to Paris?"

Did the stone crack for an instant? It was impossible to tell.

"Of course, it will be up to Monsieur de Miremont. But there's a place he knows where they'll take care of you when your time comes and help you get an education. They'll have proper teachers—not idiots like me—and, with your brains, *tout Paris* could be acclaiming your Phèdre one day."

He waited for her to smile. But after a minute or two, realising waiting was futile, he turned to the door. Then he remembered something. "Oh, by the way, please keep my watch."

"What watch? I ain't got your sodding watch, monsieur!"

He grinned to himself. So the spark was not wholly extinguished.

Although he had been too exhausted to undress or even take off his boots, sleep had proved fugitive. Indeed, it seemed as if he had only just closed his eyes when someone was knocking on his door.

He groaned and whoever it was entered. What time was it? From force of habit, he reached for his watch, forgetting as always that the Hobgoblin had relieved him of it.

"It's half past four, monsieur."

He did not feel like someone who had slept for six hours. And why was Madame Rose deigning to visit his room in person? Squinting up at her, he thought she seemed uncommonly ebullient.

"We've had some wonderful news. Monsieur de Miremont is on his way. The wire came not long after you'd gone to your bed and I didn't want to wake you. We're to expect monsieur this evening."

Max blinked. Confound Armand! Was this the old boy's understanding of 'Come at once'? To turn up when the drama was over and he was no longer needed?

"I thought I'd better come up and tell you myself. You see, I didn't want to do anything without your say-so, but the barouche was needed to meet monsieur at the station."

Max subdued the impulse to drag the sheet over his head. "Forgive me, but…"

"I'm afraid I've had to find Durand."

"Ah." Still, he supposed the little rodent could not stay missing forever. "Did you have any trouble?"

"Cousin Boniface helped with the bolts."

"No. I mean, was he… Was your husband…?"

"A bit hoarse. But meek as a lamb. And I just wanted to say—" her face broke into an expression that was not the Smile, but something altogether more roguish and spontaneous "—I wanted to say, you're a darling, Monsieur Fabien. I don't know what we'd do without you."

"Madame—"

"Not that we'll have to now, will we? Not with monsieur coming. No need for you to be going back to Paris tomorrow."

The moment she had left, he let out a soundless howl of frustration. Damn and blast the old boy. Late was by no means better than never.

Well, he would go anyway, without explanations. He would go now. Even if Armand's train was on time, the old boy would not be here before seven: that gave him two and a half hours. He would barely need to hurry. It would take mere minutes to cram the few belongings he required into his saddlebags. And, since Madame Rose was sending Pélagie up with 'something on a tray' and hot water, he wouldn't go on his way hungry and without a wash and a change of linen. While, as for his report—since he had always intended to post it to Armand, could he not just as easily write it in Auxerre?

Of course, it would be hard on Delphine. If he were leaving tomorrow morning, one of the grooms, as arranged, would drive him to Auxerre in the dog cart, saving Delphine a sojourn in livery stables and a journey home with an unfamiliar rider. But now she must make the best of it. They would have a long and tiresome ride too, for he would need to take a roundabout route across country unless he fancied encountering Armand and the barouche on the road. Still, it could not be helped. He would get out of bed and set to.

But, as he stumbled around, tripping over the coverlet and barking his shin on the bedside chair, exhaustion got the better of him. Wasn't it madness to be rushing about, simply to avoid the old boy? Weren't they, after all their time together, due some sort of farewell, however frigid and formal? Nothing could stop him leaving. What difference would it make if he went first thing tomorrow?

CHAPTER FIFTY-FOUR

On the train, Miremont had made every effort to prepare himself for finding Max gone, yet his disappointment was still acute when he was not on the platform to meet him. Perhaps he might learn his whereabouts from Durand. But the fellow, usually so free with unwanted gossip, was curiously subdued today, watching Thomas load the luggage into the barouche in surly silence. Only when Miremont was climbing into the carriage did he dare ask outright if M. Fabien would be up at the house: the reply—"Oh, he's there all right"—although oddly savage, filled him with unbounded relief.

He knew Max would be angry, not without justification; yet, when he thought of their meeting—and he did little else during the seemingly interminable drive—he could not suppress the dream that, on irresistible impulse, they would fall into each other's arms. This image was given fresh colour when at last, as the carriage emerged from the avenue, his beloved château rose up before him: while it was true that, on second glance, there was something unfamiliar, a puzzling disjunction in the view of the pantiled outbuildings beyond, the house itself—its stately portico, its stone a mellow ochre in the evening sun—reassuringly suggested peace and perpetuity. So it was a wrench to discover that, while Rosalie and the two maids were on the front steps to greet him, there was no sign of Max.

Instead, Miremont must submit to Rose's kindly fussing and to a hair-raising, if jumbled, story, muddled still further by Josephine's interpolations, of fire and narrowly averted mob rule. He was shocked to discover he had been hoped for yesterday to quell the disturbance, for it was the first he had heard of any telegram (he knew too well whom he must blame for that). However, he was delighted to hear Rosalie singing Max's praises. But where was Max himself? Apparently in his room, writing. Rose offered to send Pélagie to fetch him, but Miremont said he would go in person.

Yet in their set of rooms there was only Thomas, waiting to help him out of his travelling clothes. Nor was it just that there was no one in the bedroom connected to his own; he could see at a glance it had not been occupied, that the bed, with its coverlet flat as a pall, had never been made up. Sending Thomas away to enjoy a proper reunion with his family, Miremont went along the landing, opening the door to every suite, but found no trace of the boy. Perhaps Rosalie was mistaken.

If Max were writing, he would surely be in the library. But when Miremont retraced his steps downstairs and hurried along the enfilade, the library, like every other room he had passed through, was empty.

"Monsieur."

At the familiar voice, his heart leapt. As he span round, joyful words were on his lips. But the figure in the doorway made him falter.

From a distance he doubted he would have recognised this tall young man. A moustache and a short brown beard blurred the shape of his mouth and jaw; his cheeks—what was visible of them—were tanned, and the unkempt hair that fell across his forehead was also streaked by the sun; disdaining formality, he wore a riding jacket and gaiters, the jacket, once an exemplar of fine tailoring, now rumpled as an old blanket and torn on the left sleeve. Yet, despite his wild appearance, which might, in happier times, have stirred in Miremont a deplorable excitement, his manner was sobering: he seemed older, no longer boyish, contained, even formidable.

There was no question of an embrace. Max, too, seemed to make a tally of him as if he were a stranger, and, while his clear blue gaze was intensified by the beard, it was not warm.

"My dear boy—"

"I fear your journey is wasted, monsieur. The trouble could not wait for you to tear yourself away."

Miremont winced. "As I've told Rosalie, I never received your wire. Circumstances... Aline..." God, he was conscious of how weak this sounded. "I'm afraid any letters you have sent in the last few weeks may have suffered the same fate."

"I have not written to you. Why would I?"

"Max—"

"Anyway, I have set down the details of the disturbance." He made a small gesture with the foolscap sheets he was holding. "I hope my account is clear enough, but in case you have questions, I'd be grateful if you'd read it tonight. I'm leaving at first light tomorrow."

Miremont could not restrain himself. "But, dear boy, you can't go—not now."

Careful to maintain the distance between them, Max laid the papers on the library table. "I believe I'm free to go when I choose."

"But not... Not to Egypt."

"How the—? Oh, I see. Damn Mitya!"

"Chausson-Laurier and Selincourt won't be in the Valley of the Kings."

"I wasn't intending to meet them."

"The digging season ended last month. It's forty degrees in Luxor in high summer. Everybody retreats to Alexandria, where it's cooler."

This certainly pulled Max up. But then his chin tilted defiantly. "Very well. I shall go to Alexandria."

"Please, Max—I meant…" How had Miremont, fool that he was, thought to win the boy over by making him look stupid? "There is so much I… Surely you read my letters?"

"Yes. Of course."

"Then you will know that, while I deserve your anger—"

"I am not angry."

In Miremont's imaginings, even if Max did not forgive him instantly, he listened to his explanations: he had not counted on this icy resistance. "Please, dear boy, let us talk."

"I shall be happy to talk to you about my report. Otherwise, what needs to be said? Now—" Max turned to the doorway "—I know Madame Rose is waiting to serve dinner."

"Then perhaps over dinner we might—"

"I shall be eating in my room. If you have any response to what I have written, please send for me after you have dined."

Miremont decided to take his coffee and brandy beside the lake. His late arrival had precluded his usual stroll along its borders; besides, he hoped that, as the two of them sat together in the colonnade of the Temple of Dionysus, Max could not but recall, as he, Miremont, did, the glorious nights they had spent there.

Yet, in his impatience for Max to appear, he hardly noticed the sunset gilding the sky behind the Gothic Tower or the other evanescent beauties of twilight. He had done scant justice to Rosalie's excellent dinner and was fortified neither by the coffee nor the brandy. Nor was Max's manner encouraging when he arrived at last: although he took the seat drawn up for him at the coaching table and accepted a cigarette, he remained coldly formal. It was clear he had not relented: they must talk about his report or there would be no talk at all.

Miremont had struggled to summon the concentration to read the document. However, when the words had ceased to blur, he had found aspects of it intriguing. He had never thought Max devoid of compassion, merely that, as he was young, he tended, as youth did, to see matters in black and white; yet the report's conclusions were remarkably humane. Miremont was himself shocked and dismayed by Calvert's dishonesty; the boy, having been proved right, would surely have demanded the full might of the law. Yet here he was, advising the steward be retired due to ill health.

"Perhaps you think the suggestion impertinent, monsieur? It is, after all, none of my business."

"I'm merely surprised."

"Believe me, I'd love to see Calvert in gaol. But if you disgrace the father, you disgrace the whole family, including the son. Palmyre would never have the authority to take over the stewardship. Which would be a shame since you've paid to educate him for the job, and you set such store by tradition—aren't you forever telling me Calverts have been stewards here since your great-uncle's time?"

"Still, won't the boy find it difficult?"

"No doubt at first. But if you send the old man off to live with his mistress in Soures—out of sight, out of mind—I'm pretty sure Palmyre will establish himself. With your support, of course. But he's honest and he's mortified by his father's behaviour—I think he'll make you a worthy steward."

This testimonial, to Miremont's shame, provoked in him the old suspicion. "You seem on very good terms with him."

Max smiled. "As a matter of fact, Palmyre can be a bit of a clod. But he has some interesting ideas. I think you'll find him more open to your innovations than his father."

Miremont cherished the smile—it was the first time the boy had smiled since his arrival and, even though it meant Max had found him out, he could not but rejoice in it. Indeed, as they discussed the report, the boy's enthusiasm seemed to triumph over his reserve. When they came to the speech Miremont was supposed to have sent to M. Saint-Séverin to read, he could not restrain a grin.

"I trust you will forgive my presumption. But I felt it was what you might have said."

In fact, the speech had been another aspect of the document to surprise Miremont. Knowing as he did the frequent squabbles, from family feuds to boundary disputes, that were prone to vex the inhabitants of Beauvallon, he was astonished that Max took such a romantic view of them, wrote so eloquently of their 'heroic unity'. However, he was bound to admit that, yes, given the circumstances, this was what he might have said.

"I am not so sure, though, dear boy, about all these wrongs I have promised to redress."

Max laughed. "I think you'll find they all vanish once Beauvallon gets a new schoolmaster."

The final matter was the question of the Plibou girl. Again Miremont was taken aback, this time by the boy's vehement response to his doubtful look.

"It's not her fault she was born a Plibou. Nor is she to blame for her present condition."

Miremont raised his eyebrows.

"Don't ask me to say more. But she is another of your protégées, after all."

Miremont dimly remembered suggesting Rosalie try the girl out in the kitchen. He sighed. "Well, if you really think she can benefit from the Trust, I suppose I had better see her."

"And don't be put off if her manner is—shall I say, unpolished. She's got a good, quick mind. I've told her the charity will give her an education, so you'll have to set up that school you promised."

Miremont could not recall making any such promise; then he remembered Madame Tonton's and saw the boy was teasing him. He was far too delighted they were back on familiar terms to offer any objection.

It had long since grown dark and moths fluttered around the lantern. Beyond the colonnade, borders blurred between land and water, trees fell away into shadow, the world receded. It was, Miremont thought, the perfect setting for him to say, at last, all he was bursting to say.

"My darling Max, you have done well—extraordinarily well."

But the boy was tidying the papers into a sheaf, and when he looked up his eyes were once again cold. "I trust it will be of help to your new secretary."

Miremont stared at him.

"Monsieur Peewit, Lapwing, whatever his name is."

Miremont had studiously avoided mentioning Rossignol in his letters, for fear of precisely this misunderstanding. He could not begin to guess how Max, far away in the country, could have learned of the fellow's existence.

"My dear boy—Monsieur Rossignol is not, has never been my secretary. He is—or was—Aline's."

Max raised his eyebrows in disbelief.

"Max, you cannot think… You did not read my letters?"

No, of course the boy had not read them. Believing himself replaced, he had doubtless torn them up in anger. Yet all the same… Miremont felt sudden relief. It was easy to comprehend Max's attitude now: there had been a simple misunderstanding, simply remedied.

But the boy had not unbent. "Monsieur, knowing you as I do, I should be foolish to believe that, given a choice between me and your daughter, you would not feel bound to choose your daughter."

The tone in which he said this, carefully eschewing any note of animosity, pierced Miremont's heart. "Oh, my dear boy… I… I no longer have a daughter."

It was Max's turn to stare.

"I no longer have a family. They know."

"You told them?"

"I wish I could lay claim to such courage. They found out. Juliette found me out." It was still painful for Miremont to pronounce these last words. "I never believed you guilty, I hoped… I delayed… I thought, once she was more herself, the thing would blow over, or she'd admit she was—mistaken. But I pressed her too hard and gave myself away."

Miremont waited for Max to say something, but the boy was silent.

"As it turned out… Well, my family could not live with me on my terms, and I could not live according to theirs. So this morning I finally found the strength to tell them I loved you with all my heart—that I wanted to live with you openly, without shame, and no matter what they said, I would not change. They have left for Sainte-Fleur and I came here."

Again, Miremont waited for Max to speak. In the lamplight, with his eyes averted and his mouth veiled by the moustache, the boy's face was troublingly hard to read. Then, all at once, he said softly: "I don't want this."

Miremont's throat contracted. "My darling Max—I know I have been a coward, I know I have made your life impossible for the last six months, and even before that, with my endless conditions. But if you can find it in you to forgive—"

"You should not make this sacrifice for me."

"But I—"

"It isn't worth it."

"Oh, my dear boy—"

"It's pointless. I don't want it. But even if I did, Armand, would I wish to be responsible for bringing you a lifetime of guilt?"

Miremont began to feel encouraged again. "Yes, of course I feel guilty. But they will all manage quite well without me. Aline and I have long been separated. Juliette will doubtless marry Niversac. And Clotilde—Clotilde may even come round in the end. Naturally, if there had been any other way… But there was not. And now, whatever else I may feel, it is as nothing to my overwhelming relief. I need not lie any longer, most of all to myself. At last I know who I am."

"You?" The boy pushed his chair back with such violence that the lantern flickered and Miremont's brandy glass fell from the table and smashed. "You, Armand de Miremont, with your centuries of illustrious ancestors and your traditions and your certainties, certainties you never give a thought to because they run in your blood? You've always known who you are. Consider yourself damned well lucky! I wish to God I did!"

Miremont was momentarily stunned. But, as he sat speechless, the boy, still quivering with inexplicable rage, was rising to his feet.

"That's why all this is pointless, why I must go. I need to find something, somewhere—there must be something in this world to excuse my existence—God only knows what."

"But—my dearest Max—please…" Miremont, rising too, stretched out an arm as if to restrain him, although the boy had stepped back, beyond his reach. He was hurt and perplexed. All he understood was that they must be at cross-purposes: Max had never been troubled by his inclinations, this excoriating self-contempt had some other cause. From his words, it was most likely the difference in their rank—to Miremont meaningless, but of course the boy had borne the brunt of his family's snobbery.

"Please, my dear. You know I have always thought of us as equals. And that's how I wish us to live from now on. No pretence that you are my librarian or my secretary or anything other than my lover and my friend."

"Damn you, Armand! You don't understand. And it is better that you don't."

"But, dear boy—how can I? To say you need to justify your existence—"

"And I'll do that by letting you keep me?"

The boy's face was only partly in the light, but Miremont heard the bitterness in his voice, saw the whiteness of his knuckles as he gripped the back of the chair.

"Oh for pity's sake, Max! This is an old argument. How many times must I tell you that you give me more than I could possibly—"

"It is not about money."

"Then what? What in heaven's name is it about?"

"I need some direction—some purpose, so that I can look myself in the eye."

"And may I not help you find that?"

"Jesus, Armand!" The boy made a despairing gesture. "It is not worth it—I am certainly not worth it. Please accept that, even if you can't understand it."

But Miremont thought he understood, at last, only too well. "I see. You're happy for me to help others—Palmyre Calvert, the Plibou girl— but I can't help you, the person who matters most to me in the world. Damn you, Max! Damn you to hell! Damn you and your heartless pride!"

The boy released his grip on the chair and took a further step backwards. "We seem to have finished discussing my report. So forgive me, but I must pack."

Miremont walked with determination along the landing but when he reached the door at its end—the servant's door it had not occurred to him to open during his earlier search—he paused to gather his courage.

As he had sat alone by the lake, his anger had gradually turned to sorrow. Was he to begrudge Max his pride? It was easy for him, Miremont, to say he did not care about the boy's lowly origins, but it could not be so easy for the boy himself. After all, as Miremont knew better than anyone, while Max strove to appear impervious, the mark on his forehead was not his only scar: Miremont had held him during his nightmares; he remembered that, when they had first met, the boy had been so sensitive to the imputation customarily levelled against orphans that he had fabricated a noble father; he understood there were tender places he, Miremont, must not probe, that even Max's account of his schooldays at the monastery went no further than feigned insouciance would permit. This fragility touched him and, although it was often a source of obstinacy, it could only deepen his love for the boy.

Yet what had he done now, through his cowardice and dithering? He had left Max in a state of cruel uncertainty, subjected him to weeks of humiliation, so that the Rossignol rumour must have seemed the final insult. No wonder the boy's pride had hardened to rock.

Or was it just pride? Rosalie had mentioned that he had been ill. When prompted, she had also said he never took his meals in the dining room and, while he could have moved into his usual bedroom once the roof had been repaired, he had stayed in the servant's room from choice. Taken with his utterances, the beard and his neglect of his appearance, this suggested some sort of penance—except that Max scorned religion. Perhaps, although he concealed it, he had not shaken off his illness. Worry was added to Miremont's misery.

Max was not asleep: from the lake Miremont had seen a lamp still burning in the end window and there was light, now, beneath the door. Miremont's knock was answered after a moment or two.

"I—I thought… as you are leaving so early tomorrow… for fear I miss you—my dear boy, I could not bear us to part in anger without so much as a goodbye."

Max nodded, then stood aside for him to enter.

Miremont's first impression was of air dense with the boy's sweat and the fumes of coarse tobacco. He looked around him with dismay: perhaps it was the effect of the stained walls, bare boards, and shoddy furniture jostling for space, but squalor seemed to prevail, with papers strewn everywhere, clothes spilling out of the open wardrobe, the shabby riding jacket and gaiters tossed casually onto the floor. Although some of this might be accounted for by the exigencies of packing, such as the small pile of belongings on the bed, overall what met Miremont's eye was so contrary to Max's usual spartan habits that his anxiety increased.

Max himself was barefoot and in shirtsleeves, without a collar. He waved Miremont to the only armchair, whose upholstery vied with the wallpaper for insalubrious blotches. At least he no longer seemed angry. Seated cross-legged on the bed with his cuffs dangling loose and his throat bared, he looked young once more, very young, Miremont thought, despite the beard and the ragged moustache that marred the curve of his upper lip.

"My dear—" Miremont cleared his throat "—I apologise for shouting at you. I did not mean—I hope you know…"

"Yes. I'm sorry too."

They sat for a moment looking at each other as if neither knew how to go on. In truth, Miremont was assailed by a storm of words, but he dared not utter them for fear of breaking down. And Max? His face was opaque—the expression Miremont thought of as his footman's face.

To ease the awkwardness, Miremont rose to proffer his cigarette case. It was as he returned to his chair that he noticed the room's most disturbing feature: the glass above the washstand had been covered with a cloth.

"Max, please tell me—apart from my stupidities, is there anything else the matter?"

"No. Of course not."

"You are sure?"

The boy exhaled smoke. "Nothing whatsoever."

"Well then… I just wanted to say…" Yet he would never be able to say what he wanted. It was not merely that he feared weeping; he shrank from hearing 'fond' where he had once heard 'love'.

"My dear, I accept that you are leaving and I shall not try to dissuade you. But may I suggest—for the sake of your enterprise—and selfishly, for my peace of mind—would you consider delaying until September? If you arrive in Egypt when the excavation season begins, you won't be left at a loose end, there'll be archaeologists to take you on. You need not stay here with me. If you would rather go to Paris—the house is closed but Boussec and Madame Mercier will make you comfortable."

But Max shook his head. "That's generous of you, Armand—"

"Please, at least think it over."

"It's kind, but I would rather not change my plans."

They lapsed into silence again.

"Ah well." Miremont rose to extinguish his cigarette. "You have an early start. And you have given me plenty of tasks for tomorrow…"

Max rose too. "Armand, I…" But, although there was something in his voice that suddenly quickened Miremont's hopes, he let whatever it was die away.

With the greatest effort, Miremont composed himself. "Darling boy, for the sake of all we have been to each other, may we at least embrace as friends?"

He half-expected Max to protest, but with a shrug the boy discarded his cigarette, then moved towards him. They laid their arms awkwardly around each other's shoulders—they might, Miremont thought, have been dignitaries at a civic function. First the left cheek, then the right: the unfamiliar rasp of bristles, Max's familiar smell. Yet afterwards they did not separate as formality required; from force of habit perhaps, they continued to hold each other, indeed more tightly, and Miremont, face buried in the crook of the boy's bare neck, feeling the pulse at his throat, tasting his skin, pressed him closer and thought—no, he was sure of it—Max's body answered his. In another moment they would draw back a little and their mouths would meet.

But Max abruptly pulled away. "I can't," he said. "Forgive me, but I can't."

CHAPTER FIFTY-FIVE

After Armand had gone, Max rolled another cigarette and sat back on the bed to reflect. It grieved him to hurt the old fellow: he looked thinner, poor old boy, worn, exhausted, his lines and furrows mournful, his forelock showing the first threads of grey. Max pictured him making his confession to Aline and La Rosebud and wished he had seen their faces. But, malice apart, he was bound to concede it had been an act of valour well-nigh unthinkable given Armand's propensity for moral contortions: yes, he had been brave, poor old fellow, and what reward had he got for it?

If only he, Max, had been better able to explain himself. Oh, not about Sigismund. He shuddered to recall how, when the whole thing had been a game and he its master, he had once tried to draw in Armand by mentioning Waldavia—thank God, the old fellow had disbelieved him. But, although the truth must stay deep in the well with Westenholz's book, he might at least have made Armand understand why he must go. Admittedly, at this instant, he could not perfectly expound his reasoning, even to himself, but for that he blamed the business of Calvert and the barn: he had been so clear, so certain of his path, until he had been forced to train his thoughts elsewhere. Once he was far away from Beauvallon and after a solid night's sleep, clarity would return.

In the meantime he must bestir himself. While the old boy had been at dinner, he had visited the stables to feed Delphine a sugar lump and bid her farewell; he had stood on the Chinese bridge and watched the dragonflies dancing and convinced himself he would not miss Beauvallon; and he had at last settled on a book: true, he had forsworn literature in his new life, yet he could not imagine travelling without anything to read, and the tragedies of Euripides would remind him the gods were fickle.

Now he must deal with the trappings of his old life, fripperies like his silk dressing gown, topper and alpaca coat. He would take nothing that did not fit into his saddlebags and could not be transferred to the knapsack he would purchase on his journey. What remained he would bundle into his valise, so that Madame Rose might dispose of it as she thought fit.

Determinedly, he stubbed out his cigarette: that was the last of his tobacco, but he would buy more in Auxerre. On hands and knees, he gathered up the rough drafts of the report that littered the floorboards and stuffed them into the wastepaper basket. Then he reached beneath the washstand for his valise. As he pulled it out, something clattered to the floor. Something silver, gleaming next to the skirting. He crawled under the washstand to retrieve it.

The Hobgoblin had given him back his watch. Out of conscience or gratitude, she had crept upstairs while he was out at the lake and hidden it where he was bound to find it while he was packing.

And yet…. Had he done her an injustice? Perhaps it was true—she had not stolen it in the first place. He remembered where he had last seen it. She had been playing with it in the glass, posing as a houri, dangling it on her forehead. When he had told her to go, she must have left it on the washstand. And he—furious that the glass was uncovered—had swept the cloth back into place, knocking the watch into the gap next to the wall. Was it possible? Could it have lodged itself soundlessly where his valise met the skirting? Had it been there all this time?

He did not know, he did not care. He was absurdly, childishly happy to get it back. The old boy's watch. The watch he had admired during his nightly visits to Armand at La Boissière because it had seemed, in its lack of conspicuous adornment to shout its quality, so like the old fellow himself. It lay there in his palm, he could weigh it and feel how finely balanced it was, for all its deceptive simplicity. He wound it and immediately it uttered its discreet, reassuring tick. Shit, he had missed it. More than he could say. So much that… Oh, for heaven's sake!

He could not explain the sobs that convulsed him. He knew it was absurd to be crouched there, holding the thing and weeping over it. He knew he should pull himself together and get on with his packing. But all the same, for some minutes, the tears would not stop.

He thought suddenly of the old boy's letters. They still lay piled in the corner, next to the press. Seven in all—or was it six? He reached up to set the watch carefully on the washstand, then, still on hands and knees, crawled over to the pile. Wiping his face on his sleeve, he tore open the top envelope.

At first glance there was nothing on the paper within: no address, no date, no text, no signature. Only when fully unfolded did the sheet reveal an inscription at its centre. Perhaps he should have fetched the lamp from the chest of drawers. But no, even in this dark corner, he could read the Roman numerals.

Although some of the envelopes had not escaped his antics with the wine, the contents of the next five were the same. Just the inscription: XLVIII.

Mellitos oculos tuos, Iuventi,
si quis me sinat usque basiare,
usque ad milia basiem trecenta
nec numquam videar satur futurus,
non si densior aridis aristis
sit nostrae seges osculationis.

If I were given leave continuously to kiss
Your honey-sweet eyes, Juventius,
I should kiss them three hundred thousand times
And never seem to have my fill,
Though my harvest of kisses were more abundant
Than the ears of the ripened corn.

Only the letter at the bottom of the pile, the first, offered the excuses Max had predicted, and these were interwoven with expressions of affection that defied the old boy's usual caution.

Max lay on the floor with his knees beneath his chin. Was he truly unable to love or be loved? Suddenly it was not just his reasoning that was hard to explain, but its premise. Why must he spend the rest of his existence hiding away in the wilderness? Why must he expiate sins that were not his? Suddenly it seemed preposterous, as if he were surrendering his life for a phantasm—a country that was no longer a country, a madman long dead, a network of spies existing only in the neurasthenic fancies of two old men, Leopold and Westenholz, also by now doubtless dead. Yes, the shame of his birth was real, and yes, he would always bear it. But, in letting it rule him, did he not grant Sigismund victory?

Shame was not like leprosy: so long as Armand never knew the truth, he could not be harmed by it. And as for self-respect—wasn't the old boy right? There must be ways to hold your head up that did not demand the sacrifice of all that brought you happiness.

But here he uncurled himself. This was cowardice. No wonder he was crouched on the floor like a child afraid of thunder. Did he think self-respect would come from lounging around in luxury at the old boy's expense? There was nothing wrong with his plan: it was fine, it was pure, a life of discipline and renunciation that would test every sinew of his mental and physical strength. Besides, he wanted to go to Egypt. He was excited by the boundless sand and the barren mountains and the promise of adventure. And anyway, he had said he was going. He had said he was going and he could not back down now. The dog cart would be harnessed for five o'clock and he must be ready for it.

He staggered to his feet. He had no notion of the time, beyond that it must have reached the small hours: the watch, although it had suffered no ill effects from its dusty hiding place, could be of no help until it was correctly set. He went to the window to see if he could judge by the sky. There was still a light in the colonnade of the summer house: the old boy had not retired to bed, but had gone back to the lake. He must be sitting there, staring out into the darkness and smoking—Max thought he saw the brief flare of a match.

He carried the watch to the bed and added it to the pile for packing—not from sentiment, it would be invaluable on his travels. Now he must empty the press; it would be the work of moments to cram its contents into the suitcase. Yet somehow he could not rouse himself to action. If only he had not run out of tobacco.

He went to the window again. The old boy was still there. A memory came to him of their first summer together. He had harboured a morbid terror of spiders since his captivity in the cellar and, one morning in the Temple of Dionysus, in the aftermath of their lovemaking, a particularly noxious specimen had invaded their bedding. He had seized a candlestick to club the creature to death, but Armand had insisted on reprieving it, letting it crawl onto his palm and even admiring its markings. Then he had cupped it in his hands and decanted it carefully into the shrubbery. Max retained the image of the old fellow poised stark naked at the high back window, arms and shoulders craning out of the frame, buttocks raised, balls hanging, thigh and calf muscles straining. It was crazy, ridiculous—all to save a filthy spider. Max had been helpless with laughter. But, perhaps because it was typical of the old boy—quixotic, never standing on his dignity, tender-hearted to a fault—it had also been oddly affecting.

In recollection, it still was. Max smiled. Confound the old fellow! Would it really be cowardice, a flagrant retreat, not to leave this morning? After all, he must grant Armand's advice made sense. He could still go to the Valley of the Kings if he wanted, but later, in September. It was not as if he were making an irrevocable decision.

The simplicity of this rocked him. His lassitude vanished. He took the lamp, went over to the washstand and snatched the napkin from the glass. To hell with it, he thought, as he confronted his reflection. In the morning, when there was light and hot water, he would shave off his patchy, itchy, detestable whiskers. But now, this moment, he would go out to the lake. The old boy should have his three hundred thousand kisses—or as many as rendered both of them beyond counting, not to say speech or thought.

THE SECOND FOOTMAN

Nineteen-year-old Max is the duchesse de Claireville's second footman, but he doesn't intend to endure the indignities of service for long. He has a plan—to find an aristocratic patron to become his unwitting accomplice in an audacious fraud.

The first part of the Miremont trilogy, *The Second Footman* is a tale of ambition, unexpected passion and the frailty of human nature. The lavish nineteenth-century French setting reflects the grand but suffocating restrictions of aristocratic society—contrasting the lives of the rich and of those who must serve them.

As the novel follows the burgeoning homosexuality between an impossibly beautiful but ruthless footman and a shy but ferociously intelligent marquis, it perfectly conveys the complexities of a passionate affair that breaks the rules of both the elite and the downtrodden.

'This story is perfectly presented… A fascinating and captivating read.'
Historical Novel Society